As she l

forward, obscuring his body from her view – whereat she impatiently shrugged the garment from her shoulders, whose white perfection, set against the dark of the night and only slightly yellowed by the torchlight, now showed in brilliant contrast to the ruddier gold of his own. Her breasts were perfectly formed, their enticing curves shaped by an attentive gravity, which pulled them gently from her body as if envious to possess them, and her posteriors – seen to greater advantage by those fortunate gentlemen sitting to the leftward of the stage – resembled nothing so much as a ripe peach, the delightful flesh of which any full-blooded gentleman would wish gently to nibble . . .

Further Eros titles also available

The Eros Collection
Eros in the Country
Eros in Town
Eros on the Grand Tour
Eros in the New World
Eros in the Far East
Eros Off the Rails

The Ultimate Eros Collection

Anonymous

HEADLINE

This omnibus edition first published in 1992
by HEADLINE BOOK PUBLISHING PLC

First published in paperback in 1993
by HEADLINE BOOK PUBLISHING PLC

10 9 8 7 6 5 4 3 2 1

ISBN 0 7472 4028 0

Printed and bound in Great Britain by
Collins Manufacturing, Glasgow

HEADLINE BOOK PUBLISHING PLC
Headline House
79 Great Titchfield Street
London W1P 7FN

EROS IN HIGH PLACES

For the convenience of the reader
we here record a note of
IMPORTANT PERSONS APPEARING IN THE NARRATIVE
in the order of their appearance

Andrew Archer Esq., our hero.
Sir Franklin Franklyn Esq., of Alcovary, Herts.
Lady Margaret Franklyn, his wife.
Tabby, a maid.
James, a footman.
Mrs Samuel Treglown.
Betty, her maid.
Mrs Sophia Nelham, our heroine.
The Viscount Chichley, a friend.
M. Emile Foutarque, of the French Embassy.
H.M. King William IV.
M. le Duc de Laval, H.E. the French Ambassador.
Jacques, M. Foutarque's footman.
Mally, a rude servant.
A number of French gentlemen.
A congress of actors.
John Rice, one of them.
Anthony Treweers, a butler.
Dolly and Jane, two lady wrestlers.
Squire Dick Treleaven.
Lady Holland.
Tollersly, her senior footman.
Mrs Teazle, a lady.

Betsy Pascoe, an ancient.
Jem, her Great-Uncle.
The D*v*l.
Mrs Treleaven.
Hermes, Apollo, Zeus and Pan, four actors.
Chimaera, Dryope, Metis and Selene, four actresses.
The Rt Hon. the Earl of Stow.
Glaws, a fishergirl.
The Rev. Ebenezer Polscoe.
Flannery Fitzchrome, his lordship's racing manager.
Lady Opimion, a fool.
Six jockeys.
Six professional ladies.
Bess and Nell, two strumpets.
Betsy, a Negress.
Samuel Treglown Esq., M.P.
Maurice le Semblant.
Two French plotters.
Mrs Blowser, a Madame.
Miss Xanthe Holden, a lady.
George Float, a Negro.
Mrs FitzNott, a society lady.

Chapter One

The Adventures of Andy

At the end of my last volume of memoirs, published under the title *Eros in the Far East*, the constant reader left my friend Mrs Sophia Nelham and I in that haven of relative civilisation, Singapore, where we were intent for some weeks upon relaxing after a series of adventures which had somewhat enervated us - not surprisingly, since they had included our being captured by pirates and barely escaping execution, together with other hazards which I need not recapitulate (the aforesaid account still being in print, and available from the London firm of Headline, its publishers, upon payment of an insignificant sum).

We returned to England, and to our respective houses - Sophie (as I was privileged to call her) to her elegant domicile in Chiswick; I to the large house whose windows overlooked Regent's Park, and which I found to have been maintained in every degree as I would have wished by the small band of servants I had left there.

I had spent only three nights in my own bed, however, before the post brought a letter from my old friend (and Sophie's half-brother) Sir Franklin Franklyn, Bart., of Alcovary, in the county of Hertfordshire. I had of course sent him a message apprising him of my safe return to England and promising to regale him with the narrative of my adventures at an early date, and he wrote now to press me to propose myself to him on the earliest possible occasion – not merely because he was eager to hear my story, but because he had a favour to ask of me.

I lost no time in packing a small trunk and setting forth, and in a matter of two days' journey – with a single night's residence at the Chequers Inn at Fowlmere (a favourite hostelry, upon the same route, of the late Secretary Sam Pepys) – rode once more at dusk up that well-remembered drive of elms, to be met at the front door by my friend Frank and his wife, the delightful Lady Margaret, whose embrace was rather more than sisterly, despite the presence of her servants. (I do not say 'of her husband' for there was no combative jealousy between Frank and I; we had shared too many amorous adventures for that to be the case, and indeed, though we did not speak of it, my carnal knowledge of his Lady had by several years preceded his own!).

'My dear boy,' said he, 'come in and take a glass of wine and some food!' and swept me into the familiar and comfortable drawing-room, where we ate and drank well, a delicious fricassee of wood-pigeon being prefaced by some trout and followed by a couple of fowl.

I had some difficulty in giving due consideration to the meal amid the continual fire of questions which my host and hostess pressed upon me, and the rest of the evening proved too little time for me to detail all my adventures together with those of Sophie, who had not yet had the opportunity to convey them in person.

But what, I asked finally, was the favour my friend wished to ask of me?

Frank glanced at the clock, which now showed a quarter of one.

'Time enough for that tomorrow,' he said. 'Perhaps you will wish to sleep late?'

No, I replied; I was quite recovered from the fatigue of the journey. Eight o'clock would do for me.

'Eight it shall be,' said Frank, 'with a cup of chocolate, to which I remember you are addicted at that hour. We will see – shan't we, my dear?' he said to Lady Franklyn, with what looked like a wink, 'that it is promptly served.'

I fell into a sleep as soon as my head touched the pillow, and it seemed indeed but a few moments later that I was awakened from a dream by the sound of the bedroom door opening, and through lazily opened eyes saw the figure of a maidservant enter the still darkened room and set a tray down on the bedside table.

She then walked to the windows, and turned back the shutters. As she did so, the sun shone directly into the room – for the windows faced towards the east – and the thin gauze of her dress was turned almost transparent, revealing the silhouette of a charming, buxom figure. It was unmistakably English, if I may say so: that is, charmingly solid with generous curves of bosom and hip that contrasted with my memories of the sometimes too slim sinuosity of the eastern ladies to whose company I had recently been more accustomed.

The girl turned from the window, and strode to the bed – where to my amazement she leaned over me, and immediately planted a smacking kiss upon my lips, with the words: 'Surely you ha'n't forgot your old friend at Rawby Hall?' – and slipping her hand beneath the bedclothes laid hold upon my riding-muscle (which I must admit was akimbo, as seems invariably the case when I am aroused suddenly from a dream).

My aversion to the gentle touch of a female's hand in that quarter is not so great that I hastened on this occasion to disengage it; nevertheless, I was a little put about by the familiarity of the servant's action, and must have showed it. 'Well, I believe you ha' forgot, hoity-toity!' she said, removing her hand of her own volition, and beginning to pour the chocolate.

'A thousand apologies, my dear – but you do have the advantage of me,' I said, 'no doubt because the light is behind you.'

'Think of the laundry-room at Rawby Hall!' she said, and at that moment turned half away, so that the light shone upon her face. 'Twas that of Tabby, who had been one of my fellow-servants only five years before, when I had been for a brief time footman at the house of Lady Franklyn's father (she then being Lady Margaret Rawby, one of two sisters whose beauty and cultivated manners were equalled by the lasciviousness of their appetites).

'My dear Tabby!' I cried; whereupon she put down the chocolate cup, whisked her gown over her head, and in less time than it takes to tell had stretched herself along my own unclothed body, which was no less sensible of her country charms than it had been of those many others which had delighted me since we last lay together, which, if I remembered, had been in an attic room at Rawby a night or so before I left.

'That's more my boy!' said she with a familiarity before which our present distinction of rank became as nothing; and turning to throw herself upon her back, clasped me with arms and legs in a grasp so delightedly enthusiastic as to raise my spirits (by the close consanguinity of our naked bodies) while at the same time making it impossible (at the same time) for me to set about relieving them.

In a short time, however, by placing my hands upon her hips, I was able to contrive such a space between our bellies as enabled me to present the tip of my instrument to its proper entrance, into which it slipped with what seemed like an uninterrupted familiarity.

The reader will not wish me to detail the pleasures which followed, save to say that the intervening years had done nothing to diminish her charms – her breasts were as round and firm, her bum as fleshy and bounding, her loins as eager, as they had been years before. Removing at last her heels from my shoulders, where she had placed them in order to offer the fairest target to my advances, she ran her hands over my shoulders, which were liberally greased with perspiration (the day was already warm, and promised to be warmer), and wriggling from beneath me sat upon the edge of the bed and completed her pouring of my morning chocolate.

'My dear Tabby!' I exclaimed (the pleasure of love now to be followed by the pleasure of conversation). 'How came you here? What of Rawby Hall, and what of – what the devil was his name?'

'Tom,' she said, 'you mean Tom.'

It had been on account of the jealousy of her *beau*, one of my fellow-footmen, that I had left Rawby, his having taken a poor view of our coupling for the convenience of an elderly gentleman – the grandfather of the house – who wished to draw us in *coitus* for the purpose of illustrating a naughty book. And indeed I must confess that the pleasures concomitant with the nature of the postures we were forced to adopt were even greater than those of the guineas that Beau Rust was happy to pay us for our services.

'Tom's downstairs,' she said.

'I had thought he might have married you.'

'Not Tom,' she replied; 'or rather not me. 'Tis not that he's not asked often enough, but I've taught him in the years that I'm not for the snaring. As for how we come here – the Lady Elizabeth being commonly in London, life became tedious enough at Rawby, so, the Lady Margaret coming on a visit with Sir Franklin, I asked the favour of transferring to his establishment, which was soon enough granted. Tom followed, for where I go, he goes, though not by my special encouragement.'

'But do you not . . . ?'

'Surely,' she said; ' 'twould be out of conscience cruel to refuse him – but you know he was never the most accomplished rider in the stable, and Sir Franklin keeps an open house to visitors, some of whom are pleased to be entertained by a good countrywoman, by contrast to some namby-pamby town slut.'

Handing me my chocolate, she replaced her free hand upon my now declined instrument, which despite its recent activity swelled somewhat beneath it, at which she grinned.

'The years have not decreased your powers,' she said.

'Nor yours,' I replied, bending to plant a kiss upon one pert nipple, about which a ring of chocolate from my lips now darkened still further the shady circle which encompassed it.

We talked further as I drank; during which conversation I gathered that her favours were not denied to the master of the house. Frank having been ever a lusty youth, and now married for some years, it was no surprise to me that so enthusiastic a young woman as Tabby had found it possible to penetrate his defences; and said so.

' 'Tis not,' she said, 'that he does not love Lady Margaret; but a nightly diet even of caviare must grow somewhat tedious; and my lady understands it. In permitting my master a free rein, she feels herself at liberty to gather new garlands where she may – though being of somewhat effete tastes, the visitors she welcomes to her bed are not such as would stoke my own fires. But are we to spend the rest of the morning in mere talk?'

Taking my empty cup, she placed it upon the table, and bending over lifted my pliant tool upon the palm of her hand and took it between her lips as though it were a favourite fruit (which may not have been so far from the truth). However, though charmed by the gesture, and unable to resist a final squeeze of those delightfully full, pendant breasts, I denied her another bout, making the excuse that I had a business to discuss with Sir Franklin (which was nothing but the truth).

Tabby insisted however upon filling the large bath tub in the corner of the room and sponging my body with cool water (most reviving after our recent efforts), then drying me thoroughly with a soft towel and assisting me to dress – only then resuming her single garment. With a bob which was more humorous than deferential she left the room whereupon I made my way down the salon.

'Andy, my boy!' said Frank, who was sitting at a table upon which a map was spread. 'The sounds I heard as I passed your room half an hour ago suggest that I was right in assuming that you would be happy to be reunited with an old friend.'

My reply was simply to slap him upon the back, whereat he laughed more, and winked.

'A game one, Tabby,' he said; 'and not only game, but discreet. Mum's the word, old boy!' From which I inferred that he believed his wife not to know of his adventures with young Tabby; whereas I knew different. However, it was not for me to interfere between husband and wife.

He motioned me to a seat.

'Now, to business,' he said.

'You will not be aware – no more was I – that Sir Fitzroy Franklyn, who held this place a century ago, purchased at the same time another property in east Cornwall, near the famous port of Fowey. Upon a closer acquaintance, however, he for some reason disliked it, and visited it but the once, whereafter he let it out upon a long lease – a lease so prolonged that 'twas forgot, the income merely disappearing into our coffers. Two months ago I received notification that, the last of the line of tenants having died, his lawyers discovered that the place properly belonged to me! Now you know I have become domestic, and hate any disturbance, but I had steeled myself to the necessity of visiting the property when I heard of your return – and, knowing your predilection for continual motion, it instantly occurred to me that you were just the fellow to go down and inspect the place – to find out, you know, what condition 'tis in, whether 'tis agreeable – in short, the whole aspect.'

I instantly concurred. I had indeed had no notion of what to do with myself during the coming months, and knowing well enough my hatred of idleness, had begun to wonder what task I could set myself to banish boredom.

'I shall go at once,' I said. 'You can let me have a horse?'

'A horse!' Frank said; 'nay, a coach! But stay for at least the weekend – we haven't heard nearly enough about your adventures. And by the way' – he winked again – 'Tabby is of course at your disposal; her pleasure at my announcing your arrival suggests her willingness to entertain you and, as you well know, what's mine is yours.'

We spent half an hour over the map – which was of Cornwall and showed Vycken Hall appearing to be set in a valley at the end of a road leading nowhere else – and in looking over some deeds to the place, which revealed little except that it must at the very least be three hundred years old.

The weekend passed pleasantly enough. Tabby, however, though she brought my morning chocolate, and was friendly enough, made no attempt to renew the familiarities with which she had greeted me; and for my part I was tactful enough not to attempt them, for having seen Tom's sullen visage in the distance while walking in the grounds (he made no attempt to renew acquaintance) I assumed that my presence was the subject of altercation between him and the object of his passion – and while I knew Tabby to be a young woman of strong natural affection coupled with a will of her own, I had no wish to make trouble between them.

I was not however entirely without female entertainment for the remainder of my stay at Rawby Hall, for having spent Sunday evening in pleasant conversation with my host and hostess, and bade them good night, I had retired to my room and was about to climb into my naked bed when there came a knock upon my chamber door. Thrusting on my shirt, I opened it – to reveal Lady Margaret, herself in charming *dishabille*.

I had been offered proof, during the evening, of the warmth of her regard for me, for she had made a point of sitting upon the floor at my feet, and even of leaning back between my legs, so that her head rested just at the bifurcation of my thighs, my manhood signalling by its swelling my appreciation of her presence, and the nearness of her lips to my most apprehensive limb. Frank in the meantime sat smiling amicably, being nothing if not complaisant at the friendship between his wife and myself.

It was now clear from the panting of that bosom which she pressed against mine, that Lady Margaret was eager for a consummation; indeed, even before the door was shut, her hands had slid down the length of my back and, raising the hem of my shirt, clasped the globes of my buttocks the better to press our bodies together at the point at which such contact most readily raises both desire and confident expectation.

Thrusting the door shut with one foot, I carried madame to the bed, where, laying her upon the sheets, I opened the leaves of the book in order more closely to examine the pages, where indeed I found inscribed just that picture I recalled: viz., breasts generous, but not to excess, their pouting expressive of desire, and the beating of the heart beneath them clearly to be seen under the flesh, itself so tender and white as to reflect the golden light of the candle almost as from the surface of a burnished vellum. Then, about the shoulders, one errant lock lying high upon the bosom, were swathes of lustrous copper hair, which the lady had now grown much longer than formerly, and which formed almost a pillow upon which not only her head but my own might be cushioned. That other, smaller cushion which disguised the entrance of her cave of delights was similarly lustrous, and so tempting that (first gently removing the small white hand which lay upon it) I planted a kiss there.

I could not but fear, despite these beauties, that marriage had somewhat dulled the edge of the lady's appetite; for while at our previous meetings she had been if anything over-ready to grasp at pleasures, now she lay lethargic, almost as though disinclined for combat – though her eyes were large and deep, and seemed to draw me towards her – which invitation I was only too happy to accept, first lifting my shirt over my head, seeming to hear a quick in-drawing of breath at the concomitant revelation; and indeed before I had entirely removed the garment I felt that touch between my thighs which could only be that of a lover's lips, and which reminded me of the excitement with which this very lady, when I was but a child, had introduced me to those sophisticated pleasures with which the gentry amused themselves, but which until that moment had been unknown to me, who had been familiar only with the rougher amours of the fields, or at best the servants' hall.

'Twas now I who was confined to inaction, for Lady Margaret, once having that morsel between her lips for which she had always shown an inordinate affection, had half-raised herself from the bed and crouched in an attitude most becoming (though what attitude of the naked female body is not?) – for as I looked down, her thick hair lay along her back, parting only at the waist to reveal the lower traces of a backbone delicately marked, ending only where the globes of a full and charming bottom hung (as it were) like a peach upon the bough.

Bending forward, I could but part the hair further to stroke that long, white back and those panting sides; for the rest, I could only concentrate on reserving some of my emotion for what might be to come – for I was like to burst with the pleasure of her attentions, her lips being ever adept at the provocation of pleasure. With the palm of one hand she supported my cods, a single finger playing softly upon that small disc of flesh which lay beneath them, inherent (as she knew all too well) with the utmost sensitivity. The other hand supported, between two fingers, my delighted riding-muscle, now engorged almost to pain; for not merely contented to suck upon it as an infant sucks at the breast, she drew from time to time her lips from it in order that her small, pointed tongue might play about it, now running its length to the foot, now mounting again to the head, then flirting about the dome barely maintaining the contact; then once more embracing the whole pillar, the lips drawn apart with a seeming reluctance, so that their plump fullness allowed a smooth resistance to its entry.

At last, with a gasp, I took her head between my hand and almost with violence thrust it away.

'You must allow me, my Lady,' I said, 'to pay you a similar compliment before the pleasure of your company positively kills me!'

With apparent reluctance, yet with a smile, she raised herself upon her knees, and, transferring her hands to my shoulders, pressed a kiss first upon one pap, and then upon my lips. I gathered her up in my arms and laying her upon her back prepared to graze upon her as a grateful stallion upon the most luscious meadow.

My memory served me well as to the pleasures which most delighted her, for while every woman's body resembles the same instrument, each demands different skills from the accomplished player. My teasing of her nipples with my teeth brought forth a remembered paroxysm of pleasure, as did the running of my tongue about the little whorls of her ear; thus I progressed down the length of her body. The sucking of her toes had also the remembered effect, for after but a moment, seizing me by that apparatus which fell most readily to hand, she began to draw me back into a position which . . .

But now we both distinctly heard a cry of pleasure which had been emitted by neither of us. I caught my Lady's eye, at which a mischievous glint came into it; and putting a finger to her lips, she stood upon the bed, catching me by the hand and raising me to a similar posture. Then, turning, she drew aside a tapestry which hung above the bed head and revealed there two small holes in the wainscot, to one of which she applied her eye.

Upon my doing the same to the other, I found the next bedroom revealed to me, which was that of her husband, my friend Frank (Lady Margaret's own being beyond it again, along the same corridor). Frank's bed lay just below us, and upon it I saw – not altogether without surprise – my friend lying at length, with our mutual mistress Miss Tabby mounted upon it, and trotting at a brisk pace, the rise and fall of which was giving my friend that pleasure which had called forth the cry that had attracted our attention.

As we watched, the pace became hotter and my friend's face more and more contorted with the joy of it, until, just as Tabby herself let out that mew of bliss with which I was not unfamiliar, he lifted her body and threw her aside just at the moment when there burst from him an eruption which sent a generous fountain of the liquor of life to a height of perhaps eighteen inches before it fell back upon his belly.

My Lady was as moved by the sight as I, for, clinging to me, she drew me back upon the bed, throwing out her thighs so that I fell between them as neatly as a ball within its cup; and our own trotting match held its course for only a brief period before we, like the happy couple next door, reached the apogee of pleasure and lay in each other's arms in a fulfilled relapse.

It would have been wise – and certainly common to those practised in deceit – for us immediately to have parted; but as it was, we both fell into slumber, and when I awoke, some hours later, it was to find myself lying beside not one figure but two. Frank had entered the room unheard by me and now lay at my side, his wife cradled happily in his arms, showing, most generous of fellows as he was, not the least infelicity in sharing her with his friend.

I fell asleep again; and was awakened only by the entrance of Tabby with my chocolate, upon which I thought I descried some irritation in her at the occupation of my bed also by her master and mistress, it being more than possible that, knowing that I was departing that morning, she had counted upon a farewell buff. However, having drawn the curtains, she merely asked whether she should bring more chocolate, and having received a lazy affirmative from the Lady Margaret, withdrew somewhat sulkily, leaving we three to greet each other without embarrassment – having on more than one occasion lain between the same pair of sheets, though generally accompanied by Sophie, whose absence we remarked upon, wondering why we had received no news of her. Frank, who had looked somewhat nervously at Tabby, as though expecting some reference to the cavorting of the previous night, was quick to embrace his wife, which she returned in the friendliest manner, so that out of tact, and seeing that he was ready to prove that Tabby had not exhausted him beyond a fresh demonstration of his powers, I roused myself from the bed and made my toilet behind the screen in the corner of the room. Between the cracks in that useful structure I saw that my two friends were indeed pledging their matrimonial affection in the approved fashion.

By nine o'clock I was in my borrowed equipage, comfortable enough in sufficient space for two or even three travellers; my luggage piled upon the roof, and the two spirited horses directed by James, a young chap of about my own years, whom I seemed to recognise (and who indeed turned out to have been a footman at Rawby at the same time as myself. I recalled, when I considered it, the difficulty he had in cramming himself into the tight breeches supplied him on the occasion of the great Waterloo Ball there, his member being, if I remembered aright, of inordinate size).

Our journey on that first day was to Oxford, into whose High Street we rattled in the cool of the early evening, the setting sun gilding the tops of the honey-coloured buildings. We put up at the Mitre Hotel, a decent inn whose landlady at first assured me that there was no space, but then impressed by that readiness with coin which I generally assume in order to secure proper service, led me to a handsome set of rooms on the first floor, and upon my insistence allotted James a bed in the long room which, above the stables, served for her own servants.

I slept well, and after an excellent breakfast we were upon the road early the following morning, for Chippenham. The landlady of the Mitre having provided us with a hamper which comprised beef pasties, cold meats of other sorts, and fruit, we pressed on without pause. We had passed through Wooton Bassett by mid-afternoon, and, in sun remarkably warm for late spring, were making to Tockenham Wick when through the window, which I had fully opened in order to take the air, I thought I heard a woman's cry.

I called out to James to stop; and on his pulling up, we both heard an appeal for help issue from the woods upon our right. I took my pistol – robbers being by no means unknown upon this road – and James a stout cudgel and we descended and made our way upon a recently trodden path between bramble and briar towards the spot from which the sound issued. The cries now grew more distinct, and seemed to issue from two throats; and, breaking into a small clearing, we found indeed two females firmly tied to two small saplings which, though weak enough to be broken perhaps by the strength of a man, were sufficient to keep them in thrall.

They were clearly mistress and maid, for one was dressed in servant's clothing, while the other was wearing a gown of some elegance, though sadly bedraggled, and indeed torn so that it hung from her waist leaving the whole top of her body bare except for the ropes which crossed it – a circumstance which even in her cruel circumstances drew a blush to her cheeks as I came sufficiently close to release her, upon which she immediately gathered her clothing together and held it to conceal those handsome globes upon the surface of which livid marks had been left by the entrapping ropes.

Though distressed, she was by no means in an extreme of terror – more of anger – and indeed rebuked her maid, whose sobbing and crying had mounted to an apogee as we came into sight, and who was now in a state of advanced hysteria. The lady's calmness was such that she immediately advised me that the robbers who had tricked them from their coach were long gone.

' 'Twas a coach I hired at Oxford, sir,' she said; 'but the driver was clearly villainous, for he stopped nearby complaining that one of the horses was lame – which I believe was not the truth; and our having stopped gave his friends the opportunity to attack, to tie us here, and to make off with the coach and its contents.'

'You were not . . . otherwise incommoded?'

'Thank you for your inquiry, sir, but no. The state to which my clothing is reduced was the result of my struggling rather than of any attempt upon my virtue. Oh, do be quiet, Betty!' she said to her still hysterical maid, who, stifling her sobs, now leaned upon James's arm with a degree of confidence that seemed suspiciously admiring.

Of course, I offered the lady the convenience of my coach as far as Chippenham, where she could at least enquire about her lost coach and belongings. But what were we to do about her clothing? For it was in no state for entry to a town. I had plenty of clean trappings for myself, but, needless to say, no female clothes. Instructing James to get down a trunk, I reached from it breeches and shirt which I was pleased to offer her.

On her returning to the coach from the bushes where she attired herself, I was pleased to hand her into the coach – for she made a handsome figure, though by no means boyish, for her breasts, though no more obtrusive than was pleasant, were delightfully full, and pressed against the linen of my shirt with an insistence which revealed her womanhood in a positively provoking manner. My breeches were also at stretch across her hips – the manner in which she filled them excusing (if excuse were needed) the lack of manhood which fashion at that time insisted should be shown at that place where in earlier days a codpiece would have announced it.

With the lady sitting opposite me, and the now quiet Betty upon the box with James, we resumed our journey, and I was able to inquire more of the lady's circumstance.

Her name, she said, was Constance Treglown, and she was returning to Cornwall from the north country, where she had been upon a visit with her sister, who had married a squire in Northumberland. She was somewhat taciturn of nature, and would say little else, except that her husband was the Member of Parliament for a Cornish town – her shortness in the acknowledgement of which led me to believe that there was little love lost between them.

I asked no more, since she seemed unwilling to volunteer more.

Noting the discomfort with which from time to time she lifted the front of my shirt from her bosom, I reached for the flask of cool water with which I had supplied myself, dampened a handkerchief and offered it to her – which, taking, she applied to her breasts, soothing (as I guessed) the troublesome irritation of the flesh provoked by her bonds. Though she used a most ladylike delicacy of motion, she could not but betray a glimpse of those globes of which I had had too short a view upon our meeting, and though as a matter of course I averted my eyes I could not but hope for an opportunity of a closer inspection. Given some hours, during our drive, to talk to and look at her, I concluded that indeed I might have had a far less attractive travelling companion. She was, I believed, my elder by a few years – but of a handsome appearance which could almost have been called noble, the carriage of her head and body being poised and graceful, her speech distinctive and metropolitan with little trace of a country accent, and her manner to me perfectly assured.

By the time we reached Chippenham we were on such terms that I had no hesitation in offering her the convenience of my coach into Cornwall – for her home was upon the coast to the west of Fowey, and would be easy to reach from the road upon which I was set. Her reporting the theft of her carriage to the local magistrate met merely with assurance that 'twas a common occurrence, and that she need not expect to meet with her belongings again – which caused her only a slight impatience for, she said, she had carried nothing valuable in it apart from a few jewels; the chief inconvenience being the loss of her clothing, which however she was able to some degree to correct through sending for a local sempstress, who was able by morning to produce a gown perfectly decent though of merely rural fashion. I must confess that I regretted the return of my own clothing, for despite her most evident femininity she made a charming figure in breeches.

Setting off, then, we were most comfortable. Betty showed as little dismay as her mistress at their new mode of travel, and settled upon the box with James in perfect equanimity, if not indeed with a trifle more enthusiasm than might have been expected of a young woman forced to such familiarity with a stranger. When I came to consider, the familiarity with which they greeted each other may not have been unconnected with the fact that their sleeping quarters had been in the same area of the small inn where we had rested, and it may be that they were already greater friends than a mere twelve hours' company would have led one to expect.

Passing through Bath with only a glimpse of its delights, we entered at the end of the day into Bristol, where we stepped into the Cross Keys and engaged rooms, and after a pause for the necessary refreshment of our persons enjoyed an excellent meal of fresh fish and good boiled mutton in Mrs Treglown's private room, in the corner of which stood a large four-poster. The meal was served by a woman who clearly, by her winks to me behind the lady's back, inferred that the meal was a mere prologue to seduction, and that the juxtaposition of dining table and bed was no mere accident – and indeed might have been a convenience afforded by the landlord to any who seemed likely to make use of it. As the evening went on my appreciation of the circumstances grew keener. My companion was extremely attractive and, as our familiarity grew, gave some reason to suppose that she might entertain an advance.

I saw no ready opportunity in our conversation to suggest it, however, and when, as ten o'clock struck out, she rose and, extending her hand, supposed that we should retire, since it would be necessary to make an early start on the following morning, I merely pressed that hand with affection and planted a kiss upon its slim fingers, at which she showed only pleasure.

I was confident that her gratitude for my aid would extend to the mutual enjoyment of a more inspiriting pleasure than that of mere aural conversation, and in my own room performed my toilet with all that care suggested by the probability of intimate caresses, even summoning James to bring hot water from downstairs, which he did with an ill grace, appearing with an unbuttoned shirt and unbraced breeches – which led me to suppose that he himself had been engaged a moment previously in just such an amorous dalliance as that I was shortly to enjoy.

Having donned a clean shirt, it was with a quivering apprehension of delights to come that I stepped out of my room and slipped along the passage to Mrs Treglown's, and merely tapped upon the surface of the door with my fingertips. I found it unlocked, and slipped through it – to find the lady abed, a candle lit upon the bedside table. I stepped forward, my always ready weapon already beginning to show a happy anticipation of the pleasure which awaited it.

But instead of throwing back the sheets to welcome me, she sat up, clutching the counterpane to her breast, and with an air of surprise.

'Why, Mr Archer!' she said, with an air of surprise. 'Is there some danger that you should approach a lady unannounced, in her bedchamber?'

This, as can be imagined, stopped me in my tracks.

'Why, madam . . .' I stammered.

'Your room is, I believe, somewhat along the passage?'

She smiled in a manner which I could have believed inviting – had she not at the same time maintained a firm grip upon the bedclothes, which showed no more than those alabaster shoulders, bare to the rise of her breasts, merely suggesting other delights which were clearly not upon offer.

'I beg your pardon, ma'am,' I said, bowing with what dignity I could command. 'I was under a misapprehension which I trust you will forgive.'

I then made my exit, my tail between my legs – or, indeed, 'twould have been between my legs had its size permitted the gesture, for my rejection had reduced it to a shrunken state in which no posture other than of utter dejection was possible.

It can be imagined that I spent a sleepless night; so much so indeed that upon the following morning I was capable only of greeting the lady somewhat sheepishly and seeing to the loading of the luggage, after which I fell into a sound sleep which even the ill condition of the road towards Devonshire could not disturb.

Chapter Two

Sophie's Story

While never averse to travel, it is always with considerable pleasure that I return to London, that most inspiriting of cities; and to my home, a small but handsome building standing within its own grounds at Chiswick, which I had been able to acquire as the result of wise investments made upon the advice of a number of gentlemen friends – including my brother Sir Franklin Franklyn, and the Viscount Chichley, a nobleman to whom and to whose wife I had been of some little service in reconciling a difference between them.

I cannot say that I stirred much from the house or grounds for a week or so after my return from my recent adventures in the Far East – even neglecting to send to Frank at his house in Hertfordshire, for I was sure that my erstwhile companion Andrew Archer would have done so; and to be plain, I was exhausted both as to mind and body.

However, I am nothing if not resilient, and in ten days or so began to feel once more capable of, and indeed eager for, society – so that I greeted with pleasure my footman's announcement, at ten one fine morning, of a visitor.

Chichley strode into the room looking not a year older than when I saw him last: though he was now in his mid-twenties, his complexion was still that of a young girl, and while his body was certainly more solidly built than when I had first encountered him, under somewhat embarrassing circumstances (recounted in those of my memoirs incorporated in a volume entitled *Eros in Town*, and published some time since), a greater assurance of manner advertised that he was now a man of perfect self-possession.

'My dear Sophie!' he exclaimed, using that diminutive form of my name by which my intimates always address me; and after sweeping a low and formal bow, descended to the more enjoyable familiarity of planting a smacking kiss upon my lips, while his right hand fell, by what accident I cannot say, upon the upper reaches of a breast decorated rather than concealed by the morning-gown which it was my habit to wear at breakfast.

'I have just heard of your return,' he said, 'your man having met my own (who, you know, is his cousin) at the coffee-house yesterday.' He stood back, the better to observe me. 'Clearly your journey has been intriguing, for you look if anything more interesting than ever!'

I bowed my head; he had ever been a charming companion, able to say – and perform – just those things which delight a woman when discharged by a personable young man.

'You must tell me all your adventures,' he continued.

'Certainly!' I concurred; 'but I was about to dress and ride into town. Come into my dressing-room and talk, while I make my *toilette*.'

It may surprise the reader to find me inviting a young man to observe my *toilette*; but my familiarity with Chichley was such that he took the suggestion for what it was – the evidence of friendship; and taking my hand as

I arose, handed me into the neighbour room with the greatest ease and lack of awkwardness. There, I sat him in a chair, and while I applied those cosmetics which polite society now represents as decent, told him something of myself; then retired behind a screen to divest myself of the *peignoir* before donning my gown.

I cannot say that I was much surprised, on looking up, to see Chichley leaning with one arm upon the screen, while he inspected my person – devoid now of the encumbrance of vesture.

'You have not, I see, been able altogether to resist the compliments of the sun,' he said – and indeed, unfashionable though it is in London, I had grown somewhat fond of the foreign habit of sun bathing, or exposing my body to the comfortable rays of the planet Sol, and my skin was therefore rather browner than is normally the case with ladies of fashion. This, Chichley clearly was stirred by, and stepping forward pressed his lips to my shoulder, his hand meanwhile once more stealing to a breast, which, now unencumbered by clothing, it was able to caress with all that tender and apprehensive sensitivity of which he had been master from the first, and which was now supported by the experience of his years of manhood and an education in the courts of love in which I, myself, had been one of the tutors.

I must confess that, having for the past several months been exclusively in the company either of natives of eastern countries whose bodies were naturally darker than those of Europeans, or of men of European birth whose skins had been tinted by the fierce sun of the tropics, the sight of Chichley's body as it now emerged white as a wand from the clothing which, in his eagerness, he dropped to the floor, was as interesting to me as my darker flesh was to him; though I reflected as he took me in his arms that that limb which now knocked insistently at my belly was indistinguishable from that of any other male instrument except in those details of size and shape which naturally differentiate lover from lover.

I could not but recall, also, as, gently displacing a thigh, he presented himself at that portal which was now ready and happy to receive him, that my earlier encounters with him had been relatively brief: as a mere boy, he had been no more capable of prolonging the act than any other of his age and inexperience; and when, scarcely older, he had on his wedding night been disappointed by the coldness of pride and come to me for solace, his loving had been remarkable more for a kind of melancholy passion than for either adeptness or persistence.

I now found, however, that all had altered – no doubt as a result of that domestic happiness to which I had contributed (in the unlikely event of the reader not having perused my previous volumes, Chapter Sixteen of that entitled *Eros in Town* recalls the circumstances under which Lord and Lady Chichley were reconciled as the result of a lascivious trick). That he was strong and vigorous as ever was evidenced by his now lifting me from the floor, being careful to maintain the connection between our bodies, striding into the next room, and depositing me once more upon my bed! But once reclining, rather than that boyish force which he had previously used, the gentle and languishing sway (as 'twere) of his body now moved his prick – stern and adamant – between my lower lips with a sensation all the more stirring for its tender and leisurely motion; and continued with unrelenting softness to delight me until my bosom rose and fell with the apprehension of immediate release – when with an equal tenderness he withdrew, lying quietly at my side, merely pressing soft kisses upon my neck and shoulder until my passion had almost subsided; whereupon I raised myself and looked with a quizzical eye upon him.

He raised an eyebrow; whereat I felt myself blush (an unusual occurrence, it must be admitted) and to disguise my confusion, bent to plant a kiss of my own upon that part of his body which he had allowed to languish slightly, though it had diminished in inflexibility rather than either in breadth or length; and as I took it between my lips, I felt the tissues once more harden – the more so as I began to draw upon its length with a regular motion, encouraged by the gentle touch of a hand upon the back of my neck.

It was now my turn to bring my friend almost to the splutter; when, encouraged and warmed by pleasure, I turned my body so that he could return the compliment, feeling in a moment his tongue exploring that part but recently evacuated by the limb I was now kissing; first running this around my outer lips, he then – as I felt – parted them with his fingers so that he could reach that bud which, in women, imitates in sensitivity and even somewhat in contour the most interesting part of man; and tickling its responsive tip, soon brought me once more near my summit – while at the same time, warned by the tightening of his cods in the palm of my hand and the involuntary upward motion of his loins, I drew away, and as my own body clenched with the delight of amorous explosion, withdrew my lips just in time to see a positive gusher of liquid issue from the tiny aperture which marked the summit of the steeple.

It now being mid-morning, I rang for coffee – forgetting that Charles, the footman, had been engaged during my absence by my housekeeper, and was not used (as my household had formerly been) to my habit of occasionally entertaining gentlemen in my bedchamber: to facing with equanimity the sight of a naked couple charmingly embedded, and indeed sometimes even engaged in the lists of love. However, the man's face – which was not unhandsome – showed only the slightest tremor of emotion upon discovering myself cleansing with a handkerchief the belly and thighs of a gentleman whose contented aspect no less than the bedewed state of an only half-subdued staff betrayed a very recent happiness; and upon his return with the coffee, he set down the tray without the least sign of perturbation.

'So, Chichley,' I said, when he had withdrawn, 'tell me the story of your life. Lady Chichley, I trust, is well?'

'Very well,' he replied; 'Frances indeed sends you her kindest wishes, and hopes to see you soon. She is engaged this morning with her hairdresser . . .'

'That fact relieving you of any suspicions that she may be enjoying a similar activity to us,' I remarked – it being in general the case that hairdressers are madge culls whose interest in women is restricted solely to the hair of their heads.

'The contrary is true,' said Chichley, with a smile; 'for this gentleman is more than usually attentive – indeed so much so that Frances has had to insist that the conversation which as a matter of course takes place between them does so before her hair is dressed, lest the excellence of the one exercise should be negated by the impetuosity of the other.'

My expression must have betrayed my surprise, for he

went on: 'My indifference to the connection arises not from any lack of concern for our union; it is merely that your introducing her (as you will remember) to the knowledge of the pleasure to be found in a variety of lovers has resulted in her having much more the appetite of a man than of a woman; so that while we celebrate our happiness with regular and satisfactory union, she feels the need of a regular change of diet; and has informed me that if she is to recognise my own desire for occasional dalliance outside the marital bed, it must be in return for my compliance in a similar exchange of attentions between her and other gentlemen – which of course I am happy to agree to!'

If I was surprised by these words, it was only at finding that Frances Chichley, originally so tender, apprehensive and modest a woman, now took the same view of the matter as myself; and silently applauding her good sense, I accepted with sanguinity – after we had each enjoyed a cup of coffee – her husband's entirely successful demonstration of the recovery of his spirits.

We lunched at home, and Chichley enlarged to me the death of the late King and the accession of the new, which had taken place during my absence from the country. King William IV was proving, he said, an amiable monarch, though at first the more dignified courtiers had found him intolerable, raised to the throne as he was from a position of obscurity and neglect, of living in miserable poverty, surrounded by a numerous progeny of bastards.

If nobody regretted the passing of the late King, nobody expected much of his successor; yet King Billy had begun well, showing himself entirely lacking in false pride – and on being given the instrument with which to sign the declaration of his monarchy, merely remarked in his usual tone, 'This is a damned bad pen you have given me' – which so startled the Clerk to the Privy Council that upon beginning to swear in the members of that body, he did so in the name of 'King George IV – William, I mean,' to the great diversion of all present.

The late King's funeral was, it seems, a merry affair. In the Abbey the new King was of course chief mourner, but instead of remaining decently behind the body, darted about shaking hands cordially with his friends, waving to others, and chatting to anyone who came near. But if this behaviour seemed to some to be indecent, the man's good nature, simplicity and affability to all about him were also striking; he has rather the manners of a country gentleman than of a great monarch, while Queen Adelaide is by no means delighted at her elevation, and lives as quietly as possible at Bushy House, about a mile from Hampton Court.

Chichley promised that he would introduce me at court upon the first possible occasion, for it seems that nobility is not, there, a prerequisite for attendance, His Majesty being more interested in companions who are lively and agreeable than in those whose presence is secured by right of aristocratic succession.

We lunched in *dishabille* (I always kept at home a robe in which my gentlemen friends could attire themselves should they wish to do so, rather than resume that clothing discarded for reasons of informal conversation). Then, gossip for the time over, we retired once more to the bedroom, where we found that my new footman had carefully laid out the clothing which Chichley had in haste thrown upon the floor (that young man showed distinct promise). My friend dressed, while I completed my toilet and donned that dress which I had meant to put on some hours earlier; and we set off for town in his carriage, he dropping me – as I wished to call upon my dressmaker – at Bond Street (near the place, as he reminded me, where we had first met).

Having fulfilled my errand (having been absent for some months from the country, it was now necessary that I should order some new gowns in the latest fashion), I was walking down the Burlington Arcade towards Piccadilly when I became conscious that a gentleman was walking not far behind me and at precisely my pace.

This was perhaps not a great surprise, for the rooms behind or above the shops in the Arcade were still at that time devoted largely to the entertainment of gentlemen by ladies whose virtue could be discounted at the cost of a few shillings; and indeed some women of fashion would not have been seen there. I however cared nothing for such apprehension, preferring to walk where I liked at whatever time pleased me.

However, I did not care to be followed indefinitely by some fellow who had a false understanding of my character – for when I paused to look into a window, so he paused; when I resumed, so did he. Turning the corner into Piccadilly, towards Lord Burlington's House, I therefore suddenly stopped and, dropping a glove, made to pick it up; whereon my shadow, abruptly rounding the corner, almost walked into me, and halting in some confusion, removed his hat and bowed.

I must confess that I was not unimpressed by his appearance, which was gentlemanlike, though he was clearly foreign, being dressed in a style which was not entirely English – and indeed his words of apology for almost knocking into me were in an accent that I recognised as the French. He was dark-haired, dark-eyed, and somewhat swarthy as to complexion; his face, a little angular, was handsome enough, and the smile which played upon his lips immediately intrigued me by its decidedly sardonic air.

I made my curtsy, and accepted his apologies with a smile; and when, bending once more to take up my glove, I was forestalled by his swiftly recovering it, I accepted it with a smile perhaps as sardonic as his own – for I was convinced that he knew that I knew that he was aware that I had recognised that he had been following me, and had contrived the exchange.

'Perhaps, *madame*,' he said, 'I may be permitted to accompany you, if you are walking down to St James's?'

I bowed, and on his falling into step, enquired whether he had been long in London, receiving the answer that he had been in town for only a month, attached to the household of the Duc de Laval, Ambassador of France to the Court of St James.

I was able to exchange courtesies with him about the difference between London and Paris society, for though I had never visited the French capital both Andy and Frank had done so, and indeed Lady Margaret Franklyn, the latter's wife, had spent some time there with her sister; so that in conversation I had gleaned much information about the somewhat loose society of the place.

On our reaching St James's, M. Emile Foutarque (for such was his name) made his bow, and hoped that we might meet again. London society, I remarked, was sufficiently small that that hope might indeed be realised; whereat he bowed again, and looked as though he wished to say considerably more – but retired.

My thoughts returned to M. Foutarque from time to

time during the next two days, for while he had not that light-hearted gaiety and charm which most attracts me in the other sex, I must admit that his person had a volatile fascination for which I could scarcely account. His manner was strictly polite, yet casual almost to insult; he seemed the kind of man under no circumstances to be trusted with the person of a lady. I had almost felt that he might at any moment have seized me, and, throwing me into the nearest doorway, have ravished me in the full view of society! – something which would in all events have been unusual, if possibly with embarrassing results for my reputation, if not his own. It was an uncomfortable, but by no means uninteresting, apprehension.

However, I had fittings at my dressmaker's, appointments at my hairdresser's (not the same hairdresser, I may say, as Frances Chichley, and much more interested in the hovering presence of my footman Charles than in any part of me other than my hair), and other matters to occupy my time – for Chichley had sent to say he would present me at court at the end of the week.

This was an evening court, and took place at St James's Palace, in the presence not only of the King but of the Queen, who is very ugly, with a horrid complexion, but has good manners, and played her part well enough (though she spoke as though she was acting, and wished the green curtain to drop). His Majesty was amiable, and on my being presented said, 'Happy, very happy,' taking my hand with great affability.

Returning to my place with Chichley, who should I see standing opposite me across the room – at the side of a plump, saturnine elderly man with powdered hair, who I took (rightly, as it turned out) for the French ambassador – but my friend M. Foutarque. He bowed slightly to me, and I nodded to him; whereat Chichley looked a little startled, and said: 'Do you know Foutarque?' – and on my replying that I had met him, looked as though he would say something more, but refrained.

We sat in conversation for a while, and took some wine; when at ten o'clock His Majesty rose and said, 'Now, ladies and gentlemen, I wish you a good night. I will not detain you any longer from your amusements, and shall go to my own, which is to go to bed; so come along, my Queen.'

There was some amusement at this frankness, though it was but normal behaviour in our new monarch; but the party indeed broke up. When I had been handed my cloak and was waiting for Chichley in the outer hall of the palace, M. Foutarque approached me and asked if he might present me to the Ambassador, which took place. We exchanged a few phrases – the Duc spoke little English – then excused ourselves, whereupon Foutarque offered me the convenience of his carriage, the Ambassador leaving in the company of other diplomatic colleagues.

Chichley was now standing by, and had clearly expected to escort me; but on my glancing at him gave, somewhat to my surprise, an almost indistinguishable nod, and immediately retired. I therefore acceded to Foutarque's invitation, whereupon he offered me his arm and escorted me to the door of the palace; when after a while a carriage drew up and a footman descended to open the door and hand me in, the carriage then setting off at a rattling pace to the north.

On our turning into Regent Street, I drew to M. Foutarque's attention the fact that my house was in fact in quite another direction; whereupon he immediately apologised.

'I beg your pardon, *madame*,' he remarked; 'but I had assumed, the hour being early, that you would be happy to take a glass of wine with me at the Embassy.'

While M. Foutarque was not of such impressive parts that I would otherwise have thrown myself (as it were) into his arms, I was pleased at the opportunity of being entertained at the French Embassy, for a more or less cool relationship existed between our two countries, and the French Ambassador, perhaps especially because he spoke our language but poorly, held open house but rarely. So I chose to ignore my new acquaintance's somewhat over-ready assumption of my willingness to be kidnapped, and assented.

I did not, however, see much of the formal parts of the building; for though we entered through the main doors of the impressive building, I was hurried up the main staircase, a footman holding lights which only briefly illuminated a gilt balustrade and picture-frames, to a first floor; then up a narrower staircase to a second, where at last we entered a small but elegant panelled sitting-room, an open door suggesting a further room beyond.

Dismissing the footman with some words in the French language, which alas I comprehend but haltingly, M. Foutarque lifted my wrap from about my shoulders, pulled forward a chair and poured me a glass of claret; then, taking one himself, sat opposite me in another chair, and for a time the conversation circled about the subject of the British weather and the possibility of a warm summer, which indeed seemed in prospect, the evening even now being warm and unoppressive.

After a while, the gentleman remarked upon not

having seen me in society before, though he had been in England for some months; whereupon I informed him that I had been travelling in the East, which interested him, and provoked many questions as to the society of the nations I had visited. These questions eventually settled upon social behaviour, and, questioned about such matters as the marriage customs of certain tribes, I found myself describing a ceremony I had observed in Fiji, and necessarily going into certain details which might have been considered indelicate by a less uninhibited narrator.

M. Foutarque was now showing considerable curiosity; and with permission loosened his *cravate*, as the French call a neckerchief, and even undid the topmost button of his shirt; while when I came to the most intimate details of the ceremony (a full description of which can be found in my volume *Eros in the Far East*), he leaned forward with an intense gaze.

On my finishing, he stood, revealing by the swelling clearly to be seen in his breeches that his masculine sensibilities had responded to my story as appreciatively as his intelligence, and was now at attention in the hope of my perhaps continuing. He refilled my glass, and his own, then once more sitting at my side inquired whether my travels had enabled me to, er, examine the disparity in dimensions which were said to distinguish the citizens of the eastern countries from those of the west.

'Forgive me if I am indelicate, *madame*,' he said, 'but there is some suggestion that I might be appointed to those parts, and . . .'

'Think nothing of it, sir,' I responded (for his eager interest had given point to my descriptions, and I warmed to them).

'I have always heard,' he continued, 'that the, er, masculine appendages of the Eastern men are less impressive as to proportion than those darker African races; that, in short, while the latter are remarkably well provided for as to the magnitude of their generative organs, their Eastern brothers are relatively diminutive. Of course,' he added, 'I do not suppose that personal experience will have confirmed this; but it is possible that you may have some anecdotal evidence.'

I was able to assure him that personal experience could indeed confirm what he had heard; for I had once in my employ, when I ran a house of pleasure for ladies in West London, a young black man whose prick – though he assured me it was by no means so superior as to its dimensions to that of any other man of colour – was of a size which would certainly impress any white person. The instruments of those Eastern men whose acquaintance I had been privileged to make were (I confirmed) of a lesser bulk – but M. Foutarque would perhaps be familiar with the female opinion of the male organ, that it was the employment of it which was most important, rather than the dimensions.

'You interest me strongly, *madame*,' said the Frenchman. 'I have myself a trifle which I might perhaps offer by way of comparison,' and, standing, he swiftly unloosed his breeches and without further ado there sprung from its confinement a stout white caduceus which was certainly as lengthy as any with which I had become acquainted in Europe, though as to its breadth there was perhaps something wanted, for though it terminated in a bulb whose circumference was generous, the supporting column was somewhat slender.

Presuming that he offered congress, and finding him

not unpleasant – if perhaps a little precipitate in assuming my interest – I also rose to my feet, and stepping forward embraced him, taking his prick in my hand to discover that while it was certainly slim it was also as rigid as was concomitant with the circumstances.

To my surprise, however, he stepped back, and with a slight bow turned to pull at a silk bell-rope just behind him; then, in somewhat undignified posture – having to support his unloosed breeches with one hand – indicated the open door at the end of the room, through which we passed to a fine panelled bedroom, the main item of furniture in which was a comfortably proportioned couch towards which he bowed. Without more ado, I disrobed and laid myself down, while he too divested himself of his clothing – but refrained from approaching, which I found somewhat puzzling.

After a moment, to my greater astonishment, the door opened and the footman who had previously attended us entered the room.

I could not imagine what service M. Foutarque could require; perhaps some brandy, I thought, or even coffee – if he had indulged too freely in alcohol during the evening. But this was not the case, for addressing the man in his own language, he had scarcely completed two brief sentences when the lad bowed, removed his wig, then his coat, then his waistcoat, then his breeches – and in no time at all was standing naked before us, his tool, while by no means extended, showing some apprehension that an equally naked lady was upon a nearby bed.

Foutarque now turned to me.

'You will forgive me, *madame*, but for reasons which will not interest you, I am at present entirely unable to oblige you; but in order not to leave a lady in a state of dissatisfaction, may I offer young Jacques, who I believe is capable of fully gratifying any desire you may express.'

Of course it was open to me to take offence and to leave. However, the *monsieur* was a highly placed official in his country's service; I felt in the position of one who must offer such hospitality as would reflect well on my king and country; and must anyway confess that, lacking a regular cohabitant, and not having had the pleasure of male copulatory attention since my passage with Chichley almost a week ago, I was by now ready for a romp.

Moreover, now I looked, young Jacques, who had presented a *chic* figure in uniform, was quite as handsome out of it. Though young, he was clearly a man in all essentials, and every moment showing more evidently the signs of physical maturity. Though as slim as the wand-like youths of the East, he was entirely European, not merely as to the whiteness of his body, but as to the hair which grew upon it – which the Eastern men lack, their arms, legs and breasts being as bald as eggs. Upon Jacques' chest lay a mat of black hair, his forearms and thighs also bearing a pleasant fuzz, and from the deep dint of his navel a line of black, springy filament led down to a positive grove from which his manhood rose rampant as a young oak.

He was clearly aware of what was required from him, for without any of that embarrassment which an Englishman might have shown in similar circumstances, he stepped forward and kneeling upon the bed between my legs (which I had unconsciously thrown open to his inspection) placed a hand on each side of my body and lowered himself so that he could place his lips upon mine, whereupon I felt his tongue, sharp and lively as a young fish, playing upon my teeth and the inside of my lips with all that inventive assiduity which a Frenchman can command (the men of that race being, as to osculation, by far the most ingenious).

I will admit to my pleasure being heightened by once more feeling beneath my hands (which played now over the hillocks of his lower back) that downy covering of hair which is so attractive to some women – though lack of it in certain men (I mention the Viscount Chichley as only one example of a Western male whose person was largely devoid of it) is no mark of femininity. In young Jacques it seemed to emphasise that virility which he was soon demonstrating in the most conventional manner; my palms, resting upon the rounded platform of his buttocks, feeling a rippling of muscles beneath the hair which was conveyed through every limb.

I was conscious now, as he riveted me with energetic thrusting, that M. Foutarque, kneeling at the side of the bed, his own instrument clutched in one hand, had placed his other hand upon my thigh, pressing it downward so that he could the more clearly command a view of his footman's baton as it entered and left its welcoming sheath; at the same time manipulating his own person with a vigour which matched Jacques' thrusting. On my signalling the ultimate satisfaction, which was soon enough given me, Foutarque gave his man's bottom a slap, whereat the man with a final thrust lifted himself away, the nectar of love falling upon my body as his master, with a carefully timed flick of the wrist sufficiently adept to suggest a lifetime's practice, brought himself off; so that in a strange tableau, he sat exhausted at the side of the bed while I lay equally dissipated upon it, and the footman – whose privileges did not include the right to exhaustion - rose, fetched a towel from a nearby chair, and with the most tender discretion began to wipe the perspiration from my damp but satisfied person.

M. Foutarque showed no sign of embarrassment, politely turning his back as young Jacques (who seemed also entirely devoid of any consciousness of the occasion being unusual) assisted me to dress. A less experienced woman than myself might have been abashed by the situation, but having learned that the vicissitudes of behaviour in the human male are innumerable - nay, inexhaustible - I carried the occasion off with what the Frenchies call a *sang-froid*, and declining the offer of more refreshment, permitted Jacques (having lately resumed his uniform) to summon what I suppose was one of the Ambassador's carriages, which took me off to Chiswick. I was not unamused by the evening's adventure - my anticipation of M. Foutarque's favours not having been so keen that I had been entirely offended by his appointing a deputy in the courts of love, and that deputy having been sufficiently personable to render his service pleasant enough.

Next morning, as I was still abed, Chichley was announced, and I received him together with my morning chocolate; whereupon he enquired as to my adventures the night before.

Our relationship was sufficiently candid to permit of my describing the incident in some detail, upon which he raised an elegant eyebrow to an almost comic extent.

'This might be extremely useful to His Majesty,' he said.

It was now my turn to signal surprise and incomprehension.

'This must go no further,' he said, 'but His Majesty's Government has for some time been looking for a means of discovering the real attitude and intention of M. le Duc de Laval; and anyone who could contrive a friendship with M. Foutarque would certainly have *entrée* to the Ambassador. It may also be the case that (though our French friends are to an extent shameless in matters of love) Foutarque would not especially wish his somewhat individual approach to amour to be advertised at large to the rest of the diplomatic *corps*.'

But what was this? I asked. Was Chichley now a diplomat?

'A patriot, merely,' he said; 'and this is a sensitive time. With a new King on the throne, it is important that this country secures an advantage in matters of foreign policy. But I must not bore you – it is merely . . .'

I interrupted my friend to assure him that the fact that I was of the female gender was no index of an ignorance of politics, and that I was as great a patriot as he, and would be glad to be of service.

'Then be so good,' he said, 'as to accede to any request M. Foutarque might make – short of course of your own security, and indeed of safety and decency, for we would not wish—'

I held up a hand.

'As to safety,' I said, 'you will know that I am not unaccustomed to inconvenience and even danger; and as to decency . . .'

He smiled, and said that I need say no more. He then proceeded to question me closely about so much of the Embassy as I had seen – which was not a deal; and then as to M. Foutarque – everything he had said and done, and his personal appearance (which I was certainly able to describe in some detail) and behaviour. As to the latter, I could only say that it had been impeccably polite, and that even when entirely devoid of clothing and in a state of excitation, his manners had remained those of the *salon* rather than the bed-chamber.

Eventually, Chichley took his leave, and without any familiarity other than a kiss; remarking as he left that should I, through the *monsieur*, be able to achieve the acquaintance of the Ambassador, this would no doubt be useful; a thought not especially inspiriting, since the latter gentleman, though dignified, was of greater corpulence than rendered him obviously attractive. However, I had more than enough to think about as I rose, made my *toilette*, and considered my future life as an unofficial secret agent of His Majesty!

Chapter Three

The Adventures of Andy

A beautifully warm morning saw the enigmatic Mrs Treglown and I once more upon the road, this time for Exeter, having paid my bill of six shilling for the night's accommodation for my servant and myself, and four shilling for supper. The journey passed without incident until between Cullumpton and Exeter the road became very bad, and one of the horses fell as we came down a steep hill into Bradninch. Mrs Treglown was very alarmed and clutched my arm with an intimacy which in other circumstances would have been most promising; but though she was at all times friendly, and did not once refer to the *contretemps* of the evening before, neither was there any sign of her regarding me as anything other than a casual acquaintance – which I found dispiriting, for the more I enjoyed her company the more I warmed to her person.

The horses being unable to bear up the carriage, we were, after the accident, obliged to walk up another hill, which in the heat wearied Mrs Treglown somewhat, who was forced to lean upon me, again not entirely to my displeasure despite the fact that the exertion brought me out in a positive muck of sweat.

We reached the London Inn at Exeter at about half past six, where my first act must be to lave my body, which was already beginning to stink from the exertions of the day. The London Inn must have been used to welcoming travellers in just such a state, for the room to which I was conducted already contained a metal bath full of warm water, into which I plunged after a brief pause for the removal of my soiled clothes.

In a very short while, the water was as dirty as my body had formerly been, and not for the first time I wondered why there had not been invented some scheme which would enable one to bathe in running water, so that there would no longer be a necessity to recline in a stagnant pool. However, I had no sooner thought it, than a knock came upon the door, and, covering the bath with a towel, I called upon the visitor to open – who was revealed as a plump, cheerful Devonshire girl who bore in her arms an immense pitcher. She explained that this contained warm, clean water with which I might freshen my body before leaving the bath; and before I could enquire how this was done, she had set the pitcher down, whisked the towel from the bath, drawn up a chair at its side, and invited me to stand. I did so, whereupon she mounted the chair and poured the water slowly over my body.

It had an invigorating and exhilarating effect, and a brisk towelling was all that was now required to recover me entirely from the effects of the long journey; but on my asking the maid to pass me the towel, she rather brought it, and, placing it about my shoulders, began to buff the skin with a delightful motion. Having dried my back to the waist, she turned her attention to my bosom, then my arms, finally inviting me to step out upon the towels which were spread at the side of the bath for that purpose – and on my doing so, bent to wipe the water briskly from the cheeks of my arse, then my thighs and legs.

I am ashamed to say – but no! shame did not enter into the matter; rather, 'twas entirely natural – that after spending a dry day in close company with a beautiful but unresponsive woman my sensual apprehensions were heightened, and the touch of female hands roused me. However, I blushed somewhat at the readiness of my riding-muscle, which was now at an angle of forty-five degrees and, as she leaned forward to reach behind me, was doing its best to nestle into the cleft between her generous young breasts, the touch of which did nothing to diminish either its dimensions or its eagerness. The young lady however was no whit abashed either by the sight nor, evidently, the touch – for, while rubbing my cods gently with the towel, she took a corner of it and wiped the remaining beads of water from the device which stood so proudly above them.

She then sat back upon her heels, and examining the phenomenon quite frankly, said in the broadest of accents, 'Why, zur, 'tes a braave set o' gingambobs! Would 'ee care for a jock?'

I cannot pretend to have understood her words, but the implication was clear, for releasing the strings of her bodice, she took my cock in her hands and laid it between her breasts, when an irresistible warmth spread instantly through my limbs, and, raising her to her feet, I drew her gown over her shoulders, when its falling to the ground revealed her quite stark. I attempted to draw her to the bed, but she resisted (later, I gathered that it was a house rule that only guests should copulate between the sheets), and, gripping me by the shoulders, took me with her to the floor, where fortunately clean – though damp – towels were still spread, and there I was in a moment engulfed and at work.

It must be admitted that Mally was not the most sophisticated of lovers, her command of the amorous art being restricted to congress of the simplest form; but I was not at that moment in search of poise or discrimination, and what she lacked in this she made up for in enthusiasm – for I was forced to place my hand over her mouth in order that her yowls of pleasure should not bring in the landlord or alarm the other guests; and the seismic bound with which her apogee was reached positively dislodged me from my seat, whereupon she seized my piece with her hard hands and brought me off with a spirited and cheerful dexterity.

The dear girl rose from her recumbent position to don her clothes – or, rather, her single garment – and, positively running from the room, fetched more warm water to sponge down my body for a second time, a task she did with no less assiduity and conscientiousness than formerly, though without the same effect.

I pressed four shilling into her hand, which delighted her (I had somewhat the impression that her services might have been taken as an element of the night's entertainment, and that she was surprised that I should have been inclined to hand her an extra tip). Then, dressing myself, I took tea with Mrs Treglown, and we walked out for a while before bed time. My passage with the girl had the effect of somewhat dampening down the fire which had previously been fanned by the company of the lady, and I was able to enjoy rather her conversation, which was witty and elegant, and to take a pleasure in her appearance and deportment unaffected, for the moment, by her more corporeal beauties.

On retiring to my chamber, I undressed and put out the lamp – but walking to the window to open it against the still warmth of the night, saw across the inn yard, on to which my room looked, the figures of James, my man, and Betty, Mrs Treglown's maid, in an embrace whose passion was no doubt excused by the fact that both were bare as the day they were born. That they had been friendly, I had known; and the fact that, as they sat side by side upon the box of the carriage, they had kept their knees covered by a rug despite even the heat of midday, had suggested some familiarity; however, here was proof of a friendship which owed as much to aphrodisia as to concord.

Indeed, if further proof was needed as to the extent of their ardour, it was now offered, for as Betty drew away so her lover's grinder could be seen in all its splendour, and though he was merely a servant, it must be admitted that as to both length and circumference, his weapon was of conspicuous dimensions. I had vaguely remembered him complaining, when we were together at Rawby Hall, of the difficulty of cramming himself into the doeskin breeches of his livery; and I was now reminded why – the miracle being that such an instrument could be disguised by the loosest unmentionables.

Miss Betty did not, however, show herself in the least discomfited – which surely demonstrated that they had been intimate before; for any woman setting eyes for the first time on so grandiose a weapon might be expected to faint away at the prospect of its splitting her most tender part. She immediately knelt, and, holding it with both hands, managed with an effort to take its tip between her lips – whereupon young James instantaneously doubled up in an ecstasy which proved sadly conclusive. Betty recoiled with a furious expression, while from the end of that remarkable cylinder dripped the discharge which had done his business.

It was impossible not to sympathise with the young woman, whose expression was of a child from whose grasp a lollipop had been seized after but one taste of its flavour! She battered at James's chest with her fists, and even (I shuddered as she did it) directed several slaps at the shrinking phenomenon which, though impressive even in its relaxed state, now hung loosely between his thighs.

Those gentlemen who are of experience would have given her at least the compensatory pleasure of other attentions; James clearly knew nothing of the art of love other than simple rogering, and now merely backed away, blushing and stammering. In a moment, pausing only to pick up her clothes from the bed, she left the room, whereupon he threw himself upon it in an attitude of such despair that I could only conclude that the sad culmination of the passage I had witnessed was not unusual; and I took myself to bed with the promise that he should be educated – for we owe it to others less fortunate to communicate to them those skills which we ourselves have mastered.

I rose the following morning at half past five, and paid my bill, which was eleven shilling only – an improvement on the ever increasing sums charged by those houses nearer the metropolis. Mrs Treglown was down but a few minutes later than myself; but complaining that her maid had not yet shown her face – which was also true of my fellow: but I could guess why.

Indeed, when the couple did appear, they wore matching expressions of disconsolate misery, and each declined to address the other, which led to some difficulty and confusion in loading the coach. When Betty had almost to be forced to mount the box beside James, rather than showing her customary eagerness to adopt that position, Mrs Treglown showed considerable curiosity; whereupon I must explain to her – something which I did with as much delicacy as possible, putting Betty's disappointment down to cursory treatment by her friend, whose impatience had rendered him less attentive than a lady had reason to expect from a lover. Whether she fully understood me, I cannot say, but she looked thoughtful during the rest of the time it took us to reach Chudleigh, where we breakfasted at the Clifford's Arms, which appears to be a good house, kept by Mr Weston, who with his wife was very civil and attentive, though the place itself has not much to recommend it.

We then passed on, the bright sun with a brisk breeze raising not only our spirits but those of our servants, who we were pleased to see now held each other's hands (when the management of the horses permitted, which was often – for the roads were not only narrow but highly fenced and therefore very safe), though their knees were no longer covered by the concealing rug (whose folds, I was now convinced, had enabled Betty manually to examine the dimensions of James's better part, thus raising hope in her which had subsequently been dashed by the precipitate nature of its firing mechanism).

We changed horses at the Golden Lion at Ashburton – a good house – and were happy to get to Ivy Bridge at two o'clock, where there was an excellent good house – the London Inn – in a retired, cool and pleasant situation. Here we dined for twelve shilling, and strolled for a while along a most romantic walk on the other side of the river above the bridge, where we sat and drank tea in the garden of a small cottage – Mrs Treglown accepting my arm on our return. We stayed at the inn until seven, when we proceeded for Plymouth, which we reached at about half after nine, and upon Mrs Treglown's recommendation - who knew the place - took up our quarters at the Fountain, Devonport, where we were very well accommodated.

Devonport is that part of the neighbourhood chiefly given over to naval matters, but is now as handsome on its own account as its elder relative, Mr Foulston having designed a splendid Town Hall which proudly overlooks Ker Street Hill, and serves a population of no less than thirty-three thousand - while Plymouth itself houses twelve thousand fewer citizens. This place is still, by Plymouthians, called Plymouth Dock - which was indeed its nomenclature until a few years ago, when the King was petitioned, and Sir Robert Peel, at that time Home Secretary, pronounced that it should be known by its present name. Its citizens are very particular in the matter, and still talk of the celebrations which marked its re-naming, celebrated by a triumphal column - again designed by the ubiquitous Foulston - which soars into the sky alongside the Town Hall and offers all who care to climb to its summit a remarkable view of the surrounding harbour and countryside.

The following day being fine, we not only mounted the monument - which provoked Mrs Treglown's generous bosom to a panting highly stimulating to the observer - but walked upon the Hoe, that splendid promenade which rises above the Sound (as the stretch of water between the harbours of Plymouth and Plymouth Dock is called), and took coffee in a small but respectable hostelry upon the Barbican, or quay, near which we were informed the earliest settlers had sent out for the New World.

Apart from these pleasures, the delights of Plymouth were soon satisfactorily inspected – and a theatre being discovered at the centre of town, the lady and I took ourselves there in the evening to a moderately satisfactory performance of Mr Farquhar's comedy of *The Beaux' Stratagem*. Mrs Treglown continued to observe the strictest rules of propriety, and, while happy to lean upon my arm and to tolerate its lying along her own while we sat in close proximity in one of the small boxes of the theatre, met the slightest familiarity, the pressure of a thigh or the insinuation of a gesture, with an innocent assurance the more titillating for its being invulnerable.

We returned to the Fountain Inn late in the evening, and the lady took herself to her room, bidding me good night with (again) a steadiness which denied any attempt upon her virtue – a virtue which I was by now suspecting of being permanently inviolable.

I sat for a while, then summoned James to bring me a night-cap to my room; which, when he appeared, I encouraged him to share – my attitude to my servants always being one of friendship, and even (should they warrant it) a certain informality. James and I having been at one time fellow-servants, a natural pleasantness was to be expected, short of absolute familiarity – which he was sufficiently well-trained to avoid.

I could not but notice that he still wore a disconsolate air, and would have been glad to offer some comfort and advice, could I but think of a way of opening the matter – which must be of some embarrassment to any man. Finally, I offered the observation that he seemed to be pleased with the company of Mrs Treglown's maid.

'Oh, she's a fine girl, sir!' he replied, energetically.

'And a giving one, I would suppose?' I answered.

He nodded, but with no special enthusiasm.

'You seem in doubt of it,' I observed.

' 'Tis not the matter of her willingness,' he said, 'but of . . .' and stuttered into a silence.

'If you will forgive me,' I said, 'while I am of your own years, more or less, I am perhaps more experienced in the way of the world, and am aware of the difficulties that may arise between a young fellow and his mistress. If I can be of any assistance . . .'

'No matter who, they could not help,' the poor young lad asserted, 'for I fear 'tis a matter for a surgeon.'

'Why, you have not the clap?' I asked (knowing full well that was not the question).

'By no means, sir,' he said, somewhat indignantly; 'no, 'tis more – more – a mechanical matter.'

'Slow to stand?' I inquired (still purposely upon the wrong track). 'Well, that is certainly a serious matter . . .'

'Not that, either,' he said, with a certain indignancy. 'Rather, being too quick to stand, I be also . . .'

'Aha!' I said – 'too quick to fall.'

The lad blushed. 'Right,' he said.

'But, my dear James, 'tis a very common problem, and one easy of cure, with the help of the lady concerned. Would your maid be willing to assist . . . ?'

'I'm sure of it,' said James; and in short he went off to seek the maid, and to persuade her to come to my room, where I could offer what advice I had in the matter. I rather wished that my sister Sophie was with us, for it had been she who had imparted to me the knowledge which I was now about to share, and while I was never shy in the company of young ladies, it would have been more proper that she should have had a private talk with

Betty than that I, not only a male but a gentleman, should open it to her.

However, there was nothing for it; and by the time James and his mistress knocked at the door, I had mustered my thoughts.

I invited them to sit, which they did – James upon one of the only two chairs in the room, with Miss Betty upon his knee, while I occupied the second chair.

'My dear,' I began, 'James has done me the honour to confide in me the difficulty which stands between you in the matter of love.'

She lowered her eyes and a delightful blush suffused her cheeks, though I could tell from her demeanour that my servant had conveyed to her the matter of which I was to speak to them.

'As I have informed him,' I continued, 'it is a question that often arises (or, rather, falls) between young lovers inexperienced in the art; the young man does not realise that for a mistress fully to enjoy the act of which we speak, the passing of considerably longer time may be necessary than that which brings him to his conclusion, and that disappointment must necessarily be the result. And even when it is made clear to him that the act must be sustained, he frequently finds it impossible to contain himself and remain at a stand for a sufficient period of time.

'I do not blush to say (for it is a common fault) that I, in my younger years, faced this same problem, but happily was offered the solution by a knowing friend, and will be happy to pass the secret on to you – though in doing so I must speak more plainly than a gentleman usually does to a female, and perhaps especially to one in your station.'

Betty blushed again, but after a while almost whispered her gratitude and her willingness to hear my explanation.

I then explained, in the simplest words at my command, that the pleasure given to the male instrument by the caresses of a willing female was so acute that in no short time a pitch of delight was achieved which must inevitably end sooner than later in the flushing forth of vital fluid, and the consequent shrinkage of the conveying cylinder.

'Now,' I continued, 'this problem necessarily becomes acute when we love. In commerce with a whore – to use frank language, Betty, for you know we are at this moment friends rather than employer and servants – it is of no moment; but with one we love, pleasure is heightened, and therefore disappointment enlarged. Something may be done by eschewing those delightful courtesies – of kissing and caressing – which normally preface the act; but we must be reluctant to reject these, while at the same time anticipation is sufficient aphrodisiac to make the eventual embrace of the male part by the equivalent female part the trigger which sets off the premature explosion.'

I saw from the cloud upon Betty's brow that my words were insufficiently clear to her, and was forced to be more explicit: 'What I mean,' I told her, 'is that toying and playing, kissing and licking, so raise the heat that the pot too quickly boils over.'

She smiled at this, though coyly hid it behind her hand. The other hand, I could not but notice, lay upon James's thigh – or rather upon the bulge within his breeches which signified just that warmth against which I was preaching!

'But you know that there are various positions which can be adopted in lovemaking.'

It was a statement rather than a question – but again I saw from the cloud upon the young girl's brow that she misunderstood me, and realised that her youth was such that in fact she had not so much as considered the matter. Happily, I had the means of illustrating my statement, and going to my luggage removed from it a portfolio of drawings copied from the works of Aretino, and showing a handsome couple in those postures which the educated lover must command. Handing these to James, I permitted him to turn the pages, which I noticed he examined with an attention quite equal to that of his mistress, and inferred that he was almost as ignorant as she in the matter of the postures of love.

In parenthesis, I should say that upon considering the matter later, I concluded that my own familiarity with these same drawings – which dated from the period when I was James's fellow-servant at Rawby – was somewhat unusual in a young person of ignoble birth; I was shown them, originally, by the grandfather of the Rawby sisters – one Beau Rust – who himself not only knew and studied them, but wished to counterfeit them, and to that end had paid myself and young Tabby to imitate them, which we had done with all the enthusiasm and energy of youth, it being our first lesson in that variation which to the educated lover lies at the very heart of the successful continuation of a connection which might otherwise swiftly be vitiated by the lethargy of boredom.

James and Betty were, by the time they reached the end of the folio, both red in cheek and somewhat flustered, and James shifted uncomfortably in his chair.

'Now,' I said, 'for the purpose of this experiment, you, Betty, must assume the position in which James lies upon his back, and you mount him – 'tis shown, I believe, in the fifth of those drawings.'

They turned the pages, and Betty giggled somewhat.

'I assure you,' I said somewhat sternly – for if the matter were to be resolved this was no matter for mirth – 'that pleasure is not diminished by the posture; indeed I am assured that for the lady, 'tis somewhat increased. At all events,' I continued, 'having assumed the position, you may enjoy your congress until that moment when James almost reaches his apogee . . .'

Another blank look interrupted me.

'Until he is about to come,' I resumed, somewhat impatiently. 'At that moment, you must raise yourself from him and grasp his instrument firmly just below its head, applying a steady pressure – almost to the point of pain. This will result in the suppression of the explosion which otherwise would be inevitable; and after a while you may resume your pleasure.

'This may be repeated several times, until either you have achieved your own satisfaction, or by some accident James's delight overflows. But in any event after a few repetitions you will find that the time which elapses between the moment of your first mounting him and the collapse of James's instrument will be lengthened, and in due course sufficiently so for you to play upon each other like a peal of bells, timing to a certainty the final chime.'

There was a short pause.

'Thank you, sir,' said Betty, though somewhat uncertainly.

'You do not trust my judgement in the matter?' I asked, perhaps upon the edge of ill-temper.

'No, no, sir,' she said hastily; ' 'tis just that for folk like we 'tis much to take in at one time. Perhaps you would allow us to borrow these papers . . . ?'

But to this I could not consent, for they were bought in Italy at no small expense, and 'twas my rule never to let them out of my possession.

Betty at this point whispered something to James, who whispered back, and then in a moment turned to me, though very uncertainly.

'Betty asks,' he stuttered, 'wh – whether you might consent to – to allow us to practise for a moment under your commanding – if 'tis not asking too much.'

I could not refuse such a request, for having offered advice 'twould have been of the utmost cruelty to decline to make it clear.

There needed no pause for readying, for the moment James's breeches were off his instrument sprang up against his belly, and indeed was so emboldened by anticipation that when he was laid upon his back and Betty, bare as a bodkin, knelt over him, 'twas almost painful to him to have it raised to the vertical. That she too was prepared for the event was beyond doubt, for, lacking no lubricant, she sank upon even that giant cock without the slightest sign of distress, its length vanishing until her bush met his own in the closest conjunction.

What would have happened had I merely loaned them the Aretino drawings I cannot think, for neither had the slightest idea of how to act. Though I have no reason to doubt that James, at least, was entirely unaccustomed to swiving, this strange (to him) posture seemed to deprive him of all instinct, while Betty contented herself with a kind of shuffling movement, rubbing her buttocks against his thighs, and at the same time bending his tool in such a way that his discomfort clearly outweighed his pleasure. This in itself might as a matter of course have had the desired effect; but that was not my intention.

There was some difficulty, too, in that Betty had never sat a horse, so my instruction to her to trot on went for nothing; and in fact it was necessary for me to climb upon the bed, stand behind her, and, placing my hands beneath her armpits, to lift and drop her several times before she got the idea, and of herself took up the proper motion. Happily, when set upon the right road, instinct is quick to learn; and within a very few moments James was incoherently attempting to convey his imminent death – at which Betty showed no sign of slowing (so keen was her own pleasure), and I had once more to take a hand, lifting her bodily from him. Seizing her hand, I placed its thumb and finger in the desired position just below the handsome bulb which stood at the end of his riding-muscle.

The pressure she exerted must have been considerable, for I could see the flesh giving way to it. The expected effect was produced, and in a short time James was inviting her to ride again – until the finishing-post was once more sighted, when the action was repeated. No less than five times he refused the final jump, until Betty, with a happy cry and an increase from trot to canter and finally to gallop brought both herself and him off in happy simultaneity, both then collapsing in a happy mass of perspiring flesh.

Their gratitude need scarcely be reported; having dressed herself, Betty went off to fetch fresh linen – my own being dampened and crinkled by their actions – while James wrung my hand again and again.

The couple then left me to myself.

I must confess that I was somewhat in pain, for the exhibition at which I had been a mere spectator (though in a manner the manager) had, I confess, roused me. Yet where was I to turn for satisfaction? I would not force myself upon Betty, even if a buttered bun (as is the common parlance for possession of a woman recently had by another) had appealed to me. Mrs Treglown was no doubt in a sleep of passionate purity; and 'twas too late now to seek out a lady of the town, though, Devonport being a naval port, there was no doubt a harbourful of such pussies to be had for a shilling.

Few men will not recognise my state, nor fail to follow me when I speak of the interminable fantasies and memories which pressed themselves upon my sleepless brain – most particularly, I must confess, of the house which my friend and I had managed in Brook Street, London (an adventure retailed in my volume *Eros in Town*); being then some years younger, I had not – at least, so it now seemed – been aware of the privilege of living day in and day out in a house populated by some of the most beautiful young women in the city, each for much of the day clad in the most appealing *dishabille*, and any one of whom would have regarded it as no less an honour than a duty to have permitted me the most egregious intimacy, or to have given me, upon my request, every pleasure at their command.

What would I not have given to be for half an hour returned to that harem, to repair to the bed of Sally or Xanthe, Cissie or Rose, or the charming Ginevra, and to enjoy their practised caresses? Then there came to plague me the most vivid memories of other women – the delicious girls of Italy, of Egypt, of Ceylon, of Siam . . .

But in short, I was condemned to my lonely bed,

relieved only towards dawn by the dream of a Circassian maid whose attentions brought me to involuntary ecstasy.

Next morning, we set out for Cornwall – for it was agreed that Mrs Treglown should travel with me as far as the town of Liskeard, where we would go our separate ways. We crossed the river Tamar into that county upon a ferry rowed by eight strong men; and on the further shore our luggage was placed in a carriage commissioned for the purpose – Frank's equipage having been stabled at Plymouth Dock until I should need it for a return to London, for it would have been expensive and supererogatory to ship it across the wide river.

As we drove into Cornwall it was to the sound of the merry voices of James and Betty, singing as they sat upon the box.

Mrs Treglown in a while observed that they were more cheerful than had been their wont of late, and asked whether I knew why?

I said that I believed that their high spirits were the result of the resolution of a problem.

She was silent for a while, and then asked if I meant that their affair had progressed to the point at which James had been permitted the ultimate favour?

It was, I remarked, a little more than that.

In what way, she asked?

Whether it will be considered the conduct of a gentleman or no, I must confess that I enlightened her. Truth to tell, I was by now thoroughly tired of her touch-me-not flouncing. If she was determined to permit a gentleman no familiarity, why had she consented to travel in a closed carriage with him for several days? Was my action in rescuing her from an uncomfortable – nay, perhaps fatal – circumstance to go entirely unrewarded?

At all events, goaded by her goodness, I described in full detail the predicament our servants had faced, my advice in the matter, and the culminating passage which had resulted in their mutual enjoyment of each other, and the consequent lifting of their spirits.

It took no great powers of observation to remark that her own spirits were lifted by my narrative. Her breath now came short, her breasts rose and fell more quickly, her fingers toyed with her fan. Nor could I believe that she did not remark my distress – distress I say, for my arousal was such that my trousers, fashionably tightly cut, now painfully constricted that part of my anatomy analogous to the instrument with which Betty had so admirably coped, in James.

I could not resist it – I threw myself upon her, my hand slipping into her bodice, there to find a springy, delicious dome the tip of which was an adamant knot which almost scratched my palm, so ardently erect was it! There could be no doubt: the lady was as ready for the combat as I! Indeed, her lips parted to meet my own, her tongue as ready as mine to embrace.

Yet what was this? Once more, after but a moment, she withdrew her lips, seized my wrist and wrenched my hand from her breast. For a moment she panted, then drawing herself up:

'Mr Archer,' she said, 'I beg you, desist. Cognisant as I am of all your kindness, apprehensive of your generosity, proud to be the object of your passion – I cannot be yours. A gentleman such as I know you to be will be unwilling to take advantage of a female who cannot permit those familiarities which . . .' (her eyelids drooped to hide eyes in which, I could swear, passion still burned) '. . . would lead to a result desired only by the senses, and which would be, I assure you, tragic for both.'

I could do nothing but withdraw – though to pretend that I did so with good grace would be to put myself forward as an angel; and at that moment 'twas the Devil who would have had the upper hand, had I given him the opportunity.

We rode on in silence – I am ashamed to say, sullen silence – until, not long after midday, we drew into the main square of Liskeard.

There, Mrs Treglown descended, and had to walk but a few yards to a carriage which awaited her (summoned by a fast messenger sent the previous day from Plymouth Dock). She made her curtsy to me; I bowed to her. I was in no doubt that her feelings towards me were warm; but could not comprehend her refusal to be kind. Our parting was regrettably cold – which could not be said for that of Betty and James, whose embrace was long, and sufficiently hot to provoke encouraging cries from the yokels standing nearby.

I descended and took lunch at Webb's Hotel, while Mrs Treglown's carriage rattled down the street and down the county. I realised that I had not the slightest notion where she lived.

Finally – and after, I must confess, several glasses of claret – I shook my head, and turned my thoughts to the estate to which I must now make my way.

Chapter Four

Sophie's Story

It was not long before I heard again from the interesting M. Foutarque.

A message was brought me one morning, written upon writing-paper bearing the seal of the French Embassy, and requesting an interview later that day. I sent back by the footman (none other than the ready Jacques, who met my eye with a frankness illustrated by a smile at once friendly yet devoid of pertness) a note requesting the Frenchman to call upon me after luncheon.

He greeted me with the greatest politeness, accepting coffee rather than wine, complimenting me upon the decoration of my rooms, and not giving by the slightest hint of discourtesy any intimation of undue familiarity.

After a while, he came to the point, which was that his Ambassador wished to give an entertainment for a party of visiting representatives of his Government who (though M. Foutarque did not put it in so many words) it would be to his advantage to impress. The gentlemen concerned were young - as were many members of the Ultra-royalist party now in the ascendant in France - and it was the Ambassador's understanding that female company would be welcome to them. He - M. Foutarque, that is - had been commissioned to look about the town in quest of young persons of my sex who might be secured for some entertainment; but had been disappointed, the company most readily available being invariably of a low order, and not such as would give an impression of amiability.

I gathered that the gentlemen in question had little experience of intrigues of an amorous nature, and M. Foutarque readily admitted his own inexperience in the matter – King Louis XVIII being, as he explained, a cold and distant monarch not given to pleasure, who had collected about himself a court and ministers whose members shared his lack of interest in the earthier matters of life, which indeed had in general been condemned since the late Revolution.

However (the Frenchman said, coming at last to the point), some of the younger politicians of the age took a more vigorously amorous view of things, and the Ambassador had been given to understand (under the secrecy of his diplomatic boxes) that an entertainment of an erotic nature would be welcome to the visitors. So what was needed was someone to organise the same.

'You will correct me, *madame*, if I am mistaken, but I am given to understand that in time past you presided over a house of entertainment in Chiswick.'

I admitted it; but pointed out that it had been a house in which gentlemen were kept for the entertainment of ladies, rather than the other way about.

'So I understood,' said Foutarque; 'yet I cannot but believe that the experience must have brought you a considerable knowledge of the way in which such matters are best set about; and it is my commission on behalf of the Ambassador to invite you to arrange an evening's entertainment of a – a – of such a nature as you will understand. I need not say that any fee you may think proper will be paid to the participating ladies, and to yourself; while as an earnest of his goodwill the Duc asks you to accept this gift' – whereupon he whipped out from his back pocket a small leather pouch, and from it drew the most magnificent emerald ring, which he set upon the small table at my side.

Preventing myself – if with some effort – from diving straightway upon it, I inclined my head and said that it would give me great pleasure to serve the Ambassador, for the mutual friendship of our nations, and enquired the number of gentlemen to be entertained – which was to be a round dozen – and the date by which the entertainment must be ready – which was within the week, and gave me little time for my arrangements. I then rose immediately, assured M. Foutarque that the matter was in good hands, bade him farewell, and straightway sat down to write some letters.

My experience at Chiswick was of little use to me – but what perhaps the Frenchman had not known was that my half-brother Frank and his friend Andy had at that same time furnished and equipped perhaps the finest house of pleasure for gentlemen in town – and being of a methodical nature, I had kept about me a list of some of the ladies who had worked there, many of whom indeed I counted as friends. Though they were somewhat dispersed, there were some upon whom I believed I could count if not for their personal intervention, at least for advice. Sending out the letters upon that same day, I did not rest, but set about other matters not entirely unconnected with the coming event, which involved the bespeaking of a large room in Covent Garden and its furnishing, at one end, with a low stage; the decoration of that stage with various cloths and properties; and the provision of certain comforts for the body of the room itself.

Upon the day in question, mid-evening saw me fully prepared to receive the guests, who in time appeared, escorted by M. Foutarque and replete from a good dinner at the Embassy at which wine had evidently flowed freely – not too freely, I trusted, to have deprived the gentlemen of their sense of corporeal pleasure, for I did not wish my efforts to go unwasted.

I soon concluded that I need have no concern, however, for the gentlemen were young and lusty, and, though I understood that no hint of the kind of entertainment in store had been dropped, upon their first sight of the room I had prepared their eyes brightened, and they exchanged a number of comments in their native tongue which I understood as being expressive of proper anticipation.

The room indeed had an air of seduction. The gentlemen who had decorated the Brook Street apartments of my half-brother had hung it in velvets and silks which disguised otherwise bare, cracked walls (the room, though indeed used in general for the purpose for which I intended it, was usually contracted to the poorer sort of person, and lacked the conditions of luxury). At one end of the room stood the stage, covered with a green cloth and hung about with curtains which I had obtained from the Theatre Royal in Drury Lane, suggestive of a woodland glade. Here also were soft stuffed cushions representing little mounds or grassy banks, obtained from the same source.

The body of the hall contained twelve small gilt chairs set out in rows; but around the walls and elsewhere in the room were comfortable sophas or *chaises-longues*, together with more large cushions spread for comfort as much as decoration; and the whole lit by candles, the brightest light being at the front of the stage, where a row of candles was set out before reflecting mirrors, as used now in the best theatres – the rest of the apartment being lit merely to a soft glow.

The gentlemen were greeted with a glass of champagne, borne upon a tray by a young black boy – the son of a gentleman who had been one of the most popular stallions of my Chiswick stable; and in a buzz of interest settled themselves upon the chairs and waited with what seemed keen anticipation – answered almost immediately by the soft sounds of a guitar behind the scenes, and the appearance upon the stage of six maidens apparelled like Grecian nymphs, who disposed themselves in a pleasant group for the approbation of the audience.

I am the first to admit that my knowledge of the fashion of clothing worn by nymphs is not great, and was in this case based merely on the appearance of those classical statues upon view in the great Museum in Russell Street. I had obtained from a shop in the Burlington Arcade a length of the finest material, so thin as to resemble something spun by spiders rather than by the hands of man. This had been cut into half a dozen lengths – which allowed only a relatively skimpy portion for each girl, the material being sufficiently costly to inhibit my spending more upon it (despite M. Foutarque's assurance that all my expenses would be met). Both by its nature and skimpiness it revealed as much as it concealed; and where it concealed, did so most imperfectly.

I had been fortunate in my friends, who, though they were all now permanently retired from the profession which had first brought them into contact with me, had been from their nature unable entirely to separate themselves from the society in which they had formerly been employed, and were thus able to recommend a number of handsome young ladies whose charms were as diverse as their faces and figures: here a chubby cherub whose youthful figure was full, her breasts positively inviting the support of a gentleman's palm; there another whose torso might almost be that of a boy, were it not that her movements were clearly informed by a feminine grace; here a tall and willowy girl whose thighs seemed prolonged almost to an infinite extent; there one who could only be called plump, yet whose appeal was in direct proportion to the plentiful, rosy flesh which hung upon her frame.

There was a ripple of applause from the interested audience as the ladies took their places – when almost immediately, with a discordant note upon the guitar, an equal number of satyrs leaped rather than strode upon the stage. The reception given to them was one as much of surprise as approbation – for they seemed almost inhuman, much of their bodies covered with thick animal hair, and their male members each entirely ready for amorous conquest, so that both in their appearance and readiness they provoked as much astonishment as envy.

As to the latter, I should explain that, until a moment before the girls entered upon the stage, they had been employed – on my instructions – in provoking their partners, by various means, into the proper state of excitation, the angles of appreciative rigidity diminishing by only a degree or so before they presented themselves to the public view; and now, each making for his partner, the prospect before them was sufficiently inspiriting to maintain them in the state of arousal in which they were first seen.

Their general appearance had been achieved without difficulty. The manager of costumes at the Lane had supplied to me a large quantity of human hair, generally used for the provision of beards for those actors incapable of growing their own, and a bulk of horse-hair used for other purposes. After explaining the nature of the entertainment I had devised, I encouraged my players, first removing their clothing, to daub their bodies with a quantity of gum which I had obtained from the same source.

They at first showed considerable reluctance – but one of them, himself an actor, was able to assure the others that the gum could be easily dissolved by the application of a certain spirit (of which I also had a supply), and even demonstrated the same, whereupon they surrendered, and in no short time were using the gum to apply the hair to their own and each other's bodies, covering their legs, buttocks and lower chests with hair – so that in a brief time they bore the closest resemblance to satyrs that could be wished for. My own task was merely to provide the finishing touches, ensuring that their appearance was sufficiently wild by applying here and there an additional tuft or curl.

The ladies, when brought together in rehearsal, were at first amused and then to a degree excited by the sight of their partners – which indeed was an interesting one, for amid the clusters of hair which covered the gentlemen's bodies there soon arose, upon their closer proximity with the nymphs, an element which, while recognisably as human as it was male, was by its relative nudity even more striking than was usually the case.

Indeed, so amorous did the couples become (upon my pairing them off) that I had some difficulty in restraining their enthusiasm to the proper degree, resulting in mere excitation rather than any actual accomplishment.

Once upon the stage, however, there was no further need for restraint - and indeed that would have been inappropriate. The largest of the satyrs was a man normally engaged in delivering coals, and therefore equipped with an enviable strength (he was also, incidentally, so sufficiently hirsute that it had been almost unnecessary to decorate him with additional material!). Chosen by me for the central role of my tableau, he now seized upon a nymph and raised her into the air by the simple expedient of placing his hands beneath her buttocks. As the others formed an admiring group about the couple, she threw her legs about his waist, and he was able, simply by drawing her body towards him, to insert his powerful instrument into the sheath most appropriate for its receipt, aided by the youngest nymph, who appeared a mere child (though in fact older than she was ready to admit), who ensured that the target was properly reached by the careful manipulation of the coalman's remarkable member. Upon his fully accomplishing of his aim, there was more applause from the audience as he began by the motion of his powerful arms to move his mistress in such a way as to give them both satisfaction.

The other couples now disposed themselves in various ways about the stage. One satyr turned his maiden - the plumpest in view - so that while she bent double, holding on to the lowest branch of a tree (actually, of a chair covered with a green cloth) he was able to enter her from the rear - affording the audience an excellent view of the proceeding. Another laid himself down upon a tussock while his friend bestrode him; a fourth, over-eager for the fray, merely threw himself upon his partner in the most conventional of poses, their eagerness – her loins reaching upwards to meet his on the descend with a positive and vigorous *slap*! – compensating for the mundane nature of their action; while a fifth addressed his attentions to an aperture which, while proximate to the proper one, is more rarely used for the purpose, his friend giving a short cry of surprise which in no time turned to an expression of pleasure as the unusual friction was joined by that afforded by the application of her lover's forefinger to the most eager part of her body. The final couple took up a position right at the front of the platform, so that the candle-light burnished their skins almost to gold; here, the nymph lay upon her back and persuaded her satyr to kneel above her in such a manner that while he could pleasure her with his agile tongue, she at the same time was able to take his member between her lips while simultaneously toying with his cods in a suggestive and pleasant manner – so pleasant, indeed, that in a very short time his excitement was too great to bear, and his pleasure reached its apogee as he spent liberally upon her breasts.

At this, a young Frenchman sitting in the front row – and therefore only a short distance from them – could no longer contain himself, and, pausing only to remove his breeches, gave the red-faced satyr a push which sent him sprawling, and took his place (though in a more usual pose). In no time he was at the game, his coat-tails swinging over his bare rump as he lunged appreciatively.

I now gave a signal, and a further six young ladies, all clad – or rather unclad – for just such an evening's entertainment as was now under way, entered the room;

and in less time that I can relate, each of the French gentlemen was in Britain – or in a Briton; and my satyrs disconsolately made their way from the stage, their partners now otherwise employed.

Pausing only to see that matters were as I would wish them, I took myself to the neighbouring room, where most of the gentlemen were already removing the hair from their bodies, and moved among them with purses of guineas, which were most appreciatively received – even by the couple who, too moved by their recent experience to remain unsatisfied, lay together in a corner, pausing only momentarily in their activities to take their purses with mumbled thanks (their mothers evidently having failed to instruct them not to speak with their mouths full).

In a short while most of the gentlemen had taken themselves off; I realised then that I had still one purse with me. Searching for its owner, I walked upon the side of the stage, and saw a satyr concealing himself behind a curtain and watching with attention the scene before him (which indeed was one which, while I hesitate to describe it for fear of offending the sensibilities of my readers, was of a perfectly amorous nature).

Walking forward, I tapped him upon his shoulder, whereat he started and looked up, proving to be the most youthful of the group, a mere boy of perhaps seventeen years who was engaged by the company at Drury Lane for small parts – an activity for which he now seemed to me to be but imperfectly suited, for on his turning he revealed a part which was far from small, and indeed so distended that it must surely be positively painful to him.

I must confess that it is ever my sorrow to see hunger unsatisfied – especially in those of tender years; and stretching out my hand raised the unwilling satyr to his feet, attempting with my other hand to conceal that part of his anatomy that even two hands could scarcely have disguised. By laying my hand upon the limb in question, I at once signalled that I was not offended at its impudence, while at the same time conveying the hope that its hunger might shortly be assuaged. The satyr, young in years but clearly quick in apprehension, accompanied me without argument to the now deserted dressing-room, where, laying myself down upon a pile of spare cushions, I drew him after me, and in a moment was able to satisfy myself that the boy was as able as he was willing.

The truth was that he was the satyr who had over-speedily reached his climax, and started the party which still progressed next door; but this, it seems, must have been due to his inexperience, for the more conventional congress which now took place was quite sufficiently prolonged to satisfy me, his at first excited and febrile thrusting soon quieting itself to a sort of swinging gait which by simple perseverance raised me not once but twice to my apogee; whereat, satisfied, I brought him off by the simple expedient of twisting some of the hair which decorated his rump and tearing it away by sheer force, the sudden pain of which did his business.

On his raising himself, we found that the muck of sweat which had perforce accompanied his efforts – the heat of the candles having greatly raised the temperature of the apartment – had loosened the hair which had decorated his thighs, lower belly and chest, much of which now adhered to my body; something which caused us considerable amusement. The superfluous decoration however was easily removed by the simple application of a wet cloth, while I was forced to assist the boy by using spirit to remove the hair from his back, revealing a body as devoid of hair as a girl's, a pair of deliciously round and hard posteriors rousing my spirits so that only his exhaustion precluded a renewal of our recent enjoyment. His instrument, while enlarging itself under the pleasure of my touch, stopped short of complete rigidity, even under the attention of my lips; whereat the boy apologised prettily, admitting in the end that on that morning he had twice enjoyed a maid at his lodging house – and that the fourth encounter of the day had 'finished him'.

Needless to say, I sympathised, carefully taking a note of his name before he left, professing his eagerness to serve in any future entertainment of the same nature, for (said he) being paid to perform an action he so enjoyed was positively gilding the gingerbread.

It was past three in the morning before I was able to persuade my French guests to leave, for while several of them had by midnight fallen into a sleep comprised equally of drunkenness and corporeal satisfaction, three or four seemed insatiable, and each partnered several girls before they declared themselves contented. I could not but feel that M. Foutarque should be satisfied, as I saw the last of the girls from the now disordered room and locked the door upon a state of chaos which it would be a matter for others to clear up.

To be short about it, M. Foutarque was as good as his word – as was indeed M. le Duc de Laval, for, apart from providing the purses of gold for my performers, on the day following the entertainment he had another purse delivered at my house, which upon examination contained some fifty pounds – a payment which seemed distinguished by profligacy – so the exercise was quite as satisfactory (in a financial sense) as might have been hoped.

The week after this interesting escapade, I was invited by Chichley to make use of his box at Drury Lane – he and his wife being absent in the country – on the occasion of Mrs Sloman's performance of Juliet; whereupon, on the Nurse entering the stage accompanied by her servant Peter, I thought his appearance to be somewhat familiar to me – and on his speaking was assured that it was none other than John Rice, the young man whose attentions I had enjoyed during the closing hours of my entertainment. I found myself surprisingly pleased to see him again, and after the performance – during which he distinguished himself as much as was possible given the diminutive nature of the part – went around to the stage door-keeper's box and on slipping him a shilling gained entrance to the back of the stage and made my way, on direction, to the lad's dressing-room.

I am not sure that I could satisfactorily explain my motive in so doing – except that I had taken to the boy, which in itself is surely a sufficient motive for a lady of spirit? As I was some years his elder, it would perhaps provide the opportunity for me to help him in his theatrical career.

On reaching the dressing-room door, I knocked and immediately threw it open, revealing a number of gentlemen in, or partly in, or partly out of, their smallclothes – who nevertheless, being used to close proximity with actresses, who are as little given to the taking of offence as to undue modesty, took little notice of me, and continued their dressing and undressing.

I must remark, in parenthesis, that I have some sympathy with the late Dr Samuel Johnson, who, upon introduction to the pleasures of the theatre dressing-rooms, remarked at length to his friend Mr Boswell that he would go no more behind the scenes, lest the bosoms of the actresses arouse his amorous propensities. There is indeed a peculiar attraction about the scene, attributable perhaps to the glamour of the performances in which the actors have lately been engaged – and partly, no doubt, to the fact that for the most part their companionship is to be easily purchased by any interested party. It has been the custom for certain members of the aristocracy to introduce their male progeny to the art of love through the convenient services of actresses, who even in youth have through the moral laxity of their profession gained experience in the matter valuable to schoolboys adept at the conjugation of Latin verbs, but not in conjunction of a more corporeal nature.

The sight which met my eyes, then, was a delightful one; and when from among the cluster of male bodies my friend came forward immediately, though dressed only in his shirt (which offered entrancing confirmation of my recollection of a pair of lower limbs remarkable both for muscularity and shapeliness), and greeted me with a kiss upon the lips which I much confess to finding sweet, I was the more pleased.

'So my note reached you, Mrs Nelham!' he remarked; 'I trust it gave no offence?' – a remark which reduced me to a puzzled silence. Seeing my expression, he himself was confused, and when I informed him that no such communication had reached me, his expression changed to one of embarrassment. However, when encouraged he confessed that he had been so taken with my company (I report his words without the intention to boast) that he wished to ensure a further meeting, and had therefore invited me to accompany him to a stage entertainment on this very evening!

The coincidence was too convenient not to be meaningful, and I accepted with pleasure – at which he immediately donned his breeches, and prepared to set forth. On my inquiring the nature of the entertainment, he blushed somewhat, and said that 'twas one of which he had had no personal experience, but which, judging from the occasion on which we had met, was something in which I would be interested – that is, of a libidinous nature (though he expressed it by the statement that ' 'tis a cock-raising occasion', which was clear enough; and I did not embarrass him by pointing out that such entertainments were not the usual thing for me, outside of a business engagement).

We walked from Covent Garden to a house in the district of Soho, where, on his knocking on a street-door and exchanging a word, we were admitted to what seemed a private house, and escorted to a room on the first floor where a table was set for supper – and indeed shortly a very decent meal was served, with sufficient beer and wine.

The company was a mixed one, the other ladies present being of a somewhat lower social class than was usual with me – though agreeable enough; and at any event my own experience was such as had brought me into contact with women of every condition, all of whom I took as I found – usually discovering most of them to be good-natured enough, if unprovoked.

The feast having come to an end, we sat for a while over our wine, and John was good enough to pay me the compliment of saluting me several times with his lips, first upon the cheek, then upon the shoulder – my gown being cut low enough to permit not only this, but a further kiss upon the upper part of my breast. He was by now somewhat warm, as I discovered when, entirely by accident, my hand fell upon his upper thigh, discovering as it travelled inadvertently upwards a tumid pipette which signified the arousal of his spirits. My unconsciously pressing the same with my palm resulted in his slipping his hand, no doubt idly, under my skirts, where he soon found what he sought.

I cannot say what would next have occurred, had there not been a sudden stirring at the end of the room – when there entered a guitarist whom I recognised as the young man I had myself engaged (London is a small city) accompanied by a fellow with a tambour or small drum; and on their striking up a dance, a couple dressed in the manner of the Italian *commedia del' arte* as Columbine and Pantaloon, entered the room, leaped upon the table and began a spirited dance.

It soon became clear that their elaborate costumes were in fact ingeniously constructed, and fastened not by the usual employment of needle and thread, but by some other means which enabled the dancers to escape from them without effort – for upon Columbine reaching out, she in a second detached Pantaloon's collar; then he her *fichu*; then she one of his sleeves – then he one of hers; until, dancing the whole while, they were both reduced to nothing but a scarf about the loins, almost entirely revealing two bodies handsome enough to give as much pleasure to the eye as the most elaborately designed costume.

The rhythm of the dance now slowed, and in a languorous weaving motion they moved about each other upon the table above us, their hands gliding over each other's persons, over shoulders, under arms; one moment his hand would brush the engorged nipples of her breast, the next the back of hers would glance across his belly, whence a line of dark hairs descended into his groin, where the distinct shape of an upright staff revealed that his enjoyment of the engagement was as keen as that of any of the onlookers.

Many of the latter (though not my companion, whose youth was necessarily accompanied still by some shyness) had by now climbed or been helped out of their clothes, and were paying the dancers, without embarrassment, that peculiar form of compliment always aroused by the demonstration of beauty in action.

Finally, the dancers having performed every libidinous action which could be conceived, each at the same time, upon a peculiarly bitter chord upon the guitar, reached out and divested the other of the last covering – the lady revealing a quim entirely devoid of hair: a mouth entrancingly marked by lips of the palest pink, between which a slash of darker flesh marked the enviable entrance. Her partner, a man of uncertain years, but clearly in the greatest vigour, wore a muff which must have been carefully trimmed, for there were no random curls, but a closely cropped crown which enhanced by emphasis the base of a staff the angle of whose standing bespoke ample strength for its purpose – which was shortly accomplished, the lady merely dropping backwards so that, like an acrobat in an old picture, she supported herself upon her hands and feet, like a table, her body parallel to the ground.

Her companion now stepped forward between her open thighs, and, dropping to his knees, in a moment speared her – whereupon she threw back her head, her fine black hair falling to the very table's top, and emitted a positive yowl of pleasure, like nothing so much as that of a cat being pleasured upon a neighbouring roof-top.

Though, as my constant readers will know, I do not proclaim myself a *voyeur*, I must confess that this handsome couple, engaged in the act in such close proximity, conveyed the pleasure of it to me so keenly that I almost felt I was experiencing it: my seated position permitted me to look up between the lady's legs, where with the utmost clarity I saw her partner's member working, piston-like, at its duty, the light of the candles (almost dangerously close-by) gleaming upon its shaft, now lubricated by the natural serum of love – while the unthatched lips of her pleasure-cave seemed to embrace it almost with the motions of a mouth, for I could swear that I saw them tighten about it as it withdrew, to close again as it re-entered.

Suddenly I was brought back to reality, for – quite unconsciously, I assure you – my hand had under the excitement of the moment found its way inside John's breeches (whether unloosed by him or by myself, I cannot say) and my fingers had closed around his apprehensive part – which now, to my horror, I felt give a bound which seemed to signal the immediate downflow of those liquids whose release must deprive a lady of all further pleasure.

I whipped my hand away as from a flame – and at the same time with my other hand removed his own from between my thighs, where by an incessant movement it had, I confess, been giving me some pleasure.

The poor boy looked hurt, but by my smile I was able to comfort him by the assurance of better things to come – while at the same moment, above us, another cry from the lady signalled the culmination of the act; for, withdrawing, her partner laid upon her belly the tribute of his pleasure; whereupon a strange noise echoed around the room, a kind of soft drumming which at first confused me, until looking about I discovered that the gentlemen present were applauding the performers by knocking their distended members upon the table-top!

Some of them, the moment the table had been cleared, disappeared beneath it with their partners; others made their way slyly from the room – no doubt to other private rooms available in the house.

John looked at me somewhat confused, not knowing, I think, what to say or do. I however rose, and resting my hand upon his bade him button himself.

'I have a more comfortable place than this,' I said, and motioned him to accompany me.

The journey to Chiswick was all too long, especially as I had to spend much of the time (much against my will) dissuading my companion from those over-warm familiarities which I feared might lead to the dissipation of his energies before our arrival. Once at my house, however, my bedroom provided us with more luxury than would have been available in any common knocking shop. John's face was a picture as he saw the extent of my comfort. I am sure that he had not realised the state in which I lived; but his amazement did not last long, for in a moment he had thrown off his clothes and was bouncing upon the sheets of my bed, and clearly inviting me to join him.

However, he had not washed himself since leaving the stage of the theatre, and if there is one thing upon which I insist (if it is convenient) it is the cleanliness of my partners in the act; in the ecstasy of love we need not repine should we be led to intimate caresses the pleasure of which would be inhibited by the presence of grease and grime. (I speak, of course, for those of us for whom the rank sweat of an enseamed bed, as Shakespeare's effete Hamlet put it, does not contribute to sensual excitement.) My servants' last duty every night is to place several containers of hot water in my bedroom, in case I should have company. In the winter these are kept warm by the propinquity of a large fire; in summer, however, as it now was, the waters are of just such a pleasant warmth as to be refreshing.

John was at first doubtful of the whole matter; but on my persuading him to enter the water, I was able to show him that the very act of being sponged by an attentive lover can contribute much to the anticipation of pleasures to come; and it was indeed my own delight to ensure that the most intimate crevices of his slender body were so clean that, should I wish to kiss any part of it, nothing but sweetness would await me.

Taking the idea, he was now pleased to attend to me in turn, taking special care of my breasts, which he clearly admired – for on our retiring at last to bed, it was to these that he paid particular tribute, kissing and mumbling the nipples, softly nipping them with his teeth, taking them between his fingers almost with the curiosity of a squirrel examining a nut; and finally, kneeling astride me, tickling them by the application of his very member itself, drawing back the skin at its tip so that its bland domed end could gently buffet them. This gave me such painful pleasure that the distension could no longer be born, and, taking his staff in my hands, I wrapped my breasts about it, simply in order to prevent for a moment the tickling.

His expression at this was one of the most egregious pleasure; and in a moment he began that motion which was wasted in such a pose. I threw up my legs, and with a heave of my body I positively pinned his neck between my calves; and seizing his small buttocks forced him not unwillingly to serve me as Adam first served Eve; our joint apprehension being such that only a very few motions of his body brought us off – whereat we collapsed and in a moment fell asleep in each other's arms.

Twice that night I was roused again: the first time by his instrument growing within me, for he had not withdrawn it, and in its shrunken state it had not fallen away (our close propinquity being such); and the second time when I awoke to find him lying behind me, a thigh thrust between my own, and his member again showing signs of affection which it was my duty to return, which I soon did by the simple expedient of reaching between my thighs and persuading it once more into its proper place, whereupon, half-asleep, he reached around to seize my breasts, pressed his face into my neck, and began a rocking motion which by its very quietness aroused feelings of such tenderness that I almost sobbed with the pleasure.

I next awoke when Charles brought my breakfast tray – retiring to return with a second cup, having with his sharp eye discerned the tousled black head of my companion almost concealed beneath the bed-clothes. John, waking at this, looked confused; but, upon seeing that Charles was not disconcerted, sat up, thrust his arm about me, and gave me a smacking kiss while at the same time reaching for a piece of bread.

Though he made a pretence of ease, I could see that he scarcely knew how to address me; whereat it was my duty to place him at his ease – and in brief, to offer him the hospitality of my house for a while. This may, but need not, surprise the reader: the truth is that I had been for some time now deprived of constant male companionship – something of which I am always keenly apprehensive; this young man interested me, and apart from the pleasure of his company – which I admit I found considerable – it seemed to me that I could be useful to him in educating him in the manners of the better sort of person, which would be of help in his career (for it is to the advantage of acting folk that they can counterfeit the behaviour of gentlemen).

Though my house was somewhat distant from the theatre, its comfort and – who can say? – perhaps the pleasure of my company persuaded him to accept my invitation, and fetching his belongings (which were not so numerous that they could not be encompassed within a couple of parcels) he moved into one of the servants' rooms – to him luxurious by its space, and convenient to us both by its being separated from my own only by a corridor and a staircase, neither of which proved obstacles to his progress to my bed on frequent occasions, even after the most exhausting of theatrical performances; none of which precluded the performance of a part more universal even than that of the drama's most notable hero.

Chapter Five

The Adventures of Andy

It was clear from the moment I was driven through the park gates at Vycken that my friend had inherited a very fine estate indeed.

Passing through the town of Lostwithiel, now insignificant but once the capital of the country, we had mounted one hill, descended another, then made off to the south and entered a series of narrow lanes winding through deep, heavily wooded clefts in the Cornish hills, eventually coming to a small keeper's house where two tall granite columns surmounted by mossy balls held a pair of handsome wrought-iron gates. The hills then drew aside, as if in deference to the visitor, and a broad valley stretched before me, its floor a broad parkland, trees giving heavy shade to cattle, which stood in groups that seemed carefully arranged to give the landscape point and drama.

At length there came into view the house itself – its façade of that granite from which so many buildings of the county are constructed. Consisting of a single-storeyed central building with two wings, one at each end, it had a symmetry exceedingly graceful to the eye, and seen at its best as the pathway swung about before it, to pass through a gate-house (from the window of which an ancient retainer hung, waving a hand and shortly afterwards retiring to ring, with a fine clangour, a bell which hung above the gateway).

From the gate-house, a splendid avenue of beeches and sycamores led to a second gate, through the east wing of the house itself, where was a cobbled forecourt where we stopped before the main door, which opening now disgorged at least twenty servants who by the time I had descended had formed into double ranks through which I passed, nodding from left to right like a monarch, but without at that time being able to take note of any individual faces.

I was greeted with a low but informal bow by the housekeeper – the steward – the butler – I know not what to call him – Mr Antony Treweers, who as it was to turn out had reigned over the place for the past thirty years, since the owner himself had virtually retired from life to reside solely in his bed-chamber, a poor room at the back of the house. His mania was for complete quiet, to which end he had thick blankets hung in many layers about his room on all sides, covering even the windows, his life being lived entirely by candle-light. The candles catching light to some of the hangings, he had been smothered one night in his sleep, and the burning down of the entire building only avoided by the lucky accident of a maid, rising early, sniffing smoke as she passed down the corridor outside his room.

It was at five in the afternoon that I arrived, but on walking into the hall – set just inside the main door, and proving a nicely proportioned long chamber panelled in some dark wood – I found nevertheless a table groaning under an immense quantity of food which, after a short pause to refresh myself and answer the necessities of nature, I was glad to sit down to.

The Cornish notion of hospitality depends largely upon food, which one finds always offered in great profusion, even by the poorest family living in the utmost poverty: when potato cakes or even seaweed pie will be placed before one, and one must eat it with enthusiasm if one is not to offend.

On this occasion I had in fact a healthy hunger, and was able to do some justice to the table – despite the fact that the banquet seemed to me to be strangely composed, for rather than coming in courses, as we in London eat it, the food was all set on the table at once. Here was fresh-boiled buttock of beef with onions; squab pie (layers of apple, bacon, onions and mutton, all piled upon a young squab or pigeon); leek and pork pie – into which thick cream had been poured; goose and parsnip on one dish; giblet pie (the neck, liver and other entrails of a goose, flavoured with raisins, sugar and apples); and at the centre of the table a chief delicacy of the county, known as starry-gazy pie: that is, a pie of pilchards baked with the fish lying in it, their heads projecting through the crust and their eyes goggling at the ceiling!

My enjoyment of the latter dish, to which my attention was drawn with great ceremony, was somewhat dampened when I discovered upon my plate a fish's backbone of extraordinary hardness. The woman who had served me immediately said 'Let me see, my dear!' and seized the plate, rooted about upon it, and then exclaimed: 'Why, that edn' no fish bone at all. That's our Johnny's hair comb, what he lost two days ago – careless little emp!'

This would have put some people off their meat – and I might have been among them, had not the food been so rich and delicious, and the servants so eager and willing to please – Mr Treweers among them, who stood at my side throughout, seeing that a large tankard before me was kept full of first-rate cider, prepared upon the estate, for which it is justly famous. I might have been less inclined to consume so much as I did had I known at that time that the drink's excellence was owed in no small degree (so the master of the cider press later informed me) to the practice common at Vycken, as elsewhere in Cornwall, of always putting a toad into the cask, the cider being purified by passing again and again through the creature's body. Indeed, no cider in this county is considered up to the mark unless it has a toad to 'work' it, some toads living for over twenty years in this fermenting work (when the cask is empty the creature is tipped out through the bung-hole, and the people standing by exclaim: 'Mind the toad, mind the toad, save 'un for the next brewing!').

Mr Treweers, encouraging me to try this dish and that, finally so pressed upon me large helpings of excellent blackberry pie that I could scarcely stand when, it being almost eight o'clock, I rose and made my way unsteadily to the chamber prepared for me. I only dizzily noticed that this was a fine, great room over the main hall, with a window stretching from floor to ceiling through which I had an expansive view over the park even from my bed, before, thrusting off my clothes and falling upon rather than into the vast four-posted bed, I instantly fell into a deep sleep from which I awoke to see the sun slanting over the park as he rose, and to hear a dawn chorus which, truth to tell, sounded extremely clamorous to a brain still somewhat under the effect of the cider – a drink which, while inspiriting to a degree, is not kind to the heads of those unaccustomed to it.

I staggered from the bed to the window, squinting at the sun; and only upon hearing laughter from below the window realised that I was standing in the full view of a quartet of maidservants, who now stood quite frankly goggling at the sight of their new master displaying himself entirely uncovered, and in that state in which gentlemen frequently awake after a night's debauch – *id est*, piss-proud. It being too late for concealment, I gravely inclined my head and raised a hand in greeting, merely clutching at the window curtain and raising it, as though absently, to cover that area of my anatomy which is normally concealed from public view. The maids dropped me a curtsy and passed on, their heads together, and their laughter continuing, though somewhat stifled.

I now rang, whereupon two girls – not, I was somewhat relieved to see, from the group which had made up my audience – carried in hot water and poured it into a bath concealed behind a screen, then offering to take from me the sheet which I had wrapped about myself; whereupon I made my ablutions aided by them in the matter of washing my back. Cornish maids, it seems, grow up in so close propinquity with their brothers (most families being crowded into small households) that the sight of a naked man is no great matter to them; moreover many of them are used to helping to cleanse their menfolk upon their return from working at sea, or in the fields, or in the tin mines. The result of this is that their attentions are severely practical rather than arousingly amorous, and one of them seizing my private parts and wringing them as she might a dish cloth gave me considerable anxiety as to whether she might render me incapable of paying a tribute to any notable beauties of the country who might fall in my way.

On my breakfasting, Mr Treweers waited upon me to ask whether it would be my pleasure to be driven over the estate; and, its promising to be a fine day, I commissioned the kitchen to provide a hamper of cold meats, and we set out.

The estate was, as I had thought, a comprehensive one, the land near the house (given over to a park) maintaining cattle, while further away towards the sea (of which an occasional glimpse could be caught, the sun sparkling on the waves) it became common farm land. At the extreme southern end of the estate, my friend's land marched with that of another estate, which was that, I was told, of Sam Treglown. The name came upon me strangely; Mrs Treglown had given me no sign that Vycken (a name which I had clearly pronounced to her several times) was next her husband's estate!

We ate our lunch upon a grassy knoll near a headland called Gribbin, commanding a fine view eastwards to that arm of the land concealing the harbour at Plymouth, while beyond could dimly be seen in this remarkably clear weather a cape which Treweers claimed was Prawle Point, protecting Dartmouth and Lyme Bay; to our west lay the small bay of St Austell, the Dodman Point, and beyond it again in the far distance the Lizard, west of which only the Mount's Bay separated us from the Land's End and that vast Atlantic ocean which stands between us and the Americas.

Our lunch consisted of a pasty, or wrapping of pastry placed about meat, potato and turnip, then baked in the oven – making a pie convenient to be carried; the same invented in order to provide a package of food for the tin miners, who carry it with them for their luncheon – it being an axiom with them that the best pasty is one which can be dropped from the mouth of a mine shaft, and which upon reaching the bottom of the mine remains intact (indeed the pastry is sometimes of considerable toughness, though the contents delicious). Some Vycken cider completed the meal, under the influence of which I fell after a while asleep – to be wakened only by a number of voices; and, on propping myself on an elbow, saw a procession of men making their way along a pathway near me.

I looked about for Treweers, who had however vanished; so getting up I followed the passers-by and in a mere hundred yards found myself upon the brink of a round, grassy hollow, a natural amphitheatre, where I saw Treweers sitting on the ground a little way away. On my joining him, he explained that this was to be a Cornish wrestling – an almost weekly occurrence upon a Saturday (which this was). I was tempted to believe that he had led me this way especially in order to attend the wrestling, and was further persuaded to the opinion by his exchanging compliments with a number of other gentlemen in the crowd.

This Cornish wrestling was a curious affair from the start, and was to become more curious. The number of young men who took part were clad in a sort of baggy trousers cut off at the knee and a loose coat of cloth, and seemed intent upon destroying each other with as much celerity as was consistent with the entertainment of the crowd. Only the use of their teeth seemed to be prohibited, for otherwise they caught each other not only by the clothing, but by the hair or any other part of the body, at the same time delivering kicks of considerable violence, directed at any vulnerable area which presented itself – meanwhile urged on by the spectators with cries not only in the vernacular but in the ancient Cornish language. A great deal of money changed hands, being betted upon the fighters – and in particular upon one Ned, a fine young giant of a fellow whose limbs were like young trees and who succeeded in disposing of every rival, emerging as the clear winner.

There was then a pause, during which there seemed an air of expectancy among the crowd. After a while a stout fellow stood upon the centre of the ring where combat took place and announced the final bout, which would be – he explained – between Dolly, of Par, and Jane, of New Quay – the latter champion of her *towen* or district, and newly come to the east of the county in search of new honours. He then asked who would buy? – at which there was a clamour of voices each contending with the other.

On my inquiring of Treweers what was going on, he informed me that though 'twas frowned upon by authority, unofficial meetings such as this one often culminated with a match between two women wrestlers; and that to raise money for them spectators were invited to 'buy'. The man who offered the largest sum attached to the eventual winner became entitled to a proportion of the whole sum promised to both; while the winner took an equal share.

This seemed a reasonable proposition; and in this case I was much taken by the smaller of the two contenders who strode upon the grassy sward. One – Dolly – was indeed an Amazon, broad as she was tall, with a swart, ugly face full of malevolence – and for her there was a great rivalry of bidders. However, it was the other, Jane, who caught my attention, having a lively little monkey-face from which a pair of black eyes twinkled merrily, and whose body seemed to me, though less powerful, to be no less sturdy and capable of quicker movement than the other. I therefore bid for Jane, and after only a little opposition won. Her being from a distant place (New Quay lying upon the northern coast of the county, to which few eastern men travelled) no one knew anything of her; and her frame being so much the smaller, it was not considered likely that she could prevail.

The manager of the affair having taken charge of the papers upon which we wrote our bets, there was now a hush among the crowd, the two women stepping forward and eyeing each other with some caution, each standing with her hands upon her hips. Their clothing was the same as the men's – that is, baggy trousers and loose coats of coarse cloth, the latter cut sufficiently loosely to afford an opponent the opportunity of clutching at it in order to be able to swing the other about – the aim of the combat being (as I should have said) for one to to deposit the other upon the grass, both shoulders upon the ground, for the space of a count of three. At this point there is a general shout of *Hal*!, and a point is awarded, two points being counted a complete victory.

Now, with a movement quicker than might have seemed possible for a woman of her size, Dolly stepped forward and caught the other by the front of the jacket, sweeping her sideways and across a raised leg so that she fell to the floor. In the fall she twisted herself free of her opponent's hands, and, contracting herself almost into a ball, rolled over and in the same movement regained her feet, to cries of approbation from the crowd. Jane then danced in, and, raising her foot almost to the level of her shoulders, delivered a smart blow with the sole of it to the side of the other woman's head, which sent her staggering. She followed by catching her by one arm, swinging her about, and, grasping the collar of her jacket, pulled it down over her shoulders so that it trapped her arms. Parting her own arms widely, she brought them together so that the insides of her forearms clapped the other's head as in a vice, and she fell dizzily to the ground – at which Jane leaped upon her, turning her so that her shoulders touched the greensward. A count followed, a round of applause (somewhat mild, the victor being a 'foreigner' – from a distant place in the county) signifying the first point.

Dolly, as she rose, looked extremely displeased – as well she might – and adjusted her coat with a business-like air. (I should say that Jane's rearrangement of it had disclosed what I had suspected – that beneath their coats the women wore no other covering, a pair of white, pendulous breasts having been revealed by the slighter woman's skilful disposition of her rival).

The pair now positioned themselves for a new skirmish, Dolly this time waiting for Jane to make the first move – which in a moment she did by moving forward, ducking beneath the slow, protective movement of Dolly's arms, and throwing her own about the body of her rival. The grip was obviously a tenacious hug, for the stouter of the ladies soon grew red in the face in her attempt to break free – whereat, taking advantage of one great effort, Jane loosed her opponent, and with a skilful motion (too speedy for the eye to discover precisely how it was accomplished) swung Dolly about, and gripped her from behind, her arms beneath the larger woman's armpits, and her hands placed behind her neck – a position obviously painful, for poor Dolly groaned audibly at the pressure put upon her, her head sunk towards her breast. But then, in a moment, she freed herself by the simple expedient of throwing her own arms above her head, and throwing herself downwards, thus slipping from Jane's grasp.

There was a ripple of applause at this ruse; but now Dolly rolled away, and in one movement was upon her feet and had grasped the hem of Jane's garment. She threw her to the ground, hurling herself upon her opponent and seeking to pin her. Grasped in each other's arms, the two women rolled upon the grass, gripping each other as best they might, their coats flying open to reveal their sweating bodies – Dolly's white (though grubby), Jane's as brown as a nut, presumably from working unclothed in the open air. That this was a sight most stimulating to the eyes of gentlemen need not be said – for to the concern of speculating on the eventual winner was added the interest of observing the unclothed bodies of two females in continual and exciting movement.

The noise was by now indescribable – catcalls opposed to enthusiastic applause, shouts of encouragement to the one woman combating cries of enheartenment to the other. Not that either seemed to pay attention either to supporters or denigrators, each being entirely fixed upon triumphing over the other.

I had for a moment turned from the main spectacle to look upon my fellows – arms raised in imprecation or approval, mouths wide open the better to give vent to noise; and in short each man entirely taken up in the combat before him, and its consequence. But in the moment when my attention had been diverted from the fight, it had taken a fresh turn, Dolly having once more gained a hold upon her opponent's coat, and, twisting it about, trapping one of Jane's arms in its folds – which gave her a sufficient advantage to be able for a moment to throw the other off-balance. A quick kick to the belly deprived her of breath, and enabled Dolly easily to throw her to the ground and hurl herself across her upper body, rendering it possible for the referee – a little, squat fellow with a squint – to make the necessary count; upon which Dolly rose with a smile of triumph, and, treading upon her still winded opponent's neck with her foot as she did so, raised her arms in a gesture of victory.

There was now a pause, while two old women came forward with water and bathed the combatants' faces and necks; when the referee exclaimed 'Time!', and both women rose to their feet, Jane, with a gesture which spoke defiance, immediately threw off her jacket and stood for a moment bathed in sunlight – the very picture of some warrior from the great age of heroic Greece or Rome, when women stood by their men in readiness for battle.

After a short and sharp intake of breath through the entire crowd of spectators, there fell a moment's complete silence, even those who most ferociously supported the popular local heroine being impressed by the splendid picture made by her rival, shoulders thrown back, proud breasts, brown as the rest of her body, seeming as though carved from teak, and beneath the surface of a skin whose smoothness showed no sign of wrinkle or looseness muscles which moved like metal springs. No opponent, man or woman, could surely face such a figure without some feeling of doubt, if not of positive fear? The next moment the surmise was confirmed, for with a vigorous leap Jane rose some feet from the ground, at the same time throwing both feet out in a kick which connected with the head of the unfortunate Dolly, sending her sprawling while the leaper dextrously regained her own feet, and threw herself after the other. As she pounced, Dolly, regaining her scattered senses, moved swiftly away – yet Jane had grasped the hem of her trousers, and clutched with such a recalcitrant grip that, despite any feelings of reluctance the other may have felt, she was forced to squirm out of them, whereat with a cry of disgust Jane threw them into the crowd!

Dolly now stood, clad only in her coat – beneath the skirts of which a large and heavy-cheeked bum disclosed itself – again ready for the attack; but once more Jane was too quick for her, and this time with a movement which again was almost quicker than the eye could follow, precipitated herself at the other woman's feet, at the same time curling her body so that it was half behind the other's legs, and threw her backwards – half-rising at the same time to lift Dolly's lower limbs so that her ankles were pressed one upon each side of her neck, her shoulders firmly to the ground, and displaying to those opposite a view of the larger woman's posterior parts which was as full as it was unappealing – at least to me, though not (from the roar of the crowd) to many of the rougher sort of spectators, some of whom from the descriptive nature of their comments may have had a closer acquaintance with the generously displayed anatomy of the loser than a mere transitory glimpse could afford.

The referee – who, being a local man, was partial to the local champion – counted as slowly as he could; but was not able to deny the smaller woman's triumph – whereat she rose and with a splendid show of disdain threw her defeated rival's legs to the ground and raised her arms once more in triumph.

There was now a great bustle as the few people who had bet upon the winner surrounded the referee to collect their gains; after which he stepped to me and handed me a purse which, from its weight, comprised a considerable sum – consisting, as I have said, of a proportion of all the bets placed upon both winner and loser. Dolly, meanwhile, was surrounded by a clutch of local men intent upon comforting her, while the winner stood alone (except for her attendant crone) – whereupon I stepped up to her, and with a bow presented her with the purse.

She looked astonished, such generosity (as I guessed) being far from common in those parts, at the same time, with a diffidence that touched me, reaching for her coat and holding it to conceal her still naked body. I bowed again, and turning looked for Treweers, who however had vanished from sight – gone, I guessed, with some cronies to comfort himself with cider (for I doubted that he had supported anyone from outside his own district, being, as one or two remarks of his had shown, intensely patriotic not merely of his county but even of his parish).

I began slowly to make my way along the path back to the place at which our horse had been tethered. After a moment I felt a touch upon my arm, and turning found Jane, still looking reserved and not in the least the picture of assurance which she had appeared when ready to give battle. On my raising an eyebrow and asking whether I could be of assistance, she merely smiled and tugged again at my sleeve, turning me off the path and through a gap in the hedge into a thicket, where a small clearing was paved by soft grass; and there, without further ado, she removed the jacket which alone covered her upper body, and, throwing herself upon me almost with the same enthusiasm with which she had attacked poor Dolly, bore me to the ground, where she kissed me with a violence which was as appetising as it was eager, at the same time wriggling her body accommodatingly against mine so that I was forced to open my legs, for my own comfort, whereupon she slipped between them. Forcing her thighs beneath my own, she began with eager fingers to unloose the ties of my shirt and then the catch of my belt.

It would be a fiction were I to say that I was not stirred by this turn of events; for the recent spectacle had been one which few men could have witnessed wholly without arousal; while a closer inspection of my captor's body confirmed that it was one which must surely appeal to every masculine emotion, her breasts being sufficiently full to be entirely feminine, yet without the merest touch of that slackness which comes with greater maturity, the nipples, brown as berries, neat and peaked, her flesh firm, with so little fat that at her sides the bones of the ribs could clearly be seen, and upon her shoulders and upper arms muscles which, moving beneath the skin, felt (when I placed my hands upon them, as now I did) like little lithe animals.

She paused now in her unbuckling, as I slid my palms down from her shoulders, resting for a moment to caress those delightful breasts (which now rose and fell more swiftly, it seemed, than they had done at any moment of her recent combat) and feel the beating of her heart; then descending to her waist, where, as they slid beneath the cloth of her trousers, I could feel again how firm and unencumbered with surplus flesh her body was.

My attempt to unveil her further was disallowed, however, by the fact that she was squatting between my thighs – and indeed that fact prevented her, once she had undone both shirt and belt, from disencumbering me of my clothing; whereat what I could only describe as a grin passed over her face, and, raising herself to her knees, she caught at the legs of my own trousers, and shuffling backwards drew them off – releasing from its discomfort a part of me that had been increasingly confined since the engorgement provoked by her presence.

It was the work of but a moment to wriggle from my shirt, to kneel, throw my arms about her and to press my face to that delightful bosom – at which I discerned that it was indeed firmer than any other in my experience, and supported by muscles which were clearly the result of considerable exercise. The nipples seemed to be almost as hard as finger-nails – so much so that I could not resist taking one between my teeth and nipping at it, whereat only a little chuckle of laughter came from Jane's lips, whereas other women would have expressed discomfort or positive pain.

I could not, meanwhile, prevent my hands from sliding up her thighs beneath the wide bottoms of her trousers (which, the reader will recall, reached only below the knee) and taking in my palms the tempting curves of her bottom, my fingers straying into the cleft between them – whereat, with a simple tension of her muscles, she exerted such pressure that it was almost impossible to remove them – and again that charming chuckle of laughter was heard.

But now she bent to draw off her trousers, and as she straightened I found within inches of my eyes a quim whose shape and proportions seemed to me then – and even in memory – to represent the ideal: the mound was marked and emphasised by a covering of black hair which was caught up into curls which stood around about it as though carefully disposed, decorating the portals like the proscenium of a theatre, embellishment without concealment. The portals themselves were of a deep red darkened almost to purple, giving way almost immediately to a lighter shade that became – as I parted them with fingers which now trembled not a little – the faintest and most delicate pink, while at their top there stood that miniature facsimile of the male instrument which is present in all women, but rarely is so perfect in verisimilitude as here, even to the tiny head to which I now paid tribute by the tip of my tongue – at which Jane, leaning, gripped my shoulders with such a hold as was positively painful.

But she was unwilling to spend any more time in preliminaries: simply sinking to the ground, she rolled backwards, drawing me with her by the simple expedient of gripping my upper arms with an entirely unbreakable hold, and, throwing her legs apart and transferring her hands now to my waist, without any more delay lifted me into that position most favourable for congress – whereupon, not unwillingly, I entered her.

It would be fruitless to advise every young man at some time in his life to lie with a female wrestler, for outside Cornwall I have yet to discover any; but the experience was one which I would recommend to anyone who can command it. That control, dexterity and forcefulness which Jane had displayed in her recent combat was equally disposed in her present activity – and she seemed intent on such display, adopting figures and poses which no woman without a similar nimbleness could have achieved. Moreover, that control over her muscles which she must have cultivated for her craft extended throughout her body – I mean that those parts which in most women are either uncontrolled or (in some whores) only a little commanded, were by her entirely subdued and regulated. Not only by their movement was she able to caress my instrument in a manner I had never before experienced, positively stroking and squeezing it without any movement upon my part, but upon my showing a sign of death before she herself was ready to concede the game, by a sudden contraction of those same muscles she gripped my cock with such a painful constraint (seeming to enclose it with an iron ring) that in a moment I had recovered my equanimity and was able to continue until she was ready – whereupon, dextrously twisting her legs beneath her, she raised herself upon them and her arms, so that I was able, curling my toes and gripping the grass as well as I might, to assault her with all the force at my command. She met thrust with thrust as powerfully as I could give them, until we both cried out at almost the same moment and fell to the ground in a positive excess of pleasure.

I must confess that the nature of the fight, while entirely pleasurable during its progress, left me sore and bruised; though I did not express myself in that sense to Jane, merely dressing myself and taking my leave of her with every expression of pleasure and gratitude – which she received merely by grinning and holding aloft the purse of money I had given her; this leaving me with mixed feelings, for it was clear that her actions had been performed out of gratitude rather than any particular admiration for my person. However, the experience had been one which I would not upon any account have missed.

On our reaching the pathway, I found Treweers leaning against a post and talking to the old crone who was my companion's friend. I wondered whether he had looked for, and even found me (for in the excessive enjoyment of the time I would not have noticed the attention of an audience of hundreds). Certainly his expression left me in no doubt that he was aware of the entertainment in which I had been occupied; nor did this worry me, nor prevent me from once more taking leave of Jane with considerable affection, though this was returned only by a cheery wave as the couple made off, and we returned to the trap, which then was driven back to Vycken. There, as I drove into the courtyard, I saw a carriage drawn up.

'Ah,' said Treweers, ' 'tis Squire Treleaven come to pay you his attentions.'

One of my duties being to make it clear to my neighbours that the estate would now be managed on a more sociable basis than hitherto, I hurried into the hall to make myself pleasant to the Squire, whose estate was some miles to the east, towards Restormel. He was a plump, nay corpulent, figure, dressed in clothing of a previous age – and his acquaintance with the present day indeed was embroidered with the manners of the past, evidenced in the flowery manner of his address.

'My very dear Sir,' he said, 'a pleasure indeed! 'Tis too many years since Vycken was alive, and I cannot properly express the pleasure with which the county has heard of your presence! I have been dispatched here, indeed, by some of the gentlemen of the area in the hope that you might be persuaded to attend a supper party on Monday night, at which you will meet some of your neighbours – both gentlemen and ladies, I may say, so your good wife—'

'Alas, Squire, I am unmarried.'

'Indeed – I was not aware. Indeed, I had understood . . .'

'But have no aversion to the sex,' I hastily added (which indeed was nothing other than the truth).

Staying only to take a glass of cider, the Squire departed; and Treweers then was able to inform me that he was an influential figure in the county who had only just resigned – his heart being expressed as weakly – from the position of Member of Parliament for the town of Lostwithiel. A Tory, of course, through both tradition and sentiment, Cornwall being a stronghold of interest in landowning and merchantry rather than of the dissenters, industrialists and reformers of the Whig Party.

I spent Sunday in quiet, attending service in the small church which stood just behind the house, and which was in considerable disrepair; there was a sermon whose length was well balanced by its tedium and during which I slept like a babe in the high-walled pew which happily concealed me from the public view; and in the afternoon walked about the grounds and dozed in the sun.

Monday was spent going through the accounts with Treweers, and in writing a long letter to Frank in which I explained as best I could upon relatively little knowledge the state of the house and grounds – which as to beauty and relative attractiveness I could not fault.

On my enquiring the nature of the supper party, Treweers explained that it would be as grand as local custom allowed – which left me in the quandary of not having brought any good clothes (it not having occurred to me that I would be required to attend any social occasions). The late tenant of the estate had left a trunk full of clothes, however, from which I dug out a suit which must have been made no more recently than the 1790s, Treweers nevertheless expressing himself confident that not only would I pass in the crowd, but would be singled out as perfectly well clad. So, on Monday evening, in a coat with tails of extravagant length, boots rather than shoes, an extremely short waistcoat, a collar which towered above the back of my neck, and a neckcloth so voluminous that it rose over my chin and bade fair to conceal my very mouth, I set out for the Squire's house, which stood upon the banks of the River Fowey, some miles upstream from that town.

Squire Treleaven's house was what had once been a large farmhouse, but was now something more pretentious, a wing having been opened out from the original building, and what had once perhaps been the kitchen contrived now into a large hall.

It was a warm evening, and the heat of a room crowded with people was added to by the smallness of the windows and by the multifarious candles lit to provide a reasonable light, which soon enough fell upon a society running with sweat engendered by the closeness of the atmosphere and the confinement of their clothes – which were as elderly as those I wore, and thicker and therefore hotter than would have been the case had more recent fashions found their way into the county. The women were better off than the men, being dressed still in the *robes en chemises* which had been the fashion thirty years earlier. These, consisting as they did of high-waisted muslin, cambric or calico garments, were so transparent that they almost exposed the women's bodies to the air, and were so thin that they were almost invisible – and would have had a delicious effect had not the bodies they clothed been on this occasion matronly and stout.

The society consisted of the gentry of the neighbourhood, and was (as the reader may understand) very different from that of London. The ladies, for instance, were older, it seeming to be the case that younger women were prohibited from gatherings of this sort. In fact I later discovered that they absented themselves by choice – and could not blame them, for there was nothing to attract them except the food and drink; whereas left to their own devices they enjoyed themselves in their own way, which was often in rustic matters frequently not unconnected with sensual pleasure.

So here, as I looked about me, were their seniors: couples whose average age must have been the middle forties, but who often appeared older, sated as they were by rich food and drink. The latter here consisted more of red wine than cider, though the latter was available and was drunk in plenty by the ladies (in particular). The food was of a coarse nature, much like the feast I had enjoyed upon my arrival at Vycken Hall – but added was a great quantity of fowl, viz. duck, goose and chicken, swimming in grease which soon transferred itself to the chops of Squire, Parson and accompanying gentry.

All I could do was give myself over to the spirit of the occasion, which the application of a bottle of claret to my stomach soon made more palatable; plied on one side with food by Mrs Treleaven, I could only nod from time to time in her direction while my attention must be given to Squire and Parson, the latter the very picture of a clergyman of the hunting and drinking sort, and the two of whom were hot upon the Tory cause (though admitting reluctantly to the service performed by those

Whigs whose cooperation had resulted in the defeat of the hated Wellington and his administration). Lord Grey being sent for to form a Whig administration had set these local Tories into a sweat of fear and hatred, the mere rumour of the Reform Bill making them fear for their property and even, ludicrously, their lives! As they grew more heated, so they applied liquor to cool themselves – which in turn heated them once again. Forced to drink glass for glass, I soon found myself as heated as they, dilating at length about the good old days of Canning and his Ministry, of Castlereagh's neutrality and its effect upon Britain abroad, of Catholic emancipation, constitutional reform and the economic and social injustices of the country.

The heat grew greater, the candles guttered and leaped; I was dimly conscious that Mrs Treleaven had left and her place been taken by a large dog of strangely mixed parentage who had leaped upon her seat and was guzzling the scraps left upon her plate; the wine continued to flow into my glass, and I tore at my neckcloth and opened my collar to let the air at my body – yet there was no coolness in it. I felt a certain dizziness overtake me, and gradually slipped towards an oblivion.

I regained partial consciousness as I found myself lifted from my seat and apparently conveyed to another room. There, deposited on a sopha, I lost consciousness again – but was at the same time aware of a bustle and noise about me – and woke once more to hear Squire Treleaven in the midst of what I took to be a political speech. I forced myself to listen, made myself shift in the place and half sit up – at which a round of applause was heard – and from a great distance I heard the tail-end of the Squire's speech.

'Therefore, my friends,' he said, 'with the approbation of Parson Polware, and I hope that of all present, it is with the greatest confidence that I ask you to celebrate by acclamation the proposition that our candidate in the forthcoming by-election should be our new friend Sir Franklin Franklyn, of Alcovary and Vycken Hall, in the counties of Hertfordshire and Cornwall!'

I staggered to my feet to a cry of 'Hear! Hear!' – then, looking about me, saw nothing but a sea of faces and lifted glasses as the company tossed down their wine in a toast – and I realised that not only had they mistaken me for my friend, but that under that impression I was now the official Tory candidate for the parliamentary constituency of Lostwithiel!

Chapter Six

Sophie's Story

It was perhaps not astonishing that Chichley should, in the course of time – indeed, within a week of the most recent events I have described – procure for me an invitation to that most glittering of all London salons, Lady Holland's circle at Holland House, where the most intelligent Whig politicians mingled with the most aristocratic and literary men of London.

Perhaps the company was not as distinguished as it had once been – Lord Byron no longer limped up the steps to the grand entrance of that fine house erected soon after Shakespeare's day, with its sparkling oriel windows, its Dutch gables, its square towers, and its private park (where the Parliamentary Army had set up its chief camp in the days of the Civil War). But a remarkable number of gentlemen still attended regularly at the House for conversation and other pleasures – this had always been a society chiefly for gentlemen, since the more fastidious ladies could not overlook the fact that Lord Holland had married his wife Elizabeth only two days after her first husband, Sir Godfrey Webster, Bart., had divorced her, naming the noble lord as correspondent.

The lady had had a remarkable career. Despite the criticism to which her liaison with Lord Holland had exposed her, she had nevertheless upon repairing to his house in Kensington – to which it was already the habit of a brilliant circle of wits, statesmen, men of letters and others of distinction to repair – soon established herself altogether in control of it, and that despite natural qualities which were by no means admirable – for, polite, cold and haughty to all those she met in social intercourse, she was most offensive to any to whom she took a dislike.

Even those men of letters whose distinction marked them out for respect were belittled by her – Lord Byron himself felt the sharp edge of her tongue at a time when he was perhaps the most famous man in the country, while to Samuel Rogers she once said: 'Your poetry is bad enough, so pray be sparing of your prose.' 'Poets inclined to a plethora of vanity,' Moore once remarked to me, 'would find a dose of Lady Holland now and then very good for their complaint.'

However, Lady H. was nothing if not amiable to me – though by the time I met her she was in her sixties, when perhaps age had mellowed her. Lord Holland, I knew less of – except of course that he was one of the great luminaries of the Whigs, and estimated to command high office on their return to power. His statue, by Watts, had just been placed in the grounds of Holland House when I first entered it – and indeed that very act brought one face to face with him in effigy if not in fact, through the place set aside in the entrance hall for not only a bust by Nollekens but a portrait by Fabre, both of which are imposing. I met him but three or four times, when he impressed me as the most amiable of men – and known as a refuge to the helpless and the oppressed.

I was naturally diffident during my first two or three

visits to the house, and was noticed by Lady H. only, as it seemed to me, in the most perfunctory manner; so it was to my surprise that on my third or fourth visit I was sent for by her to the library, a handsome room at the western extremity of the house, where I found her half-lying upon a *chaise-longue*, the place where she had left off reading in a handsomely bound volume marked by one languid finger.

'My dear Mrs Nelham,' she said, politely gesturing towards a chair, upon which I carefully sat (the furniture being for the most part foreign and therefore delicate), 'I wonder if I might ask of you a favour? My senior footman, Tollersly, has unfortunately been taken ill of a bad leg, and is confined to his room. He is a man of considerable talents, but these do not include literacy, and I fear that he is extremely bored at his confinement, being usually a person of considerable activity. Would it be asking too much of you to pay him a brief visit, and to read from some improving work? I have picked a volume from my library which perhaps might be of an improving nature' – with which she passed me the volume at her hand.

What could I do but acquiesce? The lady had kindly received me at her house when others less liberal in their nature had failed to do so (on account of adventures which they considered indelicate, and which I have already related in my previous writings, a list of which may be found opposite the title page of the present volume).

Lady H. rang her bell, and, a maidservant appearing, instructed that I should be taken to Tollersly's room. Making my obeisance, I followed the girl from the library, and by a circuitous route through innumerable and warren-like passages to a back staircase, then up it and through a dormitory (by the small-clothes strewn about it and a single tousled head upon a pillow, one shared by a number of the male servants) to a door upon which she knocked, and on receiving the command to do so, admitted me.

The room was somewhat better than might have been expected to be occupied by a servant, its windows looking over the park behind Holland House, towards the rose-garden, the adjacent ice-house and the orangery. Near the window, which was open so that the sultry air of summer could waft into the sick-room, a bed was drawn up, and upon it lay the gentleman in question. By Lady H.'s words, 'my senior footman', I had expected an older man than the one I saw, who in fact was perhaps in his middle twenties. Nor did I expect him to appear half-naked, for he seemed to be clad only in a sheet thrown across the lower half of his body, from the bottom of which a foot dressed in bandages protruded. His visage was a strong one, without any sign of that weakness which marks the subservient employee; dark brown eyes were surmounted by eyebrows which in a man of superior rank I would have said were neatly plucked, while above a firm chin marked by the dint of a dimple was set a mouth whose sternness seemed set off by the suggestion of a somewhat satirical smile.

As for the rest: his shoulders were broad and well-formed, his skin white as a girl's, so that the paps which decorated a broad breast seemed by contrast purple rather than pink, and were decorated by a spring or two of hair no less black than that which curled upon his brow and fell almost to his shoulders – devoid of any hint of powder (for Lady H. was among the first ladies in

London to refrain from insisting on her footmen powdering or wearing wigs).

Clearly the man had no idea who I was; but when I introduced myself as a guest sent him by his employer with the duty of reading to him, he showed what seemed to me a proper embarrassment, attempting to lift himself sufficiently to make a little bow; an expression of pain passing over his brow, caused no doubt by his injured limb.

I waved him down; and, having drawn up a chair, opened my book: it was a treatise on Gnosticism, with special reference to the Gospel of St Thomas, which the author translated in full. I had read no more than two pages, when glancing up from my page I caught Tollersly in mid-yawn – a fact which would have distressed me more were I not by now in the same state of boredom. Meeting my eye, he I believe recognised the fact; and, whether purposely or not I cannot say, in moving himself to a more comfortable position betrayed the corner of a book protruding from beneath the sheet.

'What, Mr Tollersly!' I remarked – 'You are a reader, after all?'

'Somewhat slow, ma'am,' he replied; ' 'tis a volume a friend brought in the hope that the pictures might amuse me; the matter, however, is in a foreign tongue, and I cannot go forward with it.'

I leaned forward to take up the volume, but with a blush he seized it. ' 'Tis not a work for your eyes, ma'am!'

Which as a matter of course made me the more eager to recover it; which I did without difficulty – and found in my hands a finely illustrated edition of *Monsieur Nicolas, or the Human Heart Laid Bare* – the memoirs of M. Restif de la Bretonne – illustrated (as I could see at even a cursory glance) with the most delightful drawings, the artist not shrinking from portraying the personages concerned in the most intimate attitudes of love.

'I am sorry, Mr Tollersly,' I said, 'that your lack of knowledge of the French language has prevented you from enjoying the narrative . . .'

' 'Twould have been much the same were it in English,' he said morosely; 'for I never attended school – nor have I regretted it until the present moment. The story, I take it, is . . .'

'Of a French gentleman,' I said, 'more honest in telling the story of his life than many gentlemen are prepared to be.'

'You know it, then?'

'I saw it first some years ago, when in Paris; but in no less than seventeen volumes. This appears to be a compilation in which the editor has concentrated on those areas of la Bretonne's life which . . .' I paused.

'You are familiar with the French tongue, ma'am?' And on my nodding, 'Perhaps you could English some of it for me?'

I opened the book almost at random; its pages fell apart at that point when la Bretonne, a vigorous young man of nineteen or so, was sitting alone in his attick in Paris, with a new book which he had just acquired. I began to read: ' "A great libertine, Molet – whom I have already mentioned, and who was a fellow lodger of mine at Bonne Sellier's – had come to see me one Sunday morning when I was still in bed, and had brought me a copy of that most lascivious of books, *Le Portier des Chartreux*, which I had once glimpsed at La Mace's. Filled with a lively curiosity, I took it eagerly and started reading in bed. I forgot everything – even my mistress, Zephire. After a score of pages, I was on fire. Manon Lavergne, a relative of Bonne Sellier, came on behalf of my former landlady to bring my linen and Loiseau's, which Bonne continued to wash for us. I knew what Manon's morals were like. Throwing back the bed-clothes and revealing myself ready for combat, I threw myself upon her and with one action rent her few clothes from her body. Nothing loath, she met me with equal passion (ever ready for the game), and we played the beast with two backs in a paroxysm of energy which provoked screams of pleasure on her part and cries of delight on mine.

' "Gathering together her rended clothing, and taking with a happy grin the gold *livre* which I handed her as compensation for the damage I had done (which was no greater than many other men had done before me), she left me, and I resumed my reading. Half an hour later there appeared Cecile Decoussy, my sister Margot's companion, who came on her behalf to ask why she no longer saw anything of me. Without any regard for this young blonde's position (she was about to be married) or for the atrocious way in which I was bringing shame upon my sister in the person of her friend, I put so much fury into my attack that, alarmed as much as surprised, she thought that I had gone mad. I returned to my baneful reading.

' "About three-quarters of an hour later, Thérèse Courbisson arrived, laughing and bantering. 'Where is he, that lazy scamp? Still in bed!' And she came over to tickle me. I was waiting for her. I seized her almost in the air, like a feather, and with only one hand I pulled her under me. 'Oh! After what you've just done to Manon?

A fine man you are!' But she was caught before she could finish, and as she was very partial to physical pleasure, she did nothing more but help me. At last she tore herself from my arms because she heard my landlord coming upstairs. She went out, leaving the door open. I finished my book.

' "The bed had warmed me up; the three pleasures I had enjoyed were just a spur to my senses: I got up with the intention of going to fetch Zephire, of bringing her to my room, and of abandoning myself with her to my erotic frenzy. At that moment someone scratched at my door, which I had only pushed to. I started, thinking it was Zephire. 'Who is it?' I cried; 'come in.' 'Seraphine,' said a voice which I thought I recognised. I trembled, thinking it was Seraphine Destroches who had come to scold me for my conduct with her companion Decoussy. 'Who is it?' I repeated. 'Seraphine Jolon.' The only person I had ever known by that name was the housekeeper of a painter who was our neighbour in the Rue de Poulies, and I had whispered sweet nothings to her once or twice; but then Largeville had turned up, and Jeannette Demailly, and I had left the house. Reassured, I opened the door. It was she.

' " 'I have come,' the pretty girl said to me, 'on behalf of Mademoiselle Fagard, now Madame Jolon, my sister-in-law, who begs you to introduce me and recommend me to Mademoiselle Delaporte, who thinks highly of you and can render me a great service.'

' " 'Immediately,' I said; 'sit down, pretty neighbour.' She was charming. As she turned round, she showed me a perfect figure, her charming little bottom jutting under a thin dress, and a tiny waist showing off her hips to perfection. I seized her, and pushed her back on the bed. She tried to defend herself. That was adding fuel to the fire. I did not even take time to shut the door. I finished, I began again.

' " 'I . . . did . . . not . . . tell . . . you . . .' she cried, in time to my thrusting, 'that . . . my . . . sister . . . Jolon . . . was waiting for me!' – the last few words culminating in a squeak of pleasure.

The thought spurred me on. I was like a madman, when the door opened. It was Agathe Fagard.

' " 'Help! Help!' cried Seraphine. Lifting myself from the bed I left her uncovered, jumped up, kicked the door to, threw the lovely brunette on to my bed beside the other, and submitted her to a fifth triumph no less vigorous than the first, carried away as I was by the force of my imagination. Agathe Fagard had not yet recovered from her surprise when I blushed at my frenzy and apologised to the two sisters-in-law.

' " 'He has to be seen to be believed!' was all that Seraphine said – the two girls not being entirely displeased at the compliment I had paid them. Such is the effect of erotic literature." '

As I put the book down, I could see that Mr Tollersly's interest in it had been keen, from the light in his eyes no less than from the movement of his hand beneath the sheet, which I surmised was meant to conceal the uprising of his spirits in a form he thought might offend me – though I was conscious that my own bosom was rising and falling faster than usual – a phenomenon concomitant with the blush that suffused my cheeks – a blush less of offended modesty than of a pleasant warming from the scenes M. la Bretonne had described.

In leaning forward to replace the book at Mr Tollersly's side, my fingers inexplicably became tangled in the edge of the sheet, and on my removing my hand the sheet came with it – revealing (without my intending it in the least) that his hand was indeed engaged in attempting to subdue (by pressing it down against his belly) an engine of such proportions that one might be pardoned for supposing it capable of just such feats as those M. la Bretonne had spoken of.

The gentleman in question coloured, and now joined a second hand to the first, though both were incapable of completely hiding the instrument whose engorgement caused him such embarrassment.

'My dear Mr Tollersly,' I exclaimed, 'please do not give way to any feelings of mortification. In the first place, I am a married lady' (true, though my husband had died many years before) 'and not unacquainted with a gentleman's physiognomy; and second, it is but natural that a man should show some acknowledgement of so warming a tale as that we have just heard.'

His answer to this was immediate, and consisted of his removing both hands, thus showing his device in all its proudness – and an attractive assemblage of flesh it was, the sun as it shone through the open window giving the bronze hair at its base an almost golden glow and setting off the dark column which rose through and above it.

To allow such an implement to waste its vigour was unthinkable, and – since in warm weather I have always maintained the custom of eschewing the relatively modern fashion of wearing drawers – it was the work of but a moment to mount the bed and, throwing a leg across his body, to join our bodies in that manner hallowed by years of custom.

I can conceive that Mr Tollersly, when in full command of all his limbs, must be a man of considerable vigour; and even now, while suffering from considerable pain in his foot (the cause of which, I gathered later, was gout from making too free with Lady Holland's strawberry beds), he was incapable of remaining completely still, his thighs and shoulders combining to lift his middle body to meet my own, the rolling of his eyes at the same time showing the pleasure his action, and the reaction to it of my own person, gave.

Preoccupied with my own delight, it was not until our pleasure was some way advanced that, glancing out of the window at my side, I saw Lady H. standing on the gravel below; dressed in a day-gown and bonnet, she had clearly been taking the air, and pausing was now presented with the view of a lady (myself) whose upper person, displayed at a window, was moving with a regular motion as though she sat upon a vigorously propelled rocking horse.

I doubt not that she realised what we were at; but merely nodded in a friendly manner – to which it was impossible for me to reply in any rational manner, my emotions at that moment being at their keenest; so that all I could do was to wave at her with one hand – the other being pressed upon Mr Tollersly's belly in an attempt to relieve myself from the pleasurable but over-keen thrusting which otherwise threatened to split me open!

Such an improbable fate was of course not to be mine; and at all events Mr Tollersly had reached the apogee of his ecstasy at almost the same moment as myself (as I could apprehend from the scalding fountain which erupted within me). We lay – or rather, he lay and I sat – supine for a moment or two while we recovered our breath; after which I lifted myself from him and (he moving obligingly to one side on his couch) laid myself at his side, when he gave me a most friendly kiss upon the cheek, and thanked me for my attentions.

'Nay, Mr Tollersly; the thanks must be at least partly upon my side,' I replied; after which no words were exchanged for several minutes – when (whether or not prompted to it by recollections of M. la Bretonne's accomplishments) I felt his hand slide within my dress to caress a breast.

'Mrs . . . er . . .' (I supplied the name.) 'Mrs Nelham, might I crave the boon of setting eyes on your very person?'

It was a simple enough request, and simply enough answered by my removing the small amount of clothing necessary upon so delightfully warm a day. I noticed that Mr Tollersly was more ready in his movements than he had previously been, and wondered whether our recent bout had not been an efficacious treatment of his gouty foot; for, half-lifting himself upon his couch with no more than the merest wince of pain, he inspected me with the utmost keenness; and I could not but notice that his principal part, which had subsided to a mere squab, began to lengthen and thicken appreciably as his eyes grazed upon my body; a novelty which was accelerated as, in order that he should have a more thorough view of those pleasures he had enjoyed, I placed one foot upon the couch, thus by turning out my thigh and opening my most intimate parts first to his appreciative eyes, and then – as he raised himself still further – to the touch first of inquisitive fingers and then to the complementary touch of his lips as he planted a kiss which was meant (by the keen action of his tongue) no doubt to rouse in me those emotions recently spent, but, as I must admit, now once more mounting.

By now his engine was once more engorged – and, my palm told me, if not of such iron firmness as previously, of quite sufficient sturdiness to perform its most necessary function. I again approached; but Mr Tollersly, regardless of the pangs of his foot, now turned me with dextrous hands so that I fell upon the bed, whereupon in an instance he lay between my legs, and I felt his cock nuzzling my quim with affectionate enthusiasm.

It did not nuzzle for long: so unctuous were we both with our previous pleasure that no sooner had the shaft parted the lips of the grotto than it slid between them with almost too much ease – and it was now that the ingratiating footman revealed an uncommon side to his nature: uncommon I call it, because men of his station are for the most part over-eager to complete the act of love – no sooner in than out, no sooner up than down (as I may put it). The present gentleman, however, displayed a leisure which – whether the product of previous passages with ladies of a superior station, I can of course not say – was excessively pleasant; his motion was gentle and slow, his hips sufficiently limber to be able to withdraw his dibble almost completely from me, while at the same time the rest of his body – from upper belly to breast, from upper thighs to calves – remained fully in contact with my own. Yet again, from time to time he would lift himself upon his elbows and knees, so that the only thing that joined us was that column of flesh which all the time continued its movements with a regular and probing rhythm, arrested only at one moment by the joining together of bronze and black hair, and at another by our mutual reluctance that we should, at that point, be separated.

We climbed the hill, this time, at so laggard a pace that

it was by almost unnoticeable degrees that mild pleasure gave way to keener gratification, that to a yet sharper delight, and finally to that supreme delectation in the moment of which my limbs seemed to melt away entirely under the weight of the gentleman's body; while entirely eschewing that almost painful thrusting which too often accompanies the final throes, he accepted the culmination of the bout with a mere shuddering – the almost bulging of his eyes and the tightening of his palms upon my shoulders, however, offering indication that he was not unmoved.

Gentlemanlike, he soon relieved me of his weight, and we lay once more at each other's sides, imperceptibly drifting into sleep; from which I awakened, who knows how long later, my head upon his breast, a cheek tickled by that insignificant sprig of hair which sprung from below his left pap. My foreshortened view took in, below this, a flat belly below which the instrument of my pleasure lay contracted to the size of a thumb: and once more I wondered at the contrast which so often makes it impossible to estimate to what size the male member (when relaxed) may grow, or (when engorged) diminish.

In this case, I was in no doubt of its efficiency when in action; yet marvelled at its small size in its present state, and carefully raising myself (so as not to disturb the sleeping footman) bent to examine it – and was incapable of not smiling at the sight, for as it lay raised upon the mounds of the attendant cods (lifted as they were upon the platform of his closed thighs) it reminded me of the coarse name of *prick*, so often given it; for indeed, the skin at its head now wrinkled and lax and gathered to a point, it was of such a shape that the name was not entirely ill-judged.

Moistening a finger at my lips, I gently stroked the unconscious rod – more from affection than in expectation, for even a man ten or fifteen years younger than Mr Tollersly would be barely ready for another pass. Yet after a moment there was already a change, a slight swelling; then an acceleration, and at last a positive celebration of my touch (which must now be rather that of an entire palm than a single digit) in the complete extension of the appendage – which seemed compact and inflexible as formerly – though without waking its possessor it would be impossible to ascertain the extent of its rigidity.

I glanced at his face: there was no sign of apprehension there – he still slept firmly; and the naughty proposition came into my mind, whether 'twould be possible to excite him to the limit without waking. This is something which, I am told, occurs to young gentlemen with great readiness in their salad days; less perhaps to older men. In this case . . . I could not resist the trial.

Gently as possible, I placed a finger and thumb at the tip of his member, and with the greatest care dragged the skin downwards, revealing the pink head, bald and glistening, its single eye winking (as it seemed) conspiratorially at me from twin lids. I feared the subject of my experiment might wake as I latched the skin below the ridge – but found the instrument not yet so inflexible as to require a positive force to achieve the effect. He slumbered on – or seemed to. I raised my head for a moment and regarded him; no, the eyes were firmly shut, no hint of expression upon the somnambulant features. Lowering my head once more, and drawing my tongue over my lips, I slid them, as gently as possible, over his member.

The emotions attendant upon this action, as always, brought on a ready salivation; with the result that it was possible almost entirely without friction to convey to the surface of the pillar – whether to the column itself or to its head – the impression of a tender caress; that piece of flesh being so apprehensive that, while I would scarcely have believed it possible to produce such an effect with so little effort, I felt it harden between my lips until at last it could have been made of a warm marble – and it seemed to me that the blood within it moved rhythmically in time with my own motions, the pulse quickening and (as it were) solidifying until the hand which I had now placed upon his cods felt that tightening and lifting which was the invariable signal of a coming spasm. I lifted my head just in time, for with another tightening of his balls in my palm, there oozed (rather than leaped) from the proper aperture an unmistakable sign of ultimate satisfaction – while at the same time, with a start, my subject awoke, and gave vent to a 'Damn me!' redolent at the same time of surprise, embarrassment and – regret.

My own laughter had the result that he, too, soon recovered his equilibrium and smiled, the trick played upon him being (as he confessed) new to him – and one he would not have thought possible. Yet, he said, it seemed a pity that by my action I had deprived myself of some pleasure – my reply that the experiment had been worth the deprivation not seeming to satisfy him. But at all events, it seemed unlikely that he could recover himself yet again, this being beyond most men I had ever met; and after a further twenty minutes' dozing, I raised myself and prepared to dress, Mr Tollersly lazily smiling at me from his pillow.

As I lifted my dress from the floor where it lay, however, there was the sound of an altercation from below. Cautious not to show too much of my naked self, I climbed over the gentleman's frame and leaned my elbows upon the window-sill to watch the fun as two maids fled from another whom they had been teasing, and who was now pursuing them through the shrubbery. What was my surprise when I felt a pair of hands upon my shoulders, and the pressure against my back of Mr Tollersly's lower parts, which, though its most notable feature not yet extended to a useful degree, was none the less far from completely limp!

It appeared that, like many men, he was attached to the sight of a woman's posterior, and on my presenting him with a close view of that part of my person, he was now confident of being able to pay it proper tribute; his vigour being accompanied – unlike our last passage – by a kind of fierceness, his hands now descending to grasp my breasts, his teeth nipping the base of my neck, and his belly rubbing against the cheeks of my arse with an insistence speedily made more pressing by his member's rousing itself further, unbelievably, to what appeared to be full vigour.

Complimented by this, I reached back to grasp it and (though it bucked between my fingers with what seemed a life of its own) introduce it between my nether lips, whereupon, with a grunt of satisfaction, Mr Tollersly transferred his hands from my bubbies to my shoulders, raised himself, and thrust vigorously at me – so that gripping the window-sill with my hands, it was all I could do to prevent myself being hurled, naked and sweating as I was, on to the gravel below (where Mr Holt, the elderly butler, was at this moment walking with the housekeeper, Mrs Hacker, no doubt discussing some matter of household importance).

Bringing me fairly speedily to a conclusion, Mr Tollersly was (as might be expected) less quick to satisfy himself, his bucking continuing for rather longer than I found comfortable (my unprotected bosom pressed as it was against the wooden window frame). However, at last, with an expression as much of triumph as of satisfaction, he gave one final shove, and withdrew himself to his bed, where he lay panting (as well he might) from his efforts while I took the liberty of using the pan of cold water which stood in the corner of the room to refresh my person before taking my leave – yet not until I had complimented him.

'Yet M. Bretonne did better!' was his comment.

Frequency, I was bound to point out, was not the *sine qua non* in such matters; moreover I suspected la Bretonne of exaggeration (for no man I have experienced has completed so many bouts within so short a time – even in the early and most vigorous years of manhood). I am not sure Mr Tollersly believed me; but that he had passed an enjoyable afternoon I was in no doubt – nor did I draw attention to the fact that as I left he was not only standing but moving merrily about, on the foot injury which had formerly confined him to his bed.

Downstairs, tea was being served in the white drawing-room to Lady Holland and the Hon. Mrs Teazle, a pleasant, plump lady to whom I had previously been introduced.

'And how did you leave Tollersly?' enquired my lady.

I replied that he was much recovered.

'I make no doubt of it,' said she – but with a face

apparently devoid of irony. 'He profited, I trust, from your reading? My sight of you suggested that you found it surprisingly inspiriting.'

'What book was this?' enquired Mrs Teazle. I passed it to her.

'Why, this would recover any gentleman – or lady either,' she said, turning the leaves.

'It is a work highly recommended to me,' said her ladyship, 'by the Bishop of Durham.'

'I am almost alarmed at the liberal views of our senior clergy,' said Mrs Teazle.

'Yet they must be allowed to judge in matters of which we would as laymen be incapable of holding an informed view,' said Lady Holland.

'That is as may be,' said Mrs Teazle, closing the book with a snap, and handing it back to me – whereat with a start, I saw that I had handed her M. la Bretonne's memoirs, brought by mistake from Mr Tollersly's room. I hastily covered it with my palms, and asked my Lady whether, since I had found it so interesting, I might take it home with me for further study – permission for which was readily given; yet I cannot think that Mrs Teazle thought any the better of me for my application than of Lady Holland for her acquiescence – the latter's position in society being such, however, that none of her guests would have dreamed of questioning, much less criticising, it.

However, her disapproval was not complete; for within a week I received a message asking me to call upon her at her house in Upper Brook Street. There I found her in considerable luxury, surrounded by the most beautiful pictures and objects – her wealth being that of her husband Wellesley Teazle, Esq., who had made a fortune through the manufacture of fashionable footwear.

Mrs Teazle was somewhat slow in making it clear what she required of me. 'First,' she said, 'pray take advantage of me cellar' – and pointed to a table laden with bottles of wine and spirits.

I helped myself to a cup of wine, and asked whether I should pour her some.

'Ah, my physician forbids it, alas!' she said, but repairing to another side-table, poured herself a large tumbler of water, which she threw down in a single draught, then pouring herself another. When she began once more to address me, I could not but notice that her words were somewhat slurred; and on her approaching and sitting at my side, an overpowering odour of gin made it quite clear that she was a toper in no small way of business. And indeed during my visit she drank two more large tumblers of the liquid – enough to set most men I know beneath the nearest available table – yet her gait was sober enough, and she remained in control of her senses, though her words became less and less intelligible as our conversation continued.

In the end, however, and with many haws and hums, I understood that she wished to give an entertainment for her husband upon his fiftieth birthday – for him and a number of cronies from his club, whose interests, she readily confessed, were more amorous than artistic, or even gustatory. A feast however was to begin the evening, after which she wished some tableaux to be performed in the garden – which she then showed me: a handsome, small, terraced place, on to which large windows gave from the rear of the building.

'You will forgive me, ma'am,' she said, 'if I shay that

your reprush . . . reprutle . . . reputation has gone before you, and that I am given to supposh you convershant with the kind of entertainment of which . . .'

I let her go no further, but nodded gravely.

'There will be some expense, ma'am,' I said.

'You mean you have already some idea?'

I nodded: indeed, the sight of the four handsome statues of young gods surrounding the fountain at the centre of the garden had given me some idea. Would it be possible, I said, for me to rearrange the garden as I wished? That would be no difficulty, she replied. And as for money – that would be entirely a matter for me; such expenses as would be incurred should be paid, and as for myself, would a fee of one hundred guineas be . . . ?

It was a magnificent sum indeed; and on those conditions I had no hesitation in closing upon the matter, and left the lady leaning heavily upon a table and singing quietly to herself a chorus from *The Beggar's Opera*.

Chapter Seven

The Adventures of Andy

My emotions as I woke upon the morning after my nomination as Member of Parliament for that area of the county of Cornwall in which I found myself can readily be imagined; the tribute had been great, nor would I have repined, except that the compliment had been paid to another man, my friend and brother Sir Franklin Franklyn, the proper owner of the estate over which I was only temporarily presiding.

I should of course have made the error public upon its first being made; but once having failed to correct it, through my over-indulgence of the excellent local cider, which had followed several bottles of claret, my embarrassment, together with the friendliness of the local people, had seemed to make it impossible. That sooner or later – and, by preference, sooner rather than later – the correction must be made, went without saying; but the accomplishment of the task was clearly not going to be altogether pleasant.

The thought of all this dizzied me, and I rose from my bed to find myself dizzied in another way, my head spinning from the remaining fumes of alcohol; hanging on to the bed's end, I rang for a maid, who came with a pail of water, and kindly bathed my head before helping me to immerse myself in an almost cold bath, which restored me to some sort of equilibrium. The recovery was aided by breakfast – I found that as usual to force some food down upon my rebellious stomach was the quickest way of recovering a feeling of health, and a plate of bacon, broiled egg and mushroom followed by a steak of beef and accompanied by a pint of ale went far to recover me to full health.

I then decided upon a walk in order to complete the treatment, and set out across the estate, where here and there small cottages stood in which resided the estate workers, some of whom came of families which had lived there for as long as memory could relate. Stoutly built with walls of clay, their roofs thatched, they were pleasant places enough, and the men and women who inhabited them exchanged greetings in the friendliest way – if with accents so rough that it was impossible for me, more often than not, to tell their meaning.

I walked for two hours, until, almost at midday, and at a spot some miles from the house, I came upon Treweers, sitting on the ground with an extremely old woman whom I had seen about the place. Between them was a leather bottle, from which I was offered a drink – and which turned out to contain an anonymous liquor of such roughness and strength that it knocked my head almost back into its pre-dawn muddle, and I sat down to recover myself.

The old woman was introduced to me as Betsy Pascoe, who, Treweers later told me, was a hundred and seventeen years old – something which I might dispute were it not the case that many Cornish men and women, pickled by long exposure to alcohol and bad weather, indeed live to an extraordinary age. At all events, from the depths of a vastly wrinkled face, the happy crone conversed for some time; and upon my asking her age declined to give it, stating only that she hoped e'er long to be in Beelzebub's bosom.

'Surely,' said Treweers, 'you mean in Abraham's bosom?'

'Abraham or Beelzebub,' replied Mrs Pascoe, 'I been fifty years a widder-woman, and zo long as 'tes some man's bosom, 'tes no matter whose.'

I could not but laugh at this; it reflected well the attitude of the local people to religion – which was that it was by no means as potent as legend. Even the activities of the Nonconformist preachers have had little effect on the natural beliefs of the Cornish, which extend in the direction of superstition of every kind: ghosts and pixies, or piskies as they are known, haunted places and tormented animals of all descriptions. The presence of the Devil is strong in some places, and the belief of the people in his activities tenacious – this resulting in all kinds of pagan ceremonies intended to placate him or his officers. Mrs Pascoe was full of stories to this effect, and nothing I could say would shake her conviction – which was based, as she said, on a wealth of evidence, and on one story in particular, which she retailed with great vigour.

My pen falters in any attempt to render the dialect in which she spoke, its being so obfuscated with intrusive vowels of a strange and foreign nature – only in the interior of Ireland have I heard the English language so maltreated; so I render into a more readily comprehensible narrative the following anecdote:

'My great-uncle Jem,' said Mrs Pascoe, 'went one warm late Tuesday in the summer of 'forty-three to hear John Wesley preach over to Zennor. 'Twas a great occasion, as with all that man's meetings, and ended in an uproar of triumph and song. My great-uncle recognised a number of friends and neighbours in the crush, and among them a young woman of New Mill, his own village, who had been recently married; she was a handsome creature, and Jem was glad to see her there, for she had had a somewhat flighty reputation, and he was in no doubt that she was in need of saving, for he doubted whether her husband – a weak-bodied young man she had married more for his possessing two mules, a horse and seven acres of land than for any better reason – was capable of exercising the authority to keep her in order.

'Jem had to confess, he said later, that she was a veritable beauty, her mob-cap hanging about her neck and releasing a tidal wave of black hair which hung down almost to her waist, and the modesty of her dress was a little belied by its lightness, and the way it revealed a rosy bosom heaving with emotion as she joined in the final hymn. However, said Jem, 'twas a good thing to see her there, evidently intent on storing up weapons against the Devil and all his wiles.

'Jem, like most of the crowd, had only Shanks's pony as conveyance, and set out on his way back home to New Mill with a crowd of others, which gradually diminished as one after another of his companions turned off upon their own way until he was left alone on the moor. He came, after a while, to Chysauster, where the ancient people of the country had dug a pit in which, it was said, they had worshipped the Devil. Jem, as usual, was keeping well clear of that place, especially since the daylight was beginning to fade; when suddenly the hair on the back of his neck rose, for he heard a terrible row coming from the Devil's Pit – the sound of a woman moaning and sobbing. Cautious by nature, he fell to the ground and wriggled like the serpent upon his belly [these Cornish are full of Biblical phrases] 'til he could see into the hollow – where to his amazement he saw his neighbour's wife, her dress thrown upon the grass and now without so much as a stitch upon her body, lying upon the turf and groaning in what could have been pleasure or pain.

'Great-uncle Jem looked about, warily, wondering whether perhaps there was some lover who for the moment had left the girl friend, perhaps to answer a call of nature. But no such thing. And then, with a chill, he realised that there was an unseen presence in the little hollow, for the young woman threw herself upon her back in just such a position as to receive a man, and thrust her secret parts upwards, holding out her arms – yet at the same time seeming fearful of the weight which might be laid upon her.

'It was at that moment, said Great-uncle Jem, that he realised that the unseen man was the Devil – and that it was his duty to rescue the fair distressed. His grandfather, the seventh son of a seventh son, had been an adept conjurer, and in many a conversation had told him of the wiles of the Devil, and what must be done to defeat him, and, given courage by the words of Mr Wesley, he threw off his clothes and descended into the hollow. Standing above the girl, whose bosom rose and fell with a panting desire to be at one with her invisible Tormenter, so under his sway was she, he recited in the Cornish language a rhyme best calculated to send the horned one scampering home – and hurriedly, so as to prevent him reassuming his place, laid his own body on top of the girl's and – his pistol having cocked itself without prompting – took the Tormentor's place.

'Jem always remarked that should he have had any doubt of the Devil's presence, that action would confirm it, for, he said, no other young woman (and he was a young man not without experience) had ever bucked so violently, clawed so vehemently, received him with such heated embraces, as she! 'Twas hot as hell, he said; and having completed the act which would exorcise the unwelcome Visitor, he made to withdraw, upon which the girl laid hold of his arse and so wrapped her legs about him that retreat was impossible – for, she said, her scut itched so that more of the same treatment was required if the Devil was not to be drawn back by its warmth!

'It was, Jem said, some three hours before he was able to soothe the poor, tormented creature. But gradually, as dusk fell and the stars began to punctuate the night, she felt able to resume her clothing – as he did – and the couple walked back to New Mill, where he delivered her to her husband. Jem was ready to explain the circumstances which had detained them, but the young wife desired his silence, for, she said, it was known that the Devil attacked only the most beautiful women, and she would not wish to disconcert her female friends by a seeming boast.

'Sadly, as we can all testify, the Devil is not easily put off when he finds attractive metal, and for some years, often as much as three times a month, he would take advantage of the absence of his victim's husband to visit her. Fortunately, the smell of brimstone always preceded him, and upon smelling the faintest whiff of it, she would send a neighbour's child over to the field where

Jem was working, with the message that her copper needed stoking – which was the code they adopted, not wishing to frighten the good people of the village. Jem would then drop his task of the moment, and by a deep lane make his way to a place where, scaling a wall, he could drop down into her backyard and enter the house through the bedroom window, where he would find the victim already bereft of her clothes, since no time was to be lost if he was to be in position before the Devil's arrival.

'For some years Jem continued in this good work,' Mrs Pascoe explained; 'but doubtless through his efforts, the visitations miraculously ceased just at the time he himself got married – to a beautiful but jealous maid from Gulval; though after they had taken their own farm near Penzance, I hear that the lady concerned appealed to another neighbour to help her in the same manner, so Beelzebub may have been more tenacious than Jem supposed.

'Well, 'twas a strange story,' the old woman concluded; 'but there's no surprise in it, for where the husband is a weak thing, the Devil will try to enter, and we poor women must take what means we can to keep him out.'

Having delivered herself of the story, Mrs Pascoe fell asleep under the hedge, and Treweers and I walked back to the house talking of other things – he asking me if I would care to come, in three days' time, to see the ceremony of the Bodmin Riding, which always took place on the Sunday nearest the seventh of July. Enquiring its nature, I was pleased to note that it might give me the opportunity of returning the hospitality I had been offered, and made arrangements for the erection of a great tent and the provision of considerable quantities of our own cider, and sent out invitations to the local gentry, being specially careful to include all my friends of the previous evening.

I should explain about the Bodmin Riding: it is a custom which began in time immemorial - certainly long before the memory of the parents of the oldest man in the place - and it is said to commemorate the return to the town of the body of St Petroc, the patron saint of the parish, whose relics were stolen in the twelfth century and taken to the Abbey of St Méen in Brittany. An appeal was made to King Henry II, who sent a concourse of soldiers to St Méen and ordered the people there to give back the body, which they did, and it was returned and joyfully reinterred in the Church named after the saint.

The ceremony is not however now notably a religious one, but consists largely of the local people enjoying themselves in whatever manner most appeals to them - some of these traditional and some involuntary. I took myself off to Bodmin on the night before the Riding Day, and established myself at the best local inn, where every room was occupied, some by more than one person. Most of the people were wealthy farmers and their wives, some from as far away as St Ives in the one direction and Boscastle in the other, all looking forward to the the gaiety of the morrow, and most indulging in considerable drinking in preparation, or as it might be by way of practice.

Enormous quantities of beer are brewed in the preceding October, and kept until the day of the Feast, when in the early morning barrels of it are paraded around the town - so that I was awakened at six o'clock by a tremendous bawling below my window, and on looking out saw five young men of the town, each bearing a barrel so large that he could barely carry it, and accompanied by a band of fifes and drums and other instruments playing what I was told was the Riding Tune, halting before each house and, with a blow upon the drum, crying: 'To the people of this house, a prosperous morning, long life, health, and a Merry Riding!' – when the master of the house was supposed to descend, taste the riding-ale from a cup filled from one of the barrels, and toss into a basket a piece of silver later to be spent by the bearers.

There was then a motley procession to the Church, the men and women of the town being mounted upon any beast of burden they could find – from fine hunters to mean donkeys or mules – and after a blessing from the priest, the people made their way to the edge of the moor above the town, where the fun began, consisting of racing, the ringing of hand bells, cudgel-playing for a silver cup, jingling-matches, foot races, bobbing for apples and of course wrestling – a prize of ten sovereigns being offered for the best man, and five shillings for every standard – that is, every man who succeeded in throwing two opponents during the contest, or threw one and stood for a certain time with another. This was altogether a more violent matter than the wrestling match which I have already described, the men fighting almost with desperation for the prize, which in some cases represented their only chance of making a considerable sum in money.

I cannot say that I found this an enjoyable spectacle, for it degenerated into a fight not only with bare fists, but with metal buckles, metal-tipped shoes, and even staves; so that the contestants were frequently one mess of blood before the bout was half over. The ladies, however, particularly of the lower sort, were much addicted to the sport, the shouts and screams of encouragement from the maidservants, dairymaids and so forth spurring their favourites on, the sight of blood seeming to be an aphrodisiac of sorts, as their flushed faces and heaving bosoms testified. The winners, moreover (as I learned), could have their choice among their admirers, retiring to a nearby copse to satisfy both their own raised appetites (for physical action of the one sort engendered the other) and those of the maids for whom to have their bodies smeared with the blood of their victorious lovers was a tribute of which they boasted to their friends. Even the losers, provided their defeat had been courageously sustained, were rewarded in a similar way, having to be content however with those ladies rejected by the victorious few.

Those ladies and gentlemen to whom I had sent invitations gathered in a large tent or marquee which I had sent for to Truro, and which was fitted up in luxurious fashion, with tables properly clad with linen, with decent glasses and wine to be drunk from them, and an excellent feast of delicacies the preparation of which I had supervised in my own – or rather Frank's – kitchen, and with some homelier local food – viz. pasties and pies both of fish and of meat, with potatoes and turnips cooked with them. It soon became apparent that both the ladies and the gentlemen felt that upon this occasion they should partake of the local Riders' ale, whereupon I sent out for a barrel.

This was announced by a drum and a fife which came before it, whereupon there appeared in the entrance of the tent a well set-up young lad of sixteen or seventeen years, upon whose naked shoulders the barrel sat, and who as he walked down between the tables I was astonished to see assaulted by the ladies, who reached out to clutch at his thighs or what lay between them in an attempt to make him drop the barrel, which however (he being presumably prepared for this treatment) he did not do, and on reaching the end of the tent set it down and received much applause for his pains.

The speed with which the ale was disposed of was considerable, the lad remaining and himself taking more than one jug of it (this also being the custom). In the midst of the jollity, I announced that if the gentlemen would accompany me, I had arranged some entertainment for them, and led them to a second tent erected behind the first. There I bade them to make a circle, and that having been done gave a signal whereat into the midst of them came Dolly and Jane, who I had commissioned for the day. (They had proved, I may say, confidantes and friends, their apparent enmity being carefully rehearsed for any occasion of a battle!)

They immediately began to wrestle, and in no time had divested each other of their upper clothing, revealing to the audience (who were as pleased with the sight as I had formerly been) one body perhaps somewhat overblown, yet still in excellent condition, and one whose lithe torso and fine, firmly delineated breasts, whose back, slender yet rippling with muscles, were particularly pleasing. The weather being warm and the atmosphere further heated by the airlessness of the tent and the enthusiasm of the audience, the girls' bodies were soon running with perspiration, the sight of which, as it laved their limbs, added an irresistible glamour to the sight.

But this was not the sum of the entertainment I had

devised. After a certain time, it was clearly Dolly who was in the ascendant – which caused some consternation, as Jane, the more handsome of the two, as is invariably (unjustly) the case, was favourite. Dolly succeeded in throwing her opponent to the ground, and, sitting upon her belly, began belabouring her about the head. At this point there sprang from the audience a fine upstanding young fellow, clearly from his loose linen breeches also a wrestler, who, throwing off his shirt, hurled himself at the pair, and seizing Dolly by the shoulders toppled her from her seat. But now a second fellow, another wrestler, well matched to the first, came forth and took Dolly's part, attacking the first.

There now followed a general *mêlée*, during which it gradually became clear that the participants found a greater interest in amorous engagement than the more antagonistic sort. This was first suggested when, one of the young men being pinned to the ground by the other, Dolly turned to Jane and nodded, whereupon the former thrust her hand into the waistband of the pinned man's breeches, and found there (by her expression) a muscle as impressive as those which worked in his shoulders as he endeavoured to throw his rival off.

However, Miss Dolly's exploration had its effect, for a somewhat stupid expression of satisfaction spreading over his face, he soon gave up his endeavours, and lay without struggling beneath the body of his enemy. The latter found this puzzling enough for a moment – but only a moment, for now Miss Jane, not to be outdone, laid herself along his back, and, by rubbing her breasts against it, while at the same time reaching down to run her fingers through the fine growth of hair which decorated his chest, conveyed to him the fact that the ground of the battle had shifted.

In no time, the two men (not surprisingly, for so they had been instructed) released each other and turned their attention to the girls, drawing their breeches from them in order the better to admire them (which, by turning them about and about to explore each plane, also displayed them to the now entirely engrossed audience). Not to be outdone, the girls knelt before their swains, and loosing the cords which tied their nether clothes, drew off the breeches – not without difficulty, a serious obstruction to this course being their distended staffs, which even before the tribute of a kiss (now paid by the girls) had swelled to such a proportion as was not disappointingly at variance with the rest of their splendidly substantial frames.

There now followed a match scarcely less inspiriting than the serious display of wrestling which at the same time was taking place not far away – and which I had had some difficulty in persuading the two men to withdraw from, my argument being clinched only after the payment of a sum greater than the prize money they could have expected to win. The fitness of the couples contributed to their – and the audience's – enjoyment, for it enabled them to assume attitudes which only those fully in command of their limbs could enjoy: viz. Jane standing upon her hands while her lover, holding her legs as he would those of a wheelbarrow, eased his pego gently in and out of its natural home, each movement being accompanied by an equivalent swaying of the hips of the other gentleman, whose instrument was caressed by her lips; while at the same time Dolly, not to be outdone, hung by her bent legs about the latter's neck, her outstretched arms enabling her hands to reach the shoulders of the first man – which resulted in her quim being in such close proximity to the second's lips (do I make myself clear? – the tableau was an interesting one, but difficult to describe) that his tongue was easily able to explore it, giving Dolly such pleasure as was expressed in little yelps of joy.

By nature, such a tableau could be sustained, even by such athletes, only for moments; but its accomplishment was greeted by delirious applause just before it collapsed, and the four participants dissolving in laughter laid themselves out more conventionally, two by two, and to the continued applause of the gentleman viewers, satisfied themselves to the full in a posture more relaxed but none the less pleasure-giving.

I was glad to see that several gentlemen threw a coin or two on to the grass next the panting quartet; but before the audience could begin to disperse, I took my opportunity.

'Gentlemen,' I said, 'it seems that you have enjoyed the little spectacle which I have presented to you' – at which more cheers were heard, together with cries of 'Sir Franklin for Westminster!' 'I have, however,' I continued, 'to make an admission to you. I am not what you think I am.'

There fell an enquiring silence at this.

'I am not Sir Franklin Franklyn,' I continued; 'yet no impostor – having been commissioned by him to come among you and familiarise myself with the area. The mistake was mine in not making myself clear from the first; and for that, I apologise. I am Andrew Archer, Esquire, a gentleman of London. Yet should you wish to continue in desiring me to represent you at Westminster, I shall be pleased to do so.'

The silence which again followed my announcement did not last for long: rather, there was a call for three cheers for Mr Archer! – followed by enthusiastic huzzas. Only one man showed signs of impatience – this being Squire Treleaven, who I suppose discomfited by the fact that he had been the first to make the error of taking me for my friend, scowled and stalked from the tent. The rest seemed extremely pleased, from the applause; after which most of them, rather than turning to accompany me back to the tent where their wives and no doubt their mistresses had been left, slipped out by a side entrance, perhaps to go in search of some means of satisfying those spirits raised by the performance.

Myself, however, did return to the other place – expecting perhaps to face some dissatisfaction from the ladies, left to their own devices; but finding that far from this being the case, they had made their own fun – for I now discovered the beer-carrier spread upon a table while a young lady bestrode him, thoroughly enjoying a ride to the pleasure of which from his expression he was not entirely indifferent. The other ladies were gathered around, those who could not positively approach the couple cheering their representative on, while those nearer were unrestrained in their tormenting of the young man by pinching his nipples, scratching his flesh lightly with their nails, fondling his cods – one of them upon her knees sucking the toes of one foot, while another stood in a kind of trance while he sucked upon the thumb which she had inserted in his mouth.

The stamina of the young steed was remarkable, for he had clearly been successful so far in resisting a final ecstasy – as could be seen by the renitency of his riding-muscle as it appeared and disappeared between the caressing nether lips of his rider. However, sadly I was the destroyer of the scene, for my entrance distracted him from whatever concentration enabled him to deal with the situation, and, his eyes meeting my own, with an incoherent cry he evidently gave up his soul, at the same time however wrenching his hands from those ladies who were caressing them, to reach for the breasts of the young lady whose thighs bestrid him and squeeze them with sufficient force to bring her to an equivalent culmination, so that it was with an air of repleteness rather than disappointment that she dismounted, revealing his proud tool only a little less adamant than it had formerly been.

This was indeed so much the case that, hoping for a quick recovery, the ladies once more fell upon him, devising ever more inspiriting caresses in an attempt to raise once more his spirits – the likelihood being that they would succeed; but I turned my attention away, for at this point my eyes had fallen upon none other than Mrs Treleaven, whose eye, meeting my own, showed by the largeness of its pupil and the frankness of its gaze that she had enjoyed the spectacle to which she had just been treated – though at the back of the crowd, and so deprived of the possibility of engaging physically with the actors.

I gave her a bow. She was, as I have perhaps intimated, no longer young – perhaps of as many as forty years; but a handsome woman, her frame, though large, being by no means flaccid, and her carriage sufficiently upright to be that of a woman half her age.

She stepped towards me and gave me her hand –

pressing my own, and to my surprise lifting it to her bosom, which I found to be unsupported by any artificial means and, concealed only by a light cambric material, yielding yet firm to the touch. Even had I seen no advantage in getting her goodwill, I would not have found her unattractive; as it was, it immediately occurred to me (and I say it without shame) that it would be no bad thing to make myself pleasant with her.

'Perhaps, Sir Franklin, you would see me to my carriage?' she said. 'My husband is nowhere to be seen, and the heat has somewhat overcome me!' This with a flushed face and a panting bosom which may indeed have been the result of the heated atmosphere of the tent – though I imagined that the recent scene had perhaps contributed to it.

Taking my arm, she guided me to where, in a small stockade next the ground in which the Riding was held, a number of carriages were placed, and led me to the largest, which, though not of the proportions which would have commended it to London society, was nevertheless sufficiently capacious.

'Perhaps you would sit with me for a while?' said Mrs Treleaven; and in order to assist her into the carriage I must confess to placing my palm beneath her haunches, in closer juxtaposition to the ultimate seat of emotion than would normally be polite. That she received this without complaint gave me little surprise; nor was I amazed when, upon my mounting behind her, I found that she had already loosened the neck of her dress so that her bosom was almost completely exposed.

'You will pardon me, Sir Franklin,' she said; 'the heat is so oppressive . . .'

'Madam,' I exclaimed, 'the only protest I might make is

that the proximity of so beautiful a lady is likely to inflame my passion to the extent that I might take advantage—'

'Let the flames rise!' she said immediately; 'oh, let them rise!' – and pausing only to draw the blinds of the carriage, threw herself upon her knees before me and immediately reached for my breeches buttons, fumbling in such haste that her fingers were quite incapable of performing the task upon which she was set.

Happily, I had had no congress for some days, and on releasing my person from beneath my clothing, found the touch of her enquiring hands quite sufficient to result in an extension complimentary to the lady, whose patent admiration, and the ingenuity of whose caresses, resulted soon enough in a turgescence sufficiently impressive.

The dimensions of the carriage were somewhat confining; yet divested of the rest of our clothing, we found it possible to assume an attitude satisfactory to the lady – this consisting of her turning her back to me and resting her folded arms upon the seat opposite, so that I could guide my staff between her thighs in order to reach heaven. The ample proportions of her person were no hindrance to my enjoyment: I had quite forgot, indeed, the pleasure to be got from embracing a well-covered female, which has the effect of romping among a pile of cushions. In this case, too, the lady's appetite proved aphrodisiac, for the enjoyment she received was expressed in a controlled hysteria – so much so that after a while she was entirely unable to maintain the attitude she had adopted, and suddenly standing threw me off, turned about, and bestriding me placed her hands beneath my arse and lifted me bodily until, my cheeks resting upon the edge of the seat, she was able at her own pace to work away, my face buried in the ample convexities of her by no means unattractive bosom, and only the unusual attitude in which I found myself enabling me to keep my countenance until, her teeth nipping her lips to prevent herself crying out, she finally ceased her movements and let me fall with a thump to the floor.

It was at that moment that there was the rattle of a stick upon the door of the carriage, and a cry of 'Flora, m'dear – are you there?'

It was Squire Treleaven!

The lady showed considerable quickness. Pulling aside the blind only a little, she called out in a weak voice:

'My dear, I am a little fatigued by the heat, and taking a little rest. I will join you for dinner at the Punchbowl.'

After but a single enquiry as to whether he could fetch a glass of ale or some other comfort, the Squire left – to my considerable relief, for had he discovered that in addition to deceiving him as to my identity I had now swived his wife under his very nose (so to speak), my reputation would have become as nothing to him.

His lady had now recovered sufficiently to reach for me once more; but unsurprisingly my tool had shrunken under the effect of the Squire's appearance, and for a moment declined to rise (despite the fact that I had not participated in the consummation which the lady had experienced).

Expressing, however, no dismay, she sank to her knees and administered such attentions with her lips as the most experienced whore would be hard put to it to contrive; whereat I recovered soon enough, and was able not only to satisfy her once more, but to pay her – without any difficulty whatsoever – the compliment of a discharge sufficiently generous to confirm my admiration; indeed, her adeptness, willingness and pleasure in the game were such as to overbalance entirely the disadvantage of her years.

I had, I must confess, meant to take advantage of the opportunity to explain myself to her – in the sense, I mean, of excusing the embarrassment over my identity. Yet it was impossible to do as we both lay in that delightful lethargy which invariably follows satisfactory congress, and after a decent interval I merely assumed my clothes (having some difficulty in sorting them from the tangle of garments now scattered upon the floor of the carriage) and made my *adieux*.

That evening, I made my way to the Punchbowl Inn, where a number of gentlemen with their ladies were dining with the Squire, and screwing my courage up entered the room fairly late in the evening, when I judged that good food and drink might have lifted the heart even of the most serious Whig among them.

To my relief, I was greeted by a round of applause, as the provider of the afternoon's entertainment; and even Squire Treleaven seemed to look on me kindly, and making room waved me to a chair at his side, then rising to address the company.

'Gentlemen!' he said, 'Due entirely to an over-speedy act on my own part, I introduced this young man to you as Sir Franklin Franklyn, of Vycken Hall. It appears that this is not the case . . .' A murmur ran about the room. The Squire lifted his hand: 'But it is no matter!' he said. 'Mr Andrew Archer is a person of the utmost probity, intelligent and personable' (here I caught Mrs Treleaven's eye, and was in no doubt that she had commended me to him) 'and subject to your agreement' (he looked around the table, in the entirely confident expectation that no one would dare to cross him) 'I have no hesitation in suggesting that he should none the less be our candidate for the coming contest.'

Mrs Treleaven immediately applauded, and after the slightest hesitation was followed by most of the company – the gentlemen perhaps in part because they were in the midst of a congenial evening, and in part because they had enjoyed the afternoon's entertainment – the ladies less wholeheartedly, though led by the Squire's wife. It may be, I thought, that I should have to ingratiate myself further with the weaker sex if my position was to be entirely assured. As it was, however, I took more than a single glass of wine with the company, and sat until the candles guttered and the faint hints of dawn showed themselves beyond the blinds.

Chapter Eight

Sophie's Story

Organising the party at Mrs Teazle's was no great problem for me, since by now I had at my command a considerable knowledge of those circles in the city which could provide me with the *dramatis personae* for almost any amorous performance which the inventive mind of man – or woman – could envisage. It is also the fact that I actually enjoy the process of putting such matters in train, which in this case involved merely a visit to certain theatres in the town, both to the green-rooms where always could be found personable ladies and gentlemen happy to engage in employment outside the walls of the playhouse, and the rooms where the scene-makers could be relied upon to help with the construction of scenes or, as on the occasion of which I speak, the provision of certain paints to be applied to the skin, were it wished to give it a resemblance to the darker skins of other climes – or indeed of no known clime!

It was with some confidence that, having made my arrangements, I arrived at Mrs Teazle's house in Upper Brook Street at eleven o'clock in the morning of the day in question, just after Mr Teazle's departure for his Club; there I spent the day making my preparations, with the help of a gang of men whose first task was to remove the garden statues from their plinths, and who then helped in the decoration of the garden by hanging bands and swathes of flowers and greenery, and building *torchères* for torches which would illuminate the place.

Promptly at nine o'clock, Mr Teazle and nine of his friends arrived from their Club, where they had already spent the day celebrating the anniversary of the gentleman's birth – though not, I hoped, to such an extent that the coming pleasantries would be entirely lost upon them.

They sat down to dinner, somewhat surprised, I believe, at the absence of female company; for having heard by devious means that an entertainment was being organised, they had assumed, quite understandably, that it would include, besides meat and drink, those conveniences which permit gentlemen to satisfy other appetites.

However, the dinner I had ordered was sufficiently delicious, and the wines sufficiently excellent, to keep them in a good mood: the soup, a delicious *bisque d'écrevisses* was followed by turbot in lobster sauce; pheasant, green-goose and turkey preceded *fondue*, cabinet-pudding, orange jelly and *meringue glacés*, each with its wine; and by the time the port was circulating – a pint bottle to each man, of course – there was a general feeling of *bonhomie*. It was at this stage that, upon a signal from myself, the candles in the dining-room were extinguished and footmen drew back the curtains which had until that moment obscured the view of the garden – which was now revealed, lit by flaming torches.

At first, Mr Teazle must have thought that some Midas had been at work and turned his four garden statues upon their plinths to gold: there, in fact, stood four young gentlemen selected for their likeness to the marble effigies which I had had carefully removed and stored, to be replaced by human flesh.

Upon the first plinth was Hermes, holding his lyre – a splendid gentleman of perhaps twenty-five, slim of waist and narrow of hips, but fully developed and in the prime of young manhood; next him was a fellow of perhaps thirty and five, of a heavier build, his broad chest (normally decorated with a thick bush of black hair, which had for this occasion been shaved) expressive of the power and majesty of Apollo.

Opposite this pair stood a sturdy man fully of Mr Teazle's own age, yet preserved by action and energy – he was a professional fighter who had only recently given up the game, and whose face expressed all the burly forthrightness of Zeus; and next him the goatish figure of Pan, his horns rising out of his curly hair, his legs covered in hair, a stumpy tail perkily protruding above the cleft of his buttocks.

These gentlemen had had their bodies all gilded, even to their hair (which was painted and stiffened by the application of spirit gum, so that it looked, both upon head and body, as though 'twere made of gold thread), and were standing so still that, as I said, they seemed at first to be made of metal itself. There was some admiration from the audience, who none the less seemed to wonder what such an exhibition could have to do with them, who were not known expressly for their love of art, and were certainly not of that disposition best to be pleased by an exhibition of unclothed persons of their own sex!

But now upon the scene came four ladies, each dressed in flowing robes in the Greek fashion, sufficiently loose to reveal, as they walked, glimpses of thigh and breast – first, Chimaera, bearing her jug of wine, then

Dryope, the shepherdess, with her crook; then strode in Metis, the Titaness – a commanding figure whose burly shoulders were scarcely veiled by her flowing black hair; and finally Selene, that innocent young girl at whom Pan set his sights.

Hidden musicians now struck up an enticing air by the French musician Jean François Lesueur, and the show began. As the others held a pose at the back of the garden, before the fountain, whose drops were turned to liquid gold by the light of the torches, Chimaera approached the plinth upon which Hermes stood, and, lifting her jug to her shoulder, smiled as though inviting him to drink. I believe that some of the gentlemen in the audience believed the statues really to be of gilded stone, for there was a slight gasp as the young god came to life, moved his golden limbs, and descending from his plinth took from her the jug and drained it. The magic liquor immediately had its effect, for his legs weakened beneath him, and he swayed – whereupon the girl lifted one of his arms about her shoulders in order to support him – but was unable to hold such a weight, and the god slumped to the ground, where he lay apparently unconscious!

She stood aghast, the reduction of so promising a gentleman from vivid life to seeming death being the opposite of what she desired. Kneeling beside him, she laid her cheek against his, to discover whether he still breathed, or no; then, confirmed in her hopes at least of that, laid her hands upon his breast, which gently rose and fell beneath their palms. As she leaned to observe him, her robe fell forward over his body, obscuring it from her view – whereat she impatiently shrugged it from her shoulders, whose white perfection, set against the dark of the night and only slightly yellowed by the torchlight, now showed in brilliant contrast to the ruddier gold of his own. Her breasts were perfectly formed, their enticing curves shaped by an attentive gravity, which pulled them gently from her body as if envious to possess them, and her posterior – seen to greater advantage by those fortunate gentlemen sitting rather to the leftward of the scene – resembled nothing so much as a ripe peach, the delightful flesh of which any full-blooded gentleman would wish gently to nibble.

Now, freed from the encumbrance of clothing, Chimaera fell more minutely to examining and admiring the limbs of the fallen god, which she did with growing pleasure as her palms grazed the planes of his breast, belly and hips, then after only a moment's hesitation at what might seem behaviour improper between human and god, played for a moment among the gold curls where lay his manhood. But – alas, poor Chimaera! – what disappointment was here? – for rather than turning under her caresses from twig to tree, from acorn to oak, his shrunken piece remained so small as almost to be hidden from sight.

I must confess to admiring the powers of young Robin Phibb, whom I had found in the company of players at His Majesty's Theatre; for despite her lifting his squab part upon her palm and stroking it in the most insinuating manner with her fingers, he managed to contain himself – by, he told me afterwards, attempting to recall the entire part of Helicanus in *Pericles, Prince of Tyre*, a part of which he was memorising in preparation for a coming production of that neglected work of the great Bard.

However, such reticence scarcely contributed to the gaiety of the evening, and in accordance with our rehearsal of the scene, after a while – though his body remained still, his face expressionless and his limbs relaxed – he nevertheless showed signs of life, when the beautiful Chimaera now laid upon his reluctant firing piece a tender, exploring tongue, first gently withdrawing the skin, which disclosed beneath its gold rim an almost strawberry pink flesh, then testing it with just the hope of pleasure summer fruit would give; whereupon almost in an instant he permitted the blood to flow, and a ramrod of quite sufficient dimensions established itself between her lips – at which she started almost with fear, yet not such apprehension as prevented her being at the same time delighted.

Since the still unconscious god showed no sign of movement other than between belly and thigh, rolling upon her back the impatient maid pulled his body upon her own, opening both arms and thighs to embrace him. Yet even so poignant an invitation was ignored by Hermes, who still lay insensible, his head lolling upon her shoulder; and while a hand had fallen upon one delicious breast, it made not the slightest gesture of taking advantage of the prize within its palm. There was a stirring in the audience, and some comments to the effect that were certain humans to take his place, such reticence would be instantly banished.

But now, again disappointed, the furious Chimaera sat up, Hermes' body falling to one side – the most remarkable feature of it still extant and (to judge by her expression as she handled it) capable of performing the task demanded of men by women – yet without waking motive, inactive.

Once more taking command, and rolling Hermes upon his back, Chimaera brought things to a more satisfactory head by the simple device of mounting upon his body as upon a bareback horse, and rising upon her knees momentarily, in order to present the ramrod to the barrel, then sank upon it and with every sign of gratification began to trot – with a mounting enthusiasm which communicated its warmth to the onlooking gentlemen, who watched with keen interest as the rosy skin of a human youth began to appear upon each of still sleeping Hermes' sides, where the gilt with which his skin had been painted now transferred itself to the inside of Chimaera's thighs; and soon, indeed, the length of his swiving tool returned by exhilarating friction to the normally flushed hue of a handsomely distended prick.

To his credit, young Mr Phibb maintained until the last a pretence of unconsciousness, not the slightest flicker of apprehension appearing upon his features even when (no doubt apprehensive of the tension of his muscles) Chimaera after a final wriggle of her lower person rose, releasing from its socket the delightful wand just in time to prove by the exuberance of a suddenly released fountain that she had brought the sleeping god beyond the borders of ultimate pleasure.

The pair for a moment held the pose; then, as the onlookers broke into applause, rose to their feet and took their bow – something which no doubt broke the illusion; but it would have been unkind, even in the warmth of summer, to have them remain upon the cold flagstones during the rest of the entertainment, which followed without pause, the frozen group behind them broken by the figures of Apollo and Dryope, who moved forward, the god revealing as he strode into the full torchlight that his own torch was already burning with desire – a view of the previous combatants having been sufficient to set light to it.

In order that there should not be a climax of pleasure too soon in the evening, I had ensured that these two should present no unusual aspect: taking Dryope's crook in his hand, Apollo therefore drew her immediately towards him, and taking her by the waist lifted her upon the edge of the fountain, where, raising the skirt of her dress, he parted her thighs, and standing between them began that work which – from her silent shriek of pleasure (for my actors were strictly enjoined to make no sound which would dispel the charm of the performance) – gave her no small joy. Lifting her arms, she lost no time in tearing her single garment from her, and clutching Apollo's head directed his lips to those rosy nipples which shone upon her full breasts.

Apollo and Dryope completed their coupling in a few minutes; for I did not wish the interval of conventionality to be too long. I had anticipated, and warned them, that they would not receive the acclamation accorded their predecessors, and so having given a final thrust of his arse, Apollo placed his muse's arms about his neck, and, lifting her with his hands below her buttocks, walked from the scene – as it turned out, without either himself having reached an apogee, or giving his lady that pleasure – they being a professional couple whose participation was solely for the profit involved, while my other pairs showed an enthusiasm for the game which was the equal of, or even surpassed, their desire for monetary consideration.

This was certainly true of Zeus and Metis, who now took the stage. I have said that Zeus was a gentleman of considerable parts; but if his limbs were sturdy and his frame massive, he was matched by his companion, to whom I had been directed at a circus on the heath behind the village of Hampstead, where I found her earning coppers by the lifting of weights and the bending of iron bars.

Now, striding towards the centre of the garden, she loosed her upper clothing so that it fell about her waist, and with both hands raised a bar she had brought with her above her head and bent it with a steady motion until it was doubled. The extraordinary aspect of the performance was in the appearance of her torso, which, her arms being raised, could have been that of a well-developed man; her breasts were no larger than those rounded muscles upon the chest of a burly fellow, while cords stood out in her arms and across her shoulders which would have been the envy of many a seaman!

Indeed, the whisper ran about that she was a man – which notion however was dispelled upon Zeus stepping forward, for, immediately eager for the fray, she threw her clothing altogether aside, revealing between two thighs with the dimensions of tree-trunks a fleece of thick black hair barely concealing lips already pouting with desire as their owner's eyes fell upon the protuberance which sprouted from the equivalent area of the body of her would-be lover. His sturdy appliance seemed knotted and banded with muscles of its own, resembling ribs, giving it such an appearance as would justify some men's description of it – a weapon indeed!

I must here remark that upon my putting to her the scheme of entertainment which I had devised, Mary Morgan (for this was the giantess's name, she being of Welsh descent) had been delighted to acquiesce, for, because of her size and somewhat masculine appearance, it was (she confided) but rarely that she could entice a lover to satisfy appetites which were as keenly resident within her large frame as in that of the prettiest girl. Moreover, her passions matched her size, and lovers of conventional powers found themselves confounded, for in her frenzy she frequently did them some injury, such as the dislocation of an arm or even (on one sad occasion) a neck.

In this case, however, Metis was well-matched with Zeus: and the clashing of the two titans was like the coming together of two great jungle beasts – a bubbling sound of anticipatory pleasure boiled low in their throats as their bodies met – which itself took place with a peculiar sound, a sort of dull thud. Neither appeared to wish to give way, and for a moment they appeared like wrestlers embracing each other, arms upon each other's shoulders; then – I am convinced through desire rather than lack of strength – the titaness fell backwards upon the flagstones with sufficient force (it seemed to me) almost to break them, and threw up her legs to reveal a cavern of such dimensions that only a such a fellow as Zeus could hope satisfactorily to fill it; which, on the instant, he did, her under-thighs meeting his breast and belly with a sounding *smack!*

The appetites of this pair were as strong as their bodies; by contrast to their predecessors they engaged for a considerable period of time, the size and muscularity of their bodies giving at every turn new cause for interested attention; now he would be in the ascendant (as at first, ploughing to admiration), now she, as when with a sudden effort she grasped her lover about the hips and lifted him bodily from her, then raising him until, supporting him thus, she was able to nuzzle that massive instrument which at every moment seemed to grow more considerable, and could scarcely have been outdone in size or combativeness by those of the most prized bull of a show! Whereafter he, not to be outdone, stood, legs apart, took her by the hips and lifted her high in the air, then lowering her until he was able to return the compliment by planting an enthusiastic kiss upon that cavity which, a moment later, returning her to the ground, he again plugged with proper flesh.

I must confess that the show was as remarkable for acrobatics as for amorous play, and regarding the audience believe that they shared my own feeling in the matter, for their look was rather admiring than enthusiastic; something which however was swiftly repaired when, upon Zeus and Metis retiring (to the nearby garden shed where, ignoring Apollo, who was busy cleansing his body of gilt, and Dryope, who was engaged in sewing a skirt, they continued an enthusiastic amorous contest, their zestful enthusiasm not yet having been quenched), there now entered upon the scene the goat-like Pan, startling the virtuous Selene, who had clearly never before seen such a remarkable creature.

At first, he appeared to her with his lower person hidden behind the wall of the fountain and his hair ruffled to conceal his little horns; so that all she saw was a handsome youth, at whose presence only her shyness mitigated against welcome; though her eyes widened at his appearing, from a lack of clothing upon the upper part of his body, to be entirely naked. Upon his moving closer, she was immediately relieved, clearly believing his legs to be clad in some sort of hairy breeches, and permitted him to take her hand, and even to kiss it – whereupon, smoothing his hair with a hand, she found to her surprise those protuberances which upon closer examination revealed themselves as horns.

This clearly astonished her – yet she did not withdraw, no doubt because by now his tiny tongue was insinuating itself between her fingers, and his lips in turn sucking upon them. Transferring those lips to the back of her hand, then her wrist, and finally travelling the length of her slim white arms, he reached at length (by way of one shoulder, revealed by the fall of her tunic) her own lips, tickled the corners of her mouth, and even exchanged greetings with her own tongue, which could be seen pinkly to greet his.

But it was a different matter when, encouraged by her lack either of fear or anger, and eager to be at her, he took her hand and placed it between his thighs – for there she felt, as her expression denoted, something she had not expected: a hard yet warm prong of flesh which from its throbbing boded her no good.

She rose as though to flee: but he was too quick for her, and clutching caught the edge of her tunic, which immediately fell from her (a process encouraged by our unpicking the seams of it almost entirely before the commencement of the programme), revealing a body white as a wand, and of quite remarkable beauty, poised between the purity of girlhood and the ripeness of womanhood – she was in fact one of the most beautiful girls upon whom I had had the pleasure of setting eyes (who was, under the name of Mrs Hunbert, to become one of the admired actresses of the age, excelling in the parts of Perdita, Hermione and Ophelia). She was a person of great probity, and had only been persuaded to participate in my entertainment by the fact that she was violently in love with the young person who was impersonating Pan, and who had formerly ignored her.

I must now reveal that the actor playing the part of Pan was none other than my young friend John Rice, who but a few weeks previously had by his appearance as a satyr rehearsed for his present, more prominent – but equally hirsute – characterisation. It may be thought remarkable that I had consented to his wish to participate in the entertainment – expressed as soon as he had heard of its going forward; but my constant readers will know how devoid I am of that most wasteful of emotions, jealousy; and revenged myself somewhat upon him (if revenge is not too strong a word for what amounted merely to a prank) by appointing him a partner who I knew had for some time experienced the unrequited love of which I have spoken!

If he had previously not so much as looked at the lady, he was now – as who would not be? – struck by the loveliness of her body, its slim waist hung with generous hips below which lay thighs firm yet enticing; slight shoulders supporting arms which seemed boneless as they curved about him – and a bosom the whiteness of which was decorated by two little marks like ripe berries: and, from the tender manner in which he set them to his lips, as sweet.

For a moment, Pan forgot himself, and seemed about to treat his nymph with an unwonted tenderness; but then remembered his part, and throwing her to the flagstones – while she pretended horror and distress – knelt upon her shoulders, so that above her stood at attention an instrument so fierce-looking, being decorated with hair which had been stuck upon it with no small difficulty, that it aggravated her terror to an hysteria that only I, from my intimate knowledge, knew to be feigned.

The struggle that ensued was convincing enough to

suggest a rape; and I, knowing the secret history of the pair, realised that the passions of Pan (or rather, of my friend John) were indeed roused by the surprising generosity with which the lady not only offered him those delights of her body to which ignorance had previously rendered him indifferent, but put herself about to contribute to their coupling such inspiriting caresses that one might wonder how they came into the head of a young person who had but recently left the comfort of a Leicestershire parsonage for the more interesting but less cloistered life of the stage. I was once more impressed by the speed with which actors and actresses can command a part, speed of study clearly being one of Mrs Hunbert's many virtues.

However, to return to my narrative, the audience now saw Selene, delighted at her proximity to the person she so admired, rouse him yet further by the little bites which she inflicted upon his limbs, thus exciting him to new displays of coarseness. With an expressive display of acted repugnance, it was at first with reluctance that she shrank from the ill-manners with which he brandished his private part before her, forcing her to caress it; but gradually she seemed to find this more interesting than repellent, then curiosity encouraged her to kneel before him and inspect further such an odd device, entirely new to a maid, stroking the hair which covered its surface, and, withdrawing the skin at its end, greeting with astonished pleasure the bald head which seemed to admire her with its single eye!

After an interval, his similar attention to her own parts – informed by experience (as much the amorous experience of the actor as of the god!) – led inevitably to coupling sufficiently spirited in its vigour and exciting in its postures not only to delight the lady but to to excite the audience; and a storm of applause went out on the still night air as the torches guttered to darkness just as the embracing god and his mortal mistress with a final embrace satisfied each other.

Allowing no time for the gentlemen's emotions to cool, I entered the room from behind the screen where I had been concealed, and announced that if they would follow me to a neighbouring room, they would find the material with which to satiate any appetite raised by the spectacle. Yet there was one condition: the ladies, who were of the finest society, had asked me to spare their blushes by insisting on a paucity of lighting, and permitting them to wear masks.

The gentlemen were in no mood to argue; and followed me to a room equipped with several *banquettes* and cushions, where an equal number of ladies waited, their unclothed forms only dimly to be seen in the light shed by two candles, and upon whose bodies the amorous gentlemen fell like thunderbolts, having paused only to remove their clothing (or in some cases, merely that part of their clothing which would have hindered them from carnal connection).

The following saturnalia was satisfactory to all parties; yet I must confess it was with some anxiety that, upon the last of the couples ceasing their writhing, I entered together with three footmen bearing candelabra – whereupon the ladies, in a light now sufficient to be revelatory, removed their masks and revealed themselves as . . . the wives of the male guests!

After an initial amazement and embarrassment – some of the gentlemen having paid to their partners such amorous attention as had previously been reserved only for their mistresses – the gentlemen took the prank in good part – even those who, through some misalignment, had been the partners of each other's wives; and so delighted were the latter that the reticence with which they usually embraced their husbands gave way to unusual enthusiasm, and a recoupling was commenced – at which I retired, making my way to the shed where my actors were now resuming their day clothing, and disbursing those fees promised.

Returning to my house, my only regret – to be frank with readers sufficiently familiar with my previous adventures not to take offence at the confession – was that I had myself been unable to take part in the tableaux, for I was convinced that my own person was not so sufficiently advanced in years as not to be attractive to the discerning gentleman. Moreover, my senses had no more been dormant under the stimulation of the exhibition than those of my audience, and I was increasingly conscious that they required satisfaction.

My house was dark, the servants having permission to retire at their own time when I was from home (since there was no knowing at what time I might return). I disrobed in my bedroom, yet was confident that the arms of Morpheus were entirely unready to welcome me – and so, slipping on a *robe de chambre*, set out down the corridor and through the door beyond which lay the servants' quarters, and in particular the room appointed to John Rice, who I believed, despite his adventures of the evening, might welcome me – indeed, who had better welcome me, in view of my hospitality to him, to say nothing of my equanimity in watching his attentions to another female!

None of the servants' rooms were capable of being

locked, it not being the custom in those days to allow them that privacy which a more civilised society now permits; and the door to John's room was no exception, so on my softly turning the handle, it freely opened, and in the dim light shed by a waning moon I saw upon the bed his charming person, lying face down, the moonlight falling over his body and giving it the appearance of polished marble (though a marble here and there smirched with gold, and here and there marked by small patches of hair, which he had been unable altogether to remove).

Taking two steps forward, I stood above him, and in a moment laid my fingers gently upon that most sensitive spot just above the bifurcation of the buttocks, the slightest grazing of which raises the spirits of the most lethargic of men; and indeed, upon my merely scratching the surface of the skin with a fingernail, he stirred, and turning stretched up his arms still in half-sleep and clutching me about the waist buried his head in my lap, and murmured the name of Melody, by which name Mrs Hunbert wished to be known (her given name, Joy, being considered insufficiently euphonious for an actress). Though not resentful, this was not a sound welcome to my ears, and I could not resist the rebuke of giving a gentle twist to those twin spheres which are sensitive to such attacks, whereupon he woke completely, and had the grace to blush.

Any fears that his powers might have been exhausted by his attentions to Mrs Hunbert were within a short time dispelled. I will not detail the engagement itself further than to say that with vigour balanced by tenderness, rudeness mitigated by admiration, gentleness stiffened by determination, he entirely fulfilled – as he was always capable of – those expectations I had of him. Lying in his arms after we had both experienced the final peak of pleasure, I could not but enquire whether in the matter of such amusements as that in which he had taken part, affection could ever accompany so public a display, or whether mechanical contrivance alone produced the effect? I believe he knew by my expression what I meant, and I was rewarded by the reply (though hesitatingly expressed) that I should not be amazed that a vigorous young man should be attracted to youth and beauty – though on completing the sentence it was immediately softened by his assurance that years had by no means diminished the effect of my own charms, 'else', he said, 'how could I have raised my spirits after already twice this evening paid tribute to Venus?'

I could not but enquire, 'Twice?' – whereupon he admitted that he and Mrs Hunbert (who, I should say, is not nor ever has been married, but takes the appellation of 'Mistress' for the sake of respectability), having left the garden, had been encouraged to repeat their amorous engagement by the emotion engendered by her assisting him to remove the false hair from his loins (which I considered was taking a liberty with a young person of the opposite sex to whom she had only recently been introduced).

However, all in all I must admit that I approved the engagement; for though the young man was pleasant enough, and I was happy to continue to give him shelter, it went without saying that our connection was not such as could lead to permanence; and upon the time coming when I must ask him to leave the house, it was best he should have some companion to afford him upon a regular basis those pleasures to which I was still, for the moment, happy to contribute.

So, having given him a final embrace, and assured myself by manual examination that he was for the time incapable of renewed excitation (a circumstance for which he offered shamefaced apologies), I returned to my own bed, and fell into a satisfied and deep sleep as dawn began to rise.

Mrs Teazle was prompt in the payment of my considerable expenses, adding to them a generous fee. But the matter did not end there, for within the week a footman called upon me, asking me to attend upon the Earl of Stow, the leader of that society whose chief interest is in the breeding and racing of horses. Calling upon him at his mansion in Park Lane, I was forced to wait until a clatter of hooves in the courtyard announced his return from riding in the Park, and looking out of the window I saw a personable young man of perhaps thirty and five throwing over the back of his mount a leg of elegant proportions, and leaping to the ground with a nimbleness and athletic grace which immediately marked him as energetic and vigorous.

Upon his entering the room, this impression was confirmed – and though he apologised for his state, having been (he explained) trying out a new mount, the masculine odour of perspiration, no less than that humidity which caused his shirt (open to show the pillar of a strong and graceful neck) to adhere to a chest whose manly firmness was beyond question, was far from distressing.

His Lordship explained that, as was usual with him, he had organised a party for the Newmarket race meeting, a week hence; and that he was eager to place before his guests some entertainment for the Sunday upon which no racing, of course, took place. Such entertainment, he said, should take place in the open air – 'but will not be public' (he hastily assured me) 'for my estate is guarded by spinneys, and cannot be seen by passers-by.'

'From that remark, my Lord—'

'Call me Stow,' the gentleman generously remarked.

'—I infer that the kind of entertainment you wish—'

'—Might not be too far removed in tone from that which I understand you recently provided for Billy Teazle, who was full of praise for it at the Club.'

I bowed. 'I shall be delighted,' I said – and enquired whether he had anything specific in mind?

No, he remarked; though should it in some way include an allusion to the art of horsemanship – or horsewomanship, he added with a smile – that would not be untoward.

We discussed the matter for a while, for there were arrangements of which I had to be sure – such as the provision of hospitality for the ladies and gentlemen who should provide the entertainment; the disbursement of expenses—

'And your fee?' enquired Stow.

'I am happy to leave that in your hands,' I replied – for I was wealthy enough to ignore the matter, having been drawn into the work merely by accident and inclination, and not relying upon it for the provision of bread and wine.

Stow was good enough to offer me lunch, and having bathed himself (an exercise with which I would have been happy to assist, had I been invited, for he was an extremely attractive gentleman) we sat down to a cold collation accompanied by an Austrian wine, which we took alone, off splendid silver and from equally magnificent glasses, at one end of a long table in a sumptuous dining-room in which a hundred people could easily have been served.

During the meal he regaled me with tales of his recent tour in the Orient, which was taken for the purposes of sport, and during which (he told me with some pride) he had killed twelve brace of elephants, twelve couple of rhinoceroses, thirty-two couple of buffaloes, three camels, seven brace of ostriches, a crocodile, one hundred and thirty-seven brace of humming-birds, three boa-constrictors and two pair of rattlesnakes – upon which I expressed some surprise that any wild creatures of any sort remained upon that continent. And indeed, it seems to me curious that gentlemen should take such pleasure in the execution of their fellow-creatures. However, 'twas none of my business, and I cannot say that it detracted more than a very little from the attractions of my new friend, upon whose behalf I was shortly once more enquiring for specific talent among my friends of the theatre.

Chapter Nine

The Adventures of Andy

My passage with Mrs Treleaven, more interesting, perhaps, than positively inspiriting, seemed likely to be the last episode of erotic interest for some time, as I now found myself plunged into politicking – something of which I had no experience and in which (to be frank) I had previously had little interest.

The burning topic of the time was on the one side the popularity of Billy the King, and on the other popular dislike of the Tory Government – yet at the same time by no means a majority of people were in favour of the Whigs, most of whom were high-living artistocrats, fonder of claret and free love than of water and work.

And so I found myself a Radical, for despite Squire Treleaven (who had it not been for tradition would have been an Ultra-Tory High Churchman, but who from the accident of his birth, was a Whig Nonconformist!) this seemed the easiest way of ingratiating myself with the voters of the district. It was by no means a hardship to me, for I had much sympathy with the newly founded and growing trades unions, formed to save men from the hours of monotonous toil which made them little more than slaves.

There were no machines to break in east Cornwall, where farming and fishing were the chief occupations of the natives – yet even here people had heard of Robert Owen and what he called British Socialism, and I was astonished to find, in the hand of an artisan I encountered at the weekly cattle market in Liskeard, Lieutenant Hodgskin's pamphlet *Labour Defended against the Claims of Capital*, which, published some years previously, bore all the signs of repeated reading.

The whole county was full of election fever (I should explain that at that time the death of the Sovereign automatically dissolved the Parliament), and this persisted for some time, the polls opening in July to remain open for three weeks, during which activity was great not only in the making of speeches but the buying of drinks for voters, and even – on the part of my Tory opponent – the transfer of leases of houses, the provision of suits of clothing, small-arms, mittens and fur tippets for the ladies, and even swaddling clothes for infants.

All this I scorned (apart from any other consideration, Squire Treleaven and his cronies showed no signs of contributing funds to the election campaign, and I was certainly not inclined to squander my own funds upon it). Incidentally, I had of course sent word to Alcovary and my friend Frank of the circumstances of my standing for Parliament, and assuring him that should I obtain a seat in the Parliament, it would as a matter of course be resigned to him should he at any time require it; to which he had returned a message of congratulation and encouragement, good friend that he was.

If nothing else, my travelling about the county on this occasion taught me much about a part of the of world which I had previously been entirely in ignorance. The county is particularly marked for the splendour of its churches and the poverty of its houses, for apart from a very few (such as the one in which I was privileged to reside) the homes of the Cornish are small and mean. They are built of cob or clay, sometimes faced with local stone or slate if such is available, generally whitewashed upon the outside, and with their roofs thatched.

They look, I must admit, extremely pretty, fitting in well with the landscape, solid and foursquare, and weathered by the winds which commonly lash both coasts and inland hills. They straggle across the countryside, often isolated and lonely – for you will find them almost anywhere: tucked in odd corners by the roadside, on rocky ledges above the fishing coves, or amid the burrows and debris of the tin mines which provide (apart from fishing and farming) a chief income for the people.

They are built by the people themselves, often without the help of professional 'builders'; even the window frames are often made by the inhabitants, with such results in the terms of crookedness and small holes admitting the winds as I need not describe. Many of the cottages were built in great haste, for it was believed that any one who built a house in one night could claim the freehold of it for ever after – a belief much contested by landlords, and now beginning to be disclaimed.

Where cottages did cluster together in small groups, they made for strange villages indeed, higgledy-piggledy places with streets which so twisted and turned (and indeed so narrow) that they scarcely deserved the name: often have I ridden along streets so narrow that, by merely stretching out my arms upon each side, I could touch the buildings which faced each other. The windows of the upper rooms, which sometimes thrust out beyond the ground floor, are almost in juxtaposition, which must make for extreme ease of passage should there be extramarital concupiscence among the natives of the places.

As to the people, they are much as people anywhere else in the country, yet particularly given, as it seemed to me, to an interest in medical matters, and extremely ready to pass on even to a stranger the intimate details of their medical history. At a place called Trevarian, I was detained for an hour while two gentlemen hot in the Whig interest, and who I could not afford to offend by an over-precipitate retreat, told me of their discovery of Dr Lamb's medicines, a cure-all newly brought from Bristol, and efficacious in the curing of all manner of indigestion, bilious and liver complaints, difficulty of breathing, delicate constitutions - and above all, worms.

One man claimed that John Code, the manager of Screed Moor Clay Works, in the parish of St Austell, after taking a course of Lamb's medicine, passed a tapeworm seven feet long, with upwards of 200 joints, the symptoms of which had been pain and giddiness in the head, pain in the back and side, weakness between the stomach and the bowels, tightness across the chest, et cetera, et cetera.

No soon had I digested (so to say) that story, than I had to hear of Walter Nancarrow, miner of Mount Charles, near St Austell, who, after taking a course of the medicine, passed a tapeworm three yards long and with upwards of 400 joints - and was offered a sight of the worm, should I wish it; however I declined, and got myself off cheaply by purchasing a bottle of the medicine for three shillings - it being revealed that the gentlemen concerned were agents of the said Dr Lamb. The medicine I disposed of in a hedge directly I had turned the corner from their house.

After two weeks of riding from place to place speaking and shaking the hands of my future constituents (as I hoped) I began to fear for the health of any future pretender to Parliamentary membership, should common suffrage ever come in. Should every man have the vote, how would it be possible to survive such a campaign as would be necessary to secure election when I was exhausted almost to death even in the present circumstances – to say nothing of having to know, or pretend to know, about such matters as Mr Peel's betrayal of Protestantism, the disenfranchism of Gatton and Old Sarum, the sedition trials – and, when talking to the ladies, which perforce I must (since many of them clearly dominated their husbands to the extent to being capable of persuading them to vote for an entirely ignorant and unsuitable fellow, should he catch their eye), to discuss the present King's predilection for the actress Mrs Jordan, their *ménage* at Bushy Park, his proposal to a West Indian heiress of vast wealth but doubtful sanity, and the strange relationship of the Duchess of Gloucester to her cousin, commonly known as Silly Billy?

It will be supposed that I was more than ready for a little relaxation, and found it in the small town of Looe, which lies upon the coast about halfway between Fowey and the headland which protects the infinitely greater port of Plymouth.

Looe seems almost two places, two towns lying on opposite sides of the river from which they take their names – of East Looe and West Looe; and which, I guess, was itself named from its situation, for it runs between high hills, and the valley through which it meanders is indeed low – a word the Cornish pronounce as *looe*.

West Looe is the older place, but also the poorer; East Looe is of more recent origin, and seems a likely enough place – yet its houses seem literally to be built upon sand, for their walls are often askew and seem about to tumble. However it has lasted for some centuries, and has been of sufficient importance to be garrisoned, for the town towards the sea is faced with a garretted wall.

Thanks to Treweers – who had now become my election agent as well as my butler – I was given shelter at the Vicarage, a fine, humble house near the ancient church, and with a view over the bustling harbour which almost every tide filled with a plethora of fishing boats, some tiny, some substantial – for fishing was the heart and soul of the place.

The Vicar, the Rev. Polscoe – a local man – was a rough and ready soul, who kept a good cellar and an excellent table, rode to hounds whenever he could, and twice or thrice a week could be found, cassock about his waist, paddling in the mud looking for worms with which to bait his hooks (for he loved freshwater fish, and the river above the town was an excellent home to them).

Among the entertainment he proposed for me was to spend a day upon a fishing boat; this, he said, would endear me to the local people, and would also prove of value in recreating me, for nothing (as he said) was so calming and pleasant as a day spent upon the Channel in good, sunny weather.

I was happy to accept, and thus found myself sailing out of Looe harbour at five o'clock in the morning, on board the *George of Looe*, a hearty vessel with a crew of five men – the captain being a grizzled man of perhaps some sixty summers, his two sons of forty and five, and three grandsons, two somewhat older than myself, and one a beardless youth of perhaps eighteen years. Hoisting our brown sails, we made out into the channel until we were perhaps six or seven miles from the coast, then began to throw out our nets, and after an hour were at leisure, only having to maintain our station while the fish entered the nets.

The fishermen thereupon produced a small barrel of cider and packets of food, which we consumed sitting upon the deck in a warm breeze, with the sun beating down not so fiercely as to be oppressive, but merely pleasant in the extreme. I began to think that the life of a fisherman was not altogether to be despised (though reminding myself that it were entirely another matter in winter, when the storms in the Channel can be irresistibly fierce, resulting in much bereavement by drowning and shipwreck).

However, for the time everything was placid and recuperative, and after a while the warmth was so considerable that I followed the example of the other men (except for the youngest) and removed my shirt – they having done so long since, upon leaving port – the Cornish being a modest race, it was not considered polite to be shirtless upon land unless participating in a sport, which was considered a proper excuse.

It was, I supposed, such modesty (often accentuated in youth) that persuaded the younger man to retain his shirt, which was buttoned to the neck; yet he was not subjected to such scorn or rough humour as might have been expected from his brothers – who presumably were used to this nicety. They were a good-looking family, I reflected – rather against the grain of the local people, whose frames tended to the squat and thick, whereas these were more like the people of the eastern part of England, with long bodies, well-proportioned, though their shoulders and arms were broad and muscular from the efforts of their work (they were each to be seen upon the quays heaving baskets of fish about which would take two men of London to lift!). They seemed indeed to be of a different strain altogether, whether from their descending from another race (as, for instance, those Spaniards wrecked upon these shores at the time of the Armada, many of whom it is believed are amalgamated into the Cornish race) or from inbreeding, for as the saying is, incest flourishes where the roads are bad, and the roads of this part of England are notorious for becoming impassable in winter.

The younger brother seemed however to be slighter than the others, and I asked whether he had not been so long a fisherman as they had – receiving no reply from him, and merely a shake of the head from his brothers, which tempted me to believe that perhaps he was deficient in intelligence (as is often the case when families too closely intermarry, and went somewhat to encourage me to believe my former theory).

I was somewhat disappointed to observe that by mid-day the nets were drawn in so full of fish that the decision was made to return to port, thus cutting short what I had hoped would be a full day of relaxation, and which I had begun thoroughly to enjoy. Seeing my rather downcast visage, the old man asked whether I would care to prolong my outing somewhat, and look over St George's Island, which lies only about half a mile from the shore to the west of Looe. They needed, it seems, to replenish their supply of samphire, or *Herbe de St Pierre*, which they use for pickling. It grows commonly upon cliffs – and indeed there had been several accidents resulting in the death of those poor people who had attempted to gather it from the precipitate cliffs of east Cornwall; but it grew upon St George's Island in considerable proliferation, and Glaws was to be set ashore there, with the small coracle which was towed behind the fishing boat, to gather the herb and bring it back to Looe on the evening tide.

I agreed with pleasure, but was slightly confused at the name of 'Glaws' – but upon my asking, the skipper indicated the younger son, explaining that it was the name commonly given to her since upon her first walking she had fallen into a mess of *glaws*, this being the Cornish name for a cow-pat.

My confusion was now doubled at hearing the young man being referred to as a female; which however explained her slim figure and her retaining her shirt – and also her modesty or demeanour, rather different from the freer manners of her brothers.

On our reaching the neighbourhood of the small island, she leaped with great dexterity into the little coracle or dinghy, watching with what seemed ill-concealed scorn as I climbed more carefully into it; and then, seizing the single oar and using it thrust out behind, sped us with remarkable precipitation towards the beach, where on our landing she hauled the boat upon the sand with a greater strength than I would have given her credit for, and without a second glance at me set off around the coast, leaving me to explore as I might.

The island must be one of the smallest about the coast of England, for it is barely a half mile in circumference, rising to a low hill at the centre, and with beaches about most of its shore, though here and there there are rocks. Around the strand sea-birds breed in great numbers; they rose in great clouds as I moved about, though many declined to take notice of human intervention, so that I almost fell over them – as was true also of the conies, which played positively about my feet. Between the island and the low shoreline to the west of the town of Looe itself, is a stretch of water which is perhaps a quarter of a mile only in breadth, and now shone bright blue under the sun. It turned to a deeper blue, almost to purple, as it met the deeper water towards the south, where upon the horizon stands a lighthouse marking the famous Eddystone Rocks, upon which many a handsome vessel has foundered.

I mounted to the top of the hill, whence there was nothing to be seen – or, rather, whence nothing was to be seen except the now mild and delightful coast (turned in the storms of winter to a positive death-trap, but now most mild and agreeable). Below me, a disturbance among the sea-birds, to the south, showed me where Glaws (I knew no more elegant name to give her) was at work; and it was thence, after a while, that I strolled, eventually finding myself upon the edge of a little cliff – if a rise of but seven or eight feet can be dignified by the name – along the bottom of which she was making her way, and in a moment came to the top of, in order to reach clumps of samphire which clung to the face of the rise, and just below its rim.

For what reason she so relentlessly ignored me, I could not tell; I had not been in any way scornful of her – indeed, I had scarcely addressed a single word to her; or rather only the cursory greeting I had addressed also to her brothers. I watched her beneath lowered eyelids as she came near the place where I lay; and must admit to myself that my knowledge of her sex added an attraction which had been lacking when I had been under a misapprehension about it. She had gone so far, in acknowledgement of the sun's heat, as to undo a button or two at the neck of her shirt – but this showed, as closely as I could examine it without revealing my interest – no notably swelling bosom; however, as she presented me with a rear view of herself, on kneeling to reach over the edge of the cliff, I could not but believe that even had I not been told of her sex I would have guessed it, for her arse had that swelling roundness, almost heart-shaped, which could not for a moment be mistaken for that of a boy.

After a while, she retired with a bundle of the herb to a spot some fifty yards away, where she stuffed it into an already bulging sack, which she began hauling towards me – for the coracle lay upon the strand upon the other side of the place where I lay. With a pretence of awakening, I leaped to my feet and immediately offered to take the sack from her, which at first she refused, and then with something of an ill grace gave it over to me; whereupon I placed it upon the ground and suggested that we might take our ease for a while before the effort of rowing back to the town.

' 'Tes not so much effort,' she said, 'ef 'tis done day by day.'

Nevertheless, she did sit down, and after a moment or two seemed to withdraw her hostility somewhat – to the extent of replying, if somewhat tersely, to my enquiry about her way of life. This proved to be not so bad: the profit of the families of the place mainly accrues, as I had supposed, from the weekly markets and from industrious fishing from boats of a middle size - and I learned from her that her family's craft, the *George*, was but the latest of many of similar name, the first having taken part centuries since in a furious fight with a French man-of-war.

I could not but remark that her eyes seemed to play a great deal upon my body, which was still unclothed above the waist, and on our becoming more familiar and less constrained in our conversation, asked her why. To my amusement, a blush spread over her face - and she admitted that she had believed all gentlefolk to have white skins, whereas mine was as brown as that of her brothers!

This was not always the case, I told her, though many *beaux* who liked to think themselves men of fashion carefully preserved their bodies from the sun. On the contrary, I had from the time I was a boy enjoyed the sun, and took it whenever I had the opportunity - and took care at the same time to say something of my childhood, which, as my constant readers will know, was as far removed from gentility as her own. This she was eager to discuss; and revealed that her ambition was to 'become a lady' - which as far as I gathered meant marrying a farmer and keeping her own farmhouse; for, as it turned out, she heartily despised the fisherman's life as merely providing sufficient sustenance to keep body and soul together.

To that end, she explained, while many of her sex who worked upon the boats threw off their shirts as freely as the menfolk, she had always been careful to keep her body white as milk, for it was known that only those women who engaged in physical labour were brown of skin - and in proof, turned her back, unbuttoned her shirt entirely, and, slipping it from her shoulders, displayed a back which was indeed as white as that of any Bond Street lady.

It was perhaps natural in me to desire a view of her bosom, and taking her gently by the arm I endeavoured to turn her towards me; but she was reluctant to do so, and on my persuading her – with an insistence mild enough not to frighten her – to turn, kept her arms crossed upon her breast. It was only by taking her wrists and, with a smile, quietly drawing her arms down, that I saw before me a breast that might indeed have been that of a boy. Her breasts were little more rounded than saucers – though delightfully marked by twin nipples of the most beguiling pink, whose erect state contradicted that modesty with which she still struggled to release her arms – a struggle of such mildness as to convince me that she was by no means averse to revealing herself to me, if, from her look, fearful that she was insufficiently attractive.

'They'm too small, bain't they?' she said, finally, looking down herself at her breast.

My answer was to lean forward and plant a kiss upon each bosom in turn – at which, as though a spring had been released, she threw her arms about me and hugged me with a strength fired by eagerness. I was not averse to this, and, taking her head between my hands, pressed a kiss upon her lips – which betrayed her innocence by remaining adamantly closed; yet upon my first attempt to force my tongue between them, they not only opened to me, but soon began a most delectable sucking upon my lower lip.

That she knew to an extent what she was about was plain, for without more ado she plunged one hand into my lap and began to seek for my riding-muscle, which from its prominence was by now easily to be found. But although she was clearly no maid, it was equally the case that her experience of the art of love had been brutish and short, for her wriggling her body against me indicated that she was free from any supposition that the act might be prefaced by tenderness.

Since there were some hours still of light and warmth, and since we were in that most enviable position of being upon an island devoid of any inhabitants but ourselves (and those conies whose own amorous habits are a lesson in enthusiasm and frequency) I determined to give her a lesson in the art; first persuading her to let me go, and to recline upon the grass, where in a moment I loosened the rope which secured her breeches (no more elegant than those of her brothers) and drew them down, accompanying this disrobing by disposing a series of kisses upon the body thus revealed – the little dint of her navel, the prominent hips, the soft skin between thigh and belly, the thighs themselves, then the knees – keeping until last that most tender spot of all, guarded by a perfect, jet-black triangle, so perfectly formed that it was difficult to believe that it was not manicured.

Somewhat to my relief, her whole body was clean and sweet-smelling – from the heat of summer persuading her, as is the case with some (but by no means all) of the local inhabitants, to bathe night and morning in the sea, and then, to avert the evil effect of salt upon the skin, to wash in the clear water that springs in plenty from the Cornish earth both in running streams and wells.

It was, then, with equal delight and admiration that I continued for a while to caress her; and after a few gestures of surprise and protest, she soon became aware of the delights of a more gradual approach to love than she had hitherto been afforded, and ceased plucking at my breeches with her hands, merely reclining and allowing my lips to graze upon what indeed was a perfectly white and soft skin.

Though my perfect appetite is for a body more rounded and ample than hers, I must confess that through the charm of the open air, the novelty of her slender frame, and her own delighted approbation, my passion was much aroused, and – as is invariably the case – communicated itself to her, for as I leaned my cheek upon one breast while teasing the other with my tongue, I could hear her heart knocking within her bosom as though 'twould in a moment break out and leap away upon the hill to join the conies who gambolled there, almost within arm's reach.

My own impatience now roused, I stood and loosed my own trousers, and permitted the sun to shine upon that machinery which was more than ready for an engagement. However, rather than continuing to recline in such a position as would have invited immediate congress, the girl immediately raised herself upon her knees, and with a shyness which was infinitely more exciting than the most gross actions of a practised whore, began to examine my appliance with the most minute attention.

I must here, and in parenthesis, reveal that I later brought up with Mr Polscoe the subject of country copulation – he being a gentleman of the broadest temperament, and (as is usually the case) knowledgeable of the most intimate habits of his parishioners.

'Ah,' he said, 'young Glaws. She was, I fear, introduced to carnal pleasures at an early age. Most families here live in two or at most three rooms, and that family is no exception. The old man has his bed in an outbuilding; his two sons and their wives have their beds in one of the two upstairs rooms of their cottage, and the three cousins share a pile of bedding in the second room, where nets and crab-pots must also be stored. The close confinement of three young people must lead to an early sharing of every form of experience, every bodily habit being of necessity performed within the sight and hearing of the others.'

But, I enquired, was not incest a sin?

Doubtless, the reverend gentleman opined, that was the case, where circumstances allowed the enforcement of the strictest rules of morality.

'But it has always been my own view,' he continued, 'that where there is no evil result, animal behaviour in humans frees rather than confines the spirit; and' (he remarked, to my surprise and without the slightest hesitation) 'there are to my certain knowledge four respectable men of this town, regular church-goers and one of them a Warden, whose fathers are also their uncles, and whose brothers are also their cousins. And none of them the worse for it.'

But was this an open secret, I enquired?

'It is not commonly spoken of,' the clergyman replied; 'and you would not find it easy to extract a confession. But there are few families where occurrences of this nature are not known. The sadness is that such acts, being performed at night and in haste, do not educate these classes in those enjoyments which are the prerogative of the more educated classes. Another glass of claret, Mr Archer?'

My surprise at Mr Polscoe's openness was somewhat mitigated when, before the end of my stay, on rising in the night to make water, I heard from his neighbouring bedroom the unmistakable noises of congress, and noted next morning the late rising of Mrs Instance, the plump and pleasant housekeeper whose room was in a further wing of the Vicarage.

But to return to the island: it was with an interest sharpened by ignorance that Glaws used the bright sunlight to make a detailed survey of an area of the male body with which she had, as I now suppose, been familiar only in haste and darkness. At first she looked, only; then with an irresistible impulse laid a finger upon the tip of my cock, pressing it downwards as though to test its resilience, and at the same time looking up at me as though to enquire whether the familiarity were to be permitted. On receiving a smiling asset, she became bolder, and with the fingers of both hands assessed the thickness, circumference and length of the instrument, measured the angle of its erection, gauged the extent of its firmness, investigated the spheroids depending from its base, verified the elasticity of the pouch which contained them – and in short, so provoked and stimulated me by her touch that I was ready to burst, and had to draw away.

That this disappointed her, I could see; but, sinking to my knees, I pressed upon her shoulders with my hands, returning her to the turf, and drawing the length of my body along hers, began to pay my compliments to that area of her body similar in position, though not in landscape, to that from which I had distracted her attention.

The supposition had clearly never occurred to her that a man could have any interest in that part of her, other than to split it with his weapon; and my moistening my finger and with it caressing the most sensitive part of it, brought from her a feverish shivering which shook her whole frame; while when I followed by caressing the length of the aperture with my tongue, then flicking with its tip at that same apprehensive nodule, she let out a shriek so loud that the sea-birds rose from all over the island in a black cloud, swirling in a circle above us and casting a shadow over our bodies.

She was clearly unable to bear such pleasure longer; and myself excited almost beyond bounds, I drew myself once more upon her, and sheathed my sword in its proper scabbard, another cry and an ecstatic bounding of her loins bringing about my surrender before I could even begin those motions which normally signify congress.

My own rapture was extreme, with that almost bitter joy which marks an ecstasy too keen to be prolonged; and from her almost fainting, her upturned eyes showing white beneath their lids, from her gripping my arse with her fingers, from her fixing her teeth almost painfully in my shoulder, from her throwing her legs about my waist as though they clutched a refractory horse, I could infer that Glaws experienced the same pleasure.

Such indeed was that pleasure, on her part, that, while I would have been happy to doze in the warmth, she before long pushed me from her, upon my back, and began caressing me; an action which at first, so soon after congress, was merely irritating (though I bore it with equanimity, feeling it proper to allow her the experience), but soon once more became inspiriting, as, with my example before her, she went about to discover whether oral stimulation of the male parts could impart such pleasure as I had allowed her. The immediate recovery of my spirits, signalled in the almost instant tumescence of a limb which a moment earlier had been entirely debilitated, delighted her; and that she had an instinct for the game was soon demonstrated – for, while paying quite sufficient attention to the primary source of pleasure, she showed invention in performing such pleasurable tricks as sucking upon my fingers and toes, taking my nipples between her small teeth and giving them apprehensive nips, thrusting her tongue into the whorls of my ears, and suchlike. Finally she returned to the centre of such gratification, and taking its most prominent part between her lips, played upon it with such delicacy that she soon reduced me to just such a fever as, previously, I had provoked in herself; whereon, my exhalation of breath, and a moaning I could not control, persuaded her to relinquish her comfort and once more welcome me between those slim thighs. My having so recently given forth my soul enabled me, despite the extremity of my pleasure, to make those movements lacking from our first encounter; movements which she met with a lively thrusting of her own narrow but strong loins; our joint enjoyment reaching a culmination almost at the same moment.

We did, then, lie in each other's arms for an hour; until, the sun beginning to sink, it began to grow chilly, whereupon we resumed our clothes, and without a word descended to the beach and climbed into the coracle, which with the same skilful movements of the single oar, she propelled towards port.

Her brother – or perhaps a cousin – met us upon the quay, so that any elaborate farewell was impossible; nor I think did she expect it, for it must have seemed to her that I was so far above her in station as to make any further conversation impossible; perhaps she even believed that I merely amused myself with her – and truth to tell, that was the fact; though I flatter myself that I had been something of an education to her. I made a point of leaving a purse with Mr Polscoe with instructions that he find a way of enriching her by a gift, perhaps on the occasion of her marriage, for I now heard that there was an understanding between her and a young fisherman from Killigarth (who will, I trust, be pleasantly surprised upon his wedding night – for it is my experience that once an elaborate appetite has been awakened in a young woman, it is by no means the case she forgets how to satisfy it).

That the Rev. Polscoe guessed what had been between us, I make no doubt; but he made no mention of it, being as friendlily disposed upon my leaving Looe as he was upon my coming there, and contenting himself with the statement that his own vote was certainly mine, for he admired one who was at once free in his manners and considerate to those with whom he engaged (which indeed has ever been my ambition).

Chapter Ten

Sophie's Story

The Earl of Stow had kindly invited me to come to Catterby, his mansion near Newmarket, as soon before the commencement of the races as was necessary for the preparation of my entertainment for his guests. I travelled there a full four days before the occasion, partly for the purpose he proposed, and partly (I must confess) in order to allow myself time to become familiar with any of his guests whom it might later profit me to know. (The calculation may offend; yet even such a fortune as I had accumulated – which was not insignificant – might in time be spent, and ingratiation with the wealthy and fashionable was a form of insurance I was minded to provide for myself.)

Catterby is set between the village of Cheveley and the town of Newmarket, in a part of East Anglia with which I was not familiar, it being some fifty mile or so from the city of Cambridge, where I had spent some time in the company of my late husband, the egregious astrologer Mr Nelham (my unfortunate marriage to whom I have detailed in a volume entitled *Eros in the Country*, which must be regarded as necessary reading by those to whom my adventures have proved sufficiently amusing).

The house was first built in the time of Queen Elizabeth, but modernised by the Earl to the extent of almost excessive comfort, for he was a man not only of wealth but of taste. It is approached from the east by a bridge over a tributary of the River Kennett, and along a splendid avenue of lime trees, when through a gateway with four small, square towers one enters an open piazza or walk around which the main rooms of the house lie on the north and south side, with upon the west side is a terrace of slight elevation before the dining hall, beyond which is an inner court completely enclosed by ranges of rooms.

The great architect Sir John Vanbrugh, engaged by an ancestor of the Earl's, had in 1721 enlarged and enlivened the great hall, making a fine stone arcade of two tiers with three arches in each, from which two flights of stairs with gilt iron balustrades were constructed to lead to an upper room where it was the Earl's habit to entertain his guests before dinner, and where innumerable portraits illustrated members of his family, painted by the most fashionable artists of the times.

Stow having made it clear that his household was mine to command, and that every facility must be allowed me, introduced me to his secretary, Mr Fitzchrome – his country secretary, I should perhaps say, who resides at Catterby and looks after his lordship's interests there – including his stable, which upon my first morning I was taken to see. My interest in horse-flesh is not so keen as might be, yet even I could remark that his lordship's horses were handsome enough – some fifteen or eighteen splendid animals, cared for in the most luxurious conditions; more comfortable in their stables, where clean straw was provided every morning, and warm oats on cold mornings, than a great portion of humanity (though Stow, I must confess, made his own people comfortable enough).

Flannery Fitzchrome was a young gentleman of Irish extraction, of perhaps twenty and five years, whose duties included the running of Stow's stable, the ordering of which was the envy of the county (as he assured me). He was one of those young gentlemen whose eye immediately declared an interest in any attractive woman in his vicinity, and without the least familiarity conveyed that interest in an unmistakable manner. Being by no means averse to admiration, I got on with him from the first quite splendidly, and he was quick to answer my many queries about the running of the house and the stables. He had clearly been told the purpose of my visit, and without impertinence made it perfectly clear that he would be happy to give me every assistance.

The first request I made of him was that I might be introduced to his lordship's jockeys. Those unfamiliar with the customs of the running of an ambitious stable may not be aware of the scale upon which such things are done in the country. Indeed, it was with some slight surprise that I learned that Stow kept no less than six young gentlemen whose sole purpose was to exercise his stable and to ride his mounts at the Newmarket races, and occasionally elsewhere.

At the time when I made the request, it was impossible to fulfil it; it was late afternoon, and the entire crew was engaged upon taking the horses out of their stables in order to exercise them. The most I could do was to watch them pass by, remarking that they seemed extraordinary small gentlemen – which Fitzchrome confirmed, this being, as he said, a prerequisite, for the smaller the rider the swifter the mount. However, they were, he told me, young men who were physically exceedingly fit, having as much daily exercise as their mounts; and if I would present myself in a hour, I could confirm this for myself.

I thanked him, and for the intervening period of time amused myself by walking about the gardens, which had been laid out some seventy years previously by that excellent landscape artist Mr Lancelot Brown, and where there were several elegant buildings designed by Mr Robert Adam – two temples, a Palladian bridge, an obelisk and the Elephant Gateway, with a great stone elephant and two enormous decorative vases.

Beyond the Ionic Temple lay a beautiful Elysian Garden – a tree-lined glade bisected by a little river, which enters from the south by a rustic cascade, and runs northwards beneath the Palladian Bridge. Upon each side of the river – which here is of no great girth – run two lawns; and it immediately struck me that this was the ideal place for my entertainment, performers upon one side of the stream, audience upon the other!

An hour passed swiftly enough, and on my returning to the stables (which lie behind the house and some way from it) I was met by Mr Fitzchrome, who led me to the place where his lordship's jockeys lived. This was a long building built originally to house the servants (who now however lived in a wing of the main building). One of the Earl's ancestors, at the time of the Commonwealth, had (I was told) been much engaged in plotting to restore the Monarchy, and had become much concerned that his servants were spying upon him. He had therefore insisted that they live in one room, at the end of which was a place in which he or some trusted fellow could conceal themselves to overhear any conversation which might betray illicit purposes. This was no longer used, but (said Mr Fitzchrome) it would provide a place from which I could observe without being observed, 'for', he remarked, 'I must assume that you have in mind their participation in your entertainment?'

I could only admire his quickness, for this was indeed my purpose. So I found myself in a small, cupboard-like closet, completely dark, with an aperture in its wall through which I looked down the length of a room in which were six beds, with between them a cupboard and a low table with a washing bowl, and little else. Mr Fitzchrome excusing himself – and indeed there was room only for a single person – I settled down with an eye to the aperture, and in a moment into the room tumbled the six jockeys, who immediately – heated by their equine exercise – began throwing off their clothes and sponging themselves down.

I will not bore the reader with an exquisite description of the scene; let it merely be said that Mr Fitzchrome had been entirely in the right when he said that the lack of inches among these young gentlemen did not indicate any disproportion or stunting of growth elsewhere; indeed their arms and shoulders (through holding back and encouraging their mounts) and their thighs and buttocks (through the necessity to grip them) were developed to perfection; and I need look no further for male participants in my pageant – should they agree, which would no doubt be secured either by bribery, by their wish to remain in his lordship's employ, or – upon the nature of the occasion being explained – by simple lust.

Mr Fitzchrome was lounging against the stable wall as I descended the staircase from my perch, and on my asking readily agreed to introduce me to the jockeys. He instantly led me to their room, pausing only to ascertain (through a gentlemanly instinct which I appreciated) that they were properly clad before I entered, when I found them garbed chiefly in towels hastily taken up and girt about their loins.

'Boys!' Mr Fitzchrome said. 'Here is Mrs Nelham, a friend of the guv'nor's.'

In the respectful silence which followed, I introduced myself as someone engaged to set out an entertainment for his lordship's guests; and from the looks exchanged by the lads, saw that they were in little doubt as to the sort of entertainment of which I spoke – from which I divined that similar scenes had previously been observed at Catterby to what I now proposed.

I had in mind, I said, a pageant which would involve them and their mounts; and should they agree to participate, could assure them of five guineas each.

'This is somewhat dependent,' I said, 'upon your not being entirely averse to female company, for I must not conceal from you the fact that your skill in riding will not, on this occasion, be confined to horse-flesh.'

The boys exchanged glances which at once assured me that they would have no objection to what I suggested; and having announced that a rehearsal would be held the day before the entertainment, I left them all a-chatter and walked back to the house with Mr Fitzchrome. He was somewhat aghast at my proposal, not having had previous notice of it. He said it was usual that the lads should have no other preoccupation before the racing than riding and winning; and he ventured whether the kind of activity I had in mind might not drain the energy which would be needed to participate properly in the winning of races.

I assured him that my experience in these matters was

such that the activity I envisaged was nothing less than animating and uplifting to the spirits of young men, and that it would surprise me if it did anything other than encourage the winning spirit among them; and that in any case, Stow had given me a *carte blanche* in the matter - at which he somewhat grumblingly assented to my proposition.

Having commissioned the other participants in the pageant before removing to Catterby, I was now free for a day or so to enjoy my visit; and although I was not unused to luxury, was able once more to observe with how much ease and pleasure the enjoyment of large funds endows life.

My own apartment was comfortable enough, possessing its own side-room for dressing and bathing - hot water being continually available through the interest of a series of servants, two of whom - one male and one female - seemed to have orders to devote themselves entirely to my service. But it was enjoyment of the house itself which gave me my chief pleasure; apart from the grounds, in which it was always a delight to stroll.

It was in the saloon that I chiefly spent those hours of the day which coolness or the occasional shower rendered inappropriate for outdoor activities. This was a fine room which had been fitted out in 1785 by Sir Pothcoat Stow, an ancestor of the present Earl - the date appears over the west door, where his coat of arms and the impaled coats of his two wives are painted. The ceiling of this room is divided into compartments, the divisions marked by pendants and strapwork and the panels filled with decorative figures consisting of ships, mermaids, whales, scabbards and fabulous sea-monsters. Through the interest of these, the saloon is called, by his lordship, the Fish Room; and I was wont to spend some time lying flat upon one of the couches in order that I might gaze upward at the ceiling and enjoy the plaster fantasies proposed by the artist.

It was here, indeed, one morning, that I was lying when a maidservant entered and, having ascertained (as she thought) that no one was present – for I was concealed by the back of the sopha on which I lay – began to dust and polish. In a moment, the door opened and in came none other than Mr Fitzchrome, who, on seeing the girl, without hesitation walked up to her and, placing a hand upon her rump, greeted her with a smacking kiss upon the back of the neck.

She was not in the least discomfited, by which I assumed that such passages were neither infrequent nor unwelcome (Mr Fitzchrome being, as I may have previously noted, a fine, upstanding young man whose attentions might be enjoyed by any apprehensive female not averse to the compliments of the opposite sex).

I was about to betray my presence by a cough, not wishing to embarrass the couple, when the gentlemen followed up his first caress by slipping a hand into the bosom of the girl's dress – at which, motivated no doubt by experience, one of her hands immediately found its way to that part of his body where the most corporeal evidence of his admiration might be expected to lie.

It had now become difficult for me to show myself, for it would be apparent to them that I had seen all; and I was forced to remain out of sight while their congress developed from a relatively innocent kiss to something less ingenuous. In less time than it takes to tell, Mr Fitzchrome's breeches were about his ankles, Miss Betty's skirts above her waist, and the gentleman enjoying the lady in the simplest posture – she leaning with her arms folded upon the back of one of Stow's handsome tapestry chairs, and presenting him with a mark which (judging from her barely stifled cries) he hit at first shot, and continued to hit with each lunge of his somewhat hirsute arse.

That the pair were used to such stolen moments seemed demonstrated by the speed with which they started, pursued and concluded the business, and the adeptness with which Mr Fitzchrome resumed his breeches, while Miss Betty, her skirts now decorously lowered, thanked him with but one quick kiss before continuing with her dusting while he strode from the room – not a single word having been exchanged between them!

I must confess now that I was in something of a tizzy, for her discovery of me must surely indicate that I had been an onlooker at their feast; however, a pretence of sleep saved us both the embarrassment. They having been careful to preserve an almost total silence, it was easy for her to believe that I had slept throughout their encounter – for though I heard a quick and anxious indrawing of her breath upon her discovering me, she finished her cleaning and left the room while I still pretended unconsciousness. On my encountering her later, in the drawing-room, only a blush gave any indication of apprehension.

In the evening, on entering the drawing-room, I found Stow sitting with a motley crew of eight or ten gentlemen, together with their wives – the latter seeming however almost invisible, for the gentlemen conversed among themselves, and with so little apprehension of the presence of their ladies that not only their business but their pleasures were discussed with entire frankness, their tones so little lowered when they spoke of their whores that their ladies cannot but have been apprehensive of the details they did not hesitate to reveal, with greater colour of language than I would have permitted myself even in the drawing-room of a close friend. Upon our retiring to the drawing-room after dinner, while the gentlemen began that carousing which would in all probability cease only with their inability to remain upright, my sensibilities were pummelled by the failure of their consorts to comment upon their shortcomings.

One, Lady Indigo Opimion (whose husband was a gross, great man of seventeen stone, most of whose weight was concentrated in the region of his belly) gave the rest of us a lecture, indeed, upon the superiority of that sex to our own:

'In the character of a noble, enlightened and truly good man,' she remarked (to whom could she have been referring? – not surely to that sot, her husband?), 'there is a power and a sublimity so nearly approaching what we believe to be the nature and capacity of angels, that no language can describe the degree of admiration and respect which the contemplation of such a character must excite.'

But surely, I observed, it was not necessary to ignore those blemishes of character which in my experience flawed the most perfect character, setting it off (indeed) by contrast with entire virtue?

'No, Mrs Nelham,' was her answer; 'to be admitted to a man's heart, to share his counsels and to be the chosen companion of his joys and sorrows! – it is difficult to say whether humility or gratitude should preponderate in the feelings of the woman thus distinguished and thus blest.'

At which I made my excuses and left, saying (which was

indeed the truth) that I felt suddenly nauseous; and as I passed the dining-room, was assaulted not only by a great wave of smoke from the execrable weed tobacco – to which Stow and his friends were much addicted – but by the sound of retching and the sight of Lord Opimion vomiting into the fireplace while his friends, oblivious, continued their carouse.

My entertainment was to take place upon the day before the opening of the Newmarket races, providing as it were a preliminary potpourri which should gratify the senses of the gentlemen before they set off to watch their mounts run – heightening the pleasure if they won, compensating the lack of it if they lost.

The day before this, I went over to Bury St Edmunds in a carriage followed by two others in which the six jockeys travelled. On my explaining what would be required of them they had shown no diffidence; but this morning had become less enthusiastic, and only the threat of Stow's displeasure, together with the promise of an additional two guineas each persuaded them into the coaches.

At Bury, the six ladies whose services I had commissioned in town had been put up for the night at the Parson's Nose Inn, and it was thence that we made our way, and were shown to a large private room which I had secured entirely for the purpose of introducing the two parties. There, while I went to greet the girls, Mr Fitzchrome persuaded his lads to remove their clothing; for the sake of an immediate informality, I had decided that the excellent luncheon I had ordered should be taken by all in a state of nature – which I have ever found the quickest way of ensuring familiarity.

I returned to the room to find the six young men

huddled together at one end of it, Mr Fitzchrome alone lounging, entirely at ease, before the fire which, despite the fortunate warmth of the day, I had ordered to be lit. On my entering with the girls (clad, necessarily – for we had traversed the public parts of the inn; yet clad but lightly) the boys clustered even more closely together, endeavouring with their hands to hide from view those parts which they no doubt believed would be offensive to the eyes of the maidens – whose eyes, however (I could have told them) had seen a greater number of male appendages than most men!

On my signalling the girls, both they and I removed what covering we had and (none of us believing that our unclad bodies would be offensive) strode towards the middle of the room – which instantly resulted in the young gentlemen showing some interest, to the extent that there was an immediate and involuntary movement away from each other, and towards us.

'Mr Fitzchrome – some ale!' I directed; at which he took up a great flagon and began to fill the tankards set out on a side-table, and indicated that his boys should serve the ladies. This they did with a decreasing awareness (or perhaps simply a more natural admiration) of their nakedness, my girls continuing in their informality; and no doubt the sight of Mr Fitzchrome and myself equally unclad encouraged this – as I had hoped, though I must confess that it was he who had originally suggested that two people clothed, among others who were not, would necessarily dampen enthusiasm.

By the time each lad had consumed a pint or so of strong ale, informality had certainly increased; and on my suggesting that the meal should commence, it was natural that the sexes should be spread alternately about the table – where somewhat narrow benches ensured that it was impossible to be entirely separate from one's neighbour; even I being cheek by cheek (to use the phrase) with Mr Fitzchrome upon one side, and one of the jockeys upon the other – who found great difficulty, as I could see, in dividing his attention equally between me and his neighbour, fearing to offend one by undue attention to the other.

Mr Fitzchrome had no such difficulty, and I could not but admire his dexterity in making an excellent lunch using his left hand alone, his right lying for some time upon my thigh, and then making its way between it and its fellow – which I found not unpleasant. Upon my dropping my napkin and hastening to retrieve it, I found my searching hand, falling into his lap, obstructed by a prominent Something my accidental connection with which evoked rather the indrawn breath of pleasure than an exhalation provoked by either embarrassment or pain.

However, I was too concerned to encourage geniality among the company to be able to give myself over to sensation, however agreeable, and concentrated rather in pairing the couples in my mind's eye – something which however was no problem, for I could now see that such coupling had been naturally achieved by the instinct of the men and women concerned, each man gradually, as the luncheon continued, beginning to pay more attention to one young lady than the next, and, their spirits raised by ale, by the end of the meal being sufficiently at ease to intersperse the business of kissing with that of eating, while the occasions upon which a dozen hands were all in view above the table grew increasingly rarer.

At length the time came when a young man opposite

me actually lowered his head and applied his lips to the breast of his neighbour; at which I banged my hand upon the table, and announced that the time had come for them all to pay attention to the plan for the morrow – at which, with a somewhat comic effect, they came to themselves, reluctantly unhanded each other, and sat at attention.

My recitation of the diversion I had contrived did not take long, but certainly interested the parties most intimately concerned – not least because they by now felt a certain warmth towards each other which, had I encouraged them, would in due course have led to a natural consummation. This, however, I was determined to avoid, on this occasion, lest it take the zest from the performance tomorrow – and in any event that the jockeys should be reduced to utter lethargy before the races to come was not to be thought of, if Stow was to be satisfied by the entire outcome of the season.

So, having come to the end of my recital and the consequent instructions, and having distributed papers upon which I had roughly sketched some illustrations of the postures which I had devised and told them of, I invited the gentlemen to take leave of the ladies – a ceremony to which I had again to put a forcible end, to their regret (and indeed somewhat to my own, for, with a dexterity which ensured that his manoeuvres were not seen by the company, Mr Fitzchrome had occupied himself during my speech by investigating the extent to which he could explore that lower part of my body which was within his grasp without so distracting my attention that I broke down into stuttering and silence – which I confess almost to have done; and would with some pleasure of my own have joined in any celebration of the occasion, was not the circumstance against it).

To be short, my ladies were eventually persuaded to don their clothing, and I led them from the room, the grumbling of their male companions somewhat mitigated by the knowledge that they would meet upon the following day.

At ten next morning, Stow's lady guests were sent off in a procession of carriages to Audley End, the great house some twenty mile off, where Her Majesty the Queen was holding a reception – for King Billy had been persuaded away from his beloved billows to the unaccustomed racecourse, and his Queen to meet the local ladies of fashion at a celebration which gave her no pleasure, though it provided them with an occasion for decking themselves in their finery and behaving as though they were women of fashion (most of them however being no more distinguished than squires' wives).

Their husbands bade them farewell with equanimity – and then settled down to an early bottle before luncheon, which they took *al fresco* in just that spot I had reserved for them; they sitting upon rugs spread on the grass while the servants bore among them a cold collation of delicacies, each accompanied by its own wine. I had myself devised this feast, and with some care – for reasons of my own ensuring that they were plentifully supplied with wine. Then, at precisely half past one, there was a fanfare from hunting horns, and on to the sword at the other side of the stream came a procession of Stow's mounts, each ridden by its own jockey – as though riding to the ring before a race, but with the difference that the riders were not wearing his lordship's colours: indeed, were wearing no colours at all, each being entirely unclothed – as indeed were their mounts, which had neither saddle nor bridle. These were skilful riders who as a matter of course were able not only to preserve their balance merely by the exercise of their muscles, but to control their familiar animals without recourse to such aids as were necessary when racing.

They rode to the front of the lawn, and facing across the stream, saluted the company by raising their arms; then wheeled about and faced the thicket which backed the glade – from which, in slow and delightful procession, came my six ladies. The effect, I must admit, was an enticing one, for, clad in diaphanous clothes of white, hanging from their shoulders, they appeared like supernatural beings summoned from the shades by the horns of huntsmen. They stood for a moment; and then, as one (taking a signal from me, who was behind a bush and out of sight of the audience, but within that of the performers), dropped their concealing garments, and appeared in a state of nature. If anything they seemed yet more strange than before, partly through the unexpected sight of unclad females in such a setting (for, unlike the ladies of southern Europe or yet hotter climes, our own females are largely unaccustomed to unveiling themselves in the open air) and partly through their taking attitudes which I had taught them, and resembling those of the ancient statues of an antique age.

Both they and the riders for a moment were entirely still – then as a patter of applause broke from the gentlemen upon the opposite bank, the jockeys urged their mounts into a walk, and bore down on the nymphs, who preserved their inanimity until the final moment when, the horses reaching them, they stretched up their arms and with the help of an outstretched hand at once leaped . . . to the horses' backs, some before and some behind the gentlemen already mounted there.

The six horses now took up their stations in a semi-circle around the greensward, and one at a time came to the centre of the stage while their riders took up the attitudes I had described to them. These were sufficiently complex and precarious to amaze, no less than amuse, the onlookers – and I must confess to the reader what the audience did not know: that my six ladies had been, with some care, recruited from the same circus as had supplied the female Amazon who had performed on my behalf at Mrs Teazle's. I had, on the occasion of meeting her, attended a performance during which I had been astonished by the skills of the young Austrian riders whose task it was to show off their mounts in a series of jumps and turns, gallopings and trottings and canterings, which had proved to me an ability and tenacity in balance at least the equal of the jockeys; for which reason I remembered them on receipt of Lord Stow's commission, and secured their services at only a moderate cost, they being eager, as horsewomen, to attend the Newmarket races, which are famous upon the continent of Europe as an occasion for showing off the finest mounts and riders.

But to return to the narrative: each couple of riders, upon their mount reaching the centre of the stage, used him as a platform upon which to demonstrate a particular posture of congress – these mounting in difficulty as time went on. The first pair were content with the simplest attitude, the jockey sitting astride his mount while the young lady, facing him, was astride his thighs. In this disposition the horse was urged into a trot, the natural rise and fall this encouraged in the jockey – which will be familiar to all those who have ridden horseback – so resembling normal congress that an amused laugh rather than a sensual snigger came from the audience. This however was not shared by the performers, the motion to which they were subject being such as to give them extreme pleasure.

This was not so keenly shared by their colleagues, for the postures they adopted required more skill simply to maintain them; and indeed I wondered that the jockeys were able to maintain the extension of their most important limb, since much of their attention must necessarily be concentrated simply on remaining upon the backs of their mounts. In one case, for instance, the youngest and most daring of the men actually stood upon the broad back of his mount while his partner hung about his neck while he manipulated her lower person into such a position that, her calves clasped behind his waist and her arms about his shoulders, he was able to enter her so that they remained joined for a complete circle about the lawn.

The other four pairs were not as adventurous as this – one lady lying herself full length upon the horse's back, her companion then placing himself upon her in that most conventional of all human copulatory postures: yet so skilfully maintained during their mount's progress that they attracted much admiration. Another pair embraced each other by the simple device of the jockey mounting his partner from behind, she bending to secure her position by holding the horse's mane while he entered her from behind – the posture having the advantage that the audience was able to view the connection without obstruction. This was the case with the third couple, for the lady, with a dextrous twist of her body, stood upon her hands, bringing her intimate parts in proximity to her partner's face – he also being standing, while her lips were able without difficulty (they being of a height) to fix about his engorged prick. Thus, each entertaining the other as keenly as the spectacle entertained their audience, they rode about the ring – alas then providing an unrehearsed incident by losing their balance and toppling from the back of their steed, who continued a dignified trot while they lay for a moment, their breaths taken from them, in a tangle of limbs; then leaped to their feet to chase the steed, the jockey's quickly shrinking cock flapping in an undignified manner as he did so – which caused the kind of laughter among the gentlemen of the audience with which I have often had cause to note one male will insult another in such a circumstance. However, the man eventually catching the horse by its mane and swinging himself back into the saddle – or rather the place where the saddle would have lain had there been one – his companion in a moment joined him; though such was the young man's discomfiture that no attempts on her part to bring him back to a stand were successful, and their departure from the scene was thus a muted one.

The final tableau was provided by the most skilful pair, for the jockey was Stow's finest, much envied by the other owners of the district, while his partner was the leader of the troup of ladies. They began simply by a round of the ring during which they exposed their handsome bodies to the audience's admiration – the jockey, while being necessarily small and slender, having the finest muscular shoulders and arms, cultivated to admiration by his art, while his thighs showed by their rippling muscles the strength inherent in them, also communicated to his buttocks, which seemed to be made entirely of muscle. The lady was equally picturesque, her body, while entirely feminine, also profiting from continual exercise, so that while breasts, sides, belly and arse were all sufficiently generous to attract the admiration of any gentleman, yet there was no trace of supererogatory fat about them.

Having received the tribute of a round of applause, the jockey now took up a position upon the broadest part of his mount's back, his legs astride, while his partner weaved her body about his as sinuously as any snake, bringing (as it seemed) every part of her person in turn in juxtaposition to a piece of masculine equipment, which seemed by its resolute extension to be at least as adamant in its muscular control as any other part of his body.

Then, standing before him, her hands resting only lightly upon his shoulders, she raised her right foot and caressed his lower legs, then his thighs, with prehensile toes, before inserting the ankle between his legs, the upper surface of her foot as it were providing a platform upon which his cock and balls were happy to lie in demonstration of their size and proficiency, which she next tested by falling to her knees and proving every part with her tongue, now at the same time passing her hands behind to test whether the muscles of his arse were not, though however strong, susceptible to a soft caress – which proved so much the case that (as I could see, though the audience might not) a grimace passed over his face indicative of a keener pleasure than he would be able long to sustain. I was on the point of hissing a warning when (perhaps, I know not, from some involuntary muscular contraction) the lady became aware of the situation, and removing her lips from that part of his anatomy likely to succumb to his excitement now gave her attentions to a more general insinuation, by passing her entire body between his legs, making a point of bringing first thighs, then belly, then breasts into close contact with his most intimate parts – continued control of which he maintained only at the cost of clenching his teeth upon his lower lip, where beads of blood sprang.

Now behind her friend, the lady clasped his whole body to hers, moving her hands about his breast, then below it, rather showing off his body by her gestures than further arousing it – to his relief; now with the most dextrous leap mounting upon his very shoulders, and after one round of the ring, with a somersault landing before him and astride the horse's neck – when she had only to turn, by throwing a leg over the beast's back, to fall astride himself, so that he could bury his staff within her and bring himself the relief for which by now he was so eager that he could not restrain a cry of pleasure and satisfaction – echoed by the applause of the delighted audience.

The six couples now took their bows, each in turn riding to the front of the grassy stage; but there came a general commotion, for the gentleman viewers – who had had no way of satisfying their own sensuality except by a quiet manual manipulation of their parts (which in most cases pride prevented them from) – clearly took the view that they should be permitted to slake their lust upon the visiting ladies, and to that end three of them plunged into the water and began to swim across.

However, I had made it quite clear to my Lord that our contract did not include such an engagement; and the ladies speedily effected their escape – their partners without hesitation once more lifting them upon horseback; and by the time the swimmers had reached the bank, and the other gentlemen had found their way across the water by means of the nearby bridge, the glen was deserted except for myself and Mr Fitzchrome, whose presence restrained the ardency of the excited gentlemen; and who then announced that the carriages awaited to take them to Newmarket, where the brothel that is invariably set up in propinquity to the racecourse contained females who would be able and willing to satisfy their lusts.

Though not without grumbling, they assented; and went off, somewhat to my relief – and my admiration of Mr Fitzchrome, whose conduct had been irreproachable; despite the fact that as I had seen from my vantage-point he had not himself been unmoved by the spectacle, and even now was moving with a care which seemed to indicate an uncomfortable constriction below the waist.

Seeing the direction of my gaze, he was good enough to apologise for his state.

'My dear sir,' I said, 'what man is so incapable of feeling as to resist being engaged by such a demonstration as we have just witnessed? Indeed, what person – for as you will know, we women are not immune from such emotion.'

He looked at me with an eyebrow slightly raised, and then in silence stepped forward and, taking me in his arms, placed an expressive kiss first upon my eyes, then my lips. It was only when I showed by my responding embrace that I was not impervious to his approach that he busied his hands with releasing my clothing – and not to tire the reader with a description of the intervening action, which was of a conventional but no less entertaining description, we were in due course satisfactorily engaged, and within a short time had slaked each other's appetites. I must confess that the engagement was by no means remarkable for its ingenuity; yet performed its purpose, after which Mr Fitzchrome courteously raised me to my feet and assisted me into my clothing before resuming his own – and even began stumblingly to express his gratitude, when I stopped him by raising my hand:

'Sir,' I said, 'the day when a lady and a gentleman cannot satisfy their appetite in such a manner without one coming under an excessive obligation to the other will in my view be a sad one for civilisation.'

At which we returned to the house, pausing for a while at the jockeys' buildings in order that I should inform the ladies of the hour at which the coaches would return them to their inn, and thence, the following day, to London, and to hand them the purses in which was their fee. We found them and their friends dispersed about the room, some in attitudes merely of friendship – for whom the display had been merely a matter of technique rather than of corporeal pleasure – others more intimately engaged; I was pleased in particular to see that the couple whose misfortune had occasioned some untoward mirth were particularly lost in the digital manipulation of each other's persons, a compensation which I trusted would return the rider to such a degree of confidence as would enable him to perform with more adroitness upon his beast during the coming races.

The following day I went with his lordship to the races at Newmarket, where I had the pleasure of seeing three of his mounts – their riders clearly none the worse for their engagement of the day before – win their races.

Stow was in high good humour, and that evening handed me my expenses together with a fee far in excess of the one I had asked, and provided one of his personal carriages to take me by stages back to town – where, within a week, I was to hear from Chichley news of a most remarkable nature, concerning not myself but the entire kingdom!

Before I continue with this narrative, however, I must issue a warning, especially to my younger and more adventurous readers: serious injury could follow any attempt to counterfeit the activities which I have described, and any reader, male or female, who owns a horse and feels the inclination to attempt one of the poses with a friend, should reconsider and refrain.

Chapter Eleven

The Adventures of Andy

That I should win the election was a foregone conclusion, not only because of my superiority as a candidate – for the common sort of Cornish people found me the acme of civilisation and wit, while those who knew better were convinced that upon election I would be tractable to their wishes, and not inclined to be wild in demanding such unconscionable matters as universal suffrage.

Nevertheless, it was pleasant enough to stand upon the balcony of Webb's Hotel at Liskeard and to hear the Mayor announce that my candidature had attracted fully twice as many votes as that of my rival, the notorious and egregious Methodist Whig, Philosophy Beswarick, a thin and inconsequential little man who would in any case have been of no assistance to my Lord Grey in the administration he was now to form, and to which it was my duty to be implacably opposed.

The local Tories had as a matter of course engaged the main rooms at Webb's for a celebration of my victory, which as I have indicated was considered a certainty; and we spent some hours in a – for me – tedious round of drinking with Mr This and Mr That, supporters from the villages around (St Pinnock and Doublebois, Warleggan and Bocaddon and Penpillick) who had ensured my election through a process of persuasion and bribery (now I can admit it – though it amounted only to the buying of beer and ribbons). At ten o'clock, however, Squire Treleaven sidled up to me as I was talking to Mrs Penplodden, the wife of the Rector of Bodmin and more like a bishop than a laywoman.

'My dear Archer,' he said, 'may I draw you away? – with many apologies, Mrs Penplodden. I have a deputation anxious to meet you, come down from Plymouth.'

Bowing to the lady, whose incipient moustache quivered with disapproval at the sudden end brought to our discussion of the amendments necessary to the Reform Bill, he led me off and up the staircase to the first floor.

'You deserve a little recreation, my boy,' said the Squire; 'and I trust that you will enjoy it – at our expense. It is the best that can be secured within a hundred miles, and comes on the recommendation of Sir Brinsley Fordice, the Member for East Devonshire, who is a connoisseur in such matters.'

Upon which, he threw open a door and propelled me through it. I found myself in the chief bedroom of the hotel – which, it being by London standards a miserable establishment, consisted merely of a plain room the walls of which were hung with hunting prints, and the chief furnishing of which consisted in a great, clumsy square bed whose four posts, bearing a tattered velvet canopy, were hung with the coloured ribbons of the Tory Party, and upon which reclined not one but two young ladies whose only covering was a set of the same ribbons entwined about their limbs. They were, as I could immediately observe, of complementary form – one being slim and lithe, the other of a more rounded and chubby form. Both with an equal enthusiasm rose from their semi-recumbent posture and, approaching me, threw their arms about me and congratulated me upon my victory, accompanying their kind words with kinder kisses, and an exploratory gesture towards the fastening of my clothes, which they succeeded in undoing with such ease and rapidity as suggested that the exercise was not new to them.

Since my pleasant excursion to St George's Island, I had devoted myself with considerable attention to the duty of ensuring my election, and had therefore had no greater opportunity of carnal connexion than was offered by the cursory embracing of small children and an occasional doffing of my hat to the wife of some brewer or baker whose interest it was important to secure; so that on one of the young ladies falling to her knees before me and further fortifying by her caresses a limb already sufficiently adamant for her purposes, I realised to what extent I had missed the pleasure of the company of the fair sex.

In less than no time, therefore, I was stretched out upon the bed, with Bess and Nell (as they informed me were their names) demonstrating the extent to which they fulfilled the expectations aroused in Mr Treleaven by the praises of Sir Brinsley – praises no doubt founded in experience, the ladies in question apparently being among the conveniences offered to their Member by the Tories of East Devonshire.

It was necessary however to persuade them to modify certain aspects of their behaviour, for one of their earliest actions was to turn me upon my face, when in a moment, expecting the soft touch of lips and hands upon my nether regions, I felt rather the cutting pain of a blow from what proved to be a leather belt. Presumably this was Sir Brinsley's pleasure, and had impressed itself upon the ladies as a procedure invariably welcomed by politicians in general and Members of Parliament in particular; but as I informed them, the application of a belt to my posteriors was the speediest way to ensure the abortion of our pleasures – my member indeed already shrinking at the action, as was discovered when, apologising for their mistake, the young ladies laid me once more upon my back. However, the joint application of kisses to the offending limb soon restored it to a proper state of tumefaction – indeed, to such dimensions as brought forth congratulations from the ladies, from which I gathered that, whatever the size of his majority, Sir Brinsley was not notable for the dimensions of his manhood.

While Miss Nell, the plumper of the two, contented herself with lying at my side and admiring, with tongue and fingers, each part of my body in turn, Miss Bess was more active – unable indeed, it seemed, to be still for a moment; now bending to explore with her tongue the environs of my cods, or suck them with a most delightful sensation (at the same time presenting me with the most inspiriting view of her buttocks, the full fig of her womanhood open to my admiration), now turning to nip with peremptory pleasure at my paps, to offer to my lips her small but elegantly formed bosoms, or to (as it were) stroke my whole upper body with their tips as she slid down to such a posture as offered to the slippery caresses of her lips an organ strained almost to bursting with the desire to couple.

This indeed soon mastered me, so that without pausing to choose between the ladies, I was in a moment sheathed in a kindly orifice, the relief of an almost immediate expulsion of desire being such that in my pleasure I forgot the courtesy of ensuring that the lady in question was equally in receipt of sensual gratification. Bess (who, I now saw, was the one who lay beneath me) showed no sign of disappointment, however; from which I divined – accurately, as it turned out – that she was one of those ladies who did not find such gratification necessary; nor did my temporary collapse dismay Nell, who merely reclined upon one elbow, in the position from which she had observed the conclusion of my joy, and meeting my eye merely smiled, showing no sign that she regretted that I was now in no state to gratify her.

I must confess that I now fell into a doze, the fatigue of the past few weeks joining with the lethargy of my limbs to render it necessary; and when I awoke it was not to the renewed caresses of the ladies, but to see them rather gratifying each other, for they lay top to tail, their heads between each other's thighs, enjoying those pleasures which often compensate such women for the necessity of farming their bodies out for the pleasure of men.

They made a pretty picture, however; and even the realisation that they could not have found my person as attractive as they found each other's could not prevent my spirits rising; and indeed I was considering the possibility of intervening to play some part in the scene when I heard voices outside the door, and the protests of Squire Treleaven, who seemed to be attempting to stop someone from entering.

Bess and Nell drew apart, and I, reaching out for the crumbled counterpane, succeeded in covering myself with it before the door burst open and into the room, striding past the protesting Squire, came – Mrs Samuel Treglown!

To say that I was surprised would be to fail altogether to convey my feelings: although it would be untrue to say that I had forgotten her, I had certainly done my best to reconcile myself to never encountering her again – or if that were not the case, to regard her as a citadel impossible to conquer, since her repugnance to my person appeared to be complete. Yet now, holding the door open and gesturing to the two girls to leave – which they did, still in a state of nature (which evidently intrigued the Squire to the extent of forgetting his strictures upon her entry) – the lady stood, closing the door firmly, and for a moment simply regarded me gravely.

I must confess that I felt the blood rushing to my cheeks: had I been able to choose, would I have selected the moment at which I was abed with two whores to be seen by this admired lady? Yet she made no reproach, either by gesture or attitude; and indeed walking towards the bed, sat upon the edge of it, and reaching out a hand laid it upon my thigh (which was one of those areas of my unclothed body which was not covered by the counterpane), and smiled in the kindest manner.

What was this? Here was a lady who more than once, upon my expressing my keen admiration, had repulsed me, making it quite clear that she regretted my attachment to her – yet she was now, quite unmistakably, of an opposite view – for her fingers gently moved upon my flesh, edging upwards along my thigh in a most ingratiating manner.

My jaw must have dropped, and she was unable to repress what could only be described as a giggle.

'My Archer,' she said, 'allow me to explain myself.

You will perhaps be surprised that I now come to you in such a situation as this, when on the previous occasions when you were kind enough to express your approbation of my person, I repulsed you.'

I was able only to nod, swallowing hard as her hand now fell upon that part of me whose condition proved conclusively that my admiration was not merely retrospective.

'I must tell you that on that occasion I had left London under the circumstance of having been forced – I may even say raped – by Mr Treglown, my husband. I should explain that our marriage was contracted as the result of an arrangement by our families, made when we were still children; that we have not for some years lived together in the same house; but that my husband, in a condition of drunkenness, hearing that I was in town, came to me and insisted upon a connection; then – upon my remonstrating – positively boasted that he was poxed, and had given me the disease!

'You can imagine how distraught I was at such a revelation! And with what distraction I found myself, only a day or two later, in the presence of a gentleman whose personal attraction, and clear admiration of my person, was such that it would otherwise have given me the greatest pleasure to gratify in his desires! Yet could I do so in the knowledge that I might contaminate him? And could I explain the reason to a stranger?'

I felt my riding-muscle contract under the import of her words: was I to be invited to catch the French gout?

She must – for her fingers still lay along its length – have felt the effect of her words; for she now continued:

'Fear not! – my physicians have conducted the most

full examination, and entirely clear me of any suspicion in the matter, for signs of such a condition would, they assure me, by now have made themselves plain. My husband, with a bestiality of behaviour such as even I would have hesitated to believe possible, no doubt invented the entire story in order to distress me. Can you believe that, while it must appear unladylike, I could resist, upon hearing his words, coming to offer you at the same time my congratulations upon your election, and the opportunity, should you wish it, of . . .' But here it was her turn to blush; upon which I kissed her full upon those rosy and enticing lips – then drew back, remembering the circumstances in which she had discovered me.

'My dear madam,' I said, 'I fear that I was occupied, on your appearance, with . . .'

'Please,' she said, stopping my lips with another kiss, 'say nothing of it. A gentleman must have his amusements, and as long as your strength is not exhausted – which' (with an appreciative squeeze) 'I can tell is not the case, can I repine at others participating in that pleasure which it is now my keenest apprehension to enjoy?'

Rising to her feet, she unloosed the buttons of her gown, and, letting it fall to the floor, revealed at last that body at whose proportions it had only so far been possible for my imagination to guess. She was in every way the fruition of my hopes: her shoulders were broad, yet shaped with such delicacy that the least suspicion of masculinity was at once dispelled. Her breasts were as full as womanly nature demanded, yet were so supported by the musculature of her frame that they stood proudly from her body without the least suspicion of looseness, the buds which marked the centre of each circle erect, confirming the passion which I could see in the wide pupils of her dark eyes no less than upon her glistening lips.

Her waist was narrow, but broadening immediately to the platform of her hips, where between her thighs lay that dark triangle at the centre of which a darker cleft invited first my eyes, then my palm, and finally my lips.

It will not be supposed that I objected when she now lifted the counterpane from my body, and took her time in examining the latter, with (modesty must not prevent me from recording) many expressions of admiration, turning in time to assertions of desire; nor will the reader be amazed to learn that words only by a little preceded action – and must allow me merely to assert that neither of us was disappointed in the other during the hours that followed.

I was perhaps fortunate in that my passage with Bess and Nell had to an extent taken the edge off my passion, so that I was able to contain my emotions until I had brought the lady to not merely one but two expressions of entire satisfaction – taking, I must confess, some pleasure in bringing to her lips the shrillest and most passionate cries of pleasure. However, it will not be the reader's wish that I should detail the pleasures which followed – the strokings and scratchings, the kissings and nippings, the joinings of each part of one body with each part of the other: so that by the time the first rays of the sun fell across the square outside the hotel window, we were in an exhausted sleep, having – as it seemed – achieved within only a few hours the utmost knowledge of each other's bodies, and explored the furthest reaches of each other's desires.

It had been fixed that upon the following day I should set out for London to take my seat with the other elected members of the Parliament at Westminster; and Mrs Treglown insisted upon accompanying me (not that I made objection). Squire Treleaven was not amazed to see us together at breakfast, for, occupying the neighbouring room to ours, he had (as he told me in an aside) been kept awake for some time by the sounds of our enjoyment – until, driven by the demands of his own flesh, roused to passion by the evidence of his ears, he had sent for Bess and Nell and himself enjoyed some pale reflection of our pleasure.

We were seen off from Webb's by a cheering and congratulatory crowd (Mrs Treglown being recognised by the assembled throng, and being a popular lady through her charitable work in the county). During the following journey, broken by two charming nights at convenient inns, we got to know each other on polite as well as on intimate terms: my learning, among other matters, that her name was Charlotte, though she invited me to address her by the diminutive of 'Charlie'.

During the hours of travelling, she told me a rather alarming thing: something of which, doubtless to my shame, I was not aware: that should our present monarch die, his successor was – a woman! That is, the Princess Victoria, daughter of Princess Charlotte and Prince Leopold of Saxe-Coburg, now a young girl of thirteen or fourteen years of age and living in Kensington Palace.

You can imagine my distress at this news: that our great country should be ruled by a female – despite my devotion to the sex – is not to be thought of! Yet what can be done about it? She is indisputably heir! Charlie was much amused at my distress upon hearing this news, being of the opinion that a Queen was by no means likely to bring the crown to disrepute. The young girl, she tells me, is being well educated, taught not only anatomy but alchemy, not only English literature but music, of which she is fond; she also sketches, attends the theatre, and is steadfast in attendance at church. All this set aside, it seems to me reprehensible that no male heir can be discovered.

Upon our reaching London we went straight to my house, which had been alerted by a post rider, and where (for the sake of her reputation) a separate room had been prepared for Mrs Treglown – though not so far from my own as to render my nightly attendance upon her dependent upon too arduous a journey.

She felt it incumbent upon her to seek out her husband, who was (have I said it?) Member of Parliament for an obscure northern town, where he had recently been re-elected in the Whig interest; and met with him in a chamber at Westminster while I with a horde of other members was attending upon the Speaker of the House of Commons to take my seat, a ceremony rendered somewhat perfunctory by the great number of those participating, so that I was less impressed than I had hoped. However, I was determining to make my mark by a speech early in the Parliament – even perhaps during the first twenty-four hours – when I received a message summoning me to wait upon my friend.

I found her in the most curious state of apprehension. Reaching the corridor in which was the room where her husband had appointed to meet her, she had been shown by an attendant of the House into a neighbouring chamber, where the intervening door had carelessly been left ajar; and had overheard her husband speaking in French to someone with him. Her knowledge of the French language was imperfect, but, she told me, she had heard enough to suspect that Treglown was involved in a plot to place a Pretender upon the throne of England on the death of the present monarch – that such a Pretender was to arrive in England soon, from Calais, whereupon an insurgency would be set in motion.

I repressed my natural feeling that even an illicit King would be better than a Queen; for, after all, even from motives of concern at the crowning of a female monarch, could I not reprehend a foreign plan to interfere with the British succession?

But could it be true? Charlie was unshakeable. She had, she said, upon overhearing the gist of the conversation, betrayed her presence by a start and a small cry, upon which the person speaking with her husband had instantly ceased. Upon immediately entering the room she had seen only his back as he left, and had been greeted in the most cursory manner by Treglown, who did his best to discover what she had heard, which she disguised by saying that she had that moment arrived, and had heard only voices, not what they said. He seemed relieved at this; and after an exchange of views regarding his property in Cornwall (which he wished to sell, but needed her consent) they had parted – whereupon she had immediately sent for me.

'We must discover more,' she said; 'but by what means?'

In what respect was he vulnerable? I asked. Was there nothing reprehensible in his life, no incident which we could use to blackmail him into revealing the plot (if such there was, for it seemed to me at present to be as tenuous a matter as a fairy tale)?

Nothing, she said.

Could she not (I hesitated to suggest it) use her female

wiles to obtain information?

No – to my relief – was her reply. He had long since forsworn her bed, his recent attack upon her person being informed more by malice than by lust. From what she had heard he contented himself with an alliance with Lady Pauncefoot, a female of imperfect morals with whom he had formed an alliance some years hence, whose attentions appeared to satisfy his requirements.

Then was he not susceptible to female beauty?

No, she replied; unless it was something extraordinary.

I considered for a moment; then after some consideration put forward an idea which, after a little persuasion, Charlie agreed might extract the information we required. I left her, and making some enquiries of some old friends, then took myself to a house in Greenwich where I renewed my acquaintance with a young lady who had been, though briefly, an employee of Frank's and mine at our house of pleasure in Brook Street. Betsy is a Negress who combines an extraordinary beauty of person with a keen intelligence and wit, and indeed within three weeks of taking up residence at our house had been enticed away by a young gentleman of rank and wealth, who had established her at his house in Hampstead, where she still lived. We had parted on good terms – it never being our wish to stand in the way of our girls improving themselves; and upon my knocking on her door, at an hour when her lover was from home, she expressed herself delighted to see me, and on my explaining the matter was pleased to help us, her devotion to her adopted country (to which she had been brought as a girl by a sea captain who had rescued her from a slave-ship sailing to the Americas) prompting her to an immediate acquiescence.

Within a day, Treglown had received a simple message

inviting him to an appointment at a house in the suburb of Chelsea, where a reward would be waiting for his attentive encouragement of 'the plan we know of'. It was signed in the name of the Duc de Laval, Ambassador of France. We took the risk that Treglown did not know his signature; and were evidently right, for at the appointed time he knocked upon the door of the house which we had taken for the occasion, and was shown by a manservant (one of my own) to a room upon the first floor.

This was a bedroom which was fitted out in the most luxurious manner (it, and the house, belonged to another lady of my acquaintance, a Mrs Jopling Rowe, who used it for the entertainment of her numerous lovers). It also had – 'twas the chief reason for using it – the convenience of a neighbouring room from which an aperture carefully contrived not only afforded an opportunity to observe, but to hear, all that went on in it.

What met Treglown's eyes as he entered, was chiefly a large bed made up with the whitest of sheets, which presented to advantage the body stretched upon it, that of Betsy, now a ripe eighteen years of age, but still with the figure of a young person three or four years her junior: that is, with the full development of a female of the most luscious description, yet entirely lacking that slackness which too often is the product of a life devoted to amorous exercise (for she had kept herself solely to the young gentleman who was her friend, he being not only kindly but possessed of considerable wealth; only her debt to me, who had been the instrument of her obtaining her present position, persuading her to make this excursion).

I now set eyes upon Treglown for the first time (for, need I say, Charlie and myself were placed with our eyes at the spyholes). He was just such a man as I had imagined: coarse and unmannerly, and from his posture suffering from the effects of a life too much devoted to food and drink. Indeed, so clear was it that it was to gluttony that he was chiefly devoted, that I feared that even the sight of Betsy would not tempt him. However, here I was wrong – though perhaps as much through his pride that his employers (the French) had honoured him with such a reward, than from natural concupiscence.

At all events, no sooner had he closed the door than he began to divest himself of his clothing, all the time keeping an eye upon the prize upon the bed: which indeed was a sufficiently enticing one even to interest me, who only a few hours before had held in my arms the beautiful creature who now, with her hand upon my arm, observed the scene with an interest equal to my own. Closing the shutters, we had lit the room by candle-light, which now gleamed upon the Negress's body, laying trails of golden light upon the purple of her skin, and drawing as it were an outline about her limbs, which here and there, in shadow, darkened to complete black. As Treglown loosened the waistband of his breeches, she drew up a leg and, leaning it slightly to one side, allowed a silver of light to lie along the inside of her thigh, making yet more enticing the pitch-black shadow at its top, where now she laid a lethargic hand, as though to hide what was already obscured by the darkness.

A tightening of Charlie's fingers bespoke her approbation of the situation. When I had explained my plan, she had doubted whether any woman could entice her husband to any greater interest than he had shown, recently, in her; but in default of another plan had agreed to this, and was now generous enough to admit that she had been wrong – for Treglown, divesting himself of the last article of apparel, revealed a corporeal admiration of the banquet set before him; though not one such as would necessarily delight, let alone frighten, a woman.

His person, unclothed, was much as one would have expected from his appearance in polite society. Too indulgent an appetite at the table had thickened his frame, so that while his chest and shoulders were still those of a strong man (he was, I should have said, approaching the age of fifty), about his waist there hung those circles of flesh which thickened what had once no doubt been slender, while his belly was a converse vessel of mutton which swung somewhat as he moved.

His thighs, too, were thicker than they should have been, and there – as upon the lower parts of his arms – the skin had stretched to contain more blubber than a self-respecting gentleman would be happy with. The lack of hair upon his head, he could not be blamed for; neither was it his fault that the hair upon his chest and belly, and even that private hair below, was now grey and somewhat sparse. But was it a matter for congratulation that that chief advertisement of masculinity, confronted by such a delicious dish as was now set before Treglown, could only achieve a salute at half-mast? That even a vigorous manual stimulation, which he now applied, could rouse it only to the thickness and length of one of those cigars now imported so freely from the Americas?

It may be that, had she not been thoroughly instructed in what was expected of her, Betsy would have scorned the attentions of so poor a specimen of masculinity, so indifferent an advertisement for the sex. However, to her credit, she showed only interest – and now placed herself on hands and knees, resembling nothing so much as a handsome animal, in order to express what seemed admiration of the pathetic figure before her.

Treglown was, as she had intended, complimented by her interest – no doubt it had been many years since a woman had shown such interest in his person; and took a step towards the bed, at which she left it, and approaching him coiled her body sinuously about his own, a thigh insinuating itself between his own, her hands caressing his back and flaccid haunches, her enticing breasts pressed against his own – for his bosom was only by its pilosity different in shape to that of a woman, though one insufficiently developed for the taste of most men.

There now began a scene of such enticing voluptuousness that it roused my amorous propensities to a degree which equalled that of our victim. Betsy used all her wiles – not to entice a lover, for Treglown needed no encouragement – but to raise him to such heights of goatishness as were positively painful to him. Even his puny dangler was aroused by her attentions to such dimensions as were not entirely disreputable, while that great belly positively panted with desire; and as I saw him stretched upon the bed, his every limb tightened with unalleviated appetite, I was strung between pity and envy.

It was at this point that Betsy, carefully tutored by us, began her questioning; and such was the state to which she had reduced Treglown that the answers to her questions were immediately forthcoming. Careful though she was, I have no doubt that his suspicions were aroused; but his condition made it imperative that his body should be satisfied, and while we could not hear his half-whispered answers, the fact that in a short time she bestrode him (his person being so heavy as to make the superior position desirable as a matter of comfort) and brought him to a climax so keen that a positive wail broke from his lips, convinced us that our ambition had been achieved.

While he was still recovering, Betsy sprung from the bed, and reaching the door was through it, and had closed it behind her. On hearing it close, he roused himself – but reaching the door found it locked, and on opening the shutters found that the room looked out upon a blank quadrangle. As we left our vantage-point, he began to knock upon the door (with intervals during which he began to dress himself); but we had chosen the house with care. He could not be heard, and would only be relieved at our convenience.

Upon the landing, we met and congratulated Betsy – my own embrace being, I must confess, sufficiently keen (the young lady still being unclothed) to rouse Charlie to an uncomfortable though not unfriendly tweaking of my cods, and the reminder that we should attend to business. While she resumed her clothing, Betsy told us what she had discovered: which was the arrival at Dover in two days' time of a young man reputed to be the son of Madame de St Laurent and Prince Edward, Duke of Kent, fourth son of King George III, and father to Victoria. He was to be set forth as a proper heir to the British throne, an alternative to his sister, and an antidote to that dreadful fate, a female monarch! Since this boy had been brought up in France, and much under the influence of the notorious Charles Maurice de Talleyrand, it was hoped by the French that in placing him upon the throne they would have a puppet of their own at the head of the country which they still regard as their greatest rival in Europe.

'And while,' Charlie opined, 'so many of our people share your own prejudice against a female ruler, and since there are no other legitimate sons of George III's children, the plan has a strong chance of success unless it can be forestalled.'

The problem of achieving this was something to which we now turned our attention; and immediately took ourselves off to consult the Viscount Chichley, an old friend upon whose advice we could depend. Treglown, we left to his own devices. He was to remain for the time a prisoner; we had placed, in a cupboard of his comfortable prison, sufficient food and wine to last him for several days; by which time we trusted he could be released – if only to face trial as a traitor.

By the time we reached Chichley's house, I had devised a plan not dissimilar to that which had brought about Treglown's downfall; and Charlie had expressed her support for it, though wondering how it was to be achieved. About that, I had an idea of my own, and Chichley was quick to approve – and was able to inform me of the whereabouts of the person whose assistance was now necessary: my sister and friend Mrs Sophia Nelham.

Chapter Twelve

Sophie's Story

What was my surprise, upon my arrival at Chichley's London home, to find there my old friend Andrew Archer, together with a female friend whom he introduced as Mrs Samuel Treglown, but who goes under the name of Charlotte. She and Andy seemed upon familiar terms, and knowing my boy's delight in the companionship of willing women, I was not amazed, for she is a lady of considerable physical charms, and of just such a spirited nature as to appeal to him.

However, it was not in order to effect that introduction that I had been summoned, for pausing only to order some wine, Chichley explained the reason for my summons. It appears – and he did not explain, for there was not time, the details of the situation – that there was to arrive at Dover upon the following day, from France, a young man who was Pretender to the throne of England, summoned by a cabal of the French and English – the former eager to install here a monarch upon whose loyalty they could count; the latter eager to avoid the disgrace (as they see it) of a woman upon the throne – the present heir being the Princess Victoria.

Chichley's motives in wishing to prevent this were chiefly of a patriotic nature, as were (as I guess) those of my friend; while Mrs Treglown was of my own opinion, that there was at least a chance that a Queen might bring upon the country the same renown as that famous predecessor Elizabeth, whose monarchy was noted neither for weakness nor ineffectuality.

Andy explained to me that it was his plan that I should engage the attentions of the Pretender for a sufficient time to permit Chichley to alert the authorities to the scheme, and to arrest those culpable of it – for should the youth (of whom they know nothing) reach the capital and come into the grasp of the plotters, all may be lost within a very short time.

There were to this plan some objections: not that I was not entirely willing to devote myself body and soul to the country's good, but that we knew not the name of the Pretender, nor precisely when he would arrive; but Andy was convinced that this was no bar to the success of his scheme, and in short, upon my having consented to do what I could in the matter, it proved that he had already commissioned a coach, wherein he, his new friend and myself set out immediately for Dover, leaving Chichley to make contact with those persons in London whose loyalty could be depended upon to destroy any scheme involving a threat to the security of the realm.

On our reaching Dover – a town with which I was then unfamiliar – we found it but a poor fishing village crouched beneath tremendous cliffs of chalk, with only two inns, one of which was in such a condition that no traveller would stay there unless forced to do so. The other, to our great satisfaction, was almost entirely full, and on our making discreet enquiries of the landlord we found that no party had taken rooms for the following evening on behalf of any who might arrive from the continent (this being a less prominent port, for such arrivals, than Brighthelmstone, further along the coast). Andy and his friend bespoke the single remaining room on behalf of Andrew Archer Esq., MP, and Mrs Archer – and then set about finding lodgings for me and for my victim, and succeeded in taking a small but decent cottage on the outskirts of the hamlet; having assured ourselves that it would suit our purpose, we spent the day somewhat at ease. After an early dinner Andy and Charlotte excused themselves on the grounds of an unconscionable lethargy; the brightness of their eyes however betrayed rather a desire for carnal congress. I went to my lonely bed.

Next day we also spent in idleness, but any thought I might have had of familiarity with my friend, whom I had not seen for some time, was rendered impossible by his invariably being in the company of Mrs Treglown, with whom, on no less than two occasions, he retired to their room upon one excuse or another – returning some time later in that state of relaxation which bespeaks physical contentment. I had never seen my friend so besotted with a female – but must confess her to be charming enough.

At the hour of eight post meridian, a schooner was due to arrive from the French port of Le Havre – which, being the only foreign vessel likely to put in, must contain the traveller in whom we were most interested, and at this time, we three placed ourselves in the window of the inn – and to our satisfaction saw three men who from their appearance were more distinguished than the gaggle of other travellers who descended the gangway from the *Petite Marie* (which was the name of the vessel) approach the place.

On their entering, we saw the trio consisted of two middle-aged men, one of rougher appearance than the other, and a young man who was careful to remain as much in the shadow as was possible. Upon enquiry, finding there were no rooms available, the two older men exchanged courtesies in a tone indicative of mingled distress and anger; and one of them, in execrable English, began to enquire as to the possibility of other accommodation, which the landlord denied the existence of (he having been prepared by instruction and payment to do so).

The irritation of the two elder men now became extreme; upon which I rose from my place and approached them.

'Messieurs,' I said (addressing them in their own language, which I had some little knowledge of), 'is it the case that you seek accommodation, and cannot find it?'

They assented – whereupon I offered them the convenience of my humble home – my brother and sister-in-law (with a nod towards Andy and his friend) returning to London within the hour, there were two rooms available, which I was pleased to offer to representatives of that great nation whose recent struggle to relieve herself from the cruel rule of despots I so admired.

The gentlemen were as grateful as they were unsuspicious – indeed, I was almost ashamed at the ease with which I deceived them; and, motioning the younger man to come forward, introduced him as M. le Semblant. A glimpse of his face suggested that the task of making his closer acquaintance would not be a painful one, and his shy smile as he bowed over my hand was one which immediately engaged my sympathy – it was not the face of a villain.

To be short, pausing only for the rougher man (who seemed to be a servant) to pick up the two packages which were their only luggage, the three gentlemen accompanied me to the cottage which we had secured, my having made an ostentatious farewell to Andy and Mrs Treglown.

At the cottage I was for a time fearful that I might be discovered, for though I had explored it as best I might, I was not entirely familiar with its geography; but the travellers were weary, and almost immediately took themselves to their rooms – the two elder men to one at the back of the house, the younger to a room somewhat removed from this.

After allowing a pause of some quarter of an hour or twenty minutes I took a bowl of hot water and knocked softly upon the door of M. le Semblant's room. A gentle voice bade me enter, and doing so I found the young man sitting somewhat melancholy in the window and looking out over the sea towards the coast he had earlier left.

I set the bowl down, with the suggestion that he might wish to refresh himself after the journey; and left the room – pausing for perhaps ten minutes, and then, placing a towel over my arm, returning. This time I entered without knocking, and found the youth – for he was clearly little more – naked to the waist, having blinded himself with soap before assuring himself of a towel, and feeling about him in a state of considerable confusion.

'Monsieur,' I said, 'a thousand pardons! I omitted to provide you with the means to dry yourself!' — and stepping forward handed him the towel, with which he instantly dried his face, while I leaned to take the bowl of water.

Upon his opening his eyes, he found a sight which clearly interested him. I had now changed my formerly modest gown for one which revealed more of my person than perhaps a stranger would count upon discovering except in circumstances of some intimacy. The dress which I now wore was one of those, already out of fashion, which, being of the thinnest cotton, revealed as much as it concealed – and I took care that in picking up the bowl I allowed some of the water to splash upon its front, so that the material clung even more closely to my bosom, from which it was beyond the boy's power to take his eyes.

'*M – madame*,' he stammered, 'all my gratitude . . .'

'But, sir,' I said, 'you look melancholy' – and setting down the bowl reached out a hand and placed it upon his arm; 'you are perhaps sad to leave your home?'

'Ah, *madame*,' he said, 'I am not at liberty to explain the reason, but this is indeed a journey I had rather not make.'

'Yet,' I said, 'this is an hospitable country, in which you will find a warm welcome' – at the same time placing a second hand upon his other arm, in what amounted to an embrace. At this, a mixture of melancholy and the lethargy of the journey (a combination which must weaken the strongest spirits) so attacked him that he seized me about the waist, and in a moment embraced me with a kiss more passionate than I expected from a boy of his years.

The advantage of a French education cannot be too much emphasised where matters of love are concerned. A moment after this first embrace, he drew away, fearful no doubt that he might have offended me; but upon my showing – by the simple act of slipping my dress from my shoulders – that such was not the case, he began to prove the extent to which he excelled any English youth of his age in those arts which best please a lady.

I later learned from him that in preparation for the task he was to face he had been locked away from female company for some months, forced to memorise many facts about the English aristocracy, and in particular the royal family. Previously as accustomed to regular amorous exercise as any Frenchman of his age, his frustration had been considerable; and upon my offering the opportunity of an embrace, he seized it with the greatest enthusiasm.

I am in some difficulty in describing what followed, for to be frank my emotions were soon engaged in so vigorous and persuasive a fashion that I was in a delirium of delight such as I had not known for many months. My constant readers will not be unaware that during my years of adulthood I have been familiar with a number of gentlemen of greater or lesser accomplishment in the arts of love; yet I can say without hesitation that this boy of only nineteen – this Maurice, for that was his name – had a greater knowledge of how to please a female than any other man in my experience.

I should perhaps insert at this point a description of his life, as he later related it to me.

The question whether he is really the son of Madame de St Laurent, let alone of the Duke of Kent, must await discovery; it is what he has been led to believe, and it is clear that from an infant he was raised in the expectation of achieving the English throne. Despite this, however, and all the tuition of that villain Talleyrand, it is an expectation which provoked only melancholy, for he is by no means a person to whom rank and position offers rewards he is eager to acquire.

The reason for this disposition is not difficult to

understand, for from infancy he was treated as a mere vessel for political propaganda; his guardians, bent upon forcing him into their mould, only made themselves representative of a painful tedium. But those responsible for his nurture have been of the lower orders, whose simplicity and good humour seemed infinitely preferable – so that his personal preference was for leading a life of quiet obscurity, and his one ambition to escape the high office others intend him for.

His first memories were of growing up in a farm in Burgundy, where the first fourteen years of his life were entirely free of anxiety; he was treated as one of a family of five children, and though the others were the natural children of the farmer and wife, who played in all respects the part of parents, he was treated with the same kindness as the two boys and two girls who were in every sense except the literal one his brothers and sisters.

He was marked out from them however by being sent for, at the age of five, to the manor house of the area, where he became the pupil of a master who taught him – with the greatest kindness – to read and write excellent French, and to speak English with reasonable fluency. The purpose of this education was not revealed to him until later, and he did not allow his superior knowledge to affect his relationship with his brothers and sisters, which remained extremely close.

Indeed, as seems common with French families, it was in company with them that he made his first explorations of the capabilities of the body; he and his brothers, noting the changes which took place at the time of approaching manhood, were at one in persuading their sisters to reveal whether or not similar changes were occurring with them. They had from the earliest time been used to the differences between the male and female form, having been accustomed to share both bed and bath; and the small appendages which alone marked male from female had seemed to them of little remark. But upon the time coming when these were so enlarged as to occasion comment from their sisters (waking in the morning to the sight of three commanding extensions of their brothers' nether parts) they showed a renewed interest in the girls' persons, finding both curiosity and delight in the fringe of silky hair which now decorated portals which previously had been too naked to command anything other than slight interest.

A natural modesty prevented their doing anything other than look; and in common with other youths, it was in experiment with each other that they discovered the delights conferred by the attention of Mrs Palm and her five daughters, and were soon contesting among themselves as to who could couple the pleasure of emission with its greatest force; a game the girls soon discovered them at, and were keen spectators of.

Upon his attaining the age of sixteen, it was one of those sisters who (and how fortunate that she was not a natural sister, but one in name only!) had seduced Maurice into performing an action which gave him even greater pleasure than that of manual stimulation, and for some time (as he told me with some perturbation) he had run riot through the countryside, discovering that almost every female of his own age welcomed the attentions of his prick, which proved sturdy enough to perform several operations on the same day without diminution either of force or of pleasure.

It was on the occasion of his swiving with a maid at the manor, when he had been left alone for an hour to learn some English phrases, that he was discovered by Madame Lecouvre, the sister of the master of the house, a lady who had for some time been mistress of a gentleman at the court, and was considerably experienced in amatory art.

'She taught me,' he said, 'those skills which best please the sex.' And indeed she had taught him well, for upon the first experience of our coupling, at Dover, he proved the most splendid, efficacious, considerate and compelling of lovers.

I must first say that of all men he was the most beautiful: by which I do not mean in the least effeminate, but the possessor of limbs perfectly shaped, a torso which might have been carved by Michelangelo himself, a noble head crowned with a magnificent mane of blond hair. His hands were not only finely shaped, but admirable in conveying every shade of admiration, ready to respond to desire almost before it had made itself known to the body he caressed.

Indeed, what was astonishing to me was the extent to which the attentions of his hands were arousing – for most men are clumsy to the extent of bruising, handling a woman as they would handle a dog or a horse. Maurice proceeded with much greater care, and while fixing his lips upon my own (occasionally transferring them to the tips of my ears, my eyelids, forehead, chin – even, sometimes, descending to the tips of my breasts) his hands moved with the greatest tenderness over my body, gradually drawing nearer to that goal at which (I assumed) he ultimately aimed.

But there, too, his manners were impeccable: far from thrusting a finger rudely into the aperture, as so many men do, he stroked and caressed my jewel as if indeed it were of a priceless value, stroking first gently up and down the groove; then placing four fingers slightly above, and moving them gently; and finding the boy in the boat, gently but insistently moving his lubricated forefinger around and about, and then upon, that most sensitive zone, until I was almost mad with the pleasure of it, and finally gave way to a spasm of delight so intense that my whole body shook with it.

Yet still he persisted – now with an even more sensitive touch, so that far from making tender the source of my pleasure, he roused me in no short time again almost to the heights – then, as my panting began to signify a second culmination, withdrew his hand and in its stead juxtaposed a machine whose power I was yet ignorant of – though my own fingers had found it of significant size.

To be short about it, he proceeded to demonstrate a style of swiving which was as apprehensive of my pleasure as the preliminaries, for he fell into a regular rocking motion which would have lulled me into sleep had not the friction of his tool within me continued the raising of my spirits. At first content with a shallow penetration, so that his bulb merely stimulated the curtains of my arbour, he gradually pressed deeper, until with a splendid keenness I felt the whole length of his instrument plunging within me, seeming (no doubt through the graduality of his approach) to pierce my very vitals.

Giving myself over entirely to pleasure, and even forgetting the obligations which should have encouraged me to contribute to his enjoyment in the way of such manual caresses as were possible in the situation, I succumbed no less than three more times to convulsions of the utmost agitation before I felt the hot flow of his passion; after which he for some time still continued his movements, though with a slower and less compulsive rhythm, lulling me to the point at which I was not reluctant to permit him to withdraw.

In the light of a moon which had now risen, I could see what I had felt – that his whole body was through his efforts bathed in perspiration, and taking the towel wiped his limbs, which in their relaxed state had a beauty no less than that displayed by his previous excitement. This did not, however, prevent me from my desire to return some of the pleasure he had afforded me (apart from the fact that 'twas my duty); and driven by the ambition to prove myself as considerate and adept a lover as he, I proceeded to exercise upon him those talents which had been sharpened during the years subsequent to my first childish experiences with brother Frank, at our home at Alcovary.

I flatter myself that I was not unsuccessful; and by the time we fell into an exhausted sleep in each other's arms, we had proved to my satisfaction that we were perfectly complementary lovers.

It was with some horror that I awoke, hours later, to find daylight at the window. Opening my eyes, I found not only the sun, but Maurice's eyes, feeding on my body; and indeed on seeing me awake, he reached out as though impelled to discover whether or not the previous night had been a dream. I hastily discouraged him – and now took the great gamble of being honest with him. I have no doubt that Chichley would have been horrified; even Andy might have remonstrated; but I have always had a talent for the estimation of character, and felt in my bones that honesty was in the circumstances the best policy.

I therefore enquired, first, why he was in England; and after some hesitation, he revealed what I already knew – that it was the ambition of that consummate politician Talleyrand to prove him the proper successor to our present King, and for that purpose he was landed in England, to be escorted this day to London and the French Embassy, where a number of gentlemen in and around Parliament and the Court, who were indifferent to the prospect of a female ruler, would be introduced to him and invited to encourage him towards the throne.

And was this his wish, I asked?

Far from it, he replied. The exigencies of high office were a horror to him; all he wished for was a quiet life – and from the embraces he offered me, the company of a pleasant female.

This was my opportunity: relying upon my divination of character, I told him precisely the truth – even to admitting that it had been my intention to seduce him with a view to understanding his plan, specifically in order to frustrate it.

To my pleasure he immediately took my point, even to admitting that not only was he unsure whether his lineage was as had been described to him – but that even if it were so, protesting that he had no desire to pursue the matter! However, it was necessary to escape before the two men who accompanied him were about, for they would undoubtedly (being in the pay and much under the influence of M. Talleyrand) make him accompany them to London, and once at the French Embassy he would willy-nilly be forced to lend his presence to the plot.

We therefore rose speedily, and only pausing to make the most cursory toilet, were within half an hour at the inn and burst in upon Andy and his friend, still twined in each other's arms in a posture suggestive of agreeable concupiscence. Waking them, I explained the situation; and though Andy was clearly suspicious at the ease with which I had converted Maurice, was finally persuaded - not only by his presence but by his modesty and gentlemanlike qualities - of his honesty; while Charlie - whom I should now, in familiarity, address by that somewhat common appellation - at once took my part, immediately grasping the natural attributes of his character.

They rose with equal speed, and pausing only to leave a message for the local Watch, under Chichley's seal, which would result in the Dover magistrate detaining the two Frenchmen *incommunicado* for as long a period as authority deemed necessary, we were upon the road by six o'clock in the morning.

There had been some dispute about our destination. It could certainly not be London - but where else? It was Andy who suggested Alcovary - and once the name had been mentioned, it was clearly the proper place; only Chichley, among our friends, knew of it, and even if by some alchemy my own and Andy's identities were discovered (and it was just possible that M. Foutarque might infer it, though from no hard evidence) my whereabouts would be difficult to apprehend.

Our journey took two days; and we passed through the outskirts of London, pausing for the night at an inn at Greenwich. There, a single room was all that was available; and though Maurice showed some diffidence at sharing a bed with three comparative strangers, upon the landlord agreeing to place a truckle-bed in the room, he assented.

We were by then excessively tired, and stayed awake only long enough to take some refreshment, before taking to our beds in a handsome bow-windowed chamber overlooking the Thames, within a stone's-throw of Mr Wren's magnificent palace. Falling into a deep sleep, I believe that none of us stirred until morning; though waking at first light, at Andy's side, I saw upon his other side the figure of Charlotte, reclining upon one elbow, and regarding Maurice, who in the heat of the night had thrown off the sheet which covered him, and now revealed his figure entirely to the beholder, in utter relaxation, but as beautiful as a carved statue, his limbs perfectly white and perfectly charming.

Catching my eye, Charlotte had the grace to blush; but with a smile I let her know that her admiration was entirely understood by me, and we once more reclined, myself falling again into a slumber from which I was awakened only by the slight motion of the bed which signalled Andy's enjoyment of the body of his mistress (for they must part later that morning). He had slid between her thighs with so quiet a movement that it had not disturbed me, and was moving now with extreme gentleness in order not to wake me. However when, with that mischievousness that had always marked our relationship, I tickled his fundament with an apprehensive finger, he was relieved of the necessity for a caution which must have restricted enjoyment, and the entire mattress was soon bounding with their mutual pleasure – so much so that an uncomfortable (though agreeable) contact with their bodies encouraged me to slip from the bed and to take myself to lie at Maurice's side, who though still asleep now displayed indication of an involuntary but so far unapprehended excitement to which I felt it my duty as well as my pleasure to waken him – for we have not so long on this earth that we can afford to waste the opportunity for pleasure when so strongly evidenced.

That he was not distressed to be drawn from slumber was clear from his immediate reaction to my lips upon his admirably erect tool, which indeed justified that name, formed as it seemed to be in an ideal shape for giving and receiving pleasure. Time was short, and our preliminaries were restricted to confirming that each was ready to accept the caresses of the other – by my sufficiently anointing his instrument, and his at the same time ensuring that my own was sufficiently lubricious to receive it.

This accomplished, he was pleased to turn me upon my face, and lift my hips to address me from the rear, so that while plunging with spirited motion, he was at the same time able to caress with one hand my breasts, and with the other that portion of my inner lips not susceptible to the friction of his weapon.

The emotion resulting from this attention was sufficiently keen to make me screw up my eyes with the sharpness of it; but upon approaching an apogee I opened them to discover that Andy and Charlotte, having accomplished their own pleasure, were finding more in observing us – the latter, I thought, with peculiar appreciation; and upon Maurice courteously lowering me (our passage concluded) to the bed, and for a moment reclining upon me, they applauded us with expressions of admiration.

My lover was at first abashed, but the couple's admiration and approbation was too honest to take offence at, and he relinquished his attempts to cover us with the sheet and permitted me to wipe his body and my own before assuming (as we all did) our clothes.

On our crossing the river Andy now took his leave to make his way to Chichley in London, while Charlotte, Maurice and myself proceeded on the road towards Alcovary, which by dint of travelling all day (with a single break for luncheon) we achieved by two in the morning. It being an extremely warm day, and ourselves being the sole occupants of the coach, we were all to some extent *en dishabille*, Maurice removing his shirt and even (with our permission) his breeches, being then clad only in under-breeches, which it is the habit for gentlemen to wear in France – an uncongenial and even unsalubrious habit which I fear will eventually be assumed in this country. Charlotte and I contented ourselves with opening our clothing to the waist, allowing as much air as possible to cool our bodies, and raising our skirts above our knees.

It could not escape my eye that Charlotte regarded my new friend with an appreciative eye, the more so when he had fallen asleep, and she thought that I also slumbered. Indeed he was a picture worth perusing, and I could not blame her for wishing to study it, though upon observing her hand creep beneath her skirts I wondered whether her appreciation was entirely and singularly aesthetic.

On our reaching Alcovary, we found my brother Frank and my sister-in-law in their beds – but on being roused, as always pleased to welcome us, and keenly interested to greet both my friends and to hear our story – at which they were properly indignant, Frank, somewhat to my surprise, particularly so, for he shared my own view that should the succession fall to the Princess Victoria there was no reason to suppose that she might not prove a proper monarch, under the advice of her counsellors.

We were then allotted our rooms, Frank taking the opportunity to ask me whether I wished to share that of Maurice (for it had been clear to him, who knew me well, that I was not indifferent to the young man). I however preferred us to occupy three separate rooms, for though there was no indication that Maurice would be offended at my presence, I thought it fair that he should feel entirely free, especially in view of his position as a stranger in a strange house.

The next few days were entirely delightful, for a number of reasons. First, it was always a pleasure to be at home at Alcovary, and in halcyon summer weather; then, I had the delight of showing my friends the estate, about which we rode (both my companions being adept riders), and when the heat became oppressive made our way to the lake where Frank, Andy and I had bathed as children, and throwing off our clothes cooled ourselves in the waters, then lying upon the bank as the sun dried the sparkling droplets from our bodies.

I was not altogether surprised when Charlotte took me aside, at the end of our second day, and enquired with much diffidence to what extent I was devoted to Maurice – 'for', she said, 'I find myself strongly attracted to the young man; yet would not wish to make any move of which, as my hostess, you would disapprove.'

'My dear Charlotte,' I replied, 'it has ever been my view that what pleasure a man and woman can enjoy together, they should enjoy without the intervention of profitless jealousy. I have no rights over Maurice's body, and if he would welcome a passage with you – and I have no doubt that so attractive a lady will engage his admiration – then both he and you have my blessing; though I am not sure that my brother would say the same' (for I suspected that Andy admired Charlotte to an extent which she perhaps was not fully aware of).

Having obtained, as it were, my permission, Charlotte was nevertheless concerned not to make any move behind my back; and so it was when we were all lying together in a contented state of nature, after one of our bathes, that she whispered something in Maurice's ear as he lay face downwards upon the grass – underlining the suggestion she made my placing her hand upon his back just at that most sensitive point where the bifurcation of the buttocks offers an invariable trigger of desire.

Maurice's reply was to glance at me; and when inferring the question, I smilingly nodded my permission, he turned to take Charlotte in his arms, transferring to her breast and belly the bright green flecks of grass which had stuck to his wet body.

It was now my turn to admire the manner of their coupling; and while I knew perfectly the extent of his mastery of love-making, I was filled with a new admiration at the mixture of tenderness and insistence, of desire and restraint with which he wooed her body into a feverish eagerness to join with his own. Their mutual pleasure conveyed itself to the watcher not only through observation of their actions – which comprised every known engagement of limb with limb; not only through its prolongment – and an hour at least must have passed while they pleasured each other; but in an apprehension which combined riggishness with tenderness in equal degrees, and marked a mutual affection and respect not less keen than that which had (as I believed) graced my own passages of love with Maurice.

That I should be entirely unmoved by the spectacle was not to be expected; and in the end I was forced (lest I impose my physical presence upon the couple, which they may not have welcomed) to take refuge in the deep and cool waters of the pool, which had the effect of somewhat assuaging my ardour. It was while I was still in the water that they brought their exercises to a final conclusion, and missing my presence, were good enough to express themselves fearful that they had neglected me, and when I issued from the pool greeted me with embraces that were as warm in their emotion as in their physical expression – the apprehension of their heated bodies upon my cool one being as pleasurable, I believe, to them, as to me. While these embraces warmed me again, I was forced to restrain my sentiments, for it was perfectly clear that Maurice was now incapable of responding to them – and while I have from time to time without displeasure been the object of the caresses of another female, such was not my desire upon this occasion.

That I spent a somewhat melancholy evening perhaps need not be said. While I am the least jealous of beings, and have always believed that each individual must be free to bestow affection upon whatever object is pleasing, I had not expected Maurice to transfer his affections so suddenly and so completely to another woman; nor did it seem to me (if I must be truthful) entirely fair to Andy that Mrs Treglown, whatever her feelings towards him, should show so thoroughly the extent to which she found her new lover agreeable (even in the absence of my brother).

Nevertheless, there was nothing to be done; and the

affection shown me by the pair was only restricted by its nature – which did not embrace physical passion; and when at night I heard Maurice's footsteps pass my own door in the direction of Charlotte's, I must make as little of it as I could. Nevertheless, I could not but feel a tear spring to the eye.

Perhaps an hour after falling into the deep sleep which so often accompanies grief, I awoke to feel the familiar but unexpected sensation of an unclothed male body pressed against my own; but upon embracing it felt, rather than the lean body of the Pretender, a fuller – yet by no means obese – figure. The intruder failed to alarm me, being tender in his approaches; and my unspoken question as to whose member was now nuzzling my side was answered by a whispered greeting from Frank, my half-brother, who, recognising my dejection, had left his wife's bed (as I later learned, with her generous approbation) and come to comfort me.

I should perhaps explain that as children we had together explored the parameters of love while, ignorant of the restrictions upon familial intimacy enforced by the Church, we still believed ourselves to be the products of the same parents. Upon our discovery of society's disapproval of incest, we had ceased our pleasant games, not without a certain guilt; only to be delighted at the revelation – through circumstances which I will not now rehearse – that while we shared the same mother, our fathers were two different men. This somewhat alleviated our guilt; and indeed from time to time, when circumstance prompted, we had not hesitated to comfort each other in a manner warmer than might normally have been expected of siblings.

This was just such an occasion; and while we were not

adventurous, our conjugation was perfectly consolatory, and in falling again asleep, this time within the circle of Frank's arms, I did so with a less troubled mind, and certainly a less insatiate body, than hitherto.

I should remark that the Lady Margaret was of such a disposition as positively to welcome her husband's loyalty to an old friend, and her kindness to me at this time was entirely as marked as that of Frank; which enabled me to regard with greater equanimity, if not with entire satisfaction, the degree of preoccupation with which Maurice and Charlotte regarded each other - and to restrain both from recrimination towards the one and coldness towards the other.

More than a week had passed before, one morning, at ten o'clock, a bedraggled figure galloped up to the front door of Alcovary, his horse in a froth of sweat. It was Andy - and with a story which I can only allow him to tell for himself.

Chapter Thirteen

The Adventures of Andy

On my arrival my first action must be to report to Chichley, which I immediately did. He was interested to hear that M. le Semblant had proved sufficiently amiable to be no danger to us once removed from the influence of M. Talleyrand and his associates; and approved our plan of sending him to Alcovary, his confidence in Sophie's good sense being strengthened by his acquaintance with Frank, who though disinclined to politics is a man of some backbone, and entirely trustworthy.

The question now arose what to do about the nefarious influence of Talleyrand's friends in London – notably the Ambassador. That he should merely be instructed to leave the Court, without reason given, would be unsatisfactory, for though His Majesty, informed of the plot, would have no qualms about dismissing him, to do so without excuse would attract much unfavourable comment towards the new Government – while that the plot should be noised abroad would attract equally antagonistic attacks from those who would see it as demonstrating a lamentable lack of prescience among those whose duty it was to prevent such matters.

It was important, then, that the Duc de Laval should be discredited. But in what fashion? I assured Chichley that I believed that this could be contrived, and having made my farewells, set out that very night into that part of London where are chiefly to be found those foreign women imported into this country for the purpose of prostitution – for I could not but believe that M. *l'Ambassadeur* had his preferences in the matter of sensual enjoyment, and while I did not suppose that he would prowl the streets of Soho or the pavements of the Haymarket, it was possible that I might through gossip hear something to his disadvantage.

I met here in the space of an hour or so Spanish, Italian and Belgian as well as French women; and by dint of tipping them (from the liberal purse supplied for the purpose by Chichley, who insisted that I should not employ my personal funds for the purpose) was able to converse with them; but none had so much as heard of the French Ambassador, either by that title or by his name. This did not surprise me altogether; he would be unlikely to use either title or name under the circumstances I envisaged; but a description of his person produced equally negative results.

I then took myself to the accommodation houses of Oxenden and James Streets, of May Fair, and particularly of Curzon Street, and spoke to those women who make a handsome living by letting out their premises. The latter street contains two houses with the best-known and most luxurious rooms in the whole of London, those upon the first floors being let for as much as twenty pounds a night. I knew (through the days when Frank and I were in something the same business) the women who kept them; and one gave me some hope. She had at this moment, she said, a party going forward in her chief room, at which a foreign gentleman was at supper with some of her girls, and was sufficiently confident of my discretion to allow me to eavesdrop from the adjoining room (for all these houses have vantage-points from which their guest-rooms may be privately observed – chiefly to prevent disorder or attacks upon the persons of their girls; though sometimes, it must be admitted, upon payment of a few guineas, a gentleman whose pleasure is in looking rather than doing, may command the view).

In this case, I thought at first that I had struck home, for the gentleman whose back was towards me as I looked, seemed certainly to fit the description I had been given of M. le Duc (for, never having seen the gentleman in person, I must rely upon a sketch made for one of the public prints, and upon the fact that the Ambassador has – as Chichley had informed himself by the bribery of a footman – a birthmark upon the front of his right shoulder).

This gentleman was, as might have been expected, unclothed, and was making a good dinner off the bodies of three similarly naked young ladies. I mean, not that he was devouring their bodies (except in the figurative sense), but that upon the breasts and belly of the first were spread various cold meats, neatly garnished; upon the body of the second, a French salad – set out with much ingenuity in the cutting and shaping of the necessaries so that they did not roll from their precarious perch; while the third provided fruits of various kinds – two peaches, skinned, having been hollowed to fit over the points of her breasts, a fine melon, halved, upon her belly, and between her thighs a bunch of grapes, among which the diner was at present dabbling the fingers of one hand, while with the other he gathered the last spoonfuls of a meat sauce which lay about the navel of her friend.

The gentleman, as I have said, had his back to me; and there was no means of discovering a view of his face – but my hopes were dashed immediately by his breaking, through a mouthful of food, into exclamations in the German tongue (and indeed he later proved to be a distant cousin of His Majesty's come from Austria for the Coronation, whose introduction to the pleasures of Curzon Street made him a considerable source of income to the houses there and thereabouts).

I left my vantage-point, shaking my head; whereupon Mrs Blowser (the name of the proprietor of the house) intimated that there was a lady who might be able to help me, and escorting me to another room knocked upon the door, and on receiving an invitation to enter drew me with her into a reception room in which upon a *chaise-longue* reclined a figure which I instantly recognised: it was that of Xanthe, a lady who had been in my employ when with my brother Frank I was supervising our house of pleasure in Brook Street!

She rose immediately, and without reference to Mrs Blowser embraced me with a fervour which could not be mistaken for anything other than friendship.

'Why, Mr Archer!' she said. 'What good fortune brings you to this house! And how long 'tis since we . . .' – giving my cods an appreciative squeeze. Mrs Blowser, observing that we were not strangers to each other, tactfully withdrew; and I must confess that, what with the encouragement of the scene I had just observed, together with Xanthe's throwing off her *négligé* to reveal a body not the least diminished in attractiveness during the three or four years since we had last met, I allowed the question foremost in my mind to be thrust aside for a while, and in short permitted her to assist in the removal of my clothing and to lead me to the bed conveniently placed in the corner of the room, behind a screen which preserved the decencies on occasions when more than one gentleman awaited the attentions of whichever lady occupied the chamber.

Xanthe was good enough to compliment me upon the preservation of my own figure, and (with an appreciative caress) my apparently undiminished vigour; a kindness I was able to return without equivocation, for her slender frame remained as lithe and shapely as I remembered it – which I did in some detail, even to the mole which lay upon the inside of her left thigh, and towards the rear, which I now rediscovered in the course of paying tribute to those portals between which I would shortly take pleasure in slipping.

In parenthesis, I may say that I have always found that despite the considerable number of ladies who have kindly permitted me to admire them, my memory retains a keen approbation of most of them. I can see now, in my mind's eye, the somewhat over-ripe body of Lady Franklyn, Frank's mother (the first woman to show me, to my surprise, that an appetite for love outlasts one's thirtieth year); I remember very keenly the disparity between the bodies of Lady Margaret and Lady Elizabeth Rawby (the former now my friend Frank's wife); while even brief passages with such light skiffs as Mlle Anny, a Parisian lady of pleasure I had encountered but once, or an Arab lady whose extraordinary practices I enjoyed during one brief evening in Cairo, remain in my mind with such clarity that I am sure I would recognise their bodies were I merely to glimpse them without the protective disguise of clothing.

But I digress. Xanthe in the course of the next hour proved that her ability to please had diminished no jot; and her attentions roused me, despite a certain fatigue, to a greater degree of participation in amorous play than I would have believed myself capable of; so that in the end we lay pleasantly exhausted upon the bed, with a bottle of claret between us.

And what was I doing in such a place? she now enquired. Surely I need not purchase the favours of ladies, having always been more than capable of seduction, and being (I quote my friend, and do not assert it myself) impossible to resist, on account (she was kind enough to say) of the freshness of my looks and the enthusiasm of my play?

I explained that I was searching for someone who might have some knowledge of the habits of a gentleman of my acquaintance, a Frenchman; and described, without naming, him.

'Ah, you mean old Laval!' she said.

'You know him?' I exclaimed in delighted surprise.

'Why certainly!' she remarked; 'but not with any pleasure, and not as I know you' (bending to plant a kiss upon my now pliant tool).

My silent questioning then brought forth, without interrogation, the following anecdote:

'You remember George?' Xanthe asked.

Indeed I did: he was a young black man who had been one of the most admired hosts at the house which my sister Sophie had run, in Chiswick, for the delectation of the neglected ladies of the metropolis. The dimensions of that part of his body most admired by ladies were equalled only by his diffidence and charm, and on the winding up of the premises (as the result of a fire, a disaster my sister relates in a chapter of our adventures recorded in *Eros in Town*) he had last been seen in vigorous embrace with the lady whose head now lay engagingly upon my shoulder as she spoke.

'Well,' she continued, 'he has lately been in retirement from the profession, having employed that small fortune he saved while in Mrs Nelham's employ in the purchase of a respectable lodging house in the village of Islington, where from time to time we renew our acquaintance.

'However, his popularity with the ladies is such that he sometimes accepts the invitation of an old friend, and three months ago was sent for to Mrs FitzNott at her house in Knight's Bridge, to participate in a demonstration before a small party of ladies; and was kind enough to invite me upon that occasion to be his partner.

'On arriving at the house, we were drawn aside by Mrs FitzNott, and invited to betray no surprise should we observe anything strange about one of the observers. Nothing more was said – which of course had the effect of making us considerably more curious as to the nature of the audience than we would otherwise have been.

'Nothing at first seemed untoward: there were eight ladies seated upon comfortable chairs arranged in the chief *salon* of the house, and in a candle-light directed more at the cushions piled upon the centre of the floor than upon the faces of the females themselves.

'You will know, Mr Archer, that on such occasions 'tis necessary, especially in the opening passages of a performance, for the gentleman to withdraw attention from any other person than she with whom he is engaging; for should he be more aware of the audience than of his partner, there may be the unfortunate result that he becomes incapable of the act, which results at once in disappointment and the withdrawal of payment, and can even stimulate anger in those who have gathered to witness a performance which is then impossible.

'For the lady, however, the circumstances are not the same; indeed, upon such occasions I have always found it an advantage – however adept my partner in arousing those passions which upon a more private occasion are our particular joy – to detach myself from the proceedings in order to observe their effect upon the persons looking on; indeed, that process is productive not merely of interest and amusement, but sometimes of an inspiriting stimulation.

'On this occasion, after I had discovered to the viewers that part of George's body which invariably engages a rapt attention, and it was his turn to become the active partner, I was enabled by the circumstances, lying back upon the cushions while he grazed with his lips upon my lower body, to turn my eye upon the audience. There, it fell upon a somewhat heavily built lady who, sitting but four or five feet from us, had her eyes fixed most attentively upon George.

'This was not in the least surprising, for, Negroes being a rarity in the city, and scarcely ever to be observed in a state of nature, his body always attracts enthusiastic attention; but this lady was more considerably inspirited than her neighbours – and when again it came to my turn to revolve George's body so that that instrument whose size was the envy of his colleagues was once more revealed, and rendered yet more alert and upstanding by the attentions of my fingers and tongue, I thought the good lady's stays would burst.

'The development of our exhibition now reached the stage at which I must pay more attention to the proceedings, for as you will remember the insertion of George's prick (being of such unusual dimensions) could cause pain to those females insufficiently ready for the operation; however, I have never found it difficult to arouse my passions to a pitch at which liquefaction ensues, and (in short) in a brief time we were joined in that posture which best enables an audience to observe it; that is, with George upon his back, two pillows beneath his arse, and his hips thus elevated to an extent which displayed to advantage the pole upon which I lowered and raised my body.

'Despite the keen sensation always aroused by connection with that most splendid of lovers' (here Xanthe paused, afraid that she might have distressed me by this tribute, and afforded me the pleasure of a kiss) 'I was because of my elevation once more in a line of sight which positively forced me to observe the most prominent member of the audience, the front of whose gown was elevated, at her lap, to a surprising degree, which almost prompted me to suppose . . .'

Here Xanthe paused again; and, smiling at me, drew a finger along the length of my own riding-muscle, which (the picture she drew of the occasion having been sufficiently stimulating) was now if not adamantine, at least engorged to a promising thickness.

'You will no doubt have already guessed the identity of the woman of whom I spoke. Mrs FitzNott, after applause had signalled the end of our show and we had withdrawn, took George aside and asked whether he would be prepared to attend a lady, privately, offering a fee which was sufficiently persuasive. However, in twenty minutes, my friend reappeared in the room where I was taking refreshment, and, without himself pausing to taste anything, whisked me from the room and into a coach. It appears that upon his entering an upstairs bedroom and being embraced by the lady in question (no less than the one I had observed), he had at first been slightly repulsed by that masculine appendage, a slight moustache; yet had been prepared to believe that she suffered from that hirsute growth which can be a distressful trouble to some ladies.

'However, having permitted her to undress him, and even to address herself with enthusiasm to that part which most attracted her, and having accompanied her to the bed and begun to pay her those attentions she seemed to crave, he was puzzled to find that she made no attempt to disrobe; and on his attempting to undo her dress and stays, repulsed him – preferring merely to admire his person, which she did with eyes, hands and lips; then, growing more excited, in a panting motion clutching his body to her own and writhing in a frantic fashion, seemed to expire with such a groan as sometimes accompanies the supreme expression of love.

'Yet more puzzled, George raised himself upon one elbow – to see with embarrassment and even anger, a stain upon the front of the lady's dress which seemed to indicate that she was no lady, but a gentleman in woman's clothes; and – rather to ensure that his suspicion was justified than for any other emotion – thrusting his hand into her breast, produced a piece of cloth which, screwed up and placed there, had counterfeited a not unimpressive bosom.

'Though George has no prejudice against namby-pambies, and indeed would defend their right to take recreation with others of their own persuasion, he has never had carnal connection with one of them; and on this occasion allowed a certain anger at the impertinence of the gentleman concerned to take precedence over his generous nature. Taking up his clothes he strode from the room without even picking up the purse which had been placed for him on the bedside table.

'That the gentleman was none other than the French Ambassador, M. le Duc de Laval, I only discovered upon seeing him pass by to the Coronation, in his nation's official uniform, which nevertheless did not disguise from me his identity - but rather made it clearer, by the full-length old-fashioned wig which he wore on the occasion!'

My pleasure at this story can be imagined! - and I would immediately have leaped from bed and taken myself off to Chichley with the news - even at one o'clock in the morning, which it now was - did not Xanthe claim another passage at arms, which resulted in a sleep from which I awoke only the next morning.

Bidding her an affectionate farewell (having obtained from her news of George's whereabouts, and passing a generous reward to Mrs Blowser, to whom I felt some gratitude - though her part in the affair had been entirely coincidental) I then hurried to Chichley and laid before him the plan which had fixed itself, almost without consideration, in my mind.

The affair was simply organised. His Majesty and his Queen were pleased to accept Chichley's invitation to dine with him (for he was in great favour with the new Administration - and twitted me considerably for being a member of the loyal Opposition); and a small party was arranged, consisting of two or three influential courtiers, and their Excellencies the Ambassadors of Spain, Portugal, Italy, Austria and Russia, all of whom were accompanied by their ladies. There was some small comment on the absence of His Excellency the French Ambassador, but it was assumed that the present cool relations between England and France were responsible, the King having been heard from time to time to express the wish that he could 'blow those d*mn Frenchies out of the water!'

Chichley served a delightful meal, and their Majesties showed that cordiality which permitted them to converse with everyone present on the most friendly terms – the King showing, in especial, a talent for putting the gentlemen at their ease through memoirs of his time at sea.

The ladies were led from the room at the end of the meal, to take their ease in Lady Chichley's drawing-room, while we gentlemen took a pint or so of port apiece; after which Chichley suggested that we should repair to the neighbouring room for a game of cards.

A small procession then formed, led by His Majesty and Chichley, followed by the Ambassadors of Portugal and Russia, and at a signal from the host two footmen threw open the doors and we passed through the intervening drawing-room, and up the stairs to the card-room. Once more, double doors were thrown open, and the party passed inside – to be greeted by the sight of a lady in respectable clothing, kneeling at the feet of a naked black gentleman whose already outstanding equipment she was endeavouring by oral stimulation to rouse to an even more remarkable state of attention.

Hearing a noise behind her, the lady half-turned, and finding herself looking up into the astonished face of the British monarch, lost her balance and falling backwards upon the floor threw her legs into the air, revealing beneath her shirts a pair of white and hairy buttocks which would have seemed expressly unfeminine even without the excited appendages adjacent.

There was a moment's horrified pause, after which His Majesty (whose sense of humour partook of that enthusiastic coarseness which is the mark of Jolly Jack Tar) burst into a roar of laughter – the reaction upon which I had counted, assuming that his years in the Navy would have made amusement, rather than anger, his natural reaction.

The recumbent gentleman sat up, the female wig upon his head slipping over one eye; and to ensure that his identity was clear, Chichley stepped forward and offered his hand, with the words:

'My dear Laval, allow me to assist you!'

But the Duc, now crimson of face, ignored the hand of friendship, and, clambering to his feet, gathered his skirts about him and, making the most perfunctory bow, rushed headlong from the room.

His Majesty guffawed ('tis the only expression). 'Fortunate the ladies were not in attendance, hey, Chichley?' he remarked; but then, with a glance at George, who had retired discreetly to a corner of the room, where he was now standing uncertainly, not sure whether it would be etiquette to begin to resume his clothes in the presence of the King, he added: 'Not but what they might have enjoyed a sight of such remarkable tackle!' – and beckoned to George to approach, which he did with the utmost diffidence.

His Majesty stared for a moment at the now fallen, but still sizeable, apparatus; turned to my friend, and remarked: 'Many a vessel could make use of so substantial a foremast, hey, Chichley? Pity the lad's a sod.'

George would, I am sure, have blushed at this could a

blush have shown itself upon his dark features; but it was impossible to correct His Majesty's impression without revealing our plot; so I merely winked, and supplied some balm to George's honour, later, by providing him with a purse of more than usual weight, together with the news that Xanthe awaited him in one of Chichley's servants' rooms, where they could be pleasant together for as long as they wished.

My task was now done. The hum of conversation among the courtiers and the other Ambassadors would amplify next day to a positive chorus of gossip – and through the ladies (for what husband would not be pleased to regale his wife, upon retiring, with such a rich story?) would soon be known to all London. It was fortunate that my suspicion – that Laval's lust for George's person would be sufficiently strong to attract him to an assignation, proposed in a note conveyed to him through Foutarque – had proved correct.

Chichley having set a watch on the Embassy, it was observed that Laval made immediate preparations to withdraw from London. Unable to do so without making his obeisance at Court, he must face His Majesty once more, to take leave. The Queen being present preserved him from the chaff which would undoubtedly have been his fate; as it was, the King merely tipped him a wink which brought a blush to that cold, white and wrathful face, after which he swept from the Court, from London and from these shores.

The following day, Chichley begged an audience of His Majesty, and in a conversation to which the King alone was privy, told the whole story of the French plot. Naturally aghast, His Majesty was minded to send for le Semblant and bring him immediately to trial for treason.

Chichley at that moment, with permission, summoned me, who was able to persuade the monarch that the Pretender would be no threat to the throne or the succession; and indeed would, I believe, crave of His Majesty the indulgence to remain in England as a refugee, offering whatever securities were at his command to ensure his becoming a decent private citizen, sufficiently removed from public life to render it impossible for Talleyrand or his busybodies to discover him.

At the name of Talleyrand, His Majesty started. Was that gentleman cognizant of the plot? he asked – and on being assured that he was probably its chief perpetrator, the King informed us that the name of that gentleman had just been communicated to him by M. Foutarque, who remained in charge of the Embassy of the French, as that of the man most likely to be appointed Ambassador in Laval's place!

That that became indeed the case, everyone will know; but any narrative of his appointment and what followed should be the prerogative of historians; my concern is in more human matters – and it is a pleasure to record that His Majesty (unable to make any gesture which would make public our part in a plot, knowledge of which was to remain secret) was good enough to offer me his hand and his warm thanks, together with the confident hope of my advancement in my political career, while producing a handsome gold watch which he invited me to present to George as a token of gratitude for his part in the matter, together with his apologies for having cast any aspersion on his manhood (with the muttered aside to the effect that a single glance at his most signal masculine limb should have been sufficient to suggest that it would be the greatest waste should it be devoted to pleasuring any but the female sex). He was also good enough to suggest that should George ever be in need of employment, he should apply to the Lord Chamberlain with the word of His Majesty's interest.

This, I happily conveyed to my friend; and I may digress from the main stream of this narrative sufficiently to record that he did so apply, and in short became a footman at the Court, where he could still be seen forty years hence, a most unusual and commanding figure who filled his uniform with grace and an impressive mein; he became, indeed, a favourite with Her Majesty Queen Victoria, after her accession, who, and whose consort during his lifetime, he served most diligently, never marrying but (as rumour has it) rarely short of female company, drawn from among the minor servants of the royal household and even (it was said) some of its more senior parties – to the great distress of a cocksure Scot, Mr John Brown, who until George's ascendancy had ruled the roost where the seduction of ladies-in-waiting was in question.

Matters having been resolved, it was now my determination to travel to Alcovary, there to assure Maurice le Semblant of the King's agreement to his remaining in the country, and impatient to renew my friendship with Charlotte: an impatience the more eager because I would bear with me the news of her husband's decease – for on travelling to Mrs Jopling's house to release him, I found that he had contrived to open a window at some time during his imprisonment, and in attempting to escape had fallen and broken his neck. To suggest that this gave anyone exceptional cause for mourning would be to suggest what was not so; Mr Treglown was unpopular almost to excess not only with his colleagues in the House, but with his constituents, his election having been achieved only by enormous expenditure in the matter of bribes.

As I rode towards Cambridge at full pelt, I was almost ready to believe that I should propose marriage to the widow (being confident that the unhappiness of one union would not necessarily preclude another pledge of a similar nature). I paused, as was my wont, at the Chequers Inn at Fowlmere, where the landlord, who knew me well, had my usual chamber prepared, which lies over the main room of the inn and has as its only disadvantage the fact that it is a throughway to another room beyond it, this being an ancient house marked by its lack of corridors and passageways, each room leading into the next.

Exhausted by my ride, I partook of a hasty meal, and was not slow in repairing to my four-poster, the curtains of which I drew in order that passers-by should neither disturb my sleep nor enjoy the impertinence of observing me.

To say that I slept soundly would be to understate the matter. Indeed, I did not stir until awaking from a delicious dream of congress with my Charlotte (which I trusted would only be the pre-shadow of an enjoyment to come). I say awaking – but I was rather awakened, by the throwing back of the curtains of the bed and a touch upon my shoulder; on which I opened my eyes to find a well-shaped, dark-haired country girl of perhaps seventeen bending over me and glancing with twinkling eyes at my morning show, which was clearly presented to her through my throwing off the sheets, as is my wont when the nights are close.

That she should then place her hand upon the crux of the matter was, though uninvited by me, something which was not altogether surprising; for during the five or six years during which I had stayed at the Chequers, mine host had become aware of my appetite, which was usually sufficiently keen to prompt me to enquire whether there was an acquiescent girl in his employ who could attend to my corporeal needs – and it had been latterly his custom, without previously making enquiry, to send any promising maid to my room with my hot water in the morning, leaving it to me to decide whether to engage her in more than a light conversation.

This morning, my looking forward to renewing my acquaintance with Charlotte, and proving to her my devotion, would have precluded an interest in any other female had not circumstances been tempting, in that the young lady who now sat herself upon the bed at my side had previously had experience only with the hobbledehoys of the village, and was all eagerness to discover whether a passage of arms with a gentleman would offer any keener pleasure than with a cow-boy or labourer. To that end she did not wait for invitation, but immediately threw her gown over her head, revealing a frame the delights of which it was beyond my power to ignore – nor indeed did she give me the opportunity, for in a moment she was on top of me.

The curious thing was (and from whom she had learned such a trick it was beyond me to conjecture) that while the manner of her bestraddling my body and lowering herself upon my prick was not unusual, she did so while facing my feet! This at first discomfited me; but then I realised that the disadvantage of being denied the sight of her breasts, and indeed of the conjunction of our bodies, was somewhat mitigated by the fact that the posture enabled her to use her fingers in the most stimulating fashion upon my cods, and that area of my person immediately beneath them, to the stimulation of which I have always been peculiarly susceptible.

That young person, whatever the circumstances of her introduction to the arts of love, had an instinct for them which raised her far above the condition of other fubbsies. Upon the tightening of my person which signalled an approaching paroxysm, for instance, she immediately rose upon her knees, merely stroking my sides and thighs until the urgency – but not the desire – had subsided, then moving backwards so that she could continue with her lips the delightful stimulation while, kneeling astride my chest, she offered to my own lips that fig-like, dark and delightful fissure which I found it impossible not to taste, and which proved as sweet, as comfortable and as tender as that of the handsomest lady of May Fair!

The pleasure of such a posture was sufficiently keen to render me soon once more liable to a sudden culmination; when, sensing it, she again desisted, now merely bending forward to brush gently with dependent breasts my thighs and belly – which proved too much for my impatience, and throwing her sideways upon the bed, without more ado I fucked her in the most attentively violent manner, at which she squeaked with pleasure.

I am not usually given to that melancholy which is said to follow copulation; but on this occasion, as the girl busied herself – without resuming her clothes – in preparing the bath for my ablutions, I could not but remember that it would have better behoved me to retain those juices which had just been expelled for my so-loved Charlotte – and for some time I felt most sad. Yet then, as I stood within the copper vessel and the girl sponged my body, giving particular attention to my male member, and I regarded the delightful prospect offered by each view of her person, I felt yet again that swelling which invariably accompanies my admiration of the female form, and wondered whether it would ever be possible for me with honesty to promise to confine myself to any single female, however charming.

As if to confirm my conjecture, the young lady now dropped the towel with which she had been washing me, and with the most ingratiating smile, turned, and bending forward offered me an open target – which (the reader will guess) I had not the heart to ignore, and taking a step forward, presented myself at the mark and, my hands resting lightly upon the girl's hips, engaged her in gentle play which – the cool air from the open window upon my wet body enabling me to prolong the exercise – led to our being once more satisfied.

The remainder of my journey to Alcovary was slower than that of the previous day; indeed, often I allowed my steed to slow to a walk while I considered the difficulty before me. I was in no doubt that upon Charlotte hearing of her husband's death she would expect an offer from me. Had I the heart to refuse? Yet having accompanied her to the altar, would I be able to remain constant when so common an incident as the maid at an inn offering her body – which was in my experience a matter of course at most public inns – could lead me to stray from the basic conventions of matrimony?

I had still reached no conclusion when I rode through the gates of Alcovary Park and turned up the drive between the elms. Halfway up the drive, I heard voices and laughter from beyond the tall hedge behind which lies the lake: my friends were no doubt enjoying a bathe in the heat of mid-day – and I would be happy to join them. I tethered my steed in the spinney, and disencumbering myself of my clothing walked to the lake – and coming to it saw two figures standing in an embrace, thigh-deep in the water. Frank and his wife, no doubt; or perhaps Sophie and M. le Semblant – for it was not impossible that their obvious infatuation should have lasted this long.

But when, approaching, I called a greeting – what was my surprise (and, I must confess, in the first instance my anger) to discover that the couple who now turned their heads to me, remaining so closely glued together at the waist that one might have been forgiven for supposing that they were fully embraced, were – Charlotte and M. le Semblant!

I turned from them, involuntarily, and began to walk away, ignoring Charlotte's cry; but then I heard her running footsteps soft in the tall grass, and felt her hand upon my shoulder, and in short was made to listen. Her explanation – that she and Maurice (as I will now call him) had discovered a deep attraction, must be accepted by me; for the ways of man and woman do sometimes, and perhaps more often than we may suppose, lead to such engagements. And the nervousness, almost amounting to fear, with which she spoke of it convinced me that it was no insult to me that she should feel thus, but a true compulsion.

Taking her hands from my shoulders, where she had placed them as she spoke, I turned and walked back to the shore of the lake, where Maurice was sitting, his elbows upon his knees and his head in his hands. He must have been remembering that, with my knowledge of the plot in which he had been involved, I had doubtless the power of life and death over him.

Bending to crouch at his side, I placed my arm about his shoulders.

'Fear not, my friend,' I said; 'such an attachment as that of which Mrs Treglown has spoken must take precedence over my warm but less familial feelings. Moreover, should it be your mutual wish, I must tell you that the death of her husband now makes it possible for you to become husband and wife.'

He looked at me in bewildered delight; and at my motion rose and went to Charlie, who had remained at a distance, convinced that even should we resort to fisticuffs it was not her place to intervene. I took to the water to cool my body and, I confess, my emotions, out of the corner of my eye seeing her delight and their embrace – which gave me some pangs, though I knew that I could have done no other than what I had done.

That evening we all dined together, and I regaled the others with the adventures of which I have spoken, and was able to assure Maurice of his safety, and the fact that provided he lived in a decent obscurity every effort would be made to protect him from French agents.

'I would suggest,' I said, 'that you settle in Cornwall; for there the only Frenchmen ever to be seen are the Bretons, who are as uninterested in their national politics as any people could be. That is, if you and Charlie . . .'

Leaning across the table, she took my hand and kissed its fingers.

'How can we reward you for your loving disinterest?' she asked.

The long evening over, passed in conversation, sitting in the drawing-room through whose open windows the scents of summer swam, I took myself off to bed. As I walked down the corridor, I heard footsteps behind me. It was Sophie, who had been peculiarly quiet during the evening. She followed me into my room, where she admitted that her feelings about Maurice had mirrored my own.

'He would, I am convinced, have made an offer,' she said; 'and I am in no doubt that I would have accepted it. Yet are you and I such people as can settle into a routine of dull domesticity, even with those we love?'

I embraced her; the first embrace led to a second; and to be short, within a short time we were in each other's arms, my hands encountering the well-remembered resilience of her still firm breasts, hers reassuring herself that the body she had first excited when we were children together in this same house – indeed, in this same room – was still capable of arousal.

I had just entered her, when the door opened.

We were startled, though not dismayed. No doubt 'twas Frank, come for some purpose or another; and we three had shared the same bed too often for apprehension or shyness.

But the figure which presented itself at the bedside a moment later was a female one: that of Charlie. Sitting beside us, she laid a hand upon my shoulder, and bending forward, whispered something into Sophie's ear.

She had come, it turned out, in order that we two could say our farewells – bringing the request from Maurice that Sophie would offer him for one last time the hospitality of her bed in an adjoining chamber.

I will not detail what followed: the reader will remember what pleasures Mrs Treglown – soon to be Madame le Semblant – and I were capable of offering each other;

but I will say that the knowledge that I was taking a farewell of her body (for I was in no doubt that that was what was occurring, her moral sense being such that once pledged to Maurice she would regard me merely as a friend) sharpened my apprehension of the occasion.

Once more I was plagued with doubts: how many other women gave themselves with such freedom, such complete openness – who offered their bodies to a lover as though it were a landscape through which he would wander without restriction, enjoying in utter freedom the uplands and lowlands, the brakes and rivers, the valleys and hills? How many women explored their lover's person with such attentive admiration – yet at the same time with such a determination to afford to every surface the most signal sigh of a loving attention to the gratification of desire? With how many other women could a lover be so sure that he could make no demand, utter no request that it would not be her immediate pleasure to satisfy?

For my part, I must confess that I took peculiar care, on this occasion, to prove myself equally attentive, delaying again and again that satisfaction she craved; then offering it once more, and once more again – so that in the morning she was so exhausted that I had to leave her in my bed, while I (with a fine pretence of vigour, though truth to tell I was tired almost to fainting) took myself off, having set Maurice a standard which he might have some difficulty – I prided myself – in maintaining.

As I walked along the corridor, I saw a door ajar; and looking in, found sister Sophie abed. I entered, whereat she raised her hand in a lazy salute. I slipped between the sheets, at her side, and laid a hand upon her breast.

'Will you forgive me, sister,' I said, 'if . . .'

'Indeed, brother,' she said, 'I am limper than a dry daffodil; I believe that Maurice was attempting . . .'

'To show what you had lost?' I asked. 'I have attempted the same, I must confess, with Charlie.'

Sophie smiled, lifted my hand, and kissed it.

'Then,' she said, 'let us leave them to renew their vows – if they have the vigour.'

And turning her back upon me, she snuggled into my arms so that we lay together like a set of spoons, and we fell asleep.

EROS IN SOCIETY

For the convenience of the reader
we here record a note of
IMPORTANT PERSONS APPEARING IN THE NARRATIVE
in the order of their appearance

Andrew Archer Esq., M.P., our hero.
Mrs Sophia Nelham, our heroine.
Sir Franklin Franklyn, of Alcovary, Herts.
Sir Fyndon Trillo, a gentleman.
Ralph Trillo Esq., his nephew.
Miss Marian Trillo, his niece.
Lady Margaret Franklyn.
Lady Arabella Curryfin.
The Hon. Eliza Curryfin, her daughter.
Sir Stanley Curtis, a surgeon.
Edward Curtis Esq., his son.
A cricket team.
Their trophies.
Mlle Francine Fraudet.
Claudette, her maid.
M. Jean Villot, a music teacher.
Valentine Jeakes Esq., an adventurer.
Miss Niobe Jeakes, his sister.
William Gaucet Esq., M.P.
Dr Whilom Pettigrew, M.D.
George, a footman.
Miss Constance Gaucet.
A footman to Mr Jeakes.
David Ham Esq., an entrepreneur.
Wum Pam Fire River, a Canadian gentleman.
Jack, another.

Rob, a third.
The Duke of Genoa.
His valet.
Will Blatchford (former servant to Mrs Nelham).
Viscount Chichley.
Lionel Hamidon, a painter.
Daisy, his model.
The Rt Hon. the Lord Wickhamborough, Lord Justice of England.
Members of the Cat Club.
Their ladies.
Four harvesters.
Their maids.
A travelling French noblewoman.
Lieut. Norris Blades.
Mrs Fitful, an impressive bawd.
Filament, a footman.
Miss Tansy, a black whore.
Miss Pamela, a white one.

Chapter One

The Adventures of Andy

My regular readers will no doubt have inferred that following on my election as Member of Parliament for a Cornish constituency (an event retailed in my most recent volume of memoirs, *Eros in High Places*) the business of regulating the affairs of the country occupied my energies to a considerable extent, and such adventures as might be expected to interest them were somewhat at a premium.

Any disappointment which such friends may feel was quite equalled by my own apprehension – which was that a public life might prove irreconcilable with an amorous one, both by reason of necessary regular attendance at the Palace of Westminster (a place notable rather for the making of laws than of love) and of an increasing responsibility, which appeared to require a respectability of behaviour precluding exploits of a wanton nature.

Upon the end of the winter session – the third of my Parliamentary career – I was pleased to travel to Alcovary in Hertfordshire, the home of my friend Sir Franklin Franklyn and his wife, where we were joined by his half-sister Mrs Sophia Nelham who those acquainted with my earlier volumes will remember as the inveterate companion of my youth and sometimes of my bed.

The spring weather being charming, it was pleasant to relax in each other's company, to recapitulate those adventures which we had shared since we all grew up together, and to discuss the possibility of further exploits – though Frank and his lady were now of so sedentary a disposition that they resolutely declined any suggestions from Sophie and I that we might perhaps adventure to the continent, or to some other part of the world where we could enjoy experiences more varied and fresher than those to be found in the English counties.

Our arguments were neither prolonged nor exasperating, but neither did they lead to any conclusion. However, this was no cause of distress, for we were all content for a while merely to relax, to dine together or with a small selection of the gentry of the neighbourhood, and to wait until events – or a sudden inspiration – dictated further action.

One morning in early May, a horseman rode up to the door with a message for Frank from a distant neighbour (the inhabitant of a large house near Ely, in Cambridgeshire) whom we had never met, but with whom Frank was acquainted as a fellow magistrate. Sir Fyndon Trillo asked whether he could call upon my friend on the following Sunday, in order to consult him upon a matter of domestic importance. Frank, as a matter of course, replied in the affirmative; and at midday of the appointed day, a carriage drew up to the front door of the house, and out stepped not one but three people: a tall, somewhat thin gentleman of middle years, and a young man and woman much his junior who seemed scarcely of age, and as like as two pins. Sir Fyndon indeed introduced them as brother and sister – Ralph and Marian Fyndon, his niece and nephew.

He then instructed them to entertain themselves by walking in the grounds, while he did some business with Sir Franklin; and they strolled off, hand in hand, towards the knot garden at the side of the house. Frank in the meanwhile walked with Sir Fyndon on the south terrace – but in twenty minutes or so sent to Sophie and I to join them, where, sitting in a little arbour he had constructed, we drank some German wine together.

Sir Fyndon had put to him, he explained, a problem with which he believed we could be of assistance.

The two young people – who were twins – had been born seventeen years previously to Sir Fyndon's younger brother, the Vicar of a place in Shropshire, and were the fruit of his illicit union with the sister of the Bishop of Bridport; a union which would have caused such scandal that the said Bishop, a man of more wealth than holiness, paid the couple handsomely to conceal the fruit of their indiscretion. This they did by having the children brought up by servants in a remote mansion on the borders of Wales, not far from Llanfyllin, which together with a great estate there and in the Black Mountains would eventually be their personal property.

The choice of a governess, when the time came to appoint one, had been most fortunate, falling upon the impoverished sister of a nobleman, who had educated the children so gently and with such care that their manners (as we had observed even in our short passage with them) were impeccable, their natures sweet and open, their characters as full of charm as they were lacking in guile.

But this (Sir Fyndon reported) had brought its own problems. Their father dying of a sudden accident upon the hunting field – and their unfortunate mother having predeceased him by some years, and without being permitted to become acquainted with her children – the brother and sister had suddenly become the responsibility of Sir Fyndon; and while finding them the most agreeable of children, he had also found them entirely lacking in knowledge of the world.

' 'Tis my habit to spend half of the year in Ely, and the other half in town,' Sir Fyndon broke in, 'but the consequences of introducing them into society are not to be thought of in their present state of knowledge. They would behave well; but neither has any idea of the power (for instance) of a passionate attachment, and poor Marian would be seduced by the first rogue who set eyes on her, while Ralph would certainly fall like ripe fruit into the hands of even an indifferently handsome woman.'

It was indeed the case that they were sufficiently handsome to attract any seducer, I commented; but what harm would that do, as long as the young lady was apprised of those precautions which would protect her from the fate of her unfortunate mother?

The fact was, said Sir Fyndon, that they commanded an excellent fortune, having inherited the wealth of the late Bishop, their uncle – and so might well be subject to unfair attacks upon their emotions, should any adventurer become aware of their enviable financial circumstances.

Then, said Sophie, they should be educated in the ways of the world as soon as possible.

'Just so,' said their uncle; 'and it was in the hope

of advice as to the proper guides in such a matter that I come to Sir Franklin.'

'You need look no further than my sister and her friend,' said Frank; and went on to convince his visitor that we were at once sufficiently knowledgeable and sufficiently tactful to achieve such a task were it confided to us.

In sum, Sir Fyndon was so convinced; and it was agreed that we should escort the young couple for the coming season, introducing them to just so varied a society as would appraise them of the dangers – but also the pleasures – of modern life.

'I fear,' said Sir Fyndon, 'that . . .' – and he paused in a state of some confusion, which I was at a loss to comprehend. Sophie, however, immediately understood him.

'You mean, I think, sir, that a lady governess of such delicacy of feelings as you have described did not find herself able to convey to her pupils that information which might make them ready for the intimate company of the opposite sex?'

'Just so, madam, just so,' said Sir Fyndon, blushing the colour of beetroot.

'My friend Andy and I will not find ourselves in any difficulty,' she said, 'both of us being convinced that frankness is entirely necessary in such matters. And though in my experience there is often some difficulty where children have been permitted to reach physical maturity without such an education, I have no reason to suppose that we cannot accomplish a suitable introduction to that particular field of human pleasure.'

Sir Fyndon seemed about to say something else but was too confused to speak.

'I do not mean, Sir,' Sophie continued, 'that I should make myself responsible for the practical education of young Ralph – nor that my friend Mr Archer should teach your niece the way of a man with a maid: though I have to say that any young girl would be fortunate to have so considerate a lover' (at which I bowed, though Sir Fyndon merely looked the more embarrassed) 'but we will see to it that the service is done, and that the young people do not suffer in its accomplishment.'

To cut the matter short, it was so agreed, Sir Fyndon guaranteeing us our expenses in the matter; and the others going in to their meat, I set out to find the children and bring them in.

I did not have far to look. Between the house and the lake is a little walled rose garden which so traps the sun that Sophie and I often use it for sun bathing, a fashion more common upon the continent than in England, but which consists of exposing the body to the sunlight much as one would expose it when swimming. To that end we had had set up there a sort of platform of marble brought from Italy, which, from the sun falling upon it almost from its rising, swiftly becomes warm enough to lie upon.

There, as I turned the corner, I saw Ralph and Marian lying, entirely in a state of nature, side by side, like two carved statues on a tomb-top.

To say that I was surprised would be to understate the matter, for what I had heard of them had prepared me for a pair of ninnies likely to be more ashamed than proud of their bodies, and who had probably been taught by their lady governess that they should on no account be exposed, even to themselves (some of those maiden ladies insisting on their charges covering themselves with a gown even when undressing for bed).

No such matter, however; for not only were they now entirely naked, but their limbs were disposed in such a fashion as to be entirely open to each other's – or any chance viewer's – eyes. Their legs, for instance, were somewhat spread, no doubt the readier to allow the sun to strike upon them, with the consequence that those parts usually displayed only to lovers or to the eyes of painter or sculptor were displayed rather than concealed, the rays of the sun glinting delightfully upon the silky hairs which garnished them and (for they were both blonde as angels) gilding them as though they were spun from gold. Not perhaps unnaturally (and any lady whose eye falls upon these words will no doubt be as quick to forgive the impudence as gentlemen will be to understand the inclination) my eyes were chiefly directed towards the lady, the separation of whose lower limbs exposed a valley whose concavity was marked by a knoll or mount the summit of which was cleft by a fissure about which the golden filaments clustered, scarcely concealing lightly tinted pink lips between which . . . My heart mounted to my lips as I looked, while elsewhere I felt that aching admiration which would, had I continued to gaze, have resulted in a corporeal signal which it would have been entirely improper for me to display to a young lady whom I must teach myself to regard as a pupil!

I retired from view and coughed somewhat loudly, pausing for a moment before once more advancing; but though they were now apprised of my approach, they made no attempt to resume the clothing which lay at their side; and if they had arranged their lower limbs in a somewhat more decorous attitude, this was only for the convenience of their half sitting, reclining upon their elbows like mirror-images to greet me with open smiles as I approached.

'Why, Mr Archer,' said the young lady with a delightful smile, 'the sun is so warm we must take advantage of it!'

'It is not forbidden?' said the boy, seeing perhaps my perplexity (which was at their openness rather than their actions).

'Not at all,' I replied; 'but – if you will allow the comment – it is not common in society for a lady and gentleman to appear together clad as Adam and Eve.'

'Mrs Finch—'

'—our governess—' (The couple seemed to speak by turn.)

'—taught us that it was shameful to hide our bodies unnecessarily from God's sunlight,' said Marian.

'Indeed,' I said, 'that is a noble thought. But' (and it was as well to begin the couple's eduction while I might) 'in society this must be done more sparingly than your excellent educator perhaps explained.'

At this, Marian blushed somewhat, and, reaching for her dress, began to pull it over her head.

'Please do not think that it offends me!' I hastily added – and must admit that I was sorry to see those charmingly pert breasts, that slender frame, those enchanting thighs, all as perfectly formed as could be expected in a maiden of seventeen, vanish from sight. 'I merely report what it might be to your convenience to remember, in general company.'

The boy meanwhile had risen to his feet, looking

like nothing so much as a Greek statue, and now bowed to me with great grace.

'We thank you, sir, and will remember it,' he said, and unaffectedly resumed his own clothing; at which the three of us returned to the house.

It was over luncheon that Ralph and Marian were told of their uncle's invitation to Sophie and me to undertake their introduction to society – and received the news with a flattering degree of pleasure and acceptance. Indeed, so eager were they to begin that they pleaded to be allowed to stay on with us at Alcovary rather than returning with their uncle to his home; which, after reference to Frank and Lady Margaret, was happily agreed to, Sir Fyndon promising to send their clothing on by coach within a day. Sophie commented that it might be necessary to provide them with a new wardrobe, their present dress being too countrified to be acceptable in an urban setting.

We discussed the whole matter at length later that night, when the two young people were abed and Sir Fyndon had made his excuses and left. I agreed that I should take care of the education of young Ralph, while Sophie should look to that of Marian. She and Lady Margaret exchanged a glance at that, in which I recognised unspoken surprise that I should so readily accept the proposition; while Frank, freer with his comments, enquired whether I could be confident of not falling into bed with her at the earliest opportunity – such beauty together with the knowledge that she required to be educated in the ways of the world being an aphrodisiac which might be relied upon to defeat the good intentions of any red-blooded man. But after all, though certainly the recollection of her beauty was sufficient to send a shiver of desire along my spine as I thought of it, I was not yet entirely devoid of conscience, and it would be unfair for me to seduce her (which would certainly have been the case were I pressed into a daily closeness with her, my instincts and the extent of my self-command being about the same as those of any other healthy man); she should be shown the broad sweep of the world before being invited to confine herself to one corner of it. Similarly, if young Ralph were to fall in love (and it is in very few cases that this does not occur when young people find themselves for the first time in unrestrained propinquity with those of the opposite sex), it were better that it should not be with my delightful friend – if only that her personal charms and her exercise of them would quite possibly arouse in him an expectation of the charms and expertise of other ladies, to his later inevitable disappointment.

And where were we to take them?

Where else, I suggested, but Bath? There they would meet people of every situation, in an atmosphere where (apart from those invalids who travelled to the city for the treatment of their illness) pleasure and social intercourse were the chief, and sometimes the only, occupations of fashionable and unfashionable alike.

Our journey to Bath took place within the week. There was nothing to keep us at Alcovary, nor to prevent us setting out at once upon our proposed visit; while the eagerness of the young people to engage immediately upon the great adventure of acquainting themselves with modern manners was in itself sufficient to encourage us.

The journey was made less tedious to us than it otherwise might have been by the mounting excitement of Ralph and his sister – which grew to a scarcely containable extent upon our entering the city.

We took rooms in Pulteney Street, consisting of a handsome drawing-room and sitting-room upon the first floor, the latter capable by rearrangement of being dined in; and upon the second floor our bedrooms and two dressing-rooms, one set to be used by Ralph and myself, the other by his sister and Sophie. The brother and sister pleaded to be allowed to share a bedroom, for this had been their wont at home; but it was decided against, for perfectly obvious reasons which I need not rehearse here.

Indeed, I privately enquired of Ralph whether he had not found such an arrangement embarrassing?

But why, he asked?

I was somewhat at a loss for a reply, the answer being obvious to most young men. I finally asked if he found it difficult to conceal from his sister those changes in his body which accompanied every young man's excursion into adulthood?

Ah, he said, did I mean the standing of his thing? (He seemed unaware of any other name for it.) She had noticed the phenomenon when it first occurred, he admitted, and had been somewhat afraid for his health; but on its appearing to do him no harm, and indeed his finding that his caressing it (which, like every boy, nature persuaded him to do) gave him considerable pleasure, she had been more envious than otherwise.

But had he never . . . had she never . . .? My wonder at their innocence prevented me from putting my question into words, and he clearly failed to comprehend my meaning, while I could not bring myself to insult his innocence by making myself any clearer. However, I could not but ask whether their governess had not suggested that such close proximity between a young gentleman and a young lady was improper?

Not at all, he said; she had never spoken of it.

The lady must have had peculiar notions in education, was my unspoken comment. However, it was now time that the matter should be put into a perspective, and it was my care to explain to him something of the nature of the relationship between the sexes, not only of generation but of common politeness.

Ralph was astonished to hear the chief facts. How was it possible, he enquired, for a female to share those excitements experienced by the male, when her person lacked that chief feature upon which his pleasure was focused?

I did my best to explain that it was not entirely true that ladies lacked such a feature; merely that it was considerably less evident, and thus must be sought out by the attentive lover.

How, then, he went on to ask, was it possible that that friction readily applied by the palm of the hand was to be enjoyed by both, when the lady's thing was not of a size to be placed in juxtaposition to the gentleman's? (At this point it was necessary for me to present to him a number of terms by which men – and sometimes women – refer to the male organ, as cock, prick, hanger, riding-muscle and other more common terms; 'thing' being a word neither sufficiently forthright nor amusing for use outside the nursery.)

I need not weary the reader further with a lesson in anatomy; let it simply be said that I did my best to educate him sufficiently not to be an entire simpleton in the matter, leaving a demonstration of the mechanics of the act to whatever chance arose; and if it did not arise in Bath, I knew not where it might more readily do so.

Ralph enquired what the ladies thought of the process, and on hearing that it was by no means repugnant to them, that the female body was responsive to an act which at first seemed at the least somewhat impolite between the sexes, he was naturally excited. Being the kindly lad that he was, he was particularly pleased at the news that his sister might be brought to such a pleasure as he had experienced (if only by way of onanism). He expressed the desire to communicate this news to her at once, and was only dissuaded by my assurance that Sophie was probably at this moment conveying it. He also announced his wish to try the act at the earliest opportunity, which I promised to attempt to arrange for him, meanwhile counselling caution in any attentions he might pay the fair sex.

The first day of our being in Bath was devoted to fitting out our young friends with clothing which would render their appearance satisfactory to their peers, Sir Fyndon having immediately agreed that this would be necessary, and advancing a sum perfectly sufficient for it. I took Master Ralph to my own tailor, who had made my jackets and trousers in Bath for several seasons, and in whom I had the greatest confidence; he turned the young man out in a suit of clothing which made the most of his upright and manly figure, the collar accentuating the grace of his head, balanced as it was upon a slim neck about which his hair curled in a manner which (so Sophie assured me) would contribute greatly to his being irresistible to the opposite sex.

When all four met for luncheon, I could not but admire the manner in which my friend had had Marian dressed – for, though those materials, thin almost to transparency, were no longer fashionable which had previously clad young ladies in so desultory a manner that their bodies seemed to hold no secrets, the bodice of her dress was sufficiently shaped to her breast to illustrate perfectly its entrancing contours, while the skirt was of some material (I am not sufficiently conversant with fashion to say what it might be) that clung assiduously to her lower limbs, drawing attention not only to their slender shape, but to the grace with which she disposed them, both in motion and in stillness.

That evening we took our friends and pupils for the first time to the ballroom, which upon our arrival (carefully contrived by my friend to be sufficiently delayed to attract some attention) was crowded with the fashionable; indeed, the room was so full that we had positively to squeeze between the people already there – and I could not but notice that young Ralph took little trouble to prevent his body pressing against those of the ladies present; to such a degree indeed that I feared for him should their partners note it. I had no fear of the ladies, for, even with those who felt his proximity to be an impertinence and turned to rend him, when confronted by that open, frank and admiring visage – to say nothing of its handsome aspect – that criticism shrank on their lips; and one young lady in particular I remarked returning to our proximity, and in passing towards the neighbouring room, brushing her lower back against the boy's body in a manner which in a less crowded situation would have been regarded as outrageously provoking.

We found ourselves soon, by force of the press, separated from Sophie and Marian; I took Ralph to the card-room, but he showed remarkably little interest in what went on there – the players being entirely of his own sex; which pleased me, since gambling, never one of my own vices, was not one I was ready to encourage in him. We returned, then, to the main room, where several young ladies made it their business to stand nearby, clearly hoping to be invited to dance. But dancing was not among those matters in which his governess had instructed the boy – though from his apprehension of the manner in which it enabled gentlemen to hold ladies in their arms, often in close embrace, I supposed that he would, soon enough, be requesting me to arrange some lessons.

After an hour, it was, I felt, time for us to make our way from the ballroom, since Ralph's lacking the ability to dance, and the accident of my knowing no one in the room on that particular evening, would prevent matters from going forward. As we made our way to the door, however, I was delighted to be saluted by an acquaintance – Lady Arabella Curryfin. This was the wife of an acquaintance in Parliament, Sir Royce Curryfin, with whom – the wife, rather than the husband – I had conducted a brief and pleasant affair upon meeting her at a weekend party at the house of the Chancellor of the Exchequer. Sir Royce having been much confined by the Chancellor in discussion of Parliamentary business, I made myself pleasant to his lady, the pleasantry having extended to a couple of moderately enjoyable passages of love.

She now had in tow a somewhat plain girl perhaps of Ralph's years, whom she introduced as her daughter Eliza. The latter made her curtsy, rather more enthusiastically to Ralph, I thought, than to me. Though she was by no means as handsome as many of the young ladies in the room, she was the only one to whom he had been introduced, and they were soon in conversation, while Arabella took me to one side, and eagerly questioned me about the boy.

By an interesting and convenient coincidence, she was introducing her daughter to Bath society for the first time and she explained with that plainness which is not to be surprised at when two people have been as intimate (even upon only two occasions) as we that she was concerned that her daughter was still a virgin at an age when, she opined, no female had the right to be in that condition.

I will not conceal that had I a daughter I would not necessarily be so eager to dispose of her virginity; but Lady Arabella went on to explain that Eliza was shortly to be affianced (upon Sir Royce's account) to Lord Taliesin, a notorious rake. Should she prove entirely innocent, the latter gentleman would, she was convinced, have nothing to do with her; and so – 'Is your young gentleman . . .?'

The unspoken question hung but for a moment in the air; for why, since the offer was made, should I not take advantage of it? Certainly I would have preferred to have a longer conversation on the matter than had yet taken place between Ralph and me – but yet practical experience was worth a great deal more than any amount of talk.

We therefore made certain arrangements, and bade each other a temporary adieu – separating the young people with some difficulty.

As we walked away from the hall, I enquired as to Ralph's view of Miss Curryfin, to receive the reply that while she seemed not quite to have the looks of some other young ladies, she was agreeable enough – and after all, as the boy readily admitted, he had not the experience to say whether she was lacking in, or extraordinarily well provided with, the social graces.

But as to her person?

Well enough, said Ralph; 'Though you know, Andy' (for I had encouraged him to be so familiar) 'since I have only seen her clothed, I could not compare her with my sister, whose beauty seems to me to be a *nonpareil*.'

I could only agree, though I did not feel it proper to make the comment aloud; and merely confined myself to suggesting that he might soon have that opportunity, for Lady Curryfin invited him to join her daughter that very night in a mutual celebration of their losing their virginity.

Could this, he said, his interest now complete, really be the case? And would the young lady agree?

Certainly, I said (though whether from motives of filial devotion or of self-interest I was unable to confirm). The remainder of our walk, which now led to the house in London Road occupied by Lady

Curryfin, was taken up in my answering certain enquiries about Ralph's proper behaviour in the situation in which he was shortly to find himself. 'Twas a brief enough time for such an education; yet I trusted my answers were such as to enable him to acquit himself without too much disgrace.

Once at Lady Curryfin's, matters moved with some acceleration, Ralph being escorted immediately upstairs, while Lady Curryfin took my arm and after a moment's pause bore me up the staircase in the same direction, explaining in a whisper (as we passed a door which had just closed after my young friend) that we must keep watch, lest some accident render the occasion disastrous. She led me through the next doorway, approached a bookcase and, pressing upon it quietly, opened a door which led into the neighbouring room, emerging behind a screen through the cracks in which we could see the young people approaching each other – or I should rather say, through which we could see Ralph approaching Eliza, for the latter lay upon the bed which was the principal furniture of the room, its four gilt posts holding up a canopy of green wool hanging, and the pure white counterpane now supporting a body almost as white.

At least, I told myself, Ralph would not be frightened at the sight of a naked female, having for so long been familiar with his sister's body – though I believed him completely when he said that they were in no other way familiar, never having caressed each other, far from committing that act which between brother and sister has in Christian countries been regarded as improper (though looked upon elsewhere as vastly improving the race).

My advice to him had been to divest himself of his clothing without delay, which he now did – in so matter of fact a way that I wondered whether 'twas not anaphrodisiac; however, the sight of his body clearly pleased the young lady, a novice in such matters – yet by no means uninstructed, for on his approaching the bed with the intention of lying down beside her, she reached out and took in a tender hand that part of him, as yet completely relaxed, in which her mother had no doubt instructed her to hope.

At her touch, it almost instantaneously engorged, and, feeling for the first time the pleasure of a strange hand at that place to which only his own had so far ventured, Ralph was not slow in mounting the bed and kneeling at her side in order to enable Eliza to caress him with a more convenient ease; in a few moments he was positively panting with pleasure – but otherwise was inactive, which was not what Eliza had been taught to expect (and indeed her mother whispered to me, 'Is the boy an idiot?')

I was not able to defend him, though admitting that instinct was not so far defeating ignorance. But now he remembered the hint I had given him, and laid a hand upon Eliza's breast, moving it downwards as he leaned to kiss the bud which stood there, until his fingers reached that darker forest which concealed the solution to his problem, and he began to feel about for that nodule of which I had told him. This proved (as is sometimes the case) difficult to discover, though the young lady's wriggling, which became more acute the more exploratory his gestures, must have appeared to him to result from gratified excitement, for he soon fell upon her, and himself by dint of wriggling persuaded himself at last between her thighs, and began those movements which might be expected upon such an occasion. The girl seemed not content, however, for she grasped his buttocks and evidently tried to persuade him into a position more productive of pleasure. The emotion instilled by her clutching fingers, however, was too keen; and with a low cry, Ralph's back arched, and he lay still – though his female friend still bucked beneath him, now however seeming to give him pain rather than pleasure.

In a moment, he rose – and upon the poor young lady's belly could clearly be discerned the moist signs of his death; while, by the expression upon her face, her virginity was still intact. A tear stood in her eye, and she aimed a soft blow (which fortunately did not strike home) at the organ which, a moment ago so welcome in its approach to her person, now began to droop.

I had plainly not been sufficiently clear in my instructions – and nor had Lady Arabella, for Ralph, somewhat embarrassed, and unconscious of the fact that only a little play between them (both being young and eager) could repair the situation, now began to don his clothing.

There was nothing much to say; had we instructed either one of the young people more thoroughly, the impasse might have been avoided. As it was, I could only prepare to apologise on the wretched boy's behalf to Lady Arabella, and turned to do so – but was detained by her hand upon my arm, and her eye directing me once more to the aperture through which I had been observing the scene.

There I saw – and 'tis a tribute to the good sense

of a mother whose instructions to her daughter had clearly embraced just such a situation as had occurred – the young lady lean from her bed and catch at the tail of Ralph's shirt, through which he was thrusting his head. Pulling upon it, she succeeded in collapsing him upon the bed. The poor boy, still confused, attempted to hide himself by clasping his hands over that now much diminished limb which he doubtless believed to be permanently deprived of the ability to please; but rising upon her knees, she bent over him and gently taking his hands in hers persuaded him to remove them; whereupon she bent to kiss that sad object, at the same time gently stroking the bollocks below. Upon the chief instrument's beginning to swell, she placed it in her mouth with all the avidity a young lady of her age might have been expected to devote to a sweetmeat, and began sucking upon it with an enthusiasm that a more sophisticated lover than Ralph might have found over-rough. However, having known nothing nicer in the way of performance, he had evidently found nothing nicer in the way of stimulation, and I need not take the time to say that his recovery was almost instantaneous. Any gentleman who recalls himself at the age of seventeen will doubtless assent to the fact that at that age a fall in the bedroom can be as quickly recovered from as one upon the hunting field; and my young friend's face, first a picture of consternation and embarrassment, swiftly became flushed with pleasure, then enlivened with new excitement.

His instrument having recovered its former dimensions, he would immediately have resumed the interrupted business; but Miss evidently had a taste for her work, and for a time refused to retire from it – so much so indeed that I feared his firing-piece might again too expeditiously discharge.

However, Ralph was a quick learner, and employing a tender force threw the lady once more upon her back, and this time, by dint of holding his body somewhat aloof so that she could with her hands direct his approach, in no short time was again at work, this time – to judge by the lady's panting pleasure – with a proper connection properly established.

At the cry which signalled Miss Eliza's first experience of entire joy, Lady Arabella led me from the scene; and, shutting the intervening door, expressed her pleasure in the scene by offering a celebration as perfectly attractive to me as to her.

On our walking home, an hour later, Ralph asked why I had not disabused him of the notion that a single course was all that could be achieved in one sitting? I had no answer to that, other than that he must not expect to understand everything at once; to which he assented – and was kind enough to express his regret that I had not been able to enjoy a feast similar to that in which he had partaken; adding however that he supposed that at my age the heyday in the blood was much diminished. This from a boy only eight years my junior! Well, it was perhaps not the time to instruct him otherwise. He still had much to learn; but his openness, frankness, liveliness and enjoyment of life were such that I was under no illusion that it would be a trouble to teach him.

Chapter Two

Sophie's Story

A perusal of the opening chapter of this record will have informed the reader of the two young people who were presented to my friend Mr Archer and myself, in the hopes that we could improve them; and indeed, this seemed a probable task, for neither of them appeared to know anything of the ways of the world, either as to fashion, behaviour, or indeed the art of living.

It being my task to guide, in particular, Miss Marian Trillo, it is of her whom, in particular, I shall speak – though the reader need not suppose that I did not join my friend in admiration of her brother, who indeed was a picture of manly beauty the more beguiling for its innocence.

It would be difficult to conjecture which of them, the young man or his sister, was most excited by our arrival in Bath, the appearance of which, with its bustle of the fashionable and the disreputable, the miserly and the respectable, was more variegated than any scene which had hitherto been presented to them. A hundred questions were asked of me as I took Miss Marian about, upon the day after our arrival, in order to get her supplied with accoutrements which should represent her youth and beauty in their most advantageous light.

Already, by the time we set out from Pulteney Street at nine o'clock, the invalids had returned from the baths, and the quack-doctors had tired of pursuing them with their infernal remedies – of new-gathered earthworms, black tips of crabs' claws, goose dung gathered in the springtime and dried in the sun, seahorse tooth, frogs' livers and man's bones calcined. The young men of fashion were already making their way towards the coffee houses or the bowling-greens, and in the flowered walks were strolling to greet the lovely fair, who were equally abroad, all a-twitter with their admiration and their dislike.

Marian, as can be imagined, was agog at the little shops, with their displays of ribbons and gloves or fans for the ladies, powdered coral to whiten their teeth, cake houses with shelves of fruit-lulibibs and Spanish wines and Hydromel. By the mid-afternoon we were exhausted and, the day being warm, returned to our rooms to refresh ourselves; and after we had bathed our limbs we retired to my room, where we reclined upon my bed – a circumstance which I myself arranged in order that I might converse for a while with my pupil, in order to attain a comprehensive view of the true extent of her knowledge and understanding of the world.

I was able to lead to the subject through introducing Marian's request, made when we had first arrived at the rooms, that she should share her brother's bedroom. It was, I explained, considered improper by most people that having attained a certain age, two people of the opposite sex – even (or especially) if they were brother and sister – should share the same room, much less the same bed, unless they were joined in matrimony. She argued custom, for such had been the case since she and Ralph had been infants – for as long indeed as she could remember. Why should they suddenly cease so friendly an intercourse?

I was somewhat hard put to it to explain the reason to one so innocent. But, I said, she must surely have noticed that some little time ago their bodies had become susceptible to certain changes? Ah, she said, blushing slightly; did I mean the blossoming of . . . and with a hand indicated her nether regions and the down which grew there.

Partly, I said.

Or perhaps I referred to . . . and she touched her breasts, which seemed to palpitate with a sudden acceleration of her heart.

Again, this was partly my meaning. But it was more of her brother that I spoke.

Here she blushed indeed (an indication that even innocence apprehends, perhaps unconsciously, those facts which even in the educated are but rarely spoken of).

Yes, I continued, I meant the sudden prominence of a limb which, in his childhood, may have seemed scarcely worthy of notice, but which upon the attainment of man's estate had become considerable.

My having gained her confidence through a blend of kindness and frank speaking, she admitted that she had been strangely affected by the change I mentioned, which had first been apprehended by her on waking one summer's morning, when they had thrown off their covering, and seeing between her brother's thighs what appeared to be a pole of flesh, quite out of proportion and almost threatening in its demeanour – despite the fact that he was still asleep.

On waking, he had seemed embarrassed, turning upon his face and with some difficulty – even amounting to pain – concealing this new growth between his belly and the sheets, and declining to rise from bed until she had left the room. On their meeting at breakfast, she discreetly examined the front of his breeches, but could see no bulge in them which might conceal the phenomenon – which, though they always talked between themselves with complete freedom, she felt strangely inhibited from mentioning.

But though she respected his silence in the matter, their living in such close quarters naturally resulted in other sightings, and she realised that while at some times his thing (as she termed it) was almost as small and shrunken as when he had been a child, at others it attained these remarkable new dimensions – apparently without cause or purpose. Chiefly, she saw it in such a state when he was asleep; but soon she noticed that it would raise its head on other occasions – sometimes, though perhaps it was a coincidence, when she was dressing or undressing, which as a matter of course she did in her brother's presence, without shame or attempt at concealment, as had always been the case.

This was a strange story, and I must confess that I felt a considerable respect for the young man who was able to bear such a temptation as the sight of this almost excessively beautiful young woman in a state of undress – be she a thousand times his sister. For she was extremely lovely, as I was now able to see her; I had set the example of declining to cover myself after our bathing, and we were both in a state of nature; I leaned upon the pillows of the bed in a half-reclining posture, while she lay upon her side, her head raised and propped upon one hand.

She was of course still very young; yet even for one so relatively lacking in years her person was exceptionally compact, no hint of thickness about a waist which was creased only by the effect of her trunk being at an angle to her slim hips, and her breasts not in the least dependent from her torso, but standing proudly, their elasticity exhibited in the fact that they were not even slightly pendant, like fruit upon a bough, in the manner which one often begins to see in the female frame even at so young an age.

I must now explain fully to her the true nature of what she had seen; and did so as gently as possible – yet still she was reluctant at first to believe it, for (as she said) Ralph had never shown the slightest indication of wishing to approach her in the manner which I now explained was the prerogative of the male with the female; yet she was slowly convinced, and while (on my praising Ralph for his forbearance) she was properly thankful that a natural instinct had forbidden him to love her, she admitted to me that she had from the first felt a strong wish to caress the thing she had seen, and even – she whispered it – to kiss it, as she was used to kiss his lips upon greeting him each morning.

I had at this moment to inform her that *thing* was not a proper appellation for the *membrum virile*, and that, though not in polite society, in conversation with myself or (should the occasion arise) with other ladies, there were a number of synonyms which could be more aptly employed – as *cock* or *prick*, the most common, but also perhaps *gaying instrument, lobcock, plug tail, sugar stick, Thomas*, or *tool*. This information she received with interest, and made me promise to write her down a list which she could memorise.

But to return to my narrative. She asked many questions of me regarding the method of concubinage, and was keenly interested by my replies; yet remained confused by the fact that pleasure should be given either to man or by woman by what seemed to her a mere description of a strange sort of athletics. (It will be an opinion familiar to any adult who has attempted to describe the Act to a person of tender years; but it is with remarkable celerity that the contrary view is taken, upon the achievement of the earliest experience!)

Was she not conscious, I asked, of a pleasurable sensation even in talking of these matters?

'Why yes, Mrs Nelham,' she admitted (on which I invited her to call me Sophie, the difference in our ages not seeming so considerable as to warrant such formality).

'And is this not centred . . .' – and I made a gesture towards her nether parts.

On her nodding, I explained about the boy in the boat – that miniature prick any friction of which must be pleasurable; whereupon she began fumbling about her parts in an attempt to find it, looking appealingly at me the meanwhile.

'My dear, lie still!' I finally said in pity, and reaching down, parted her lower lips and laid my index finger upon the important part. At this, the most astonishing scene occurred – for upon my digit merely grazing the spot, her entire body seemed to levitate from the bed, curved like a bow, while from her lips came almost a scream – a gasping exhalation of every breath in her body, and at the same time tears spurted from her eyes in a positive fountain.

I was somewhat alarmed by the phenomenon: but a moment later was caught up in her arms as she hugged me, covering my face, then my bosom with kisses, and in a moment descending so that she could plant further caresses upon my thighs, and then – my lacking the sense (or I must confess the desire) to dissuade her – between them, until her tongue found there the simulacrum of the part which had afforded her such pleasure, and played upon it with such enthusiasm yet at the same time such tenderness that I myself felt a pleasure almost as intense as that which had seemed to destroy her senses!

For a moment I wondered whether I had discovered in her that instinct which turns some women towards femininity and the embracing of their own sex; but I did not believe so, for now Marian, the first flush of our emotion over, was full of apologies, dreading that she had offended me, or that her behaviour had been unladylike.

Not in the least, I assured her; it was such as was common in most female societies where young ladies were separated from the male sex, either for reasons of politeness, or because they were judged not yet ready for it; and in my view such entertainment was infinitely preferable to the self-pleasuring which was the fate of more lonely females – though that, I hastened to add, was by no means to be despised; for in caressing one's own body one best learned how it was best pleased.

By now it was high time that we made our way to the ballroom (though first it was necessary once again to refresh ourselves, bathing in particular, in cooling water, those nether regions still inflamed with the afterglow of pleasure). Marian was a picture of handsome young womanhood in the clothes which I had chosen for her, and I was conscious (if she was not) of the admiration of many young gentlemen in the crowded ballroom – where although some requests were made of her, she was unable to dance, neither she nor her brother ever having learned the exercise. She was delighted to look on, however, and was especially pleased at the minuet.

Andy and Ralph, who had accompanied us to the rooms, soon strolled away – first to the card-room, and then to the main room (where from time to time we caught a glimpse of them). We remained only for an hour or so, and as we left caught sight of our friends leaving with the Lady Arabella Curryfin and her pale daughter, neither of whom seemed likely to excite the interest of either. However (as the reader by now knows) I was on this occasion wrong, and by later in the evening Marian's brother had lost his virginity (I must say that I would have been happier had he done so to a more experienced and indeed a handsomer girl; but she seems to have been kind enough, and it may be, after all, best that the first step should be taken without recourse to an over-experienced woman who might startle the tender proclivities of a tyro).

Upon the following day, Marian was eager to visit the Pump Room and baths; both of which as a matter of course attract most visitors to this city. We took a dish of tea there upon its first opening – and indeed a glass of Bladud's celebrated medical water, whose taste is sufficiently horrid to convince the imbiber that it must in the natural course of things be good for him.

As to the baths, I explained to Marian that there were five, including the Leper's Bath; but that of these only two were fashionable and frequented by the society of the time – the King's Bath and the Cross Bath. These were surrounded by buildings, from the windows of which anyone was at liberty to watch the bathers – this resulting in a considerable profit to the owners of the overlooking properties, many of those immersing themselves preferring to have no covering other than a towel with which the more nervous of them concealed their bodies while walking to the bath's side from the rooms in which they left their clothing.

It was to the Cross Bath I first took my young friend, for the King's Bath was frequented more commonly by those who bathed from a desire to cure some sickness, rather than for a social pleasure; and I cannot deny that these were sometimes an unpleasant sight, their skins and even bodies often unsightly through some disease.

At the Cross Bath, on the other hand, one bathed to be with one's equals – or perhaps one's betters – in an atmosphere of informality; and I cannot but confess, sometimes for amatory reasons, for the bath was famed more for pleasure than for cures, so that here (in the words of an earlier visitor, a Mr John Ashton)

> was performed all the Wanton Dalliances imaginable; Celebrated Beauties, Panting Breasts and Curious Shapes almost expos'd to Public

View; Languishing Eyes, Darting Killing Glances, Tempting Amorous Postures attended by Soft Musick enough to provoke a Vestal to forbidden Pleasures, captivate a Saint or charm a Jove. Here the different Sexes from Quality to the Honourable Knights, Country Put and City Madams, wade about like Neptune's Courtiers, supplying their Industrious Joints; the Vigorous Sparks presenting them with several Antick Postures, as Sailing on their Backs, then embracing the Element, sink in Rapture!

Mr Ashton, I dare say, did not approve – for he ended his description with the warning that ' 'tis a Valley of Pleasure, a Sink of Iniquity; nor is there any Intrigue or Debauch acted in London but is mimick'd here.'

It will not be supposed that I described such a scene to Marian in detail; yet to present her with a view of it would, I thought, give her an idea of the tone of some elements of Society here, both as a warning of the attempts which might be made upon her virtue by those incapable of polite restraint, and as a recommendation of the pleasures which, when proffered in kindness and tenderness, may be enjoyed without reprehension.

The Cross Bath was full when we arrived there, and shown to the small changing-room by an attendant, we could hear in the distance a buzz of conversation which inferred that there was a crowd present. Marian showed, somewhat to my surprise, no hesitation in disrobing, nor any in making ready to leave the shelter of the room; however, I remembered that she and her brother were wont to be naked together without any suspicion of impropriety, and supposed that she believed other men to be as indifferent to the presence of an unclothed woman as Ralph was to her bare self – an opinion of which she would at some time, and I hope not too cruelly, be disabused.

We stepped, then, from our small room into a corridor full of men and women coming and going, some with towels wrapped about their persons, others carelessly trailing them over one shoulder, or even failing to make even so mere a gesture of concealment, having left their towels at the bath. Pressing through the crush, it was impossible not at some time to come into contact with other members of the public. As I had noted upon previous visits, it was almost invariably the limbs of the gentlemen present who brushed against ours as we walked, while the ladies managed to keep themselves apart. It was no surprise to me that those gentlemen glanced with more than usual appreciation at my companion, some of them pausing, turning and reversing their progress to follow us to the bath's edge, where as they had doubtless hoped, they were rewarded by my friend's dropping her towel to her feet and for a moment standing in the costume of Eve before descending the steps into the waters of the bath, too muddied however to afford them a view of her limbs once she was submerged.

I too entered the waters, and purchased from the attendant boy two trays of sweetmeats which we floated before us, occasionally placing one between our lips; my purpose partly being the simple pleasure thus accomplished, and partly the fact that the trays provided a kind of protection against any untoward incident resulting from the too close approach of a gentleman.

Even with most of her body submerged, Marian was a delightful sight, the upper parts of her breasts revealed by the lapping water – and even her nipples sometimes rising into sight by result of some movement, or a small wave resulting from the passage of another person, nearby. It was noticeable that everyone present paid her attention; not only from looking, but upon her moving from the side of the bath, by one or two gentlemen contriving to get behind her, and entirely by accident to collide with her, upon which they were forced to bow in acknowledgement of their discourtesy, which afforded them the opportunity to examine at closer quarters such portions of her person as were exposed.

I did not follow her too protectively, but merely kept an eye towards her in case my protection should be required; and in doing so came at a particular point in collision with a gentleman who was standing in a melancholy pose behind me. I turned in acknowledgement and apology, and on seeing his face was pleased to recognise it.

'Will Langrish!' I remarked – and immediately took him in my arms and gave him a smacker upon the lips!

'Why, Mrs Nelham!' was his returning greeting, a smile for a moment crossing over his features.

Will, I should explain, had been employed by me as a stallion in the house of pleasure for ladies which some years ago I established at Chiswick (an event chronicled in our previous memoir, *Eros in Town*). He was the son of a prominent churchman, himself studying for entry into that profession – yet conscious of a proclivity for sensuality, which I too recognised, and for that reason employed him; when he showed considerable ingenuity in devising new pleasures with which to stimulate and satisfy the ladies who were attracted to my house – some of whom made him a favourite, despatching messages to insist that he should not be enjoying a day of recuperation when they particularly wished to be entertained.

I was sorry to see him evidently weighed down by care, for after the brief pleasure of our meeting a melancholy once more settled over him; and upon my enquiring he confirmed that he was somewhat sad – and after further questioning invited me to take coffee with him, when he would confide in me as in someone who might be of assistance to him.

I therefore persuaded Marian to leave the bath – somewhat reluctantly, for by now she was surrounded by admiring gentlemen who, though not in conversation, were full of glances and admiring gestures; on her leaving the bath, which she did at a corner opposite the exit, she bent to pick up her towel, but with a coquettishness more conscious than unconscious (she was a quick learner) merely threw it upon her right shoulder, where it half-concealed one delightful breast. In such a state of provoking nature she strode around two sides of the place, all male eyes (and some jealous female ones) following her; but none of the gentlemen daring to leave the water, perhaps – I conjectured – because their bodies would then too openly express the admiration clearly seen in their eyes. Though the atmosphere of the Baths was the opposite of anchoritic, there was a general rule that gentlemen whose pricks were incited to a stand by the not infrequently lubricious displys of femininity should remain veiled by the waters until by an exercise of will they had reduced them to a less provoking condition.

I was somewhat surprised, indeed, that Will climbed the steps at my side, but a glance informed me that his person had been entirely unaffected by my friend's beauty; and even while we followed her, that long and willowy back, those broad hips, those full thighs between which, as she walked, could be glimpsed an entrancing bush, seemed to have no effect upon him. Only a few years ago, I reflected, that would certainly not have been the case.

Sending Marian home in a chair, I repaired with Will to a coffee-shop, where he obtained upon payment a small room where we could be private. I wondered somewhat at his motives – we had been familiar in the past; was he perhaps unable for some reason to come at female company, and wishful for mine? I could not believe it – though I would have had little objection, for he was a most personable young man (as had been all the members of my Chiswick stable). That it was not the case became obvious when, ignoring the sofa which lay invitingly along one wall, he sat me in a chair, and himself took a seat opposite, the table between us bearing a coffee pot and two cups which, filling, he began his story:

'After the unfortunate fire at Chiswick, when you were forced to relinquish your business, I kept company for some time with Polly Playwright – who, you will remember, was a servant of your brother's in Brook Street. (I did indeed: and a bouncing girl she was.)

'After two months, however, she returned to Lavenham, where her home was, and I was for a time at ease, not repining at a lack of female company – for as you will know, I had been for almost a year engaged every evening upon pleasuring some lady or another, and the satisfaction which this gave me (as I trust, them) was such that to be without a bedfellow for a while was no distress to me.

'However, in due course an opportunity presented itself in my juxtaposition at an evening party with a lady of the most engrossing beauty – just such as most appealed to my senses, which by now were at a point when I relished the prospect of a new connection. This person was a Miss Sally Dordi, then employed as a milliner; and on my offering to walk her to her home, she accepted with that alacrity which seemed to promise a speedy consummation of my wishes. Indeed, on our reaching her rooms in the village of Knight's Bridge, she was quick to invite me into them for some refreshment, which consisted of her immediately removing her clothing and inviting me to do the same.

'You will forgive, Mrs Nelham, my frankness in describing what followed. That I was not slow to accept her invitation will not surprise you, nor that in a short time we were enjoying that activity in which you yourself largely tutored us – the giving of pleasure to the gentler sex. Miss Dordi received me with every display of delight, opening herself on the fairest terms, and proving altogether as charming in person – when that person was fully displayed to view – as had been promised by her public appearance.

'Her enjoyment seemed unalloyed; and after some thirty minutes of enchanting play, I began to lead her in the direction of a consummation. But though I employed every art at my command, I could raise her enjoyment no higher than it had been from the beginning – that is, she showed in very limb the keenest apprehension of pleasure, yet all my efforts could not bring her to a culmination; and though I delayed my own expiration until my entire body shrieked almost with the pain of it, on my collapsing in exhaustion, my person drained of life-giving fluid, she continued to thrust her body against mine in the most libidinous manner; and every effort I continued to make, both while recovering myself, and later in a second passage of complete connection, failed to satisfy her.

'After some two hours, during which I employed a hundred debauched and lickerish tricks, she continued unsatisfied; and when, finally, entirely pooped, I left her, it was with the most scornful laughter.'

At this point I interrupted his story, with the exclamation that it was not unknown for some women to be to that extent inexhaustible in passion; but that any decent person would have refrained from blaming their disappointment on so admirable a lover as, I was convinced, Will was. But he continued:

'That is not all; for I found upon my next engagement, which was with an old friend visiting the metropolis, who on such occasions relied upon me to give her some relief from the tedium of an ancient and impotent husband, I was at first unable to stand, and then upon my entering, immediately expired – which upon each connection since that date, now for some months, has been the case. My former powers seem entirely to have left me, and I am no longer capable of giving any lady more than the expectation of pleasure – for upon the first moment of my prick touching a cunny, it discharges; a fact which even my oldest female friends find risible and frustrating.'

My old friend, on reaching this point of his narrative, paused, overcome by emotion. I reached out and took his hand. This was, I told him, merely the result of a single incident to which he had afforded too great a significance; his failure to please one insatiable female was, he should know, no mark of a general defeat.

But, he said, not only his waking but sleeping life was marked by it. His rest was haunted also by the incident; he slept poorly, and on sleeping often fell into terrifying or distressful dreams – as a night or two ago, he had found himself journeying through a valley between two great hills, whose regular swelling sides culminated in a pair of circular turrets or gun emplacements, looking threateningly down upon him. Emerging at last upon a plain, he skirted a pit which seemed to lower dangerously before him, then reached a dark thicket of impenetrable wiry brambles, through which he forced himself with difficulty, these tearing at his clothing until it was rent from his body, and marking his flesh with red weals from some of which the blood streamed.

Eventually, he found himself standing at the end of a gully or gulch, the edges of which were of dark red earth, and slipping upon the greasy ground saved himself only by clutching with both arms a knoll which stood up between the lips of the gulch – and which, when he threw his arms about it, had the soft and yielding consistency of flesh. This knoll now became, as it were, a living thing, which seemed to embrace him as he embraced it, thrusting itself at the bifurcation of his limbs until despite himself he felt the discharge of his passion – whereat his grasp failed, and with a fearful cry he fell into the chasm below, and, losing his senses, found himself awake in his naked bed, bathed in perspiration and the liquor persuaded from his body by the circumstances of his fantasy.

In the telling of this sad story, I could see that Will's distress was accompanied by a certain rush of sensation; and through pity and friendship determined to do my best to help him, and – feeling a certain lack of confidence in the safety of the sofa of the coffee-shop (it not being unknown that such places offered to customers the opportunity to view, through concealed apertures, the activities of those in such private rooms) – invited him to accompany me to Pulteney Street, which after a formal protestation, he did. Once there, I invited him to divest himself of his clothing and to place himself in my hands. This he did without demur, for he understood that I wished only to be of assistance – as I must be to so old a friend.

His disrobing revealed a body whose features I remembered well: his person was almost hairless, slender and shapely, his arms almost like those of a girl, his breast muscular, his belly flat and without a trace of fat, even after the elapse of the several years since I had last seen him. His prick was loblolly, of which I was glad, for too much excitement at the beginning would have made for an additional difficulty. At my own disrobing there were proper signs of interest, and an attempt at an embrace – from which I dissuaded him, persuading him rather to lie upon the bed, whereat I caressed or massaged him (as the French express it) by passing the palms of my hands over his limbs, approaching but not touching the most tender parts; and on his beginning to breathe deeply and to show signs of complete repose, myself lay at his side and invited him to pay similar attentions to me – after a while simulating a growing pleasure (without difficulty, for he was a man whose attractions were undiminished either by too great an accumulation of years or by those appetites which result in thickening of the limbs).

On the time seeming right, I threw open my lower limbs, and invited him between them – his prick now being, as I could see, of just such a proper elevation as promised a satisfactory union.

But alas, the result was just what he may have feared: for as the plump and promising bulb which crowned his affair nudged at the door which I offered, I felt a shiver run through his entire frame – and politely throwing himself away from me and upon his back, he expired, the generous expulsion of sap displaying virility, but its too speedy discharge being expressive of just such a failure as he had already related.

The reader will apprehend that I showed neither anger nor disappointment, but rather an entire sympathy; first fetching a cloth and cleansing his limbs, then exercising those arts of which (in honesty) I must describe myself as mistress – at first giving my attention to persuading him of my entire admiration (which was not difficult, through – as I have said – his retention of all the good looks of a boy in his earliest years of manhood, while at the same time being without doubt an entire man) – then rousing him after a due time to a new expression of desire – only, on offering connection, to suffer with him from the same over-speedy culmination.

His disappointment weighed equally with his gratitude, tears seeming to well in his eyes as he thanked me for my attentions, but convinced that his days as a lover were over: for what woman, except one of the streets, could pretend to be satisfied with a person unable to retain the power to please for more than a moment or two?

I did my best to reassure him. After all, as I reminded him, it was possible through the passionate employment of other limbs than the most sensitive one – the lips, tongue, fingers – to bring about the consummation of a woman's pleasure; but could not pretend that that would be entirely satisfactory to himself. We drank together a somewhat dolorous cup of coffee – but in the midst of it, there came to me the recollection of my short passage, upon that same bed, with my young friend Marian. Could it be that the solution to Will's problem might lie in that direction? It might, might it not, be so?

Chapter Three

The Adventures of Andy

It was but a week after our arrival in Bath that I encountered at the Pump Room Sir Stanley Curtis, a surgeon with whom I had exchanged pleasantries upon previous visits to the place; he was imbibing a glass of that quite amazingly unpleasant water dispensed in metal cups from the fountain which overlooked the bath, and which is said to be an encourager of health and general ability – though with what degree of confidence I cannot say; it has been hinted that he is retained by the Lord Mayor at a considerable stipend to drink there daily in order to encourage others to credit the liquid's curative power.

He is an amiable enough person, whose geniality mirrors his considerable wealth; and upon this occasion was good enough to invite myself and Sophie to witness a game of cricket at a ground newly laid out for that pleasant sport upon the outskirts of the city. This was to be a contest between players from Bath and others from the city of Winchester. He himself, he said, would not be present, for he must travel to Bristol upon business; but his son Edward, who was to be captain of the Bath team, would be pleased to receive us. On my explaining that we were entertaining two young people, he was kind enough to extend his invitation to them.

I was happy to accept his invitation, for I knew that neither Marian nor Ralph had ever seen the game in play, and since the weather was warm and settled, and a day's relaxation of that sort seemed to promise well, I considered that such an outing would be extremely agreeable.

Sir Stanley was delighted, and the more pleased when I introduced him to the twins, whom he found to be both presentable and polite. Making an excuse, however, he then beckoned me aside, leaving his lady wife talking to the others, and produced from his pocket a parcel of papers which, he said, he had discovered in the library of a recently deceased gentleman of Bath.

'Knowing your interest in the subject,' he said, 'I have preserved them for you; but indeed, they are historical documents of some importance, which I shall see deposited in the King's library. They preserve an account of a series of lectures given in Bath some decades since by my old colleague Dr Aloysius Plumtre – a friend of the Beau Nash.'

I took the papers, placed them in my pocket, and promptly forgot about them – until, undressing at home that night, they came once more to my hand. Opening them, I found a brief prefatory note in Sir Stanley's hand. Dr Plumtre had been approached, it seems, by Nash, who had become concerned lest the increasing popularity of Bath as a place of recreation should bring about a concomitant lowering of general standards of behaviour, particularly among the young blades and men of fashion, some of whom had more money than education, and were concerned more with enjoyment than with decency. Some of these blades the

Beau could – and did – control by the simple expedient of personal example and public notices; their private behaviour, however, presented a problem – and he received many complaints from ladies that young gentlemen promising agreeable companionship proved rough and uncongenial under circumstances of intimacy.

In an attempt to remedy the situation, he had engaged his friend Dr Plumtre to present three lectures, privately, at his house, upon the subject of lovemaking. Sir Stanley had come into possession of the doctor's notes – which are quite sufficiently interesting for me to place on this occasion before the reader, having slightly amended the language to dispose of some of those phrases which the passage of time has rendered obstructive to the understanding.

The notes bore the title *Plumtre on the Conventions of Amorous Behaviour*, and began:

'I need not devote much time to advising a young gentleman upon the seduction of a young lady. No such matter has ever happened at Bath! An exchange of eyes at a ball, the laying of a hand upon an arm, a lifting of the eyebrow or an inclination of the head has sometimes drawn a young lady from the ballroom floor into a corridor, where an appointment has perhaps been made for later in the evening. But as for *seduction* – why it is as undesirable as rape, for the term suggests undue persuasion, whereas it is a mutual spark which must draw a couple together, the lady being as desirous of an union as the gentleman.

'But how can a young man be sure that such a spark is fanned to a fire? First, should he be hopeful of an amorous connection, he must take care that his personal appearance, while not necessarily lacking in display, should not be ostentatious: viz, his hair should be neatly dressed, and not over-lengthy; his eyebrows plucked, his beard – if he wear one – trimmed. His clothes must be chosen to present with the utmost charm his best characteristics, while his attitude should be one of attentive solicitation for the pleasure of the lady he is accompanying. Extremes of fashion, whether these consist of a shirt collar too high or a coat too loosely cut, a waistcoat too colourful or boots badly made, must be avoided. As to his person, exercise and a reasonable diet should ensure a lack of that superfluous flesh which, overlapping at the waist or gathering below the chin, can make a sensitive female positively ill at the sight of it. A concern for the shapeliness of his form does not disgrace any young man; and it should always be remembered that be he of what build he may – muscular or effete, large or small, tall or short – he may please any lady by ensuring that he carries himself well.

'It is well for him to remember also that should he succeed in his ambition, he must unveil those parts which, in a public place, will not generally be seen. This must concentrate his mind on ensuring that he does not offend, in the process, the susceptibilities even of the youngest and least experienced of females. He must first of all be assured that the age has passed which paid no concern to personal cleanliness. A lover must now find it advantageous to wash his person thoroughly before any appointment which he suspects may end in amorous pleasure. If self-respect does not dictate such a process, he should remember that lack of dirt, and – especially in summer – as little perspiration as is possible (though this cannot always be avoided) – will commend him to his mistress, who will then be freer with her embraces than would otherwise be the case; in especial, she will be more willing to pay the tribute of a kiss to those private parts where such a caress is most welcome, if they are free of any odour but that of freshness, though a little perfume may be employed; be sparing of it, however, not least because the alcohol used in its manufacture may be uncomfortable to sensitive areas of the skin.

'Within an established partnership, one may throw off one's clothes without thought for the action; indeed, husband and wife will perhaps only exceptionally pay attention to the unveiling of each other's bodies, be he as handsome as Apollo and she as desirable as Venus. The enjoyment of the process of discovering the sight of a new mistress is, however, of the essence of a conquest; as (the gentleman will do well to remember) should her first sight of his own person – which may under some circumstances dictate her emotions and actions both. Upon a first meeting, then, it is well to consider a number of matters: whether, for instance, too abrupt an unveiling may disconcert the female (who, if of tender years, will scarcely have seen a young man unclothed, except it be her brother). It should be remembered that a too sudden exposure of the organs of generation, especially if these are in an animated state, may surprise even a female warmed to such a degree as to wish for the sight: education in these matters being omitted from young ladies' academies, they frequently know not what to expect – and you should mark well that their notions may lie upon either extreme: that is, rumour may have raised their expectations so high that the most generously hung stallion appears to them disappointing; while those who have never discussed the matter even with another female will find the sight of a modestly endowed lover as shocking as the French or Americans find their first glimpse of a good British cannon elevated for action!

'Remove, then, the nether garments first. Our shirts are still of such a length as naturally to conceal all that need be concealed, while being short enough not entirely to conceal the suggestion of what may be hidden. Now, offer a fresh embrace to your mistress, who will not be disinclined to accept it; and, curiosity being a chief characteristic of most women, their apprehension of a Something beneath your shirt will attract her attention, and very possibly her hand. Should she herself be so bold as to venture to touch your person, your problem is at once, in all probability, at an end; if shyness prevents this, continue your embraces, and draw her into a reclining position when, as if by accident, your shirt may be ruffled to expose the limb in question.

'Before I continue, I must speak of the preparation the civilised lover, eager to be approved, must find necessary before such a scene. This must necessarily involve your yard and the adjacent and decorative features of your lower person. First, it is advantageous to remove any superfluous hair. This is not to say that a generous growth is not admired by many females: but this admiration extends, on the whole, only to that cluster of curls which lies at the root of the Member. The testicles are shown to a better advantage without too generous a cloud concealing them; quite apart from which it will be found that an absence of thatch lays the cods open to a more apprehensive caress.

'As to the decoration of the pubes, which certainly need not – should not! – be omitted or neglected, there are, happily, barbers in Bath well practised in the art of enhancing that area of the body by shaping or curling, and who upon special commission will trim to what degree they are instructed. Dying or colouring is not advised – except in the case of the elderly, white hairs in this place being less an advertisement of vigour than grey hairs upon the head are of wisdom. It has been brought to my notice that some barbers who discreetly advertise this service were brought to it by such a keen interest in their fellow men as too often results in attentions which, welcome to some, are offensive to others; and I need not warn that the shaving or shaping of hair in this region may become positively dangerous should it be conducted by an over-excited person.

'A recent habit is to deck the male member or the curls surrounding it with ribbons. This is largely a superfluous folly, rather suggesting femininity than masculinity – although it must be said that rules in this entire area of human life are to be regarded as supererogatory, behaviour only being reprehensible which displeases one of the partners concerned. It may be found that the lady is similarly trimmed to perfection; and her wearing of ribbons may be greeted as an advertisement of a desire to please and also, it is more likely than otherwise, of a greater experience in love-making than you may previously have apprehended.

'As to the presence of hair upon the limbs – viz., the arms, legs, back and buttocks – this must remain a matter of individual taste: for what it is worth, it is my observation that those who, like Esau, are hairy men, long for smooth bodies; while those whose skins remain as devoid of hair as a girl's, often into extreme old age, would rather they were thatched! Those who would wish to have been devoid of it will do well to remember that to some ladies a strong growth of hair upon chest and arms, at least, is a *sine qua non*; however, too great a proliferation may be governed by the use of a razor – though again with the warning that in re-growing, the hair of the body may cause some discomfort, as in pricking and irritation.

'Once you are exposed, take careful note of your mistress's response. Should she show signs of fear, be not too rough: do not immediately offer to spear her – for this, if she be a virgin, will terrify her; and if she is experienced, may still frighten her – any lack of forwardness may be taken to suggest a possibly unfortunate experience. Go gently at her, until you are sure of a kindly reception.

'I should say a word or so of the male member, which upon the first acquaintance may be found appalling by the innocent female. The most ingenuous, however, will apprehend something pleasant of it, and it is therefore important that it should seem divest of any violent intention. This may partly be achieved by such a careful grooming as has already been mentioned – the trimming of surrounding hedges, and a perfect cleanliness. If it is possible to retain a shrunken dimension in the first instance (though I do not underestimate the difficulty), the lady will be pleased that it is her touch that raises your creature's head, and the consequent engorgement will be (as a compliment) less fearful to her. Be prepared for her to wish to examine the instrument, whose construction she will naturally find interesting. In preparation for this inevitable display of curiosity, the application in private, before the encounter begins, of a manual technique to milk yourself of a first throwing will be found useful, in that your *penis* (to apply the proper Latin term, no doubt rejected by you young men in favour of all sorts of babyish terms – though I do not object to the good old Anglo-Saxon names for the instrument) will then be less sensitive to her enquiring touch, and less likely to give way to a precipitant explosion under her caresses (interesting though she would no doubt find that phenomenon).

'In parentheses, I cannot too strongly stress the wrongheadedness of those who claim that *self-abuse*, as they mistakenly call it, is improper or damaging; on the contrary, *self-love*, as I prefer to call it, is the young man's best friend, relieving him of the heaviness attendant upon longings which by nature of extreme youth cannot be satisfied, or but rarely; while in learning to please himself, a young gentleman may learn how best to conquer that over-speedy precipitation of passion of which I have spoken, while providing himself with information which, upon his teaching it to an apprehensive lover, will give him the utmost delight.

'Gentleness must be your mark in persuading the lady to relinquish her own clothing. You will, in early embraces, have placed a hand upon her breast; and few women will be repelled by this, or discourage the gesture – for why otherwise should they be so ready to expose to the view those bulwarks of womanhood? Indeed, a fulsome compliment paid by the eyes if not by the lips will be first to convince her of your admiration. But there is a difference between such a compliment, paid in a public place to a figure ill-concealed, and an attempt to gain access to a view of the whole!

'Your conduct must be regulated by the young lady's behaviour. Should an attempt to relieve her of her clothing be kindly received, few activities can so warm a pair as that act; however, should she wish to retire behind a screen, or to turn her back, her reticence should be observed, lest the occasion be soured by what she may regard as an untoward lack of gentility in a lover. We have no reason to suppose that you will be disappointed in the result of the unveiling, especially should the vision now afforded you be your first sight of a woman unencumbered by clothing. If this is the case, it is best to make an attempt to refrain from a goggle-eyed peering – a display of wild surmise akin to that of stout Cortez on first observing the Pacific ocean (to paraphrase the late Mr Keats, a medical man like myself). And it need not surely be said that you should be free with your compliments – which may as well be paid by the lips and eyes as by words.

'A young man's first engagement with a person of the opposite sex must result in a passionate inquisitiveness which he should nevertheless satisfy with tact; falling upon her nether parts with the apprehensive curiosity of a monkey examining a nut will only in a small degree be taken as a compliment – besides betraying an inexperience which may be regarded as denigratory. It will naturally be your wish to examine that part of woman the achievement of which will no doubt for some time have been your aim;

but do so gently, without unnecessary fumbling, and above all with such an air as will convince your mistress that your interest is in herself rather than in an universal attribute of femininity which might belong to any other woman. This, while being no more than mannerly, will have the effect of a compliment which can do nothing but redound to your credit.

'It is not my intention to enlarge upon what my hearers will know, by instinct if not by experience – the private conduct of a lover with his mistress. But the younger gentlemen among you are to remember, should the experience be your first, that it is possible your mistress compliments you by offering you her virginity; and that if such is the case, you must be particularly cautious in your approach to the ultimate pleasure. In your excitement, do not batter at the gate like a bull; for should it be fastened, undue force in breaking the lock will result in a discomfort which will relieve the lady of all pleasure, and may encourage her to be less obliging to you in future. A cautious approach will render her grateful, and – her enjoyment being at best equal to your own – will enable pleasure to outweigh discomfort.

'A young gentleman has asked for my view upon a certain procedure which, upon his desiring a young lady to employ it, led to her scornful dismissal of his courtship: viz., his desire that she should whip him. Some of you may share this taste, which seems markedly peculiar to this country, often being early instilled by the masters of our public schools. In such a case, it is well not to invite a lady's participation upon your first becoming familiar with her; females rarely experience the same coarse treatment in early years and so rarely share the taste either for whipping or being whipped. There are of course exceptions; but a desire for such treatment is best satisfied at the hands of an experienced whore. The best-educated and most modest young ladies, however, sometimes enjoy other irregularities: such as dressing a lover in her own clothes, or wishing herself to don his clothing – or other less simple pleasures.

'My view, since I am asked for it, is that none of this signifies except to the persons concerned; but that it is best, should the irregularities be sufficiently unusual to cause surprise, that they be not introduced until the happiness and permanence of the union is assured. Upon that first connection it is well for the lover to give an impression of more knowledge than he may possess – as in the matter of French kissing (employing the tongue as eagerly as the lips), and in a variation of posture which, while not so obsessive as to seem boasting, will persuade the young lady that he has the means to please.

'As to the use of looking-glasses – this too may be a mistake with a tyro pair; for the young man will spend too much time admiring himself, while the young lady may, in catching a glimpse of herself in attitudes which she must believe unbecoming, may be rendered unwilling or in the extreme even incapable of such relaxation as must be commanded if the connection is to be a satisfactory one.

'I am asked to say a few words about the class of female I mentioned but a moment ago: viz., those ladies whose amorous services can be bought, no less here in Bath than in any other city in this country, for sums varying between twenty pounds and twenty pence.

'I need scarcely say that I do not commend the latter, for the first notable warning must be of disease, and those unfortunates who find themselves in a profession which often repels them, and has been adopted through simple want, frequently are the communicators of disease. Yet it must be remarked that among the highest class of prostitute (and it is no less the truth that here as in other transactions the customer receives goods of a quality directly proportionate to the fee he is prepared to pay) there is great attention paid to hygiene; being by the nature of their employment more thoroughly versed in the sport than other females, these know how diseases are passed from female to male, male to female, and take great care to avoid either catching or transmitting them. You will find, for instance, that upon your first presenting yourself to them in a state of nature, they will at some point, before the ultimate connection is made, find some opportunity to examine minutely your organs of generation for those sign of illness which are well-known to them – and some will insist upon washing your amatory equipment in a solution of water and potash, the better to ensure that neither they nor you are in the least danger of a venereal infection.

'My advice has been, and remains, to any parent not devoid of means, to send his son to a first-rate brothel for his first experience of congress with the opposite sex. Not only will he be enabled there to lose his virginity to a lady whose person is pleasing to him, but she will be sufficiently experienced to smooth the way, and he will emerge from the occasion with his susceptibilities undamaged either by the fear that the lady has been disappointed, or having experienced disappointment himself. That, alas, may come later, with less amenable and amiable females than those who, often shunned by the rest of their sex, provide such an admirable service.

'I would even go so far as to suggest that any gentleman of means who can afford a sum in excess of two guineas (which must be considered the minimum sum to procure a lady of discernment) should repair to these ladies rather than attempt to seduce some young woman who . . .'

Here, the doctor's manuscript broke off: but not before exhibiting such wisdom as made me convinced that Ralph would profit from a sight of it – and indeed from an additional sheet which bore, in another hand, some copies of postures which I recognised as being among those illustrated by the Italian Aretine, and showing some of the attitudes possible to young persons engaged in amorous congress. I carefully put the manuscript away in a drawer, for further study with my pupil.

On the following day, we four – myself, Sophie, and the twins – set off in a hired carriage for Twerton, outside the town, where we found a small select crowd attending the two teams of players. Ralph, on the way to the ground, had questioned me about cricket – of which indeed I knew little other than that it had been played in England for over a century; I had seen my first game only a year or two before the present date, when the Londoners and Dartford men played each other for a considerable sum of money, which the Dartford men had won. But I knew that the King was a follower of the sport, and when a naval man had organised many a contest. However, as to the rules, I had no knowledge of them other than that it was the purpose of the members of one team to run between two sets of stumps at which the others must aim a ball, from which the first protected it with the aim of a bat. The niceties, I explained, the pair must discover for themselves.

Sophie and Marian laughed merrily at the idea of grown men engaging in so notably silly a game as that; but their laughter was moderated on their arrival at the game, when they found that many members of the two teams – to the number of eleven in a side – were sufficiently handsome to engage their admiration! I introduced myself to Edward Curtis, my old friend's son, a boy of perhaps twenty and two, who received us with great pleasure, and was particularly kind in assisting Sophie and Marian to seats in an area marked off by a rope for particular friends.

There we sat while the game commenced, which was not without interest, though ineffably slow and lacking in excitement (as I thought, though a collection of gentlemen from Bath found it sufficiently inspiriting to mark it from time to time with applause and shouts of encouragement).

Upon breaking for luncheon, I was led to believe that the team from Bath was losing, for young Edward led his team off into the small tent or pavilion; and on following him I found him giving them words of encouragement, with enjoinment to remember what a prize awaited them should they win. On my remarking, when he had left off, that I did not know that this was a prize match, he reddened slightly; and only on my encouragement admitted that a private wager was under consideration – 'to brighten the match', as he put it – consisting of eleven maidens who even now awaited the winning team at his father's house, and whose duty it would be to pleasure the winners. The losers, as he said, would make do with what they could find!

This amused me considerably, but consideration for my host disallowed me from letting Sophie know the cause of my amusement, as we joined the party for a little cut meat and some wine, participation in which I offered the captain, who was no less pleased to accept than to take his refreshment while talking in an animated manner to Marian, at whose side he sat, attentively picking the best pieces of meat and fruit to hand her; she being as full of admiration for him, as it seemed, as he for her.

Too soon for either, the second half of the match commenced, when Edward must stand before the wicket. The third ball bowled to him bounced unevenly upon a turf, and struck him a blow too near the groin to be comfortable – and indeed he fell to the ground in pain clutching that area of his person inappropriate to such unkind attentions. After a while he rose, but could not stand unattended, and was helped from the field by two friends – when Sophie and Marian jumped to their feet and immediately went to attend him (with an eagerness which said much of the impression he had made).

Ralph and I remained where we were, and were surprised that our two companions did not return – even when, after what seemed a hard-fought match, the Bath team were returned as winners, and the gentlemen from Winchester took themselves disconsolately off. Our men, however, seemed no less disconsolate; and upon my enquiring the reason, I was told that while they had been told of their reward, they knew not where it awaited them, and Edward, their captain, was nowhere to be seen – for they had looked in the tent, and he was not to be found there.

Fortunately, I knew Sir Stanley's house, which was in the Circle, in Bath, and was sufficiently confident to suggest that they should accompany me there, young Edward having (I was sure) been detained in the service of my sister and her friend. So we collected ourselves together, and set off in several carriages, arriving in half an hour at Sir Stanley's, to be admitted by a servant who clearly understood the situation.

We were shown immediately upstairs, where in two rooms a number of baths were set out, and the players were happy to remove their clothing and bathe themselves. Meanwhile I took it upon myself to enquire of the servant what further arrangements had been made, and leaving young Ralph with them (whom they welcomed, being much of his age, by ducking him with water, and attempting to relieve him of his nether clothing) I was shown across a corridor into a large room which my have been Sir Stanley's bedroom, but which now – though the bed remained – was furnished in addition with a great number of cushions, upon which reclined what seemed a crowd of young ladies. Where Edward had found these beauties, I could not know; but they were extremely handsome, not giving in the least the impression of blowsiness or age, and being clad in dresses whose flimsiness failed to disguise those limbs which confirmed an impression of freshness and beauty, producing an effect of gaiety and vigour. Young Edward must, I reflected, not only have access to the best source of beauty in the neighbourhood, but possess the purse to command it.

My eye had scarcely time to take in this sight, when the door behind me burst open and in came the eleven young gentlemen – or, rather, the dozen, for in the midst of them I saw young Ralph, who like them was now utterly in a state of nature. Without pause, the entire team fell upon the young ladies like rutting bulls upon a herd (if with less violence, certainly with an equal anticipation of pleasure). Nor were the ladies slow to respond: indeed, their gestures were so welcoming that in less than no time the entire room was full of embracing couples and it became clear that the numbers were equally matched, and that young Edward had engaged eleven players for his eleven gentlemen – his own absence meaning that one was available for a guest, Ralph now lying upon his back under the admiring gaze and in the attentive grasp of a lady of perhaps nineteen, whose raven hair fell over alabaster shoulders, and the whiteness of whose body was in delightful contrast to his own bronzed limbs.

It would take a more talented pen than mine to describe the scene which followed; and indeed so multifarious were the couplings, so inventive the attitudes, so engaging the attentions, so considerable the enthusiasm which I saw before me that I found it impossible not to wish that I, too, could participate. My face must have betrayed my disappointment, for young Ralph, looking up from his recumbent position (his gaze for a moment released from admiring his partner, now engaged by the application of her lips in an attempt to render even more adamant the wand which sprouted from between his thighs) cried 'Hey,

Andy! What's your lack?' and drew his partner's attention to my plight, whereat (whether to his temporary displeasure or not I cannot say) she left him, and coming up to me attempted to relieve me of my breeches; a task in which I was obliged to assist her, for reasons of impatience.

Despite her youth, this lady proved perfectly capable of satisfying two lovers – certainly where one was as inexperienced as Ralph. He had grown somewhat glum at the sight of Miss, kneeling before me to pay some attention to my laggard equipment, which through lack of obvious opportunity had been slow to respond to her initial caress; but on her leading me by the hand to a position at his side, recovered his brightness, though still clearly uncertain in what manner a young lady could pleasure two gentlemen simultaneously. However, this she did with entire ease – by lying him upon his back and lowering herself pleasantly upon his staff, while encouraging me to take an attitude with my knees contiguous to Ralph's shoulders, in order that her upper lips could perform for my pleasure much the same task as her lower lips performed for his.

Despite my strong belief that no action which a man performs in the course of his life which is not dictated by ignoble or unkindly motives can be shameful, I must confess that even in the midst of my enjoyment (which was keen) it occurred to me to wonder what the young man must think, who had but a week ago been entirely innocent, and who now found himself regarding, from a distance of no more than twenty inches, the yard of another being voraciously consumed by a female to which neither of them had been properly introduced. However, upon glancing downward, I saw that he was far from concerned at the spectacle, his gaze being equally divided between that prospect, and the engagement of his own person with the lady's nether regions; and indeed in catching my eye, he grinned with unconcealed pleasure, and, with a degree of wicked mischievousness of which I would not have suspected him, reached up and grasped my cods in his hand, giving to them so inspiriting a tickle that my business was done; and for the moment retiring from the fray, I lay at their side while my friend and his temporary inamorata continued their engagement.

Young Ralph was evidently a naturally speedy learner, for (no doubt warned by his over-quick expiry on the occasion of his engagement with Miss Eliza) he now took the lady by her hips and lifted her bodily from him, then drew his partner upon him so that their entire bodies were in proximity, encircling her with his legs so that his heels were tucked into the delightful, deep crease of her bum; whereat a certain wriggling of her person denoted pleasure, and a surprised look about her eyes seemed to indicate that she was unused to dealings with a young man prepared to show her that degree of concern for her own pleasure which Ralph now exercised, in caressing her back and sides, and stroking with the soles of his feet her thighs and calves.

Looking about me, I could understand the lady's satisfaction; for the ten young gentlemen who were also at work were clearly concerned only to satisfy their own lusts, and many of them, already requited, were now lying in a comatose state upon the cushions, their erstwhile partners looking decidedly glum – though two, disconsolate at being left with an incomplete apprehension of delight, had turned their attentions to each other, and were completing with the help of fingers and tongues that task which should have been accomplished by their inexpert swains!

Ralph's lady was now grown impatient, and struggling to release herself – but he was not inclined to permit her once more to mount him (though showing no signs that this would be unrewarding); instead, he threw her – with more affection than violence – upon her back, and with a dexterity surprising in one so inexperienced, placed himself with his shoulders beneath her legs, and raising his body at the same time raised hers, so that he was able to engage in a position which (regarded by some as indelicate) has certainly been known for two thousand years, being recorded in ancient manuscripts and upon the side of Grecian vases.

The spectacle was so pleasant that it re-engaged my own interest, and I was encouraged to reach out for one of the young ladies nearby, who, kneeling with her back to me, was engaged in conversation with a friend. At first surprised – for she had believed that all the gentlemen in the room, like her former lover, were entirely exhausted – she was only too pleased to feel my riding-muscle nuzzling at her rear. She lightly raised her arse and encouraged me to enter and pleasure her, which I did to an extent which provoked no complaints, and indeed soon drew from her lips a series of sharp cries which attracted the attention of those about her; and the sight of Ralph and I so pleasantly engaged encouraged an unexpected recovery among the other youths, so that once more the room was soon a scene of what can only be called debauchery – though I use the term in an entirely uncritical sense, everyone being similarly minded.

It will not have escaped those readers who are of a mathematical mind that, as has been remarked, there were eleven ladies and twelve gentlemen present; and indeed it occurred to me – but the place was such a tangle of limbs that it was impossible to comprehend who was engaged with who, and in what manner; all I can say is that there was no sign either of a lady or a gentleman disengaged from pleasure, so that by hook or by crook (or some other means) the odd man out was clearly as satisfied as the rest of us.

The scene settled, after some time, into a still life; and it was half an hour or more before any of us stirred – but then were surprised by sudden hunger and thirst. Donning my clothes, I took myself off to discover the servants; found none – but in a downstairs room, a buffet of cold meats and salads clearly intended for the team. I summoned them to it – first taking the precaution of closing the shutters and lighting the candles (though 'twas not yet entirely dark); which was as well, since a number of Edward's guests chose not to resume their clothing, while others merely wound a towel about their loins; and a view of the party might have somewhat shocked the more sedate dowagers of Bath, on their way home from the Pump Room.

I was myself satisfied with two engagements; but was interested to see that already Ralph was showing signs of a renewed interest in the ladies, having (by accident or design) taken a seat next to a young lady whose golden hair was in contrast to the night-black tresses of his former mistress. By his third glass of claret, indeed, he had drawn her upon his knee, and a disarrangement of the towel which had lain across his lap seemed to suggest that she was becoming acquainted with a persuasively pert prick, attempting to find its way between her thighs; not that, I hasten to remark, she showed any apprehension at this, or indeed anything but pleasure – which she illustrated by interrupting their eating and drinking to offer her tongue as an additional course, between the sweetmeats.

I was wondering how far this new exercise would go – not in apprehension, but merely in interest (recalling the day when I was Ralph's age, and could perform my duties almost at will, and to the extent of perhaps five or even six passages in twenty-four hours), when the door opened, and admitted Edward Curtis, upon whose arms were Sophie and Marian!

I was not apprehensive that the scene would disturb my friend, whose view of such conduct was decently founded upon the precept that love was free and should be unfettered; but it did occur to me to wonder whether young Marian would not be shocked by the revelation that the act to which she was yet to be introduced was not invariably performed in private.

However, she showed no such concern; and indeed rushing forward pressed a kiss upon her brother's brow, and immediately began removing her clothing! Catching Sophie's eye, I could not but signal surprise – and met in turn a look which seemed a mixture of amusement and resignation, while young Edward showed a similar disinclination to amazement – even when, having arrived at a complete state of undress, Miss Marian began to walk about the room, first to one young man and then to another – few of whom were, by now (with wine and concupiscence) capable of showing any interest even in so delightful a prospect as her naked self; until at last one was found who at least caught at her hand and pressed a kiss upon it whereat she positively threw herself upon him, and sitting astride his knees, bounded with such enthusiasm that I feared for his equipment – though not for long, for after only a quarter of a minute, there came from the girl's lips a shout of triumph, and clasping her goggle-eyed lover in her arms, his face pressed against her breasts, she indicated that her course was run.

My friend now drew me from the room, and announced that she was in some trouble with the young lady whose access of enjoyment we had just witnessed. What that was, I will allow her to explain; myself, having listened with sympathy, but being unable to counsel her, I returned to the dining-room, persuaded young Ralph into his clothes, and drew him home; where I had to help him to his room, remove at least his outer clothing, and tumble him upon his bed, where he was by the time his head touched the pillow in the kind of deep sleep which can only result from a combination of vinous and copulatory satisfaction.

Reaching my own room, I noticed that the drawer in which I had placed the good Dr Plumtre's lecture was slightly open; and that the sheet of drawings which accompanied it was out of place – from which I was able to solve the mystery how my innocent young Ralph had come by the attitude he had adopted in his recent amorous passage (though at the same time full of admiration for one who could so dexterously reproduce it at a first attempt).

Well, I was not displeased; the doctor's words were

admirable advice, and I had intended showing them to the boy – but at the same time must clearly be careful in the concealment of any material which it would be best, for any reason, he should not see!

On the following morning, I was awakened by Ralph himself, who had taken from the servant my morning tray of chocolate, and brought it to my bedside.

'I have a confession to make,' he began; and went on to inform me that searching for a cravat which he had mislaid, and thought might have been confused with mine, he had come across Dr Plumtre's lecture, and read it with interest – finding the advice it gave eminently practical; would (he said) that he had had such an instructor years before; which amused me, for how much younger could he have been, in order to put such advice to practical use? The reader will understand that I assured him that I had intended to show him the notes, and was pleased that they had been of use; pressing him indeed to make a copy and keep them permanently by him – and indeed to copy the drawings, also; which, blushing, he admitted he had already done (something I had of course been suspicious of).

Throwing himself upon his back at my side, he confessed that had never believed that life could become so interesting as – translated from a country life in the exclusive company of his sister – it had now become; and hoped that she, too, was profiting from it. 'I dare say,' he said (clearly remembering the scene of the night before), 'that it is entirely possible!'

Chapter Four

Sophie's Story

After my encounter with Mr Langrish, I found Marian sitting somewhat disconsolate in her room, and upon my persuading her she reluctantly confessed that she had been somewhat out of temper with me for sending her so soon from the baths, where not only the female but the male form was to be seen clad only in vestigial garments, and upon occasion even without these – for, she said, she found the sight compulsively interesting, her observations having hitherto been confined to her brother; and had been surprised (in so far as he had been able to observe them) at the difference in contours between one human form and the other – more marked perhaps in the female, but still notable in the male, form.

There would be ample opportunity in the long life which lay ahead, I assured her, of making similar comparisons; indeed, she might in the course of time conclude that she had seen rather more of the unveiled bodies of gentlemen than she now wished; her disbelieving look reminding me, however, of the eagerness of my own youth, so that I smiled and, taking her hand, promised that other visits would be arranged. But had any special offer of pleasure been made, to make her particularly sad to leave the baths?

No, she said; but it had been her impression that a number of gentlemen were ready to pay her the compliment of conversation, one in especial (who, she confessed, had been of particular beauty, resembling the medallions recently struck of the late Lord Byron) having been of particular assistance when her towel had accidentally fallen to the floor during her walk to the dressing-rooms. Bending to pick it up, he had returned it with particular solicitude, placing it carefully about her shoulders. But he did not, she was sure, mean any impertinence by the action. (I did not know whether to suspect her of naivety or equivocation; it was difficult to believe that she did not connect his attention with a desire at the very least to observe her person at closer quarters; yet it must be recalled that she was used to appearing naked before her brother, and he before her, without either, it seems, showing more attention to the other than if they had been fully clothed.)

But now I must open to her the matter which had been preoccupying me since Will's visit.

'My dear,' I said, 'you are eager, are you not, to discover the precise nature of that alchemy which draws men and women so strongly together?'

'Indeed, ma'am . . .'

'Sophie,' I prompted her.

'Indeed, Sophie, I am,' she said. 'You have been most kind in explaining to me the mechanical nature of the union, and my imagination has been strangely worked upon by your words; moreover, the pleasure given to me by your digital demonstration of two day's hence was such that I have not been able to resist . . .'

Here, she coloured and hesitated; but I was quick

to reassure her that any experiment she may have made in self-pleasure was only to be expected, and was certainly not a matter for reprehension.

'But we can do better,' I said. 'I have it in mind to introduce you to a young gentleman of my acquaintance, whom I think you will not find unpleasant, and who is of considerable experience in the matter of which we speak. While no doubt in an ideal world the first exchange of passion between two young persons will be the resolution of a period of mutual attraction and love, it is in the nature of things the case that young gentlemen are first introduced to the passions in connection with women whose profession it is at once to satisfy their lust and to teach them something of the skill necessary for the satisfaction of the female sex.

'It has always seemed to me inappropriate that a young woman, entirely innocent of love, should first experience the act at the hands of a person as innocent as herself – or at least whose experience has been at the hands of a person whose care in teaching him has no doubt been in strict proportion to the fee received; the result of which can be to persuade the young female pupil that love-making is at best dull and at worst a positive pain to women.

'Mr Langrish, for that is the name of the gentleman of whom I speak, has a considerable knowledge of amatory matters, and while I would expect neither you nor he to form a permanent attachment to each other, I would count on his introducing you to the pleasures of the bed with a tenderness and an enthusiasm which will persuade you of the continual joy which such entertainment can offer.'

Marian shyly accepted the proposition; and offering a few words of advice, I left her to prepare herself for an encounter that evening; first speaking to my servants and bespeaking a decent small dinner for two, and then taking myself off to Will's lodging, where I had promised to meet him – and there informed him of the appointment I had made.

Clearly grateful for my confidence, he nevertheless demurred.

'You have had a first-hand experience,' he said, 'of my inability to maintain a stand long enough to give a lady the satisfaction she merits; to offer a young person such a disappointment upon a first engagement must run the risk of setting her against similar pleasure . . .'

But taking him by the hand, I expressed my certainty of his proving an entirely satisfactory lover; and left him, though in some doubt, at least promising to keep the appointment.

I must now describe the evening as he related it to me, for I took myself off to the card-rooms sufficiently early to be clear of the house by the time he arrived at it. He had made just such an effort in dress as I would have expected of him, his linen being sweet and clean, his suit cut to display his person to its best advantage; and he confessed that, as she made her curtsy, he saw by the gleam in Marian's eyes that she did not entirely despise his charms.

A table had been set in the dressing-room next to our bedroom, and upon it some cold meats and salad and a fine bottle of French champagne set upon ice; of which they took a glass or two, which as I had supposed drew them to an ease in each other's company which enabled him to propose the removal of his jacket. This, his shirt being untied, gave an impression of informality almost to provocation, considering the manner in which a fine column of neck, joined to a promisingly full expanse of chest, was exposed; while Miss Marian had donned a dress which was unusually cut to display the swell of her breasts (fashion sadly now tending to the entire covering of the bust, a disappointment both to gentlemen and to those ladies possessing a figure worth complimenting; though of comfort to the flat-chested).

Will had to make most of the conversation, but happily was able to speak both of Bath society and of that of London of which he had some experience (having been employed for his lickerish powers by a number of the great ladies of town). Marian, he told me, listened with apparent interest; but he could not but be conscious that under cover of lowered eyes, or while he was paying some attention to his food, she was examining his person with more than a slight interest; and upon their ending their meal, when he stretched out a hand and took one of her own within it, she did not demur, but allowed it to lie there.

'My dear Miss Trillo,' he then said, 'we must now be frank. We both know for what purpose Mrs Nelham contrived this evening; but I must now offer to withdraw if for any reason you find my company repellent. I need not say that if such is the case my disappointment will be severe, for I must confess that your youth and beauty are such that I can scarcely command my heart, so quickly does it beat at the prospect of our friendship warming to something more intimate.' At this point he lifted her hand and placed it upon his breast (in which, he told me, his heart was indeed beating with more vigour than common – but less from excitement than from the apprehension of failure).

Marian's reaction was all that the most ardent suitor might expect upon a first trial. On feeling the beating of his heart, she gasped with pleasure, and slipping her hand within his shirt, placed her palm upon his skin, as though to apprehend more keenly his ardour, then making a brief excursion to feel beneath that palm the pleasant prospect of his manly bosom. This level plain was interrupted only by a pleasant pair of low convexities at the centre of which small nubs of flesh, surrounded by a slight mist of hair, indicated by their erection an excitement not far from her own. At this (he confessed) his caution failed him, and clasping her in his arms, he planted his mouth firmly upon her own, catching her lower lip between his and sucking upon it in a manner which might have been a matter of concern to a girl as innocent as this one; but, he said, she showed no iota of dismay, but on the contrary gave every sign of pleasure, to the extent of applying the whole of her body to his own.

This must have made her the more apprehensive of his passion; yet the most obvious sign of it dismayed her no more than the kiss which had been its first overt signal. Indeed by pressing the centre of her body to his own, she seemed to seek out and encourage a contact with it. In short, she was all liveliness, and rather than half-fainting in his arms and encouraging him to carry her into the bedroom, she released herself from his grasp and positively led him thither.

'Shall we rid ourselves of these unnecessary

encumbrances?' she then said, laying hold of his shirt with so eager a grasp that two of the buttons were immediately rent from it. It goes without saying that a mutual unveiling soon occurred; and his pleasure in the prospect then set before him was equalled only by the interest she showed in his figure. This, I had no reason to suppose was different from what I remembered.

Marian demanded (Will told me) a full survey of the land before beginning her exploration of it, encouraging him to turn this way and that before her. Passing her hands over his broad shoulders, she showed surprised delight at the manner in which his paps, erecting their tiny centres, mimicked the pleasure which had upraised her own, remarking with admiration upon the evident strength of the muscles of his arse, and laughing with unconcealed amusement and pleasure at the manner in which, by a contraction of his muscles, he was able to make them jump beneath her palms; and finally going down upon her knees the more completely to survey the ultimate scene of his masculinity. It was at this point (he said) that Will felt all his old apprehension returning; as her slender fingers travelled the length of his instrument, drawing the skin back frcm the bulb to contemplate with admiration the purplish head, weighing each cod in her palm as though testing the resilience and ripeness of plums, he was in a renewed agony of fear that on being called to exhibit the machinery in action, he would prove a sad disappointment to one whose expectation was clearly mounting by the minute.

Soon enough he felt that even another moment of such venereal caresses would result in a calamitous collapse; and lifting her in his arms, he conveyed her to the bed, and without a moment's pause – apprehending quite correctly that her interest would sufficiently have lubricated that orifice to which he now presented his pego – plunged within her. As he feared, the inundation was almost immediate – yet to his relief, the mere touch of his wand as he entered seemed to bring her to the peak of sensual gratification; while it seemed improbable, so lacking had he been in nursing her pleasure, the manner in which her loins lifted to his own, the flush which coloured her breasts and cheeks, the vigour with which her fingers clutched at his crupper all indicated such a height of gratification as a half hour's wooing is frequently too brief to achieve!

His relief and delight were equal in intensity: what he had feared had come about – but without any misfortune, for the lady was as satisfied as any whom he had spent a full hour in the gratification of; and Marian now showed her delight and gratitude by the many kisses which she showered upon his face, holding it between her hands and entwining her hair in his fingers. The very keenness of her pleasure rekindled his own, and to his astonishment (for his recent difficulties had communicated themselves also in an inability for speedy recovery) he was aware of a re-stirring at the root – which Marian also felt, for his instrument had remained sheathed in its delightful socket; and complimented him by her expression of astonishment – for, she said, she had understood that while ladies were instantaneously ready for the next engagement upon completion of the first, gentlemen needed time to re-prime their weapons.

Will's answer was a gentle movement of his arse which communicated to both parties, on this second course, a gradually increasing buoyancy of spirits; and upon this reaching a point at which my old friend was confident of his powers under no circumstances diminishing, he withdrew himself from his position between her thighs – a fact which so dismayed Marian that she did her best to restrain him; but in a moment was reconciled, for kneeling between her legs, he lifted her so that she too was upon her knees, but now stretched astride his own – a position inspiriting from the additional depth to which he could plumb her, and frcm the freedom it gave his hands to caress her breasts – a merely feathery touch upon the petulant tips of which was enough to make her positively squeal with pleasure – her back and the cheeks of her arse; all movements which she was quick to imitate, showing (he tells me) a quickness of wit which promised to make her a mistress worthy of any man's metal.

This time, Will was happy to note that he was able to restrain his coming off to a degree which in the past had been usual for him, but more recently had been shortened. His partner, he said, remained peculiarly sensitive in her reception of his toying, assuring me (in the expectation of my incredulity) that she reached an apogee of pleasure (signalled by those portents which he saw, heard and felt) no less than five times before he himself was again exhausted.

Will now felt that it was time for a rest, and reclining upon the bed drew Marian down beside him so that she lay within the crook of his arm – where she was content for half an hour to rest, until, while he was yet in a doze, she felt the need of a further exploration of the new country which had been opened to her. He woke suddenly to the sight of the globes of her bottom as she leaned over him in a position from which she had evidently for some time been applying herself to a more leisurely survey of the landscape – which, finding him waking, she now enlarged from the ocular to the oscular form (I mean, turning from the tribute of her eyes to those of her lips).

She was somewhat disappointed to find that the instrument of her impalement, reduced to an unimpressive miniature of its former grandeur, remained at first disconcertingly flaccid under the touch of her lips; then in her impatience ceased merely to press them upon it, but lifting it upon her palm, took it entirely within them, and sucking upon it with the enthusiasm of a hungry child for the teat, at the same time mumbling at his cods with her fingers, she succeeded in arousing it to the beginnings of a recovery.

The action of lowering her lips to such a degree elevated still further that delicious rump, and without difficulty Will drew one leg across his body so that they were head to tail, and by raising his own head was able to return her compliment in a manner which provoked an immediate orgasm so keen that for a moment she forgot herself, and positively clenched her teeth about his baton – the pain of which made him in turn, without intending it, bring his own teeth together upon an adjacent fold of flesh; which, far from distressing her, activated an even keener pleasure.

Her apologies, when she realised the discomfort she had inflicted upon him, were expressed with such tender and comforting gestures that it was soon forgotten; and while their expression of their pleasure in each other's bodies was now demonstrated in a more leisurely fashion (even by herself, who was nevertheless as quick to pleasure as ever) it was none the less excellent as to its quality; and to be brief about it, it was dawn before Will could persuade himself (even then against Marian's expressed wishes) to leave her room.

On his way, he was good enough to enter my own room, and to wake me by placing a hand upon my arm, eager to tell his story. Waking suddenly, and supposing in my half-awake state that I was in the company of a lover, I automatically reached towards him in a gesture which might under other circumstances have resulted (Will's blood always being easily heated) in an embrace; but on this occasion he was too milked of all pleasure to respond; and in any event I had by then fully awakened.

He looked so weary that I immediately invited him to bed – an invitation which, after a moment's fear that I was anticipating a service which in all probability he would not be able to perform, he accepted, collapsing with a sigh upon the counterpane and almost immediately falling into a deep sleep, from which he awoke only upon the appearance of my tray of chocolate, which he shared while retailing the incidents of the night – a narrative I have no doubt imperfectly replicated above.

His pleasure in his own part in the scene was clear; and I was happy also in having been the instrument of the recovery of his spirits: I had, as the reader will have apprehended, been confident that Miss Marian's emotions, running so high, would result in her being satisfied much more quickly than a female more familiar with the arts of love; and hoped that that speedy response would recover Will's confidence – which had been the case.

He was grateful, though I believe now apprehensive of the dual nature of the arrangement I had made – for I had been confident that in introducing her to the pleasures of the bed he would be at once spirited and kindly. He did, with some hesitation, offer the opinion that Miss Marian might be one of those ladies who, once aroused, would prove difficult to satisfy; her eagerness for the game and her quickness in learning its rules were, he said, uncommon even in his own considerable experience, and he was apprehensive that he might have set light to a fire which would prove difficult to control.

However, on the whole I was extremely happy at the result of my machinations; though there was a moment's consternation when Marian knocked upon my door and asked for an audience. It seeming at least possible that Will's presence in my bed so soon after he had left hers might lead to a misunderstanding, he took refuge beneath it; where, in contrast to the old saw that eavesdroppers hear no good of themselves, his face must have burned with a mixture of pleasure and embarrassment as Marian spent half an hour in continual praise of his arts as a lover, and the expressed wish that they might meet again at an early date.

Having sent her off to her *toilette* and dismissed Will with my thanks (he declined the payment I offered him as a professional gentleman, saying that the events of the night were sufficient reward in themselves), I was treated again to a long expression of Marian's delight in the new recreation to which I had introduced her, and her repeated implorings that Mr Langrish and she might soon be reunited. I explained however that the sea was full of fish, and that it was a mistake (as in feasting) to confine oneself to one particular species; suggesting that she should look about her for a while and consider a broader menu.

She was unconvinced, but for the moment reconciled.

It was within a few days that, as Andy has already related, we met his acquaintance Sir Stanley Curtis and were invited to a cricket match. My own experience of this game had been limited and, truth to tell, I was unenthusiastic about it as a way of spending leisure, there being little interest – as it seemed to me – in watching young men throwing balls about; there was also the problem that I found the phrases associated with the sport gave rise to inappropriate mirth, having on my single previous experience of the game (watching with my brother Frank at Alcovary) disgraced myself by falling into a fit of hysterics when, a large and vigorous player having been struck in an unfortunate area of his body, the umpire cried: 'No ball!'

However, the weather being fine, the prospect of a lazy afternoon lying in the sun did not seem entirely disagreeable, and so Marian, Andy, Ralph and myself made our way one afternoon to a small village just outside Bath, where twenty-two youths in white clothing were gravely discussing the conduct of the game. Sir Stanley's son Edward, our host for the afternoon, proved to be a youth in his early twenties, and I must admit an extremely handsome one, whose blond, almost yellow hair curled about a neck bronzed by the sun, and whose elegant figure was emphasised by the costume he wore – consisting of a loose white shirt and trousers, white dress being obligatory, it seems, for the game of cricket.

Marian and I spent most of the morning half-awake, a state of affairs unlikely to be discouraged by the agreeable luncheon which we then took; though the presence of young Mr Curtis at least to a degree engaged Marian's attention, for she seemed unable to take her eyes off him. In return, except during a brief absence when he must address his players, he was most attentive to her, selecting for her the best morsels of food, keeping her wine glass full, and not taking particular care to avoid brushing her naked arm with his own, or indeed to prevent his eyes falling upon her bosom – which, I must confess, by my advice was revealed rather more freely than present fashion dictates, by the simple stratagem of failing to connect a button with its hole at the neck of her dress.

The afternoon's portion of the match had scarcely begun when a hulking great villainous fellow from the opposing team was set to bowl balls at Edward, defending his wicket with what seemed a very small bat. The third ball sent by the blacksmith (as I believe he was) seemed to strike the batsman about the leg, for he clapped a hand to his thigh and fell to the ground in apparent agony; rose after a while, but was then helped from the field by two fellows. I must admit that both Marian and I leaped to our feet on observing the incident; she in sympathy with his pain, I with a more apprehensive fear – for the ball seemed to me to have struck very close to that area of the body designed as much for woman's pleasure as for man's, and I was aware not only of the extreme pain that might result, but of the inconvenience that could be concomitant.

Scarcely pausing to make our apologies to Andy and Ralph, we went to meet the young captain and – his fellows eager to return to the match, and dismissed by him – encouraged him to lean upon us as he limped to a small tent behind the main pavilion. There we laid him upon the ground, and set about persuading him to dismiss any embarrassment and remove his trousers in order that his injury might be examined. I offered to prevail upon Marian to leave the tent, should he be flustered by her presence; but with remarkably good sense in one so young, he declined to allow bashfulness to stand in the way of a practical care for his injury, and raising his bottom from the ground enabled us to draw his trousers from him, revealing that he was wearing those underdrawers which had relatively recently been introduced from the continent, and were all the thing with the young blades.

Handsome though they might be, and convenient in that young men may strip to them for boxing or fencing, when they offer greater freedom of movement, they did – reaching almost to the knee – make it impossible to discover whether the blow he had suffered was a severe one; and undoing the strings which confined the drawers at the waist, with his aid I was able next to remove them, revealing upon the upper thigh almost at the bifurcation of the limbs, an already livid bruise at whose black centre was a distressing and angry smudge of livid colour.

The slightest touch upon it bringing forth an

indrawn breath of pain, I took from a hamper which lay handy some butter, and applying it to the palm of my hand, laid this as gently as possible to the bruise, moving my palm in a circular manner about the area. This immediately, from his expression, brought relief; but so strong is the rude instinct of young men that it soon did more. I was unfortunately unable to attend to the sore spot without my fingers brushing against the adjacent bollocks; whereat a distinct stirring took place in the instrument above, though by applying a slightly greater pressure to the painful area I was able to prevent any further development.

After a while, 'I hope, my dear ma'am, that your kindness is not exhausting you,' he said.

'Oh, yes, Sophie!' said Marian; 'do let me help!' Buttering a palm, she laid it upon his thigh – though upon the uninjured one. On my drawing attention to this, she nodded thoughtfully, and by the application of an elbow dislodged me from my position and took my place.

I was too amused to be annoyed; and watched with some admiration (I must confess) as she tended the injured spot. In her innocence, however, she was not aware – I suppose – of the nearness with which pain and pleasure are allied, and did not take such care as I had employed to avoid brushing those accoutrements whose sensitivity resulted in the former giving way to the latter. Indeed, far from avoiding them, she unconsciously approached them more nearly, slipping her palm as it circled the bruise ever wider, so that it now passed to the inside of the thigh, the fingertips moving between it and the cods, and the back of her hand necessarily brushing the young man's blow stick, not yet erect but somewhat swelled, and growing by the moment larger.

This seemed to signal to Marian a decrease of distress, and no doubt in order to encourage the recovery, she began to allow herself more lenity; and with the pretence of making it easier to attend to the wounded area, placed her other hand upon Edward's male equipment and eased it to one side. The grimace which passed over the young man's face was to me less indicative of agony than of ecstasy, and indeed somewhat to her surprise Marian soon found that her left hand was of insufficient dimensions to conceal an instrument whose head now forced its way from beneath it and seemed to wink at us.

Edward's eye now catching my own bore an expression unmistakable in imploring me to allow him the convenience of a private consultation with Marian; and I noticed indeed what had previously been unseen by me – the fact that his right hand had disappeared under her skirt, and seemed likely to be engaging in the treatment there of some inexpressible ailment of her own.

I rose to my feet, I really believe unnoticed by Marian, and slipped from the tent; forgetting however my reticule, and returning for it found that my young friend had already discovered how to ride a man with the same confidence (I assumed) that she would ride a horse, for though in her hurry she had omitted to remove her clothing, the posture she had adopted was certainly one which would bring the elements necessary to coition into juxtaposition, while the expression upon Edward's face was indicative of a pleasure sufficient to make him forget, for the time, his injury.

I remained on guard outside the tent for half an hour, during which time no one approached, and only the sound of bat striking ball was to be heard. (I closed my ears to sounds indicative of another game being played in the near vicinity.) I then grew somewhat bored, and, assuming that the couple would by now have completed their experiments, with a loud cough re-entered the tent. I need not have bothered to announce my entry, however, for they were still in an enthusiastic coitus which precluded them from noting any less severe disturbance than a volcanic eruption of peculiar force. They had now – with an alarming lack of caution – entirely removed their clothing, and the view was one of Master Edward's smooth buttocks dancing between his mistress's knees. Believing ever that there are times when a lack of ceremony is necessary, I approached and gave his inspirited arse a smack with my hand, the sudden shock of which (as I had guessed it might) startled the lover sufficiently to trigger an immediate conclusion to the act. His woeful face as it was turned towards me was sufficiently amusing to make it difficult to refrain from smiling; but I apologised, saying only that it appeared to me that the cricket game was coming to an end, and that they had better clothe themselves if there was not to be a scene embarrassing to my friend if not to Mr Curtis.

The latter had the grace to take my point; and, I was happy to see, was quick to help Marian to her feet and into her clothes, before drawing on his own. He then announced that he would be happy to entertain us to supper. At his home, I asked? But would that not be an inconvenience to his father? No, for the latter was away from the city on business. Nevertheless, a party having been organised at Sir Stanley's house for the winning team (whichever that might be), we would be better at an hostelry; and in short, taking us to where a small curricle stood with a pair of spirited horses, he whisked us off to the Green Man upon the outskirts of the city, where he was so respectfully and readily greeted that I could not help but suspect that this was a common place of assignation with him – an opinion confirmed by my overhearing the landlord ask (with something of a leering look towards us) whether Mr Curtis would be requiring his usual room for the night.

However, I could have no complaint of the meal we were given, the roast beef being excellent and the claret first-rate. Neither was Edward backward in paying us all the polite attention any female guest might expect, nor – apart from the disappearance from time to time of one hand beneath the table in a position approximate to Marian's thigh – was there any undue sign of lasciviousness; though from her glances she would not have disapproved had there been such.

At last, there was some hemming and hawing about its perhaps being time for us to withdraw – Edward, I was sure, hoping that by some pretext he could keep Marian in that place for longer, if not indeed for the night. However, on my insisting that the young lady should not be deprived of the benefits of restful sleep, he reluctantly paid the bill and escorted us once more to the curricle, which he then whipped up; and passing through the elegant centre of the city, we came to the Circle, and to number twenty-four, which was Sir Stanley's house. On Edward's inviting us to take a final glass with him, we entered, and heard a subdued noise of conversation. 'Well!' he said, 'the party is not yet quite over.' Opening a door he revealed a room in which were the ruins of what had clearly been an extensive buffet, and where a scene of only moderate debauchery was in progress. Fragments of food lay upon the table, and plates and glasses were strewn about the room – which otherwise was occupied by a number of young gentlemen, many of whom I recognised as members of Edward's team of cricketers. Two of them were yet more familiar, as being my friend Andy and his charge, young Ralph – the latter engaged in an amorous embrace with a young lady whose clothing was as vestigial as that of everyone else in the room, a number being bollock naked, and others with their limbs only imperfectly concealed.

My immediate thought was for young Marian: what view would she take of a scene so lascivious? I need not have worried on the score of her taking offence, for a single glance at her face showed it enlivened by a smile, and if also coloured by a blush, by one as much an advertisement of admiration as of any other emotion.

She immediately brushed past me and planted a kiss upon her brother's forehead, at the same time reaching down to pat upon the rump the young lady seated across his knee. But to my surprise, and the greater surprise (and, I suspected, something to the distress) of Edward Curtis, she then in a moment divested herself of the clothing which no doubt he had hoped to be the one to be permitted to remove, and walking about the room positively advertised herself to the young gentlemen there – most of whom were, through liquor and exhaustion, in no condition to take advantage of even so excellent an offer.

One, however, did rouse himself sufficiently to take her hand and plant a kiss upon it; whereat she immediately knelt at his side, and using the same pleasant caresses as she had employed with Edward, soon roused him to such an extent that she was able to bestride him; at which sight Edward, understandably, left the room.

Andy had meanwhile donned his trousers and shirt, and was at my side. Drawing him from the room, I announced that I was of the opinion that trouble was in store should we not be able to instil in young madam some rather more respectable behaviour. But, he said unkindly, this was my responsibility; I had introduced her to pleasure – now I must convince her that it should be governed. And he returned to the room in hopes of persuading Ralph that it was time to return to Pulteney Street. Meanwhile, I must wait until madam had finished her bout; and to do so, retired to a room at the other side of the hallway, where I found young Edward, sadly regarding the wallpaper.

I commiserated with him, doing my best to explain the situation; Marian had not, I was sure, intended an insult to him – much less to his powers as a lover (which had clearly been his first belief). No one, I opined, could consider him as anything but a young man of considerable powers – and indeed, I could not but envy my friend . . .

Was that perfectly so? he enquired, getting to his feet. And upon my confirming it, planted a grateful kiss upon my lips, the embrace becoming warmer upon my apprehension of his vigorous body against my own.

Not to be tedious in the description, he was soon proving to me that our mutual young friend had not exhausted those powers which enabled him to compliment a beautiful woman; nor, I must confess, did I repine at his approaches, having myself been somewhat warmed by the events of the day, and possessed of the knowledge of my present lack of a lover, was only too happy to make him free of my person. This offer he was generous enough to accept, to compliment, to pleasure, and finally to satisfy; his enjoyment not being spoiled – though perhaps very slightly mitigated – by the sudden appearance in the doorway of Marian, just in time to witness the completion of our enjoyment. She applauded this scene with a little jump of pleasure, proving what I had suspected – that jealousy was something she had yet to learn, believing (and may it remain an unshakeable conviction with her) that a loving congress is to be enjoyed in the same manner as a good meal or a good bottle. I must nevertheless talk with her about this matter – a sufficient number of people not being of her conviction to make it in some circumstances a danger.

Chapter Five

The Adventures of Andy

My intention being to introduce young Ralph to every polite entertainment which might fall in the way of a young gentleman of fashion, I took two tickets for a recital of piano music to be given at the Assembly Rooms by the sensation of the season, Mademoiselle Francine Fraudet, a young lady whose talents were celebrated throughout her native country of France, who had played in London, and now undertook an engagement in Bath.

Ralph was by no means devoid of interest in the arts, and was himself no mean performer upon the pianoforte (of which his uncle possessed a fine early example); he was entirely happy to attend with me a concert whose programme promised to be of interest, including as it did, besides music by J. S. Bach, Jean Philippe Rameau and Tommaso Albinoni, a number of modern works by Franz Peter Schubert, an Austrian composer, by Carl Maria Ernst von Weber, a German, and (in compliment to the pianist's hosts) by William Shield, Henry Ripley Bishop and François Cramer, the latter recently appointed Master of the King's Music.

Upon our arriving at the rooms, Ralph was particularly interested to examine Mlle Fraudet's instrument, which he explained was an admirable example of the 'portable grand' piano, framed in iron, and evidently made in the factory of John Isaac Hawkins (the inventor of the ever-pointed pencil). It seemed to me almost to resemble an encoffined harp, for the case was turned upon its end so that the strings extended to the floor, the keyboard being at right angles to it. My interest being somewhat less technical than Frank's, however, I must confess that my thoughts somewhat strayed as he gave me his lecture on the development of the instrument, there being in our vicinity a number of the most beautiful ladies of Bath. Having lived as an eunuch since we had arrived in the city – with the single example of the connection I had made at Edward Curtis's cricketing reception – my spirits were somewhat raised in the presence of so many naked arms and shoulders, and the promise of more delicacies unfortunately concealed beneath the dresses of the female part of the audience.

My reverie, which had gone unnoticed by Ralph (so considerable was his interest in the pianoforte) was disturbed by the entrance of Mlle Fraudet, who, having been greeted with considerable applause, now took her seat at the instrument and began to play. My pleasure in music is considerable, and indeed I am a not untalented guitarist; but I must confess that upon this occasion my attention was soon concentrated on the pianist's person rather than either her performance or her programme. She was an enchanting young woman of perhaps six-or seven-and-twenty, with raven hair which fell over her shoulders, half shading flesh which was almost opalescent in its whiteness. Her expression was grave, as she concentrated upon her music-making; her eyebrows, splendidly curved and plucked to a slender line, were set above dark eyes the pupils of which seemed extraordinarily large, and which when they caught the light of the candle set by her instrument seemed of a depth sufficient to swim in. Her lips were full and sensual, and a slight smile from time to time curved about them as she brought off some passage to her own satisfaction.

She wore a dress which was somewhat out of the fashion, being cut close to her figure – presumably in order that folds of clothing should not encumber her as she sat; made of some light material, it clung to her limbs, embracing the curve of a breast fuller than would have been admired by many men, but to me in excellent proportion with the rest of her body; then marking the line from waist to ankle along limbs which must surely be most handsomely shaped. Her arms were bare, and the sensitive and graceful way in which her hands rose and fell at the keyboard, turning at the wrist with the most delicate movement, could not but suggest that their employment in a more personal context would be extremely grateful to the fortunate recipient of her attentions.

Ralph meanwhile was entranced by the performance of the music itself, almost (as it seemed) failing to breathe for fear of missing a period; and from time to time whispering his admiration at my ear.

At the end of the concert I suggested to him that we might pay our respects to the lady – something regularly done in London, but a compliment not so often paid in the provinces, where after a performance players both of the stage and of the recital room are left too often to themselves, applause soon fading in their lonely ears. And indeed, we found Mlle Fraudet sitting solitary in a room behind the stage, only too pleased to receive our homage, which on Ralph's part was concentrated on her musical powers, while I have no doubt that my eyes spelt out a more personal admiration, and by the hints every gentleman has at command (as, holding her fingers a second longer in my own than might have been expected; or, holding her eyes with mine; or, taking care that my foot should accidentally fall into contact with her own) I made it clear, as I believed, that she was to me as admirable as the music she had performed to such perfection. I flattered myself that the message had been clearly received, for while she was entirely polite in receiving Ralph's homage, her eyes when they caught my own seemed to send out flickers both of desire and of invitation.

After ten minutes, we made our excuses and left; but as we walked down the corridor, we heard in a moment footsteps pursuing us, and the elderly maid we had seen preparing the pianist's day clothes in a corner of the room came trotting after us carrying a note. I held out my hand for it, but, after a moment's confusion, to my chagrin she pressed it into Ralph's hand. Upon opening it, it was found merely to give the name of the best hotel in Bath, the number of a room, and symbols marking the hour of ten o'clock. I must confess to considerable envy of my young friend – but the message intensely surprised him. Was it possible, he asked, that, impressed perhaps by his knowledge of music, she wished to consult him upon the composition of her programme? Surely no respectable female would make so overt an approach to an unknown gentleman?

The former was almost certainly not the case, I opined; he must realise that performers travelling the continent from one place to another, alone except for a companion of the same sex (who being most frequently a servant was out of the question) were often extremely lonely, and that it was by no means uncommon for them to solicit liaisons – indeed, they were a capital prospect for the single gentleman in search of a temporary engagement of the amorous sort.

What was he to do? Ralph asked. Why, respond to the invitation with all the ardour expected of him, was my reply; to which idea he was certainly, when the first shock of it had passed, by no means opposed, and indeed became quite cheerful at the prospect – as well he might.

It being now almost nine o'clock, we repaired to the hotel in question, and bespoke there a light supper; and as we were concluding it, saw the lady and her maid pass through the main door and up the staircase, at which Ralph seemed to me to become somewhat nervous. On my questioning him he admitted that he felt a considerable disproportion between the engagement between himself and the two previous females whose company he had enjoyed in the city, and an invitation to visit a woman of such charm and personality as Mlle Fraudet. I pointed out to him, however, that it was she who had made the appointment, and that he, with youth and a handsome appearance on his side, should merely be happy at the prospect before him.

Taking a final glass of brandy, he could muster no contradiction of my view; and on the clock in the dining-room striking the hour, took his leave and went upstairs. I remained, taking another glass of wine; in a somewhat melancholy frame of mind, I must confess. Were the years beginning to take a toll? Separated by less than a decade, was Ralph now to gain, as a matter of course, the prizes which would formerly naturally have fallen to me?

I was feeling, I confess, extremely sorry for myself; and had almost resolved upon repairing to some brothel (of which establishments Bath had several superior examples) when I was conscious of a female making her way towards me, and recognised Mademoiselle's maid. For a moment I thought that she had perhaps been dispatched as a consolation prize: but then, in a mixture of bad English and imperfectly understandable French, she began gabbling some message at me. Making her sit down (though with difficulty) and calming her, I eventually learned the import of her message: that she had answered the door to Ralph, who had strode past her and into the inner room where Mlle Fraudet was – and that she, Claudette, the maid, had been unable to stop him.

But why should she wish to do so? I asked.

Because, Claudette tearfully confessed, she had made a mistake – her mistress's note had been meant not for Ralph, but for myself; and what was she to do?

I hesitated only for a moment. Ralph, I explained, was in my care; it would be perfectly proper for me to inform him of the error, should the lady for any reason decline to do so; and the more quickly I substituted my presence for his own, the less embarrassing the whole matter would be for those most intimately concerned.

On my entering the outer room of the lady's apartment, I found it empty; an inner door was ajar, but I could hear no sound of conversation, and approaching it as silently as possible, applied my eye to the crack in the door. Through this, I saw the unexpected sight of the pianist, less formally clad than at her concert – indeed, to be frank, not clothed at all – playing a solo upon the body of my young friend, those susceptive fingers thrumming upon his chest and thighs with an enviable lightness of touch, pausing from time to time to pay passing attention to one special major key whose quivering seemed to indicate that the right chords were being struck – indeed to such an extent that the piece might be over before either of them were ready to reach the closing bars.

It seemed to me improper to interrupt them, and I turned to leave; but unfortunately collided with Claudette, who in following had approached too near to me, and in the confusion lost my footing and fell into the bedroom. My embarrassment, as might be expected, was considerable; but Ralph, with that good nature and humour for which the boy will ever be dear to me, rose from his recumbent position and came to my aid, pulling me to my feet and dusting me down – while the lady, far from showing either discomposure or anger, on the contrary fell into a fit of laughter.

This slightly irritated me, I must confess; through her maid's mistake I had been put in a most humiliating position. However, on seeing a shadow of anger pass over my face, she herself now rose, and approaching me dropped a curtsy (a most charming sight), and offering me her hand (which I kissed) begged me not to be angry.

'My dear monsieur,' she said, in the prettiest imaginable of accents, 'do not repine that I should so speedily have adopted the substitute whom you sent to my bed. One must always be free to accept or to reject the advances of a lover; and this charming young gentleman (she bowed to Ralph) was—'

But I must interrupt her.

'Mademoiselle,' I said, 'you wrong me. I would never have dreamed of rejecting an invitation from one so beautiful. The mistake was another's. But the accident was clearly insignificant. It is my present interruption which has put a period to your pleasure, and I will happily now withdraw—'

'No, don't do that!' said Ralph, who had been following the conversation with attention; 'it is I who should withdraw!' – and crestfallen in more than a single way, he bent to begin recovering his clothes, which were scattered about the floor in a manner which told of some haste in their disposal.

'Neither need withdraw,' said the lady, taking him by one arm and myself by another.

It is the case, then, reader, that I shortly found myself, clad as my mother first saw me, upon one side of Mlle Fraudet, while my young friend lay upon the other; the lady demonstrating the remarkable manual dexterity which she commanded by moving the fingers of each hand about our persons in a manner entirely independent of each other.

That her person was as beautiful as I had conjectured might go without saying; yet I will still pronounce the fact. It was true that her breasts were indeed larger than would commend them to some tastes; yet they were perfectly formed – and changed form in the most delightful fashion as she adopted the various postures of amorous play, adopting the shape perhaps of bells, or even of ripe pears hanging upon a bough, so that it was impossible not to take one of their nipples from time to time into one's mouth, so entrancingly appetising did they appear. The rest of her body was as has been already described; plump without any hint of corpulence, even about the hips, which nevertheless were full enough to be entirely indicative of femininity; and between her thighs lay another female attribute, unquestionable in sex and charming in appearance.

Those to whom circumstance has never afforded the experience of sharing a lady with another man may suppose that such a situation will invariably lead to tears; and this may be so when the first is a rival for the lady's favours, is envious of the powers of the second, or for some other reason is at odds with him. Ralph however was as conscious of his friendship to me as I was of mine to him, while the lady – although her feelings to me were such that I had been her first choice as a night companion (it was my additional years which chiefly commended me, or so I later understood) clearly bore no resentment towards him; we therefore set about pleasuring ourselves with the best will in the world, and accomplished it without difficulty. I will not say that the situation did not provoke me to display, in Ralph's presence, some of that superior adeptness in love-making which must naturally be the product of my additional years of experience; while the lady proved sufficiently knowing to match trick with trick; but I believe she apprehended that Ralph's innocence was matched by his enthusiasm, for she allowed him every familiarity, and did not permit herself to be offended by the closeness with which he observed our own behaviour – indeed was at pains so to place her body that he could see clearly the manner in which we had connection (which included a number of those attitudes he had copied from Dr Plumtre's manuscript).

He had no notion, I believe, of it being possible for Mademoiselle to please us both simultaneously, except perhaps by oral meals (in the situation in which he had found himself placed at Edward Curtis's reception) and on her turning him upon his back and lowering herself upon him, he looked at me almost with pity; but she winked at me and lifted her rump slightly – upon which, entirely apprehending her purpose, I freely moistened my ready riding-muscle and applied it to that fissure which, giving to a man a pleasure only secondary to the primal connection, affords to some ladies an additional titillation unequalled in its effect.

That this form of congress was not uncommon with her was signalled by my ease of entry (the French, as I believe, regarding this form of congress as almost an everyday matter); but that Ralph was surprised at it was plain, for at first he knew not what was happening – and then on feeling the juxtaposition of my cock to his own, separated as they were merely by a tissue of flesh, by inserting his hand between Mademoiselle's thighs discovered how things lay – and seeing from her expression, which was of a pleasure almost to fainting, grinned broadly and relaxed; when my careful movements, encouraged by her own, provoked that degree of enjoyment which inevitably culminated in a mutual threefold pleasure.

That we spent more time, during the following hours, in making ourselves acquainted with each other's tastes, needs no rehearsal; by morning we were so replete with sensual satisfaction that I was content to lie back half-asleep while Ralph and Francine discussed musical matters, and he again complimented her upon her performance upon the platform.

'I sall play happier tonight,' she said in her very attractive mock-English, 'in resulting of our *jouissance*,' and went on to admit that corporeal pleasure invariably had an enlivening effect upon her playing; and upon Ralph's retiring for a moment to supply a need of nature, confessed to me that upon contemplating a performance one of her prerequisites was, if possible, to form a *liaison* with a gentleman who could satisfy her bodily needs – though preferably upon her leaving the platform after the performance; the prospect of a performance not either prefaced by a satisfactory connection or with such a pleasure in prospect would render her execution of a programme dry and sterile, *sans la passion propre*, as she put it.

She therefore persuaded me to attend her at the concert hall on the three following evenings immediately after her performance; when I invariably found her in a state of nature, her evening clothing being carefully folded by Claudette, and reclining upon a sofa which she had commissioned from the management, which while not of enormous size was perfectly capable of holding the two of us, though it was necessary to eschew any remarkable feats of love-making for fear of throwing ourselves to the floor.

On the last evening, having engaged for some time in a most feverish series of embraces, I took the liberty of enquiring how it was that the requirements of her art demanded the promise of a concomitant act of passion in order that an audience should be assured of the perfect performance of a concert.

'The connection,' she told me, 'was made in my youth – not my extreme youth, when from the age of about three I am told I showed remarkable promise as a young musician, so that I was set to learning first the flute and then the piano from that early age; but from the time when I was fifteen and my parents engaged a teacher to tutor me for some hours every day in the pianoforte.

'My father,' she went on to explain, 'was a banker in Lyons, a city of considerable wealth, but one in which the arts were not cultivated with any real attention, so that upon the organist of the Church of St Pierre – an elderly gentleman who until that time had been my musical mentor – informing my father that I not only required but deserved further musical education, he sent to his friend the Marquise de St Jacques, at the Vendôme, who recommended a teacher who, she said, would be entirely suited to educating a young lady in musical art. I have confirmed since that the Marquise and my father had been acquainted from an early age, and that their relationship was a close one (I speak of the time before my father had met my sainted mother); and there can be little doubt that she, a lady of great intelligence, beauty and acumen, had it in mind that it was time for a provincial girl to be introduced not only to the great composers and their works, but to the art of living. She may also have wished to rid herself of a young man who was too much engaging her own emotions. But whatever the explanation, the gentleman who arrived at our house one spring morning was a considerable improvement (to my mind) on eighty-four-year-old M. Cassilot, the organist.

'Jean Villot was tall, slim, dark and nineteen years of age – close enough to my own years for us to be in instant *rapport*, yet distant enough for me to respect him as representative of a world of which as yet I knew nothing: viz., the world of fashion and of sophistication. He was himself a brilliant pianist, and startled me immediately by the performance of music by living composers of whom I had never heard, and whose discords, while they excited me, alarmed and discomfited my parents, who considered these pieces unfit for the human ear and prohibited M. Villot from playing them in public.

'However, I must confess immediately that it was his personality and presence as much as his musicality which captivated me. With his elegant manners and carriage, he was very different from the *jeunesse dorée* of Lyons, and my attitude to the sex changed overnight. I will not say that I had been entirely uninterested by the young men around me; having no brothers, I was curious enough to regard with some attention those whom I met – but these were very few, and seemed rough and unpleasant, staring at me with what seemed an undue insolence, and often retiring to exchange between themselves jokes which, while I could not hear them, from the coarse laughter they provoked must necessarily be rude and offensive to female ears.

'As to the most significant difference between the sexes, will it be believed that I had reached the age of fifteen without being aware in the least of what it consisted? My mother was so shy that it remains a mystery to me how I was conceived; she never spoke to me of the relations between men and women, except to enjoin me to keep as much distance between myself and any male person as could be contrived; while for my unmusical education I was put in the care of the local priest, an elderly gentleman of unprepossessing appearance and great sanctity, who went so far as to cut from the Bible with a scissors any allusion to procreation (the Old Testament as a result being rather severely truncated), and when I enquired what was meant by the virgin birth, remarked that this was an ecclesiastical mystery too complex for the female mind to comprehend.

'Imagine so innocent a girl suddenly thrust into the presence of an elegant and worldly young man! My mother almost fainted away on first seeing him; my father, however, though extremely protective of me, made no objection to M. Villot, and went so far as to instruct the household that on no account should our lessons be interrupted, even for the most urgent reasons.

'My new tutor treated me with the utmost respect, impressed by my talent, which included the ability to play even the most difficult piece of music immediately, at sight; but after a week or so, it was clear even to my innocent eye that he had become as interested in myself as in my performances at the keyboard. This was perhaps not surprising, for although I cannot say it without perhaps the appearance of an indecent self-regard, I was a handsome creature, well-formed and with natural grace, and moreover, living in the provinces, was dressed in the manner of a somewhat earlier generation – that is, in loose-flowing gowns which often revealed more of my body than might be considered proper in the presence of a susceptible young man. Added to this, my very innocence precluded me from adopting that attitude of reticence or modesty which would have been more decent, if less interesting to him; while not purposely exhibiting my breasts or lower limbs, I took no care to conceal them; and should my gown, through my leaning forward, fall away and thus reveal the greater part of my bosom, or through some accident slip from my thigh, I did not even take care to turn away.

'This, as of course I now realise, but then was ignorant of, was tinder to a spirited young fellow – which M. Villot certainly was; and it is a wonder to me that he was so long able to maintain a distance, or that rather than throwing me to the carpet and ravishing me upon the spot, he should have approached me so tenderly. Even now, I remember keenly the first occasion on which he touched me. I had through improper teaching formed the habit of staring down at the keyboard while playing, and had proved unable to avert my eyes; so that M. Villot was forced to help by placing the back of his left hand under my chin, and gently holding it up. This still did not prevent my attempting to lower my head, at which he placed the fingers of his right hand about the nape of my neck, in order the better to support my head in the proper position.

'It was the first time that I had ever been touched in a familiar way by the hands of a gentleman; and to my amazement a sort of electric current seemed to spring from them, and pass from my neck down my entire body, seeming to culminate at a point below my stomach. I began, indeed, to shake; at which M. Villot became concerned, and in a natural reaction let go of my head, placing his right arm about my shoulders and instinctively (I do believe) rather than with any carnal purpose allowed his left hand to fall upon my breast where, my gown as I have explained being a loose one, it met with bare flesh.

If his first touch had somewhat alarmed me, his second threw me almost into an hysteria of pleasure – but one which I knew not how to satisfy; and my panting and shaking now so alarmed him that to my regret he let me go altogether, and leading me to a couch, left the room, returning with a servant and some cold water, which eventually recovered me.

During the night which followed, I lay awake in my bed, recapitulating again and again the events which had so amazed me; and, nature being so excellent a teacher, by morning had reached the conclusion that the only way in which I could come at a solution to my curiosity as to the nature of my disturbance was to provoke a similar incident.

'On the following day, M. Villot was his usual elegant, civilised and amusing self – while expressing concern for my health. Assuring him that I was well, I played my pieces with even more than usual brilliance – and, upon his applauding and crying *Bravo!*, I reached out, took his hand, and laid it upon my bosom, within my dress. Nature being entirely in command, my body reacted to his touch in a manner of which I was unconscious, and my tits stood proud, in a manner only hitherto provoked by the application of cold water – suggesting to him, no doubt, even a conscious longing for attentions the nature of which I in fact was unaware of.

'He had, as I think I have hinted, a reticence, gentleness and experience quite beyond his years (the Marquise de St Jacques, if I am correct in my supposition, had taught him well), and showed the most delicate care in meeting my approaches – now carefully lifting my skirt and placing his other hand upon my thigh, which he stroked with a tender concern, each stroke of his palm proceeding a little further north, until it reached that area the mere suggestion of an approach to which laid me once more upon the edge of that hysteria which the previous day's much less adventurous stimulation had provoked.

'Meanwhile, I merely sat upon the piano stool, accepting his caresses, and knowing not how to return them. Apprehending that my inaction proceeded from ignorance rather than lack of interest, he took my face between his palms, and leaning forward, kissed me upon the lips. My parents had of course kissed me before, but scarcely to the same effect; for he drew my lower lip between his own, so that I could feel the prickles of his slight moustache; and, moving his lips gently upon mine, then to my delighted astonishment inserted his tongue into my mouth, when on its meeting my own, just such another electric shock as had previously excited me was again provoked.

'As if this were not enough, he now took my hand and gently laid it upon his thigh; when what could I do but imitate his own action? – eventually finding the progress of my palm halted by a limber obstruction in a shape not unlike that of a bread roll, and of about the same size; yet upon my pressing it, it obviously possessed no crust, for although to an extent hard, it gave way slightly under the pressure of my fingers – at which M. Villot winced slightly, startling me into removing my fingers.

'He now got to his feet, an action which I imitated; and lifting his hands to my shoulders, loosened my dress so that it fell down my body to the ground – at which he drew in his breath in so feverish a manner that I feared for a moment he had caught the sickness which had previously disabled me; but happily he recovered, and bending forward, placed his lips in turn upon the tips of each breast. But now, in one movement, he tore the shirt from his body. What this revealed was no surprise to me, for I had often seen the workmen about my father's estate stripped of their shirts when the time of the vine harvest came. His body, however, was almost entirely white and smooth, only a few hairs set abut his paps, the pink shade of which was startling against the white skin. It was an entrancing view, which brought me yet further along the road of discovery down which I was so happy to progress. On his going further, and removing his breeches, he revealed a new turn of that road, and a landscape entirely foreign to me.

'What, you may ask, did I expect? The answer must be that I expected nothing; or if anything, a body somewhat like my own – for you must remember that I had had no information at all upon the subject either of the physique of gentlemen or of the means of the procreation of the species. The object which I had felt was now revealed as a sort of tubular construction or tower of flesh, of the thickness almost of my wrist, which stood at an angle which almost laid it upright against M. Villot's belly. (This, upon my thinking the matter over, later, must explain how it could be concealed by his dress; it must usually lie, I thought, up against his belly in just this manner, there disguised by the lower part of his waistcoat – for, for some time, it was my illusion that the instrument was always in a state of uprightness; something of which I was disabused in due course, under somewhat disappointing circumstances.)

'What could be the purpose of this surprising object? That it was the visible sign of some kind of excitement was clear, for with an emotion of its own it almost quivered, while from a small aperture not unlike an eye, set in the centre of a bulbous tip, a tiny tear fell. Almost instinctively, I reached out to touch it – but then drew back; at which my teacher took my hand and placed it upon this strange limb. It was warm, almost hot, to the touch, and on my moving my fingers the skin which clad it moved also, and I felt beneath it what almost seemed a set of miniature ribs. M. Villot was clearly not unaffected by my exploration, gasping with what seemed pleasure as I attempted to discover more clearly in what this manifestation consisted.

'My curiosity was now so great that I could not resist falling to my knees, the more closely to examine the phenomenon; and on doing so, saw that at its base there hung a small bag, closely drawn up, within which (on my placing my hand upon it) could be felt two spheres of slightly disparate size, one hung slightly higher than the other; these seemed, on my exploring further, to be attached to the gentleman's body by strings – but at this point my exploration clearly became somewhat painful, for M. Villot reached down and removed my hand, instead now taking his tool (as I learned to call it) in his hand and seeming to offer it to my lips, whereat in imitation of his earlier action I gently kissed it; an action which was greatly appreciated, for with a gentle pressure it nudged at my lips until I was forced (with what pleasure it would have embarrassed me to admit!) to open them, whereon it nestled between them, and I found myself, in the most natural way imaginable, sucking gently upon it.

'That this was pleasant to us both goes without saying; but to my disappointment M. Villot too soon raised me to my feet and led me to the couch, where he stretched me out and kneeling at my side began to kiss first my lips, then my shoulders, my breasts, my sides, my thighs, taking between his lips my fingers and even my toes, so that in a short time my entire body was aflush with pleasure; though when I attempted to reach between his own thighs, he moved away (no doubt fearful of too early a culmination), and all I could do was stroke his shoulders, back, thighs and the cheeks of his arse, which were as smooth as my own, but to my amusement smaller and rounder, while when I passed my fingers between them, I felt about the bag which hung between them a little cluster of hair which sprang like wire beneath my touch.

'When this had continued for some time, M. Villot permitted himself, after kissing my belly and exploring the dint of my navel, to run his lively, pointed tongue downwards, and gently parting my thighs with his hands, to approach that part of me previously untouched by anyone other than myself. Like every young girl, I had of course been aware that some pleasure was to be gained from this area; but never had that pleasure been so obvious, so keen, so exciting as upon the first approach of his lips, and when, parting the folds of skin there, he enabled his tongue to touch what seemed the very centre of it, I actually for a moment lost consciousness.

'That a young man in his position should be courteous enough to refrain from an immediate rape is truly remarkable; nevertheless, it was the case – and I have never ceased to celebrate my good fortune in being introduced to the pleasures of love by one so considerate! Upon its being clear that my sickness was merely an excess of pleasure, he continued, until (I suppose) he realised from the liquefaction which generously occurred that a more intimate approach would be without pain, and upon that point knelt upon the couch between my legs, and spitting upon his hand lubricated his tool generously before presenting its head at that door the lock of which had previously remained untried.

'It was my good fortune that, while perfectly adequate to its purpose, his instrument was by no means a vast one; and also that so thorough had been his preparation of the ground, so well had he oiled the wards, that the insertion and turning of the key was almost entirely comfortable – the bulbous tip passing into my body with much more pleasure than pain – indeed, so relaxed was I that even the sharp discomfort consequent upon his breaking the barrier which separates virginity from experience was outweighed by the joy conveyed by that movement, at first gentle, with which he moved his tool within its socket. The pleasure was so keen indeed that I could not have too much of it; and upon feeling the manner in which I instinctively lifted my body to meet his own, he increased the rhythm of his movements until he was positively thrusting himself into me; whereupon a great wave mounted and drowned me, so that I fell into the very depths of liquid delight, this time remaining unconscious for perhaps half a minute and recovering to find him relaxed and supine, though preventing his weight from smothering me by reclining upon his elbows, placed at each side of my body.

'The tender kiss with which he greeted my return to life signalled his complete satisfaction. I, too, was satisfied; though upon his attempting to withdraw, did my best to restrain him between my thighs. This, however, he argued against; for, he said, upon first introduction to that activity which had just been concluded, it was wise for a young lady to be sparing if she was not to suffer injury through her own experience. Reluctantly, I allowed him to leave; whereupon he produced a handkerchief and wiped first my body and then his own, showing me with a smile a small spot of blood which decorated it, and which, he said, was the signal that I had truly become a woman.

'That I concealed what had occurred from my parents goes without saying; but they were amazed at the progress in my performance upon the piano – as was my teacher, who swiftly found that its excellence seemed to be connected with my enjoyment of my new-found pleasure, and that the prospect of this activity upon the conclusion of my music lesson produced from me feats of musicianship which were astonishing. It was even the case that the promise of a new embroidery upon the original theme would in itself be sufficient to provoke a more inspirited attack upon a particular difficulty of execution or interpretation – though in the nature of things my tutor found that his repertoire of erotic delights was exhausted while he had still some way to go in teaching me all the techniques a commanding musician must acquire.

'It was thus very early in my career,' Mlle Fraudet concluded, 'that I discovered that to play at my best, the prospect of sensual satisfaction must accompany a performance; and separated from my teacher, who cannot always accompany me upon my journeys, it is necessary for me, if I am to impress, to discover a gentleman who will afford me this satisfaction.'

It was indeed ironical that she should be expressing gratitude to me, when the boot should be on the other foot; for she was a mistress whose activities off the platform quite equalled her performances upon it; and I was sad that she should, after the term allotted to her performances in Bath, take herself off to Bristol, whence I had a great mind to follow her had not it been necessary for me to stay in Bath with Ralph – who, incidentally, had come to every concert, admired more and more Mlle Fraudet's performances, and envied me my private discussion with her on musical subjects (for I did not think it necessary to divulge to him the more corporeal nature of my nightly conferences with this most remarkable of performers).

Chapter Six

Sophie's Story

It was necessary, as the reader may suppose, that I should take an early opportunity to have a few words with Marian on the subject of the enthusiasm with which she now seemed to be pursuing any human being of the male sex.

'But,' she said when I raised the matter, 'can there be any objection to a connection when both wish it?'

'None in the world,' I replied; 'but it is not always the case that gentlemen *do* wish such a connection as you mention.'

'I have not yet observed it.'

'But you have not been moving long in the world of fashion,' I remarked; though conscience forced me in honesty to add that it was true that it was exceptional for a man of spirit not to respond to the advances of a beautiful woman. And, it was often the case that those who did so were either pledged to marry, or actually in the married state, and felt that they should at least temporarily restrict their adventures.

It was at the very least the case, I opined, that connection with such men, who might indeed succumb to her youth and beauty, would not in general meet with the approval of the other woman in the case, and that considerable complications might thus arise.

Marian expressed herself amazed at the fact.

'Why should I object to a gentleman taking pleasure with another woman simply because we were pledged to some future union?' she asked. 'Were I in such a position, should I object to his taking tea with another woman, or talking with her, or raising his hat to her in the street?'

Some women would even object to such innocent encounters, I said; but pointed out that there was in most people's view a difference between a gentleman's raising his hat to a woman, and raising something else which should not be mentioned in mixed company.

Marian laughed merrily at this; but then seriously enquired in what the difference consisted? – to which I could only reply that the strength of feeling aroused by intimate contact was such that it engaged those emotions unconcerned by more innocent exchanges. And (as she tried to interrupt me with more questions) I must be serious with her, and warn her of the difficulties which would arise from too free a setting of her cap at any gentleman who took her fancy. After considerable talk, she expressed herself as understanding my advice as revelatory of the general state of affairs in society, while not understanding the premise upon which it lay, which she described as excessively stupid and likely to deprive her – if not her prospective partners – of much innocent entertainment.

I had an appointment with my dressmaker that morning, so Miss went off to the Pump Room by herself, and there – it seems – had a chance encounter with Mr Edward Curtis, who, admiring her greatly, and with memories of their encounter upon the cricket field (or at least upon the periphery of it), made the suggestion that they should retire to his rooms 'for a romp', as he expressed it – whereupon, with my advice fresh in her ears, she made an excuse which clearly did not satisfy him, for he became pressing, and it was only by walking away that she was able to free herself from his attentions (which she did not do entirely without melancholy, as she told me; but determined to follow my advice).

I had not heard of this meeting when, at midday, following a knock upon my door, my servant announced a caller – who turned out to be young Edward. He was a charming figure, dressed in the finest fashion of the time; and if he had looked fresh and almost innocent clad in the white clothing of the game of cricket, the clothes which he now wore announced him as a young man of sophisticated taste; while by their very nature they flattered his fine upright figure and noble carriage.

He bowed, and expressed the hope that I was well; and went on to make several perfectly proper comments upon the weather, the prevalence of drought, the popularity of the card-rooms, the new practice of serving tea in the Pump Room at four o'clock, and the farmers' desire for rain.

I was somewhat at a loss for an explanation why he should wish to engage me in a meteorological discussion, when after a moment's confusion he went on to ask whether I had enjoyed the cricket match.

I had not, I confessed, been entirely engrossed by it, for it had struck me as a somewhat dull occupation for spirited young men.

Ah, but it had been followed, had it not, he said,

blushing only slightly, by exploits manly enough to satisfy me that he and his companions were sufficiently valorous to impress any female?

I made a little curtsy by way of acknowledgement.

'I trust – if I may open the subject to you – that I did not offend, during the afternoon, by my exclusive attention to Miss Trillo?' he said.

I made no reply.

'I fear that it was a case of her enthusiasm meeting my own, to the exclusion even of such delightful company as yours,' he went on.

I bowed my head.

He now seemed confused.

'I felt I should apologise that our subsequent engagement, though charming, was so brief – and indeed, would not wish it to seem the result of mere pique at having been disappointed in a renewal of my addresses to your young friend. I should perhaps offer – in case you might be offended . . . that I should now present myself in case . . . in order that . . .'

He stumbled to a stop, whereat pity made me assist him – which I confess was no great trial, for he was an extremely attractive young cub.

'You feel, sir, that you should suggest some kind of recompense for what may have seemed too perfunctory an encounter?'

He sighed with relief.

'Exactly, ma'am,' he said.

I must confess that I made no very obvious attempt to prevent his slipping his hand into my bosom as his lips complimented my own, despite the fact that it occurred to me that I was not perhaps entirely following the counsel I had given my ward; but after all it was surely not proper that I should offend so charming and kindly a young gentleman, and thus perhaps encourage him to believe that women are not pleased by a man's desire to ensure that his neglect has not injured our susceptibilities?

I therefore enquired after his health, and the state of the unpleasant bruise which had been given him by the cricket ball; and with one thing (as I confess I had anticipated) leading to the next, was invited to inspect it, and accepting the invitation led him for convenience to the bed chamber, where the maid left her making of the bed with that bland absence of surprise at our appearance which is the best signal of an admirable servant.

His speedy divesting himself of his trousers (he had on this occasion, I was glad to see, eschewed the silly and dirty habit of wearing an additional cotton garment beneath them) revealed that the bruise had indeed almost vanished, a bluish patch of skin merely indicating the damage; indeed, when on his invitation I pressed the flesh with my fingers, he expressed himself as feeling no pain whatsoever, though the stirring of an adjacent spur suggested that pleasure was certainly involved.

The view of his person necessarily exposed by the removal of his lower clothing indicated that he had been at the barber's; for though the golden hair which decorated the area below his belly was plentiful, it had clearly been carefully trimmed and shaved both from the area below the navel (to a point perhaps an inch above the limb which it surrounded), and also, upon my being curious enough to examine more closely, from the pouch containing his cods.

Seeing my approbation, he invited my comment; and upon remarking that he seemed to me to display great taste, opined that the only problem attached to the present fashion was that a man must place himself in the hands of a barber; whereas a pretty woman – such (he said) as myself – adept with scissors and razor could perform the necessary trimming quite as well, making the occasion a pleasure as well as a necessity.

During the course of his discussion, perhaps partly as the result of my passing my lips over the skin of his scrotum in order to confirm that the closeness of the shave was such as my fingers had already discovered, his most interesting part had gradually thickened, and now was risen to what might be described as an attentive loll.

Perhaps, he suggested, it would be more comfortable were we both entirely to eschew clothing? 'That is,' he said, 'if, as I suppose, you are inclined to grant me the privilege of paying my respects to a lady the delights of whose person I have only, so far, imperfectly inspected?'

I was by no means inclined to refuse his request; nor were his reactions upon the revelation of my body, when we were both stripped, any less admiring than his attitude had been courteous. While with Marian he had been all eagerness and speed – provoked no doubt by her own fiery passion – he now showed that most gentlemanlike of all qualities, the ability to take his time; and in doing so admired each part of my form, first sitting upon the edge of the bed in order to enjoy a view of the whole, and then, reclining at my side, giving his attention to each part – not only breast but hand, wrist and arm; not only that part in which gentlemen always show an engrossed interest, but the turn of my ankles, the swell of my calves; and only then were his compliments paid by the art of touch as well as the pleasure of sight, to the centre of my being.

Though I presume that he was no less interested in his own satisfaction than other men, any attempt upon my part to caress him was, if not repulsed, at least discouraged; for he wished, as it seemed, to concentrate entirely on pleasuring me, first by caressing each part with fingers and tongue, then by lying upon me and as it were massaging my whole body with his own; and, in short, driving me finally almost to the edge of frenzy, so that, with a strength I almost thought myself incapable of, I threw him from me, and falling upon him devoured him as though he were a feast, sucking at his fingers and toes, nipping his ears, licking at his sides, and finally taking between my lips a prick grown so adamant by desire that it seemed a bar of iron. So much a man was he, that even at this he was able to contain himself, permitting me to spend as long in embracing him as gave me pleasure, and only then, with a gentleness allied strangely but admirably to his strength, turned me upon my back and entered me.

The scene which followed will be of interest to no one, and I will not describe it at length; suffice to say that time seemed to stand still – for how long, I cannot say – while the universe revolved about that single pole which is the delight (though sometimes the sad disappointment) of very complete woman. After a series of mounting waves of pleasure, each of which burst in its own scatter of foam, I finally felt that scalding flush within me which signalled his release, while beneath my palms the small earthquake of muscles beneath the skin of his arse further expressed the paroxysm.

So intense had been our pleasure that it took us some while to recover. I rang for tea, which we took upon our naked bed; and it was as we had consumed our second cup that the door opened to reveal – Marian! returned from town, and surprised to see Mr Curtis in a state of nature, imperfectly concealed by his swiftly pulling a corner of the sheet across his lap, reclining at my side.

I must confess to a blush; but Marian coloured too, realising no doubt (as I, later, did) that it had been her own refusal to entertain his advances that had sent Edward straight from the Pump Room to Pulteney Street – a fact that might have diminished the extent of my welcome, even had I been conscious of the splendid extent of his *repertoire*. However, she now recognised that a magnanimous gesture was in order, and walking towards us enquired whether she could share a cup of tea – but then, noting that there were only two cups and that the pot was in any event empty, suggested that she should share some other inspiriting refreshment, the nature of which was clear from her slipping out of her dress and mounting the bed, stretching across my body to lift the sheet from Edward's and take between her palms his still fallen pole.

Such is the power of recovery of the male sex that this almost immediately stirred, and within a short time resumed its height – if not, as my testing it showed, a solidity equal to what it had formerly shown. This however was shortly attained through the remarkable persistence of Miss Marian, whose efforts almost confounded me by their ingeniousness and facility – so much so that it was difficult to believe that she had not been instructed by someone, rather than being, as I knew to be the case, a tyro whose experience of sensual pleasure had been strictly limited, if not altogether non-existent, until a few days previously.

Her adeptness was a tribute to the instincts which, if we will allow them, introduce us all to the means of heightening the pleasures of ourselves and our lovers. No one, I am convinced, had actually taught the girl that the caressing of a man's nipples by soft, feather-like touches, is at least as interesting to most members of the sex as his attention to the female equivalents is to the other; she merely assumed this to be the case (as we know to be the truth). No one had informed her that almost any attention paid by a female to the male buttocks is highly inspiriting – and since this is by no means as true with the female sex as the male she could only have intuited it; but that her instinct was a proper one must have been confirmed to her by the wriggling and moaning, the lifting of his crupper as though begging for a yet more interesting touch, with which Mr Curtis greeted this particular nicety. Finally, no one had given her a lecture on the manner in which to rouse the utmost joy in those parts where such joy is most happily focused; but again Marian's instinct led her aright, and it was not long before it became obvious to me, if not to her, that if she did not desist, Edward would in no short time experience such a height of pleasure as would make the probability of her matching it unlikely.

However, again her instinct came to the rescue; for, lifting her head and regarding his instrument, swollen almost to pain from her attentions, she caught his eye and now throwing a thigh across his own introduced her cup to his bowl and squatting over him veiled his now most prominent feature from my (I confess it!) interested gaze.

I must have shown to some extent my disappointment, for (perhaps remembering our early familiarity) she now reached out and placed her palm over that part of my body which felt most strongly my lack of male attention. This, she could not supply; but by lowering herself and planting a kiss upon my bosom, hinted that at least she might go some way to supplying the want, and on my rising to my knees, did so – showing that, short of the attentions of a man, any female might present herself to my friend (I cannot say pupil!); who, if she preferred the attentions of the other sex (and her spirited rising and falling upon Edward's body suggested that such was the case) was by no means unwilling to substitute for him as best she might.

Indeed, her best was good enough; and I conclude my account of this interesting meeting by observing that none of we three was, in the end, unsatisfied; and that on Mr Curtis's leaving the scene of the battle, Marian threw herself upon her back and, smiling up at me, asked whether it were still my opinion that restraint was a necessary attribute to ladylike behaviour. My reply could only be to join in her laughter, though I still reserved the intention to tutor her a little in that necessary attribute of polite society.

After a couple of hours, we took ourselves to tea

at the Pump Room, where a number of those whose acquaintance we had made in the past few days bowed to us, or paused to exchange a word, while upon a little platform at the end of the room, placed in front of the great clock, three musicians played, a delightful accompaniment to the clatter of cups and saucers.

The company was much as might be expected at tea time in an English watering place: that is, a majority of ladies, somewhat of the extremes of age – that is, rather elderly, and excessively young; those men who were present similarly tended to be old, fat, lethargic and uninteresting, or extremely young, over-excitable and uninteresting. However, after we had been there for three-quarters of an hour, Marian dug me in the ribs with her elbow in a manner which both bid fair to raise a bruise, and seriously threatened the cup which I was raising to my lips. On my turning to ask what she meant by the action, I was greeted by sealed lips, and a movement of the eyes in the direction of the door.

When I followed her glance, I was rewarded by a sight which resulted in my immediately understanding her excitement – for there stood just such a man as a young girl might dream of when first awakening to womanhood; or might, indeed, wish to awaken her. Indeed, I would go so far as to say that he was just such a man as a woman of any age would be pleased to see, in or out of a dream; and a sudden silence as a number of other females about the room caught sight of it, confirmed my opinion.

He was perhaps of twenty-eight or thirty years, tall, slim and dark – his colouring set off by the black coat he wore, by a white shirt which almost dazzled, so well had it been laundered, and by the high white collar which rose from it to meet the raven locks which, somewhat long, curled about his neck almost to his shoulders. A single lock of that same hair fell across his forehead, below which a pair of eyebrows marked out eyes which, from this distance at all events, seemed quite as dark. An aquiline nose, high cheekbones, and a mouth stern but yet with lips sufficiently full as to suggest passion, made for a face at once striking and interesting. His skin was sufficiently dark to suggest some foreign interference with the course of a merely caucasian nature; his hands were slim, the fingers long and sensitive; and he stood with all the ease of a man sure of his place in any society, one hand resting on a silver-mounted cane, and surveyed the room. As his gaze raked it from side to side, there was a rustling as the ladies turned their heads away, as though to claim that they had not seen him – which he must have known to be untrue.

'Who is it?' demanded Marian.

I had to admit that I did not know; and that I was sorry I did not know, for I found him as fascinating as she. He evidently saw no one whom he wished to see (though I fancied, perhaps out of wishing, that his eyes rested for a moment longer upon us than seemed the result of a mere survey) and now walked from the door across the room in front of the musicians to the window commanding a view of the bath, where for a moment he paused, before turning through the door leading to the dressing-rooms.

To say that there was a rush for that window would be perhaps to accuse the ladies of Bath of a greater preoccupation with the sex than they would think proper; however, it was the case that a number of them strolled in that direction; and it was also true that Marian and I were first to reach the vantage-point. In the waters below us, and below the tablet to the memory of King Bladud, the founder of the medicinal baths, were a few ladies and gentlemen, whose pale white bodies, somewhat misshapen from the ripples upon the surface, were not sufficiently attractive to detain the eye.

After perhaps five minutes a gasp from some of the women around us (though not, of course, from ourselves) greeted the appearance of the stranger, now looking like some actor in the role of Antony in Shakespeare's *Julius Caesar*, for he was wrapped in a towel which had just the style of the Roman toga. He walked with measured step to the edge of the bath, with not a glance to left or to right (let alone to the gallery from which he was with so great an admiration observed), and then, scorning to debase himself by attempting those awkward contortions with which some people attempt to conceal themselves at such a juncture, simply dropped the towel to the tiles, and continued his measured tread down the steps and into the water.

The body he thus revealed was only partially viewed, since he had his back to us; but its resemblance to a noble statue was sufficient to make me catch my breath, while Marian tightened her grip on my elbow almost to pain. His skin was, as his face had hinted, somewhat darker than common; but his frame entirely European in its proportions, with a long back marked by a backbone of which (though he did not want flesh) every dint could be seen, to the point at which, below narrow hips, that pleasant bifurcation of the frame separated the globes of his backside, perfectly round and neat, carried by splendidly sturdy thighs.

A collective sigh once more ran around the little group, and several of the older ladies turned away as though the sight was too much for them to bear, as he struck out in gentle and lethargic strokes for the other end of the bath, the water dividing on each side of him, then flowing back to move caressingly along his sides. He was careful, upon turning, to observe the decencies by remaining face downward; to my disappointment, and I dare say that of the other ladies present.

Marian now turned to me with every indication of despair: 'I must know who he is!' she cried.

'We will certainly attempt to discover,' was my reply, and I led the way through the door and down the stairs to the rooms behind the bath whereupon payment of threepence we were allotted a changing-room in that half of the establishment reserved for ladies. These all gave on to a corridor leading directly to the bath, while opposite lay the range of gentlemen's rooms. We hurriedly divested ourselves of our clothing and wrapping ourselves in the towels provided made our way to the bath, where without any great contrivance for avoiding exposing our persons to the gentleman upon whom our attention was focused, descended into the water – conscious that he had not, as far as we could see, given us so much as a glance; but rather was standing at the other end of the bath, his arms outstretched upon either side of him along its edge, and his eyes apparently firmly shut.

We remained immersed for some time, making our

way to and fro and endeavouring to be in the stranger's vicinity as much as possible, in case he should waken from his daydream and make some motion which would provide an excuse for us to address him. This did not occur, however – and at the moment when he did move, which was to turn and mount the steps nearest him, we were at the other end of the pool, and our only reward was a closer glimpse of his person as he passed, which merely confirmed the fact that he presented a representation of the acme of masculine beauty.

We did not long remain after his departure but climbed out ourselves, and dressed as hurriedly as we could. He was nowhere to be seen as we left our room, and making our way to the small hole in which lived the cantankerous old woman who attended the visitors, we pressed a sixpence into her hand and asked whether she knew anything of him. She did not – or said she did not; and even an increased bribe of a shilling got nothing from her.

Reluctantly, we left the bath – but had paused only for a moment at the milliner's across the road from the entrance to the Pump Room when once more Marian attacked my ribs with her elbow, this time signalling that (as she had seen in the window's reflection, made a mirror by a convenient display of bombazine) the gentleman had strode out of the Pump Room, and was now walking across the square towards the Abbey.

The dexterity involved in following him as discreetly as possible was not great, for he walked at a leisurely pace, from time to time pausing either to look into a window or merely to admire the river along whose bank for a time he made his way, before turning up towards the town. Halfway up the hill, we saw Edward Curtis descending towards us, and to our intense interest saw him bow slightly to our quarry as he passed. Need I say that we detained him, and eagerly questioned him as to the gentleman's identity?

'I know nothing of him,' was the reply, 'except that he goes by the name of Valentine Jeakes, and resides in rooms in the Circus; we exchanged courtesies yesterday afternoon, upon leaving our respective front doors, and I believe he has just arrived in town; but as to anything else, I am as ignorant as yourselves.'

Disappointing as the information was in extent, it was better than nothing. 'Surely,' Marian said when we had bid Edward *adieu* and proceeded up the hill, 'surely he will attend the ballrooms, and we shall see him there? Let us go this evening and be attentive!'

That she took more care of her *toilette* than was usually the case, it is perhaps needless to remark; that I did the same, I am not ashamed to assert – for while it was nothing to me if Miss Marian had decided to set her cap at Mr Jeakes, it seemed to me that as a gentleman of more than tender years he was more likely to have an eye for a woman of experience than for one who, however young, and despite an experience which was surprising for her years, could not match myself in knowledge of the world.

However, I was certainly not disposed to quarrel with my young friend unless the positive necessity arose; and we set off together, as amiable as sisters (or more so) to the most fashionable Rooms, which by nine o'clock were ablaze with light and already sufficiently warm to make dancing a real exertion.

There was no sign of Mr Jeakes – nor indeed of our friend Mr Curtis; and we were merely able to exchange a nod or two with those few ladies whose acquaintance we had already made. By ten-fifteen we were already weary – there never being sufficient seats to enable one, unless well stricken in years, to rest one's limbs – when framed in the doorway we saw our victim. Marian immediately started forward; but I took her by the arm.

'What do you intend?' I asked.

'Why – to contrive a meeting,' she replied; at which I let her go – for should I wish myself to attract the attention of this splendid stranger, 'twould be done in a more subtle manner than she would devise; and it would be best to allow her to make her own attempt – which, rejected, would make way for me.

Marian walked straight across the room, and without for a moment halting in her stride, positively barged into Mr Jeakes; then, in well-pretended confusion, dropping him a curtsy and evidently apologising – too prettily for my own comfort, for, somewhat to my surprise, I saw him take her up, and evidently inquire solicitously whether the collision had injured her; next, to my amazement, escorting her to a vacant seat which – alas! – appeared as if by magic in the vicinity. Seating her there, he conversed for a moment, and then with a bow withdrew.

To say that I was annoyed would not be true; the world is too wide for the poaching of any fish at which I intended to cast my line to be a matter of great concern. But I must say that I was surprised at his attentiveness. Marian, as I have perhaps described, is a girl the freshness of whose youth must certainly be attractive to any gentleman, especially since that attraction is supported by a charming figure, sparkling eyes, an excellent sense of humour, and (to be entirely frank) a taste for male company which betrays itself immediately, as such carnal matters do, to the instinct of any aware gentleman.

Yet I had been convinced that Mr Jeakes was a man whose experience of life, whose very demeanour, would allow him immediately to be aware of so obvious an attempt to scrape an acquaintance; and I was keenly disappointed that he should be such a fellow as to succumb to it – even to the extent merely of finding her a seat, and being as solicitous of her comfort as he had shown himself to be.

Crossing the room, I found Marian fanning herself assiduously with her programme.

'He has gone to fetch me an iced drink,' she said; 'oh Sophie! he is yet more delicious than we thought – his very tone, his expression, his manners!'

Words failed her.

I must admit that I was somewhat terse, bidding her take her fortune, and that I was for my bed; and before she could argue – not that, I believe, she would have attempted to detain me – left the room.

In descending the staircase to the hallway, I must pass the small room where refreshments were prepared, and glanced through its doorway on my way – where, indeed, I saw Mr Jeakes. He was holding a glass, indeed, in which there was some liquid; but he was holding, also, the wrist of a woman of about his own height, with hair as dark as his own. Her back was towards me, but the turn of her neck and the shapely curve of her shoulders bespoke considerable beauty, the perfect whiteness of the latter thrown into relief by a perfectly round, dark brown mark or mole just upon the right one. Her left hand was lying upon his shoulder, and now, as I looked, was raised so that her fingers could caress his cheek.

I continued to the street in a thoughtful mood, and returned to Pulteney Street and to my bed, quite expecting the door of my room to admit, later, a tearful Marian, baulked of her prey. But this did not happen: I heard the door of her room open and close, perhaps an hour later – but she made no attempt to discover whether I waked or slept, and it was not until the next morning that I was able to question her upon the events which had followed my leaving the Rooms.

Chapter Seven

The Adventures of Andy

Two or three days after Mlle Fraudet's departure from Bath, I returned one evening to our rooms in Pulteney Street or rather, early one morning after dining with friends and sitting late over our wine – to discover young Ralph lounging in the common dressing-room which we shared, and where we sometimes sat and talked during those relatively few hours of relaxation when we were neither at meals, at play, or in our beds.

He was looking, as I told him, somewhat tired.

'Do not wonder at it!' he replied; 'you have just, yourself, recovered from those attentions you paid so regularly to Mlle Fraudet (yes, though you were most discreet, we live at too close quarters for such matters to go unobserved!).'

'And your present lethargy is the result of a similar *régime*?' I enquired.

'Not entirely so,' said Ralph; 'or at least not so consistently so – but . . .' And he went on to relate the following narrative:

'I was standing in the card-room (he observed) early this evening, watching a game at *écarté*, when to my astonishment – for the people surrounding me seemed of the utmost elegance and indeed prudence – I became conscious of a hand exploring the lower rear area of my body. I started, and looked about; but there was no one in the close neighbourhood who could be suspected of such indelicacy. On my left stood Rear Admiral Sir Townsley Phipp, a gentleman whose whiskers alone would disqualify him from any suspicion of being interested in young gentlemen, despite those suspicions which must naturally attach themselves to members of His Majesty's Navy; while on my right was a lady whose carriage was so noble, whose features so composed, that one could not harbour either the fear or the hope of her making so intimate a contact with a stranger.

'Puzzled, I returned my attention to the table, where Lady Pluvium had just discarded no less than four cards, and received in return (as I, standing behind her, was able to observe) three queens and a knave, thus entirely upsetting her opponents' attempt at a *jeux de règle*. But at that very moment, I felt once more, and with an insistence that ruled out any possibility of there being a mistake, the palm of a hand applied to the left cheek of my backside, where it passed over the surface with the kind of lingering persistence that suggested an admiration which did not run short of desire.

'This time, forbearing to move, I turned my head and met the eye of the lady standing behind me, and to my left. My eyes meeting hers – and the latter were of quite remarkable beauty – I saw she was, altogether, extremely handsome. As I looked, I felt the no longer mysterious hand insert itself into the division where, had I not been standing and clothed, its fingers would without doubt have discovered my danglers.

At this, I turned, and bowing bade the lady good

evening in just such a manner as would suggest to anyone listening that we were already acquaintances; whereat she curtsied, replied that she was well, but went on to remark that it was a hot evening, and that she would be grateful if I would accompany her in search of some cold refreshment.

'You will not be surprised to hear that I was quick to offer her my arm, and without exchanging another word we left the card-room and mounted to the refreshment-room, which at that time of the evening – still relatively early, and still (despite her remark) relatively cool – was empty, apart from the two servants behind the table. I fetched madam a glass of lemon and sugar water, which she sipped, then, placing it upon a table, remarked that she would be grateful for some air – and led the way to that window which, you will remember, stands in a deep recess looking out into the courtyard at the rear of the rooms.

'I held the curtain for her, and she passed into the recess, then drawing the curtain behind her. – and, barely glancing to see that there was no one in the courtyard to observe her next action, threw her left arm about my waist, pressed her lips to mine and glued her body to my own with a passion which was none the less exciting by her at the same time attempting to undo the buttons at my waist. This proving a difficult task for her, I soon relinquished her lips (though not without regret) and completed the task on her behalf, whereat, the moment my engine was free of its protective clothing, she hitched up her skirts and affording me only a glance sufficiently revelatory to make it clear that she wore nothing beneath them, threw one leg up and passed it with great dexterity about my waist, thus presenting me with the opportunity – nay, almost the necessity – of a carnal embrace.

'As you will realise, the achievement of such an embrace while one is standing upright is not an experience I have hitherto enjoyed. The effort required of me was merely to stand still: my shoulders against the wall, I projected my middle parts as determinedly as I could, while the lady thrust her loins against mine with a ferocious eagerness, at the same time addressing me in such terms as I have only previously heard from the lips of the village boys at home, from whose company I had always been kept, in so far as that was possible, by my guardians.

'I need not say that I found the occasion extremely enjoyable, and indeed so stimulating was it that I fear I reached my apogee rather sooner than the lady may have hoped (provoked in part by the sudden appearance in the courtyard below of a lad – a stable-lad, I believe – bearing a box of rubbish, who, placing it upon the tiles, paid us the compliment of giving us his whole attention, one hand upon that part of his body which he would have been pleased to employ in a similar manner, while he held his other arm upright, moving it in the manner of a plunger, a broad grin upon his face as, no doubt understanding from my sudden change of expression that my means of pleasuring the lady was ended, he let that same arm droop to his side – then with a wink vanished through the door whence he had come, before my companion could observe him.

'I was left, by this incident, in a considerable state of confusion – but certainly when the lady, having dropped her skirts and rearranged her hair (which had been somewhat ruffled by the encounter) and professed herself ready to be escorted home, I was not slow to take the hint, accompany her to the street, and help her into her carriage – a handsome equipage which stood waiting for her.

'There was little conversation during the journey, of about twenty minutes, which followed: I longed to discover whether this strange lady achieved the company of young men in this manner as a matter of course; or whether – as my vanity prompted me to hope – it was my particular self which had attracted her to that degree that it was impossible for her not, even at risk of her reputation, to throw herself upon me. But even had I plucked up the courage to ask such questions, it would have been difficult to do so, for drawing the blinds (it was already dusk) she drew me to her and engaged me in a bout of kissing during which it would have been difficult for me to swear, from moment to moment, whether her tongue was exploring the interstices of my mouth, or mine hers, while I had positively to discourage her hands from again uncovering me, lest I should lose what control I had, and again exhaust myself before (as I was now convinced would be the case) the opportunity arose to love her in more convenient circumstances.

'In time, the carriage came to a halt after a short excursion upon loose gravel, and (it now being almost dark) I fleetingly saw the shape of a large mansion as I followed the lady from the carriage up a curved flight of stairs, into a dark hall, through a sitting-room dimly lit, along a corridor and finally – with what surprise you will realise when you hear a description of the place – into a large room the centre of which was occupied by what seemed to be, in so far as I could see it in what was again a very dim light, a replica of one of the Roman baths of this city.

'The lady, whose name I still did not know, went straight to a bell-pull and tugged upon it; there was no responding sound, but in a moment a footman appeared, and she gave instructions to bring candles. Without waiting for them to arrive, madam again threw herself into my arms – or rather took me into hers, for I was still too surprised by the continuing marvels of the evening to take any initiative – and now began to undress me in earnest, so that by the time the footman appeared bearing two candelabra, which lit the room to a warm glow, both of us were half-naked – a thing which appeared not to amaze the servant, who gave no indication of my presence and, I was amused to see, bowed to the lady with his eyes closed.

'I was scarcely able to examine the room, so pressing did her attentions now become; but I will describe it, none the less, from my subsequent view of it. It appeared, in the candle-light, to be furnished almost entirely in blue: deep blue carpets, blue silk hangings upon the walls (which incidentally at no point betrayed the presence of windows, these having as I later discovered been bricked up); and the bath, which was perhaps ten feet square, was paved with tiles of the most cerulean blue, so that the water sparkled with a hundred points of light, where the flames of the candles (placed at each side) caught it. A low bench or *chaise-longue* stood at one side of the room, near which had been placed a generous pile of the softest towels – again dyed a light blue. A small table stood nearby, upon which were flagons of wine and two glasses, and plates of ripe fruit. The whole scene was reflected in a great, dark mirror which filled much of one wall, beside the entrance.

'But as I say, these details escaped me, being much more intent, now that we were both unclothed, in examining my mistress, who revealed to me a body which I scarcely know how to describe: it lacked altogether the slimness, almost boyishness, of extreme youth – yet certainly was also without any of the slackness which I assume accompanies age. The bosom was full, yet entirely supportive and without the slightest hint of sagging; the stomach flat, or at least only very slightly convex; thighs ample, but what no one could call fat; while between them the mound which normally is veiled was – astonishingly, to me – entirely naked, every vestige of hair having been removed, leaving a bareness which for a moment shocked, then violently excited me, so that almost without knowing what I did, I discovered myself upon my knees saluting those smooth lips with my own; whereat from between their upper cleft immediately sprang a small, thumb-like protuberance of flesh which I suppose I unconsciously recognised from your lectures upon the subject – for from instinct alone I found myself giving especial attention to it, which resulted in the lady's showing signs of considerable pleasure; eventually to the extent that she almost collapsed with delight, and (on purpose, I am sure) rolled over and over with me upon the thickly carpeted floor until with a splash we both fell into the central pool.

'This might have ended our congress had it been chill; but the water proved to have been warmed, I know not through what agency, to the point of comfort (though not to that of lethargy); and immersion in it had the advantage of rendering the body weightless; an advantage particularly efficacious in sensual gratification, as I discovered, for, when lying upon her back and placing her hands in two brackets conveniently situated at the side of the bath (a convenience, I am convinced, carefully planned for just such occasions) madam threw her legs apart and encouraged me to swim between them. I found that – a connection once made – we were able to lie there, my hands entirely free to busy themselves about whatever areas of our persons seemed most in need of stimulation.

'Should some supernatural being suddenly remove from earth the heavy effect of gravity, what charm there would be in swimming thus in air! – for the contact between us, relieved of the necessity to support ourselves, varied between so light a touch as to be that of a feather and caresses as firm as we cared to make them, while our attitudes could be as various as contrivance could invent: and without the slightest difficulty we could adopt the most strenuous postures depicted in Dr Plumtre's catalogue, which under normal circumstances must surely require so considerable an employment of energy as to take from that energy later required in satisfying a partner!

'Having pleased ourselves and each other to a point of satisfaction, we removed ourselves from the pool, and wrapped in soft towels reclined upon the *chaise-longue* and refreshed ourselves with fruit and wine, after which I will confess to finding myself drowsy and in a while fell asleep in the arms of my remarkable new friend – to awake almost instantly (as it seemed, though perhaps some time had elapsed) with a most languorous sensation in my nether regions, provoked (I saw in opening my eyes) by the lady, who, now kneeling at my side, had taken my temporarily flaccid pego between her lips, and allowing it to lie upon her tongue was merely passing her upper lip across its tip; which even before my coming to consciousness had resulted in a certain recovery in dimension, and now in my cock springing once more to a full size; which she greeted (on its becoming too large for her to retain at full length) by taking it between her fingers and playing upon it almost as upon a flute, changing the apprehension of pleasure from moment to moment by passing from tip to root and pressing one moment that bulb which marks the swelling diapason of delight, the next caressing that bellows which conceals the twin stones which contribute the essence discharged at the triumphal culmination of an anthem.

'Although you have remarked to me upon the pleasure to be derived from the company of an experienced mistress, Andy, I must confess that I had not supposed that the difference could be so great between a young girl such as Eliza Curryfin (whose enthusiasm is great but whose knowledge is small) and a lady whose vigour is matched by her experience! It may be that in an ordinary congress there is little to divide them – and indeed that the activities of the elder my seem less to be desired, in that her limbs are likely to be less firm and limber; but as far as the giving of delight by more subtle means is concerned, there can be no doubt which is preferable!

'Partly to return the favour, and partly as an excuse

to remove my member from that delightful irritation which would too soon have done my business, I persuaded the lady to permit me to practise – as inspiritingly as could be, considering my relative inexperience – those favours with which she had delighted me; and found that provided attention is paid to the reception of a caress, it is perfectly easy to understand what does, and does not, give pleasure; and I must confess with some pride that in no short time madam's body was writhing with what seemed (if there was no pretence) to be quite as inspiriting an enjoyment as had been mine; and when, a short time afterwards, we were once more joined together in a full celebration, we cried out in an ecstasy which was as keen as it was mutual.'

In telling the story, Ralph had been lost in the memory of his pleasure – to the extent that a very obvious mark of it appeared in a swelling in the area of his lap, which he attempted to conceal by gathering the folds of his dressing-gown about it; then, seeing my eyes upon him, smiled weakly and gave up the idea of concealment, merely laying a hand upon the offending portion of his body as though to comfort it, while going on to relate how, bidding him farewell with a smile, the lady had wrapped a towel about her person and, almost before he knew it, had vanished from the room; whereupon he had plunged into the pool once more to refresh himself, and dressing had pulled upon the bell-rope, summoning a footman who with attentive politeness, but without words, had guided him to the door, where the carriage waited, and as he stepped into it pressed into his hand a folded paper. The carriage returned him to Bath and (on his direction) to Pulteney Street.

Hurrying upstairs (for the carriage was unlit) he had unfolded the paper, which merely bore upon it the words: 'Tomorrow – Pump Room – 6 p.m.' and the initials N.J.

What name could those initials signify? young Ralph asked – but I could not advise him, for they meant nothing to me, and I could do nothing but congratulate him on his good fortune – and congratulate myself, also, for in introducing a young man to the pleasures of love there is no substitute for an experienced woman. His introduction to *amour* had been easily accomplished, but I had been uncertain how this was to be extended into a proper knowledge. I had considered searching the brothels for a tutor; but this would have been an expensive business, for in this matter there is no substitute for purchasing the best, if one is to avoid both the vulgar and the diseased. Now however the problem appeared to have solved itself, and I could only encourage Ralph to accept the invitation to another meeting – while not failing to warn him of the possible pitfalls: as of falling in love, or of becoming besotted with a lady who was clearly a kind of adventuress. (I began to fear the worst at that point, for my words were greeted with a frown, as though he had already begun to admire the lady to a point at which any criticism was regarded as insulting. However, I could but state the warning.) Nor should he, I suggested, be so delighted with her expertise between the sheets that he begin to feel there was no substitute for it, living for his next encounter with her; for, as I remarked, there was in my experience no woman living whose skill in making love was not to be counterfeited elsewhere. However, I must hope that the lady was as discreet as she was experienced, and that rather than being an adventuress she was simply (as is the case with many females in this place) in search of innocent amusement.

In the meantime, as I explained to Ralph, I was under the necessity of spending a day or two in London upon Parliamentary business and intended to set out upon the following day on the morning coach; and now took myself to bed, leaving Ralph to what I feared would prove an uneasy couch (as I judged from the continued protuberance yet imperfectly concealed by his robe!).

I was in course of packing my bags early next morning, when I heard a terrific clangour upon the front doorbell, and in a moment the servant announced my acquaintance William Gaucet, the M.P. for Bath, and leading magistrate of the town – a gentleman whom I knew from our mutual presence in Whitehall, and had seen about the city with a charming young creature whom at first I took to be a mistress, but later found to be a daughter. My introduction to her had been the occasion of my foreseeing some difficulties for Mr Gaucet, for her pressure of my hand no less than the sparkle in her eye seemed to me to betoken a spirit which, as it so often does in young ladies of seventeen or so, seemed to me to be at the point of explosion – and while Mr Gaucet was clearly convinced of his child's perfect innocence and obedience, from the glances which she covertly gave to the young gentlemen about the place, I believed that she would soon break out.

And now it proved that such was the case: her maid had come to Gaucet that morning having found her mistress's bed unoccupied and certain of her belongings missing; this, together with the fact that the window of her room was open and the marks of a ladder upon the sill, suggested abscondment. Poor Gaucet was in the utmost distress, and paid me the compliment of asking me to attempt to discover whither she had fled.

But why, I asked, should he come to me?

The reply was (of course) that my reputation was of a man learned in the ways of womankind – and I cannot deny that there is some truth in it. I therefore said that I would do what I could, imploring Gaucet to take himself to his club and remain there until he heard from me – for I did not want him blundering about the place making a row which would only disturb Miss Constance (as his daughter was called) should I discover her, and encourage her to flee entirely from the neighbourhood (should she indeed still be at Bath).

Having cancelled my place in the London coach, I went first into Gaucet's rooms, and – having a note of permission from him – into Miss Constance's bedroom, where I conducted a close search. There was little here other than the bits and pieces collected by a young person of more innocence than experience; until upon the floor under the bed, carefully folded but perhaps dropped, I discovered a printed flyleaf:

Il Convito Amoroso,
or a Philosophical Lecture
on the
Causes, Nature and Effects of Love and Beauty at the Different Periods of Human Life, in

Persons and Personages, Male, Female and Demi-Charactere; and in Praise of the Genial and Prolific Influences of the Celestial Bed.
As delivered by Hebe Vesteria
The Rosy Goddess of Youth and of Health
from the Electrical Throne,
in the Great Apollo Chamber at the Temple of Hymen, in London.

'Before a glowing and brilliant Audience of near three hundred Ladies and Gentlemen, who were commanded by Venus, Cupid and Hymen to assist in Joyous Assembly, Various Young Persons were introduced to the pleasures of Love, at the Temple in London last month. Now, the Celebrated Celestial Bed, as recommended by Emma Lyons, afterwards Lady Hamilton, will be in station in Bath, and on Tuesday the 5th August, will be at the Command of Whoever desires its Effects, upon payment of ten guineas – such effects guaranteed to allow the persons commanding such a sum that Bliss remarked upon by the Poets, and now offered to the Commonalty.

'Published at the earnest desire of many of the Company and to gratify the impatient and very intense longings of Many of the Cognoscenti, *et de les Amateurs des délices exquises de Venus.*'

Dr Whilom Pettigrew, M.D.

Below this had been added in pencil an address; and it was to the place named that I now took myself – though in little doubt that I would be too late to prevent mischief, this now being the morning of Wednesday, August 6th.

The Hymeneal Temple at which I found Dr Graham, owner of the Celestial Bed, was set up in a house in the Crescent, a very fashionable part of Bath – an indication that he had had some success in separating ladies and gentlemen from their money. On ringing the bell at midday, I was greeted by a footman fully powdered and ceremonially attired, despite the early hour; who, simpering, ushered me into a waiting-room where I was seated and, during the next few moments was at liberty to look through a number of flyleafs similar to that I had discovered in Miss Constance's room, some offering various medical cures by means of Electrical Aether, Nervous Aetherial Balsam, Imperial Pills, Liquid Amber and Restorative Balsam, some of which were offered at reduced prices which could not (Dr Graham asserted) be equalled by any of his rivals: 'The bottles, marked and formerly sold at one guinea, may now be had at half a guinea; the half-guinea bottles at five shillings and threepence; the five-shilling bottles at two shillings and sixpence, and the two-shilling-and-sixpence bottles at one shilling and threepence.'

I had just finished reading this when the good Doctor himself appeared – a plump person of perhaps fifty years, with every sign of affluence in dress and manner, who immediately began to congratulate me upon the cure for my ills which I would soon be offered – without taking any care to enquire what they were.

Soon, however, it appeared that he assumed I was present for one reason only, for he began to assure me that my difficulty in establishing what he called a firm communication with the ladies would soon be over.

'I do not enquire how the problem began!' he exclaimed; 'except that a gentleman of your presence and person can scarcely have been troubled with it for long – am I right?' – and without pausing for a reply, continued: 'It may be that some sad experience has had this result, or that it is merely a practical problem; but the Celestial Bed is never known to fail – and as it happens I have a nymph' (here he closed his eyes in a parody of inexpressible pleasure) 'who cannot fail to raise your spirits, however crestfallen. The fee will be ten guineas, paid in advance.'

Had he not mentioned a particular nymph, I might have left at that point; but some instinct told me that his words were not unconnected with the disappearance of Miss Constance, and without a word I placed my guineas upon the table, at which he rubbed his hands together with a pleasure which seemed more genuine than that which he had parodied a moment before, picked up the gold pieces and rang them together with what was evidently a satisfactory clink.

'Please to follow me, sir!' he said – and I did so; up the handsome staircase, and into a nicely furnished room where half a dozen empty chairs stood in a row, while on a dais was a naked Venus in plaster.

'You are fortunate,' remarked Dr Graham; 'you are our first client of the day – by mid-evening this room will be crowded with ladies and gentlemen—'

'Ladies?' I asked.

'Indeed,' he replied; 'I have two young male assistants whose duty it is to apply themselves to those females whose desire for congress has diminished – for though they have not the same practical difficulties as we gentlemen' (he gave an inexpressibly offensive wink) 'it sometimes becomes a trial for them to entertain their lovers when the wish for it has gone. Then, some come merely that their first experience of *amour* should be satisfactorily concluded – and in the case (as with yourself, good sir) I am sometimes able to match them with gentlemen visitors, whose experience – and I can see that you are no novice! – satisfies their curiosity, while their freshness and longing for the Act almost invariably raises the spirits of even the most lethargic of our sex. I may say that the Celestial Bed – which my Lady Hamilton commissioned for just that purpose – has never been known to fail in efficacy in either case. But please follow me!'

In the next room stood the Celestial Bed itself: which looked no different from any other similar piece of furniture – large, with four posts from which handsome hangings depended, and dressed with perfectly clean clothes.

Going to another door, the Doctor clapped his hands, whereupon a young man instantly appeared, clad in a loose white smock. For a moment I wondered whether the doctor had mistaken the nature of the problem he assumed had brought me thither; but 'George will assist you,' he said; 'if you would be so good as to divest yourself of your clothing and establish yourself in the Bed, your Attendant Nymph will shortly appear.' Whereat he vanished.

George took each article of clothing from me carefully as I removed it, folding them with great care and placing them upon a chair; then lifting back the bedclothes handed me upon the bed, drew its curtains and took himself behind a large screen which stood perhaps five feet away. No sooner had he vanished, than the door through which he had entered opened once more, and a young lady appeared, led by an older woman. (The vision was clear, I should explain, because the curtains were of a material sufficiently thin for me to see through them, though the darkness at the back of the room I suppose was sufficient to conceal me where I lay). Constance's fair hair was loose about her shoulders, and her person covered with a gown of white silk. I was immediately sure that it was she, from her resemblance to Gaucet; and indeed, when she showed some hesitation in approaching the bed, her attendant muttered some words to her of which 'Miss Constance' seemed to be two.

Her hesitancy in approaching brought her to a complete stop when, standing at the side of the bed, the beldame threw back the curtain, revealing my figure. I assumed what turned out to be the truth – that the young lady had never seen an unclad gentleman before; for colour immediately came to her cheeks, which deepened when, releasing two pins at her shoulders, her helpmeet allowed her gown to fall about her feet – whereupon she raised one arm to cover her breasts, and lowered her other hand to conceal her most intimate part, thus resembling that statue of Venus which the Greeks gave to the western world as a picture of such ideal beauty as to suggest perfection in womanhood – a replica of which indeed stood next door.

Gently but firmly, the older woman now insisted that Constance (who I had as well call by her name) lie beside me; and pulling the curtains once more, left the room. We lay for a moment motionless as two statues, neither willing to be first to move or to speak. But then the strangest thing happened: for as the sound of mysterious, ethereal music began to sound – played, I assume, by musicians in a neighbouring room – the whole bed seemed to begin to quiver, not so much shaking as trembling beneath us with such an intense yet narrow vibration that in a moment it had just that effect upon me which for once I least wished: the excitation of my member, which from remaining squab upon my thigh, now thickened and raised itself in so determined a manner that I immediately (if silently) congratulated Dr Graham upon his invention, which I had no doubt frequently proved efficacious in the arousal of the dead!

Miss Constance could scarcely have been aware of the phenomenon; but her head being sufficiently raised by the pillow, and catching a glimpse of movement, she lifted it the better to observe, and then, while studiously avoiding my eye, was bold enough to lay her hand upon my member.

I now found myself in a quandary, for while I had certainly been invited to find Miss Gaucet, if I could, it was no part of my contract to seduce her; yet her touch, which had all that nervous tentativeness which made it the more tender, could not but excite my spirits, while her person was certainly not such as, by its ugliness or coarseness, was likely to lower those spirits. However, by exercising considerable control, I was able to refrain from any movement towards her.

She clearly found this extremely disappointing, raising herself upon her elbow and regarding me with some scorn, before, with a tremble of her lip and what seemed almost a tear in her eye, addressing me for the first time:

'I am sorry, sir,' she said, 'that my attractions are not such as to permit you to caress me; for my part I must confess that your person is just such as provokes in me those emotions which I have longed to experience – but which must, it seems, remain unfulfilled!'

Could any red-blooded man accept such a rebuke, especially when it was accompanied by a clear sphere of salt water, rolling down a cheek upon which the bloom of youth was accompanied by a blush of shame?

Raising myself in my turn, I laid my hand upon her bosom and kissed her upon the mouth – whose dormant lips spoke of entire innocence. At this, I would once more have desisted, had her touch upon my nether regions not now grown much bolder as the lady began to explore the shape of things unknown to her – and had she not then, with a small moan, thrown herself upon me and with a wriggling movement begun to rub her entire body upon mine – at which the shuddering of the bed increased (the mysterious coincidence being explained when I caught sight beyond Constance's shoulder of the moon-face of the servant appearing above the screen, red and with perspiration bedewing his forehead – at which I guessed that he was in some way responsible for the movement of the bed, which I believe was indeed so, through an ingenious arrangement of levers and cables).

The knocking of my now adamant member against her belly throwing the young lady into a paroxysm of pleasure, I could think of no way out of the situation other than through satisfying her; and, to make the story short, having to her great displeasure persuaded her to relinquish her position on top of me and permit me to lay her upon her back and deploy my body between her legs (which she found no great discomfort once the idea had communicated itself) in the most obvious and convenient posture for the task in hand, I deflowered her with, I trust, that tenderness and tact due to a virgin, while at the same time giving as much pleasure to her (and incidentally, to myself) as was possible under so unusual a circumstance; the vibration of the Celestial Bed, I must confess, contributing something to the latter, which from her expression and the exclamations which fell from her lips, seemed to be considerable.

She was all eagerness to continue; but I now had some explanations to give, and with (I confess) some confusion, admitted that I had been dispatched by her father to find her, explaining the circumstances which had led me hither. She took this amazingly well, admitting that (her mother having died while she was yet young) the mysterious yearnings which had tormented her recently upon the sight of the more agreeable members of the male sex, together with curiosity aroused by some etchings in her father's library, had made her determined to penetrate to the centre of the mystery which she felt sure must lie behind those casual exchanges which were all she was permitted to observe of the relationship between the sexes, and had for that reason approached Dr Graham, pretending that she was an experienced woman who had for the time taken no pleasure in men; the very vague expression of that difficulty had led him to promise his assistance, which could not be given upon her immediate approach to him the night before (the Celestial Bed having been kept busy by a succession of couples) – but which had been promised for the present day, the doctor having been confident of a presentable male visitor before that was out – Bath being full of invalids of one sort or another, and of the venereal sort as much as any.

I was unable to fault the Doctor on this occasion; he had clearly divined the true nature of Miss Gaucet's disease, and had certainly supplied a remedy more than adequate. The Celestial Bed was certainly also to a degree as efficacious as it was ingenious – so he could scarcely be described as an entire quack. I persuaded Constance to leave with me, and on the way home we concocted a story which innocently explained her absence – invoking a young female friend whose invitation to spend the night she had inconsiderately accepted without informing the household of it.

This Gaucet accepted without questioning, his anger at the girl's alleged lack of feeling being quite submerged by his delight at her uninjured return. His gratitude to me was considerable and embarrassing; I shook it off as soon as I could, and caught a late stage to London, reflecting that my life seemed, these days, almost exclusively taken up by educating the young, and reflecting that perhaps it would have saved Sophie some trouble if I had applied myself in a similar manner to the education of young Marian. However, it was too late for that: and perhaps, after all, it was as well!

Chapter Eight

Sophie's Story

Marian, when we met for breakfast the morning after her encounter with Mr Jeakes, looked like the cat who had had the cream – and I was inclined to believe that he had bedded her as satisfactorily as she might have wished. Such proved not to be the case; yet far from being dismayed by the fact, she seemed to regard it as a compliment.

'He is the most perfect gentleman,' she said. 'I had begun to believe that every man had but one end in view to any meeting with a young girl. But Mr Jeakes, while making it perfectly plain (indeed in so many words) that he found me amiable and handsome, neglected to do more than take my hand.'

'How very slow of him,' I drily remarked, remembering his behaviour with the unknown woman in the refreshment rooms.

'Ah, but he left me with such compliments, and so complete a notion that we should meet again, that I could not but be confident that he admired me – nor that that admiration will, if I nurture it, lead in the direction of just such an encounter as (I must confess) I look forward to with increasing anticipation' – and she blushed, a phenomenon which indicated to me that despite her recent experiences she was still in character if not in fact an innocent girl.

'So when do you meet again?'

'Not for three days at least,' Marian said, 'for he has business which removes him from Bath; but he has taken a note of the address of these rooms, and has promised to send a message upon his return.'

I expressed no feelings either way upon the matter, no doubt to Marian's disappointment, who was waiting to be complimented upon capturing the attentions of so notable a figure. However, I wished neither to congratulate nor to denigrate; keeping to myself the private opinion that there was something a little mysterious about Mr Valentine Jeakes.

Leaving Marian to her late breakfast, I made myself ready for the streets, and walked down to the coffee-house by the Pump Room, where I knew that Edward Curtis took refreshment in the middle of the morning. Sure enough, he soon entered with a small crowd, and I succeeded in drawing him aside.

'I know very little of the man,' he said when I introduced the subject of Jeakes; 'he talks big – of Lord This and Viscount That – but without so much knowledge as to convince one that he knows them well; he speaks of a house in the Park Lane, but declines to give its full address – and knowing little of London I have no means of telling whether he is honest in that matter—'

'Have you heard of a wife?' I asked.

'Certainly not; but he has been seen about the town with a tall, dark woman, of whose true relationship with him I am entirely ignorant.'

'And they both stay in the Circus?'

'He has rooms there . . . but he seems to reside

chiefly, no doubt with the lady, at Pendlebury Manor, some five mile from here, towards Bristol; at least, it is from that place that he dates his letters.'

I thanked him, took a dish of coffee with him, for the company, and afterwards went straight to bespeak a curricle and invite the somewhat surly driver to take me to Pendlebury.

'At St Loe?'

'If that is where it is, then that is where you should drive,' I responded, at which he scowled but set off at a rattle, so that it was not twenty minutes before, passing through a mean village, we turned into a drive.

'Stop, driver!' I cried. ' 'Tis such a charming afternoon that I will give myself the pleasure of walking up to the house, lest the weather turn off later.'

He brought the curricle to a halt, and I descended, handing him some small change and recommending him to try the liquor at the Boot, a public house I had observed standing in the village, whence I would make my way when I wished to return to the town. He brightened at this, turned the horse, and was quickly out of sight. I walked on up the drive, but keeping to the grass verge rather than the gravel, in case it should be to my advantage to arrive unobserved.

The house was not a specially grand one, but with a curved flight of stairs rising to a door set beneath a small portico. I rang at the bell, and after some time a footman appeared – a dark young man, unpowdered and with livery showing signs of being hastily donned.

'Might I speak to the master or mistress of the house?' I enquired, confident that Mr Jeakes was certainly not at home, for I had seen him in the distance at Bath a half-hour ago.

'Neither are at home, madam,' the footman returned.

'How teasing,' I responded; 'for I had hoped to beg the favour of being allowed to look over the house, which I have heard is a fine one.'

The fellow hesitated, but only until I rattled my reticule and fixed him with a pleading eye.

'I am sure my master would wish me to admit you,' he said with a smile, and standing back invited me to enter the hall, which was spacious if somewhat dark, rising a full two storeys to a domed light in the ceiling.

'Perhaps you would care to step into the sitting-room?' the man said, and conducted me into a sufficiently pleasant room, whose furniture was undistinguished and whose pictures were without peculiarity, but whose proportions were fine and the plasterwork of whose ceiling was sufficiently remarkably formed for comment, so that I had something about which to speak with approbation.

An open doorway at the far end of the room led to a corridor, into which I stepped, despite the footman's clearing of his throat and attempts at a speech, which I drowned by a continual babble as I walked down the corridor – where within a door left (as I take it) carelessly open was a room completely dark, but which seemed to have a floor largely covered with water, for the light coming from behind me sparkled upon its surface. There being no other illumination, I could see no further; and the footman went so far as to take my arm to draw me back.

'This seems a somewhat peculiar room,' I remarked.

'A foible of the owner,' he remarked, but made no

further comment. I dutifully followed him into a drawing-room and thence into a dining-room, neither of which were remarkable. He then escorted me again to the hall.

Here, I set my foot upon the lowest stair.

'I hear,' I remarked, that the chief bedrooms are astonishing for their beauty.'

He gave me a blank look.

'I have never heard of it,' he said.

'Of course,' I said, 'the beauty of any bedroom must depend upon the occupant . . .' and lowered my eyelids at him, whereupon the fellow reddened.

I must admit that in following him from the dining-room, I had loosened the strings of my bodice so that it now showed perhaps rather more of the upper globes of my breasts than would normally have been acceptable in the company of a servant, and made sure that in panting slightly these were seen to admiration, while in pressing the skirt of my dress to my thigh I hoped to show to advantage the curve of my waist.

Almost as though in a dream the fellow opened his mouth – but no more intelligible words emerged from it than might have come from that of a goldfish; and it was in silence that he began to mount the stairs, myself following behind.

The reader will apprehend that I was determined to use the fellow to find out what I could about Mr Jeakes. That this would not be too arduous a process I was convinced; had the footman been old and ugly, I might have hesitated longer, but he was a spruce young fellow in his prime, upright as an ensign, and to a degree handsome, with a long back, pleasantly rounded haunches, and a decent open face.

He led me first to the chief bedroom, unexceptionally furnished, but clearly occupied by the master and mistress of the house; then to a lady's dressing-room – where the silver combs and brushes bore, I noticed, the initials N.J. – and to three less handsome ones, which I admired with a distant air. Then:

'And I trust your master looks after his men,' I said, 'and that you are handsomely housed?'

'Um – um – er,' replied the man.

'Your bedroom is no doubt snug?'

'Er – er – um,' was his comment.

'I suppose that it lies behind this door?' I said, trying one covered in a green cloth, which seemed to lead towards rooms above the offices at the rear of the house.

'Hah – uff – um,' he explained, following me.

'This, perhaps, is the room of which we speak?' I said, turning towards the first door I came to.

'No, no!' he said, amazing me by his loquaciousness, and rushing past me made to a door further along the passage and threw it open. This revealed a small room, neat enough except that the bedclothes were rumpled upon the bed.

'Dear me!' I exclaimed, 'I believe that I interrupted you in a slumber! How sad. But how easy the bed appears!' – and throwing myself upon it, gave the impression of great comfort, though it was in truth hard almost to excess, seeming to consist of simple boards upon which was laid a pair of blankets.

There was now a pause, myself lying upon the bed and showing no positive intention to move – the footman standing at its side and regarding me with an expression notable chiefly for its entire lack of understanding of the situation. Clearly, I must be the first to take the situation further, if we were not to remain in that posture for the indefinite future.

I therefore sat up and remarked, with what I trusted was a winning smile, upon the clemency of the weather, and the consequent warmth of the room.

'It is altogether too close for comfort,' I continued, 'and I find my constitution revolts at the evil effect of a confinement for too long under such an atmosphere. Perhaps you would not object if . . .' – and accompanied the words by further unloosing the cords at my breast, and shrugging the confining material from my shoulders, thus completely revealing that bosom which (as I cannot deny) has been much admired by connoisseurs of that special object of male admiration. His eyes, I may say, started almost from their sockets at the sight; and started even more when with a wriggle I sloughed the rest of the artificial skin in which we confine ourselves, and lay bare as a salmon upon his bed.

He was, as I think, still too dumbfounded to make a move, and seemed rooted to the spot. (I was fast reaching the conclusion that the man was a booby!)

'Do you not find it remarkably heated?' I asked.

His Adam's apple gave a great gulp, but no sound emanated from his lips.

'I really think,' I said, 'that you too would be the better for shedding some of those swaddling-clothes, which seem to me to be altogether too warming for the hour.' At which, I stood up, and while he moved no more than was absolutely necessary to enable me to do so, removed first his footman's coat and then his shirt, which was imperfectly stuffed into his white doeskin breeches.

Doeskin has a remarkably pleasant texture, over which it is impossible not to pass one's hands. The extent to which in this case it was stretched over the footman's lower limbs rendered it difficult to do so without imparting some sensation to the body beneath it, which perhaps accounted for his breathing growing somewhat noisy, especially when I contrived to release the buttons securing the flap at the front, and then to draw the garment downwards, sinking as I did so to my knees, the more easily to enable me to help him step out of it.

If the man's mind was slow to grasp the situation, his body certainly was not, for the contraption I now saw before me was anything but listless, and indeed was extended to a degree which laid it vertically upon his belly, revealing a sack rather larger than average which, being devoid of hair, presented itself to the lips with a kindness that suggested a textured velvet, it being peculiarly pleasant, and the contained orbs sufficiently small to enable them to be drawn entirely into the mouth – an action which drew a moan from the gentleman to which they were attached, and at last persuaded him to act – for, like a spring suddenly released, he reached down, took me under the armpits, threw me upon the bed, and without more ado penetrated me with an enthusiasm that was in the first instance somewhat painful, though the vigorous action which followed through the usual agreeable friction soon roused my spirits to the extent of enabling me positively to enjoy the situation rather than merely suffering it.

In no short time the passage was over, however; upon which the young man withdrew himself, and without so much as a glance lifted himself from me, threw himself face downward upon the bed, and seemed immediately to fall asleep. This, apart from the discourtesy involved, was not to my point, for I had hoped to extract from him in the *extremis* of his enjoyment some information about the household; which seemed not, at the moment, to be possible.

I propped my head upon my hand and regarded him for a moment – not by any means an unpleasant sight, and like most servants neither sufficiently well fed nor provided with so much leisure as to encourage the accumulation of over-much fat, his waist being marked only by the very slightest swelling at its sides. I considered, his sleep seeming to be sound, dressing myself and going upon a further excursion about the house; but what would that accomplish? Better wait until another assault might prove more efficacious. I therefore laid myself down once more, my cheek upon one of those accommodating buttocks, and allowed myself to fall into a doze.

How long this lasted, I cannot say; but a slight stirring beneath my head seemed to indicate at least the beginnings of a recovery – so I set myself to take advantage of it, lifting my head and replacing it with the palm of my hand, stroking his bum with a feathery touch, and gradually sneaking my fingers between his thighs, where they brushed against the equipment there, at present in a dormant state. Before long, there was a response to this, in his lifting his hips slightly, to allow my fingers to progress more deeply, taking his cods between them, and then stroking the very root of his tool, which almost instantly began to grow and harden. In time, with a heave, he lifted his whole middle self from the bed, and planted it down again so that his instrument (as far as my hand was able to accommodate it, which was incompletely) lay within my palm.

The time seemed right to come to my purpose. I placed my lips against the man's ear, and after giving its lobe a little lick, remarked: 'You will forgive my familiarity, but I was ever the victim of my passions where so brave a fellow was to be found!'

He grunted, and pressed his body more firmly against my hand.

'But you must have many admirers – perhaps even including the lady of the house?'

He gave a short laugh.

'No?' I enquired. 'It is rare that a woman of spirit, in these days, is entirely faithful to her husband.'

'Rare indeed!' he said, 'and not the case here, for only the other evening she and a young man of the town were playing in the pool below – a fellow who'd not been seen before or since – and her man likely to return at any moment!'

I inserted my tongue into his ear, at which he squirmed a little; and enquired whether his master and mistress were wealthy.

'That is as may be,' he said; 'he pays us as little as he can, and the tradesmen nothing; time and again I've had to turn away those whose only concern has been the payment of some overdue account – and there are batches of bills in the *escritoires* all over the house . . . But ma'am,' he went on, 'if you could see your way to it, my balls ache something fearful, and . . .'

It seemed only proper to give him his reward, which this time I accomplished in a convenient manner by turning him upon his back and, taking his sword between my hands, stroking it into submission – a process which is efficacious when a lady does not wish the inconvenience of a more intimate contact, and which if dextrously performed does not disappoint the gentleman.

I then rose, dressed myself, and left him, bidding him farewell as amiably as might be. I stepped from his room almost into the arms of a lady's maid, who regarded me with some surprise and no little displeasure, then burst into tears and rushed into the room I had just vacated, where, if the hysterics, the sound of which followed me down the stairs, were of any significance, she received my naked friend's attempts at an explanation with less than complete satisfaction.

At the Boot, I found my coachman half-in and half-out of liquor; but he drove me home with solemn care at an exceedingly slow pace (for which I was most grateful). At our rooms, I ate a late and light lunch, then spent the afternoon in a brown study. Except that he was strapped for cash (and there were many in Bath whose pockets were all but empty, and who lived on the credit of unfortunate tradesmen) I still knew nothing against Mr Jeakes – yet still it continued to appear to me that there was something mysterious about him and his wife (as the black-haired woman must be, not only on the evidence of the footman but of the initials on the silver).

It was in the late afternoon that Marian presented herself, in a state of some mystification. She had taken tea with a new acquaintance, Lady Brownlow, and upon leaving the tea-house had been approached by a fellow – not unhandsome, and of a respectable mien – who bowing had suggested that a bill which he handed to them might prove of interest, should the attractions of Bath be palling upon them. Marian now produced this interesting piece of paper, which simply announced that

Mr DAVID HAM
formerly of the London Theatre and late of Canada
is able for a sennight only
to produce before the Ladies of Bath
for their approbation
the finest Specimens of the Male Creatures
of that Colony
whose Generous Parts and Particular Forms
may be freely Inspected
by those so Desirous.

There followed an address unknown to me, and the injunction to present the invitation at the door together with a fee of two guineas.

'What can it mean?' asked my young friend.

Though not entirely certain, by applying my mind I could make some guess at it, and supposed that the occasion would provide an evening's spirited entertainment, while also further educating Miss Marian; so I suggested that we might perhaps attend it, if she was willing to take the risk of its being, perhaps, a little vulgar.

She was not particularly depressed at that possibility, and to cut the story short, having dined, we set off in two chairs for the address upon the handbill, which proved to be in a somewhat disreputable part of town, down by the river, where we were set down outside a bare wooden door with a grill from behind which a pair of eyes stared out. On our showing the invitation, the door was immediately opened, however, revealing a gentleman of perhaps five and twenty and of no mean appearance, who courteously took our guineas – seeming, as I thought, to look keenly at my face, as though almost he knew me – before leading us up some tumbledown stairs to a room where only four other ladies were gathered, and where he seated us in the two vacant chairs which stood about a low dais. The doors being closed, some candles placed immediately below the dais were lit, and others about the room extinguished so that a pool of light upon the stage was the chief illumination.

There now began a somewhat strange tune upon a flute and drum, placed behind a screen in the corner of the room, and the gentleman who had admitted us strode upon the stage. He was in a form of dress which was somewhat of a previous age, and yet had some touches about it of the present; in short, it seemed almost a theatrical dress – and his form of speech was rather that of the theatre, also.

'My Ladies,' he began, 'it is with pleasure that I welcome you to our Exhibition, trusting that your evening will be as pleasurable as it is educative!

'Having spent some time in the northern Colony of Canada, I have been struck by the manner in which those few ladies of this country who have visited that northern portion of the Americas have viewed the young gentlemen of the place, whose notoriously wild upbringing, though subjugated in their youth to a certain civilising influence, has often resulted in fine specimens of manhood in whom are combined great strength and gentleness.

'Noting that admiration, I have persuaded a number of my Canadian friends to accompany me upon a short visit to their Mother Country, in order that they should represent before you those who so bravely took the British side during the late rebellion, and who are ever ready to serve the gentler elements of Great Britain!'

At which the flute and drum briefly struck up the tune of 'Rule Britannia!' and the gentleman strode from the stage. From behind the screen, his voice was then heard to announce: 'First, Wum Pam Fire River, a native Indian!' – and on to the stage strode what was indeed a fine example of manhood, whose skin (even without, I guessed, the additional golden glow of candle-light) was of a delightful amber hue, and was stretched over a frame tall and broad, yet at the same time fine, well-proportioned and without brutality. It was possible to inspect this with a degree of freedom, since apart from a head-dress which seemed constructed of coloured feathers, he wore only some kind of animal skin about his loins, his chest, arms and legs being bare. He lifted his hand in salute, and slowly revolving offered his audience the opportunity of observing with a degree of freedom the extent to which his frame was an improvement on that of the average young gentleman of Bath – which was considerable.

Now, the flute and drum, which had been extemporising some strange music, which I supposed was characteristic of the tribe of Indians to which this brave fellow belonged, changed; and on his taking up a station at the rear of the stage, the Master of the Ceremonies now announced:

'Here is Jack, from the Province of Alberta!' – and on came a young trapper, dressed from head to foot in skins – something disappointing, for from what could be seen of him, he was a well set-up fellow, with a broad chest and muscular arms, whose person it would have been a pleasure to inspect. Yet what was this? – after a period of his walking to and fro, he slipped from his shoulders the skins which lay about them, exposing a chest which was indeed as broad as had been suggested by his first appearance – though so thatched with black hair (as were his arms and even the backs of his hands) as almost to be clad despite his nakedness!

He walked for a while about the stage, and then – not entirely to my surprise (for by now I had fathomed the kind of entertainment to be offered us) – loosening the leather ties at his waist, allowed his trousers to slip to the floor, remaining clad only in a slim strip of fur which concealed his male parts; yet still covered by fur of his own – for that thatch which covered his chest now proved to be equally thick upon his thighs and calves, and on his turning, upon that part of his arse which was as yet revealed to us.

Marian had, on his first uncovering, grasped my forearm with fingers which now tightened almost feverishly upon it – her excitement (as I guessed) being the product of her never previously seeing a man's body so generously covered with hair, and so approaching the condition of a wild beast. This appearance is never, to me, excessively charming; but I could well remember my own surprise at first seeing such a body – and indeed my eagerness for a closer acquaintance with it, to test whether the wildness of that appearance might be linked to an equally wild sensuality (which somewhat too rarely, in my experience, is the case).

The furry gentleman now retired to the back of the stage, and another appeared – announced as 'A Young Gentleman of Winnipeg!' – this time a young man clad in city clothes, though, from their being ten years out of the fashion, I presumed to have been the product of a colonial tailor. This young buck was but a moment or two upon the dais before, to the tune of a civilised gavotte, he slipped his coat from his shoulders, then his shirt, and with a slowness that was inspiriting (being a well set-up creature whose appearance it was a pleasure to observe) removed, in time, all his clothing save that undergarment now sadly becoming fashionable, which consists of short trousers cut to just below the knee and made in a white linen, and which disguised just that portion of his body which would otherwise have been the focus of attention – though not entirely so, for perhaps through his seeing our interest, a certain shape beneath these drawers (as they are popularly called) denoted its presence in a manifestation promising as to shape and interesting as to a growing size.

To the disappointment of the audience, these three gentlemen appeared to be the entire show; the buzz of disapprobation which followed resulting in the appearance on the stage of the manager, who, holding up his hand for silence, regretted that since the colony from which they came had as yet a small population of gentlemen, these were the only examples who could be spared for even a short excursion to the Mother Country.

'However,' he said, 'in order that there may be no disappointment, the payment of an additional guinea will ensure a fuller and closer inspection of three gentlemen whose characteristics have never yet failed to satisfy the demands even of the most ambitious of ladies!'

At this, the ringing of several coins upon the stage answered him; and after a pause during which the manager collected these and counted them to ensure that each female had contributed her guinea, he left the dais, and the flute and drum began again – whereat the three gentlemen came forward and began a slow dance, weaving their limbs in the most intriguing manner (and incidentally proving to me that far from being mere labourers, they clearly had some experience of the theatre) – the young Indian being especially lithe and supple, his hips seeming unattached to the upper part of his body. The other two gentlemen were almost equally dextrous, though the larger of them – he whose heavily furred body still clearly interested Marian the most – moved more deliberately and heavily, yet with a sort of ponderous grace.

I believe that he must have sensed my friend's interest, for he seemed to direct his movements more and more at her, and even sank to his knees directly in front of her – then, to her astonishment (if not to mine, who now expected just such a thing) unfastening some ingenious catch at his waist and in one movement whisking away his last remaining covering.

That he was less excited by the interest of the audience than they were by his own appearance was clear from the fact that his implement was unready for any material participation in the entertainment, almost entirely hidden by that great mass of hair which seemed to grow even more thickly about the middle of his body than elsewhere – so thickly indeed that Marian clearly found it almost unbelievable that it should be natural, and instinctively put forth her hand as though to touch it; then coming to herself and withdrawing it with a blush – seeing which, the huge man smiled, and reaching forward took her hand and placed it upon his thigh, where she was able to thrust her fingers within that thick pelt, assuring herself that indeed it grew upon the flesh as naturally as the pelt of an animal.

Her gentleness and shyness (for she, despite her recent activities, retained a degree of uncertainty as to the behaviour to be expected of her in situations new) clearly interested him, for within the darkness which lay between his thighs there was now a movement, and there appeared a pale something which was not – as far as could be ascertained – clad in anything but skin.

However, he now rose to his feet and, retiring to the back of the stage, gave space to his Indian colleague, who entirely without hesitation, tore his loincloth from him, revealing a person so shapely and elegant as to remind one of the finest of those sculptures so beloved of our Italian cousins – somewhat too fine and elegant for me, indeed, whose admiration is reserved for somewhat earthier and more masculine figures than this; though no one could withhold admiration altogether from such a youth, whose member, though in such a state as to disqualify him from any present lustful emotions, was none the less worth examination, being of a most tasteful slenderness, gathered to such a point as to justify the name of *prick*. The third gentleman, however, was more to my taste – and may have seen it, for, striding now to the front of the dais and laying his fingers upon the buttons which held that ridiculous nether garment at the waist, looked straight at me and raised his eyebrows in enquiry.

Never one to refuse a challenge, I rose to my feet, and easily undid the button, then slipping my hands beneath the drawers, aided their descent to his feet – and revealed in doing so a body much more to my inclination: thighs which while slender were muscular and strong, a waist thicker yet without indolence, and a tool which, while squab, was of proportions sufficient to promise that in extension it would not be far short of that nine inches which, as the Scots poet has it, will always please a lady.

But what was this? After a final turn which enabled us to inspect them from every angle, and after a final *tableau* consisting of their standing, legs apart and hands upon hips, they now strode from the stage, and the manager was once more assuring us of his respect, and of the troupe's remaining in Bath for three more days should we wish to advise our friends, or even ourselves return for a second view.

'I had hoped . . .' whispered Marian; but then fell silent. Indeed, the other ladies clearly shared her disappointment that no one was to have the opportunity of a closer inspection of the participants in the exhibition; but nevertheless collected themselves together.

We, the last to leave as last to arrive, made our way to the door – but there were drawn aside by the manager, who placed his hand upon my arm.

'You will pardon me, ma'am, but surely I address Mrs Sophia Nelham?'

I looked blankly at him. How could he know me? And yet was there not something familiar about him?

'You have forgot me!' he said accusingly, though without spite. 'We met at your brother's, Sir Franklin's, house of pleasure in Brook Street; I was able to be of assistance to him when a Signor Carlo Gaskill became troublesome to him . . .'

Of course I remembered: who could not remember a murder, and one conducted in such an unusual setting as a set of hot baths constructed in the cellars of a London town house? (The circumstances, the curious may find related in my previous volume, *Eros in Town*, which that admirable firm of publishers Messrs Headline keeps conveniently in print.)

'My dear Mr Ham!' I said; 'Marian, Mr David Ham, an old friend of my brother and myself.'

The couple shook hands, and David revealed that he had returned but recently from Canada, where he had met Andy during his own tour of that country two years previously. And what, he enquired, did we think of his show?

Was it, I asked, profitable?

Indeed it was, he replied.

And were there no riots when the ladies of the audience discovered that their eyes were the only portions of their bodies allowed in proximity to the actors?

'Ah,' said David, 'well, that is not perhaps entirely the case; usually, the evening ends with an auction during which any ladies who wish may bid for the attentions of the players. But this evening, seeing you enter, I determined that should you wish it, you should be free of my hospitality. So perhaps . . .?'

'How exceptionally kind!' I remarked; 'and indeed, my friend Miss Trillo would, if I am not mistaken, welcome the opportunity of a closer inspection of the person of that amazingly hirsute gentleman who—'

'Ah, Jack the Trapper,' said David; 'yes, I find that a great number of English ladies find him especially attractive, his appearance being fairly unusual in this country . . . And you, yourself? Might I suggest my friend Rob.'

'The Indian?' I enquired.

'The other,' he said, shaking his head; 'I think Rob would satisfy you to a more considerable extent.'

He retired behind the screen for a moment – during which Marian enquired whether he really meant that . . .? I assured her that he did; and indeed in a moment he returned.

'If you would care to come with me, ladies,' he said – and led us through a doorway behind a screen, and into a room where three compartments had been roughly constructed within one large room, each marked out merely by hangings, and each containing a comfortable mattress. Here lay the young gentlemen we had previously admired, none of them having troubled to replace their clothing (the evening being more than commonly warm, and the candles having warmed the first room to a degree almost uncomfortable).

'I apologise for the meanness of the accommodation,' David said; 'but the chief hotels of this place are strangely antagonistic to members of the theatrical profession; and this is the best we can do. However . . .' And he motioned Marian towards the end compartment, where her admired Jack lay, a figure resembling almost that of an ape – save that his great, square face wore an expression of the utmost benevolence, a broad smile crossing it as he rose and took Marian by the hand and, as she placed her palm upon the great expanse of his furry chest, lifting her skirt to stroke her bum with his spade-like hand as he at the same time released the front cloth which fell to conceal them both.

David now directed me towards the centre compartment, where the young man called Rob lay somewhat like an animal upon display – but one whose properties I was certainly happy to try; so stepping inside and myself lowering the concealing curtain, I was out of my clothes before he could assist me; at which point, however, no doubt eager to demonstrate that he was a man, and not merely a player, he took me somewhat roughly and, thrusting me to the mattress (which was much more comfortable than might have been expected) began to tease me with his tongue in a manner which was as delightful as it was unexpected (gentlemen in his position usually offering only the convenience of their pricks, and a rude and swift congress which upon occasion even leaves the lady unsatisfied).

No complaint could have been made of the

treatment I received from him on this occasion – which may have been the result of his being invited by David to please me to the best of his ability – yet it seemed to me that he so enjoyed the work that he would need little persuasion; his tongue was well-educated in the skills which best please, and for a time he even resisted my attempts to return his favours, forcing me to relinquish my tender grip upon his tool almost before I had achieved it; and enduring only for a minute or so the delightful agony of my sucking upon it, before drawing himself away in order to perform a similar compliment to the equivalent part of my body.

In time, however, when (rightly) judging that the time was right, he allowed his instrument to explore that cave where it could expect to die; and had so well prepared me that only a few strokes delighted me to the point of near exhaustion (whereupon, accelerating his movements only for a moment or two, he also represented himself as entirely satisfied).

Lying still for a moment, I become aware of certain sounds which represented an equal enjoyment in the next cubicle, and could not resist lifting the drapery which alone separated it from my own; however being presented with an unexpected sight, for I was gazing not into that space occupied by Marian and her friend the Trapper, but into the other – where I now saw the delightful Indian boy, upon his back, his legs thrown over the shoulders of my friend Mr Ham, who was engaged upon plumbing that orifice which is the chief delight of those gentlemen who are less interested in the company of ladies than of their own sex.

Meeting my eyes, David gave me an enormous wink;

at the same time withdrawing his prick (which was of sufficiently considerable proportions to persuade me of the wastefulness of its being so employed) from his friend's arse, and laying it in close juxtaposition to his own, gathered both in his hands and, briskly rubbing them together in his palm, in a moment produced a mutual eruption which swamped the boy's belly, giving ample proof of that pleasure which is clearly not confined to more conventional congress.

Blushing (though I had remembered David's tastes) I let the curtain fall, pleased that the youthful catamite had had his eyes closed – whether in pleasure or pain, I knew not – and had not observed my inquisitiveness. In the other cubicle, all was quiet; and lifting the edge of the intervening curtain, I saw the delightful picture of my friend asleep, her lying astride (as it were) her lover's thigh, her breast against his side, and her head pillowed amid the generous black curls which blanketed her lover's breast, while he gently stroked her hair.

I let the curtain fall again, and myself drowsy, nestled my head upon the arm of my own partner, and fell asleep.

Chapter Nine

The Adventures of Andy

Having conducted my business at the House of Commons – in a matter concerned with the Agricultural Implements (Section 5, Use of Pitch Forks) Bill, the complications of which were sufficiently boring to make me yell, and which in consequence I will certainly not visit upon my readers – I found myself at leisure, and was happy to comply with the invitation of my friend Viscount Chichley to visit with him the annual exhibition of the Royal Academy of Arts, which the interest of King George III has converted, besides being a show of pictures, to an occasion which is also a show of the most fashionable people in town.

Half an hour of the press there, of exchanging greetings with this Countess and that Lady, with never an opportunity (so great was the crowd) of seriously examining a single painting among the many works of art upon show, I determined to leave – Chichley being entirely of my opinion.

As we made our way through the crowd to the exit, however, a momentary gap gave me a view of a portrait which stopped me in my tracks. This was a picture of a woman in Greek costume – that is, in a sort of toga which, falling from one shoulder, left the other bare except for a single strand of black hair which fell over it. It was a portrait which had the most immediate effect, ironically expressed not least in people's seeming to avoid looking at it – for should a gentleman pause to admire, his partner would immediately take offence, its attraction plainly being to those senses which most women decline to recognise when directed at any female but themselves; and it followed that no lady would be seen to admire so singular a display of it.

The picture was perfectly decent, in that the woman's body was completely covered (upon the walls there were many pictures within view in which entirely naked female bodies were to be seen), but the artist by some alchemy made the onlooker aware in the most vivid manner of the body beneath the folds of the toga – the flesh almost seemed tangible, its glow almost to warm the material which concealed it from the viewer; while, glancing towards the onlooker, slightly over her shoulder, the model held his look with two deep, dark eyes which vied for attention with the perfect whiteness of the skin of her bare shoulder, marked only by a black mole upon its round extremity.

'Ah!' said Chichley, 'the remarkable Niobe.'

I enquired with the lift of an eyebrow who it was he meant.

'Little is known of her,' my friend explained; 'except that the artist, Lionel Hamidon, R.A., has been heard boasting of her beauty for some time, claiming that a sensation would follow upon the exhibition of his portrait of her – which as you see is not far from the truth.' (Indeed, as one looked about, one could not but be aware of the slanting glances of the men who were accompanied by females, and of the outright admiration of those who were not.)

'She is indeed a beauty,' Chichley said; 'and I am not surprised at Hamidon's painting her – only perhaps at his reticence; though should he have depicted her unclothed body with the skill and admiration he has expended upon this draped view, some kind of public riot might indeed have followed!'

I had not heard of Mr Hamidon; but on my enquiring, Chichley explained that he had spent a lifetime in painting the undraped female form, for which he had an admiration which did not stop at its depiction in oils, for as far as was known he had never painted a woman without fucking her, and had rarely fucked a woman without painting her, both his artistic and sensual lives having been extremely active. On this occasion it would be difficult to say – putting oneself in his place – which would be the greater pleasure – the painting or the fucking.

And was it the case, did he suppose (I asked Chichley) that the lady was, as it were . . .

'Open to the attentions of admirers? I cannot say,' he replied. 'It has been impossible to discover from Hamidon whence she came or indeed whither she has gone. It may be that she resides with him in Hampstead; that she is received in society, I cannot believe, for it were impossible for her not to have been recognised and named by someone here were that the case: whereas she is merely known by that name, Niobe, which you see is inscribed upon the frame of her picture.'

I expressed myself as being tempted to discover more, being at leisure for a day or two.

'Well,' said Chichley, 'you could take yourself to Hamidon's studio, I dare say; he's an approachable fellow, and not normally jealous of his doxies, as I hear – though the relative modesty of this painting suggests that his interest in Niobe may be somewhat more tender than usual.'

On a pretence that I wished to enquire about available works for sale, I acquired Hamidon's address from the Secretary of the Academy, and bidding Chichley good morning immediately walked out to Hampstead, now somewhat more than a village if somewhat less than a town, and in due course no doubt to become part of the great Wen itself.

The house to which I made my way, in what is known as the Vale of Health (through its being situated near a series of strong-smelling and insalubrious ponds) was little more than a cottage, whose door stood open; but no amount of row created by my fist, my stick or my voice could raise any attendant – so I walked in. There was a short corridor, off which were several rooms; then an open back door giving into a long stretch of garden at the bottom of which stood a large shed or construction with, again, an open door, and a roof largely made of glass. No doubt the artist's studio.

I walked down the path, and taking the open door for an invitation to enter, strode through it. Immediately within stood a screen, and in common courtesy I looked through the gap at its hinges before taking myself into the body of the studio – for that is what it proved to be: a large, square room with a raised platform upon which the artist's models could be posed; an easel with a painting upon it and a three-legged stool before it, with a case of paints and a bundle of brushes. The painting upon the canvas was little more than a sketch: an outline of a slender female figure posed upon a grassy bank.

The fictional nature of the bank was clear from the fact that the raised platform had upon it a small hillock of pillows covered in a green baize cloth; but upon it reclined a girl who was real enough – a pretty young person of perhaps seventeen years of age, whose head was thrown back, her face turned up towards the light which poured in through the skylight, and whose breasts, somewhat raised by her pose, were pert, round, luscious and perfectly unclad, as was what could be seen of the remainder of her body.

I say 'what could be seen' for much of it was concealed by the body of a gentleman whose large and unclad buttocks were towards me, while his head was thrust between the girl's thighs, which his massive hands caressed rather than forcing them wide – for she showed no disinclination for her position, which enabled (no doubt) his tongue the more thoroughly to reach the most tender parts of her nether regions (the reason, I was not slow to apprehend, for the delight which was visible upon her features).

The gentleman so engaged, I assumed, was Mr Hamidon himself, performing one of his two most favoured functions. It would clearly have been improper for me to interrupt the proceedings, so I remained in concealment, merely keeping half an eye on the artist and his model. The artist was clearly of some experience – an experience perhaps which matched his age, for from the greyness of the hairs which covered his arse, he was no longer a youth.

However, that his years had diminished neither his vigour nor his expertise was clear from the expression on the face of his young mistress, and the urgency with which she now attempted to persuade him to give over his consumption of the first course and approach the main dish. Like all good lovers, he did not allow himself to be hurried, however; and it was not until, somewhat raising herself, the girl leaned down and raked the skin of his back lightly with her fingernails, that he transferred his kisses first to her upper thighs and the adjacent region to her belly, then to her breasts, to each of which he gave inspirited attention which at once raised her feelings higher and sharpened her impatience. But at last the necessity of raising himself in order to reach her lips brought his lower body into such a position that, however he may have wished further to prolong the congress when she positively threw her legs about his waist, congress became inevitable, and that instinct which in the end must always prevail expressed itself in the lunge with which his loins thrust against her own, calling from her almost a scream of pleasure; and from him a roar which indicated that the climactic moment of her delight had been joined to his own.

After a moment or two, the artist raised himself, and sitting upon the edge of the platform seized a rag from the floor and wiped a tool which, though beginning to droop, was still of notable dimensions – then throwing the rag to the model, who, declining it with an expression of disgust, took a handkerchief from the small pile of her clothes which lay nearby, and made herself comfortable before naturally re-adopting the pose which Mr Hamidon was already impatiently awaiting.

I still hesitated to announce myself, for (it being a sufficiently warm day) the artist had not troubled himself to resume his clothing, perhaps in his impatience to resume the picture, and stood naked before his canvas, an imposing figure, his broad chest covered with a mass of grey hair still matted with perspiration. Now that I saw him entire, it was clear that he must be well into his sixth decade, though his body was as strong and vigorous as that of any man half his age.

Since he was clearly not intending to dress, and since there was no bell to ring, I coughed once or twice, and then rapped upon the doorframe with my stick – receiving immediately an invitation to enter.

Hamidon continued to paint as I stepped in, merely glancing towards me.

'Don't mind us, friend,' he said amiably; 'we're simply Adam and Eve, you know!'

'Mr Hamidon?' I enquired.

'The same,' he said. 'And this' (gesturing towards the young lady, who with perfect equanimity maintained a pose that was as revealing as it was charming) is delightful Daisy.'

Daisy winked, but otherwise did not move.

'I have come from the Academy,' I said, 'where I have been admiring . . .'

'My Niobe,' said Hamidon.

'Ah,' I said, 'that Niobe turned to a column of stone upon Mount Sipylus, in Lydia?'

'No,' the artist declared. 'No one so august. Simply, Miss Niobe Jeakes. The price of the canvas is one thousand guineas.'

'Ah,' I said, 'I had hoped to make an offer, but that is far beyond my means.'

'I am glad to hear it,' said Hamidon; 'forced by the Academy, as a condition of hanging the picture, to offer it for sale, I have put a price upon it which I trust will repel collectors. It is a picture that I wish to keep. You ask me why?'

I had indeed been about to do so.

'Sentiment, sir, sentiment. The lady is not only beautiful, but was the best lay I ever had. And I have had many. She has a talent for the act which, could it but be made available to the public as is a talent for music or dancing or reciting, would slay in its thousands.'

Consciously or unconsciously, he patted with the palm of his unoccupied hand that part of his person whose acquaintance with Miss Jeakes had clearly been even more intimate than his artist's eye.

'I understand, Mr Hamidon,' I said.

'Indeed,' he remarked, 'I have the distinct apprehension that you did not come here intending to acquire the canvas as much as to acquire knowledge of the lady.'

I had to admit it.

He laid down his brush.

'Daisy,' he said, 'run across to the Arms and fetch us two tankards of porter.'

He threw her a coin, which she caught, then slipping into a tattered gown and making off.

'Well, now, Mr . . .'

'Archer.'

'Well, now, Mr Archer; you have seen my Niobe, and you wish to test wether she is likely to be, er, approachable?'

I remained silent.

'You may be frank, sir,' he said; 'I am no prude. However, you are not under the necessity to answer, for your interest is plain, as is your motive.'

Hamidon walked over to the model's platform and threw himself upon the cushions, waving me to his side.

'The answer is, I fear, that your success depends upon the depth of your purse. She appeared under the most surprising circumstances, coming to me here and offering herself as a model. She believed, she said, that if I painted her and exhibited that painting it would enable her to make a match within the nobility, or at least within the wealthy classes – something she needed, she said, having been impoverished as the result of some family calamity. It was clear that she was a cold-blooded fortune hunter – cold-blooded, however, only in that – for on my hesitating, she immediately asked whether I did not find her sufficiently beautiful, and in a moment had divested herself of her street clothing and was standing before me in just that costume in which you have discovered us this afternoon.

'Her body was as magnificent as I had supposed; and agreeing to paint her, as a matter of course I intended to have her – I find the process is unrivalled as the inspirer of excellence in portraiture. I assumed that I must court her; but on my agreeing to her proposition, she immediately proposed that she should express her gratitude, which she did in such a manner as I have rarely experienced. Whatever man, or men, taught her the art of love, had a pupil whose arts must soon have outstripped his own: declining to allow me to pleasure her, she refused every move I made, forcing me (on peril of her giving over the occasion) simply to recline while in turn she reduced every part of me to a shivering apprehension of pleasure. You will perhaps not believe me – why should you? – when I say that I am by no means a tyro in the art of pleasure; nor, at my age, am I quick to arouse – one of the advantages of age is that one is no longer as sensitive as a boy in these matters. One of the disadvantages is that it is no longer easy to climb again, within any brief time, the hill from the summit of which one has just discharged a signal of delight. Yet by her arts she escorted me to that peak no less than four times; latterly so swamping my senses that I could not describe how it was done – merely that I was drowning in a sea of love.'

The artist fell silent for a moment, clearly indulging his memory – the effect of which could be seen clearly among the grey hairs which clustered between those tree-trunk thighs.

'I painted her, as you have seen, with her body largely concealed – a trick I perform only with the extremely beautiful, when concealment feeds rather than mitigates the carnal emotions. So, I believe, I have been able to show something of her nature.'

'The picture is a masterpiece, sir,' I said – which was no more than the truth.

'It is,' the artist agreed; 'and you wish to meet the original. Well, I am not a jealous man; if it would be to her advantage, I would gladly give you an introduction. But sadly, she has vanished. I have not seen her these two months. That is nothing to me: I am an admirer of the sex, but do not wish to own a single element. I would have painted her again, and perhaps more than once; but on the last occasion we met, she was collected from my door by a young man much of her own age and condition; they drove off together; and I have not seen her since. This is curious, for in vanishing she has not been able to take advantage of the sensation which her picture has caused – and I may say, Mr Archer, that you are not the only man, nor I dare say the wealthiest, who has come here to enquire her whereabouts.'

Daisy reappearing with two tankards, I stayed for a while and drank with the man; and persuaded him to draw a sketch of Miss Niobe Jeakes for my private collection.

'I am sorry,' he said, 'I can be of no further help. You could perhaps help me?'

The man had been friendly enough. How could I be of assistance, I asked?

'By fucking Daisy,' he answered with refreshing frankness. 'The picture upon which I was engaged has been commissioned by a nobleman for his bedroom, and is to show a nymph and a hero in congress. I must confess that just before your arrival, I was attempting a sketch' (I now saw, at the side of the pile of cushions on which the pair had been lying, a sketch pad and pencils, while at the side was a large mirror) 'but the act is, with me, always too engrossing in itself to allow of a simultaneous exercise of art. If you would consent merely to a short congress?'

It would have been churlish in me to refuse, and though the slightly confusing exercise of removing my clothing and placing myself in intimate juxtaposition with an entirely unknown young female in the presence of another man at first resulted in my being incapable of flying the flag, young Daisy, by dint of a delightful manipulation of my cods by fingers no less expert from being young, resulted in my giving a lively impression of interest, and upon our being joined her subtle provocations enabled me to remain engaged for the ten minutes or so during which Hamidon occupied himself in sketching us.

'Right,' he then said, 'finish the cully off, Daisy, and we'll let him go to his supper!' – at which the young minx at once bit me upon the lobe of my right ear, tweaked my left nipple with her nails, and thrust a digit into my fundament – whereat an eruption occurred which satisfied us both. As I rose, Hamidon, still in a state of nature and now in a state of some arousal (no doubt from the necessity to observe us closely while making his sketch) took my place, and was still swiving merrily away as I took my leave, giving me a cheerful wave with an unoccupied hand, as I took myself off.

My friend Chichley was interested to hear my story, and I think as disappointed and intrigued as myself to learn of Niobe's inexplicable disappearance. However, a pint or so of claret disposed of any remnants of regret I had upon the subject, while my memories of my engagement with the charming Miss Daisy were sufficiently inspiriting (though I did not communicate them to my friend) to keep her warm in my recollection.

Chichley was good enough to invite me to take dinner with him the following evening at the Cat Club – a private dining club he attended regularly in Of-Alley, off the Strand, not far from the cellar where my Lord Rochester was wont to carouse in years gone by. Spending the day on the tedious business of my constituents, a number of whom had written to complain about tithes and similar matters, I was pleased enough to look forward to an evening in congenial company – which indeed proved the case, for on my arrival at the rooms whence I was bidden, I found a considerable number of admirable gentlemen gathered, some of whom I knew, and some of whom were merely names to me. Chichley was the only one with whom I was on intimate terms, but he introduced me round – most notably to the Rt Hon. the Lord Wickhamborough, Lord Justice of England, whose stern visage I knew from representations in the public press, and who looked quite as forbidding, when he took his chair at the head of the long table, as he must do when sentencing some poor rogue to transportation to Perth or such another Godforsaken place for the unutterable crime of poaching a pheasant.

The table at which we sat was of splendidly polished but worn and much bruised oak, perhaps six feet wide and twenty long – so long indeed that it was a puzzle to know how it had been got into the room, or whether perhaps the room had been constructed around it; indeed, its end was set up against a gap in the wall – once a doorway – which clearly led to the cellars and kitchens, for the food was passed through it directly on to the board, where it progressed by the hands of the diners to the top of the table, there to be carved or distributed by His Honour.

The meat was excellent, and the wine even more so; and after an hour's good company, we who had formerly been strangers to each other were talking and joking in a state of complete equanimity; Chichley had seated himself at the head of the table, next to the Judge; and the pair seemed to be enjoying themselves considerably, exchanging nods and winks such as (had it been possible) might betray some private communion.

It was when the cheese and fruit had been withdrawn from the table and the port had been placed upon it, that I was surprised by a cry of: 'Gentlemen! – hands upon the table!' – a cry which seemed to be in pursuit of some ancient custom, for all about me placed their palms flat upon the oak, only moving them in order to convey their glasses to their lips.

It was at this point that I became conscious of something brushing against my knees. At first I ignored it, but then once again was aware of some movement beneath the table – a movement which at first was scarcely a sensation, perhaps as of a dog or cat walking past, merely disturbing the air. Then I sensed something very much more corporeal; a pair of hands upon my knees, gently easing my thighs apart. I glanced at my neighbours and the men across the table: from their expressions, which varied from the agreeably surprised to the somewhat apprehensive, it was clear that some were as surprised as myself to share the experience; others – the Judge, Chichley and four diners who were regular attenders at the dinners – though silent, smiled in a sort of happy acquiescence with whatever was occurring beneath the board, and had clearly expected it. The action now, in my case, comprised the gentle undoing of my trousers, so that I soon felt cool fingers about my private parts.

The major element of these, I may admit, was still shrunken and inactive; for (think of it, gentleman reader!) it was not entirely pleasant to have that most vulnerable area of one's body opened to action by some unknown person, the etiquette of the occasion making it impossible either to discover the nature of the examination or the character of the person performing it.

It was with a somewhat increased apprehension, then, that I felt the unseen hands extracting not only my unextended jock but also my cods from their protective covering. But after a moment, upon the tip of the former came the soft, wet, warm touch of what could only be a pair of tender lips. So delicious was the sensation that, I must admit, I lifted myself sufficiently from my seat to enable the unseen angel to drag my nether garments about my ankles, this enabling her to ply the more readily about my private parts with her dextrous digits – and, again sparing my companions a glance, saw that they, too, shifted in their seats with various degrees of freedom, and for the same purpose, no doubt, as myself, while their hands were now for the most part no longer lying relaxed upon the table top, but clenched together; and a sharp *crack!* from the other side of the room accompanied the action of one gentleman whose pleasure (I presume) was so great that he had snapped the stem of his wineglass clean through.

It was a strange experience to find myself roused to the extent of positive exultation by a female I could not see; the abstract nature of the delight not, however, diminishing its keenness, the unseen lips now moving over the head of my cock with that delightful, slight suction which seems to denote a pleasure in the operator no less than that of the recipient, while her fingers strayed upon the stalk of my instrument and stroked the cods and thighs, and my knees, now uncovered, were brushed by something soft and warm – or a pair of somethings: could it be that the lady was naked, and her breasts those objects which now pressed themselves against my lower limbs?

A cry now sprang from the lips of the large, apoplectic gentleman directly opposite me, whose face had reddened and whose eyes (as I looked at him) were turned upwards in their sockets so that only the whites showed. The cause was obvious from the great sigh he immediately gave; and his action was soon echoed elsewhere along the table – and neither too soon nor too late by myself, as my very soul was drained from me by those unseen lips.

There was now a banging of a decanter upon the board from the head of the table, and a cry of 'All rise!' from the Judge, who suited the action to the word by springing to his feet, showing the lower parts of Justice to be as bare as truth, the judicial mace somewhat drooping but revealing by a thread of liquid the fact that the occupant of the highest bench in the land had not been exempt from certain activities taking place beneath it. The rest of us somewhat sheepishly followed Justice Wickhamborough's example, and in the way of nature a somewhat crestfallen group we appeared; the ready laughter of the Judge (who now looked almost cordial) and the others who had been in the secret – together with a refilling of the glasses – nevertheless returning us soon to an excellent humour; completed now by the emergence from beneath the table of a number of unclad young ladies equivalent in number (save one) to the diners – the exception being in the case of the corpulent gentleman opposite, whose unseen companion proved to be a boy – and one whose beauty was such that his victim's fallen staff immediately showed signs of a renewed interest.

It was clear (as it must be to the attentive reader) that these young ladies had entered the room beneath the table from the door where, at its top, the food had been served; and that the purpose of the club was not merely eating and drinking, but the keenest of the remaining pleasures known to man. It was peculiar, however, in that rather than retiring – as I had imagined we would – to another room where we could take our ease in more comfort, the diners now in ascending order of their ages (it being supposed, correctly, that the younger of us would more quickly recover from our former exhaustion than the older) must pleasure themselves upon the table before their companions. I was the third of those gentlemen present to be pressed into this circumstance, and I determined to give a display worthy of the occasion. Rendering myself naked, I stood upon the table and (having warned her of my intention) grasped my young friend's fortunately light person about the buttocks, lifted her right leg and assisted her to curl it round my waist, while I lifted my left and placed it behind her, at the same time slipping my prick (which she had well lubricated with saliva) into her person.

This was a position I had learned to adopt in Arabia (my erotic adventures in that part of the world having been recorded in the volume entitled *Eros in the Far East*). I would not commend it as one likely to give inordinate pleasure, too much attention being necessitated to maintaining the balance and the proper positioning of the lower limbs for that; but it is inspiriting to any observer, and indeed a round of applause greeted us when we accomplished it – a sort of dull thudding rather than clapping, which was occasioned (as I now observed) by those gentlemen still awaiting the exhibition of their pleasure thumping the table with their extended members!

I must admit that we were forced to adopt a more conventional attitude before I could attain complete satisfaction; which we did by sinking to the ground, myself in a kneeling position, and my partner astride my thighs; in which position we both, I believe (from her expression and the involuntary tightening of the muscles of her arse) reached a happy culmination.

Other gentlemen adopted other means, most stripping as bare as the ladies and laying themselves out upon the table, often two at a time, in a variety of positions chosen less for comfort than for pleasure – the hardness of the surface being ignored by them in the excess of their enjoyment.

Some of the *tableaux* were as a matter of course less to my taste than the others: one gentleman's insistence that his partner puncture the skin of his buttocks until the blood flowed with one of those new-fangled forks (eating implements lately imported from France) exhibited for instance a pleasure in pain which I certainly do not share – yet clearly raised his own spirits (to such an extent indeed that he reached his apogee without his prick having come into contact with any part of his lady's body). Nor did my florid neighbour's delight in consuming his boy's prick give me as much pleasure, in the contemplation, as it clearly gave the latter (the relative absence of teeth from the old gentleman's mouth no doubt contributing to the effect).

Despite my twice having paid the goddess of love a generous tribute, the sight of these varied pleasures somewhat aroused my spirits, my own partner doing nothing to diminish the effect by sitting upon my knee so that my member stood erect between her thighs, which she moved gently one against the other in a manner scarcely calculated to teach me restraint! However, it would have been the height of ill manners to insist upon a third encounter, in the presence of those less happily endowed with high spirits; and I restricted myself to observation of the doings of others – which culminated in the Judge merely sitting upon the corner of the table without removing the upper constituents of his clothing, and, his shirt tucked up, permitting himself to be mounted by a plump nymph of some forty years (I would judge), whose efforts to please were accompanied by his quaffing port in generous quantities from a continually refilled glass.

I am pleased to say that at the end of the evening His Honour was generous enough to congratulate me upon my contribution to the entertainment; he had observed, he said, my readiness to return to the witness box, and admired the restraint with which I declined to indulge in boasting – an activity as much frowned upon here as perjury in court! Though I had a word or two to say to Chichley, later, about the propriety of inviting a friend to such an entertainment without any kind of warning of what was in store, I had to confess that I had enjoyed the evening, and learned with some pleasure that I was now an honorary member of the Cat Club (a fact testified to, later, by my acquisition of a membership card depicting an enormous phallus with black ears and whiskers!). It is always pleasant to have a restful place in which to entertain one's friends.

On our returning to my house for a late drink, Chichley now asked a favour of me: which was that he could impose his company upon me during my journey back to Bath, his wife being upon her usual seasonal visit there. I expressed myself surprised at not having seen her – though perhaps thirty thousand persons visiting the city during the course of the summer, it was not altogether astonishing; and of course, in any event it would be a great pleasure to me to have his company on the journey, and I agreed to call for him the following morning at 6 a.m., when my coach would convey us both once more westwards.

Chapter Ten

Sophie's Story

Poor Marian's passion for Valentine Jeakes was something to be pitied: despite all the diversions to which I introduced her – and Bath is a city where diversion is more easily come by, in the season, than in perhaps any other city in the country – despite the introductions I procured to many of the numerous presentable young gentlemen of Bath – despite excellent food and wine and sufficient fine clothes to make any other young girl happy for life, she continued to pine after that one individual young gentleman.

Whenever she found herself in the same gathering as he, she stared moonily after him, followed him from room to room, watched over his shoulder at cards, contrived to sit behind him at the theatre, and every way put herself in his view. But despite the fact that she was often clearly the most handsome young woman in the crowd, he ignored her as much as was in his power without giving actual offence: begging her pardon when, through her care to be in his close proximity, he stepped upon her foot in turning; bowing briefly to her when through her throwing herself in his way they met in a doorway or a corridor; but despite her fluttering eyelashes and gowns cut so unfashionably low that almost the entirety of her breasts was thrown into view (giving serious offence to ladies not so generously endowed as herself) he seemed to take the most determined care not to notice her.

His treatment was so cool, indeed, that she was barely able to restrain herself from a public outburst, and more often than not relapsed into tears the moment we had returned to our rooms and closed our door.

It was certainly a puzzle what to do. The question why Mr Jeakes was so painfully indifferent was a large one, and susceptible, it seemed, of few answers. It was certainly not the case that Marian could be positively repulsive to him, for her person was, if experience was to be counted upon, particularly lovely, and was enhanced by (though I say it) my own skill in presenting her in just those fashions most flattering to her face and figure. Nor do young gentlemen come to Bath for the season to conduct themselves like eunuchs; and he seemed to me to have the air of one to whom the satisfaction of his senses was by no means unimportant to him (as, I must confess, it was to some of the more effete dandies of Bath).

Neither could I believe that he was so strongly attached to his wife (for I took the dark lady whose cheek I had seen him caress, and in whose company I occasionally saw him, to be his lawful spouse) that he would not be happy, like most gentlemen, to relax occasionally in the company of another. I had little enough sympathy with Marian, in one sense; I have never myself seen the necessity to pine after a gentleman whose interest I could not command at an early attempt – that, in the old adage, there are plenty more fish in the sea has ever been my own view, and I have consequently shown no hesitation, should my net come up empty when thrown to starboard, in throwing it over to port, when a catch of one kind or another has invariably come to hand. However, I must remember that my young friend *was* almost laughably inexperienced, and that the pain and insistence of love are not to be under-estimated when those involved are not yet aware that that emotion has many forms, none of which are determinate.

Casting my mind about for ways in which to advise her, however, I recollected an incident that had occurred to me in the city of Lisbon, upon my visit there some years previously (and which, incidentally, I believe I failed to set down in my memoirs of that time, *Eros on the Grand Tour*).

By that time I was already (as I told Marian) a lady of some experience, having been introduced at an early age to the pleasures of the flesh without at the same time being taught that they were either sinful or dangerous; and therefore had had no hesitation in indulging myself in the company of any gentleman whose person was sufficiently attractive to strike a spark in my bosom which was met by a reciprocal explosion in his own. My personal witchery was such (I am forced in the interest of veracity to claim) that I was infrequently refused the company of such a gentleman. Indeed, that is an under-statement; I can recall no occasion, up to that moment, when an offer of mine was declined.

The beautiful city of Lisbon, as I have recorded elsewhere, is the epitome of the most civilised qualities of Europe; in formality, at the opera or at a formal ball, its people are the equal of any to be seen in another capital; but as a result of the climate's being warm, neither ladies nor gentlemen are under the necessity, in going about their daily business, of wearing a greater amount of clothing than is positively necessary for decency's sake. While formal dress is of course worn on great occasions, it is a commonplace to observe both ladies and gentlemen going about the streets clad only in a simple shift or shirt, while upon casual walks upon the banks of the river Tagus or the coast near the city, the less fashionable are often to be seen in clothing so informal that some of my fellow-countrywomen might have been tempted to regard it as indecent, while both boys and girls up to the age of thirteen or fourteen are to be seen, even in the streets or market places, almost entirely unclothed – a freedom also enjoyed by adults when swimming or taking the sun. Such freedom was formerly the case in England, in seaside communities; and is still sometimes to be found at Brighthelmstone and other coastal resorts on those rare occasions when the weather is sufficiently clement.

As is often the case in warm countries, the strictness with which morality is observed seems in disproportion to the heat of the sun, and it is taken for granted that a wife shall have as many lovers as she requires for the satisfaction of her carnal needs – indeed, a husband is positively flattered should his wife have a number of them, for this marks him out as possessing a consort whose pleasure in the game is no doubt enhanced by an equally great aptitude in giving satisfaction.

This is perhaps beside the point, except that it

convinced me that I would have no difficulty in enjoying any man whose person tempted me during my stay in the place, which had begun (through circumstances I will not now recapitulate) in poverty, but soon became more comfortable, on the arrival of funds from England. My success with the gentlemen indeed was considerable, and I had several adventures as enjoyable as they were easy of arrangement – a simple exchange of eyes or a touch upon the elbow being enough to attract the attention of any gentleman who had not already signalled an interest, and the passing of a note being sufficient to make an appointment for the happy satisfaction of a mutual attraction. These matters are much more easily and freely arranged abroad, than in England, where they still tend in some quarters to be reprehended.

However (and I come to the point of the story) the course of true lust does not always run smooth. I was walking one morning in the Praca do Comercio when I saw, sipping at a glass of iced lemon, a young gentleman of really very considerable charm; and immediately seated myself at a table which, providentially, was placed opposite his own. He was, from his complexion, an Italian, for his skin had that olive sheen so common in both the ladies and gentlemen of that country; black curls fell about his shoulders, where his shirt lay negligently unbuttoned; his hands, resting upon the table, were beautifully shaped, the fingernails carefully trimmed, and the fingers which bore them slim and tapering (remind me sometime, my dear, to address you on the subject of the alleged resemblance between the shape of a gentleman's fingers and of his *membrum virile*). I happened accidentally to drop my handkerchief, and on bending to pick it up, was able to observe a narrow waist and sturdy, long legs.

I ordered a glass of that same iced lemon which he was enjoying (a drink commonly favoured in southern Europe, and consisting of the sugared juice of two or three lemons, with water added and cooled by ice – of which, inexplicably, they seem to command an inexhaustible supply), and in commissioning it from the waiter and thanking him for bringing it, did my utmost to speak in a voice sufficiently soft and tuneful to be interesting.

Certainly, the young gentleman glanced in my direction; and on my raising the glass to my lips, our eyes met, and he bowed his head slightly; but then, before I could make any gesture suggestive of serious interest, turned once more to observe the passing scene, and paid me no more attention. On his rising to his feet, I asked him in imperfect Italian if he could inform me what time of day it was, to which he replied with perfect courtesy but some coolness that it was approaching midday; and then strode off.

I hastily paid my account, and followed him at a distance until he entered the portals of the Farrone Hotel in the Praca Rossio – providentially the very same in which I and my servant had a set of rooms, and where I made it my business to enquire his identity of the *concierge*. He proved to be the Duke of Genoa, a young man of eighteen years of age travelling with but one servant. The maid who was my informant (and who with that prescience shared by most European servants was instinctively aware of the nature of my interest) assured me that the Duke had no female travelling with him; nor had she seen any enter or leave his room – and she knew the identity of most of those respectable whores who might have been summoned to cater to the vigorous lusts of a young male traveller to whom the expense of hiring them would be no inconvenience.

She admitted, upon my pressing her, to an admiration of the young gentleman, and proved to have arranged, one morning, to substitute herself for the manservant who normally took a tray of coffee and pastries to the Duke's room in the early morning. On entering the bedroom, she said, she had found him asleep. With the sheet thrown from the bed, his masculinity had appeared undoubted (here, she raised her eyes appreciatively to the ceiling, and kissed her fingers in a meaningful gesture); and on her awakening him and taking care to appear interested in rather than repelled by his open display of masculinity, a glance had been exchanged between them which betrayed no repugnance on his part to the expression of sensuality; but on his manservant then entering the bedchamber, the matter had been aborted – which had clearly disappointed her.

On my enquiring whether it was really the case that a young man of such rank should be so much under the thumb of his valet, she said that she assumed that both the Duke and his servant had been warned of the necessity to avoid casual connections, on the grounds of health; for which same reason, she supposed, the valet, an extremely melancholy fellow, intercepted her at the door on the following morning, and took the tray of coffee from her, so that she had had no further opportunity of approaching his master in similarly inviting circumstances.

This intrigued me further, as you can imagine; and I took care to put myself in the young man's way by bribing the major-domo to place me next him at supper, by contriving to put myself somewhat in his way at other times of the day, and once by stumbling upon the staircase giving him a view of rather more of my lower limbs than could have been exposed without remark on any other occasion.

But the Duke, while perfectly polite, and even admiring (for I believed I saw in his eye a gleam, imperfectly concealed, which betrayed an interest) remained in his behaviour perfectly cool, and more respectful than I would have had him be.

I therefore contrived the following plan. Remarking that at a particular hour of each day he walked alone in a small park not far from the Tower of Belem – a park normally deserted, through being too formal for the Portuguese taste (having been laid out by an English lady half a century before) – I made arrangements to be there some ten minutes earlier, with my servant Will Blatchford.

I must at this stage say a word about the latter, who was then (though now settled in domesticity elsewhere) my companion. A servant of the most respectable character, he had shown himself truly my friend, protecting me from the rough attentions of a sea-captain who would have subjugated me and set me in the position of an unwilling concubine – though all this has been related elsewhere, in a volume which is readily obtainable. Our relative positions as servant and mistress had, for the reason of his devotion – but also, I readily admit, through my invariable admiration for a well set-up young man – given way upon occasion to a closer one; and though we could not be described as lovers, it was the case that from time to time I enjoyed his attentions in that capacity – and no doubt he mine, though he never approached me without invitation, having no difficulty through his admirable carriage and looks in achieving satisfaction with young women of his own class.

Happily, he had not a jealous bone in his body, and on my explaining my plan was happy to participate in it. He therefore accompanied me to the park, and some minutes before the Duke was to appear we placed ourselves in a small glade where, I had observed, the young man generally took his ease for a few minutes at the halfway point of his morning walk, before returning to the Praca do Comercio for a refreshing drink.

Having stripped ourselves of our clothing, we now lay down together upon the soft, parched turf – at which a certain difficulty arose, in the sense that nothing else arose. My plan was to be executed in cold blood, and Blatchford, though perfectly acquiescent, found as most gentlemen perhaps would under such circumstances, that without those preliminaries which raise the pressure of the blood, that part of him which must necessarily acquire a certain tumescence before the conversation I required could begin, remained limp and inoperative.

The sun however was warm, my person not unattractive, and the juxtaposition of our bodies suggestive; my attentive palm soon felt beneath it a stirring indicative of interest; while on my replacing my fingers with my lips, but a brief space of time passed before I was accorded the compliment of a tool as ready for work as any woman could have wished. Indeed, I feared for a moment that we were too quickly about it, for I could not be perfect in foretelling the moment of the Duke's appearance; and his coming upon us either before or after congress would be unfortunate – for in the former case politeness would require his withdrawal, while in the latter the spectacle would not be sufficiently interesting to provoke the response for which I hoped.

However, as with a quick flickering of my tongue upon the dome of his prick I kept Blatchford alive, I heard the crackling of sticks beneath approaching feet; and quickly raising myself, placed myself astride my servant's body, and lowered myself upon him. Despite his now raised spirits, he could not resist a cry of pain; for my concentration – I admit it! – had been upon making him ready for the congress, and this had been done with such a reservation of my own feelings that my person was not in that state of liquefaction which under normal circumstances would have eased his entry. However, it was the work of but a moment to raise myself once more, thus permitting Blatchford to spit upon his hand and anoint his tool so that a second presentation resulted in its comfortable disappearance within my muff.

I had, you understand (I told the still attentive Marian) considered most carefully the posture we should adopt on this occasion. Under normal circumstances lovers will fall into that posture which they mutually find to be provocative of most pleasure at a particular moment, or which expresses that variety in congress which is both necessary and desirable to keep interest alive during a second or a third passage.

Here, however, the effect upon a spectator must be considered – and, especially, the effect of as complete a view as possible of my own body, which I wished to commend to the Duke. I had therefore placed us so that Blatchford's head was in the direction from which the Duke was expected to appear; and so it was that the young man, coming around a corner masked by a thick shrub, saw before him the prospect of a woman the whole length of whose person, from head to knee, was to be seen: I threw my head back, so that the line of my throat was clear, and the tension of the skin raised my breasts, the pink buds of which were now closely gathered into knots; and stretched myself so that my waist seemed long as it was slender.

That my thighs were not only slim but muscular could clearly be seen from the rippling of those muscles which raised my body and allowed it to fall; while I took care to lift my body to such an extent that merely the tip of Blatchford's wand remained nestled within me, then slowly allowing it to fall until that instrument, embraced by pink lips glistening with a liquor distilled not only from my immediate pleasure but from the prospect of that delightful youth who stood rooted to the spot, unable to lift his eyes from the scene before him, disappeared completely from view, the black, wiry curls about its base meeting those softer curls which would normally have veiled portals now stretched to admit a prick admirable in thickness as in length.

I had not at that time been long from England, and my body had not been exposed to the continental sun. Blatchford, on the other hand, was used to working in the open air, with a minimum of clothing; so while the only band of white upon his body was that which covered a line from hips to groin, my own skin was parchment-white, and by contrast to his own appeared the whiter.

The effect upon the young Duke was almost laughable. While no doubt the instincts of a gentleman told him to turn upon his heel and leave so intimate a scene, he remained incapable of retiring, his eyes wide with interest and – I was sure – a quickly apprehended passion. I met them with my own, and as I continued to rise and fall, held them in a gaze which was as inviting as I could make it. Beneath me, Blatchford now groaned and tightened his hands upon my waist, and I felt within me the scalding proof of his pleasure; yet though I was apprehensive it must cause him some discomfort, I continued to rise and fall – and so virile was that excellent man that he did not fail me.

It seemed an hour, but was perhaps only two or three minutes, before I put an end to the *tableau* by quickening the pace of my canter, and, throwing my head back again, let out a little cry of pleasure – though I must confess that so much energy had gone into the artificial performance with which I hoped to impress, that I must counterfeit my orgasm (a skill which every woman should be capable of employing, as I will explain to you, dear Marian, upon some other occasion).

The Duke now immediately found himself once more in command of his limbs, turned, and positively ran from the scene. I rose and thanked Blatchford for his cooperation, apologising for any pain I might have given him by prolonging the action which had previously been so pleasurable. He replied that this was not a matter for apology; and indeed his tool remained at such an angle that I recognised a renewal of his interest – and now myself felt a renewed passion, no doubt provoked partly by my apprehension of the attraction my little scene had had for the Duke. I therefore once more lowered myself to the ground, and with my arse this time pressed to the prickly grass welcomed my faithful servant again between those thighs which had recently ridden him; this time permitting my feelings free rein and enjoying those rough and vigorous attentions which, while perhaps somewhat lacking in that delicacy and ingenuity which refine the attentions of a more educated man, can always be relied upon to satisfy – as indeed they now did.

That evening, the Duke appeared as usual at dinner, his servant standing behind his chair, intercepting the dishes as they were brought, and inspecting them before laying them before his master. The former glanced from time to time in my direction; but now, in contradistinction to my former behaviour, I took care not to catch his eye, even when he grew bolder in his attempts to persuade me to notice his presence. At length, after partaking of his food and a small amount of wine, he rose to his feet and left the room – this time pausing by my table and bowing slightly, so that I must take notice of him at least to the extent of recognising his respectful attention.

I sat for a moment or two over my own wine, then as I got to my feet saw the Duke's servant enter; upon my turning to the door, he came up to me and addressed me in imperfect English, managing at the same time to give the impression that he disapproved entirely of the message which it was his duty to communicate.

'His honourable the Duke of Genoa request milady in the honour of a glass.'

Presuming the man to mean a drink rather than a mirror, I bowed and followed him from the dining-room, up the central staircase of the hotel and along a corridor on the first floor to a door which opened into what I guessed was the finest suite in the place – handsomely furnished in the most polite style, at least as far as I could gather from the drawing-room at whose door I was announced; when the Duke rose from his seat to greet me with a low bow, holding out his hand, which I took and pressed gently as I made my curtsy. He then spoke in a heavily accented Italian to his servant, who asked me if French champagne would be to my taste.

I smiled and nodded, at which the man turned to a large silver wine-cooler and took from it a bottle, filling two glasses to the brim. I took mine, and lifting it wished the Duke all happiness.

It was clear that he spoke no English, for he simply made an acknowledgement in his own language, which his man translated as 'The happiest wish His Honour give on you.'

We drank in silence, and though our eyes now (as I believed) exchanged wishes for a more intimate expression of our mutual goodwill, the circumstance of the valet standing between us, an expression of profound indifference and haughtiness upon his face, was not conducive to intimacy.

After a while the Duke smiled at me, and made a remark to the servant, who bowed slightly, and turning to me conveyed the information that His Honour wished the knowledge in case of the lady's permitting an intimate congress of persons. The words, spoke in the most funereal tones and in a manner suggestive of the valet's considering them entirely unwise, could not but make me laugh; which the young man interpreted as a rebuke, for he sprang to his feet in embarrassment, his sallow face reddening; but I hastily rose to my feet also, and stepping forward took his hand and pressed it to my bosom – which at once corrected, consoled and inspired him; and taking me by the arm he hastened me towards a door which led directly into the neighbouring room, which unsurprisingly turned out to be a bedroom in which a large bed stood beneath a canopy of silk supported by an enormous structure of carved and gilded wood.

Somewhat to my surprise, the servant followed us into the room, and immediately began to assist his master to remove his clothing – an action which though no doubt a commonplace in every nobleman's life was not in my experience one which naturally occurred when a gentleman was contemplating a connection with a young lady.

My own clothing being sparse, and not being of a mind to allow the presence of a servant to prevent a circumstance which I had taken some trouble to organise, I was lying upon the bed in a state of nature while Mario (which was the man's name) was still carefully folding his master's trousers, the latter meanwhile standing in his shirt, his arms raised above his head, waiting for it to be removed!

That there was something ludicrous about the scene I cannot deny; yet upon the valet standing behind his master and lifting the shirt from his body, the vision revealed (as though upon a stage the curtain was raised) was sufficiently pleasant to make me immediately forgo any tendency to laughter. The body so uncovered was of a perfection of form remarkable even among his countrymen (who are often of a spectacular beauty when young, and often retain their handsome physiques even into old age) – slim without being effete, shapely without being effeminate, and as to its manly parts, provocatively delightful, a show of gleaming and apparently soft curls coiled about the base of an instrument which though at present unaroused and consequently relatively diminutive (perhaps through a certain nervousness on the Duke's part) was delightfully formed.

Stepping forward, the young man looked down at me with (I can say without confusion) some admiration; but then, directing his glance at his own still flaccid part, addressed a remark over his shoulder to his man, who took a pace towards the bed and remarked: 'His Honour has the wish you would eat his, er . . .' – his vocabulary clearly lacking in any English expression for the limb to which he wished to allude.

Delighted though I was that my ruse had brought about the situation in which I now found myself, I was not pleased by the prospect of having the resultant union presided over by an interpreter – for I fancied that two such young people as we could do without such assistance. I therefore rose from the bed, and walking straight to the servant placed my hands upon his shoulders, turned him about, and – meeting with no resistance, no doubt due more to his surprise than his acquiescence – marched him to the door, pushed him through it, and turned the key in the lock.

I then returned to where my would-be lover stood, his lower jaw somewhat fallen in shock that a female should so take charge of the situation, and with equally firm hands pushed him so that he fell upon his back on the bed.

If anything, he was now in lower spirits than ever; and on my kneeling at his feet and, lifting one of them in my hands, nibbling upon his toes, his amusing reaction seemed to lie between confusion, wonder and pleasure – the latter however swiftly becoming the predominant emotion as I passed my hands up the calves of his legs, smooth as a baby's, then over his knees and thighs, gently pressing these apart so that, sliding on my stomach upon the bed, I could follow them with my lips, pausing from time to time to plant a kiss upon that deliciously smooth young flesh.

By the time I approached his groin, there was evidence not far above that even should I proceed no further he would be capable of a connection; indeed, reaching down to seize my shoulders, he showed some impatience for it. He was not, however, to escape so easily; and coming now to the place which showed the only growth of hair upon his body (other than that upon his head, a thread or two about his paps, and a single curl beneath each armpit) I lifted the pouch which hung there, merely dusted with the lightest down, and with that care especially requisite if the action is not to give more pain than pleasure, took the smaller of his cods into my mouth.

At this motion, which I accompanied by allowing my fingers to play about the base of his prick, he gave an immense sigh, and releasing that hold which he had maintained upon my shoulders, fell back upon the pillows as though struck down by some blow to the heart, deep, shuddering breaths only signalling the fact that he still lived!

Having sufficiently mumbled his cods (care must always be taken, my dear Marian, that a pleasantly warming emotion is not disturbed by too coarse an attention to a sensitive area) I turned to that delicious cranny which lies between them and the thighs, taking upon my tongue that faint salty taste which is to be found upon the hide of a young man who, preparing for congress, is careful to cleanse his body in every particular – yet refraining from dousing it with those perfumes which, pleasant in the ball- or dinner-room, confuse the senses in a more intimate circumstance by obfuscating the natural aromas which otherwise are stimulating.

Having allowed my tongue to play along the gap from the point at which that rich though sparse crop of black curls began down to the area where the inner thigh broadens to the first hint of that curve comprising the buttocks, I now approached at last the tower which now stood where a mere limp thumb of flesh had formerly hung. Supporting it with a kindly hand – and it was now so muscular that considerable force was necessary to raise it from its horizontal posture on the belly – I allowed my tongue to mount from base to top, pausing where the bulb began to swell in order that I could draw down the foreskin, stretched now almost to painfulness, revealing the head, which I was able first to tickle by the faintest touch of my tongue about it, then in pity (the young man's gasping becoming almost frantic) to wet my lips and pass them over it, so that first it, then the better part of the whole manly apparatus, passed into my mouth.

To those females who find it uncomfortable or even repulsive to hear such a manoeuvre described, let alone to think of performing it, let me remark that few things are more delicious, once the first step has been taken, than the placing between one's lips of the instrument of a young man of parts – provided always that such measures have been taken as make it inoffensive in the matter of cleanliness (should this not have been done, the precaution should be followed of thoroughly washing the part in question – this itself being often something that will give both parties some pleasure). It is, certainly, not easy to define the pleasure: but the keenness of the emotion thus communicated to your lover must be a part of it, together with the obligation thus conferred upon him to ensure that your own pleasure at least equals his own!

In this case, I imagine that the Duke's former love-making (and his previous experiences had clearly been negligible) were lacking in such tenderness, for within a moment or two – and too suddenly for me to prevent it even should I have wished – a sudden muscular spasm, which I felt through my fingers (placed about his fundament), shook him, and with an unconscious upward thrust of his loins, his pleasure culminated, the proof of it being the expulsion of that tasteless, slightly salty liquor, too bland to give offence.

I must now act speedily if, embarrassed, believing himself to have offended me, or simply exhausted by the extent of his emotion, my friend was not to think it proper to summon his servant and invite me to retire! I therefore slid up his body until we were length to length, and planted a kiss upon his lips – the very fact of which proved both my indifference to what had just occurred and my pleasure in having pleased him.

That he was relieved by this was reflected in his immediately returning the kiss; and if he then turned upon his stomach and fell asleep in my arms, his face pressed against my breast, it was what was only to be expected in one so young and (I believed) inexperienced. I was happy to allow him to slumber for twenty minutes or half an hour; but that being an entirely sufficient period for recovery (in one so young), then through the gentlest movements of my hands over his back, those charmingly rounded buttocks bare of even the finest hairs, aroused him – at which, finding a nipple within an inch of his lips, he fixed upon it, and an almost subconscious shiver of pleasure passing through my body, continued to suck and play, at the same time beginning to explore my body with his hands.

That I was now ready for him to reciprocate that pleasure I had given him, was quite apparent; nor did I attempt to disguise it – and by the subtlest suggestions possible, directed him to such a posture as made it possible for him to approach that area of my person where such attentions would be most acceptable. Like most of those young gentlemen whose education, lacking in sensuality, has been excellent in theory, he was quick to learn, assuming that such care as had been devoted to pleasing him could not but please me, were he to attempt it; so he now explored with his tongue any and every plane where he supposed he could delight me, fixing in the end upon that miniature prick which marks the apex of the cave where pleasure lies; and by an avid attention to it – sharper and more attentive, the more apprehensive he became of my delight – brought me once, then again, to an apex of joy; by which time he was himself roused by the aphrodisiac effect of my delight, and in fine penetrated me with his prick, and this time was so much slower to approach the *dénouement* that I was a third time gratified before he fell upon my body in a state of even greater exhaustion than before.

I tell you this story, Marian (I concluded), only to show that no young man is in my experience unconquerable, and that a little demonstration will often attract even those who seem so. I think that perhaps Mr Valentine Jeakes is in need of just such a show of your indifference to him, and your attraction by another; and rather than passing the remainder of the evening in stupid despair, we should spend it in planning his downfall. Do you not agree?

She did.

Chapter Eleven

The Adventures of Andy

The morning proved clear, bright and brisk. We started our journey inside the carriage, since though the day promised well, it was still sufficiently near dawn for it not yet to be sufficiently warm to sit outside with comfort. At first, as we rattled along the road past the villages of Knight's Bridge and Kensington – where Lord Holland's fine herd cropped the grass around the gates of his drive – we were silent, still somewhat drowsy from the earliness of the hour. However, after the first hour or so, when we had passed Syon House and were towards Egham, we fell into a conversation.

In due course this led inevitably to the matter of my temporary ward. On hearing the name Ralph Trillo, Chichley gave a low whistle.

'Not the nephew of old Sir Fyndon?' he said.

I assented.

'At his majority, he will be one of the richest men in the kingdom,' Chichley averred. 'Even without his uncle's fortune to add to his own, your young friend is able to buy and sell King Billy several times over!'

It was my turn to purse my lips in astonishment. Though Sir Fyndon had been generous enough in his promise of covering our expenses, and indeed in provision for matters in hand, I had not supposed my ward to be in his own right a rich man.

'No doubt the fortune is one of the reasons why the boy was brought up in a certain innocence,' said Chichley; 'though that has its dangers. However, his uncle's choice of yourself as a mentor should lift him from any danger, for I know not a better fellow, nor one who has the world in more balanced perspective than yourself!'

I was of course proud to hear him speak in such terms, and without immodesty was bound to agree with him, though forced by common politeness to deny his words.

'No, no,' repeated Chichley, 'it is the simple truth. You will forgive me for reminding you that you grew up in straitened circumstances, and therefore know the value of money – yet have never learned to love it beyond all else. You are well travelled; you know the ways of the world and of women – and that most delightful of ladies Mrs Nelham has been sufficiently your companion to teach you the pleasures of a faithful female friend, even if you have never felt the temptation to establish a permanent household. How, by the way, is that lady?'

'Well,' I said, 'she also stops at Bath, with Miss Trillo, and will be delighted to see so old a friend as yourself.'

I disclosed at this point that she had the care of Ralph's sister, Marian; at which Chichley was pleased to say that she would prove as satisfactory a mentor as myself – having, as he said, through her unfortunate matrimonial experience learned while still almost a child the lesson that men will marry for other reasons than love, and since her own unsatisfactory alliance proved that it is possible for a lady to live in the utmost independence of spirit provided that her wits are about her and she is prepared to ignore the current foibles of fashion, and build her life after her own inclinations.

'The two young people are fortunate indeed. And how do they fare? They are agreeable?'

I was able to tell him that indeed they were a charming couple, and that I thought they did well; keeping to myself my suspicion that Mr Ralph was a little more passionately engaged with his mistress than I would have wished in a young man of no previous experience.

We jogged happily along thereafter, until the sun attaining its zenith suggested that it was time for some refreshment, and on our reaching the top of a low hill upon the outskirts of the village of Weyhill, I called up to John, on the box, to stop in the shade of a group of elms, when we would climb down and refresh ourselves.

He did so, and we were pleased to stretch our legs after the confinement of the carriage over a parcel of roads even rougher than common. The air outside the coach was still and warm, for it was a cloudless, hot day, and one ideally suited for a meal *al fresco*, as the Italians have it. So walking a few yards from the road, we spread a cloth beneath the elms, and left John to lay out the pies and pasties we had brought, while we strolled a little further, relieved ourselves, and then coming to a hedge looked through it to discover that we had chosen a picnic place just beside a field of corn which was being harvested by a group of farm workers – four men and four girls.

I say that they were harvesters; yet at the moment they, like us, had stopped for some refreshment, and having taken food and drink – as was evidenced by the remains of a feast lying beneath a stook of corn, great stone cider jugs lying empty upon their sides – were now engaged in a form of recreation more spirited if no less satisfying than mere eating and drinking; for four pairs of male buttocks were busily working away between four pairs of thighs at a task which, from the muffled cries and groans both of the grinders and the grindstones, was agreeable to all!

I must confess that the scene was somewhat comic. Though while one is engaged in it the act of procreation is without doubt one unsusceptible to laughter, there can be little doubt that in itself it is an act which can to the cool non-participant be amazingly amusing: in this case, the scene might have been carefully staged as farce – for the country copulatives (as Shakespeare terms them) seemed to have taken their places in order of size: on the left-hand was a big fellow who, if his arse was any indication of the size of his belly, must have weighed quite seventeen stone, so that had the red face of his companion not been split by an enormous grin, one would have feared for her safety as he heaved and grunted, his huge white buttocks shivering and shaking as he worked, and his mistress's hands almost vanishing into the blubber as she clutched at it.

Next him was a man who might have been his father, for his bald head was surrounded by a crown of white hairs denoting some age; yet he was swiving as vigorously as the other, and was almost a replica in little, his person being shaped much like the first's, as round and plump, though far less portly. Then came perhaps the son of the first, a man of middle years with the body of a workman in the prime of his life, his legs and bum white as milk (for the people of this class are not given to exposing their lower limbs to the sun) but sturdy and muscular and covered with a mat of coarse brown hairs. His mistress, whose mop of black hair fell upon every side of a face agape with pleasure, was perhaps the most fortunate of the four women, for his movements, while vigorous and lively, were controlled and careful; he was not going to exhaust his pleasure in a brief assault, and lunged at his target with an easy, swinging motion which seemed likely to continue for as long as either participant required for their complete satisfaction.

Upon the far right, was the grandson (I speak of the men in this way because their age suggested the relationship); a mere boy in his teens, whose short, sharp jabs even as we watched culminated in a sudden leap, after which he lay still, a complaining wail emerging from the lips of the young woman beneath him: 'Jem, you never . . .!' – slapping his arse vigorously with a hand, and at the same time diving with the other between their bellies, no doubt in the hope of reinvigorating a weapon which, I would guess, had been too recently discharged to be capable of re-cocking in less than half an hour.

I was about to turn to Chichley with some comment upon the *scena* before us, when I felt a hand fall upon my upper thigh; not, I immediately assumed, that of my companion, who no extremity of desire would, I was convinced, drive to a connection with the male sex. And indeed, I was right, for upon looking over my shoulder, I saw that we had been joined by two young women – young women? – girls, I should rather say, for both had the clear complexions and slim figures of extreme youth.

One was fair, the other dark; both had faces rosy with a sort of excitement which seemed to me to indicate that they had also been watching, over our shoulders perhaps, the scene which we had witnessed. That this was so, and that they were invigorated by it, was immediately confirmed by their throwing themselves upon us and smothering us with kisses.

I will not say that I (and I dare say I speak for Chichley also) did not find it pleasant enough to feel a warm female body pressed upon my own, especially since the warmth of the weather had derived us of the necessity to wear any clothing other than shirt and trousers, while it became clear that the young women's bodies were covered only by a single thin smock. Nor can I do other than confess that their passion communicated itself instantly to us, for they wriggled in a most enticing way, thrusting their middle parts against ours, and upon apprehending – no doubt – our response from the swelling of those parts which invariably respond to such approaches, became yet more excited, and now, with as little separation of their bodies from ours as could be contrived, removed their single garments.

It was at this point that I became uneasy, for while from their actions they were ready to offer some consolation for our being merely observers of the act in performance just over the hedge, from their appearance it was clear that they were sufficiently young to make any gentleman hesitate before taking advantage of their eagerness – though certainly not sufficiently young to be ignorant of passion. I glanced at Chichley, whose attacker had now seized his shirt and torn the buttons away so that his chest lay bare, and bending over him was lavishing her kisses upon his chest. He caught my eye, and I could see that even in his enjoyment of the moment he shared my own misgivings; for from the body of the girl who bent over him there hung no full breasts; his nymph's torso might almost have been that of a boy, indeed, the pads of flesh upon it being perhaps only of the thickness of a man's hand – though at their centres the pertness and ripeness of the rosy buds of May bore witness to emotions better suited to July. The sun, falling upon her body and that of the friend who crouched over me, gilded their fresh young skins with a light which appeared to turn them almost to transparent gold.

My own attacker herself had indeed meanwhile not been inactive, and in the moment when my attention had been distracted had undone my breeches and now, before I could grasp them (and I had the instinct to do so, if not the power) had with a surprising strength wrenched them from my body, revealing my person in that state in which it was capable of addressing a riper target. I now began to try seriously to escape – for though, to be honest, I was aroused to almost a painful extent (as which man would not, in similar circumstances?) it was not my wish to deflower a young girl of such tender years as this one appeared to be – was she fifteen? – fourteen? – thirteen?

Of whatever age, she was seriously interested in what now stood before her, and though for a moment she simply stared, as it seemed struck in a heap by the sudden juxtaposition of the primary male form, fully at a stand, she now leaned over it and seizing it began to handle it in a manner at once insistent and infinitely titillating, so that for several reasons I found it impossible to interrupt her – first through her evident wish to examine something so new, then through fear of disappointing her, and not least (I must confess) through the pleasure her gesture, though rough, gave me.

Chichley was subject, as I saw, to the same examination – and to my astonishment and, I may say, envy, his girl (who seemed of an age with mine) having lowered her head and sniffed at the apparatus between her hands, now began to taste it with her tongue, and finding it pleasant was sucking upon it as, not much more than a decade and a half previously (as I would guess) she had sucked at her mother's teat. I must confess to an envious desire that the young miss whose fingers were at that moment somewhat over-eagerly moving the skin over the surface of my prick as though preparing (I shuddered at the thought) to skin it like a rabbit, would emulate her friend – but a more serious situation now developed, for feeling no doubt the instinctive urge which results in the copulation of beasts, she raised herself upon my body, and was rubbing her lower parts against my own, a rosy pair of lips about whose portals a faint down only announced the approach of womanhood, lying as it were astride my prick, positively stimulating that instrument which it was increasingly difficult to restrain from its natural desire – to introduce the young person to that ultimate pleasure for which she evidently pined.

I must confess myself at that moment ready to permit it: but the danger was providentially averted; for as I raised myself upon my elbows (whether to push the young person away or to embrace her was a moot point) there was a furious shout, and looking up, I met the eyes of the younger of the three mature men who – perhaps attracted by some noise, for I could not swear but that the girls had expressed their interest in appreciative sounds – now looked through the hedge to see, perhaps, his daughters in a situation which he deprecated.

The girls did not stay to argue, but in a moment rose and fled naked into the copse; while Chichley and I, hampered by the fact that our trousers were about our knees, struggled also to rise – then, the other two men appearing, this time armed with pitchforks, simply tore the offending garments away and fled.

Happily, our pursuers – which comprised the middle-aged man, the boy and no doubt the elders in as far as they were capable – were hampered by the fact that the hedge was partly composed of briars, unkind to their still naked flesh; so Chichley and I were able to make some way before they, with cries of mingled anger and pain, crashed through; and by the time they had done so, John, our driver, had been astonished to see his employer and friend, bare as bodkins, trample over the cloth where pies and pasties were laid out, and race towards the carriage.

Happily, he was quick-witted enough, hearing the shouts of the pursuers, to follow our example and, neglecting the luncheon viands, to leap for the box; and we were able to close the door behind us and, looking out of the window as the carriage was whipped up, to see two men brandishing their weapons (I mean, their pitchforks) after us as we went. Turning the corner, we also saw, half-concealed in the hedge, two young ladies equally unclad, who waved to us as we passed in a manner sufficiently merry to suggest that they were unworried about the possible consequences of their curiosity.

We now found ourselves in some difficulty, for we had no spare clothing, and the spectacle of two entirely unclad gentlemen descending from a coach might be counted upon to alarm the inhabitants even of the tolerant city of Bath. However, fortunately our purses were where we had left them, upon the seat; and the possession of sufficient funds would no doubt go some way to provide a solution to the problem.

It may be supposed that we discussed the incident with some interest. I must admit that had we not been interrupted, the maidenhead of my young seducer would have been in serious danger of damage.

A virgin, said Chichley? He very much doubted it.

'Even ignoring the probability that some country lad had them months ago, incest, you know, my dear Andy, flourishes where the roads are bad, and there can be few young girls over the age of twelve or thirteen or even younger who are not entirely familiar with the male anatomy, through the close proximity of brothers, cousins, uncles – even, I fear, fathers. And from what you know of the functions of that anatomy, can you doubt that they know also the practical use of it? Did they look frightened by our apparatus, or alarmed at the contours to which their attentions raised it? Can you not suppose that they were teasing us towards a full display of that act their elders were so enjoying, and of which doubtless they were jealous?'

I could not dispute it; for in my own extreme youth, abed with two brothers and three elder sisters, I remembered the girls insisting on a close examination of my person long before the age at which such an interest would have stimulated any unbrotherly emotions; and doubtless only my removal from my mother's cottage had precluded their instructing me in the employment of an appendage which up to that time I had regarded as useful only for the disposal of waste product.

As to whether such an introduction, at so early an age, would damage either boy or girl, Chichley opined that desire must be the signal for its own satisfaction – a rough and ready guide which I take with a pinch of salt; and – especially perhaps since the appearance and intent of the pitchforks had driven any thought of erotic satisfaction from my mind, as from my loins – I persuaded myself that I was glad that I had been interrupted before the opportunity arose of discovering whether my young spoiler was, or was not, a virgin.

By five o'clock we had had enough of our journey, and when, entering a hamlet called Seend, we saw a cottage, rough and threadbare thatch almost falling to the road, which announced itself as an inn, I instructed John to stop, to go into the place and to purchase some clothing. He emerged, after a while, with two pairs of trousers in which a generation of country folk appeared to have toiled, and which had the appearance of old-fashioned night-shirts. Needs must when the Devil drives, and attiring ourselves in these costumes we descended and bespoke supper –

a mess of boiled beef with carrots and potatoes which was rough but satisfactory, and together with plenty of country ale encouraged us towards the single (fortunately large) bed the place afforded, where we slept like babes.

We woke, next morning, late; and rising made an excellent breakfast of raw milk and a mess of cooked eggs. There could be no question of our assuming our usual mode of dress, for the nearest town boasting a decent tailor must be either Devizes or Trowbridge, and neither could be relied upon to produce clothes of any style. We therefore decided to waste the time until late afternoon, for Bath was only four or five hours distant, and arriving there after dark we could enter my lodgings under cover of night, when I could lend my friend a suit of clothing until he was able to bespeak his own.

We strode out about the countryside, which was extremely pleasant; in our rough clothing we positively felt part of the agricultural scene, and those few men and women we met gave us a comradely greeting, which we returned in tones appropriate to our appearance, it seeming a shame to put on the gentleman under such circumstance. After lunch, I left Chichley dozing on a bench in the back yard of the inn among the chickens and rooting pigs, and myself set out along the road towards Trowbridge, feeling somewhat in need of the exercise (due perhaps to my rough upbringing, my energy has always been more highly charged than that of most men – and the comforts of a life well provided for have not reduced me to the lethargy of the born aristocrat).

After a mile or so in the heat I sat myself down on

a milestone and rested; hearing, after a while, in the distance, the clatter of horses' hooves and the rumbling wheels of a coach – when soon, around the corner, lurching in and out of the pot-holes (the road surface being as bad here as anywhere else in the country) came one of the largest equipages I had ever seen – the size, it almost seemed, of a small house; with wheels fully six feet across, a row of windows, a door which almost demanded a portico, and a platform (for that, it almost was) upon which sat two drivers to command the four fine horses which pulled the *ensemble*.

Four outriders trotted past me, stirring a fine dust; then the coach itself, at one of the windows of which I seemed to see a face.

Almost immediately it had passed, the coach began to slow, with an application of brakes and the neighing of restrained steeds, and within fifty yards came to a stop. Its door then opened, and two men climbed down and at a trot came back towards me. I rose to my feet as they reached me, but had no time to speak before, one taking each elbow, they frogmarched me towards the carriage, and before I had time to protest had propelled me up the steps and into the vehicle.

My bewildered senses now took in an interior hung with rich, red velvet; windows the glass of which was in some way obfuscated as though by frost; and a large couch upon which reclined, rather than sat, a female clad in silks, before whom I was now held, willy-nilly, at attention, one man at each arm.

The female looked me up and down with an appraising eye, and then nodded to the fellows – one of whom reached out, and having produced a leather bag, jangled it before me, opened its neck, and reaching inside produced a handful of gold coins in a currency I did not recognise. I was about to enquire what he meant by this, when the woman spoke in a language I immediately recognised as French, and over which I have some command. I would have taken advantage of that familiarity to address her and enquire what she meant by this arrest of a British citizen upon the open road, were it not that the words she spoke instructed her servants to unclothe me!

Such was my surprise that before I came to myself, the rough smock in which I was clad was whisked from me, and the tattered and dirty trousers similarly removed, leaving me naked as the day I was born, and unable – the servants holding my arms – to make the slightest gesture of modesty.

The woman now enquired (as I understood it) as to my cleanliness, and one of the fellows, leaning over, seized my private parts in no gentle a hand, and lifting the entire assemblage subjected it to as close an inspection as he could make in the relatively dim light of the coach, then announcing his satisfaction as to its state. I was about to protest – but it occurred to me that the lady of course took me for a member of the working class; and instantly realised that she was probably one of those grand ladies for whom congress with an underling provided that *frisson* lacking in a respectable *liaison*. And now that I looked, I found her not unattractive; indeed, as she stood and, unloosing her gown, permitted it to fall to the floor of the coach, revealing her unclad form, she was far from disgusting, her figure though full being shapely and firm, and her avidness for congress – ever an aphrodisiac – being clear from her eyes, which fixed themselves on that part of me which, as ever, was quick to respond to a display of female charm – the more so, perhaps, after my disappointment of the previous afternoon.

Well, I decided, if the lady wished to taste the delights offered by the English peasantry, I should not disappoint her; and with one sudden exercise of my muscles threw off the two servants, and hurled myself upon her.

It has been, since my extreme youth, my habit to take as much time in the wooing of women as in the ultimate conquest; more often than not slower to arouse than men, they should in courtesy be afforded that leisurely attention which results in the sharpening of their appetites to the point at which their satisfaction is as keen as that of their lovers. On this occasion, however, no such delicacy seemed called for – indeed, I doubted that any was expected, since the lady had taken care to cull from the very hedgerow a member of that class with whom copulation was likely to be nasty, brutish and short.

I therefore lost no time in preliminaries, but parting the lady's legs (which, I must confess, took no great effort) thrust my member immediately into her – finding the receptacle sufficiently slippery to receive me without pain, and the lady from the eagerness of her embraces clearly pleased by the approach. So fierce was the combat that followed that though they were doubtless accustomed to such scenes I was almost embarrassed for her servants, who merely stood by, at attention (inasmuch as they were capable, for being men they were naturally affected by the scene, their footmen's breeches, tightly fitted in doeskin, being strained almost to bursting).

Madame, as I rogered her (for only so coarse an expression reflects the true nature of the engagement) delivered herself of a continual stream of chatter in French, the meaning of which I could only guess at, since my own conversation in that language, which had been moderately expansive, was on the whole of a nature more polite than this, and most of her words were obscure to me (though from their context and intonation their nature was clear enough).

Throwing her legs about me, she used them to sharpen, if possible, the spasms with which I thrust at her, seizing the cheeks of my arse to pull at them in a positive frenzy. The resulting friction seemed to enliven rather than satisfy her, for now, releasing me, she caught at the hairs of my head and forced it downwards to her middle parts, which she raised to my lips as though in an attempt to force a horse to drink.

This style of congress is not (I remember thinking even as the affair went on) one which commended itself to me. Though the frenzy of passion is by no means outside my experience, I prefer to take my love in a more leisurely and may I say affectionate manner; for it seems to me that even with a very whore, it becomes the gentleman to show a respect for the body whose delights, by the invitation of the female in question, he is tasting. But I found myself, somewhat to my own surprise, nevertheless excited by this remarkable war in which the Frenchwoman seemed to regard me more as enemy than friend; and now was filled, despite myself, with what I recognised as an emotion akin to that of those men whose pleasure is to force the unwilling – and releasing my hold, suddenly withdrew, stood up, and looked down at her with what must have seemed a mixture of threat and contempt.

Far from frightening her, this seemed the more to excite her – which sharpened my own lust; and bending, I seized her and turning her upon her face grasped her hips, raised her arse towards me, and with one lunge plunged my instrument into it.

The cry which emanated from her lips was so loud that I feared for a moment that I had done her a serious damage, and paused; but the immediate wriggling of her posterior against my belly disposed of that suspicion – the cry had indeed been one of abandoned delight, and reaching back to take my hands she placed them upon her breasts, yet another cry of pleasure mewing forth as I positively clawed at them with my fingers.

To cut short a scene which I fear may give offence to those of a gentler disposition (or those perhaps who have never experienced the excesses to which females, as well as males, may be drawn by love of the game), it was not long before my business was done; at which, no doubt apprehending the fact, the lady drew my hands downwards to her middle parts, where a moment's caressing of that centre of pleasure which under more normal circumstances would have been occupied by my manly root, brought her to the same release.

She now fell forward on to the couch, my still extended cock reappearing with a comic *pop!* like that of a cork being drawn from a bottle. The two men standing behind me now handed me my smock and trousers, which I shrugged on (there had been no requirement for me to remove my boots). Meanwhile, the lady lethargically turned, raising herself upon one elbow, and without troubling to cover a body whose whiteness bore here and there signs of a bruising which, delivered at my hands, was what she had required, gestured towards the bag of money, which was then handed to me, and the door opened.

I drew myself up, made a slight bow, and with every attempt at the accent of a gentleman, remarked in the French language:

'I am infinitely obliged to Madame for the entertainment she has offered me, and will be pleased to attend her ladyship in Bath, should she wish to renew an acquaintance which has, I trust, been as pleasurable to her as to myself. Her kind gift will be distributed, of course, to the deserving poor. *Au revoir*.'

Her astonished face was the last thing I saw as I descended to the roadway. One of her men, closing the door and hoisting the window, gave me an enormous grin and a wink before shouting to the coachmen, who whipped the horses into a slow amble, then a trot, the heavy equipage lumbering off towards Bath.

I returned, more than a little exhausted, to the inn, where I found Chichley still somnambulant among the chickens; and making my way to our room, fell upon the bed and into a deep sleep from which I was awakened only by my friend's announcing that it was time to make for the city.

I did not apprise him of the incident which I have described: there seemed no point in disturbing him, and since I knew him to have some prejudices against the French, I did not wish to provide him with ammunition against the ladies of that nation, whom I have found to be no more and no less amiable than those of our own. But I spent some time pondering the event, which had revealed to me a susceptibility to violence in the act which I had not previously suspected in myself – and which made me wonder whether all men have not the capability of being so aroused; perhaps dangerously so, should the occasion occur. In attacking Madame so fiercely I had been encouraged by the fact that by her choice of a random roadside vagabond she had positively seemed to expect it; so I had perhaps little enough with which to reproach myself. Nevertheless, I could not but wonder whether such a woman might not in due time invite a violence such as might be dangerous to herself, and which, should her servants not be within call, might even prove fatal.

As we had calculated, we entered the city of Bath in darkness, and drawing up at Pulteney Street slipped into the building unseen – but in the corridor met Sophie, who dissolved into laughter at the sight of us (though at first somewhat alarmed, through not recognising me, and believing that two rural roughs had found their way into the house).

Our first requisite was to bathe ourselves – the inn having provided merely a bucket of cold water; Sophie remaining and chatting to us while we did so (I should explain that Chichley and she were old acquaintances, and the sight of his unclothed body was by no means unfamiliar to her; and we, of course, had grown up together, and were entirely familiar). She described the continuing story of Marian and Mr Jeakes; the name now striking a chord with me and with Chichley. Could there be a connection with Miss Niobe Jeakes, whose portrait had been so much admired? There was certainly, Sophie confirmed, a dark woman seen frequently in his company: and she mentioned a daring visit to his house, and the revelation that he appeared to be in a state of financial uncertainty.

This was a little worrying. Could he have heard of Marian's fortune? Was his indifference calculated to sharpen his interest in her? It was something to be thought of. Meanwhile, I asked, what of Ralph?

The latter, Sophie said, had been seen but rarely since my departure for London; she believed he was spending more and more time with the mysterious woman with whom he was increasingly besotted. She had not, she feared, discovered anything about her – even so much as her name – having been more concerned with looking after her own ward.

Well, it was clear we must both spend some more time in examining the circumstances of our young friends' *amours*. Meanwhile, it being too late for Chichley to disturb his own household, Sophia invited him to share her bed for the night (there being no spare one in the house).

'I do not ask,' she said with that frankness which is one of her most attractive features, 'for those attentions which are more properly directed to Frances . . .' (Frances being Lady Chichley, the wife whose happy reunion with her husband Sophie had been, some time since, the cause of).

'Frances would be sorry indeed were I not to return your hospitality by offering those courtesies ever due to a friend,' replied Chichley, whose unclad person began, at the thought of such attentions, to display the means of conveying them.

I left them at this point, being myself exhausted by my afternoon's activities and eager for bed – a bed unoccupied by anyone but myself – between the clean sheets of which I was soon asleep and dreaming of being pursued across the Abbey square at Bath by a naked Frenchwoman brandishing a pitchfork.

Chapter Twelve

Sophie's Story

I found Marian peculiarly impressed by my story of my seduction of the Duke of Genoa – as well she might be, for it carried a lesson which will be of service to all my female readers, very few men being unsusceptible to jealousy, which while in itself no doubt an ignoble and wasteful emotion may nevertheless be effectively employed as a weapon in the courts of love.

My friend realised this immediately, and nothing would do but that we should put into effect a similar plan in order to ensure an interest on the part of the enigmatic Mr Valentine Jeakes. We therefore went off to the Eagle, one of the middle class of inns at Bath, neither frequented by the best sort of person nor by the entirely impecunious. There, we took a room for the day in the name of the Misses Ponsonby.

It was the best room in the place – which does not say much for it, but at least it was situated on the first floor, its door right at the side of the main staircase, and therefore exceptionally easy of access. It contained only the bare necessities in the way of furniture – a dressing-table, a washing basin concealed by a screen, a couple of chairs with an occasional table, and a handsome bed without hangings (at the period of which I write, beds in public hotels were often equipped with generous hanging curtains which those of a nervous disposition could draw in order not to be observed by the servants when they came in the morning with hot water, or to mend the fire, or for the purpose of performing some other task).

All was well, then, as far as the setting was concerned; and one of the actors was ready to play the scene – but how to cast the other? This was a question which concerned us in no small degree; for while for such a purpose Marian declared herself ready to accept the attentions even of a very Caliban, the gentleman concerned must not be so ugly as to convince Mr Jeakes that she was susceptible to the approaches of any Tom, Dick or Harry; while were he to be too handsome, the opposite effect might take place, and he might take her affections to be so completely engaged that his own would as a matter of course be refused, and retire from the contest before the starting pistol had been fired!

The servants at the Eagle were, of course, disqualified by their position from employment in the matter: not that several of them were not sufficiently personable, but that Marian should not be seen to consort with menials. (It is of course a commonplace that gentlemen may, and frequently do, employ the women servants of public inns in the capacity of temporary mistresses; but those females who take a similar line with the male servants are generally supposed either to be far gone in their demand for somatic pleasure, or are utterly blind to the effects of their action upon polite society – for they are then generally considered by every man who comes into contact with them as a common slut available to all – a mare for everyday riding).

We considered summoning young Edward Curtis – but then remembered that he was occupied upon his father's business in Bristol. Marian suggested that her brother Ralph would be happy to pose as her lover; but that seemed to me to be a suggestion prone to difficulty, and I rejected it.

We were sitting by the window of the room, drinking a dish of coffee and discussing the matter, when into the street below came a young lieutenant of artillery, brightly garbed in his best uniform, and with all the bearing of a gentleman.

'The very person!' I remarked – for to my knowledge the regiment to which he belonged was upon the very next day leaving to march to manoeuvres upon Salisbury Plain; so there would be no question of his remaining in the town to become an embarrassment to us while his situation in society was ideal – neither sufficiently high nor sufficiently low to give us concern upon either account.

I therefore hastily rang the bell, and sent the servant into the street to invite the lieutenant to wait upon us – 'two ladies,' the man was to say, 'who in a temporary difficulty prayed that he would be of assistance to them.'

The young man, when he was announced and strode into the room, was sufficiently good-looking to give me some misgiving, on the ground I have already mentioned; it seemed entirely probable that any young woman to whom he paid the compliment of giving his attention could very easily find her emotions engaged. Tall and slender, he had a fine, narrow face, straight but fine, brownish hair, and a figure which his admirably cut uniform threw off to distinction. He seemed to be no more than twenty years or so in age, and when we enquired his name, clicked heels and announced himself as Lieutenant Norris Blades of the Duke of Cumberland's 23rd, and at our service.

'Pray, sit down, Lieutenant,' I said; 'and unless you would prefer a stronger drink, take some coffee.'

I then explained the situation – altering the circumstances only to the extent that I described Mr Jeakes as Marian's affianced lover, who had been unfaithful to her, and who, I believed, would be brought to his senses by the apprehension of her attractiveness to another man.

The officer looked somewhat puzzled.

'So you wish me perhaps to escort the young lady to the Pump Room, or an Assembly?' he said 'where Mr—'

'Jeakes.'

'Where Mr Jeakes, seeing us together, will through feelings of jealousy once more declare himself for her? Would the motive be sufficient?'

'Certainly not,' I said; 'which is why we have a rather more intimate circumstance in mind.'

'You mean . . .?'

'I mean,' I said, becoming somewhat impatient with the dull fellow, 'that he should find you abed with her.'

There was a silence, and Mr Blades' cheeks coloured.

'Come, Lieutenant,' I said; 'a member of your regiment can surely not have reached your rank without . . .'

'No, no!' he said hastily; 'but if you will forgive me,

ma'am, I have yet to hear the young lady herself upon the subject. One so beautiful (if you will forgive the impertinence) can surely command a gentleman in a more exalted position than myself.'

Marian smiled.

'Should you agree, sir, to assist me,' she said prettily, 'I assure you that your attentions would be no pain to me, for your person is no more repulsive to me than mine to you.'

He brightened somewhat at the pretty speech; but then asked whether such a situation, discovered by a passionate lover, would not be likely to lead to a duel? – which would not be acceptable to his Commanding Officer, and would seriously damage his prospects in the regiment.

I assured him (perhaps libelling Mr Jeakes, or perhaps not – I cannot say) that Marian's lover was not the fighting sort; and (hoping that 'twas true) that I could absolutely guarantee that 'twould not come to a duel.

Marian, seeing that the lieutenant still hesitated, rose to her feet and taking his hand sank to her knees before him.

'I hope, sir, that no motives of respect for my person, however complimentary, will stand in the way of your granting our request?' she said, and pressed his hand to her bosom, much of which was revealed by her semi-recumbent posture.

With such a heaven to tempt him, and the promise of its successful attainment, what could any young man of spirit do but agree?

Upon his concurrence, I seated him with Marian upon the window-seat (where I soon observed her hand steal into his own, and smiled to myself at the speed with which my pupil was learning to exert the wiles of womanhood), sat down at a side-table, and wrote in my finest calligraphy a note to Mr Jeakes, informing him that should he present himself at the first room upon the staircase at the Eagle at two o'clock that afternoon, he would learn something to his advantage – a note signed only by A Well-Wisher; and sent it off to the Pump Room, where, unless he had suddenly departed from his normal custom he would at that moment be found: and was, for the servant returned almost immediately to inform us of the safe delivery of my missive.

Meanwhile I ordered a cold collation and a couple of bottles of German wine, strong enough to loosen the lieutenant's somewhat formal manners but not sufficiently strong to fuddle him. And indeed, as he drank he became somewhat more enthusiastic about the scene in which he was to be an actor. Despite the difficulty of doing so, he retained Marian's hand within his own while they ate and drank, and I could not but notice that in due course he contrived, without obviously doing so, to move his seat so that her right thigh fell in a closer proximity to his own than was entirely necessary.

It struck me that it might have been best simply to encourage the lieutenant to believe that Marian was one of that band of eager, solitary ladies of Bath who were ready to prostitute themselves to members of the Military in return for a suitable gift of money; but apart from the very good chance that he might have declined her services, he did not appear to me to be likely to command much coin, especially since his regiment had been for some time in Bath, a city which in one way or another was likely to have parted him from much of his cash. No, the present way was the best – though as the clock turned twenty minutes to two, I began to wonder whether the gentleman would be up to the task which we had invited him to perform, for while he showed signs of partiality, he had so far taken no steps likely to lead to a more intimate connection.

I tipped Marian a wink, at which: 'Mr Blades,' she said, 'it is time that we repaired to bed!'

At this, he blushed strongly. The ninny! Had I captured a mere butterfly, I wondered? Or perhaps he was much younger than he looked? The latter, I am inclined to think, was the explanation, for while he had been pleasant enough with her, and certainly seemed to enjoy the proximity of their bodies, he showed neither signs of pleasure at her touch, nor any intention to take the matter further – despite being entirely apprised of our intention.

There was nothing for it but to force the issue. I therefore got to my feet and held out my hands to Marian.

'Come,' I said; 'allow me to be of assistance' – and on her standing before me, turned her about, undid the back of her dress, and lifted it over her head. Since she had (on my encouragement) not yet succumbed to the foreign fashion of wearing drawers, my action left her entirely unclothed save for her shoes and stockings; and – as I could see in the mirror behind the lieutenant as he in politeness also got to his feet – a very pretty picture she made, with her slender waist, broad (but by no means pursy) hips, and pert breasts sufficiently rounded to cry out for a caress, while not yet of such weight as to be heavily pendant.

The lieutenant, who I had rather hoped might be brought to some action by the display, remained where he was; his eyes, certainly, now somewhat round and protruding (I trusted, in admiration), his hands clenched before him. However closely I observed, I could see no sign beneath his nether garments of an excitation; though it was possible the constriction of such tightly cut breeches was sufficient to make such a display painful enough to be self-defeating.

I now led Marian to the bed, where she laid herself down, one arm beneath her head, in a pose which I would have believed capable of impressing (or perhaps distressing) a saint; yet which – though he could not take his eyes off her – appeared not to have any notable effect upon Lieutenant Blades.

'Come, sir!' I cried, ' 'tis too late to retreat!' and going to him, took him by the hands and attempted to draw him to the bed; yet he resisted – not forcefully, but simply by failing to follow my invitation, or rather Marian's, who by holding out her hand towards him plainly indicated her willingness to receive him.

The clock now showed almost ten minutes to two, and the situation was becoming urgent. I therefore turned my attention to the lieutenant's uniform, and happily (since I had in my time had some experience of such apparel) managed to unfasten the jacket with relative ease, after which it was a simple matter to remove the shirt. This left only the breeches, which proved a more difficult matter. Kneeling at the gentleman's feet (a position which is not one I readily adopt except in amorous play) I was permitted to remove his boots and stockings; but then on reaching to his waist, he began to obstruct my hands as I attempted to undo the buttons there.

Finally, I lost my temper and administered a sharp slap to his hands.

'Fie, sir!' I cried; 'would you insult my friend by refusing the offer so generously made?' – and positively forcing the buttons from their seating hauled his breeches about his knees and ankles, at which with an indifferent grace he stepped out of them.

It was now clear why he had been so slow to agree to a divestment, for where another man – presented with such a charming picture as my friend made – would by now have been more than ready to prove his admiration, the lieutenant was clearly incapable of anything more than a look: his prick was just that – a mere needle, almost hidden in the cluster of brown curls about it, smaller indeed than the pouch which hung beneath it.

'I – I –' he began to stutter, no doubt in excuse. But now I heard footsteps upon the stair: 'twas too late for argument or persuasion or anything other than action. I gave the lieutenant a push which landed him upon the bed beside Marian, and, hiding myself behind the convenient screen, hoped that she would have the wit to present the situation, somehow, in the light which we had planned.

The screen faced the door, and when, in a moment or two, it opened (for it was unlocked) I saw through a crack in it Valentine Jeakes standing in the doorway, an almost comical look of surprise upon his face. Curious as to the picture my friend was contriving, I peeped around the edge of the screen.

She had acted speedily: it being out of the question for Lieutenant Blades to mount her with any impression of verisimilitude, she had clambered on top of him, with her back to the door, and had buried her face in that part of his body where expectation had been defeated by primness, finding it necessary – as she later confessed – to take not only his dangler but also his cods between her lips, in her effort to disguise his lack of interest.

Jeakes, therefore, upon opening the door, was presented with the view of her delightful arse – plump and pink, looking like nothing so much as a delicious peach, a fuzz of brown hair throwing into relief (rather than concealing) that cleft which any right-thinking man would wish to seal up either with a kiss or a more invigorating embrace; her thighs tapering to the point, just above the knee, where the white stockings which still decorated her calves were secured by a pair of light blue ribbons.

Despite what fears or apprehensions the lieutenant might have had, the touch of Marian's lips speedily disposed of them; between her lips, his cock swelled almost instantaneously (she told me) to a more than respectable size, and, deaf to the sound of Mr Jeakes's entrance, he now raised his shoulders, reached down, clutched Marian beneath the arms, and drew her upwards until thrusting at the bed with his feet he could lift his middle parts and present his armour at the breech – an operation all too clearly discerned by Mr Jeakes, who I now turned once more to observe.

A cloud like thunder crossed his face; he took half a step forward, his hand falling to where, had he been wearing a sword, its handle would have hung; then turned on his heel and slammed the door at his back.

I burst from behind the screen in triumph, and turning towards the bed was ready for congratulations upon the apparent success of my scheme – only to find both the actors so immersed in their parts as to be unconscious of anything else – the lieutenant's feet almost beneath his thrusting bottom, his hands clutching Marian's hips, and she, eyes closed and face screwed into a picture of the keenest pleasure, supporting herself only partially on her knees as his action lifted her, time and again (so vigorous were his actions) towards the ceiling.

If he had been slow to arouse, the lieutenant was now equally slow to satisfy. My friend – who, readers will remember, was remarkably speedy in her response – shrieked time and again with an enjoyment unfeigned and almost painful. Indeed, when she had thrice seemingly fainted from the waves of pleasure which swamped her, I began to fear for hysterics, and since the lieutenant showed no sign of reaching his own climax, applied some stimulus of my own – pinching one of his nipples between my fingers as hard as I could, while at the same time running my other hand down his spine, and on reaching the bifurcation of his buttocks, continuing until my index finger could insert itself in his anus, where an invigorating and rhythmical probing finally resulted (though it took more time than I would have thought possible) in his giving a roar and collapsing upon Marian's body.

It took a little time to persuade him to move, for so vigorous had his attack been – once mounted – that he seemed completely exhausted, and his entire body so slippery with perspiration, 'twas impossible to get a grip upon it when I attempted to lift him from the form of my friend. Seizing a sheet, I wiped him with it, upon which it became possible to grip an arm and turn him so that he fell face upwards beside her – his instrument, though it had been used to such effect, not yet even half fallen to such a size as would enable him to replace his uniform. (It has often struck me that those gentlemen who are slowest to arouse to passion, once provoked are equally slow to satisfy: a more reliable rule than that which seeks to equate the size of a man's most private part with that of his nose or its length with that of his fingers. This, on the evidence which has so far been available to me, has proved a fiction. But I digress.)

Marian clearly admired her new friend's stout constitution, and was perhaps even ready for another bout, for she cast an admiring glance between his legs and even made half a gesture with her hand in that direction; but I shook my finger at her, raised the lieutenant to his feet, and marched him towards his clothing, which he resumed with quite as much reluctance as he had used when I attempted to divest him of it.

Our thanks to him were unfeigned; as were his protestations that the opportunity afforded him had given him nothing but pleasure (which I believed). He was clearly sorry to take his leave – as was Marian, for some time (on his going away) admiring him to me in tones which suggested that Lieutenant Blades, had he wished to do so, might well supplant Mr Jeakes in her affections should he care to essay the attempt.

I will not disguise that this gave me some cause for

some irritation: my efforts had not been made in order that Marian should transfer her affections from one young man to another – I had acted upon the understanding that she would die of frustration were she not to be Mr Jeakes's bedfellow before the week was out, and was more than a little dashed by what seemed a suggestion, now, that failure in this would not, after all, be fatal.

However, after an hour or so, and our return to our rooms, Marian seemed once more subject to her original wishes, and was conjecturing what effect the scene had had on Jeakes; whether indeed he would be jealous, and now make an obvious attempt to engage her affections – or whether he would consider her worthless, and become even more distant?

I was not prepared to join her in this guessing game; for in such situations one must always wait upon events. But my best supposition was that Jeakes, if he was at all like most of the young men of Bath, would be vain enough to find it impossible to tolerate the success of a handsome young lieutenant of artillery in winning so beautiful a prize ahead of himself, and would indeed at this moment be laying plans for her conquest.

We had not been in Pulteney Street an hour when Andy appeared, having arrived late the previous night with Viscount Chichley (who, however, had now returned to his own rooms). He told me, during the few moments we were alone, his news of the richness of our wards' estates, which somewhat surprised me; yet I understood why their uncle had thought it best not to reveal this to us, for though he patently trusted us, great wealth often arouses notions of villainy even in those who are ostentatiously honest.

Needless to say, I told Andy of our latest escapade, which at once amused and interested him – and Ralph, who entered when we were halfway through the narration. I would have refrained from the story on the grounds that the brother might take offence at the sister's going to such lengths to capture a lover; but far from it – she insisted that he should know all, and he was as amused and interested as Andy. Whether or not the plan would succeed divided opinions, Andy being somewhat of the opinion that we might have frightened the gentleman off – and I was interested to observe that Marian's eagerness in the matter still seemed somewhat mitigated; perhaps her passage with the good lieutenant had gone some way to convince her that it was early days to be thinking of setting her sights so very decidedly upon one lover.

Ralph had an appointment that evening – as always – with his friend; and we all four made our way in the late afternoon to the Pump Room, where he had engaged to meet her, and had promised to introduce us, the affair having reached (as he thought) that stage at which such a courtesy was demanded. I do not believe that Andy had talked to our young friend about his intentions with regard to this lady – but it was clear he was completely infatuated with her, and it somewhat disturbed me that he should be so; even the idea of marriage might have entered his head – for he had had little experience of the world; he and his sister were in the same boat, as far as that went, and I determined to discuss it with Andy. Perhaps our removal from Bath might even be necessary as a cure; but we were perhaps both somewhat to blame in permitting things to get out of hand, and should have concentrated on introducing our wards to a greater variety of personable young people of both sexes, thus preventing their minds from centring so decidedly on single targets. However, it is often my observation that young people kept from the amorous affections of their contemporaries for too great a period after their puberty, often do fix upon lovers somewhat older and more experienced than themselves; it was this tendency from which at present we were all suffering (though to be sure the sufferings of Ralph appeared to be such as most young men might envy).

At the Pump Room there was the usual fashionable press; into which Ralph plunged without hesitation, finding his way to a particular woman, whom, having kissed her hand with the most devoted attention, he brought to us. She seemed to be considerably older than his years – though not so greatly so as to provoke comment; handsome, certainly – and distinguished by an uncommonly bold and resolute face. You will be as surprised as I, dear reader, when I tell you that she was the woman I had seen in conversation with Marian's beloved, and was introduced to us as Mrs Niobe Jeakes! Whether the title of Mrs was an honorary one, or whether they were husband and wife, I could not say; Ralph was besotted enough to believe the former – which indeed I feared, for the thought that she was an adventuress intent on his fortune could not be dismissed by me. Nor, perhaps, was Andy unaware of it, for he regarded her with peculiar attention (rather as I did, though I hope I was more circumspect, and did not stare so).

When Ralph and the lady had taken their leave, and

strode from the room (whence, I did not care to enquire, though his flushed face and eager eyes suggested that he anticipated some conversation more inspiriting than mere talk) I asked my friend what he thought?

'Most interesting,' was all he said; then asked Marian whether she would not like to take tea with Viscount Chichley, who was standing not far from us. She was delighted to be introduced; and I to greet him again (though as an old friend taking the opportunity to suggest to him, in confidence, that he refrain from interesting Marian too keenly, knowing that his devotion to his wife did not preclude an occasional amorous adventure, and not wishing to confuse matters more than they were already confused!).

On their taking themselves off, Andy immediately revealed to me the fact that he had recognised Ralph's friend as a woman whose portrait had been greatly admired at this year's Royal Academy exhibition.

Well, was my response; and what of that? Was it not more a matter for congratulation than otherwise that our young friend had been able to capture the attention of one so formidably equipped with beauty and poise?

Andy replied that he was not positively worried; but that he knew from conversation with the painter of the portrait that the lady was impecunious, and I believe that the knowledge of our friends' riches was preying upon his mind, as indeed it did upon mine.

What did I know of Mr Jeakes, he asked? (for he had apprehended Ralph's friend being connected with Marian's love). Little enough, I admitted; but told him in detail of my visit to Pendlebury Manor. He admired my venture anew, but, 'What,' he said, 'if we make another examination?'

Would that not be rash, even dangerous?

But we had been entrusted with the care of these two young people, and every effort upon our part should be made to ensure that they came to no harm – which included protecting them against adventurers.

To be short, I agreed; and leaving Marian in the care of Chichley, we commissioned a carriage and in no long time were at the entrance to Pendlebury Manor where we dismissed the driver to the Boot and walked to the front of the building, dark except for the windows of the sitting-room.

'Let us try the back door!' said Andy, and led the way around the side of the house.

There we found a single, lighted window; and on approaching softly and looking in, saw my friend the footman, *en déshabillé*, slumped at a table with a bottle before him, and looking as though an earthquake would not disturb him. The back door proved bolted; but next to it was a window an inch or two open at the bottom. It slid up easily under my friend's hands, who wriggled in, motioning me to wait – and in a moment, the back door opened quietly.

We made our way along a corridor which led towards the front of the house, and in a moment were through a green baize door and in the darkness of the hall. Thence I led the way to the sitting-room. Two candles only burned here; and all was quiet – but in the distance came the sound of voices. I turned to the corridor which led out of the room to the east along the corridor which led to the strange room which I had glimpsed in my previous visit. The door to it was closed but from behind it came certain noises suggestive of enjoyment. I put out my hand to the door-handle, but Andy held me back – and instead tried the handle of another door, on our right. This opened without difficulty, and we found ourselves in what seemed to be a small gaming-room, for there was a table at which cards could be played; yet the four chairs which would normally have served it, with two more, were set not about the table but in a row facing a tapestry hanging from the wall.

This, while well enough, was not especially interesting, and I could not conceive why anyone should want to sit and contemplate it at length; but Andy knew better, as was immediately to be seen from the grin which split his face. He felt about at the side of the tapestry, and there discovering a silk rope, pulled upon it – whereat, lifted by a counterweight, the tapestry rose, revealing a window which looked upon the next room.

I stepped back, for a moment afraid of revelation; but then remembered just such a window which had separated two rooms in the house of entertainment for ladies which I formerly ran at Chiswick. This (it is more fully described in the account published under the title *Eros in Town* by the reputable firm of Headline, from their address in Great Titchfield Street in London) was so that visiting patrons could view, without themselves being seen, the gentlemen I had engaged for their enjoyment: these latter, in relative light, could be seen by the ladies, while those visiting females, sitting in an unlighted room, were unobserved by the men. Just such a arrangement was before us: installed, no doubt, by the owner of the house.

Whether or not the Jeakeses were aware of it, I could not say; but at all events, Mrs Jeakes was not at the moment giving any of her attention to the possibility of being observed by anyone other than my young friend Ralph, who in turn was as entirely engaged by his companion.

Andy told me later that the room had been described to him at length by Ralph; and since he has recounted that adventure in a previous chapter, I need not recapitulate. But to me, who knew nothing of it, it was a fascination to observe the two lovers, bare as fish, their wet bodies shining in the xanthous light of half-a-dozen candles, half-in and half-out of the water, Ralph lying with his upper body reclining upon folded towels, his arse, upon a ledge, just submerged – while Niobe, who I must confess was exceptionally handsome, almost floated before him, her body, rendered weightless by the water, merely brushing his own, his upstanding bodkin caressed in turn by her breasts, then her belly and thighs as she swung to and fro above him, pinioning with her hands those arms which otherwise would be thrown about her.

As we watched, however, he succeeded (in an ecstasy of emotion) in freeing himself, and standing, swept her from the pool and carried her to a pile of cushions on a nearby bench, where he began to smother with kisses every inch of her body – she at the same time passing her hands over his shoulders and back, down his spine, over a pair of charming nates where water sparkled in golden drops upon a thin pelt of hair . . .

I must confess that I could have stayed to watch the further developments, so charming was the picture; but that Andy took my arm and dragged me somewhat unwillingly away, through the door and along the passage, and then invited me to take him to the upstairs apartments. Seizing one of the lighted candles in the sitting-room, I did so.

The main bedroom remained much as I had seen it. Telling me to keep an eye out in case, unlikely though it seemed, Mrs Jeakes broke off her engagement and made her way upstairs, Andy began to work with system at examining the room, going through the drawers of the table and dressing-table, turning over every paper with care, while I stood in the doorway.

He had just opened a small *escritoire* by the bed, when I heard a noise upon the stair, and saw the early hint of an approaching light. Whispering a quick warning, I slipped from the room into the passage and, in the darkness, closed the door behind me. The light, as I had hoped and expected, was that of a candle borne by my old friend the footman, staggering slightly. He passed the end of the passage, and turned towards his own room; the door swung shut behind him. No doubt within a few minutes he would be sleeping like the dead.

Now, the bedroom door opened behind me, and Andy emerged, clutching a piece of paper. Without pause, he took me by the arm and hastened me towards the main stairway. Just as, descending, we reached the half-landing, we heard a door open, downstairs. Andy quickly pulled me into the shadow of a large carved marble urn that stood on the landing, almost (but happily not completely) filling a niche in the back wall.

No footsteps were heard; but there was a low murmur of voices – and through the ornate handle of the urn which concealed us, I saw Ralph and Niobe coming up the stairs. Their feet were bare; as, I assumed, was the rest of them, for they were wrapped in a single, large towel, beneath which certain movements suggested that the mere act of climbing stairs was not being allowed to interrupt those caresses which resulted, on their reaching the landing, in our young friend stopping in his tracks and slipping to the carpeted floor, dragging the lady with him.

Throwing off the towel, they now began a course of love-making which suggested that their bathtime pleasures had been merely a preface to the book they now intended more fully to peruse – but the pages of which they began to turn with such speed and enthusiasm that they seemed scarcely to allow themselves time fully to examine them. Thus Ralph began, in his eagerness, by throwing himself upon the lady in that pose which records confirm is most common to us; his face buried in her neck, we could clearly see by her expression that, while by no means averse to his attentions, she was not as lost to reason as he, and had the situation well in hand.

The next moment, by simple means of pushing him to one side, she threw one leg across him, and reaching down to ensure by the pressure of her hand that they remained engaged, began a swift series of changes of posture which reminded me of nothing so much as the Poses of Pietro Aretine, recorded in his *Ragionamenti* and illustrated by Marcantonio Raimondi in order to inform and instruct adepts in the possible postures of love.

I must admit to admiring young Ralph's stamina, for though the lady's attentions were sufficiently lubricious to arouse even my spirits (who had seen it all before!) he succeeded in keeping his countenance – and more than that, to refrain from the final throe; a fact which seemed to rouse her almost to desperation, for, throwing him on his back, she now rode him with an increasing fierceness – then dismounting, turned so that she was able to caress with tongue and lips his recalcitrant instrument: at which, far from succumbing, he took the opportunity to reach with his own tongue that tender spot in her which now reacted to his attentions with even more readiness than before – Niobe in a while being forced to remove herself and once more leap into the saddle, where this time a few minutes' riding sufficed not only to content the steed, but – as I guessed – the rider.

They lay for a moment exhausted – and I became conscious that Andy's body, pressed against my own from his position behind me, now boasted a protuberance which demonstrated that he had been as interested in the scene as I.

But this was certainly not the time to consider placating either his desire or my own. We must remain still for the while; fortunately but for a few moments, when the couple before us lethargically rose to their feet, and leaving the towel where it had fallen, went hand in hand on, up the stairs; when we heard the door of the bedroom close behind them.

Quietly, we took ourselves off, letting ourselves out at the front door. At the bottom of the drive, we were just passing between the gates when without any warning other than a scatter of hooves, a carriage rounded the corner, a running footman bearing a torch. We had nowhere to hide, the shrubs being behind us; and for a moment I met the eyes of Mr Jeakes – and could swear that he recognised me.

Well, there was nothing to be done about that.

We found our coachman at the Boot, and were returned to Pulteney Street. Andy was ungiving when I asked what he had found in the bedroom, and would say nothing – until we were alone in his room, when he produced a piece of paper and placed it before me: it bore a long list of names, largely unfamiliar, but including those of Ralph and Marian Trillo – the latter two pricked out in red.

What, I enquired, could be the meaning?

'This,' Ralph said, 'is a list of some of the richest young persons in England. I only know some half dozen of them – all young, all unmarried; and would guess that the persons whose names are unfamiliar to me are in a similar case.'

The inference was an obvious one. Except that there was one perplexing matter. Two adventurers aiming to seduce, then presumably marry a young couple for their fortune – this was neither uncommon nor difficult to credit. But that such adventurers should not only already be married, but be husband and wife! What could be the meaning?

Talk though we might, far into the night, we could not imagine an explanation.

Chapter Thirteen

The Adventures of Andy

Our difficulty now was in finding a way of discouraging our young friends from their too close interest in Mr and Mrs Jeakes. While it was impossible to discover what intentions the couple could have towards Ralph and Marian, it seemed perfectly clear to us that they were connected with the youngsters' considerable fortune, and the means of converting it to the Jeakeses use.

It would be easy enough to summon our wards and, informing them of our discovery at Pendlebury Manor, to invite them to consider their situation. Yet, rightly or wrongly, we believed that this course would have the opposite effect to that which we wished – for young persons are notoriously persuaded to be faithful to those they consider their friends, above those they consider their guardians; and while we had been fortunate in establishing a close relationship with the brother and sister placed under our guard, we could not but fear (I, in the case of the besotted Ralph, in particular) that any advice of ours would but persuade them to an opposite course. We had in some way to trick the Jeakeses into losing their footing and falling prone at our feet in a manner which could not be misinterpreted.

I will not disguise the fact that the matter quite defeated us; for the moment, we would continue life as usual, Sophie certainly attempting to distract Marian in order that her thoughts might be as little as possible drawn towards Valentine Jeakes, while I should, by arranging the most interesting possible entertainments and invitations for Ralph, distract him to the extent that his preoccupation with Niobe Jeakes might be less all-consuming. We were, as we perfectly knew, unlikely to succeed: the first romantic preoccupation of the young is one of the most intense in life, and the most impervious to distraction.

For that reason, our attempts at providing our friends with more engrossing entertainments were not very successful: we took them to a number of admirable concerts – but the trio-sonatas of M. Michel Pinolet de Monteclair and the cantatas of M. Joseph Bodin de Boismortier, even when played by the most admirable instrumentalists, lacked excitement when compared with the pleasures (even, in Marian's case, the apparently unattainable pleasures) of love.

We took care also to provide them with the kind of company which might be expected to divert them: a succession of young ladies whose easy virtue was matched by their personal attraction were unsuccessful, despite the most evident blandishments, in keeping Ralph from the arms of Mrs Jeakes, while though our young friend Edward, when he returned from Bristol, was extremely happy to give Marian dinner, and upon his making the most tentative of advances was welcomed to her bed with an enthusiasm which gave us hope that she had finally despaired of Mr Jeakes – yet from the eyes she made at the latter next afternoon, this was not the case. She was indeed clearly about to throw caution to the winds and make an overt approach, when providentially Chichley swam into view, and appealing to her sense of decency I was able to pair him with her, and he took her off to the Paragon for a game of *écarté* – at which Jeakes threw me a glance of absolute dislike from which I gathered that he and his wife perfectly understood that we had a clear view of their aims, and were unanimous in standing in their way.

Another incident occurred when Sophie and I took the siblings to the Bath Pleasure Fair, an annual event which – designed for the commonalty – was attended by ladies and gentlemen of fashion, though pretending (by dressing with less than usual formality) to be above such matters as booths in the streets, toys and sweets, noise and clatter, shows of monkeys and wild boar, a Zulu Caffir, a fat woman performing juggling tricks, and the like. Ralph and I were pleased with the dancing-booth, in which four uncommonly handsome young ladies – black-eyed girls in tawdry bright attire – performed eurhythmics of a surprising nature; while for Marian nothing would do but having her fortune told by a brown old witch in a tent, who informed her that her fate awaited her outside – and on leaving, a young gypsy man, lithe and tall, a wonderfully handsome animal like a black panther, approached her and announced that he would be pleased to show her the wonders of gypsy conjuring for a guinea (including, he said, tricks but rarely performed in company).

His meaning was perfectly obvious, and it was clear to me, catching Sophie's eye, that in the first place she wondered whether her ward should be allowed to experience these tricks, and in the second place regretted that the gypsy's offer had not been directed to her (but perhaps, since she left the fortune-teller's tent a pace behind Miss Marian, she had been mistaken for her maid – a suspicion I kept to myself rather than insult my friend by voicing it, which she would certainly not have approved of!).

At all events, upon Marian raising an eyebrow, she received a nod of approval, and in a pretty gesture laid her delicate hand upon the swarthy forearm of the gypsy, as thickly furred as the limbs of the beast to which I have already compared him, whereupon he led her off behind the fortune-teller's tent (whom I strongly suspect of being his mother) – at which very moment, turning away, I found myself looking once more directly into the angry eyes of Valentine Jeakes, who had the perfect appearance of wishing to murder me; and from time to time during the course of the afternoon, I saw him in the distance, watching us, and in particular seeming impatient upon our being rejoined by Marian, whose usually rather quiet demeanour had been enlivened at her gypsy friend's contrivance, for she was now flushed and spirited.

Ralph and I parted from Sophie and Marian at supper time; and I attempted to persuade Ralph to spend the evening with me at Bellamy's (a club where gaming took place, though within those financial limits which made it possible for me to participate without the fear of bankruptcy). However, he cried off, saying he had an engagement elsewhere – which, I suspected, was not unconnected with the vision of Mrs Jeakes which I saw in the distance, by the Abbey, when we parted.

Not caring to go to Bellamy's alone, I decided to sup at Tawson's, a public eating house upon Pulteney Bridge; and having made a decent meal there, left and took a stroll upon the river's bank in the cool of the evening, just as dusk was falling. There, on coming round a bank of bushes, I heard a voice crying for assistance, and saw a ruffian attacking a young female, who was clinging on to her reticule with great courage. I naturally went to her assistance – whereat, seeing me approach, the cowardly assailant left his prey, taking to his heels.

I could not resist a few words to his victim on the inadvisability of so young a person walking in so relatively remote a place; but she replied that she had been visiting her grandmother who, being sick, had prayed her to remain until the candles were lit, which had made her later than usual. Her way taking her near Pulteney Street, I naturally offered to walk with her, and she gratefully accepted my escort, taking my arm with a shy grace which was extremely becoming.

Her age was difficult to assess in the somewhat dim light (I speak of a time before street lighting was common except in the most populated streets); she might perhaps have been seventeen; her voice was low, and she kept her face somewhat averted (no doubt through shyness); her figure was slim, and she moved with a gait which was more assured than her bashfulness might have suggested.

She was, she told me, a sempstress, living in Bath with her younger brother, whom she had cared for since her parents' death in an epidemic of cholera which had struck the town two years since. She talked cheerfully of her life, and on my enquiring whether she had a gentleman friend, replied that she had, but that he (being a driver on the stage from Bath to Nottingham) was frequently absent, so that she felt the lack of masculine company. She stammered somewhat over the last phrase, which convinced me that she was not as innocent as her demeanour suggested – an impression somewhat confirmed when she stated, in a hesitant voice, that she hoped she could reward me in some way for my timely assistance – her hand tightening upon the back of mine, as it lay within my arm, in a manner highly suggestive.

Upon our reaching the door of my rooms, the reader will not be surprised that I asked whether she would do me the honour of accepting a cup of chocolate before we parted; to which she readily assented, and we mounted the stairs together. On entering my rooms, I went to light the candelabra – but she prayed that only a single candle should be lit, for (she said) her profession had affected her eyes, and a bright light peculiarly distressed them.

I naturally assented to this; and we sat by the light of one small flame while she accepted a glass of brandy in the stead of chocolate – a suggestion to which she assented with a pretty hesitation, chocolate (as she said) falling heavily upon her stomach so late in the evening (though it was scarce ten).

She drank down her glass with ready enjoyment, and accepted a second almost with eagerness; which seemed to give her courage, for she now rose and approaching my chair placed a hand upon my shoulder, then touching my cheek with the back of it, asked whether she could not show her gratitude for my action and her pleasure in my company, in a manner which would give me more satisfaction than the mere sharing of a drink?

Seizing her hand, I pressed my lips to it, and standing, clasped her in my arms and transferred those lips to her own – which immediately confirmed my suspicion as to her experience by allowing my tongue to taste the sweetness of her own. Picking her up in my arms, I then strode into the bedroom, and placing her upon the bed began to unloose her clothes – whereat, to my irritation, she stopped me, positively pushing me away (and with surprising strength).

'Sir,' she said, 'forgive me – but this is not a common matter with me, and I must confess to a modesty which our longer acquaintance will no doubt dispose of; however, in this instance, might I pray you to leave me to unclothe myself in private?'

Again I naturally concurred with her wishes, pleasant though it always is to assist in unwrapping unfamiliar gifts; and taking myself once more to the sitting-room, occupied myself in removing my own clothes, then standing all a-shiver (it was not a warm evening) behind the door and waiting my summons, which soon enough came, in that low, almost hoarse, highly individual voice of hers. It will be imagined that I was not slow in accepting the invitation, and slipping between the sheets was happy to warm my cool body against her own, which though slim seemed almost feverish with warmth. When I once more clasped her in my arms, she was without her clothes even slimmer than I had previously observed, her breast against mine seeming almost to lack those protuberances which naturally cushion an embrace; however, her lips were as welcoming as formerly, and her hands immediately embraced my shoulders and back with a tender and rousing aptitude.

My own hands, running down her back, encountered a backbone so distinct that every nodule of it could be separately felt; and the globes upon which my palms now fell were smaller and harder than common, while surely the down upon them was thick enough almost to counterfeit the hairiness of a man's arse? And what was it I felt pressing against my belly? A dreadful suspicion began to dawn on me. With difficulty prising our bodies apart, I brought a hand between us – to find, in that spot where a welcoming cranny was anticipated, a male organ which to my touch was as hard and ready as my own!

With an oath, I drew away. Though from unusual circumstances which I will not now describe, a male bedfellow was not altogether outside my experience, I have never positively sought one, while those kind of Amy-Johns who commonly dress in women's clothing were positively repulsive to me. Throwing back the bedclothes, I was on the point of leaping from bed – when there was a sound of breaking wood as the outside door was forced, and in a moment three fellows bearing lights came into the room – revealing the coiner and myself in a state of nature, and in my own case a state of some embarrassment.

The men were constables; and immediately, and despite my protests that I had been deceived, arrested us both, and scarcely permitting us time to resume our clothing, carried us downstairs. Outside the house was a prison coach, into which I was thrust – at the same time hearing a scuffle, and cries which proceeded from my seducer breaking away from his escort and taking to his heels. He was pursued some little way by one of the three constables, who (too swiftly, it seemed to me) returned to announce that he had got clear away. The coach then wheeled off to the gaol, where I was thrown into a filthy cell, alone, and left to consider my situation.

This was not happy. Though it may by some be considered unjust to punish men and women for proclivities which, while against the normal run of behaviour, are none the less natural to *them*, it is a fact that I was in danger not only of loss of reputation but of suffering a severe penalty at the hands of the law for being found abed with such a fellow in such circumstances; despite the fact that it was clear to me that I had been manoeuvred into the situation with some care – for while such a queen might solicit my attention for money, he would not have gone to the trouble of setting up a rescue in order to attract my attention.

No, I had been – in common parlance – thoroughly bamboozled; and I could guess by whom. If I was not much mistaken, Mr Valentine Jeakes was behind this. The knowledge somewhat comforted me, for Sophie at least would believe me, and it might well be possible for her to procure some proof of the plot – supposing I could get a message to her. As to what Jeakes hoped to achieve by his scheme, that I could only guess: my removal from the scene was no doubt the chief aim – but as to the rest . . .? Did he perhaps intend to seize Marian and hold her to ransom? He could not marry her, being himself already married – though since he was able to contemplate with such indifference his wife's affair with Ralph . . .

There was no point in considering the matter further. Clearing some filthy rags out of the way, I lay down upon the wooden bench which was the only furniture of the dank cell in which I was confined, and with surprising celerity fell into a sleep.

I was awakened early in the morning by a loud clatter which, when I recovered my senses, I saw had been made by a tin cup of water thrown to the floor of my cell by the gaoler; when I protested that the accident had left me nothing to drink, the reply was that a duchess like myself need expect no favours of him. I did not protest: my (happily) small experience of prison suggested that there was nothing to be gained by expostulation, and I suspected that in any event before long I would be provided with the opportunity to protest my innocence.

There was nevertheless what seemed a long wait before, at midday, the door of the cell was thrown open and without ceremony I was hauled to my feet by a burly fellow the size of two, dragged along a corridor without the opportunity to put my own feet to the floor, and propelled up a narrow staircase which led into the dock. There I found myself in a courtroom facing a bench upon which – I must confess, to my relief – I saw that the presiding magistrate was none other than Mr Gaucet, to whom I had been of assistance so recently that surely he could do nothing but assist me in my predicament.

However, I had counted without the exigencies of the law and the intractability of the magistrate's personal opinions. My name and occupation (gentleman, and Member of the Parliament) having been recited – and I was extremely grateful that there was no one present in the courtroom likely to report the fact at large – I was charged with committing the unnatural act of sodomy with another male person. This brought from me the immediate and passionate declaration that no such act had taken place – but one of the officers who had arrested me (I suppose generously paid for it) declared that upon entering the bedroom he had clearly seen myself buggering the other offender, and would be prepared to swear to it. On Mr Gaucet enquiring as to the whereabouts of my partner, he was informed that unfortunately the latter had escaped from police custody, and that there seemed little chance of apprehending him.

The seriousness of my position was now perfectly clear: the offence with which I was charged was a capital one, and should the officer perjure himself at my trial with sufficient persuasiveness my neck would be in danger of breaking at the hands of the public hangman!

My hopes of assistance from Mr Gaucet were swiftly dampened, also; for clearly he was one of those gentlemen to whom the offence of which I stood accused was anathema. Though he saw with surprise the identity of the prisoner who stood before him, he was clearly disposed to believe the officer speaking against me; and without giving me the opportunity to comment further, gave out that I should be confined in the prison until a date for my trial could be fixed, for male connections of this sort, he said, were becoming so prevalent that before long the act would be a more fashionable device than simple fornication, and the tendency must be put an end to. He then made a dismissive gesture, and I was seized to be taken below.

I did however manage to gasp out an appeal to be heard – for, I said, I had after all been of some service to the magistrate. The appeal struck home, and after a moment's pause he agreed to see me in his 'chambers', which proved to be a room the size of a broom closet, behind the courtroom. There, I do believe that I managed to persuade him that I was not guilty of the offence with which I had been charged; but this was so grave, he said, that he could do nothing but keep me confined – there was no device by which I could be freed.

He agreed to inform Sophie of my predicament; and I could only trust that her intelligence – which I knew to be of the highest – would provide some means of escape. I was then returned to my cell and possessed my soul in such patience as I could command. At least my gaolers had clearly been instructed to treat me with more courtesy, for not only was I removed, in a while, to a more convenient room of detention (one generally used for common debtors) but was permitted to send out for food and wine.

It was early evening before the door of my cell was opened. Sophie and Marian entered, and to my surprise invited me to accompany them, which I did – the gaoler outside, a lean and hungry fellow whose face was unfamiliar to me, leading us along a series of dank and gloomy corridors which culminated in a ramshackle door giving on to a mean and narrow street at the back of the courthouse. Here, a closed coach was waiting, into which we all bundled except the gaoler – who, having received a purse from Sophie, made off in the opposite direction with remarkable celerity.

Query seemed superfluous: it was obvious that bribery was again at work, this time on my account. How my friends planned to relieve me of the necessity to remain for the rest of my life a man hunted for the most serious of crimes remained to be heard, and at the moment, breathing in the fresh air of freedom (remarkably pleasant after the fetid atmosphere of my prison cell), I was indisposed to ask.

Making the most of the air, I was almost hanging from the window as the coach made its way through the back streets of the city (though careful that my face should not be too plainly seen by curious passers-by).

It was thus that my eye fell upon a figure lounging at a street-corner, the sight of which made me cry out to the coachman to stop – which he did, pulling his steeds up so short that they reared almost out of control. Before the wheels had stopped turning, I was out of the vehicle, had swooped upon the astonished figure, and whipped it into the coach, which immediately began again to move.

I had recognised, despite his now being dressed in man's clothing, the gay deceiver of the previous evening, whose pretty face, now smudged with dirt, was clearly that which had with an embarrassing ease seduced me. My companions, at first startled by my action, needed only a few words to inform them of the reason for the kidnap; and, the boy showing some disposition to cry out, was gagged with his own handkerchief and restrained until we reached the countryside, when I instructed the driver to turn into a remote lane and stop.

There, I questioned him. The interrogation was not prolonged, he being insufficiently courageous to stand out for more than a minute against my threat by a simple operation to remove from him those masculine attributes whose presence had so surprised me on the previous evening, and which appeared in his opinion not to be as superfluous to his pleasure as others might suppose.

In short, he confessed almost immediately that he had been bribed by a man certainly answering to the description of Valentine Jeakes to place me in the uncomfortable position in which I had been discovered – Jeakes having also ensured by a present to one of the constables that my seducer should be permitted to escape. He pleaded poverty and the state of orphanhood, and professed complete repentance; and since he was indeed evidently poor (a state with which I have been personally acquainted, and know the horror of) and terrified, and no doubt had learned his lesson, I insisted that he should be released, and he ran off into the countryside with many expressions of sorrow and gratitude. I had a fear that he was unregenerate; but which of us would not be so, being born to the condition with which he must struggle?

We now held a counsel of war, and I heard what I had not previously known: that Ralph, whose absence from the carriage had somewhat perplexed me, it seeming more likely that he rather than Marian should with Sophie play a part in my rescue, had not been seen since the previous evening, when he had had as usual an appointment with Niobe.

Well, I said, there was probably no time to be lost: if Jeakes had been so eager to have me out of the way, it seemed most likely that some untoward contrivance was reaching its culmination. Fortunately, we had come out of Bath upon the road westwards – and I now instructed the coachman to make all haste to Pendlebury Manor.

We reached the house by ten o'clock, to find it almost in darkness. I led the two women immediately to the back, and, spying through the window the footman whose vigilance had been so lacking upon our previous visit, this time knocked upon the door. After some hesitation the fellow opened it, to find Marian, apparently in some distress, enquiring whether he could inform her of the way to the village, since she had lost her way. On his stepping from the door, it was a simple matter to throw my coat over his head and to bind him about the arms with a belt; after which I marched him some distance from the house and set him free to blunder around as best he might, his muffled cries too faint to rouse anyone in the house.

Returning swiftly, I then led the way into the house, and through the silent interior to the hall. A light once more stood in the sitting-room, and on our passing through to the corridor, once more there were audible sounds from the bath-room at the end. Softly, we let ourselves into the side room, where the tapestry remained as we had left it – the Jeakeses presumably not having since entered the place. As we stepped towards it, the room next door became clearly visible, and a little shriek from Marian indicated that the scene before us was one which was as unfamiliar to her as it was unexpected to me. I shall not describe it, for such scenes are best left to the imagination of those who wish to visualise them; I will merely say that the central figure was Mr Valentine Jeakes, and that he was entirely preoccupied with two young gentlemen of ages between eighteen and twenty-five, like himself bollock-naked, and indulging in that form of conversation which (though the instruments of speech, viz. the lips, were certainly employed) is not verbal, the three forming a perfect triangle the major points of which were their pricks, and the scene strongly resembling those orgies regularly depicted upon the sides of Greek vases, and presumably familiar to those who painted and possessed them.

It must now be clear to Marian, as it was to Sophie and me, that it was unlikely that she could continue to seek the amorous attentions of Mr Jeakes without an exercise of hope over experience too extreme to be likely.

We did not stay to observe the scene (though Marian's curiosity, she not having any previous knowledge of what gentlemen of Mr Jeakes's persuasion do together, was obviously considerable). Instead, we retired to the hallway and proceeded upstairs, where a dim light from beneath the door of the main bedroom was all that was to be seen. Here, I presumed, Mrs Jeakes was ensconced with the unfortunate Ralph. I must say, I began to sympathise with her: for what could be expected of a lady whose husband's tastes ran so exclusively to boys, other than that she should seek consolation where she could find it? But there was still Ralph's fortune to be considered – and the list which I had found in the very room before us continued to suggest that Niobe's affections were not merely erotic.

Without hesitation, I threw open the door. There before us, on the bed, sprawled the figure of Ralph – but alone! I strode over and shook him by the shoulder; he stirred slightly, but did not wake. I shook him again, more violently. Still, there was no response. Bending over him, I sniffed at his mouth – a strange fragrance hung about it. Clearly, he had been drugged. I instructed the ladies to bathe his head with cold water, and in a fine fit of temper rushed down the stairs and into the room where Jeakes was still enjoying himself with his catamites.

To be entirely frank, I cannot remember either what I said or what I did; but that it was effective is signalled by the fact that, having merely been given the time to wrap himself in a towel, Jeakes was within a few moments upstairs with me, where Ralph was beginning to show signs of recovery.

This somewhat alleviated my anxiety, and I was able to give cooler attention to Jeakes, who I must confess seemed as surprised as we were to see my ward's state – and professed to have no knowledge of Niobe's whereabouts. But here came the great surprise: when asked about Mrs Jeakes's absence, he replied that he thought his 'sister' would have been in the bedroom with her young friend.

His sister! But we left the conundrum, and concentrated our attention upon Ralph, who was now almost entirely brought to consciousness by the application of some salts discovered in a drawer by the bedside. He seemed as confused to see us, as we were at his condition; and it was some time before he could be rational – but then could throw little light upon the situation, except to say that he had accompanied Niobe as usual to the house, that they had engaged in their usual passionate embraces, but that he had then fallen asleep – to be awakened only by us.

It seemed clear that the woman had drugged him while he slept. But to what end, we could have no notion.

In a while, we encouraged Ralph to resume his clothing, which lay scattered about the floor of the room, evidence of the speed with which he had thrown it off in his passion. I quietly invited him to assure himself that any cash he had been carrying was still in place; and indeed it was – but in searching for it, he found a folded letter in an inside pocket, which he averred was in his mistress's writing.

'My friend,' it began, 'I ask forgiveness for the manner of my leaving; and invite you to believe that my course of action is taken only because my efforts to leave would otherwise be frustrated by your affection . . .' and went on to state that Niobe had, with her brother, positively planned to seduce Ralph, as a means of getting at his fortune; that originally the plan had been for Valentine to make a similar attempt at Marian – but 'his natural proclivities forbade it', and the fine pair had decided to rely upon the sister's persuading young Ralph into marriage.

However (the note continued) his frank and open nature, the intensity of his emotion and the pleasure they had enjoyed had been such that Niobe now found it impossible to continue the plan; she was, therefore, leaving him, in the hope that the memories he would retain of her would not be altogether unkind.

At first shocked by the revelation, Ralph was almost immediately devastated at his loss – for, he said, did the note and the woman's action not demonstrate the innate goodness of her character? Taking Valentine Jeakes by the shoulders, he shook him vigorously and entreated to know Niobe's whereabouts – which Jeakes claimed to have no knowledge of, seeming by his attitude rather to disapprove of his sister's generosity of spirit; though I wondered whether 'twas not a ruse to make more sure of Ralph's affections.

However, it was clear from Ralph's attitude that he would not give up the idea of tracing the lady; and it seemed my duty to discover whether this was or was not a good plan, and if good, to lay some rational plan for finding her. Leaving Marian and Sophie to comfort Ralph as best I might, I therefore took Jeakes into the neighbouring dressing-room, and there questioned him closely for almost an hour; at the end of which I had arrived at the supposition that his sister's letter could be taken as honest – for from his words she seemed to have retained a natural element of kindliness, though poverty and the demolition of her prospects (a fine marriage falling through because of the groom's discovery of Jeakes's unnatural disposition) had driven her to the plot to which she herself had confessed.

They had taken this house, he said, as part of the scheme; and now must find themselves all the more impoverished by reason of the money they had pledged for it, and that which they owed in Bath – Niobe's desertion having clearly resulted in the collapse of their plans. (He did not say this with particular regret, I must confess, but as a matter of record.) His anger at me had been generated by my obvious suspicion of him and his sister, and by his apprehension that she was becoming genuinely fond of Ralph; and a combination of these circumstances had led to his reprehensible engagement of one of his paramours to seduce me in the guise of a woman.

It was difficult for me to forgive this potentially extremely damaging – indeed dangerous – jape; yet Jeakes, I must confess, was somewhat less objectionable the more I spoke to him. I was indisposed to blame him for his attachment to his own sex, which seemed to me to be no more blameworthy than the colour of his hair; and in declining to take advantage of Marian's clear admiration, he had done her and ourselves a great favour.

Questioned about his sister's possible course of action, he could only suppose that she had made for London, the town which above all others she knew best; there, he said, there were a number of friends who it was possible might know of her whereabouts.

I now encouraged him to dress himself and make ready to accompany us immediately towards the capital, and he having taken himself off (no doubt to dismiss his young lovers) I returned to the bedroom and revealed what I had learned to my three friends, all of whom agreed that we should make an immediate start for London – which, in short, we did.

Whether this was wise, subsequent events only could show; what was clear was that whatever I did or said, Ralph was sufficiently besotted to chase after Niobe, if necessary alone; far better that their meeting, should it be contrived, should take place in such circumstances that I and Sophie could be privy to it, and if possible guard against the worst result of it.

Chapter Fourteen

Sophie's Story

We are now at a stage in our story when my narrative and that of Andy must inevitably overlap; and the reader will understand that I shall not recapitulate the incidents which he has just described – except to add that while Marian and I were awaiting the full recovery of her brother and he was interrogating Mr Jeakes in the neighbouring room, she questioned me keenly upon the scene which we had witnessed downstairs – for a lady (even one less innocent than herself) an unusually graphic view of an orgy between the gentleman and his catamites.

Was it the case, she enquired, that such men (of whom she had heard spoken, but only humorously and without detail as to their habits) spent their entire amorous lives in the pursuit of those of their own sex?

It was, I must tell her, in general the case, though some to my knowledge were capable of entertaining feelings of almost equal enthusiasm for both ladies and gentlemen – one sex, however, being usually preferred by them when a final choice must be made.

And were there any so unregenerate (she then enquired) as to be incapable of persuasion? In short, could they not be saved by the love of a good and enthusiastic female?

I replied that in most cases, that was not the case. It was easy to see how her thoughts were tending, and I found it my duty to do my best to persuade her to detach her hopes of happiness from a contemplation of the reformation of Mr Jeakes, who it seemed to me was from every sign he had given unlikely to respond to her blandishments: would he not have capitulated by now, had he been capable of responding to her obvious enthusiasm for his person? And even should he do so, was his character such as honestly to commend him as lover or (much less) husband?

She merely shook her head, and I fear was unconvinced – a fear which became keener when we had established ourselves in our carriage and were making for London, whence it was generally believed that Mrs Jeakes – or perhaps to avoid confusion, I should merely refer to her as Niobe – had fled. (Incidentally, was our situation not the clearest argument for relinquishing the silly habit of affording ladies of a certain age the dignity of the title of 'Mistress' or Mrs? While such confusions may occur as had dogged us, there can surely be no excuse for clinging on to this ancient custom.)

But as I was remarking, Marian's deportment in the carriage convinced me that she had by no means given up the prospect of seducing Mr Jeakes; for she contrived to be seated by him – and since the carriage was somewhat cramped and its passengers confined in closer quarters than would ideally be the case, they were fiercely thigh by thigh in a propinquity which would have delighted most men but was evidently a matter of indifference to this one – if not of evident irritation. He did his best to ignore her rather than positively to be insulting (no doubt in part because he feared the reaction of her brother and friend should he step beyond the line of polite behaviour); but his haughtiness in itself was offensive to me (together with his arrangement of a plot which could have cost Andy his life). I could not like him; and by the time the carriage stopped, perforce, in order to enable us to have a few hours' sleep, I began to think that Marian herself had begun to realise of what sort of metal he was made.

This became more obvious when we had settled into our rooms – Andy and Ralph sharing one with Jeakes, while Marian and I were abed in a smaller room. Thoughtlessly, perhaps, being exhausted by the day's activities, I swiftly threw off my clothes and tumbled between the sheets; Marian took longer to prepare herself and stole into bed when I was half asleep – and it was only upon awakening some little time later that I realised, feeling the bed shake and overhearing little moans, that she was weeping bitterly.

I immediately caught her in my arms and hoped to comfort her; but the tears continued, and indeed the dampness of her cheeks soon transferred itself to my breasts, upon which her face lay. Gradually, however, she grew quieter; and upon my stroking her shoulders gently, I felt her body relax – though so heated by emotion that I must thrust the sheets from us, the night being warm, though the windows were open.

Half asleep, I next felt a tender nibbling at my nipples, and realised that the poor girl, no doubt in an access of grief (so near that other passion, of love) was transferring to me some of the emotion which was wasted upon Jeakes; her desire for comfort was so great that in a while her tender lips sucked upon me like the gentlest baby, while a hand stole upon my thigh, and meeting no obstruction then rose to lie as lightly as a feather upon my belly, one finger gently insinuating itself into those curls which lie below it.

I could not be so rude as to push her from me – besides which, any comfort I could offer was only her due, since a closer watch on my part – and perhaps less encouragement to suppose that all men were as easy targets for love as she had been taught to suppose – might have avoided the *contretemps* in which she now found herself. I therefore did nothing to dissuade her from finding what comfort she might in caressing me, and in turn did not desist from quietly fondling her own body, though since she lay face downwards half upon me, this could consist only of continuing to stroke her back and buttocks. She assisted me, however, by spreading her legs so that upon my hand reaching the point where the cheeks of her bottom divided, I could, inserting my hand, place my palm upon that spot in which (had he been a man) Jeakes might even now be rooted; and felt from its liquidity what I had suspected – that Marian had worked herself into a passion from which she could only in one way be released.

I herefore persuaded her upon her back, and so twisting myself that I was lying head to toe with her, began, kissing first her thighs, then her lower lips, to offer such a release. She, rather relieved than otherwise, at the same time seized upon my proper person, parting with her fingers those outer portals which lead to heaven, and seeking within them with her tongue lighting upon that little turret of flesh where loving feeling is centred, and by a slow and insinuating preening, stoking the fires which now began to set me ablaze.

I must once more suggest what my lady readers may already be apprehensive of: that only a woman can know with untutored instinct what best satisfies another woman – just as it may be that only a man knows, without being taught, what best pleases a man. The early practice of onanism informs us of those caresses which give us most pleasure; but male and female being different in the apprehension of delight, such caresses when merely transferred from the male to the female body (or *vice versa*) can tend to bring less enjoyment to a partner than might be supposed. When the whole of nature conspires to bring male and female together, it may seem a complete oddity that they must *learn* what pleases each other; but so it is – and while I would never claim, as some inverts do, that no commerce between the opposite sexes can reach the height of pleasure exchanged between male and male, female and female; yet that there is some fragment of truth in the statement cannot, surely, be denied.

I believe that Marian felt this also, as our passions mounted to a mutual peak; when, quickly reversing our postures, we embraced breast to breast, the middle parts of our bodies thrust violently together, now writhing so that the very friction, while incapable of directly stimulating the centres of our being, brought us off in the same heart-stopping moment.

We lay for a moment still; when, in a tearful voice, Marian asked whether I thought that such a passion was experienced by Jeakes in the arms of one of his boys? To which I could only reply that I supposed so.

'Then,' she said, 'it is of such an intense nature that I understand it, for while in some respects I delight in the touch of a man, your own body is so pleasant that to enjoy it seems completely natural to me.'

This worried me considerably, as might be supposed; was the girl to be turned into a Sappho? Another weight of responsibility upon me?

'However, I must confess that I could never deny myself the pleasure of a male embrace,' she continued (and I could feel, though not see, her blush); 'there is something indispensable which . . .'

I assured her that I knew what that thing was.

'Nevertheless . . .' She sighed again, and kissed me upon the lips; whereat we fell asleep in each other's arms, awakening next morning, with a start, to see Ralph and Andy standing over us and regarding us with considerable interest, naked as we were, and in so intimate a pose.

Andy immediately leaned over to give me a morning kiss, as was our custom; and if his hand fell upon my breast, this was nothing to startle me, for we had been intimate since childhood, and while we but rarely shared a bed, it was by no means unknown for us to do so – with the consequences that might be expected to follow. As he straightened up, Ralph came shyly forward and asked whether he might be permitted the liberty? – and similarly saluted me.

Of course I acquiesced; though not expecting him to follow to the letter my friend's example in laying his palm upon my breast; nor can I say whether it was by intention that he so placed his body that my arm fell upon his thigh adjacent to that part of his body which suggested that he was not repelled by the sight of two naked nymphs. I will not swear that it was not by an instinctive movement of my own that the latter accident occurred, for I confess that I was not unmoved by the handsome youth, though strictly speaking I should no doubt have been impervious to the charms of one to whom I was, to all intents and purposes, *in loco parentis*.

However that may be, not only did his palm close upon my breast with a firm pressure, but I felt his lips part upon mine, and thought I apprehended the movement of his tongue between them . . . However, at that moment Andy took him by the shoulders, and suggested that it was time we were moving. The boy instantly moved to the door – but I could not swear that he did not give me a regretful glance; nor could I swear that Marian (whom Andy had saluted, though perhaps with somewhat less warmth) did not cast her eyes on my friend with a certain regretful admiration. It was perhaps as well, I thought as I dressed, that Andy had taken the positive step of removing himself and his ward from the room at the moment he had chosen; otherwise an already complicated situation might have become yet more labyrinthine.

All such matters however must be secondary to our reaching London, for Ralph was determined to find Niobe – whose action in leaving him he now saw as the noble consequence of an upright mind. So within less time almost than it takes to tell we were once more encoached, and by dint of much whipping up of the horses, and two changes of steeds, reached the city in the late afternoon. I had had little time to exchange words with Andy; but had learned from him, while Ralph and Marian were dozing and Jeakes as usual staring coldly out of the window, that he considered it best that the boy should be encouraged to find his late mistress, and that some accommodation (short, it was hoped, of marriage) should be worked out between them; otherwise, Andy was sure, Ralph would spend the rest of his life in a passion of regret which could not but injure his prospects of happiness.

He went straight to Andy's house, where there was of course sufficient space for us to be properly provided with rooms of our own (again, I could have sworn that Mr Ralph would have welcomed some other arrangement, for from time to time I caught his speculative eye resting upon my person – a consequence no doubt of his having for the first time seen it unclothed: an occurrence which must suddenly have shown him that someone he had hitherto regarded as a surrogate parent was in fact a woman, and one capable of arousing certain emotions in the male breast!).

On the following morning, as soon as it was open, we took ourselves to the Academy exhibition, there to see Hamidon's portrait of Niobe; which indeed was as fine as had been reported to me. Jeakes, I may say, we had left at home (where Andy had given the servants strict instructions to keep an eye on him; for we trusted him no further than we could have thrown a Waterloo cannon). I was not perfectly assured that he did not think we contemplated some action against him, at law; and should he choose to take himself off, that was an arrangement that would have suited me, as long as he left my friend's belongings behind him. Andy however took the view that Marian must finally be taught to forget her ambition to conquer him, before he could be allowed to leave the field.

Both brother and sister admired Niobe's portrait, the latter swearing it was like life; while the former spent some time staring at it, and then conveyed to Andy his wish to buy it – whereat the latter smote his forehead, and remarked that he was an ass! On our enquiring the reason for this judgement, he said that he dare swear he knew where Niobe would be lodging – and swept us downstairs, into a carriage, and away to the studio of Lionel Hamidon, the painter.

Ralph was silent upon the way, though from his clenching and unclenching his hands he was by no means as much at ease as he wished to appear. On our climbing out, he moved without urgency, as though he now found that he was less eager for the reunion than he had earlier seemed.

The door to Hamidon's cottage was open, and without knocking Andy strode in, waving to us to follow. Through the house he went, and down the garden path to a building which I supposed to be the artist's studio. The door to this place was also open, and Andy paused to look in at it; then beckoned us forward. There, upon a sort of low platform, where no doubt the artist placed his models, lay the woman we had come to seek; she appeared to have prepared herself to sit for a nude study, for she was unclothed. However, she was at present assisting to put the artist in the mood for his work, for he lay, similarly unclad, upon his back, a phallus of notable dimensions mounting from a cloud of grey hair between his thighs, the tip of which my poor young friend's mistress was gently stimulating with lethargic movements of a pink tongue.

I stole a look at Ralph. He had turned pale, though more with shock than fury. A sharply indrawn breath came from between his lips, which both the figures before us heard. Hamidon lifted his head, but upon seeing us failed to react either with anger or embarrassment. On the contrary, he merely sat up, and not troubling even to cover himself remarked that he took it somewhat ill of us to appear unannounced before him; but that if he could be of assistance . . .

Niobe, however, I must confess did show a vestige of modesty, reaching for her dress and holding it up to conceal as best she might her handsome breasts – and I must admit that as far as her body was concerned, and provided that one was impressed by solidity and amplitude, it was sufficiently impressive to attract men more experienced than Ralph; it was no wonder that, with all the inexperience of youth, he had formed an attraction to her. However, his opinion of her had clearly received a blow for –

'Do not concern yourself, ma'am,' I heard him say, in a shy but cool voice; 'I am familiar with the landscape, as you know.'

The lady now got to her feet, and dropped her clothing to the floor, exposing herself as fully to us as to the artist for whom she was to have posed.

'To be sure,' she said, calm now, and (I must confess) extremely dignified. 'I wonder, ladies and gentlemen, whether you would grant me the favour of a moment or two with Mr Trillo? Lionel – if you don't mind?'

'Not a bit of it, my dear,' the artist said; 'come,

ladies and gentlemen – let me show you some paintings in the next room.'

'Nay,' said Ralph; 'anything this lady has to say may be said before you all, or not at all.'

We halted uneasily, as you may imagine. Niobe shook her head; then said, somewhat haltingly but with the greatest conviction:

'Very well. I assume by your presence that you have uncovered the plan which my brother and I made to secure for ourselves an income? Yes, it is true; impoverished by our father's unconquerable passion for gambling, it became necessary for us to marry wealth, if we were to continue to live in that relative comfort to which a large fortune (before its dissipation) had accustomed us. We set our eyes upon Mr and Miss Trillo, after a careful consideration of the available bachelors and spinsters possessed of large property, and coldly set out to capture them.

'My brother, as you must now know, is not the marrying sort; and while he had at first convinced himself that he was capable of wooing a young lady to the extent of marriage, when he found that Miss Trillo was likely (from his observation of her education at the hands of Mrs Nelham here) to require proof of his passion before promising her hand, he retired from the contest; and it was left to me to secure, by marrying Mr Trillo, a fortune which would be sufficient for us both – the gentleman in question clearly being sufficiently honourable not to let his brother-in-law starve.

'However, one misfortune put an end to the plan: that is, Mr Ralph Trillo's person. Had I not become so engaged with him, had I been possessed of the good sense to keep him at arm's length until I had snared him, all might have been well; but a close association with that young man entirely dissuaded me from my intention. Such innocence, such good nature, such – nay, I will say it! – such love, made it impossible that one such as I should drag him into a contract which would have led both of us into a slough of misery.

'I therefore entertained him to what I intended to be a final meeting; administered a drug which would enable me to make my escape; and the rest you know. I cannot prove that what I have said is the truth; however, Mr Trillo and his friends may assure themselves that I intend now (with the help of a loan from my good friend Mr Hamidon) to leave this country for ever.'

Saying which, she turned her back on us; and stood, waiting no doubt for us to retire.

For an instant, no one moved; when Ralph took several steps forward, and placed his hand upon her shoulder. She started at it, and turned; and in a moment they were in each other's arms.

I was not entirely happy at this turn of events; neither, I could see, was Andy. But the two principal actors were now so engaged, their lips so closely embraced, their arms so closely wound about each other, that it would have been impertinent to interrupt them. We therefore stole from the room, accompanied by Hamidon – who, in the cottage, assumed a smock before opening a couple of bottles of claret, from which we drank several glasses while being careful to talk of something else.

It was almost an hour before Ralph and Miss Jeakes rejoined us; both now clothed, though from a certain new carelessness about Ralph's dress it seemed the case that there had arisen some circumstance which had necessitated its rearrangement.

'I am convinced,' he now said, 'as who would not be? – of Miss Jeakes's honesty; and we have agreed to part. It is not' (and here he looked somewhat sadly) 'my wish, but her own; and since she is immovable upon the subject, I must agree. However, I have convinced her' (here he turned to the artist) 'with your permission,.sir, that I should make myself responsible for allowing her such financial assistance as she needs, and have asked that she should accompany us back to your house, Andy, where we can reach some mutually agreeable conclusion in the matter.'

So, taking our leave of Mr Hamidon (whose embrace of Miss Jeakes was sufficiently warm further to impress Ralph – as I believed – that she was not entirely devoted to himself, other than financially), we returned to Andy's house, where we found Mr Jeakes contemplating a book of views of Italy, which was open at the pages illustrating Michelangelo's statue of David, which I believe he took as evidence of the general physique of the young men of that country; a matter on which I did not think it proper to disillusion him.

Chapter Fifteen

The Adventures of Andy

I must confess that supper that evening was not particularly high-spirited. Though Mr Jeakes did his best to be pleasant, he clearly laboured under the apprehension that I intended to have him prosecuted for setting up those circumstances which had placed me in jeopardy of the law, and after an initial forced cheerfulness consumed his food with an air of melancholy which could not but communicate itself to his sister, who though she had brought off her *coup* against all the odds, was also I believe affected by the gloom with which Ralph contemplated her going abroad – though the sum of money which he was determined to fix upon her was such that he need not have feared any ill consequences for her for the foreseeable future.

Marian, meanwhile, though she must accept Sophie's explanation of Jeakes's nature, still looked upon him with a wistful air, as though hoping for a last minute conversion to an admiration of womanhood (entirely lost on the fellow, whose eyes were more upon the thighs of my footman than upon the eyes of his female admirer).

Sophie and myself attempted some merriment; and with reason – we had managed to save the two young people placed in our charge from the worst of fates – in both cases marriage to a fortune-hunter, and in one, marriage to a buttercup.

I should mention here that it had proved impossible not to discuss with the two young people their circumstances; and on bringing up the subject, we learned that they were entirely aware that their individual fortunes, upon their attaining the age of twenty-one, would be considerable; that Sir Fyndon, their uncle, had impressed upon them the impropriety of discussing this with us; and that he, a most kindly guardian, had assured them that should they require any portion of their funds for a proper purpose of their own, before reaching their majority, they had only to make application.

Ralph had therefore that evening sent to his uncle a long letter of appeal, which he had asked me to support, for the money with which to provide his mistress with a competence; and I had privately drawn up an article – to which Ralph was not privy – which the lady had readily agreed to sign, to the effect that she should not attempt to see the boy again for five years. Her readiness to put her name to such a condition confirmed me in believing her still an adventuress at heart; though her claim of some real affection for young Ralph could not entirely be dismissed; certainly she showed much unwillingness to allow me to believe that she was not sincere in her admiration, and that at a time when there would have been nothing to be gained on her part had she shown herself entirely worldly.

The lady and her brother expressing the wish to retire early, and Sophie and her ward seeming happy to remain in the house, I suggested to Ralph that we should go into the town – for I was determined to take him out of himself to provide some recreation which would enable him for the time at least to forget what he was losing – merely a female whose appeal was her willingness to please (though he believed otherwise). I walked him off down Regent Street and through Hanover Square to Brook Street, where I knocked on the door of a house which was familiar to me (and will be familiar to those faithful readers who are following me through these chronicles) – i.e., that in which my friend Frank and I had, a few years previously, established the finest house of pleasure in London.

Our old servant Blatchford, who had been a faithful friend and companion of Sophie's on her travels, had for a time run the place when Frank and I relinquished a personal interest in it; but it was now in the hands of an admirable lady, Mrs Fitful (gentlemen still being, at that time, denied by law the right to run such establishments) – while my friend and I took a sufficient rental from her to make our continued investment in the place financially satisfactory, and retained the right to interfere should standards be permitted to fall.

Ralph had no notion of the sort of place to which I was taking him, believing I suppose that it was some sort of gaming house. This expectation was not at all diminished on the door being opened by a decently caparisoned footman, who showed us into the hallway, where we were greeted by Mrs Fitful, a handsome if large lady with the air of at least a Duchess.

'My dear Mr Archer,' she said; 'it is too long since you visited us. And your friend . . .'

'Mr Trillo,' I said, 'whom I trust you will afford your best hospitality.'

'To you both, the best the house has to offer!' she said. 'Please to accompany me upstairs.'

We followed her up the fine staircase – still decorated as we had planned, those years since, but so cared for that it showed no sign of wear – and into the sitting-room, the shutters closed against the light so that only candle-light glowed softly upon the skins of the ladies waiting there to greet us: eight in number, and of every sort. I was glad to see that the house still followed what we had considered an important rule: that the women employed there should be as varied in character as possible, so that men of every inclination might expect to find one to their taste.

So, here was one well into her middle years, statuesque and graceful, though to my idea more resembling mother than mistress; here, at the opposite end of the scale, a young girl who looked only perhaps sixteen (though to my knowledge the rules of the place accommodated young persons no younger than eighteen). She was slim and boyish; while a sister only perhaps slightly older was plumper, her breasts almost peeping out from the low neck of her gown. Ralph, I could see, was fixed on another, however – a young negress whose white dress accentuated the almost purple-black of her skin. Clearly, he had never seen a black girl before – at least, one who was not in an entirely menial situation (one or two black persons being employed by the quality at Bath, in the position of running footman or maid).

He now, it seemed, began to realise what the place was; and certainly must have done so when Mrs Fitful, seeing his glance, said: 'Tansy, come forward. May I present, Mr Trillo, young Tansy, who has recently joined us from the Indies? She will be glad to accommodate you if it should be your wish.'

Ralph looked comically at me.

'Yes,' I said smiling; 'I should no doubt have told you. You are free of any of the young ladies here – and from their look, any of them will be happy to be chosen by so personable a customer!'

He blushed at this, and half-whispered to Mrs Fitful that he would be glad if Miss Tansy would care to, er . . .'

Mrs Fitful smiled: 'You have chosen well,' she said; 'Tansy knows exactly what's what. And you, Mr Archer?'

I had my eyes on Pamela, a young lady whose favours I had from time to time enjoyed upon previous visits, and who indeed had anticipated me by rising to her feet and coming forward.

'Filament!' called Mrs Fitful – and instructed the footman to show us downstairs. There, in a dressing-room, we removed our clothing and were given two large towels in which to wrap ourselves, then escorted by the two girls, now similarly clad, into that set of rooms which in my day had been entirely unique in town and which, though later imitated elsewhere, was still the finest of its kind – and certainly one which astonished Ralph, who had never seen anything to equal them.

They consisted of a hot room, where steam rose from water running in channels beneath the floor through carefully placed apertures to heat the air; next to this was a warm room, where massaging could take place (and other exercises which often followed); and finally the bath rooms, where a sunken bath sufficient to accommodate perhaps six persons had been constructed. I was happy to see that these rooms had all been kept in admirable condition, and were as clean and fresh as when friend Frank and I had laid them out and had them constructed.

Sitting upon the benches placed about the walls of the hot room, we almost immediately began to break out in a healthful perspiration, which soon began to stand out in beads upon our bodies and run down our arms and breasts. Upon Ralph lifting a hand to brush away a tickling runnel, Tansy, sitting next to him, leaned over and took up with her tongue the drops upon his chest. This attention, he received with surprised delight, the application of her tongue to his breast and paps clearly being a pleasant stimulation; in turn, he lifted her head, and bending began to lick between her breasts, where the salt water ran; at which she arched her back with a little mew of pleasure, raising her upper body so that he could scarcely neglect paying attention to a pair of charming breasts, the tight nipples positively offering themselves like ripe raspberries to his lips, which instinctively made towards them.

I was at this point myself somewhat distracted by Miss Pamela's taking her cue, and while kissing me full upon the lips, passing her hands over my body – her own being, as I discovered, as wet and slippery as my own. It was a positive effort not to persuade her to the bench and take advantage immediately of that perfectly accessible cleft the rim of which, as my fingers discovered, would present no obstacle to the entrance of my engorged prick – which itself was neither diminished in eagerness nor rendered less ready for congress by the exploration of Pamela's hands, which had made their way – or rather, I should say, had slid thither – over the buttery surface of my chest and belly.

Tansy now had the same idea as her friend: that if we remained as we were for a moment or two longer, enthusiasm would overtake will, and we should be joined in a congress which would be too speedily concluded for the pleasure they planned to give us to reach its proper height.

They rose, then, and taking us by our hands led us into the baths, where we entered water heated only to such a degree as to be comfortable – in order that any lethargy introduced by the considerable heat of the previous room should be dissipated.

Here, when designing these rooms, Frank and I had contrived a somewhat brighter light: in cold blood, I may say, so that the ladies of the house should be able to inspect the bodies of their customer's – without of course seeming to do so – in order to discover signs of any disorder which might make it unwise to accommodate them further. On this occasion, needless to say, the situation did not arise; but the additional light did afford Ralph the opportunity to see the person of his friend more clearly – and with both interest and pleasure. She was indeed extremely beautiful, her skin clear and unblemished, and stretched almost to tightness over a body which was different from that of a white girl of her age only in its being perhaps more muscular, and longer – her legs in particular being lengthy almost to an extraordinary degree, her thighs slim and well-set, and her haunches (as she turned and bent to step into the bath) somewhat lengthier than usual.

More astonishing to Ralph was the fact that she was entirely depilated – so that the only hair upon her body was that upon her head, itself cut short and extremely curly. Her armpits were (as Ralph could not help but confirm with his tongue) entirely smooth; while between her legs there was no sign of that moss which more usually is to be found there. Catching his eye, the girl was pleasant enough to spread her thighs – when there was to be seen a perfectly bare cleft, most beautifully shaped, neither gaping nor tight, but so relaxed as almost to seem to smile.

Ralph could not take his eyes from the sight, which indeed was a pleasant one; and seeing this, Miss Tansy now sat upon the edge of the bath, and encouraged her admirer to kneel before her, in order that he might make a more intimate examination of the phenomenon – which after some initial hesitation he did, parting the skin with his fingers (to reveal, between ebony lips, deep red flesh like that of an unusual foreign fruit, which he could not but taste – an action which I could see gave Tansy as much pleasure as he).

Once more, I now found myself in some difficulty in continuing to observe (and the reader will perhaps find it possible to forgive what may seem too great an interest in the matter; but to be honest my young friend's pleasure was such that one could not but delight in it) – for Pamela, no doubt feeling that any inattention on her part would be to deny her contract, was, beneath the surface of the water, manipulating my prick and cods in a peculiarly interesting manner – two fingers finding their way along the channels at each side of my groin, while her thumb was at the base of my cock, and with a regular pressure was bobbing it in such a fashion that its movement through the water caressed it more softly than any human agency could do.

Not to continue a description which must be wearying in its detail, in time we found ourselves in the warm room, where we were encouraged to recline while the two girls caressed every part of our persons, first drying them, then dusting us with a white powder which removed the final traces of our sweat; and only then permitting us to begin that final act which was the apex towards which all their attentions had been directed.

It may be considered a fault, but I persuaded my partner to kneel with her arms upon the bench, while I entered her from behind; not merely because I must confess to a partiality for this position, especially when so physically heated that a more complete connection between two bodies makes for some discomfort – but also because it enabled me to observe Ralph and his friend. She, realising perhaps that he was not as experienced as myself, had persuaded him to remain in an horizontal position, while she stretched herself along his side, her head to his toes, and was playing upon his tool as if upon a musical instrument – stopping its tiny aperture with her tongue, surrounding the dome with her lips, moving the skin about with one hand while the other manipulated his cods, then paying attention to that happy point between cods and arse-hole where the most alarmingly delightful sensations seem seated; this final action being the last straw – for, raising his head from between her thighs, where he had been drinking from a well he found enchanting, he screwed up his face as though sucking a lemon, and a series of shudders ran through his body as Tansy milked from him to the last drop the proof of the collapse of his powers.

The sight, I must confess, was sufficiently stimulating to allow me, with a couple of final thrusts, to reach the culmination of my own pleasure; whereafter the girls, complimenting us upon our powers (something which I always take with a pinch of salt, though upon this occasion they had seemed sufficiently to enjoy themselves) once more wiped our bodies, and all four of us – the house being quiet, and the young ladies' services not elsewhere required – relaxed and even slept.

For how long we slept, I know not; but when I awoke, it was to see, over the head of Pamela, who was asleep beside me, that Ralph was once more engaged with his black beauty – this time copying my own previous stance (which he must have observed – though I suppose he may have been introduced to it by Miss Jeakes, whose love-making was clearly of an ambitious and informed kind). A convenience of the posture of which I speak is that the gentleman is able to observe his piston disappearing, then reappearing, between his mistress's lower lips (and it should always be remembered that sight is a great contributor to the excitement of congress – a circumstance which makes it the more remarkable that so many of the commonalty insist upon making their love in the dark; though the Church, insisting often upon it, is able thus to set up another barrier against the enjoyment of an act which so many theologians regard as one to be performed with as little pleasure as possible).

However, in the present case Ralph pursued his pleasure with a fine, swinging regularity – his expression being one of great interest, as though he had doubted whether his instrument was indeed capable of such a vigorous application! Meanwhile, when they were not resting on her hips to help govern his action, his hands were busy about the body of his partner, soothing her sides, exploring the crack of her arse, caressing her breasts . . .

From the pleasure on Tansy's face (her eyes shut, and a beatific smile upon her features) I imagined that Ralph's previously expressed pleasure had dulled his senses in a manner which had allowed him to continue his present motion for some time – and she certainly showed no signs of wishing to cease from it!

The sight was one which moved me, and since only a slight movement was necessary to bring my body into contact with Pamela's, and that contact roused her, we were soon gratifying each other in a similar, but I must confess less energetic, manner. As is so often the case when one indulges one's passion immediately upon waking from sleep, I slid into orgasm without a long time elapsing, Pamela I believed enjoying the mild pleasure of contributing to my enjoyment without either attaining or envying that climacteric which was her right: happily for many gentlemen, and contrary to a popular belief, it is not invariably necessary for their comfort that ladies must be raised to that pitch of heaven which exhausts all feeling (while it is equally the case that they must regularly enjoy that elevated feeling, are they to be happy). Ralph was still engaged as we parted, and rising quietly to my feet, I gave him a wink and a slap upon the buttocks, and took myself off to the dressing-room. Though on returning home I was wakeful for some time, I did not hear him return – and in the morning a pair of red eyes suggested that his night had been a long one.

Within the following week letters of credit had been received from Sir Fyndon which enabled Ralph to give the Jeakeses their *congé*; and the parting between the two pairs of siblings was less painful than I had supposed – Marian apparently now entirely reconciled to Valentine Jeakes's disinterest in her sex, and Ralph able to part from Niobe without repining – I think partly from his realisation, proved by his night in Brook Street, that her love-making was not so singular that enjoyment quite as keen was not to be found elsewhere. Miss Tansy had also, I believe, done much to impress upon him the pleasure afforded every gentleman by a periodic intimacy with an unfamiliar lady, and disillusioned him of the utter conviction that a partner with whom an intimacy is formed at eighteen can necessarily fulfil every imaginable amorous desire for the following sixty years. However he might now feel about Miss Jeakes, Ralph never thought of withdrawing his offer of financial support, and any regret Miss Jeakes may have felt at parting from him was certainly much mitigated by the clink of coin in her purse, for she and her brother left Dover with a sum of money far greater than they deserved, Jeakes himself having as a condition signed a letter confessing the plot against me, which I promised would only be shown to the magistrates at Bath (where the case against me was still upon the court books) after he had left the country and the jurisdiction of the English law.

Sir Fyndon had announced his intention of coming to London, whence he would escort his nephew and niece to the great house which waited them at Llanfyllin, where they must now learn how to manage the establishment, and take their places as the natural leaders of the neighbourhood. (I had my doubts, however, whether either Ralph or his sister would settle very happily to life on the Welsh borders, having enjoyed in so spirited a manner those pleasures available in more socially advanced places.)

The night before Sir Fyndon's arrival, we four dined together, recalling in some detail those pleasures and their outcome, and the couple taking the opportunity to question us upon morality, and in particular upon our own attitude to those amours which (as they said) we both seemed to enjoy so freely. Was there no circumstance, they asked, which might stand between the happy joining of a lady and a gentleman who mutually desired it?

Our answer can be inferred by the reader, and was given with some enthusiasm, for both Sophie and myself had seen the consequences of men and women being deprived of the expression of their passions under the influence of puritans or theological argument.

And was age no bar? they then asked.

Far from it, we replied; both of us having had experience of congress with ladies and gentlemen both much our elders and considerably our juniors, the former (in time now considerably past) having indeed had much to teach us in the technical expression of amorous talent.

Brother and sister seemed at this to exchange significant glances. Both were prolific in their gratitude to Sophie and me – more so indeed than I felt was proper, for we had been sufficiently lax to allow them to place themselves in situations which might have proved most difficult. But they would not have it: we had introduced them, they said, only to such problems as young people must eventually face, and our guardianship had been more like friendship than supervision.

'Indeed,' said Ralph, 'we have had some difficulty in considering how to express our thanks – for a gift of money would be out of the question. However, I believe that we have fixed on an accommodation which would certainly delight us, and we hope may give you some pleasure.'

He had some difficulty in proceeding further; but his sister, rising to her feet, came round the table to where I sat, and leaning over, kissed me upon the cheek, and whispered that they wished to spend their last evening with us in a more intimate situation than dining- or drawing-room could afford.

Neither Sophie nor I for a moment thought of insulting our young friends by declining the compliment. In short, in a very brief time we were all four upon the large bed which I had established for myself (any bed less than five foot square being in my estimation too small, no less for slumber than for erotic athletics – and this one nearer six!), and our bodies no longer encumbered even by the relatively casual dress we had adopted for dinner.

I had had the opportunity of examining young Ralph's person, just as Sophie had upon many occasions observed his sister in a state of undress; and just as I supposed that Sophie would be pleased by the spare and muscular slimness she now saw laid before her, she (as she later told me) did not apprehend that I would be disappointed at young Marian's appearance – both young people being sufficiently personable to raise any member of the opposite sex to admiration (indeed, for a moment it crossed my mind that I had reason to be grateful that Mr Jeakes had not set his eye on Ralph, who was certainly sufficiently attractive to have besotted him; a situation might then have arisen which might have been difficult to resolve, little though I suspected young Ralph of any preference for his own sex – a fact now demonstrated by his admiration of Sophie's body, which he was regarding with a pleasure which he soon expressed more positively than by the eye alone).

Meanwhile Marian proved that, apart from the bloom of youth which added a lustre to her natural charm, she had an instinctive knowledge of what best pleases a man. As to herself, I had learned from Sophie of her being quick to please – but even so was surprised when on my planting a single kiss upon her lips and starting to caress her nether regions, she began to wriggle with pleasure like a fish upon a line; such a response being as aphrodisiac as can be imagined, I can only say that we both found a complete satisfaction in the night's work, and that our pleasure was repeated as often as both of us wished. Ralph, in the meantime, I believe surprised Sophie by his sophistication (for I had not thought it necessary to inform her of his night's tutoring in Brook Street) – and in next to no time had placed himself upon all fours and was complimenting her most tender part with kisses, while presenting her with a view of his pendant cods and a cock so far from pendant as to be almost threatening; but which, she being no tyro, was soon arousing to an even more adamantine state by a combination of tongue, lips and fingers.

Our pleasures continued for as long as all four

desired; and eventually we fell asleep wrapped in each other's arms, and without conscious knowledge, I believe, of which errant limb belonged to which of us.

During the hours of darkness, this matter was sorted, however; and I woke at first light – perhaps five o'clock in the morning – to find Sophie, raised upon one elbow, casting her eyes over the body of her companion, evidently exhausted by his pleasures, one hand carelessly lying upon his mistress's thigh. His sister, meanwhile, was sound asleep, her head upon my breast. They were both perfectly a picture of youth and beauty – the boy's breast almost entirely devoid of hair, except for a light down upon his lower arms and thighs, and shading about his pink paps, while a mere trickle of filaments led from the dint of his navel over the slightly convex platform of his belly to a cluster of tight curls at the base of an instrument now so innocent that the most modest of ladies would not, I believe, have shrunk from observing it: a tender white skin gathering at its tip to a pinkish point.

His sister was just such an Eve as to match just such an Adam: her breast almost as flat as a boy's, her normally full breasts lacking the tissue to raise them much above the surrounding flesh; the two paps however, even in sleep, erect and proud. Her waist was pinched to what seemed merely a hand's span, hips then jutting almost horizontally before rounding and falling over full thighs, and promising a bottom so delicious that I could scarcely resist reaching out to turn her on her face, in order to cover them for a last time with kisses. Yet that would have been to hide that charming aperture which had so welcomed me on the previous night – and now, couched between a more generous muff of fair hair than her brother could yet boast, seemed ready to welcome me again.

I believe that both Sophie and myself felt a pang: seeing in the two sleeping children perhaps images of what we once were – yet after all we were but eight years older than our young friends, and neither exactly decrepit. Indeed, perhaps seizing my thought, Sophie stretched out a hand and took one of mine; and seeing her familiar body stretched out beside me, I felt a movement below which was proof that I was not as drained of all feeling as the sleeping Ralph.

We stole from the room, and made our way to Sophie's bed, where, not to be tedious in the telling, we embraced each other with that leisurely and familiar warmth with which true friends can easily re-invest old favours; and, in short, made each other happy before falling again asleep – and remaining so until Ralph and Marian woke us, fully dressed and evidently amused at the situation in which they found us.

Sir Fyndon had arrived, they told us – the three had breakfasted, and were about to leave. At our invitation, Sir Fyndon entered and paid us his compliments – being, as I think, sufficiently warmed by the sight of Sophie in a pretty *déshabillé* to wish he was thirty years younger!

Standing at the window of the bedroom, a sheet around our shoulders, we waved as their carriage made its way down the drive and through the entrance to the Park, before turning to the west. Had we taught them well? Had we prepared them properly for what at least one area of life would bring them? The reader must judge.

TALES OF EROS

Contents

For the convenience of the reader
we here record a note of
IMPORTANT PERSONS APPEARING IN THE NARRATIVE
in the order of their appearance

Andrew Archer Esq., our narrator.
Mrs Sophie Nelham, his companion.
Jem Rackham, a coachman.
Mrs Ellen Rackham, hostess of the George Inn, Stamford.
Johnny, Fred and Ben, her brothers.
Three friends.
Lieut. Raphael Rymer, R.N.
Three midshipmen.
Mrs Fossick, of Valetta, in Malta.
Her young ladies.
Lieut. Robin Spencer, R.N., surgeon of the *Leopard*.
Mrs Rose Allbig, a cook.
Michel, a country lad.
M. de Bernouailles, a young nobleman.
Mlle Cotteret, his friend.
Michel the younger.
Edward Chaunter, a tutor.
Sir Witley Johnston, a Scottish Gentleman.
Peter and Paul, his sons.
Amabel and Nicola, his daughters.
Miss Elena Stanbury, a governess.
Martin Eckersley Esq., her uncle.
Mrs Mary Eckersley, his wife.
Jack Nicolls, a farmer's son.
Paul Hawthorn, a poet.
Mr Pennyford, a schoolmaster.

Master Henry Fillip, a schoolboy.
Betty, a maid.
Lord Infermine, of Blatchett Hall.
Lady Infermine, his wife.
The Hon. Carola Infermine, their daughter.
General Sir Amis Quartermaine, her *fiancé*.
Miss Rosario Nephrosyte, a dressmaker.
Lady Darcy, a client.
Lord Pemberley, another.
Gabriel Shore, a gardener.
Lillian Gandy, a maid.
Oswald Manship Esq., a gentleman.
Davina Dance, an actress.
Lydia Kelly, another.
John Baldwin Buckstone, an actor.
Amelia Ormidale, an heiress.
Roger Fitzwilliam Esq., a gentleman.
Robert Cross Smith, or Tarantabobus, an astrologer.
Two persons from Soho.
Mrs Phillida Madden, a respectable lady.
Lord Mars and Lady Venus, two aristocrats.
Mrs Aspasia Ryves, a clergyman's widow.
Mr Albert Cowland, a kindly pimp.
The Very Rev. Bruno Ryves, a rural dean.
Gerry Trustworth, a.k.a. Geraldo de Hoyas.
Mrs Vashti Treleaven, an unsatisfied wife.
Doll, her maid.
Miss Amelia Rodesley, an unsatisfied spinster.
Sir Franklin Franklyn, Bart.
St John Fenmore Esq., his acquaintance.
Fence, his man.
Richard Trevithick Esq., the celebrated inventor.
Dick Trevithick, his son.
Lord Nettlesburn, a peer.
Maggie, an actress.
David Ham, a friend.

1

The Hostess's Tale

Some of my readers – those at all events who are not to be shocked by forthright accounts of amorous adventure – may be familiar with the *Decameron* of Messire Boccaccio, an Italian work which reports the anecdotes related, to amuse themselves, by a number of ladies and gentlemen confined together while escaping from the plague.

There is no similar English work; and perhaps it might not be thought there could be one, for British ladies and gentlemen, though no less given to bawdy pleasure, are on the whole less forward in confessing than their continental neighbours, and while it is my considered opinion that (contrary to the popular view) they are as capable of amorous enjoyment as those, they are less disposed to boast of their conquests.

After some reflection, I have decided to produce (and, in the volume now in our hands, take pleasure in laying before you) a volume of a not dissimilar character, collecting together a number of adventures enjoyed by a random selection of English ladies and gentlemen of no exceptionable character; each entirely credible (for I heard them at first hand) and the whole showing, as I take it, that as a nation we are no slower to enjoy occasional dalliance with the opposite sex than our brothers and sisters of Italy or France, Spain or Germany.

The occasion of my hearing these tales was as follows.

Some years ago, I and my friend Sophie (Mrs Sophie Nelham, with whom I have in the past shared many escapades, some of which at least will be familiar to readers of the eight previous volumes of memoirs for which we have jointly been responsible) were invited to spend Christmas with Sir Josiah and Lady Conrad, whose estate in Northamptonshire marches with that of Sir Clifford Chatterley (the scandal of whose wife's adventures with her young footman was still much talked of in society through the explicit accounts published of their affair).

As we set out from Charing Cross on December the twenty-second in a public coach (my carriage having been incapacitated some evenings previously by an adventure with a brewer's wagon while crossing Richmond Bridge) the day already displayed that slight mitigation of intense cold which suggests snow, and as dawn came up and we started our journey proper along the Great North Road, heavy storm-clouds began to pile up ahead of us, and one of the two ladies who shared the inside with us began to grow extremely nervous, having once, as she explained, been marooned for forty-eight hours in a carriage snowed up between Greenwich and the city, incapable of rescue despite the nearness of civilisation. And what, she asked, would be our fate if we were to encounter a heavy fall of snow on some open stretch of road miles from any human habitation?

This lady was clearly of a nervous disposition, though dressed in the finest dispensation afforded by contemporary fashion – a fact which could be confirmed by the occasional glimpses of furbelows to be seen under her heavy cloak. I did my best to reassure her, and Sophie to distract her attention from the much-feared predicament by talking of the coming trends in dress, of new productions at the theatres, and other matters. The second lady was rather more handsome than the first, and infinitely more appealing to myself (no doubt through her being particularly attentive to me when I spoke to her, and from a pair of dark eyes whose flashing, even within the necessarily gloomy confines of the carriage, seemed to light the air about her). She remained perfectly calm, and declined to entertain feelings of alarm; for, as she said in an undertone, life was too short an affair to spend time either fearing for the future or regretting the past; and the warmth of her glances and the pressure of her thigh against my own (which, though necessitated by the closeness of our confinement, seemed nevertheless peculiarly constant) suggested that she would not necessarily regret any delay which would result in our having to spend additional time in each other's company.

Our first day was devoid of any such delay except that necessitated by the scandalously poor state of the road; and after a brief few hours' sleep in an indifferent inn north of Cambridge, we made off again, the clouds seeming heavier than ever. Soon enough, on our passing Godmanchester, snow indeed began to fall in giant flakes, some of which seemed several inches in diameter; and I feared that the outside passengers – though they had of course provided themselves with all that additional clothing necessitated by an outside journey in winter, and to the northwards – would soon become snowmen and snowwomen, while I wondered that the horses could see sufficiently well to continue their steady progress along a road the verges of which were swiftly becoming indistinguishable from the fields which lay alongside them.

Our pause for a meal at a mean inn at Conington was as brief as could be, for Rackham, our coachman, was eager to press on; the weather, he suggested, was likely to get worse before it got better, and he was eager to reach a place of superior accommodation lest indeed it proved necessary for us to contemplate a prolonged stay; and in the late afternoon, after mounting the hill beyond Wittering, a sharp turn to the right and the application of the brakes persuaded me to contrive with a wetted finger a hole in the mist which occluded the window glass of the coach, through which I saw the long wall of a great estate, and caught a glimpse of a fine gateway and lodges before, after another half a mile, we swung round a corner and into the forecourt of an inn.

The few clues I had discerned through my spy-hole had not permitted me to identify the place other than to see that it was a town of some distinction. On descending from the coach – a matter involving some skill in the disentanglement of cloaks and rugs, the discovery of small luggage and larger (those of us inside seemingly forming at last one homogeneous mass of humanity and detritus), I found myself to be standing in the courtyard of a handsome Tudor inn which announced itself as the George of Stamford, an hostelry well-known to travellers to the north as a place of distinctive accommodation and cheerful hospitality – a claim now demonstrated as no less than the truth by our being welcomed by a cheerful and bustling hostess who ushered us into a room where a great fire burned in a broad fireplace, before which we speedily divested ourselves of our outer clothing.

The landlady, for so I took her to be (there being no sign of a male host), was immediately outside in the yard again, busying herself about the unfreezing of the four outside passengers who had become stiff as boards, and were now lowered to the ground with the help of the coachman, almost indistinguishable as to sex and for the time incapable of speech.

The hostess now returned, and asked whether we would object to these fellow-passengers entering the room that custom would more normally designate for inside passengers only. Could any of us contest so humane a suggestion? In no long time, our four unfortunate fellow-travellers were beginning to recover, permitted the best part of the fire, before which their outer clothing soon began to steam, then to bend, then at last to resume some likeness to cloth rather than metal; and eventually it was possible for them to remove several layers, revealing themselves indeed as human.

One was clearly the maid to the more nervous of the two ladies travelling with us; for whose comfort she showed much more concern than she received, for the moment she was unfrosted the girl began to fuss about her mistress, the latter showing no concern whatsoever lest her servant had been affected by the ordeal of an outside journey in such inclement weather. That the girl's recovery (she was little more than a child) was relatively speedy, I took to be the result of her having been seated between two of the gentlemen who travelled with her, and who now were revealed as a Naval lieutenant (a handsome fellow with flashing eyes and curly hair, who immediately took Sophie's eye) and a sallow fellow, also quite youthful, of a reserved, though not uncheerful, disposition; neither of whom however refused – as did none of us – the steaming tankard of hot ale brought to us by the hostess. The third of the outside passengers was perhaps the more remarkable: a seemingly elderly man with a straggling, full greying beard, eyebrows of the beetling kind, and a taciturn air nevertheless susceptible from time to time to a brilliant smile – nay, a grin – which split his otherwise unpromising countenance, and was invariably directed at one of the ladies in his vicinity. At all times, he clutched to himself a bag made out of carpet or some such material, the weight of which, together with its shape and the strange bulges in it, suggested that it was full of books.

We were now ready for food, and the smell of roasted meat suggested the immanence of a meal, when there was the sound of clattering wheels, and into the forecourt swung a second coach – just able to pull up before colliding with our own (whose horses had fortunately been led away to stable, only that fact permitting sufficient space to accommodate the new vehicle). This, we soon learned, was the mirror-image of our own equipage, bound south as we were bound north; and it soon began to disgorge passengers in just such a sorry case as we had been.

There was now some additional delay, impossible to avoid since clearly the inhabitants of the second coach were in need of just such immediate succour as we had been; and the men among us volunteered immediately to assist in the distribution of that smoking hot sack which began to recover the new guests with the same speed at which it had comforted ourselves.

The chief room of the inn, though large, was now positively crowded, and began to resemble a giant Christmas party. The common difficulty in which we found ourselves made instant friendship advisable, for clearly, judging the manner in which the snow was now banking itself against the windows and scurrying into the yard (such was its assiduity that it was necessary to close the great doors against it), it was likely that we must spend much of the festive season together.

The second coach had brought eight new passengers: inside were four ladies. One was a buxom character who seemed enormous even before she removed her upper clothing, and scarcely less large when this had been accomplished; the roundness of her limbs and the rosiness of her beaming face being nevertheless far from unpleasant to the eye. Next my glance fell on a pretty woman of early middle age, neat and meticulous in her movements, then on an equally pretty, younger woman whose attitude seemed somewhat stern and unbending, but whose face in repose suggested a more outgoing disposition. The fourth of the inside ladies was as great a contrast as could be imagined, for she was of the most forward manner imaginable, at once making it her business to introduce herself, and busying herself, without invitation, in helping the hostess to dispense more tankards of grog.

Of outside passengers, the second coach bore four: the most feverish among them being a gentleman who clearly believed himself to be hard done by through an uncommon exposure to the weather: for, forced to travel by that coach, he was equally forced (through the inside places having been taken, and by ladies) to travel outside; and was belabouring his unfortunate servant or valet with complaints about everything in and out of view. The two others were quieter and of less rumbustious disposition. They were perhaps in their mid-twenties or younger; the first clearly, from his appearance, a gentleman (though of less elevated a condition than his less pleasant fellow); the second perhaps still a student, or perhaps a schoolmaster; at any rate, if I was any judge, of a studious and bookish disposition.

Our hostess's difficulty in bedding so sudden an influx of guests was no small one; maid and mistress, valet and gentlemen, clearly must share accommodation. I was able to take the lady aside and inform her that Mrs Nelham and I would happily share a room or even if necessary a bed, for though we were not (as I readily admitted) man and wife, our familiarity as friends was such that we had no secrets from each other. She was extremely grateful at this, and, showing not the slightest sign of surprise or disapproval had us immediately taken to a pleasant room overlooking the courtyard where, our baggage brought by an overworked boy, we were pleased to bathe ourselves in the hot water which, despite the crowd and the unexpected emergency, the house provided – the earliest but not the last mark of an excellent inn.

By now the smell of food had become irresistible, and hastily redressing ourselves, we made our way to the dining room, where already several of our fellows had gathered. There we made ourselves free of a first-rate table, with roast beef, pork and fowl competing for excellence with fine platters of vegetables so well kept that it might have been spring rather than deep winter!

Later that evening, we seemed to resolve ourselves into one large family, sitting together in the great room, the fire if anything burning brighter than ever, and most of us in spirits all the higher for the consumption of a few bottles of excellent wine. The one dampener was that which will be familiar to any Englishman or woman who has experienced the circumstance of being thrown together with a company of strangers: that, despite our relatively good spirits, we remained somewhat aloof, one from the other, Sophie and myself being the only couple sufficiently easy to carry on a conversation (the servants clearly not being on terms sufficiently friendly to be able to converse freely with their employers).

'Come, come,' I said after twenty minutes of almost perfect silence, punctuated merely by the crackling of the fire, 'we seem likely to be here for several days, and cannot remain thus uneasy. Might I suggest that we introduce ourselves by telling the brief history of our lives, or perhaps relating an incident which is likely to entertain the others? Thus we will become friends as well as fellow-passengers, and moreover pass the time pleasantly.'

My suggestion was welcomed by the company with all the cheerful acquiescence with which an inspector of taxation meets with an indifferently formed excuse. The uneasy silence continued. Then it was broken from a somewhat unexpected quarter: our hostess, who had been quietly busying herself in making sure that glasses were full and that the fire was a-roar, asserted that my idea was an excellent one.

'And since,' she said, 'there seems some backwardness in offering the first tale, why do I not first tell my own story? That is,' she added, 'if, Jem, you give me your accord?'

The last remark was addressed to none other than our coachman, who was seated in a warm corner near the door, where, I had not failed to notice, he had been served with titbits of special delicacy, and his tankard attentively filled and refilled.

'Ay, girl, why not?' he remarked. ' 'Tis not a tale which is common; and if it is not of interest to most here, I shall be much surprised.'

And so it was that we heard The Hostess's Tale.

'I was born Ellen Pawley,' she said, 'the only daughter of an innkeeper and his wife at Southwark, and the first fourteen or fifteen years of my life were spent – after only five or six devoted to play – in a hard but happy round of work. The inn was not in a particularly good way of business, and, my father and mother being able to afford few servants, their places were taken by me and my three brothers, all of whom worked a great deal harder than employed men, and for almost nothing.

'Every possible room at the inn being set aside for the housing of members of the public who frequented it (chiefly, the lesser sorts of merchants on their way to and from the city), I shared a single large room with my brothers and my parents; the latter sleeping behind a blanket strung from the ceiling, the former sharing with me a single bed.

'The scheme worked well for some years, my mother and father being sufficiently cool-blooded not to engage more than once or twice a month in those pleasures which are enjoyed between man and wife, and then doing so in a silence which betokened no strong enjoyment. They betrayed only by an occasional grunt the fact that they were waking rather than dreaming.

'As to myself and my brothers, we were far too tired at the end of a day's work to regard bed as a place for anything but exhausted slumber; though it had become a habit with me, no doubt in unconscious regard for my virginity, to ensure that my youngest brother – some years my junior – lay next to me in the bed, rather than the two who were my elders; as a matter of course, I would first take my place next to the wall with little Johnny by me, leaving the outer space for Fred and Ben. The latter, if they noticed this phenomenon, did not comment upon it, and kept any conclusions to themselves.

'The safety could not last, however; for we all grew at the same rate, and at a time when I was fifteen, and my two elder brothers seventeen and eighteen, it was not to be expected that the difference between us would long go unremarked by them (or indeed by myself, for I had for some time been conscious that, despite their exhaustion, certain games would from time to time be played between them, to the intimacies of which I was not privy). While familial piety might have resulted in my elder brothers continuing to content themselves with attempting to spy on me as I washed myself, or as of a summer's evening I sometimes lay naked upon the bed when I believed that no one was about, it did not restrain little Johnny, who I naively believed would ever remain so much my junior that his feelings towards me could be nothing but brotherly.

'I was disillusioned of this upon waking one hot morning in June to find that the sheet which covered us had been thrown from the bed, that in my sleep my night-gown had ridden up about my waist, and that (consciously or unconsciously) my younger brother's hand had slipped between my thighs, where it now lay in a not unpleasant position, cupped about that part of my person which had recently been the cause of emotions at once strange and delightful.

'Not only that, but Johnny had wriggled out of his night-shirt, and his still unformed body, slender and unmuscled as that of a young kid, now lying upon his back, showed that in one circumstance at least he was no longer a boy but a man.

'I must confess that the sight was not uninteresting to me; occasional glimpses of the same phenomenon as affecting Fred and Ben had already suggested to me something which might prove worth investigation; and this would have been easier with Johnny than either of his elders. However, there was no possibility of this at present, for the latter were at the moment kneeling at the side of the bed, all smiles, and as interested in my own perfectly displayed nakedness as I might have been in theirs; Ben even going so far as to advance a hand in order to lift Johnny's palm from the spot in which it reclined, the better to lay my person open to examination.

'What might soon have occurred I know not; for at that unpropitious moment, my mother, rising for her morning work, stepped from behind the curtain to discover the *tableau*, and seizing the first weapon that came to hand – an unfortunately brimming night-jar – scattered us and set us about our work. Two days later, I was disposed of to a colleague of my father's in Wapping, who was happy to exchange me for a daughter of his own in similar circumstances. My sorrow at leaving home was somewhat mitigated by the fact that Mr Jeavons, my new master, had three sons just of the age of my brothers. I dare say that Kitty, their sister, found her enforced banishment to Southwark similarly alleviated by the presence of my brothers, though I never had the opportunity of discussing the fact with her. However, she became within six months my sister-in-law, and within nine was delivered of a fine boy; so her presence scarcely went unnoticed by at least one of my siblings.

'For myself, I can never be sufficiently grateful for the fact that the young men with whom I was now in close proximity were, despite their low birth, gentlemen. I had been allotted, for a sleeping space, the little nook or shelf where their sister had lain, and which was reached by mounting a short ladder at the side of the bedroom where they lay. From it I had a view, as from a theatre box, of the room below; and upon my first night watched, though somewhat nervously, as the three boys came to their room (having in a manly fashion allowed me to retire somewhat earlier) and divested themselves of their clothing – which they did without any attempt at concealment, thus allowing me to confirm that my brothers had indeed been typical members of the male sex (though somewhat to my disappointment, the major or most interesting features of their persons were devoid of any unusual proportion, perhaps through nervousness at my presence).

'The three lay themselves down to sleep upon their bed, which, standing inside a window, and the summer's night still being bright, was lit, as were their bodies as the light in a theatre illuminates a scene. They lay still for some time, but I believe could not but be conscious of my bright eyes, which I could not tear from the sight; for in time one began to nudge the other, then to giggle and whisper; and finally the eldest was almost thrown from bed by the poking which he received from the others.

'Finally, he rose and nervously approached, and standing upon the lower rung of the ladder and thus being able to address me in a low voice, requested unsteadily the pleasure of my company upon the bed below. For, he confessed, neither he nor his brothers had had any experience of the opposite sex, their sister of course having been out of the bounds of any physical examination (another example of their natural gentility; incest not by any means being unknown in Wapping). Though she had not been so modest as not to permit them occasional glances of her person, the female body was a landscape of which they cordially desired further exploration.

'My inclination to concur came as much, I confess, from my desire to familiarize myself with the male person, as any eagerness through politeness to comply with their wishes; and my quickness at joining them, while somewhat unladylike, may perhaps be understood when it is remembered that I was at that age when many girls are already mothers.

'It need perhaps not be said that our mutual explorations were as thorough as they were enjoyable; the boys almost fought for a vantage-point from which it was easiest to examine my person – while I was more fortunate in that with three of them jostling for position, there was no time at which at least one set of balls was not within close range; these being surmounted, as I soon saw, by wands now grown to admirably mannish proportions, and pleasingly susceptible to the caress of inquisitive fingers.

'On that first evening, the freshness of the prospect before us was such that a survey alone was its own reward, accompanied by only the simplest manual manipulation of parts – which none the less led to the (to me) interesting evacuation of that liquid whose expulsion accompanies masculine satisfaction. However, because these explorations continued night by night, it was not long before mutual discussion of the purpose of this thing and that thing resulted in the inevitable suggestion that the cranny or chink which was the main characteristic of my nether regions seemed made for the insertion of the upright instrument which proved the boys indeed to be of the opposite sex; and a short step to their contesting who should attempt to prove the theory in practice. The breaking of my hymen, which shortly followed, proved less painful than might have been the case, and while the younger boy (to whom the honour fell of taking my maidenhood) was done in less than no time, the fact that he had two brothers eager to follow where he had led meant that I was more satisfied by my first passage of love than many a girl dependent upon a single lover!

'None among this company will be so naive as to suppose that our experiments ceased upon that first attempt; nor did my father's friend or his wife attempt (though they must have known how their boys and adopted daughter were spending their nights, from our drowsy appearance during the day!) attempt to interfere – until the elder announced his intention to marry me; which threw them into a seizure, for they were depending on joining him to the daughter of a neighbouring innkeeper, and thus enlarging their business. I was therefore immediately dispatched in the direction of Northampton, to my employer's brother's inn in that city.

'My sorrow at leaving was not connected with any disappointment of an ambition to marry, for I did not love the brother who had offered for me; I was however sorry to leave a household where three lovers nightly competed for my favours (and mostly succeeded in enjoying them, in one order of precedence or another) – having been in the happy circumstances of enjoying corporeal pleasure to the keenest extent at just such an age when the appetite is ambitious but complete satisfaction usually lacking.

'Having spent two days upon the top of the coach, in scorching weather and without the company of a gentleman (my fellow-passengers outside all being female) I was beginning to miss my night-companions; and on stopping at this very inn, on the second night, had determined to do something about the circumstance. I had to this end spent the last twenty miles or so sitting upon the box next to the coachman, a finely set-up young man of perhaps twenty and five, who had not been slow to accept my suggestion that I should join him (though 'twas indeed against the rules of the company which employed him). My presence I believe was not unpleasant to him; and when, upon the coach lurching into a particularly deep pot-hole, I accidentally placed my hand upon his thigh in order to retain my balance, he did not repine; and indeed made no attempt to remove it when, in forgetfulness, I permitted it to remain there.

'I had now some hope of the night to come, for, on my moving my palm somewhat upwards, a swelling beneath his breeches seemed to promise a manifestation worth further exploration. Our arrival at the George necessitated our parting, for Jem must occupy himself in unloading those customers and that freight destined for Stamford. He found time, however, to ensure that I was provided with a room under the roof, cheap but extremely pleasant, and in relatively close juxtaposition to his own; whence I took myself after supper to await events.

'It was still relatively early when a soft knock came upon the door, and (not to my surprise) the coachman appeared, to enquire with a nice diffidence whether I had everything I wanted.

' "Not, perhaps, everything, sir," I replied; and stepping forward and raising myself upon tiptoe planted a frank kiss upon his lips. This led to other familiarities, and in short to our engaging in that act which I was so sadly missing. I was delighted by my lover, whose body was much sturdier than that of either of the three brothers who had driven me down the same route. I was surprised for instance at the growth of hair about his chest and haunches, which was in complete contrast to the smoothness of those masculine limbs which I had so far observed, and which had been decorated only beneath the arms and in those secret areas to which I had been privy. While Jem's hands were stronger and more capable then those of my infant lovers, they had all the softness concomitant with his commonly holding reins determining from the soft mouths of horses, while the muscles of his thighs – no doubt cultivated by the common feat of balancing himself upon a leaping coach's board – enabled him to thrust and bound with such invigorating force as soon raised me to a height of pleasure which was considerably greater than I had previous experienced.

'His apology – for the act concluding sooner than he had anticipated (though I had twice enjoyed a particular spasm of pleasure in the mean time) – made, he lay at my side, the coarse hairs upon his chest in a lather of perspiration, and complimented me upon my frankness.

' "Nay," I said, "I see no reason to hide the fact that I enjoy the act; is it not a chief pleasure in life?"

' "Few young ladies," he said (dignifying me with a title

to which I would not, alone, have laid claim), "would be happy to fall upon a bed with a stranger in quite such freedom."

'And why not? I enquired.

'Some men, he said, were villains, and would take advantage of such freedom to their own ends.

'I had, I said, yet to encounter them; but was confident of my being able to deal with them should the necessity arise.

'At this stage, I must confess, it occurred to me that a second bout would be pleasant; and turned my lips from speaking to a more lascivious pleasure, first paying a tribute to those sturdy paps which marked a firm and muscular breast and, having roused them from flaccidity to hardness, then devoting my attention to his riding-muscle, already half-risen and soon, under those attentions which I had taught myself to give, becoming sufficiently adamant for me to raise and impale myself upon it; a posture which he found surprising, never perhaps previously having been ridden rather than riding.

'We slept little that night; and in the morning, after greeting the dawn with what must alas be a final tribute to Venus, he enquired whence I travelled; and having heard I was destined for an inn, asked whether I was indeed committed to employment at that place in particular.

'No, I answered – for I travelled merely on the suggestion of my previous employer, no contract having been exchanged.

'Then why, he asked, should I not remain here, at the George? He himself spent a night at the inn once in every three days, so the pleasurable contact between us (and here he placed a kiss upon my breast) could be maintained, while the innkeeper, he knew, would be delighted to employ so eager and lively a girl as myself.

'In short, I agreed; and to cut what would otherwise be a tedious story short, with Jem's approval I devoted the next five years to the work with which I was already familiar, and – since I am being frank – somewhat to the innkeeper, a widower otherwise devoid of female company. He was undemanding, and a visit to his bed once a month or so (during which a comfortable and quiet embrace was preferred to more strenuous acrobatics) resulted in his becoming sufficiently fond of me to name me in his Will, so that on his death I inherited the inn, where I have remained ever since, devoting myself upon the one hand to the provision of excellent accommodation for travellers, and upon the other to the entertainment of my coachman friend, whose visits continue to be as pleasurable to me as upon that first appearance.'

The whole company now turned to stare at our driver, who lifted his hand in acknowledgement; and, upon turning again to the hostess, we found her pointing to a band of gold upon her finger which indicated a bond between them stronger even than that of the mutual pleasure which (from their eagerly taking themselves, a little later, to bed) they still enjoyed!

2

The Lieutenant's Tale

If fate decides it is necessary that one is detained for some time, against one's will, in a strange place, there can be few establishments in the country where that inconvenience may be sustained with more equanimity than at the George Inn at Stamford, where the rooms are comfortable, the fires always roaring, and there is a plentiful supply of food and drink.

The rigours of our journey resulted in Sophie and I sleeping like dead things from the moment we placed our heads on adjacent pillows; we awoke indeed only upon a maid entering in the morning to ensure that the fire in our room was refreshed (it had burned all night, thus obviating the unpleasant necessity of loading the bed with blankets). I ordered up breakfast, and spent the time waiting for its arrival in paying my friend the compliment of an assault upon her body with a weapon roused to vigour by an excellent night's rest. She, for her part, offered little enough resistance – and since, our association being long, we knew just those amorous tricks which each found most agreeable, by the time the maid returned with a groaning tray, I had been milked of those liquors which build up a pressure during the hours of darkness. In parenthesis, I cannot entirely dismiss the possibility that madame used her arts in order to bring about my collapse as swiftly as possible; for I have often observed that ladies are by no means invariably as eager as gentlemen to make love immediately upon waking. Some have said it is because our faces, being rough (our not yet having shaved), are uncomfortable to their cheeks, and indeed to any other part of their bodies with which they make contact).

The maid, a pretty, pert and no doubt willing girl, was no whit disturbed to find Sophie and I lying, in a state of nature, still clasped in each other's arms (and in a position highly suggestive of the occupation we had just concluded). She placed her tray upon the bedside table, and withdrew politely – though with a gleam in her eye which seemed to me to confirm at least one of the adjectives I have just applied to her; and which Sophie also noted, for administering a slap to my unprotected arse, she prompted me to refrain from complimenting one woman (if only by a glance) in the presence of another whose favours I had just enjoyed!

We laughed together, and set about our stirred eggs with cream, newly-baked bread, and dishes of coffee; after a while summoning again the maid and ordering up hot water, which was brought with remarkable promptitude by a manservant who then drew aside a screen to reveal a large tub which he almost filled, and at which we made our oblations to the god of cleanliness. So, by ten o'clock, we were downstairs in the main sitting room, where already most of our fellow-travellers had gathered, somewhat glum, staring out of the window at the whirling snow, now so thick as to make impossible more than an occasional glimpse of the opposite side of the street, and an unmistakable announcement that any thought of our leaving Stamford until after Christmas was too optimistic to be confirmed by good sense.

The same kind of distant silence was observed as had pertained at first on the previous night, which was now interrupted by Sophie, who, determined as ever to woo the party to a more friendly atmosphere, asked whether it was not time for one of our friends to relate the story of his or her life?

There was a silence at this – until, after a moment, a man's voice spoke out. It proved to be that of a young man who at first we did not recognize, but who proved to be the

Naval lieutenant who had at first been dressed in his service greatcoat and naval jacket, but who now stood revealed as unquestionably a gentleman, in a handsomely cut dove-grey topcoat and a shirt with a sufficient show of snowy (if somewhat crumpled) linen.

'Madam,' he said, addressing Sophie, 'I will be happy to volunteer a tale – for I have one to tell which is perhaps remarkable, though I must confess not entirely free of circumstances which might make it injurious to the sensibilities of ladies, for, although a narrative of simple truth, it is revelatory of a perhaps surprising though none the less interesting aspect of human nature.'

The suggestion that The Lieutenant's Tale might contain some colourful material clearly did not offend anyone among those present; indeed, the ladies seemed if anything somewhat eager to hear it (not only, as I suspect, from its possible content, but from the fact of the lieutenant being an exceedingly handsome young creature). And so a ready silence fell, which invited him to begin.

'My name is Raphael Rymer,' he said, 'familiarly known as Raff, and I am the third and youngest son of Sir Osbert Rymer, of Kelso, in the county of Northumberland. My elder brothers having gone, respectively, into the Army and the Church, there was nothing left to me but the Navy – a fate which I looked upon without undue regret, having been fed to happy repletion upon the stories of heroic Nelson and Trafalgar.

'My romantic notions received something of a blow upon my taking up my position as midshipman on a 74-gunner out of Portsmouth; for my rank was only somewhat above that of the rats who scuttled about the lower decks – and though it was unquestionably above that of the men who served there, most of whom had been pressed into the King's service unwillingly and from occupations which unsuited them for a life at sea, they and the lower ranking officers were pleased at the opportunity afforded them of treating with contempt the sons of gentlemen far above them in condition.

'Though I found my companion midshipmen reasonably pleasant, the conduct of the officers immediately superior to me was less so; though nimbleness of wit and a willingness to endure being the butt of rough shipboard humour soon won me a certain respect and even rough affection. I also managed through an inherent manliness to escape the fate of the prettiest of my young friends, who was adopted by the First Lieutenant as a substitute wife, and was so used by him as to be on occasion worthless about his work, through an enervation of spirits resulting from the sleepless nights he spent in the former gentleman's bunk, where . . .'

The young man paused, evidently hesitant to describe in the presence of ladies those customs which, at sea, have been raised by tradition to a degree of normalcy unsuspected by many landsmen, let alone by females. After a confused pause he continued, somewhat haltingly.

'My regard for my person persuaded me to avoid any seduction into sodomy; though the vigour which my body developed as a result of the healthy life I led encouraged me to enter to some extent into those lesser intimacies with which young boys counterfeit the amorous exchanges freely enjoyed between the sexes upon land. I had however a kind of natural delicacy which prevented me from exploring too deeply into such matters. My father had failed to converse with me on the matter of love, and I was entirely ignorant of the venal act (as indeed was the case with my fellows, who exchanged crude jokes about the matter which bore little relationship to the facts).

'It was the day after we had docked at Malta that upon the Captain's instructions (it was a custom he invariably encouraged) the Bo'sun, a kindly and fatherly figure, took we four midshipmen (who were all of about the age of fifteen) ashore, and promised us an entertainment which would "set us right", as he put it.

'The place to which he took us was of course a bordello; but since none of us had a notion of such a place or the purpose to which it was put, we did not of course recognize it as such. We were all the product of homes where neither of our parents would have been prepared to admit that such things existed, much less to explain the nature of those desires which rendered them necessary to single men, and on occasion even to husbands!

'It merely appeared that we had been taken to a rather splendid house to be entertained perhaps to afternoon tea: for this was no low place of converse, but one furnished with great taste by its Madame, an Englishwoman of some parts – the middle-aged widow of a businessman who had attempted to establish a vineyard on the island, without first assuring himself of the probability of success; on his dying, Mrs Fossick had turned to making her living as best she might. She had contrived an unofficial agreement with the Admiralty which resulted in her customarily entertaining His Majesty's officers upon special terms, and in particular undertaking through the young women she employed the education of the King's midshipmen, their Lordships believing (and who is to contradict them?) that the sooner young men are informed of the nature of sexual congress, and warned of the possible concomitant dangers, the better, since such an education is most likely to render those dangers least likely to injure them.

'We entered the house through a hallway with a floor of admirable white marble, then, leaving the Bo'sun below, were escorted by Mrs Fossick, an elegant lady, up a wide curved staircase; there then appeared a double doorway through which we expected – or *I* expected – to find perhaps a sitting room with tables bearing fine china, and was looking forward to some cakes which bore a resemblance to home comestibles rather than to those sawdusty biscuits, speckled with the occasional weevil, which were all too common on board ship.

'However, upon passing through the doorway I was confronted by a tableau which resembled the classical scenes with which I was familiar through those etchings in my father's library: the full glare of sunlight was excluded from the room by long shutters through which the sun, his direct light diffused, threw a low, white light over the scene. This suggested, rather than fully illuminated, the presence of several female figures in the room, who at first seemed to be wearing classical dress, resembling Roman togas.

'We took off our hats as one man, and must have made a pretty sight, standing in a row like stuffed dummies – though the ladies concerned must have seen a similar sight before, and were far too gracious (or, I dare say, too conscious of their position and duty) to laugh. As my eyes became accustomed to the gloom, I saw that there were six females present, the youngest of almost my own age, the eldest old enough, as it seemed to me, to be my mother. They were dressed in simple white shifts, which, to my amazement, I saw, as they stood to greet us, were sufficiently diaphanous to outline figures which seemed almost of heavenly beauty. Never having seen a woman's body before, except when fully clothed in those garments suitable for the northern British climate, the sight was to me a fascinating one.

'We four boys remained rooted to the spot as the ladies made us a curtsy; and whereas any one of our seniors would immediately have offered a hand to the female of his choice, we had no such notions. Behind our backs (as I guess) Mrs Fossick gestured to the four youngest of the six, who now approached, and held out their hands – which we took, expecting I suppose a handshake; but instead finding our hands firmly gripped as we were led towards a doorway, the opposite side of the room, and once through it into a corridor, and each into a separate small room leading off it.

'To my astonishment, I now found myself in a bedroom: or at least, in a room with a bed or low couch, at the side of which stood a large mirror, and at the foot of which was a basin of water and some towels. My first instinct was to explain that I had already bathed (for one of the first consequences of making landfall had been the provision, for the first time for weeks, of sufficient fresh water to enable us to refresh our soiled bodies). However, the young lady who had led me thither was already (to my astonishment) unbuttoning my tunic, and I was too well-mannered to protest. It had not been many years since my nurse had performed the duty of helping me to dress and undress, and, during my first separation from home and family, there was something comforting and reassuring about the action: moreover, this young person's attentiveness had something decidedly pleasant about it – as indeed had her person, for I had already discerned beneath her shift curves and protuberances which I found peculiarly interesting.

'Speaking not a word (indeed, I doubt that she had any command of English) the young lady helped me off with my jacket, and then turned her attention to my breeches, which in coming off revealed my untrained cock in what might be described as a state of semi-readiness. This may have been seen by her as an insult – but was actually the result of my being entirely ignorant of the nature of the prospect before me – and indeed of a certain nervousness and uncertainty as to my situation. My inappropriate lack of tumescence did not disturb me, for I saw no reason why a lady should expect any different state of affairs. Why should a female be interested in that particular part of me – either in that fully erect state which it sometimes assumed, or in a condition of flaccidity?

'My attendant nymph, however, now whisking off my shirt, seemed to expect something different of me, for looking down she tut-tutted, and to my utter astonishment laid her hand between my thighs – an intimacy which, however unexpected and shocking, gave me nevertheless a shock of unusual pleasure which so weakened my knees that I collapsed with a gasp upon the couch! She no doubt took this for an invitation, for taking the hem of her shift she raised it above her head, and allowed me only a moment's opportunity to see for the first time a naked female figure before lowering herself upon me and beginning with the most lascivious motion to wriggle her body against my own.

'Had she been any less experienced, despite being of no great age, my business would immediately have been done; for the combination of the apprehension of her person and the sight of it in the mirror, so angled to reveal to my gaze the most delicious pair of posteriors, thrilled me almost to distraction. However, no doubt apprehending the keenness of my emotion, she now threw herself to one side and with an adept skill turned my body so that I lay above her, when embracing me with her thighs, she guided my adventuring prick for the first time into harbour.

'I was, though delighted by the new sensation, sufficiently puzzled to find it impossible not to raise myself upon my elbows and gaze down towards the point at which my new sensation was centred – and to my astonishment saw that my cock, that obstreperous lower limb which now seemed the very centre of the universe, had apparently entered the very body of my companion, a fact which was perfectly inexplicable to me, since I had no notion of the female shape. My puzzlement did not however prevent my enjoyment, for instinct now took command, and in a moment I was swiving as to the manner born, the young lady uttering squeaks of pleasure – which, whether (as I now guess) assumed for the purpose of making me pleased with myself, or genuine (for I was a well set-up lad) had the effect of persuading me that she was enjoying the occasion as much as I.

'To cut short a description which must be tedious, our first embrace was concluded long before I had experienced enough of this new pleasure, and recovering with the speed of youth I persuaded the young lady to a second passage; after which a knock upon the door summoned us, wrapped in two towels, to the sitting room, where lemonade was served to cool me and my friends, who, similarly clad, showed that they had all been equally pleased. On our way back to the ship, we exchanged views of our experiences, which were enthusiastic to a degree. Even the First Lieutenant's catamite had not been disappointed. His companion, finding him disappointed that she had no instrument with which to penetrate a bum which had been taught to receive as well as give pleasure, had seized a dildo (an instrument whose purpose and very existence I was then unfamiliar with) and plunged it into his arsehole, while at the same time teaching him the more conventional use of his prick; the result being (as young Master Bobby described it) his complete ravishment.

'We were all ready – nay, eager – to renew our experience upon the morrow – but sadly learned that our new young friends, who apparently had enjoyed our companionship almost as much as ourselves, required payment for their services. We had no money – and the sum extorted by the Captain from our fathers upon some excuse (as lessons in the use of the sextant) would allow of no further expenditure; upon which we stood sadly at the rails and watched the harbour of Valetta fall away behind us, incapable of guessing when we might renew our experience of the sex, only Bobby being somewhat comforted by his regular assignations with the First Lieutenant, who he now found a reasonable substitute for female company, being one of those unhappy, or perhaps happy, young men to whom any port is welcome in a storm.'

The narrator paused here, and there was a stir as though his tale was over; but he held up a hand.

'I have more to tell,' he said, 'indeed, this has been a mere prologue, interesting perhaps to those who are not aware of the circumstances of the amorous education of the young gentlemen of the Service. What comes now is another matter, and I shall be surprised if anyone here can offer a story as interesting.

'My true narrative begins ten months ago at Portsmouth, where I joined the *Leopard* as officer in charge of navigation. She was a particularly happy ship, under a Captain of extraordinary diligence in his calling – and a diligence which happily extends to the care of his crew, whose health is of paramount importance to him, and is assured by the taking of as much fresh food as can be carried on board, including fruit, at every stopping place where it is possible – and by the presence of a first-rate ship's surgeon, whose cabin I found to be next my own, just below the Captain's, and looking out on the wheel-deck, so that merely stepping from my door I was immediately behind the steersman – a convenience excellent in good weather, but less to be commended in a storm, when great waves crashing upon the deck rendered the place almost uninhabitable.

'The surgeon of whom I have spoken was a Lieutenant Spencer, who on my introducing myself greeted me with a firm and manly handshake and a friendly, if strangely disconcerting, look from peculiarly light blue eyes. I calculated he was of rather less than my years with a fine, upright carriage, his head held high and his shoulders well-set. We immediately struck up a friendship as close as could exist between two men of unequal rank – his position placing him, in any case, rather outside the hierarchy of naval discipline, for it is often the case that medical men serve merely for a few years on board ship before taking up positions ashore (Robin, however – as he permitted me to call him – being the exception, for he seemed entirely devoted to the Service).

'I have spoken of our Captain's care for his ship's company; and he is indeed one of the most enthusiastic naval officers in insistence upon proper living conditions for his men. This however does not mean that he does not impose proper discipline – and though no consistent flogger (there still exist such commanders) was brought, on a voyage to Constantinople, to the position of ordering a man to sustain thirty lashes for breaches of discipline too persistent to be neglected.

'The ship's company was summoned to the quarterdeck in the late afternoon to witness punishment – the Captain having chosen the time in order that the pain of the offender should not be exacerbated through the heat of the Mediterranean sun. I need not, perhaps, describe the scene minutely, for I cannot imagine that the gentlemen present will not be aware of the details, while the ladies will perhaps not care to hear them. I need only say that the Bo'sun wielded the cat with a proper power, and that the offender sustained his punishment with as much equanimity as could be expected; but that the scene was one which I hope not to see again, the man's back being laid open after the first six or seven lashes, the remainder reducing the skin to tatters, the blood freely running to the deck.

'It was the duty of the surgeon and myself to accompany the victim below decks, where my friend bathed the raw back and tended it as best he might. I was amazed to become aware that Lieutenant Spencer was clearly affected by the admittedly unpleasant sight of so much bleeding flesh, and even began to waver upon his feet as we returned to our cabins, staggering and almost falling. Such unmanly conduct was surprising – yet, I told myself, so young a man could not have seen action, and it may be that the extent of the injury he had just witnessed was the worst with which he had come into contact, while the manner of its infliction was also sickening to those who had not previously witnessed it.

'Upon our reaching his cabin, for a moment he actually lost consciousness, and I lowered him to his bunk. Nearby stood a flask of brandy. I poured him a glass, and meanwhile loosened the neck of his shirt to allow such air as there was in the close cabin to refresh him.

'What was my surprise and horror to see, as I undid the buttons, that his chest was bound up by bandages which were laid in such complete swathes that they must surely conceal a fearful wound. But now, opening his eyes, he threw down the brandy in a single swallow, gathered his shirt about his neck, and turning away from me did up the buttons.

' "Thank you, my dear Raff," he said. "I am ashamed of such weakness; but I have been much in the sun today, and I fear, suffer from a touch of heat exhaustion."

'Within ten minutes he appeared completely to have recovered, and I thought no more of the affair; nor did I have the temerity to mention the wound upon his breast, which seemed not to incommode him, for his movements were as free and unconstrained as any man's.

'Upon the ship laying to on the Golden Horn, we went

ashore together at Constantinople. There, we visited the famous Blue Mosque and the great church of St Sofia – after which I must admit (the ladies in the company will, I trust, excuse the confession) I was eager to experience the comforts of the famous Turkish *hammams* or hot baths, where I had been told one might be entertained by charming young ladies of the city the beauty of whose persons together with their adeptness in giving pleasure was said to suggest that they might have received some training in the Sultan's famous harem at Topkapi palace, were it not that no female had ever been known to escape that place, once taken to it.

'On my suggesting this, however, Robin begged to be excused, explaining to me quietly that his having so frequently treated men for the complaints which were too often the result of such entertainment had entirely persuaded him to avoid brothels of all descriptions. He failed to persuade me to neglect the opportunity – nor did he persuade me to make use of that form of protective covering or *cundum* which, while unquestionably reducing the risk of infection, also reduces the pleasure of the sensations accompanying coitus.

'I thought no more of this – but in a week's time, when we were again upon the sea, making back for Italy, was seriously troubled to wake one morning and find a strange inflammation about my private parts: immediately, of course, remembering Robin's words, I feared that my rashness had resulted in my contracting some fearful disease, leaping to the conclusion that the young woman with whom I had spent an expressively enjoyable hour had not been as healthy as she had been handsome.

'Not caring to broadcast my condition among my friends, I made a private confession to Robin, who invited me to present myself at his cabin that evening, when he would make an inspection (assuring me that even should my suspicions prove correct, except in the most unusual cases a cure was possible, if not entirely pleasant in its execution).

'On my removing my trousers and lying upon his bunk, he lifted my prick and balls, looking carefully at the red blotches which marked the skin of my thighs and belly and parting the hairs with his fingers the better to examine them; he then gently drew back the skin to reveal the head of my prick, which he studied with the closest attention.

'He did all this with such tenderness that to my embarrassment I found the touch of his hands so pleasant that for a moment, closing my eyes, I could almost believe that I was being handled by a woman. The thought was fatal to me, for despite my best efforts I felt my apparatus swelling as it might under the attention of a loving female. It can be imagined how ashamed this made me feel: for Robin could scarcely fail to notice my reaction, and I had no wish to spoil our friendship by persuading him that I thought of him in any other way than as a comrade.

'Noting the reaction of my person, however, he seemed almost to encourage it, by a kind of stroking of the barrel of the gun, and at the same time a light squeezing at the base which almost instantaneously resulted in an elevation sufficiently handsome to impress any female! Now, a new concern struck me: I remembered that Robin had avoided accompanying me to the bordello in Constantinople in my search for female company. Was *he* one of those men – not infrequently found on board ship, despite the opposite conviction of their Lordships of the Admiralty – whose satisfaction was found in the intimate company of their fellows?

'I was somewhat comforted to observe – which in my reclining position was easy – that there were no signs of excitement about my friend's own crutch: his tight trousers would surely have revealed that swelling which in the male is concomitant with desire. Yet he continued to examine my private parts with a tender care, and his voice when he spoke seemed to tremble with emotion in an almost girlish fashion.

' "This is merely a local irritation," he said, "the cause of which may merely be in the over-tightness of our clothing in such hot weather. I advise your removing your lower clothing in the privacy of your cabin, and bathing the whole area with fresh water . . ."

'As he spoke he still stroked my person, ostensibly, it may be, to comfort the slight irritation of the skin, but in fact conveying another form of irritation which was so extreme as to produce at the tip of my cock a little bead of moisture – seeing which, as though in a dream, I saw to my astonishment the doctor lean to take it up upon the tip of his tongue, going on to kiss, with the most careful fondness, the place from which it had sprung.

'Despite the fact (and I must admit it, even had not my narrative made it sufficiently clear) that I had not been impervious to his ministrations, he had now gone too far. I sat up suddenly, throwing him back against the wall of the cabin, and swung my legs to the floor.

' "Forgive me, Robin," I said, "but my inclinations do not lie in that direction."

'At this he blushed like a girl, but then, drawing himself up, lifted a hand:

' "One moment, Raff," he said; "it is not what you think" – and began to unbutton his shirt.

'Once more I made as though to stand – yet something in the expression of his eyes detained me. Beneath his shirt, as I had remembered, his chest was tightly bound by a bandage which he now began to unloose. I was at once horrified and confused: what distressing injury was he about to show me? And was he about to attempt to convince me that out of pity I should submit to that illegitimate desire which he had conceived?

'My amazement may seem naive to those of you who have already guessed his secret: what was revealed as the bandage fell away, was as perfect (though small) a pair of woman's breasts as any man could wish to see.

'For a moment (and again my auditors may think me a fool) my horror was intensified: what kind of freak stood before me? But the few seconds it took him to throw off his breeches revealed the truth – which of course was that Dr Spencer was, in fact, a woman.

'Any desire to hear the circumstances of his presence on one of the vessels of His Majesty's navy was, I confess, subjugated on that occasion to a desire of another sort; and he – or she, as I must now say – met my own eagerness for congress with an equal enthusiasm, sharpened as I believe by the unusual nature of the occasion to a fervent fire. Deprived as she had been, through circumstances, of intimate male companionship while continually in exclusively male company, her senses had throughout the course of the voyage been excited to almost an unbearable degree by the necessity of intimately examining, from time to time, the bodies of a group of healthy young men any one of whom would have been for her an agreeable companion in the act which we now performed, not once but several times, in as energetic a manner as the confinement of the doctor's cabin allowed.

'When we were persuaded through exhaustion to desist for a few moments from these delights, Robin explained that she had been brought up by her father, a retired surgeon who himself had served under Lord Nelson, and he had told her such inspiriting stories of life at sea that she would think of nothing else but the Service; and how, with his assistance, she had first obtained such knowledge of medicine as would impress an examining board, and had then practised such wiles as would permit her to impersonate a man.

'This single voyage would, she believed, exorcise her longing for service at sea, which only the lack of intimate male company had rendered less enjoyable than she had supposed.

'Having penetrated her secret (in every sense), I now found it difficult to imagine how I could have been deceived in the matter of her gender. Though her figure, especially when bound up, was sufficiently boyish, it seemed to me even when clad in uniform to betray her female form in every movement – and particularly in the aspect of her rear; time and again, watching her walking upon the deck in her tight, white trousers, I could not credit that I could ever have mistaken those slightly elongated, full female haunches for the tighter globes of a male arse.

'However, she kept up the deception until we docked once

more at Portsmouth; and in the mean time by my assistance, which I was by no means hesitant in offering, was able to dissipate those energies aroused by the necessity of being in close proximity to the unclad male form (for, apart from medical occasions, in hot climes the men were clad in as little clothing as possible, and frequently cavorted upon deck washing themselves from great pails of water and skylarking in a manner which would frequently be regarded as obscene by those onlookers unused to the coarseness of the lower deck).

'She was good enough to suggest that my attentions removed altogether the temptation which might have led to her discovery through just such a gesture as had revealed her secret to me. I must be immodest enough to say that she claimed to have found my unclad and excited person so attractive that she had been unable to refrain from that gesture, for (she said) the size and perfection of my . . . But no, I find that after all, modesty demands that I should not repeat her words. Sufficient to say that our regular meetings now defused a situation which might otherwise have been dangerous – though even so there were occasionally moments of some danger, as when she was consulted about some minor genital irritation by the Bo'sun himself, whose equipment (she told me) resembled rather that of a bull than of a man, and who became aroused at her touch even more readily than I. It was clear from his glance he was ready to use it upon any living creature in the vicinity, and only the swift application of a somewhat painful astringent lotion reduced the danger of rape.

'This extraordinary story, ladies and gentleman,' Lieutenant Rymer concluded, 'seems likely to continue – for as our voyage grew towards an end my friend confided that she found the prospect of leaving the Service impossible of contemplation; moreover, the Captain expressed himself so satisfied with her conduct (being, of course, entirely deceived as to her sex), and so willing to recommend her reappointment, that it seemed unnecessary to decline to continue so promising a career. As far as I know she will, after the expiration of the present period of shore leave, once more embark upon the *Leopard*. At present, it seems most likely that I shall join her – which is not a fate I regard with any regret, for I must confess that long confinement on shipboard without the solace of female company is not something which is particularly agreeable to me. Marriage to the ship's doctor will be healthful in more way than one – though how long Lieutenant Spencer will be able to deceive the generality of her fellow-officers and men is another matter: and I must confess that the scenes that will follow such a revelation will be well worth witnessing!'

With this, the lieutenant concluded his tale – which was received with much laughter and applause, and confirmed my own view that in this world nothing should be taken at face value.

3

The Cook's Tale

After the lieutenant had ended his story, there was a general buzz of conversation – and indeed of congratulation, for he had held every one of his audience captive by his extraordinary narrative, which would have been difficult to credit had he not given the impression of being entirely truthful.

There was now, once more, a silence – broken suddenly by a passenger from the second coach: that robust, rosy-cheeked lady of considerable size, whose attractiveness was that of a merry and cheerful character, reflected in every glance of a pair of humorous eyes.

'I will be happy to entertain the company with a relation of my history, should it be agreeable,' she said. 'It will perhaps contain elements unfamiliar to most of you, for my occupation is one which is for a woman relatively rare in England, though less so in my native country, which is France.'

There was a stir of surprise at this, for her previous conversation, though marked perhaps by a very slight accent, had provoked no extraordinary suggestion that she was of foreign birth.

'I see I surprise you,' she said: 'and indeed I am usually now taken for an Englishwoman – but that is through long residence in this country, together with a talent for languages which has always gone hand in hand with my profession. There will therefore perhaps be no hardship in your listening to The Cook's Tale.'

We did not demur, whereupon she began:

'My name is Rosalie d'Albignac – but upon my first coming to this country that proved to be too trying to the English tongue, and I very soon learned to announce myself as Rose Allbig, a sobriquet now entirely suitable to my frame.' She shook with laughter, her large body veritably quivering with good humour.

'This was not always so,' she continued; 'when I was a child I was *petite* and elegantly formed, and one of my first memories is of being displayed upon a table to some ladies and gentleman, made to stand quite still, for my body was covered with a white paste which, if I moved, would crack and spoil the effect. I can only have been three or four years of age at the time, and I now realize that the white material was of course icing sugar, and that I was the centre-piece of a table decoration – for (no doubt you will have guessed it) my father was the master chef of a great household – that of the Viscount de Bernouailles, near Vichy, who was given to extravagances of the kind.

'I grew up in the kitchens, where my mother – once a simple kitchenmaid but now my father's irreplaceable aide – was held in a respect almost equal to himself; because of which the other servants permitted me a licence which would have been denied to most children. By the time I was ten or eleven, I was helping my parents to prepare some of the simpler dishes which were served upstairs – *oeufs à la tripe*, for instance, or hard-boiled eggs served with fried onions, nutmeg and cream; *pigeons aux petits pois*, or pigeons cooked with a little diced pork, seasoned with parsley and spring onions, garlic and bay leaf, and served covered with a litre of little new peas; or perhaps – a favourite of my lady's – *truite à la montagnarde*, or trout cooked in white wine, with onions, garlic, cloves, thyme, basil and butter.

'These dishes I found easy to prepare, and had from the first a talent for arranging them upon their dishes so that they looked as charming as they tasted. So, from an early age it was clear for what profession I was destined – though from the first it was assumed that I could never be more than an assistant in the kitchen, because for a woman to be in entire charge of such a male domain was at that time believed impossible!

'My fascination with every aspect of cooking made me an attentive student, and from making the simplest dishes I moved on to assisting my father with more complex and difficult tasks – the making of sauces, for instance, which in France is always a matter of the greatest concern: by the time I was fourteen, I was able to turn out a reliable *béchamel*, blending the cream with such patience that it never curdled, or to make a *sauce à la maître d'hôtel froide* in which there was the most perfect balance between the parsley and tarragon, the balm, the lemon, the verjuice. I was even permitted to make that grandest of all sauces, the *espagnole*, ensuring that the knuckle of veal was of a size proportionate to the amount of bacon, that the pieces of partridge, rabbit or chicken were sufficiently succulent to release reliably rich juices, composing a bouquet of basil, shallots, bay, garlic and thyme which was of just the right composition, and finally binding the sauce with a *roux* before adding madeira, champagne or burgundy according to milord's taste.

'All this left me little time to worry about any other aspect of growing up – though if you are pitying me for my lack of young companions and my entire ignorance of any conventional schooling – indeed of any life outside that of the kitchen – please refrain; for I was entirely happy.

'It was quite by accident that, at the age of perhaps fifteen, I quite suddenly made the discovery that there was another great pleasure other than the cooking and eating of food (for as you may perhaps guess from the proportions of my frame, I have always been as delighted to consume a dish as to compose it!). I was one day engaged in preparing some long parsnips for the luncheon table, scraping and trimming them. I was alone except for one of the kitchen lads, a bright spark named Michel, who was cheerful and willing, but would never be more than a washer-up of dishes, a fetcher and carrier of coals, a performer of the roughest sort of tasks. Nevertheless, it was impossible not to like him:

he always had a cheerful smile upon his face, and had never been known to refuse to do anything asked of him. He had lately been particularly attentive to me, taking my arm (quite unnecessarily) to help me up if I had been choosing and picking beans, and offering to assist me to put on or remove my apron. I regarded this with some impatience; yet as I say, it was impossible to be angry with the lad – who was now engaged in cleaning potatoes at a tub next to that in which I was trimming the parsnips.

'Quite suddenly, he began to laugh until his face was quite red. On looking up, I discovered that he seemed to be amused by something I was doing – and on my raising an eyebrow, he pointed at the parsnip on which I was at work. This was indeed a somewhat distorted one, which I was about to trim to a more conventional shape: it tapered not to a point but to a blunt, round end; and at the thick point where the leaves had been, it was decorated with two spherical bulbs attached to the main stem.

'I smiled at Michel, but could see nothing to laugh at.

' "Don't it remind you of somethin'?" he asked.

'I looked at the object, and shook my head.

' "Oh, my!" he exclaimed. "You mean, you never saw nothin' like it before?"

'I had not, I said; and had no idea what he could mean.

'He had now stood up, and dried his hands, and was standing behind me. He reached over my shoulders to take the vegetable from my hands – pressing as he did so his body against my own, producing a sensation of warmth and pleasure which surprised me, no person of the male sex having ever taken such a liberty (there had been some in the kitchen who, as I now realize, may have been tempted to do so; but the commanding presence of my father no doubt deterred them).

'Michel now held the parsnip in his left hand, and closing his right hand about it, moved it up and down, so that its end first appeared and then disappeared within his palm. I had not the faintest idea of his meaning; but was now conscious of something hard yet somewhat malleable pressing against my lower back. Michel thrust the middle part of his body forward in order to make me even more aware of this thing, which now seemed to be trying to nudge between the cheeks of my arse – though not, I must say, in a painful manner. What could it be? I reached around, and he immediately withdrew his body from mine sufficiently for me to thrust my hand between us and seek out the intrusive object, which fell into my palm as though placed there.

'It being summer, none of us wore more than a minimum of clothing, and Michel was clad only in a thin shirt and a loose pair of linen trousers, which concealed little to the sight, and disguised nothing from the touch: I immediately understood, from the shape of the thing I felt, his former merriment: what was now beneath my palm seemed to be a similitude of the vegetable which was again in my other hand!

'It was my turn to laugh – but in a somewhat confused manner, and it was evidently clear to the boy that I had not the slightest understanding of the situation. He took me by the hand, and drew me from the kitchen into the dairy – without any resistance on my part, my curiosity having been thoroughly aroused. In a corner of the dairy was a screen set up to divide the main body of the room from a corner in which was a stock of paddles for butter-making, pots and churns and other miscellanea.

'Here, without more ado, Michel unloosed his trousers and let them fall to the ground, raising his shirt to reveal to my astonished gaze a thing almost the model of the rude parsnip which I still clasped! I fell to my knees to compare the two. The parsnip was admittedly a little smaller, but the only other difference between the two objects was that that attached to Michel's body, at the bottom of his belly and between his thighs, was decorated at the base by a cluster of fair hair.

'What could be the purpose of this object? I looked at it closely, reaching out to part the hair and discover that it was indeed attached to his body both above and below.

As I passed my hand beneath the two round protuberances (which, unlike those attached to the base of the parsnip, were somewhat loose, and appeared to be joined to the remainder of the apparatus by two cords which lay beneath the skin), Michel drew in his breath sharply, and clasping my head with his hands attempted to draw it towards this peculiar limb. As he did so, I saw that there was a tiny hole which could be seen at the tip of his parsnip, from which now oozed a tiny drop of whitish liquid.

'I looked up at the boy, upon whose face there was now an expression rather similar to that of someone who had just tasted the first spoonful of a delicious soup.

' "What can it be for?" I asked.

' "You don' know?" said Michel. "You want me to show you?"

' "Please do," I said – at which, to my astonishment, he drew me to my feet, and asked me to turn about and place my arms upon the white marble top of a table where butter was sometimes mixed. He then lifted my skirt, and I felt a pleasant draught of cool air about my loins – which I must confess seemed somewhat more heated than was concomitant with even such warm weather as we were experiencing.

'What happened next was even more surprising: for I felt him introducing his parsnip into that cavity between my legs which I had previously believed was formed for only one purpose. He then began to move so that the object first penetrated and then withdrew from my person – in just such a manner as he had moved the vegetable within his palm!

'My first instinct was of surprise, and something of distaste, and then of a sharp pain which made me wince: and yet there was after all something remarkably pleasant about the sensation produced by the friction – a feeling almost as good as that produced upon the palate by a first-rate dish. I could now hear little moans behind me which at first I thought to be expressions of pain, and wondered that Michel continued his movements; but soon I recognized that he shared my own pleasure, for the gasps and groans were just such as I heard my mother make when testing a spoonful of *grenadine* which she had just made, or a particularly delicious *gâteau* of my father's.

'Just as is the case as one eats a first-rate dish, the sensation was sustained while the action continued – and even mounted; until the warmth which I had felt became almost a fire, and I could not resist thrusting out my bottom to meet those lunges with which Michel was now causing his belly to smack against the cheeks of my arse. Just as it seemed impossible that my emotion should grow any keener, Michel reached around to thrust his hands beneath my dress and clasp my breasts – which even at that age were sufficiently large to be well worth clasping; this gave me an extraordinary thrill of pleasure, and resulted in what seemed a veritable explosion of passion within me, while at the same time a muffled roar came from Michel, and giving a final thrust he laid himself panting along my back.

' "Well," he said some minutes later, when we had returned to our tasks in the kitchen; "now you know the purpose of parsnips." I could only smile, and though I carefully disguised the particular vegetable which had led to the discovery, could not but blush when I carried the dish of those vegetables to table that afternoon, leading my mother to suggest that I was over-heated by the fires in the kitchen, allied to the heat of the day, and make me lie down in my room – causing me some irritation, for I had hoped to explore a little more the matter of parsnips and their extra-culinary use, and enforced leisure only led me to remember the extraordinary emotion to which I had been introduced, and to long to re-experience it.

'Happily, there were many opportunities for this; and I became somewhat notorious with my parents for my interest in a vegetable which, though popular, did not seem to them to merit the extraordinary attention I gave it – for sometimes I was known to spend more than an hour seeking for parsnips in the kitchen garden, and preparing them in a quiet corner of the outbuildings. Michel often helped me, though I found that other young men attached to the *château* were equally enthusiastic about the vegetable, and discovered that, just as with the original, parsnips were variegated in shape and quality: some long and straight, some thick and ridged, some of a generous size and some less so – but all capable of conveying pleasure.

'My interest in cooking and in that other pleasure which I have named henceforth ran side by side; and I could not resist the attempt to bring the two together. The first opportunity for this came when my father and mother had accompanied the Viscount and Milady to Paris for the season, leaving me for the first time in charge of the kitchens which they felt confident in, since the only person to be served (outside the servants' hall) was the Viscount's son, M. de Bernouailles, a young man of eighteen years.

'He summoned me one morning, and informed me that he was to dine that evening with Mlle Cotteret, the seventeen-year-old daughter of a local notary, with whom it had been rumoured he was carrying on an assignation. I could not resist giving him a quizzical look – we were on terms which allowed it, for he had done me the honour of allowing me to taste his parsnip (he having come across an under-footman and I dining upon each other's bodies, *au natural*, in a wood on the estate, and insisted on sharing the feast). I may say that this was not of astonishing proportions; yet despite my being a servant he had taken care that I should be provided with a full meal rather than a snack – and indeed the repast he provided was considerably richer and more varied than I had received from any fellow-servants.

' "I would like you to provide a small feast suitable for the occasion," he said; "you will perhaps understand my intention – but the young lady is, as I believe, innocent, and will need careful wooing. I leave the menu to you – but it should perhaps be a little more subtle than, er . . ."

' "Than unadorned parsnip, Monsieur," I said, and curtsied.

'It was an interesting task, which I performed with considerable care and thought. I had to consider that some dishes might suit the case because of their appearance, others for their taste, yet others through their traditional association with the arts of seduction. At eight o'clock, just before Mademoiselle was due to arrive, I took up to Monsieur a dish of two dozen molluscs from the oyster park at Marennes, which he ate simply with a few drops of lemon juice. It is said that oysters increase fecundity; I have not found this, but perhaps by suggestion they certainly seem invariably to increase venery, and I was confident would have that effect upon Monsieur – not that, in my experience, the encouragement was particularly necessary.

'At ten o'clock, I donned my best gown and accompanied the footman to Monsieur's chamber with the first course. He and his friend were at their ease, having consumed already most of a bottle of champagne. Monsieur rose to his feet (clad, I saw, in the most elegantly ruffled shirt and breeches of black silk) and handed Mademoiselle to the table. I must confess that she made a pretty picture, her gown sufficiently low to disclose almost half of her pretty, firm breasts, all the whiter against dark brown silk, while the grace of her movements somehow suggested that her lower limbs, concealed beneath a flowing skirt, were rather slimmer than my own – which were more substantial, if capable of giving no less pleasure to the discerning lover.

'The first dish I set before them was a mussel soup, the mussels having been cooked in their shells in a *bouillon* made with tomatoes and white onions, and a little garlic (when two lovers eat garlic, the effect is strangely to bring them together; when one only has consumed that delightfully aromatic vegetable, the result can sadly be the opposite). There is an ancient tradition (perhaps something to do with the shape of the mussels, or clams – with which the dish can also be made) connecting this soup with a magisterial swelling of the male parts; whether for this reason or because of the dish's delicacy, both Monsieur and Mademoiselle devoured it voraciously, and turned then to the second course.

'This was laid before them beneath silver covers,

withdrawn to disclose a dish of fine asparagus, brought that week from Marchiennes: the stalks thick and firm, the heads slightly enlarged, round and purple, and dressed with fine melted butter. Having set the dishes down, I signalled to the footman to retire, and myself stepped behind a screen which performed the dual office of removing me from the sight of the young diners while at the same time permitting me to observe them – not, you understand, for any reason of lechery, but in order that I should note their enjoyment or otherwise of the dishes.

'My observation of Mademoiselle's manner in eating asparagus convinced me that she was not as innocent as perhaps Monsieur might believe – nor could I conceive that she would be difficult to conquer; for she lifted the stalks with the fingers of her right hand, laying them across the palm of the other, then, raising them singly to her lips licked the butter from the tip of each with a delightfully pointed, pink tongue – looking the whole straight at Monsieur, who had the grace to blush at her glance.

'The pantomime which followed was distinctly amusing: first, Monsieur, lifting a stalk to his lips, inserted the tip between his lips and slowly eased the entire piece into his mouth, then swallowing with an appreciative rolling of the eyes. Mademoiselle, not to be outdone, parted her lips just sufficiently to insert the empurpled bulb between them, easing it into her mouth, then withdrawing it, sucking every drop of rich liquor from it before swallowing it, with a delightful stretching of her slim neck. Some drops of butter rolling from her under-lip down her chin, dropped upon her breast and descended to the very edge of her gown – whereupon, drying her fingers upon her napkin, she lifted the edge of the dress and pulled it away from her breast, then taking up the buttery drops from where they had come to rest, against the delicious rosy nodule which was as swiftly disclosed as it was, once more, hidden.

'I cannot speak for Mademoiselle – or indeed for Monsieur (though I can guess at the emotions of both) but by the time the dish was finished, the idea of *parsnip* was by no means far from my mind, and I suspected that it was a case (as we say in the kitchen) of *feu dessus, feu dessous*, or "heat above and heat below". However, no such crudeness could be allowed on this occasion, and at a signal the third service was brought to table.

'Since this was only a light meal, this dish consisted of my *gross pièce*, or most effective creation: it was a pie, the pastry top of which I had carefully decorated with a scene from Aretine, the great Italian libertine, showing a man and woman enjoying each other. I had gone to some trouble to ensure that, while there was no doubt as to the activity in question, the *bas-relief* was not sufficiently lubricious to give offence – nor did I allow the diners more than a glimpse before I removed the dish in order to open the pie, which was of pheasant – but decorated with *croutons* cut in unmistakable shapes; so that while this main course was designed for consumption rather than for suggestiveness, the *dénouement* of the meal could at no time be forgotten.

'The diners having signalled that they had done, the final touch was eventually produced: each of the two plates now set before Monsieur and Mademoiselle consisted of a banana, at the base of which a peach, cut into two halves, lay beneath a small thicket of spun brown sugar. Bananas, the fruit, you know, of a tree formerly to be found only in the East and West Indies, had recently begun to be cultivated in Tunisia, and were just being seen for the first time in France. They are considered by some to be the forbidden fruit which our mother Eve bit into; and the very shape indeed suggests that this may be the case.

'Mademoiselle was intensely curious – yet what was evidently her first sight of the fruit filled her with confusion – and this time it was her turn to blush. She laid a gentle finger along the banana's length, as though to test its texture and firmness; then inserted it beneath the little curls of spun sugar, as if to tickle the peaches, one of which she then lifted to her lips, sliding it between them with a movement which struck even myself as ostentatiously libidinous. The manner in which she then lifted the plate so that she could nibble at the sugar nest; her toying with the second peach; and finally the manner in which she caressed with tongue and lips the banana, finally convinced Monsieur that any subtlety of seduction was unnecessary – and ignoring his own plate, he leaped to his feet and approaching his mistress, bent over her to insert his own tongue into that delightfully voracious orifice into which my meal had vanished, at the same time taking the opportunity of passing his hand into her bosom, drawing down her gown to reveal once more those small buds which like wild strawberries bloomed upon her white breasts.

'Whether her eagerness in reciprocating by passing a hand between his thighs was connected with any desire to discover the dimensions of the fruit contained there I could not, of course, say – but when (as happened within a very few minutes) they had assisted each other into a state of undress and placed themselves upon a convenient couch, she showed no hesitation in tasting the viands upon offer with an enthusiasm at least equal to that she had shown in the consumption of the meal I had so carefully composed, her admiration of the purple head of his staff being no less (and no less practically expressed) than of the similarly robust tip of the asparagus which had been laid before her.

'Many writers have noted the similitude between the act of love and the act of eating; I will pursue the comparison no further upon this occasion – and in any event it breaks down at the point when the former act becomes robust, as now it did; however, that Monsieur and Mademoiselle received great pleasure from both experiences went without saying, and the fact that a generous sauce of perspiration set off their final consummation will be the last simile I will make.

'The occasion pointed out a way by which I believed I could make my fortune; and Monsieur shortly afterwards succeeding to his father's title, moving to Paris, and there starting a salon which drew most of the fashionable ladies and gentlemen of the town, offered the occasion of my preparing many similar feasts – not only in his own house but in those of his friends.

'The unfortunate events which brought the age of aristocracy to an end in France also provoked my departure from that country, for those who had been my patrons became much more occupied with the problem of keeping their heads upon their shoulders than with amorous feasting. However, I was fortunate in that Lord Clavering, a friend of the Regent, had dined at Milord's on one occasion when I provided the menu for a party of a dozen, at which as a final dish one of our most attractive young courtesans emerged from a cake, covered from head to foot in a brandy in which cherries had been steeped – a liquor removed by the diners by application of their tongues. I applied to Clavering upon my arrival in London, and he kindly sponsored a dinner at which I demonstrated my skills to a number of his friends – an introduction which made my reputation among a small but generous circle. Since then I have travelled from house to house, devising upon commission entertainments of a similar nature. I shall of course be glad to do so here, should I be invited.

'But you my ask,' our narrator went on, 'what of my own corporeal satisfaction? Does this refer entirely to the provision of amorous entertainments for others?

'For some time it was indeed the case, my fascination with the art of the kitchen quite precluding an interest in the art of the bedroom, despite the fact that my early experiences had shown me that the latter pleasure can easily equal the former. It is also the fact that in common with most cooks, I have a considerable appetite, which had resulted in my frame being generous – and the fashionable taste of most gentlemen of our age has been for female bodies which are slim almost to excess. By the time I had been working in this country for a decade, I had quite concluded that mine must be a life deprived of any sensual pleasure except that of taste; and was not, truth to tell, too sorrowful about the fact, for it seemed to me that the effect upon the palate of a *grosse pièce d'agneau aux tomates farcies* or a *caneton de Rouen à l'échalote* was quite as delicious as the most cultivated taste for parsnip (or, for that matter, for asparagus or bananas).

'However, the time came when I was cooking a special dish for the Regent at his strangely decorated Pavilion at Brighthelmstone, and after the considerable effort (Mrs Fitzherbert, the Regent's friend of the time, being highly critical) strolled down in the early evening to the harbour, where a small ship from France was putting ashore some of those refugees from my sad country which at that time were still from time to time making their way ashore.

'What was my astonishment to see, leaping nimbly ashore, none other than my young friend of the kitchen, Michel! Before I knew it, I had cried out his name! – whereat he turned, looked, seemed puzzled, but on seeing me staring at him with such attention, made his way towards me, a pack slung over his back his only luggage.

' "Madame?" he said.

' "Why, Michel, do you not remember me – Mlle d'Albignac – and the parsnips?" But then I stopped, and blushed: for of course this could not be Michel, who upon that celebrated occasion could not have been less than sixteen years of age, and that was now over twenty-five years ago!

' "My namc is indeed Michel," said the lad, "but I fear I do not recognize you – nor do I remember anything to do with . . . parsnips?"

'The likeness to my old friend, and the similarity of the name, seemed too much of a coincidence to be explicable by mere chance; and to cut a long story short, upon taking the youth away to a meal (he proving excessively hungry), after some talk, I discovered that indeed he was the son of the boy who had, all those years ago, been the subject of my first experience of amorous play! He could almost, in fact, have been my son; but was rather the offspring of my old friend and a milkmaid on Milord's estate, who had both at the time of the Revolution been driven from it and into considerable penury; their son had been separated from them in the general confusion and had determined to make his way to England, where he believed it would be easier to make his fortune than in a country still so uncertain as to its future.

'Did I know, he asked, where I might find employment? He had, he asserted, an interest in culinary matters, and some ambitions to become a chef – but this was an art which he knew nothing of, nor could he imagine where he could learn it, for he had always understood England to be a culinary desert.

'You can imagine that I was happy to be of assistance to him, and promised him immediate employment, offering him accommodation that night at the lodging provided for me by the Regent's Comptroller, in a house near the palace. This comprised only a single room; but the boy – who was then perhaps seventeen or eighteen years old (he did not know his precise age, nor could we ever discover it) – tactfully left the room while I prepared for bed, and only entered it upon my calling out that I was ensconced beneath the sheets.

'The moon was full that night, and shed into the room a light as bright as that of a number of candles; so that upon his undressing – which took no long time, his clothes being less than elaborate – there could be no question of concealment, though he kept at first his back to me; nor, I must confess, did I refrain from looking beneath my lids, curious whether the resemblance between Michel and his father was as impressive in body as in features.

'There was revealed the most delightful sight – at least to me, who, perhaps because my own frame is a large one, admire a somewhat unsubstantial frame in gentlemen. The boy's legs were slim, the thighs strong and muscular but lithe, and in handsome proportion to a long back which tapered to a narrow waist, while below it was the most charming arse imaginable, the cheeks round and firm, without a trace of hair upon them, a faint down only catching the silver from the moon's rays; and between them could just be glimpsed that pouch containing the organs of generation.

'My pleasure in the sight was not long-lasted, however, for, dropping his clothes to the floor, he hesitated only a few seconds – then, turning, with a bound was upon the bed and between the sheets. I, who had arranged a couch for him, assuming that he would occupy it, was surprised – but had only a moment in which to wonder whether this was wise, before I felt his lips close upon mine, and his body writhing upon my own.

'I will not disguise the fact that what followed was entirely pleasurable. I had, of latter years, assumed that my person was unattractive to most men, and certainly to those of relatively tender years; yet here was a mere boy whose pleasure in it was so obvious that it struck from me such a spark as I had not felt for a very long time. I felt almost instantly the sudden starting from between his thighs of a prick which seemed hard as iron – yet could not dispel a certain disappointment at its size, for upon his leading my palm to it, I found it to be virtually the size of my thumb!

'However, the disappointment was only temporary, for just as in cooking freshness and preparation are all, so in amorous matters youth and simple pleasure are the greatest appetizer. Soon I was being played like some instrument by this young performer: his tongue found out the whorls of my ears and tasted my underlip; he buried his face in my breasts and adventured upon my body like some little barque sailing upon substantial, buoyant waves – and delighting in the venture, for he played with my bubbies with what seemed complete happiness, laying his body upon my own, wriggling upon me like a slippery and eager eel; taking my nipples in his mouth, he sucked on them for a while like a voracious babe – then, in a moment, reversed his posture so that he could tease them with his little cock, which felt almost like a hard beak, pecking at my softest flesh – while when after what seemed an age of pleasure, he parted my thighs and dived between them like a young swimmer, immediately finding with that remarkable organ the centre of my being and, applying it to my most sensitive point, matched my increasing ardour with his own.

'Nor did his attention cease after that first night, for I found in him a constant lover who after ten years still delights in my person with just such enthusiasm as on that first occasion. Fearing to lose him as I grew older, and no more shapely, I have made it clear to him that I do not forbid his homage to other ladies – but he has always maintained that my pastures are those in which he feels most at home, and I have no reason to believe that matters are otherwise, for he appears to be one of those young men for whom a mistress must resemble a mother. He has given me the devotion not only of a lover but of a son, with the advantage that the latter attitude does not in the least preclude the attentions of the former.

'I wish, ladies and gentlemen, that I could produce him for your inspection: but alas, he waits for me in Nottingham, where he proceeded a week ago to prepare for a banquet I was supposed to arrange for the Lord Mayor, upon Christmas Day.'

The cook looked for a moment sad; but then brightened, her eyes again shining with merriment.

'Yet,' she concluded, 'I have no doubt that he will welcome me with a warmth that will send both of us into a deep sleep – if only after some hours of mutual delectation. In the meantime, I am at your service – and if our hostess will allow, I shall be happy to prepare a Christmas feast, which I trust will prove memorable even within this obviously admirable hostelry.'

At this, the cook ended her story – to applause which congratulated her no less upon its originality than upon that complete happiness which has rewarded goodwill.

4

The Tutor's Tale

In a good, humorous mood after Mrs Allbig's story, the company dealt heartily with an excellent luncheon of venison pasty washed down with a Burgundian wine – after which we were good for nothing, for several hours, but nodding in front of the generous fire which was always kept burning in the large public room.

By about three o'clock, however, most of us were astir, if not particularly lively. Several of the men were beginning to feel the lack of exercise, and attempted an excursion; but having fought our way from the front door to the shores of the nearby river Welland, we found it frozen solid – yet the snow still beat down so thick that no body ventured upon it with his skates, for the surface was too soft for that pleasurable sport. So thick was the air with frozen rain that only the nearest of the town's six church spires was to be seen, and that imperfectly. Frozen almost to the bone by the keen wind which blew the snow before it, we turned and hastened back to the comfort of the inn.

As we fought our way out of our topcoats and shuffled about in front of the fire, the youngest of us, beating his hands together, remarked that it was almost as cold as it had been when he had arrived to take up his first position as tutor, some four years ago, at Caskieban Castle near Inverurie in Aberdeenshire – a place, he remarked, known for the inclemency of its weather. Yet . . . and he paused.

If any words were cue for a story, these were, and the ladies sitting around the fire demanded it. The young man shook himself, and blushed.

'I fear' he said, 'that my tale may perhaps shock those of you who are mothers. Yet it may, on the other hand, be of an educative nature. So, if you will permit . . .'

No permission was necessary, and encouraged by the entire company, the young man was ushered into a chair at the centre of the fire, and after but little humming and hawing, began The Tutor's Tale.

'My name is Edward or Ned Chaunter,' the young man said, 'and I am the son of a parson with a living in Dorsetshire, whence I was sent, as early as was convenient, to the University at Oxford; and had no sooner obtained such qualifications as would suit me for a Church of England living than I reached the conclusion that such a fate was not one to which I felt greatly drawn. My father, disappointed, was not inclined to support me in idleness nor indeed was I inclined to such lethargy. The remaining possibility was a career in some corner of education.

'My success at Oxford had been considerable, for I was an eager and quick scholar (if you will allow me to boast), and I was offered positions at two of our great public schools; but one visit to each of them was sufficient to inform me that I would be happy at neither – for the boys looked miserable and were meanly kept, and the teachers clearly held to Dr Johnson's definition of the term *tutor*: "one who treats his pupils with superiority or severity" – and followed that definition not only by their attitude to the boys in their care, but by beating them with great regularity and enthusiasm; something I could not convince myself was either desirable or necessary to the communication of information.

'I therefore placed an advertisement in the public prints, setting myself forward as a private tutor who could be engaged at a reasonable recognizance, and waited on events.

'Within a week, I was summoned to a meeting in Oxford with Sir Witley Johnston, a Scottish gentleman, who proved to be a man of good sense and reasonable education. He was a descendant, it appears, of that Arthur Johnston known as "the Scottish Ovid", who, educated at Aberdeen, cultivated the study of Latin verse at Padua before returning to Scotland, where his reputation as a classical scholar was but little damaged by the circulation, under plain covers, of verse in English in which he celebrated carnality with wit and vigour.

'Sir Witley had come to Oxford especially to find a tutor for his twin sons, Peter and Paul, who were ten years of age. He made an excellent offer which embraced both the hospitality of his home and an income entirely commensurate with the position. I accepted it without argument and on terms of cordiality, and within a fortnight had set out on the long journey north.

'This was in the first week of February, and my travel was plagued by increasingly bad weather, so that it was only by good luck and the skill of the coachman that I arrived at Caskieban merely a day late. The snow was piling itself against the walls of the castle as I trudged up from the road with my bags; and the butler opened the front door only a crack more than was absolutely necessary in order to admit me and my luggage upon a draft of cold air laden with white crystals.

'Sir Witley gave me a warm welcome, and after being so good as to show me, personally, to my room – which was a decent one, rather better indeed than I had expected – introduced me to Lady Johnston, a sallow but pleasant lady of retiring disposition, and to my two pupils, handsome and charming boys, pretty as angels and (what was unusual) of dispositions not so far removed from the angelic – yet robust and boyish enough to remove any suspicion of mawkishness or sentimentality about them.

'I began their lessons on the following day, and found them not only eager but quick to learn – so that at supper that very first evening, after but a little effort on my part, they were able to recite to their father one of the Latin epigrams of his distinguished ancestor (I had thought it tactful to begin by talking to them of Mr Johnston, in order that his example in learning might be a model for them).

'For a week, lessons continued, the schoolroom barely

warm enough despite the heat of a good fire, and excursions into the gardens out of the question through the thickness of the snow and the hardness of the frost. On the eighth day however a sudden thaw set in, and almost overnight the weather was so much on the mend that the boys were able to show me the grounds, and traffic once more began to be heard upon the road on the other side of the high wall which ran round the estate.

'I had overheard Peter talking to Paul about Amabel and Nicola, and thought little of it; but on overhearing Sir Witley asking one of the servants whether the girls' rooms were properly heated against their return, I enquired of him who they might be. The reply was that they were the boys' sisters, also twins, and now seventeen years of age, who had been about to return from a visit to their aunt in Craiggiecat when the sudden storm postponed their departure.

'In the late afternoon of the following day, a disturbance at the front door drew me to the window of the schoolroom, and I saw a coach setting down two young females – at the sight of whom the boys begged to be allowed to greet their sisters. Permission was of course granted, myself following the boys, curious to see the new arrivals.

'When Sir Witley told me about them it was clear from the manner of his speech that he was one of those gentlemen who believed that daughters merited a degree of education. Indeed, he remarked that it was not impossible that I might be required to teach them the rudiments of literature or the history of art.

'Amabel and Nicola had not then been made privy to their father's intention; but nevertheless had from the moment they heard that a tutor was arriving at the castle been harbouring just such a hope; and thus remarked at table that evening upon their aunt's cleverness and education, on the fact that they had been quite incapable of conversing with her upon any topic of interest, and asked me whether I did not think that it was wrong to suppose that females should not be in command at least of a certain knowledge of music, literature and drawing.

' "Why, Mr Chaunter would no doubt be happy to make you free of his knowledge," cried Sir Witley. Then, turning to me, "What say, Mr Chaunter? Mind you, I can afford no higher stipend than you now command – though I dare say a present can be found to acknowledge any additional work which may be required – which I cannot think will be considerable, for I never met a young girl of seventeen yet who stuck to her school desk longer than it takes to tie a granny knot."

' "Oh,' cried Nicola, "we'll find some way of rewarding Mr Chaunter, if . . . Mr Chaunter, say you'll agree."

'What could I do but consent? – and I must say that the two young ladies who now sat before me were not only extremely attractive but had qualities of quickness and intelligence which, I was sure, would make it a positive pleasure to inform them. It was therefore agreed that henceforth lessons with the boys should cease at three in the afternoon, and the hours between then and five should be occupied in giving their sisters as thorough a grounding in literature as could be managed. (I cried off from teaching them either music or drawing, being myself not proficient in either art.)

'We started by reading through some Shakespeare – for like every right-thinking person, I consider the Bard of Avon to represent the very apex or apogee of literature. The girls had glanced at the works, it seems, but were on the whole ignorant of them, so that on almost every page – nay, in almost every speech – it was necessary for me to explain some turn of language. Soon enough they understandably tired of this, and requested that we might ignore the niceties and concentrate on the plots of the pieces, after which things went more speedily, though from time to time either Nicola or Amabel would stop to ask me to explain the meaning of one word or another.

'This soon became somewhat embarrassing for me, a young man unused to the company of ladies (I had had no sisters, and at Oxford had felt it my duty – being destined as I then thought for the priesthood – to abstain from that commerce with the loose women of the town, which, for many of my contemporaries, resulted in a broadening of sexual experience all too often accompanied by venereal infection.

'I therefore found myself in some difficulty when I had to explain what was meant by the *amorous rites* in *Romeo and Juliet*, and what a *concubine* and a *lecher* were – terms appearing in several of the plays. But none of this was so difficult as Nicola's enquiry as to what was meant by a man's *pipe*, a query I ingeniously deferred when we were reading *Much Ado about Nothing*, but which was insisted upon when we came to the same word in *Romeo and Juliet* – a play so fraught with innuendo that I regretted ever embarking upon it.

'I was finally forced to be so clear as to say (with a necessary blush) that by *pipe* Shakespeare meant the male organ of generation. But what, the girls asked, was that? The query was put with such slyness that I was half-sure that they knew perfectly well what was meant – and yet I did not wish to be unjust to them, for I could not be sure how far their mother had explained to them the difference between the sexes.

' "Is it," Nicola enquired, "the thing that Peter and Paul have between their legs?'

'I nodded.

' "But how can they generate anything," asked Amabel, "being so tiny and so insignificant."

'And so before I was aware what was happening, I found myself in the middle of a lecture on procreation – and moreover one delivered without embarrassment and even with a certain amount of enjoyment, for their heightened colour as they listened, and the rise and fall of their bosoms (seeming to denote a certain excitement) communicated their own interest to me – with the inevitable result that my own organ of generation began to show a more distinct interest in the matter than was entirely proper in the company of two maidens *in statu pupillari*.

'I do not believe that either of the girls was aware of the

tumescence; yet it was without a great deal of hesitation that Nicola asked whether it would be possible for them to have a sight of my own *pipe*, the which, they said, would immediately dissolve their complete ignorance upon the subject.

'You will understand that I felt it improper to acquiesce in such a demonstration; not only had I never been familiar with any female since I left my mother's knee, but it seemed to me entirely improper to illustrate such theoretical knowledge as I felt able to convey in so forthright a manner. However, it would be true to say that I was not unaware of the suggestive charm of such a demonstration as the girls suggested. Have I said already that they were two extremely handsome young persons? Amabel, the senior by (I am told) two minutes, was by a hair the taller; though they seemed alike as two peas – both dark, both with raven tresses falling over their shoulders in the same manner, both with the same deep and sparkling eyes (sparkling, as it seemed, both with humour and – as I now understand – a kind of amorous invitation).

'The girls were modestly clad – which I found no bar to my admiring them, for I had never lived in circumstances where low-cut dresses or material of lawn revealed female limbs; the freedom and ease with which they moved was by no means incompatible with the loose, slightly heavy clothing they wore (clothing appropriate to the cold weather, for the rooms of the castle, apart from those in which we lived during the day, were sufficiently cold to make it necessary for both sexes to wear thick breeches, skirts and coats). Indeed, the very completeness with which their clothing covered their bodies made these seem the more mysterious and exciting – a circumstance I commend to those ladies who go out of their way to appeal to the masculine senses through immodest dress. Such senses are not always best served by revelation: concealment can be as complete an aphrodisiac.

'However, all this in parenthesis. I swiftly made an excuse to end a lesson which was becoming somewhat over-stimulating to my senses, and after supper took myself off to my bedroom, where, sitting at my desk with a single candle to write my daily journal, I soon cooled to a degree at which I was able to contemplate without sorrow the fact that my sentimental education was not to be acquired at the expense of my pupils' sisters!

'I took myself in due time to bed. There, however, the warmth which my body engendered beneath the heavy bedclothes also heated my senses – to an extent that was dangerous to my equanimity: for I began to realize that however I might argue against myself, I would very much have liked to know what forms lay beneath the girls' clothing. As I say, my experience in that area of study was nugatory – the only naked bodies I had seen were those of the gentlemen disporting themselves at Parson's Pleasure, by the river at Oxford; the only amorous play I had observed was that between the elderly and portly sodomitic dons and their young catamite choristers there – play which was never, as it so happened, a great temptation to my senses, even if my religious calling (which I was then certain of) had not suggested that such activities should be denied me.

'As I lay abed, Amabel and Nicola inhabited my imagination so keenly and to such amorous purpose (despite my ignorance of women and their ways) that in a very short time my prick had grown to such a size and such a solidity as was positively painful, and I began to think it necessary to quiet it by those means of which every innocent, solitary child is naturally aware.

'Just as I laid my hand upon it, however, I apprehended rather than heard (so little noise was made) the door of my room open, and in a moment against the dim light thrown through the window by a gibbous moon saw two figures at my bedside. I opened my mouth to shout, fearing intruders – but they were not of so fearful a nature as to cause prolonged distress; for in a moment I saw the silhouettes turn from black to a dim, glowing white as they removed their clothing; then there was a disturbance of my bedclothes, and in a moment against my warm body I felt two cold ones clinging to me upon each side; the flesh of both rough with goose pimples – and clearly, from the bosoms which were pressed against each upper arm, feminine.

'That my visitors were none other than Amabel and Nicola was certain: Lady Johnston was extremely unlikely to climb into bed with her sons' tutor, much less accompanied by another female! Nor, should she have done so, could I imagine her to be so bold in examining my person as these two, who, growing warmer by the minute, now busied their hands about me, passing them over my bosom, my face, my head, my belly, my thighs, my . . .

'Their plain purpose was, it seemed, to allay their curiosity as to the design of the *pipe* so venerated (according to our Bard) in ancient Verona. They positively contended for its possession, and if one captured the main stem (as it were), tested the rigidity of the body and experimented with the movement of the skin, the other took the testicles in her palm, separating and weighing them, examining the sack which contained them and its jointure to the groin.

'It will be no surprise to my gentlemen auditors that a young man in the full vigour of life, who had never in his life come closer to a young woman than to kiss her hand (and that with extreme nervous delicacy) was not long able to contain the excitement of such a situation; with all the velocity of a long pent-up river or of a lake bursting a dam, and with a shout which I was only able to muffle by stuffing the greater part of a sheet into my mouth, the liquor of life was expelled in an unstoppable fountain, the flowing of which amazed and somewhat discomfited the girls.

'I was quick to apologize, and to explain – during the pause necessitated by the collapse (though only partial) of my generative organ, which also excited astonishment and extorted comment. My explanation of the physical attributes of the organ (which I now felt free to give in some detail, since the excuse for not doing so no longer held) was followed by the girls' eagerness to test each statement. This resulted in my *pipe* recovering its former dimensions – but not (though it might have been expected) in a practical demonstration of the act of coitus. This may seem surprising: but apart from any feeling of honour which might have dissuaded me from rape (which, despite the girls' clear willingness, would in fact have been an accurate term) of my employer's daughters, it must be remembered that my knowledge of the act of love was severely restricted – in fact, to reading and to certain obscene illustrations which had been shown me by my rougher companions at university.

'I went out of my way, then, to conceal from my companions the nature of the act which I now longed to perform; and they, driven almost wild by a longing they knew not how to express, perforce confined themselves to wriggling their bodies against mine, one upon each side, and to kissing every part of my person which they could reach – not excepting that prick which was now itself once more swollen with desire, and which – for after some time I could again no longer contain the urgency of my need – again in time exploded.

This second fulmination was not so startling, but was no less puzzling to the girls than the first; they discussed it with serious interest. I kept mum, however – even when driven a third time to extremes by their continuing titillation of my person – which, poor things, was inevitable, for they were still frustrated by my failure to comfort them. In the end, they seized my hands and conveyed them to their own sweet parts, which (whether or not I imagined it) seemed to radiate a positive fire of desire. Feeling beneath my fingers such delightful mounds, such soft, fresh moss, such welcoming and slippery lips, I conceived it only a kindness to stroke and caress them until, accompanied by little wails of pleasure, the girls' bodies relaxed; and I guessed that in some way they had obtained at least a modicum of satisfaction – though at that time I could not have explained how.

'By the time Amabel and Nicola slipped from my bed it was almost dawn; and I fear that Peter and Paul received less than complete attention to their schooling on the following day, for despite the fact that I was exhausted both physically and emotionally, my thoughts kept returning to the sensations I had experienced; and I found myself counting the hours (though with some apprehension) until I could tell the boys to shut their books and dismiss them – the time having come for their sisters to enter the schoolroom.

'Despite the fact that only a small fire was lit there, the girls now appeared wearing dresses which revealed more of their persons than I had hitherto seen; and my imagination was not slow (from my recollection of the contours of their bodies) to fill in that part of the picture which was still concealed. Nor were the sisters slow to show that their principal interest was no longer in an analysis of the Duke's motives in *Measure for Measure*, for sitting one upon each side of me they soon began to attempt those liberties which they had taken the previous night, even struggling to unloose the buttons of my trousers.

'This might be fatal: for it was not unknown for Sir Witley to visit the room during our lessons; and (though with great difficulty, not only physical but emotional) I restrained them from actions which might too soon have terminated our connection.

'At last, they consented: but upon one condition. Their imaginations had been so heated by their turn between my sheets that they now longed for the evidence of their hands to be joined by that of their eyes. The house being so cold, the only room where this would be practicable was the hall, where a roaring fire was maintained day and night. This being normally occupied by the family, I agreed to meet the young ladies there at two o'clock in the morning following – when, I agreed, they could examine my person and satisfy their curiosity.

'As to the consequences of this agreement, I was in a turmoil of confusion; I was in some doubt of my steadfastness in continuing to be capable of respecting the persons of two young ladies so eager to initiate themselves into a full enjoyment of love – in particular when I was myself almost equally eager for a similar initiation. However, I thrust this consideration to the back of my mind, and spent the intervening hours attempting to forget the trial or delight awaiting me. Commanding a servant to prepare hot water, I thoroughly bathed my body before retiring to bed, where I hid beneath a mountain of bedclothes in order to keep myself as warm as possible while waiting for the chapel clock to strike each hour: eleven – twelve – one and having estimated as accurately as I might the passage of time between one and what I reckoned to be a quarter to two, then climbed from bed, threw on shirt and trousers, and in bare feet (the more easily to tread quietly) made my way as swiftly as possible through the chill corridors to the hall.

'This, like all the rooms in the castle, was large; but its size was matched by that of its fireplace, where flames burned low but steadily, logs having been piled up by the butler to keep the fire in until morning. Taking a poker, I stirred them until a positive blaze burst out, and sat before it on a thick rug, in the small square formed by two chairs and a couch.

'In a few moments, and just as the clock struck, the door opened and the two sisters walked in, clad in heavy dark cloaks. They came towards me – stood over me: and with a delightful suddenness that matched all the excited imaginings I had been unable to suppress, threw their cloaks to the couch, their long white bodies emerging from the blackness with all the drama of a scene in a theatre, illuminated now by the rosy glow of the fire, its light falling over their breasts, bellies, thighs, and lighting them as though with an affectionate fervour.

'Naked themselves, they were of course not long content that I should be clad, and in next to no time had reduced me to a similar state, when, eschewing any romantic preparations, they positively fell upon me and began to examine first that part of me in which they were most interested (and which had instantly sprung to an attentively upright position, the formidable sturdiness of which they greatly admired). Feeling already a mounting excitement which could only lead to a too precipitate inability to maintain a stand, I dissuaded them from any further manual manipulation; and though regretting this, they moved away to examine the rest of my body – for, though I presumed they must have seen their brothers, and possibly other men, stripped at least to the waist, they had clearly never had the opportunity for any close examination of the male form, and were interested to scrutinize the extent to which (for instance) my limbs and torso were hairier than their own, exclaiming over the sprigs which grew about each pap, and the trail of fibres which led from my navel to the root of my prick, and, turning me about, admiring the thin pelt which shaded the cheeks of my arse, which they admiringly smoothed with their palms until I purred like a cat.

'It will not be supposed that my eyes were not at the same time busy about their persons, which were as similar as their faces: each pair of breasts a similitude of the two others, each waist pinched to the same delightful slimness, arms and thighs of the same dimensions, so that 'twas almost as though a mirror was placed between the two girls, so similar was one to the other. Nor will it be imagined that the faculty of touch was entirely neglected in favour of that of sight; the experience of lifting for the first time a handsome bosom in the palm of my hand, of caressing the length of a back (the bones of the spine a charming roadway to the cleft dividing two enchanting globes, below and behind), of venturing between readily parted thighs gently to tickle the entrance to . . . In short, I almost fainted with the dual pleasure of exploration: of examining and being examined.

'But the problem which I had anticipated now arose: for Nicola, perhaps the quicker of the two, was suddenly aware of the coincidence that where her body was concave, mine was convex; that where she had a cleft, I had a projection. Did it not (she thought) seem that the one might be made for the other? And taking advantage of the fact that Amabel was half lying upon my upper body, the better to taste with her tongue the tiny nodule of a nipple whose similarity to her own (despite being a miniature) fascinated her, her sister threw a leg across my own, and with a hand laid my delighted prick along the length of her cunny.

'This was, naturally, excessively delightful – certainly to her, and partly to me – though since I could not see precisely what was occurring, I only experienced the pleasure of a warm something embracing the length of my weapon. That pleasure, however, was not sufficiently keen to persuade Nicola that it could be complete; and wishing to experiment further, she raised herself slightly, and, placing the tip of my prick within the portal sank down upon me with a cry at first of apprehension, then of slight pain, and finally of delighted satisfaction.

'Her sister, hearing her cry, sat up, and turning was in time to witness the strange sight of my joint gradually vanishing within her sibling's body; and to see with what increasing pleasure Nicola began to raise and lower her body so that my cock was as it were first welcomed, then rejected; each movement clearly being as productive of pleasure to her as to myself.

'Jealously, Amabel reached out to thrust her sister from the seat which she envied; but just as she laid a hand upon her shoulder – horror! – the door burst open, and in strode their father, Sir Witley! Nicola's body contracted with surprise and fear – her entire body, so that I felt as though a soft vice had closed about my prick, provoking despite my apprehension an explosion of the most intense pleasure (which, however, I found it impossible to enjoy as thoroughly as I might have done in other circumstances).

'Sir Witley strode immediately towards us; Nicola threw herself from my body, and she and her sister scrabbled about, pulling their discarded cloaks over their bodies to conceal an improper exhibition to their father, leaving me only a corner of one to cover my most vulnerable part (now, as might be expected, becoming by the second less visibly impressive).

' "Sir Witley, sir," I stammered, "please forgive this

familiarity. I cannot too regretfully express my embarrassment at . . ."

'But he interrupted me with an amazing geniality.

' "Not at all, my boy," he said. "I am greatly obliged to you. I have been aware for some time that my girls have reached an age when it is necessary that they should learn what they are to expect of their husbands, and I am delighted that they should be taught by so personable a young rogue. However, the hour is extremely late, and . . ."

'Swiftly recovering from her fear, Amabel, with a grimace, exclaimed: "I hope, father, you do not intend to send us to bed!" – then giggled, and added: "at least, not to our solitary beds – for so far 'tis only Nicola who . . ."

' "Ah, I see," said her father; "the lesson is only half done. Then I shall retire and allow the master to continue – perhaps with the aid of a little liquor to encourage him . . ." And striding to the cupboard where were kept those wines in daily use, opened it and taking a bottle of brandy set it down at our side.

' "Now, good night," he said, and carefully shut the door behind him. The two girls collapsed upon their backs, almost helpless with laughter at the (I do not doubt) ludicrous expression upon my face. Not until I had the opportunity of a conversation with my employer did I learn that he, quick of apprehension in these matters, had closely observed his daughters' behaviour in my presence, and had intuited that they would very likely make use of me to learn more fully the lesson only half-broached by that tender but modest person, their mother. Though ignorant of our previous meeting, he had heard his daughters leave their room, and following them had allowed just sufficient time for us to get on familiar terms before bursting in on a scene the constituents of which were no surprise to him.

'The sisters were not inactive for long after Sir Witley's departure; and I, having recovered my assurance through a draught or two of *aqua vitae*, was soon capable of proceeding with my practical demonstration – based, though the girls did not know it, on an ignorance almost as complete as theirs. However, I was able to elaborate somewhat upon the lesson I had given Nicola, for from those improper prints I had seen, I now recollected that it was not invariably the man who lay beneath the woman, and encouraged Amabel – at first much against her will – to recline upon her back, and, having first and instinctively planted a kiss upon those parts most eager for an encounter (a thing which greatly pleased her), laid myself between her thighs. Nudging in an amateur manner with my newly distended prick, I discovered to my delight the ease with which entry could be gained, and with which congress could subsequently be carried on in a comfortable and convenient position – while, provided that I supported some of my weight upon my elbows, Amabel seemed to experience no discomfort.

'Nicola meanwhile took a keen interest in the proceedings, eagerly observing our congress, to the pleasure of which she contributed in no small manner by stroking my back and bum in a delightfully free manner, which grew more and more salacious as our activity increased; and finally thrusting a hand between our bodies and interposing it at just that place where we were joined, both instigating a new friction to my member and (no doubt not by accident) contributing a delightful irritation to that particular area of her sister's quim in which the female emotions are centred – an action which, though we would not have been without it, contributed to our activity reaching a somewhat premature conclusion.

'I am in little doubt that she intended just that; and now nothing would content the girls but that Nicola must enjoy the experience of lying beneath. Amabel, not wishing to lack pleasure, with an instinct no less accurate for being entirely innocent, meanwhile knelt by our heads, and, since my hands were occupied elsewhere, manoeuvred so that her knees lay against my shoulders and my head between her thighs, and I could shower kisses first upon them, and then, with a daring I would not, only an hour before, have possessed, could apply my tongue to her most tender part

– which appeared to afford her, if anything, a pleasure even greater than her sister was experiencing by the plunging of my loins.

'My youth, and the fact that I was experiencing my first full act of rutting, enabled me to maintain a stand which would have been no disgrace to the most active Lothario, and by the time we finally repaired to our beds, we were all three not only exhausted but satisfied.

'I remained at the castle until the end of April, when it was decided that Peter and Paul were ready to attend the grammar school in Aberdeen; and, their sisters having by general consent – even that of their mother, whose approval I took care to cultivate with all the charm at my command – come to my bed by turn and turn about every night (except that once in ten days or so I needed a night of unbroken sleep, to recharge my libidinous forces), it was considered that their education had also been completed to the point at which their proposed and long pre-arranged marriages – to two local landowners' sons – could take place without their disgracing the marriage bed through ignorance.

'Sir Witley was so impressed by my performance as a tutor that he had spoken freely of it to a neighbour, a Mr MacCatterey of Whiterashes, who gave out that I was to come to teach his daughter Latin. Miss Cecilia MacCatterey proved an enthusiastic and apt pupil, and conjugated the verb *amo* with an enthusiasm I could not fault, and eventually with an expertise at least the equal of my own – the latter having improved immeasurably: which considering that I began in utter ignorance, was not surprising, though at the same time demonstrating that any full-blooded young man needs no manual or textbook to enable him to devise and elaborate on this particular form of pleasure.

'My success at Whiterashes led to a situation at Kirkton of Strathmartine (Miss Olive MacMottran), then another at Fairmilehead in Edinburgh (Miss Kirtie MacKnicker); and so I gradually worked my way south until my Lord X (for I must not give his full title) engaged me to oversee the sentimental education of his three daughters at his place in Hertfordshire.

'This last almost killed me through the young ladies' insatiable appetite for the game, which once aroused I found it almost impossible to satiate, and was extremely relieved when the time came for their triple marriage, a month ago after which I took myself off to Oxford and spent six weeks in simple relaxation, taking the opportunity however to effect some research among the shelves of Bodley's great library, studying such works as Aretino's *Flagello de' Principi*, Ferrante Pallavicino's *The Whores' Rhetorick*, and the secret works of the Earls of Rochester, Roscommon and Dorset, together with other less famous volumes on the venereal act, which I trust will further my career in a department of education which has proved as profitable as it is pleasurable, and which will lead me the moment this weather lifts, to the town of Grantham, where Alderman Sir Dudley Roberts has engaged me to attend upon his daughter Margaret – though for a fee so considerable that I fear it may conceal some general deficiency of feeling in her which it may prove difficult to overcome. However, I am certain 'twill not be beyond me.'

And with a smile which bordered on the self-congratulatory, Mr Chaunter here brought his tale to an end, among congratulations from the company upon his good fortune and the quickness of wit which had enabled him to put his luck to such good use. Gracefully accepting the thanks of his audience, he received the particular compliments of one of the ladies, a pretty little fairhaired woman perhaps in her late twenties – an age far above that of his usual consorts, no doubt; but she was sufficiently charming for him to kiss her hand with considerable attention – and on the company dispersing to prepare for supper, I noticed that the two left the room together, and that when they reappeared they were arm in arm, and showed a familiarity which suggested that they had become more closely acquainted during the intervening hour or so.

5

The Governess's Tale

After Christmas Eve supper, remarkable for good humour and good eating, it was not long before the company gathered once more before the fire – and it became clear that everyone was now thoroughly minded that we should continue to entertain each other, and expected another story. As usual, however, no one was eager to take up the custom – and it was Sophie who decided to end that problem once and for all by proposing a lottery: numbers should be written upon pieces of paper and these drawn in turn out of a basin which the hostess provided. These numbers would denote the order in which our fellows would be called upon to give us their narratives.

This being acceptable to all, the lot fell upon the handsome young woman who had been my neighbour in the coach, and with whom I had from time to time during the day exchanged such glances as seemed to promise (should I care to propose it) a greater degree of friendship than is necessarily concomitant with a random meeting at an inn – at least, between lady and gentleman.

The lady was somewhat abashed at being chosen as narrator, but, having agreed to the process, must acquiesce: and so announced, after settling herself in the central chair placed directly before the fire, that she was by profession akin to the previous speaker: that is, a governess – but that the subject of her tale would not be connected with any of her pupils, but had taken place some time before she adopted her present profession.

'My name is Elena Stanbury. My childhood was

unexceptional, and until I was fourteen I was placidly happy. Then, however, both my father and mother were carried off by the cholera, brought ashore to Southampton (where we lived) by a sailor who had caught it in the East. An only child, I was kindly taken in by my mother's brother, Mr Martin Eckersley, who had a small estate near Chichester. He and his wife, my Aunt Mary, were kindness itself to me, and I soon recovered my spirits, being of a naturally cheerful disposition, and though at first I of course missed my parents sorely, I lived happily enough in a household which was not large, but in which there was no lack of comfort.

'My uncle and aunt had one daughter, some ten years older than myself, who had some months before my arrival been married to a clergyman, and lived in a village a sufficient distance from her previous home to make her visits irregular and sparing. She had been a particular favourite of her father, who missed her sorely, and immediately adopted me as a surrogate, allowing me every leniency as to keep and education, and treating me with the utmost kindness.

'My aunt was similarly loving, though perhaps a little more distant in manner. She was more reconciled to her daughter's absence, and, finding additional companionship less necessary, entertained little, and made my uncle's life, I fear, somewhat lonely – an additional reason why he spent a considerable amount of time with me, educating me with the help of his considerable library. I should mention here – in case those of you with minds tending to the lascivious (which, from your reception of previous tales, seems to be considerably the case) – that our relationship was as innocent as that, indeed, of father and daughter; you are to expect no tale of incest from me!

'My uncle's house was set by a river, and the garden – scarcely large enough to be called an estate, but sufficiently large to seem, to a young girl, handsome – ran down to the water, which, at the lawn's edge, swept in a handsome curve, the horns of which were protected by trees, so that it was secluded from the public view. Across a stretch of deep, still, dark water undisturbed by any current, was a little patch of grass entirely surrounded by bushes and tall shrubs – amelanchier and laburnum, forsythia and buddleia, syringa and caryopteris. These had been planted by my uncle with the permission of the farmer whose land lay across the river, in order to form a sort of backdrop (as they say in the theatre) to the water, closing the prospect of the garden in a delightful manner.

'This small secluded lawn was a considerable temptation to a young girl – especially during the hot days of summer; and I soon learned to swim across to it, and discovered that it was possible to lie there in a sort of shady crypt, within sight only of our own garden – and of a part of it where my uncle and aunt, and even their servants, very rarely walked.

'The metamorphosis from girl to woman, at or about the age of fifteen, passed, in me, with painless ease. My aunt was severely practical in the matter, and explained simply and without drama the changes which were taking place in my body – though she stopped short, through a natural reticence, of any description of the act of love which now became practicable, merely commenting that I was ready for marriage – though my uncle, overhearing the comment, said that it was not necessary to think of it for some years, no doubt hoping to retain my presence and companionship for some little time to come. I fancied that my aunt's face darkened somewhat at this, and seemed to notice a touch of jealousy in her when – as was often the case – my uncle took me into Chichester on market day (where he would frequently buy me some inexpensive frippery, or perhaps a book, for I had an interest in literature, and in general showed the effects of an education which continued now on two days a week at a local school where it was already thought that I might become, myself, a teacher). However, as I have said, any suspicions she may have entertained as to our relationship were completely unfounded and indeed it never seriously occurred to me that she could harbour them.

'Though I was as aware as any other young person of my age of some immature and vague longing not unconnected with that part of my person upon which recent physical manifestations had necessarily focused my attention, I had no means of discovering their purpose or meaning; my uncle's library contained no erotic material, there was no handsome young servant who might have introduced me to love [Miss Stanbury stole a sly look at Mrs Allbig, who had the grace to blush], and a parsnip might have taken any shape it pleased without any association other than nutriment!

'However, it was not probable that I should for long altogether escape some connection with the opposite sex; and this occurred one summer's afternoon as I was lying in the sun upon the little spread of grass opposite our garden. As was my custom, I had swum across in my shift, having been brought up in the notion that the unclad body was to be exposed as rarely as possible even to the daylight, much less to any other person. My clothing was scarcely dry, so that (I have no doubt) it not so much concealed as emphasized the shape of my person. I was half asleep in the warmth, and the slight sounds of breaking twigs and rustling leaves scarcely roused me. It was the passing of a shadow across my face which made me open my eyes, when a figure passed between me and the sun.

'Never having been threatened by any person, and always shielded from any tales of violence, I was by no means alarmed; and squinting beneath my eyelids was not in the least troubled to see that the newcomer was a young man. I was perhaps very slightly surprised that he should stand so still, staring at me; but having no experience of the opposite sex except in the most conventional of circumstances, it did not occur to me that (what was the truth) I presented a picture which could only be calculated to arouse physical excitement in any man of spirit. I have no doubt that it would have been extremely difficult for him to avert his eyes from the sight before him: of a young girl in the first bloom of youth, her breasts rising and falling beneath the damp material of a gown which might have been transparent for all it concealed, the nipples of her breasts still tight and pert from the cool water of the river.

'However, I do not doubt that the pause which preceded any speech was not so long as it seemed, and in a moment there was a mumble of " 'Scuse me, ma'am," and the figure began to move away.

' "Please, sir, do not go, for me!" I said. I knew not why I spoke so hastily; but no doubt it had something to do with the fact that upon his moving I was better able to see the young man, and found his open, frank face, set under a broad forehead and low clustered yellow curls, so far less dangerous than appealing. He was dressed in a white shirt and what had once been white trousers, now none too clean, perhaps, but clearly dirtied only by proper toil, for the stains upon them were only those of grass and earth.

' "Oh, well . . ." He hesitated. "I have been at work in the field just yonder" (he gestured behind him) "and 'twas my purpose to cool myself by bathing in the river."

' "Then, sir, please do," I said; "the waters must be common to all – and if anyone is a trespasser, it is myself, for this is not our land but the neighbouring farmer's – perhaps, indeed, your father's?" – for it occurred to me that I had perhaps seen the young man in company with an older, who I knew to be the owner of the farm whose acres marched with the boundary of my uncle's land.

'He smiled and nodded at this – but hesitated still, no doubt because I showed no sign of averting my eyes, being far too interested in this stranger, who represented the first adult male person of almost my own age with whom I had had the opportunity of conversing at any length. However, the heat which had provoked that dampness which I now saw stained the arms and breast of his shirt, and the deep black cool waters so near, decided the matter; he turned, and in a moment slipped from his shirt and trousers and with three running steps dived into the river almost without a splash.

'Spluttering and blowing, he came to the surface, and

grinned at me before turning to swim away, inevitably if perhaps unconsciously allowing me a glimpse of a pair of handsome buttocks, about which the waters caressingly played as his body slid about and beneath them. Then, he turned upon his back, and my eyes were drawn to a fair shadow between his thighs where there seemed to be an attachment of some kind, looking somewhat like a thumb, but less rigid and bony, nestling in a patch of yellowy hair.

'I did not wish to appear familiar, and so lay back and closed my eyes; and no doubt this fact enabled him without undue embarrassment to leave the water after a while, when he threw himself face down upon the grass some three or four feet away from me. After a while his regular breathing seemed to suggest that he slept.

'I cannot think of any sum of money which could have persuaded me not to open my eyes sufficiently to examine the prospect before me. I know not how many young women grow up, in this so-called enlightened age, without seeing so much as a copy of a Greek statue; but I must be believed when I assert that I had had previously no notion at all of the shape of any other human body than my own, and that only imperfectly examined in a mirror. I was perhaps fortunate in that the young man who now lay before me was an excellent specimen of his kind: his shoulders and back broad and muscular, no doubt from the nature of his work; his legs long and slim, though again with strong muscles to be seen in calves and thighs; his waist and hips narrow and without any trace of plumpness, and – most delightful and attractive – swelling to those two charming globes upon which my eyes fixed themselves with a gaze which I found impossible to avert, despite the suspicion (founded only upon instinct) that so close an inspection might have been considered rude by the object of my gaze. Unlike my own bottom – in so far as I had been able to discern it – his consisted of two halves of a perfect circle, each in itself beautifully rounded and raised, and dusted with a golden flush of fine hairs, so fine that they resembled almost the bloom upon a peach.

'As I watched, the small beads of water which at first stood upon the skin or adhered to the almost imperceptible hairs of his arse, occasionally, as he breathed, trickling down his sides or vanishing into the cleft between those entrancing hillocks, gradually dried and disappeared, leaving the whole surface of his body as smooth and velvety as my own.

'So entranced was I that unconsciously I leaned forward, and even raised a hand as though to caress . . . but then remembered myself, and reluctantly lay back. But my movement had disturbed him, and turning his head he allowed my eyes to meet his own – bright blue and with the black pupils large and liquid. Reaching one hand behind him, he brushed his back with his fingers, as though to ascertain whether it was dry, as, now, it was.

' "Would you object if I turned over?" he asked, with a look which seemed almost mischievous.

'Will any lady be surprised that I gave my immediate permission?

'My first sight of that instrument with which it is man's nature to compliment women, was innocent enough; I was not disappointed, for I knew not what to expect. But that I was interested was certain. I assumed that this object was a superfluity of nature, meant only for decoration – for it did not occur to me but that there must be beneath it another aperture similar to my own through which he could pass water. Yet, as I looked, the small object which at first lay quiescent upon one thigh, began apparently to change shape – the small, pointed end where a little pucker of skin gathered into almost a spout, now swelled somewhat, and from beneath the hood of skin appeared a rounded head in which was a tiny aperture – at which point the thought occurred to me that perhaps this superfluity in fact was employed for the use to which indeed it is regularly put; though I had of course no notion of its amorous connection.

'I must not libel the young man by suggesting that he consciously wished to startle me by the sight of his instrument in erection; but I cannot now find it surprising that in such a situation the phenomenon began to occur –

the simple fact of my so closely inspecting the object could not contribute to its remaining inactive, while the fact that I myself was so lightly clad must encourage a show. Of course once the process of enlargement had started there was no stopping it; and though I did notice that the young man clenched his fists and screwed up his face as though with some kind of an effort, the metamorphosis continued until, in place of the innocent object which had at first showed itself, there lay back upon his belly a piece of work a good eight or nine inches long and perhaps three in circumference, with a dome-like head which had entirely emerged from a shrouding circle of skin which now lay in a tight and almost painful-looking noose about its neck.

'My new friend now did look somewhat embarrassed when he caught my eye; and mistaking the situation through my naivety, I said: "Sir, if you wish to make water, please do not hesitate upon my account – the river is free to all!"

'The excuse clearly pleased him, for, reddening slightly, he once more arose and dived in, the coolness of the water doing its work, for, upon his emerging some minutes later, his article had returned to its former dimensions (which only had the effect of convincing me that its enlargement had indeed been connected with the need to urinate).

'After drying his lower limbs upon his shirt (being careful, I noticed, not to look at me while doing so) he now pulled on his trousers, and took his leave – rather too abruptly for my pleasure, for I had hoped to further the acquaintance – and indeed I will not say that it was without hope of seeing him again that I continued to swim across the river; nor was he reluctant to appear. I discovered that his name was Jack Nicolls, and that he was as I had suspected the son of the farmer who worked the land which marched with my uncle's. He was eighteen years of age, and an extraordinary young man with a strong natural sense of what was proper; for though I took no care to be particularly modest, and after the first two or three occasions did not hesitate to strip to bathe with him, and indeed to lie quite naked while the sun dried our bodies, he at no time sought to pay me those attentions which perhaps the more libidinous of my hearers may expect to hear of.

'I say, at no time. This is not entirely true, for (and this is a tribute rather than a criticism) his tool frequently became tumescent, I at first assuming my former belief about it to have been correct – until, after we had become more familiar, he stutteringly confessed that such an extension was not for the purpose I had supposed, but in order to give pleasure to ladies. This seemed to me to be ridiculous! – but he insisted that if I would permit him to place it between my thighs, adjacent to my belly, I would experience a pleasure which would delight me.

'Jack being a humorous and lighthearted lad, I assumed that he was joking, and made no more of it, merely laughing. I have often since marvelled that he was able to refrain from the rape of so silly an innocent as myself – though I found later that at the time he was regularly enjoying the nocturnal company of not one but two maids from the neighbouring farms, which no doubt made it easier for him to refrain from that intimacy which my behaviour might well otherwise have provoked, for it must have seemed to him that I was what is vulgarly known as a prick teaser. Perhaps my relationship to my uncle, who was much respected in the area, played a part in persuading or enabling him to keep his distance. At any rate, he played the part of a friend rather than a lover, and our companionship most resembled that of Adam and Eve before the fall.

'The situation obtained throughout the summer, and though it may seem almost incredible to some doubters among you, by the autumn I was no better informed as to love-making than I had been in the spring – and thanks to the uncommon natural gentility of my friend no nearer losing my maidenhead. I believe, mark you, that I was by now beginning to grow a little impatient for I knew not what – and had perhaps even begun to suspect that Jack's explanation of the purpose of his tool (it was the word he used for it) might be nearer the truth than I had at first supposed, for the idea of its nestling between my thighs seemed by no means as silly or absurd a I had at first found it. Nor could I refrain from inspecting it as closely as possible at every opportunity, especially while Jack was asleep, when I approached my eyes to within an inch or so of it – until, by its sudden jerking, as though possessing a life of its own, I was frightened away (no doubt my friend was less soundly asleep than I supposed!). However, before my increasing interest could lead to action, a new situation arose.

'My uncle suffered somewhat from insomnia, and had recently acquired from a wise old crone in the neighbourhood a pillow stuffed with herbs which was supposed to provoke, or aid, sleep. This he had found a great convenience, and was given to claiming that he could not sleep without it. What was my irritation one evening, upon retiring to bed, to find that some stupid new girl employed about the house had in remaking the beds placed this pillow in my room rather than my uncle's, which was next along the hallway. Believing my uncle and aunt still to be downstairs, for I had retired somewhat early, I seized the pillow, and, dressed as I was – which is to say, not dressed at all – I slipped from the room, meaning to place the pillow in my uncle's bed and take my own back.

'Entering his room, I found the curtains drawn about his bed; whisking one back, what was my surprise to see my uncle, clad in his night-shirt, lying upon the bed; what, indeed, was his surprise, on hearing the curtain drawn, to open his eyes to see his niece in a state of complete undress standing before him, her modesty protected only by the pillow she was clutching to her bosom!

'Before either of us could stir a limb, a cry behind us announced the fact that my aunt had entered the room, and was as surprised as either of us at the sight that met her eyes.

'My attempts at explanation were as fruitless as my uncle's. It was impossible (he said) that she should suppose that even had he desired an incestuous connection with his niece, he would have chosen the moment before his wife might be expected to retire, in which to attempt it. My own protestations had the force of utter innocence, for I was not only ignorant of the meaning of the word *incest* but even of the nature of the act which it described! Yet my aunt would not listen, and after twenty minutes of berating us took herself off in high dudgeon to a spare bedroom upon the other side of the house.

'I was completely confused, and seeing my uncle's distress climbed upon the bed and embraced him, meaning to comfort him; I was once more fortunate in that he, while still a man of vigour, was able to resist the temptation to make good his wife's accusation – for I doubt that it is unknown that a man finding a pretty unclothed young girl in his bed may fall into temptation, despite a blood relationship between them. However, in this case my uncle merely kindly invited me to cover myself – and then, in order that I should understand the situation, undertook an explanation of just what occurred between a man and woman – of the act which my aunt suspected us of performing. This seemed to confirm the suggestion Jack had made of the pleasure to be found in the juxtaposition of male and female bodies; though I still did not understand the situation as to morality, and even asked whether my uncle could not undertake some kind of a practical demonstration – for I could not but notice that beneath his night-shirt there was a sign of a disturbance which suggested that his tool was in a condition which would enable it. It is another measure of my uncle's self-control – and indeed of his affection for his spouse – that he explained that this would not be proper – which somewhat disappointed me (I should explain that my uncle, being my mother's younger brother, was not so many years older than myself, and by no means unattractive).

'After some thought, I enquired whether my aunt had never herself committed any act which might place her in danger of being misunderstood? To which the answer was in the negative. But what, I asked, if she did so? Would this not make the situation more equal, as between her and my uncle? But, he claimed somewhat glumly, this was extremely unlikely.

'I did my best to comfort him in turn; but then made my excuse and went to my own bed, for I had the beginnings of an idea which I wished to think out.

'The following afternoon I repaired to the river, and after a while was rewarded by Jack's arrival – whereupon after we had swum, and were lying as usual in the sun, I related the occurrences of the night before – which he found extremely amusing; and I was forced to join in his merriment, for now that I had had time to recover from the drama of the situation, it was clear that it had its humorous side. When we had sobered, I put to him the plan I had devised for the recovery of the situation. His first reaction was that it would be dangerous to him, for his father was a tenant of my uncle's, and there was surely the possibility of the tenancy being withdrawn should he offend. My having reassured him on that point, he asked – with something of a twinkle – what would be his reward? Prompted by the new knowledge so recently acquired, I reached out a hand and placed a finger upon his thigh, trailing it upwards until it reached the base of his tool, which immediately nodded in recognition of my interesting gesture, while a shiver ran through his body.

' "I shall not be ungrateful," I exclaimed.

'Why, again, he did not rape me upon the spot, I do not know; but there are young men in this world whose naturally gentle qualities enable them to resist those instincts which prompt others to an extremity of violence. In short, he agreed to my plan. Returning to the house, I now laid it before my uncle, who at first resisted it vigorously but on my explaining that I had already commissioned an actor for the scene, eventually and somewhat reluctantly consented that it should go forward.

'At ten o'clock that evening, then, two figures – one of them myself – slipped up the back stairs. Half an hour later my aunt, who had been sitting by the fire without addressing so much as a single word to my uncle or myself (to whom she had not spoken since the affair of the night before) rose, and with a deep and melancholy sigh made her way upstairs to the spare room which she insisted on occupying. I glanced at my uncle, and we quietly followed, remaining at the bottom of the stair until we heard the bedroom door close behind my aunt. We then crept up, and my uncle applied his eye to the keyhole, through which he saw his wife, now clad in her bed-gown, approach the bed and reach up her hand to draw the curtain. At this, we opened the door – and simultaneously my aunt drew back the hanging: to see before her, face downward upon the bed, my friend Jack – that delightful bottom fully exposed to view. My friend had apparently fallen asleep while waiting for her to come to him!

'My aunt's vapours were equalled by my uncle's outrage: he railed against that deceiver, his wife, against her paramour, against that fate which had linked him to the one in order that he might be cuckolded by the other! To my aunt's protests he would give no credence: and ordered me to take her from the room – whereupon, on our closing the door the most fearful noise was heard: Jack's cries topped by my uncle's roars, added to which was the unmistakable noise of blows, of furniture being overturned . . .

'After a while, the noise ceased; the door opened, and my uncle appeared, holding Jack beneath his arms whose body was black and blue, and down whose face blood was coursing in a red mask. My aunt was immediately struck by renewed hysterics – which did not however affect her husband, who merely continued down the stairs; and after a while we heard the front door slam. My aunt meanwhile had somewhat recovered, and while continuing to protest her innocence could not prevent a certain light of admiration appearing in her eyes – admiration for her husband's violence in revenging himself on a supposed lover. On his taking her arm, she accompanied him upstairs without a murmur.

'I must confess to sneaking to the keyhole ten minutes later, through which I could hear sounds the significance of which escaped me; and through which I could see only two pairs of feet projecting from the bottom of the bed – one pair upturned, the other, between them, facing downwards. The latter appeared to be my uncle's.

'Next morning, he greeted me at breakfast with an enormous wink; while my aunt, meek as milk, served him with the utmost placidity and kindness, pouring him more ale before the first glass was finished, cutting his meat for him, and apparently unable to keep her hands from his body, now caressing his neck, now putting a hand on his shoulder, now standing so close behind him that their persons were pressed together. Her manner to me was also just as it had been before her unjust suspicions had made her cold.

'As we had arranged, I met Jack later that morning by the river. He had already bathed, and was stretched upon the grass as I climbed the bank from the water. He had made, it seemed, a complete recovery; the bruises had vanished, and there was no sign of a cut upon his face. To what extent this was the result of his washing coal-dust from the former and the juice of blackberries from the latter, I cannot of course say.

'I greeted him with thanks – which he scarcely paused to acknowledge, but instead, sitting up, reached for my hands and pulled me down on top of him. I must confess that the sensation of my naked, wet, cool body pressed upon his own warm one was very pleasant – so much so that I could not but wriggle with delight, the writhing of my body having the effect – as I could feel – of waking to full vigour that instrument whose purpose I now understood. Rolling over so that he lay on top of me, Jack now endeavoured to perform the act which my uncle had described. But I must admit to being somewhat nervous of this; and pausing violently, threw him off.

' "But wait . . .!" he expostulated, thinking perhaps that I meant to renege on our bargain.

' "No – no," I said; "lie still – I merely wish to examine the goods before purchasing them!" – and took in my hands his admirable tool, and leaning meanwhile upon one elbow made a more open inspection than had earlier been possible. This proved most interesting, as did Jack's reaction to my manual exploration. Upon my grasping the bulbous tip of his instrument he seemed to experience some discomfort; but on my wetting my fingers at my mouth, I found that a tender stroking of it gave him extraordinary pleasure – and when, interested by this, I went so far as to pass my tongue over its surface, his entire body seemed to leap with joy. Quick to take a hint, I then moistened my lips and slid them over the head, gradually taking as much of the fleshy fruit as I could into my mouth, while keeping my lips in contact with its surface.

'Whether in revenge or by way of returning the compliment I cannot say, as I did so I felt one of Jack's hands slip between my thighs, and his fingers attempting to enter that verge within which no doubt he would later wish to place that wand which now throbbed against my lips as I first withdrew, then again embraced it. On my moving my limbs to enable him, he positively slipped two fingers into the fringed aperture – and on my quickening the movement of my lips, his instinctive response was to plunge them yet deeper: whereupon a sharp pain for a moment gave me a shock of unease – however, on his apologizing and attempting to remove his hand, I found that my discomfort was not so great that I desired its absence, and by tightening my thighs, retained his fingers within me, when by gently and rhythmically caressing me he gave me considerable pleasure.

'It seemed to be a pleasure that he shared; for after a while I heard him panting, and indeed saw his belly rise and fall with increasing pace – until in a moment, with a gasp, the middle part of his body threw itself upward in a paroxysm, and reaching down he dashed his tool from my lips. My protest died as I saw to my amazement a fountain of whitish liquor start from the aperture at its tip, with so forceful a motion that it splashed upon my breasts.

'For a while I feared some calamity – my uncle's explanation of the act had been superficial, and had not embraced the description of such an eruption. However, though Jack swore to himself as though disappointed, his demeanour was not that of one who had been injured; and on seeing my amazement he comforted me, and taking a handful of grass considerately wiped my body.

'Seeing, I suppose, the disappointment of an ignorant girl at seeing his tool now shrunken, he kissed me upon the lips and assured me that not a long time would elapse before he would be recovered; and indeed whispered that if I cared to pay him once more the compliment of a kiss . . .

'Leaning towards him, I kissed him again upon the lips; whereat he somewhat sheepishly remarked that he had meant . . .

'At first his tool lay like a dead thing upon my palm; but the soft attentions of my lips gradually awakened it, and Jack assisted by taking my hand and placing it upon his breast, where I found that on my pressing his nipple between finger and thumb the business of recovery was much accelerated – indeed, on my accidentally twisting it (in an excess of pleasure consequent on his finding with his forefinger that place between the upper lips of my cunny where, I recognized, a soft spot might well prove my undoing) the real pain I appeared to give him resulted in an immediate and most admirable extension.

'To make the story short, in a little while he placed me tenderly upon my back, when it took no great persuasion to encourage me to open my limbs and welcome him between them – his tool slipping within me with an almost entire absence of pain, arousing a pleasure that was greater than I could have imagined or would have believed had it been described. It astonished me then, and has continued to surprise me, how much sharper is the pleasure of a touch in those parts which is the result of the presence of a prick, than can be instigated by the most considerate and sensitive application either of lips or fingers!

'Relieved by his former explosion of over-eagerness, Jack was now able to control his pleasure to such an extent that I was fully introduced to the pleasures of love – which so affected me that I became like a wild thing, bucking and rolling, so that we flattened the grass around us. Once, then again, I reached the heights; and would have done so a third time had a peculiarly active thrust of my lover's loins not provoked such a leap of our bodies that we lost our balance and rolled down the bank and into the river – surfacing with a splutter of laughter rather than that irritation which might have been provoked by the accident had I not been confident that a sufficient time was left for us to recover and enjoy yet another bout.

'The remaining three years that I spent in my uncle's house were the happiest I had yet experienced. The time I did not spend with Jack was spent in study, so that by the date of his marriage – which took place to the charming daughter of a neighbouring farmer – I was ready to earn my living by seeking an appointment as governess to some young lady or another. Jack, I have every reason to suppose, has been happy in his connubial relationship; and though I had no desire to shackle myself for life at that age, I cannot but envy his wife the attentions of a young man the vigour of whose manly parts was accompanied by sensitivity and kindness uncommon in country men and rare enough in any, and whose natural talent for giving – indeed, for receiving – amorous pleasure I have yet to find the equal of.'

Applause greeted the story which concluded with those words; and the party now dispersed. I made it a point to congratulate Miss Stanbury on her narrative, and to enquire how it was that so amiable and beautiful a young lady had not agreed to one of the many proposals of marriage which she had no doubt received.

Her reply was that she valued her freedom too much to be shackled even to the most admirable of men; while as to physical pleasure (she was sufficiently frank to use the words) this was to be found in plenty when a woman was devoid of those inhibitions which prevented her from denying herself.

It will perhaps be believed that I was not slow to take the hint, confiding that her tale had made me envious of her friend Jack to a point at which I longed, should she consent, to sample those pleasures which had made him the happiest of men. I will not describe what followed; but merely state that Sophie enjoyed the convenience of a bed to herself, while I was able to assure myself that Jack – if he was as honest a man as I supposed – however happy his state of connubial bliss, would probably from time to time remember with mingled pleasure and regret the ministrations of a lady whose skill and enthusiasm for the act of sensual delight was as great as that of any other woman with whom I have enjoyed the pleasure of dalliance.

6

The Poet's Tale

I must confess that a certain lethargy delayed my awakening on Christmas morning, for I had spent some good portion of the night endeavouring to prove (I trust to Miss Stanbury's satisfaction) that her youthful lover Mr Nicolls had no monopoly either of gentlemanlike behaviour or of manly vigour.

So satisfactory had my endeavours been (as I may claim without boasting) that neither I nor my companion felt the impulse or necessity to engage in a further, *ante meridien* bout of those enjoyable activities which had reduced us to our present languor; we merely took an easy breakfast, and I bade my friend farewell and returned to my own room – or rather that of myself and Sophie, who waking as I entered felt no need to enquire where I had spent the night, but merely enquired (with perhaps a slightly feline lift of her eyebrow) whether it was my view that the governess had anything worthwhile to teach. I greeted this sally with a smile, knowing that there was no malice behind it, but merely the twitting of one friend by another.

The second full day of our enforced imprisonment was just as inclement as the day before; even as I performed my ablutions, in a room distinctly chill despite the blazing fire in the hearth, I could see the snow beating down into the courtyard below, where an unfortunate red-nosed boy occupied himself in trying to hammer a hole in a bucket of water which (I could have told him) was in fact frozen solid).

The usual large fire greeted us on our descent, together with a side-table groaning under the usual breakfast of broiled bacon, beaten or fried eggs, hogs pudden, pork and beef sausage and freshly made chocolate and coffee. Gradually, the full complement of guests gathered, and breakfast over we began to eye each other with expectation; and finally one stood and announced that through the operation of the lottery it was his turn to attempt to engage our attention with a narrative.

'And,' he said, 'the extent to which it will be found amusing is perhaps considerable, for it involves a description of a habit of which many present may be ignorant. So it is with pleasure that I put forward the anecdote, which I entitle – to keep the pattern which has so far been followed – The Poet's Tale.'

The speaker was a personable young man of, I should guess, twenty and three, somewhat sallow, with dark hair worn long and free about his shoulders, and with a thoughtful mien, who had not yet been seen without a book – and indeed had sometimes been seen to insert his nose into one while half-listening to one of the stories with which we had already been entertained. He always carried about his person a loose sheaf of papers, neatly tied together at one corner, in which from time to time he was seen to write a line or two, carefully stuffing it out of sight should anyone approach sufficiently near to be able to read it, even inadvertently.

'The story must begin with my childhood,' he said 'for reasons which will no doubt become apparent as it continues. My name is Paul Hawthorn, and I am the son of a merchant of Peterborough, who unfortunately died not long after my birth, and of his wife, who he left well provided for, so that neither she nor I wanted for anything; and I certainly did not want for affection, for all that which she had previously lavished upon a dearly beloved spouse, she now turned upon me.

'The recipe is one which might have led to my being completely spoiled and indulged, had my mother not had too much good sense for that. I was kept in check whenever my self-regard might have led me to become selfish, and was from a very early age tutored in good manners and consideration for others, whether my social superiors or inferiors. When I misbehaved, my mother would seize me, place me across her knee, pull down my small clothes, and apply the flat of her hand to my naked bottom. The cries which followed (which were not the result of any great pain, for I must admit that the chastisement was as gentle as it was unwillingly inflicted) resulted in her immediate repentance, when she cuddled and cosseted me, positively smothering me in the warmth of her maternal bosom.

'I cannot say at what period of my life I began positively to court her rebukes: nor when I began to enjoy the chastisement as much as the subsequent comforting – but I fear that by the time I was seven or eight I was beginning to distress my mother by the regularity of the small misdemeanours which I committed in order to court her admonitory rebukes. Having stolen a cup of milk from the pail in which it was lying in order to raise the cream, or having wickedly pulled the tail of our cat, I would happily receive the summons to her room, where even before she had come to me I would have removed my lower clothing and be waiting by the stool upon which she sat to spank me.

'Whether or not she eventually suspected my motives, I cannot say; it may be that the idea of continuing to punish in such a way a son who was so rapidly gaining in height as to be almost as tall as herself, struck her as ridiculous, but at all events when I was ten years of age she sent for me to her room and announced that while she did not consider me a wicked boy, the regularity of my misdoings was such that she must now put me to a master. On the following Monday I was to attend the local grammar school, where I would sleep during the weekdays, though returning to my home at weekends.

'My tearful protests were unavailing. On the following Monday morning I was presented at the school, where I was greeted by Mr Pennyford, the master. A small school, it employed but himself to care for the twenty boys who attended; and it will be believed that he must employ strong measures to maintain discipline. That he did so was an undoubted fact, for there was for the most part perfect silence when he spoke, and equally perfect attention to any task which he set us. There being no advantage now in being naughty, I was myself impeccably behaved, and for three days engaged in a not unenjoyable process of learning – during which Mr Pennyford began to perform a service for which I shall never cease to be grateful – introducing me to the pleasures of English poetry. He was a great enthusiast for the work of the poet Herrick, and even when he was teaching the use of the globe, the intricacies of Latin verbs, or the use of algebra, he would break frequently into quotation – not always, or even often, apposite quotation, but quotation merely for the pleasure of it. Sometimes it would be ''Sadly I walked within the field,'' sometimes ''Among the myrtles as I walked,'' sometimes ''If that my fate has now fulfill'd my year'' – but frequently a verse hardly apposite for the ears of young boys tottering on the very edge of manhood: on hearing him quote the verse

'I could but see thee yesterday
  Stung by a fretful bee;
And I the javelin suck'd away,
  And heal'd the wound in thee . . .

we could but titter at the idea that a man should apply his lips to the breast of a lady in order to suck out a bee's sting – though something in the notion seemed attractive to us.

'Our laughter did us no good – or rather, did no good to one Master Henry Fillip, who failed to cease his grinning before the master turned around and caught him at his smiling – immediately summoning him to the front of the class.

' ''So, Master Fillip,'' he said, ''we smile, do we, at the words of the bard? We must make sure that his lines are in future regarded with proper seriousness.'' And he reached up to the wall and took down a branch of birchwood, stripped of its twigs and leaves, and pointed with it to the master's bench.

'Young Fillip blanched, but knew he must obey; lowering his trousers, he laid himself over the bench, presenting to the class and to Mr Pennyford a pair of unmarked white buttocks. The master, taking up a stance before his victim, then recited the whole of Mr Herrick's poem, punctuating the prosody with switches of the cane upon the unfortunate lad's arse, as –

> I *could* but *see* thee *yes*terday
> *Stung* by a *fret*ful *bee*;

and so continued to the end:

> What *dis*mal *stor*ies *will* be *told*
> Of *those* that *cruel be.*

'I could not but admire the master's skill – and not only in recitation, nor in his understanding of Herrick's prosody, which resulted in his conveying immediately both the full beauty and the meaning of the poem. What impressed me even more was his use of the cane, which was employed with a force insufficient to injure the boy, but sufficiently severe (as he intended) to impress the lesson on his mind with the same force and nicety as the strokes which marked those formerly pallid cheeks with thin red lines.

'Unlike some masters, he was not hardhearted enough to lay each stroke precisely in the path of the previous one, thus exacerbating the pain; rather, he took care to place them parallel – fifty-six strokes in all: which would seem excessive except that they were applied, as I have perhaps indicated, with just sufficient force to be mildly painful, yet so far from disabling that I am convinced that young Fillip was nowhere near as hurt as his cries might have suggested to the uninformed looker-on.

'My own reaction to the scene was unmixed: I envied Fillip to the bottom of my . . .'

A laugh ran about the room as Mr Hawthorn stumbled, aware of a semantic simile which was extremely suggestive. To do him justice, he himself smiled, before continuing:

'Had the punishment been cruel, had the blood run, I should have been horrified, for cruelty entirely disables my emotions; but as each stroke fell upon the fortunate Fillip's posterior, my own longed to feel the tickling sensation of the stroke, so that by the time the scene ended I was in a positive sweat of envy. At the same time, I was perplexed – for I felt between my thighs a strange sensation of warmth, and my toy (which was the word my mother always used for my *penis vulgaris*) swelled to an unconscionable size – indeed I feared it would almost burst, so resolutely did it strain against my trousers, as though positively to wish to escape from their constriction.

'Fillip's dismissal to his desk (having resumed, somewhat gingerly, his trousers) and Mr Pennyford's continuation of his explanation of the properties of an equilateral triangle, bringing in some allusion to the sum of the squares upon its sides, quietened my person. However, that night, lying in my small hard bed in a room noisy with the breathing of my small colleagues, my remembrance of the scene – which I could not keep from my mind – provoked the same strange distension; and I discovered that upon rubbing the limb in question, the sensation of pleasure I felt became almost unbearable – reaching a culmination as I heard inside my head Herrick's lines and saw in my mind's eye the master's cane reddening the white skin of young Fillip's bottom (he, himself, I may say, meanwhile sleeping, as uninjured as he seemed innocent, two beds away!). The fact that I later found my belly to be damp and sticky, I set down to perspiration, only time and experiment revealing that the enjoyment I felt was linked to the expulsion of a liquor of some kind from the end of my enlarged *toy* – which I kept to myself until my observation of the other boys revealed that too large a number was given to similar nocturnal tricks to make it seem any longer a singular event.

'The very day after young Fillip's punishment, in the

middle of a lesson in history, Mr Pennyford in describing the dress affected by the supporters of King Charles II in the late civil wars, was tempted to comment that in his view, and Mr Herrick's,

> A sweet disorder in the dress
> Kindles in clothes a wantonness . . .

whereat alone in the class, I let out a guffaw of sufficient loudness to attract the master's attention, who turning expressed himself sorry that a new pupil should so soon have descended to the level of the others.

' "I fear, Mr Hawthorn, that it is necessary to teach you the lesson Mr Fillip learned yesterday." And seizing the birch cane, he gestured to the stool. With an eagerness which might have betrayed my true state of mind to a suspicious observer, I walked to the front of the class and divested myself of my breeches, leaning over the bench with heart beating so strongly that it almost choked me. I heard the swishing of the cane with the keenest anticipation – and it fell upon the emphases of Herrick's iambic tetrameters with the most delightful consistency. Only those who have experienced the same pleasure could share my delight, could share the pleasure which each stroke upon my bare posterior gave as it marked one of the poet's delightful periods.

'My only regret, in short, was that the poem was a short one – the same length, indeed, as that which had marked Fillip's punishment. But it was a more delightful poem, and though I was still far too young to have experienced any corporeal passion for the fair sex, the poet's references – to lace, stomacher, flowing ribbands, a tempestuous petticoat – invoked in me feelings which I could not as yet explain.

'I did realize, though unconsciously, that I must to some extent restrain and indeed disguise my emotions – for I somehow knew that should I, on rising, exhibit to Mr Pennyford a *toy* in any other condition than complete relaxation, my punishment would take on an entirely new dimension; gaining permission to go to the jakes (clutching my breeches to my front to conceal my embarrassment) I was able, still feeling the delightful stinging of my nether cheeks, to relieve myself of an enjoyable but inconvenient tumescence by that means I had so recently learned.

'During the next several months, I learned to associate most of the poems of Herrick – but also some by Dryden, Chaucer, Byron, Chapman, Jonson, Gay and even the immortal Shakespeare with the keenest pleasure; and was led to attempt to express myself also in poetry, at first in the clumsiest of metres, but gradually becoming more skilful.

'Sadly, as time went by, the opportunity for matching poetry with the pleasure of corporal punishment diminished; Mr Pennyford was unwilling to cane boys much past the age of fifteen, and the copying out of lines of literature was substituted. This, while furthering my knowledge and understanding of English poetry, was by no means as welcome to me as his former attentions, which I now saw inflicted upon younger newcomers who, I fear, failed to appreciate them with the keenness which I felt, and to my mind were unworthy of them. Nor did I join with any great enthusiasm in those nocturnal games with which my contemporaries allayed their adolescent emotions – as mutual play, or contests to discover who could project to the greatest distance the liquor called forth by sensual pleasure (though indeed I discovered that by allowing my mind to dwell on those lines of poetry most keenly, by means of whippings, associated with such pleasure, I invariably won such contests – my record being in reaching a distance of four feet and three inches, from a seated position).

'Shortly after my sixteenth birthday, I was invited by my master – so quick and good a scholar was I – to assist him in school; which I did for a while by teaching literature and language. As part of my duties I was encouraged to enforce discipline in the manner tried and tested by Mr Pennyford (though with many warnings not to injure the boys). My first beating I remember keenly – the use of the cane seeming as natural to me as the use of the pen, and the skills called for seeming as easily mastered as those of poetry; the laying of those mild pink weals on to that innocent backside gave me an almost equal pleasure as that obtained by my receiving the stripes – though I was astonished to find myself, in the middle of the punishment, wishing that the bottom upon which I was laying the strokes of the cane was that of a young woman: in particular, of Betty, a rosy-cheeked and buxom young maid of much my own years, recently taken into service at our house.

'I had by now learned what are euphemistically called "the facts of life", which had been explained to me, at my mother's behest, by Mr Pennyford (essentially a kind man, and an admirable teacher). These facts somewhat confused me, for I could not associate them with pleasure – and certainly not with that onanism which continued to be my only expression of my masculinity, and which was invariably connected with a mixture of poetry and the memory of corporal punishment. However, my attention having been drawn to the existence of the female sex (my companions up to that time having been exclusively male), when the school closed for the summer holidays just before my seventeenth birthday, I found myself spending as much time as I could in Mistress Betty's company – which was not too difficult to contrive, since the garden in which I spent much time reading was very near the kitchen, and she would venture forth often, shelling her peas in the sun, hanging out her washing, or about other small tasks. However, I found it difficult to make any move in her direction – partly through natural shyness (I had had no contact with the fairer sex, other than with my mother) and partly through the fear of being rejected.

'However, one afternoon when my mother had gone into the town and the other servants were occupied elsewhere, I was occupying myself with turning over some waste ground with a spade (though we had a gardener, I found work in the garden pleasant, and often indulged myself there), while Betty was washing clothes in the scullery nearby. I had removed my shirt, the sun being hot, and my back had reddened in its rays – almost painfully, though I was not for the time conscious of it.

'Betty, on coming out to hang up the clothes, found the line broken and trailing upon the ground, and my additional inches of height prompted her to ask me to hang it for her. I picked up the loose end, and was stretching up to pass the loop over the crook which was fixed at the top of the pole, when she exclaimed:

' "Master Paul – how red your back be; is't not painful?" and passed her hand over it.

'I shivered at the touch – not only because the skin was indeed sensitive, but at the feel of her horny palm, hard with housework; I had often privately admired their roughness, and imagined how pleasant it would be to feel those coarse palms smacking down upon my fundament – a fantasy which had often tormented me during my sensual imaginings.

'Having hung the clothes upon the line, Betty now asked to examine more closely the skin of my shoulders and back, and tut-tutted; then said that, should I not cool the skin, 'twould blister and slough like the skin of a snake.

' "Butter-milk's what's needed," she said, and invited me into the dairy. There, she went to a huge churn of butter-milk, ladled out a small bowl, and taking a cloth dipped it into the liquid, and began to apply it to my back. The coolness was immediately pleasant to my scorched skin – as indeed was the sensation, and the feel of her left palm against my side, as she steadied me.

' "Look, Master Paul," she said, in a moment, " 'tis running down to your waist and will soil your trousers. Best take them off," – and stepped back, expecting me immediately to comply.

'I cannot, now, but suppose that she was signalling her compliance, should I have wished to make an amorous approach to her, for my trousers were already so torn and soiled (kept as they were for rough work) that another stain would have been nothing. However, at the time I thought merely that she was being considerate, and standing unloosened my garment at the waist. I wore nothing beneath them, the French habit of wearing drawers not having at that time caught on in the country – yet so ignorant was I of any danger such a circumstance might signify between two young people of our age, that I ignored this, and removed my breeches; not, however, revealing a sight which might have encouraged the young woman, for though somewhat aroused by the situation, my *toy* was no more than half-enlarged, and still hung in place rather than standing to attention ready for any combat for which she might be inclined.

'However, she said nothing, and inviting me to sit once more, continued to bathe my back. The presence beneath her hands of a young male body necessarily had an increased effect, however, and she gradually strayed from the particularity of her task, dropping the cloth and passing her hands not only over my shoulders but my breast (where the sun had not particularly burned me); not only over my back but down as far as she could reach, to the very swell of my buttocks where I sat. This was too close to home to be ignored, and I could not but rise from my seat in order to enable her palms to slide over my very arse – when, to my astonishment, not content with that she reached about and took my *toy* between them.

'The strangeness of the matter was that though the pressing of her body against me was delightful and the touch of her hands not unpleasant, my reluctant tool remained entirely limber, and the fondling she gave it had no effect other than a slight warming.

'I assume, considering the matter in retrospect, that she had had some previous experience, for she was kind enough to whisper a word of encouragement in my ear, and standing away for a moment, removed her single garment (which indeed had little enough prevented an apprehension of the warm softness of her body); then, turning about, leaned forward with her arms upon the dairy-table, allowing me my first sight of a naked pair of female buttocks – at once similar to those of a boy, and entirely different from them, being shaped more like a peach than an apple, with – rather than the dependent cods and prick, a dark slit-like aperture in which, from the small information I had been given upon the subject, I supposed that I was expected to sheath my *toy*.

'This however was the last thing which came to my mind: the sight of an unprotected naked arse had precisely the effect that might have been expected upon a mind which inevitably connected such a prospect with correction. Above the table upon which Betty leaned hung an implement for lifting cream from the surface of the milk – a cane with a flat, spade-like wedge attached to its end. Without thinking twice, I reached up, took it, stepped back and began to apply it with enthusiasm to Betty's posterior.

'From her reaction I almost immediately realized that this was not an action she had expected of me. With a shrill cry, she straightened up, seized the cream-ladle and wrested it from my hand – and would I believe have run from the dairy had she not seen the effect my action had had upon me: for the moment the first reddening of her arse resulted from my earliest stroke, my *toy* had straightened into an upright position, where now it stood positively trembling with emotion. Jumping up upon the dairy table, Miss Betty threw open her thighs in invitation . . .

'But the matter was not to be simply resolved, for to my disappointment – to say nothing of my companion's – on being invited to perform its proper function, my tool bowed and retired, declined to re-erect itself to the degree necessary for its insertion, even though my friend was by no means so impatient as to be discourteous; turning, she sank upon her knees and took the recalcitrant instrument between her lips. This was such a shock to my system – it had never occurred to me that such an action was possible – that my *toy* shrank to even smaller dimensions, and all Betty's mumblings, accompanied by the busyness of her hands about my lower parts, failed to have any effect upon it – nor indeed had the sight of her body, which was by no means unattractive, her breasts full and round, her haunches generous, her legs strong and willing. I attempted to arouse myself by considering the pleasure of her applying her palms to my fundament – and had I had the courage to invite it, the affair may have had a different resolution.

'That was impossible, however, to one so shy and inexperienced; and after a little while the girl simply gave up the effort, and with a mixture of impatience, disappointment and scorn, seized her clothing and took herself off in silence. No doubt she would have wished to comment, but she also wished to keep her position in the house, and I was after all her employer's son. I resumed my own clothes in the most crestfallen state you can imagine.

'From that time on I led a celibate life – which I found (it may surprise you to hear) to be less trying than one might imagine. My devotion to learning the craft of poetry – for it was my ambition to perfect myself in it – was no doubt helpful, for its intricacies kept my mind well above my breeches: engaged upon the definition of pleonasm and enallage, synaeresis and diaeresis, in exercises in trochaic dimeter, iambic hectameter, anapaest and dactyl, I had little time to contemplate what I was missing – and what to most young men would have been essential. All my passion was released in verse.

'It is perhaps not surprising that with the passage of time my verse became excellent. At first confining myself to exercises, I began soon enough to write verses celebrating events which took place in neighbouring families – marriage, death, the birth of children; and I soon had enough for a slim volume which was published by Mr Anderson, a local printer, under my own aegis. This sold well to those whose family history was commemorated in it, and I began to receive commissions from others who believed that a set of verses especially composed for them gave them a particular *cachet* – as was indeed the case.

'Within two years, I was complimented to receive an invitation to attend upon Lord and Lady Infermine, of Blatchett Hall, not far from Cirencester. Their elder daughter, the Hon. Carola Infermine, was shortly to be married to Sir Amis Quartermaine, a general officer in His Majesty's Army. It was suggested that I should stay at the Hall for some few days, in order that my verses should be informed by an understanding of the noble beauty of its gardens, lake and park, and so could place my verses securely in the context of the individual landscape.

'It can no doubt be imagined that my mind, during the short journey to Blatchett was occupied by those phrases which immediately offered themselves to me – as:

> O fair CAROLA! – mistress of the glades!

or

> CAROLA on whose bosom, beauteous rare,
> The honour'd MOON is pleas'd to shed her light . . .

or

> The nuptial hour of lovely CAROLA
> Invokes the muses to a joyful dance . . .

'On my arrival at Blatchett I was greeted not only by Lord and Lady Infermine and Lady Carola, but by Sir Amis. The bride would have fulfilled all the hopes of a more experienced man than myself: she was a vision of maidenly beauty – her raven-black hair setting off a pair of the deepest black eyes imaginable; her body almost insubstantial, so slim was she – yet she moved with so natural an apprehension of its beauty that one was immediately impressed by the knowledge that she was completely naked beneath her clothes.

'She greeted me with a shy smile, her eyes downcast – in contrast to the greeting of her husband-to-be, a great hulking fellow with moustaches and side-whiskers, fierce enough to frighten a whole army of Frenchies. He clearly felt that he had not waited all his life for the moment when he might be introduced to a mere poet, and after bruising my hand to such effect that it seemed unlikely I should ever be able to hold a pen again, he contented himself with glowering at me from a distance, exchanging not a single word, and making it plain that he could think of a hundred and seven better ways of spending twenty guineas than upon commissioning someone to write an epithalamium, however fine.

'Lady Carola was as quiet as her *fiancé*, though with no ill will (as it seemed to me); her parents treated me with some disdain, but with the respect due to a tradesman from whom they were making a purchase.

'On the following day I was invited to stroll about the grounds and take in the delights of the landscape, which it was confidently expected that I would wish to describe in my verses. It was a fine park, the lake

> (O flattering waters: with CAROLA's eyes,
> Thy waters clear and dark cannot compete!)

the fair lawns

> (The finest grasses, the most lush of lawns
> No rival are to pale CAROLA's hair!)

and a fine obelisk (which I despaired of including in my work except in a rude compliment to the bridegroom which would perhaps not be welcomed by his parents-in-law) were all handsomely assembled in one of the finest products of Mr Capability Brown's elegant imagination.

'I enjoyed the gardens for about an hour, and then, turning once more towards the house, was strolling along an avenue of handsome shrubs when I heard cries coming from a short distance away – the cries of a man who appeared to be in distress. Quickening my pace, I hurried towards the sound – and coming around the corner of a hedge, quickly concealed myself: for the scene before me was not what I had expected.

'I had thought that perhaps some poacher had been caught

in a man-trap (for Lord Infermine's keepers still set those infamous machines). However, before me in a confined glade, the sun slanted between leaves to throw its light upon a strange tableau. At the centre of the sward stood Lady Carola, clad in a white gown; at her feet cowered the figure of her *fiancé*: his uniform was thrown about the ground beside him, and, entirely devoid of clothing, he knelt before his love, presenting to her the unedifying spectacle of a hairy bottom too large and cumbersome (it seemed to me) for the admiration of any sensitive female. Lady Carola was, however, not called on to admire it. Far from this, she held in her hand a birch switch which she was bringing down with the utmost severity upon that bare back-side.

'The force she exerted was not, however, sufficient for the General. Used, no doubt, to the severity of similar punishment handed out to miscreants in the army, or perhaps to the beatings he was able to purchase from those whores who specialize in such matters, he looked around at her with flushed face, and cried, "Harder, you soft-handed bitch, harder!" as the birch fell upon his skin – which, tough though it no doubt was, had been broken in several places by the force of the blows, so that lines of blood started from the weals.

'Raising herself to her full height, Lady Carola now put all her strength into two or three concluding blows – the final one bringing from the General a cry which was half of pain, half of ecstasy. He threw himself to one side, falling half upon his back; and from a prick which seemed of the dimensions of a horse's, a flow of semen marked the apogee of his pleasure. Lady Carola meanwhile looked at him in haughty disdain – and something, I thought, of disappointment and even disgust.

'Sir Amis somewhat sheepishly got to his feet, gathered his clothes and got himself into them, all without reference to the lady; then muttered some words of acknowledgement which I could not fully hear, and made off – at which the lady sank to the ground and dissolved into tears.

'The spectacle of her dejected beauty moved me strongly. I could not – my hearers will believe – but be envious of the General; I would have given much to have changed places with him – and yet I flattered myself that I would not have left her so entirely uncomforted. Dare I . . .? Would it be improper to . . .? I did not allow such questions to do more than half-form in my mind, but stepped into the glade and approached the lady.

'My footsteps on the grass were almost silent, and she did not apprehend my presence until I was upon her; when it was impossible for her to conceal the tears which flowed from her eyes. Bending, I took the liberty of brushing them from her cheeks with the back of my hand, and murmured some words of comfort.

' "Thank you, sir, for your sympathy," she said, after a while.

' "I long to offer more than mere words," I replied.

' "Sir, you cannot know how impossible that would be. My problem is more deep-seated than you can know."

' "Forgive me, my Lady,' I offered; "but I came upon the scene some while ago, and was the reluctant witness of . . ."

'She coloured.

' "Can you understand so gross an impertinence?" she said. "This is the man I must marry – a man whose only pleasure is in being beaten; and whose selfishness is such that he is incapable of offering the least consolation in exchange! Can you understand such a fellow?"

' "I can understand no man capable of leaving so beautiful a woman in such distress," was my careful reply; "but it is within my experience that some men do require the infliction of violence before they are capable of—"

' "Sir Amis's capabilities stop short of offering any satisfaction to his mistress," she replied. "But" (and she looked at me with an interest that was touched, it seemed, with some diffidence) "am I to suppose, sir, that you . . ."

'I nodded.

' "I must confess to being subject to the same desires as

Sir Amis,'' I said; ''but the result, if I may say so, is rather different.''

'Of course the latter part of this statement was based only on my own imagination; for on the last and only occasion on which I had had the opportunity for congress, poor Betty had been left at least as frustrated as Lady Carola. However, I saw with a mixture of pleasure and apprehension that her hand had moved towards the switch which she had employed upon Sir Amis. Her eyebrow lifted a fraction. I nodded.

' ''If you would care to try . . .''

'She rose to her feet. In less time than it takes to tell, I had discarded what clothing I had, and stood naked before her – my prick leaping fully extended from my trousers, for even had I wished to do so I could not have restrained it from its appreciative anticipation of what was to come. I fell to my knees before the lady, my buttocks seeming of their own accord to thrust themselves towards her.

'There was a pause. I glanced around, and saw that she was gazing in what seemed to me to be some appreciation at my figure – I later learned that I was the first man other than her swart and stout *fiancé* who she had seen unclothed – and was much the prettier sight. However, she recalled herself, raised the switch, and in a moment I felt it fall upon my bottom.

'She did not – I am glad to say – use the full violence with which she had beaten the General; my pleasure is more in an inspiriting tickling than in positive pain. Perhaps the truth was that her arm had been somewhat tired by the beating she had been persuaded to give him. Now, she directed her efforts with more elegance than force, distributing the strokes so that each fell upon a different area of my bum – some from side to side, laying a stripe (as it were) from hip to hip, some almost vertically, so that the tip of the switch curved to flick between my thighs and inflict almost a pricking sensation just at the base of my cods.

'I could stand no more than perhaps ten or fifteen strokes before I was overcome by a feeling of lust which surprised me by its violence, and brought me to my feet almost before the notion of moving had conveyed itself to my mind. Turning, I seized the switch from the lady and sent it soaring through the air; then I seized the bosom of her dress and with one effort tore it from her body – thrust her to the ground – and without even that pause which might have been expected of one unfamiliar with the practical business of congress, had sheathed my prick in a scabbard well lubricated by the oils of desire.

'Happily, I found that the beating, while instigating the violence of my attack, had prepared me for congress rather than milked me of the desire for it; and I was able to maintain a stand for several minutes, during which my determined lunging provoked cries from the lady so piteous that any hearer might have thought her in distress rather than in the throes of pleasure.

'The crux of that pleasure was reached by both of us almost at the same moment; and we lay afterwards upon the cool grass – which I found grateful to a backside now a little sore. After a while, she persuaded me to turn over and, distressed at the redness of the skin, cooled by the application of her lips and tongue the irritation of the more prominent weals; that tongue finding its way eventually into areas less injured and more appreciative of its explorations – which in turn led to a renewal of an activity new to me, but one which I found I enjoyed with an almost alarming fervour; with, indeed, so keen a delight that it might have been frightening were it not the fact that Lady Carola was as delighted as I by its novelty.

'The remaining ten days I spent at Blatchett were exhausting ones; for not only was I engaged upon my Ode, but on the regular satisfaction of Lady Carola. Upon her proving curious, I even introduced her to the pleasure attendant upon slight pain, and although a whipping did not delight her to the extent to which it roused me, she confessed that she was not indifferent to the stimulation of it.

'She blossomed as the result of my attentions to such an extent that Lady Infermine congratulated me: she had noted her daughter's depression, and I suspect inferred (though with no particularity) its cause, being no more an admirer of the General than the bride – it being Lord Infermine who insisted, for political reasons, on the union.

'My Lady's gratitude to me for my effect upon her daughter did me a service, for it was she who suggested to her husband that it would behove so important a man in the county – he had recently been appointed His Majesty's Lord Lieutenant – to support the arts, and to become my patron. His Lordship accordingly offered me a house in his grounds, and allows me a certain competence; so that I have remained ever since at Blatchett, writing verses on several occasions – and now travelling north to attend his Lordship on an embassy he has to His Majesty in Scotland.

'The marriage of Sir Amis and Lady Carola took place as had been planned – the bride being much comforted by her husband's departure soon afterwards for the West Indies, a place whose climate is so poisonous to the fair sex that it could not be expected she would accompany him. Lady Quartermaine thus lives at home, and with an interest in poetry which has grown keener within the past few years, frequently does me the honour of visiting me at my house, where I am able to give her lessons in rhythm and form which, frequently instilled with the aid of the cane, are received with the utmost enthusiasm.

'For myself, I find my capability of satisfying the female sex no longer dependent upon beating – though it remains a pleasure which I do not go out of my way to avoid, the use of the birch, in moderation, being a titillation which adds an unmistakable *frisson* to any amorous occasion. I have indeed a set of verses, privately printed, in which I invite the attentive parent not to despise the use of the cane in the education of a son – and the son to be aware of the pleasure such a policy may bring:

'It wouldn't, I may say, be proper to spare
So invitingly tender a bottom, when bare –
So temptingly slender a bottom as yours

Provokes the infliction it braves and endures.
It is ever a pleasure to feel the swift flick
Of a birch twig whose pleasure's to swell a fine pr*ck . . .'

Laughter and applause at this point interrupted the recitation – and pausing only to observe that copies of the poem might be obtained of him, privately, upon payment of one penny, Mr Hawthorn concluded his tale, leaving the company cheerful and much entertained by his frank exposition.

7

The Dressmaker's Tale

The pretty but slightly nervous young lady who confessed to having been designated as our next story-teller at first begged to be released from the necessity to entertain us – for, she said, she was but a simple dressmaker, and had nothing extraordinary to relate. However, after a while Sophie intervened. Was Miss Nephrosyte (the lady's somewhat uncommon name) not known to her? she enquired. The latter, blushing somewhat, denied it. But surely (Sophie continued) the name was familiar to her as that of a lady who served certain members of the aristocracy by devising costumes of a superior and interesting kind?

Miss Nephrosyte, catching my friend's eye, was forced to admit it – for Sophie clearly knew more of her work than she would otherwise have confessed; and she now found herself under the necessity to tell her own story, for otherwise (she said) it would have been told for her, and perhaps with some inaccuracy.

'The first eighteen years of my life were so mundane as not to be worth relating,' the dressmaker said. 'I grew up in Soho in a small house in Frith Street, the daughter of a milliner and a tailor, and it was naturally assumed that I would follow them into the profession of making clothes for the upper classes – though my parents' business was confined to, at best, aldermen and impoverished knights, their powers never having been so excellent as to attract the attention of the true aristocracy.

'At an early age I discovered in myself a talent for cutting and shaping garments, and from merely assisting my mother soon found myself in demand for making ladies' dresses, and with recommendation from one to another built up a regular business among what I suppose might be called the upper middle class of persons, so that it became possible – nay, desirable – for me to have my own workroom, which I took at some distance from that of my parents; not through any ill-feeling between us, but for the natural reason that I began to feel the constraint of always being under their eye.

'My work was entirely with ladies, though wives occasionally invited me to perform some minor task for their husbands – as, mending a glove or cutting a shirt, where it was to be specially decorative (for I was an excellent needlewoman, and it was no problem to me to produce work of such neatness that gentlemen who prided themselves on their appearance found it entirely satisfactory).

'One day a gentleman who, through his wife, I had served in such small matters came to me with a great length of soft, black leather which he had obtained from Florence (for in Italy the production of good leather is something of a specialty) and asked me to make a coat of it. This I was easily able to do, for it was as pliable to work with as linen. The result pleased the gentleman greatly, who not only paid me well, but made me a gift of the remaining leather, which lay in my room for some weeks, since I was unable to think of an immediate use for it.

'There then came to me my Lady Darcy, upon the recommendation of Mrs Alderman Willoughby, for whom I had recently made a gown. My Lady wished to commission clothes for a ball to be held at Hornyby House, in Chiswick, which was to be a masquerade, and an occasion upon which some originality of dress was invited, through the hostess's preoccupation with fashion. I made several suggestions which fell upon stony ground – when my Lady sees on a table in the corner the black leather for which as yet no use had been found.

'Picking it up, she was astonished at its softness and captivated by its appearance.

' "What a pity," she said, "that it is impossible to fashion women's clothing from such a splendid material; why should men be the sole benefactors?"

'It would be easy enough to make anything from such fine material, I observed; it was simply that it was not the recognized custom for women to wear it.

'My Lady thought for a moment, and then asked whether it would indeed be possible to make a dress for her from such material?

'Perfectly so, was my reply; but in fact, there was not enough of it.

'She was extremely thoughtful, holding the material up against her body and examining it in my glass; and then took her leave, without giving me that commission for which I had supposed she came, which was depressing in the extreme, my business recently having suffered from the lull which often affects the trade during the last days of winter.

'However, within a week, Lady Darcy returned – with a length of soft black leather which, though shinier than the first, was almost as pliable. What did I think of this, she asked?

'It would be difficult (I observed) to shape a bodice from such leather; but quite possible to make a skirt – and indeed it held its folds with such nobility as to promise extremely well.

' "Right, Miss Nephrosyte," she said, and stripping immediately subjected herself to my measuring tape.

'The number of fittings required for the task was somewhat more than usual, for there were certain difficulties of construction to be overcome; and the material proved somewhat intractable in handling, so that more attention had to be paid to the rounding out of the clothing than is usually the case.

'However, at the final fitting the result surpassed all my expectations – and from her satisfied air, even those of my Lady. The skirt, she had insisted on being cut close to her figure, and the leather lay over her hips, thighs and buttocks with almost that clinging affection with which it must have protected the body of the animal from which it had been derived; while the bodice, in the softer material, embraced her breasts – which were full without being shapeless – and seemed to stretch and lift as naturally as her skin to their rise and fall, while the blackness of the material (so much darker than any cloth could be) set off the whiteness of that skin to such a degree that it resembled ivory.

' "My dear Miss Nephrosyte," she said, "a positive triumph. We shall make a sensation. But you will have to dress me, for I cannot trust the matter to my maid; and perhaps it would not too greatly inconvenience you to attend me to Hornyby House on April the nineteenth? – I would be reluctant not to have you upon hand in case some adjustment becomes necessary."

'I was of course happy to comply: I had never attended such a gathering, and apart from any particular pleasure, it would be useful to me to be able to observe the dresses of the fashionable women there.

'We approached the house in a closed carriage, and despite the warmth of the evening and of her costume (for one of the inconveniences of the latter was that the leather proved, after a while, to be reluctant in allowing the body to breath) Lady Darcy entered the house under a cloak, and we went immediately to a changing room set aside for the ladies. All our attempts at privacy then ended, for the room was full of other ladies readying themselves for their first appearance in the ballroom.

'On my Lady reluctantly setting aside her cloak, a gasp went up from the others, who crowded around to examine the uncommon garment which she wore. I could not but discern more amusement than admiration in their eyes; but my Lady – though I believe she similarly observed it – made no account of it, paying more attention to the elegant setting of the dress than to any opinion of those about her.

'As we were almost ready, the room emptied – and it was clear to me that the ladies had gone downstairs in order to observe the impact made by my Lady's entrance in so curious a costume and to gather other parties to observe it

– and I must confess that, while I was proud of my handiwork, it occurred to me to wonder whether my reputation among the aristocracy might not be ruined before it was established – for should my Lady be a laughing-stock the denigration would undoubtedly be conveyed also to the maker of the garment she wore.

'Accompanying her to the top of the staircase which swept down to the hall, I concealed myself behind a convenient pillar as my Lady began her descent. The hall was crowded with those I recognized as the cream of London society – though perhaps chiefly of the raffish kind; husbands and lovers had been collected by those ladies who had been led to believe that a walking laughing-stock was about to entertain them.

'Lady Darcy descended the staircase slowly and deliberately and with admirable coolness, one hand upon the balustrade. On her first being seen at full length, a gasp went up – for (someone later told me) the dress was so perfectly cut to her figure that she appeared almost a naked blackamoor except for the perfect white of her uncovered arms and the swelling of an ivory bosom. A hiss followed – which at first I took to be an expression of disapproval. But if disapproval it was, it came (it was soon clear to me) only from the women – for the men were speechless, and bereft of words through admiration rather than horror.

'On my Lady reaching the bottom of the stairs, there was a pause and a silence; until there stepped forward from the front rank of men, my Lord Hornyby – a handsome man in his middle fifties, whose wife looked as black as my Lady's skirt at the eagerness with which he offered her his arm, and led her to the supper table.

'Through being decently dressed in one of my own creations, I was able to mix with the crowd – and even, I may say, attracted some admiration myself: but it was nothing to that bestowed upon Lady Darcy, the gentlemen vying with each other to dance with her, and finding it, it was clear, quite impossible not to place their hands upon the leather which clad her body – even though it was difficult to do so without indelicacy: the temptation to feel beneath their palms the texture of that almost living black material was too much, several of them being careful to contrive to work their way, during a dance, into a corner, where believing themselves to be unobserved they passed their hands over my Lady's back parts – at which I expected her to protest; but she took their rudeness without offence, even smiling at it.

'One extremely handsome gentleman was in particular most assiduous in his attentions, and towards the end of the evening positively monopolized my lady, rather to the ill-temper of the others; I learned through conversation with one of the footmen that 'twas my Lord Pemberley, one of the richest young gallants in the kingdom, usually celebrated for his ineffable boredom on such occasions. Boredom was not an emotion shown by him this evening, however; on at least one occasion I saw him with his lips glued to my Lady's bosom – and without a great deal of attempt at concealment (his rank and wealth making this, no doubt, superfluous).

'Later, the two of them vanished, and despite my best endeavours I could not contrive a sight of them. After some time I made my way upstairs, where I intended to wait for my Lady in the room where she had left her cloak. Passing a door, however, I heard – or thought I heard – my Lady's voice, and softly opened it, intending to ask at what hour she wished to depart. The sight which met my eyes was not perhaps remarkable on such an occasion as this, but was uncommon where I was concerned – and considering the brief time my Lady had been known to Lord Pemberley would have been remarkable, I believe, even to those more used to the ways of the world than myself.

'My lady lay upon a *chaise-longue* beneath the window, my Lord – entirely unclothed – reclining upon her and wriggling with delight at the sensation of the leather of her dress against his body. His pleasure was so intense (I was relieved to note) that he did not hear my approach, while my Lady, meeting my eye, did nothing more than lower an eyelid in a ribald wink, at which I could not but smile, while being shocked that so interesting a scene should be taking place in so relatively public a setting, upon which anyone, after all, might have walked in.

'I confess to being rooted to the spot by the fascination of the *tableau* before me; for Lord Pemberley – perhaps cognizant that his merely wriggling on top of her gave his partner less pleasure than himself – now rose to his knees, and, clutching at the skirt, attempted to rend it from her body. The material, however, being considerably stronger than common, resisted his attempt – so that he could have no other recourse than to raise it (my Lady lifting her body to assist him) above her knees, then roll it to her hips, rendering available to him that prize which he now proceeded to enjoy, while at the same time rubbing his face, his hands, and his upper body against that crumpled gathering of leather which lay between him and his mistress.

'I remained for some time, interested by so uncommon (to me) a spectacle; but then withdrew. My Lady, when she eventually came to collect her cloak, ventured no comment other than to say that she would without doubt be visiting me on some future occasion. She then handed me a folded paper which contained a banker's draft for twice the sum I had suggested as a proper fee for my services!

'A month then passed by – when one day I was astonished to have delivered to me, without message, a large consignment of fine black leathers, a quality at least as good as that with which I had previously worked, but of different textures, from the fine to the coarse and stiff. In mid-afternoon a week later, a carriage drew up, and into my workroom came not only my Lady, but a gentleman who I recognized as Lord Pemberley, who was most condescending, and joined enthusiastically in praising my work for Lady Darcy.

'There was then a silence for a while, which was eventually broken by Lady Darcy.

' "My lord," she said, "wondered whether you would be averse to doing some more work in the material which he has I believe sent you." (And indeed, it stood nearby.)

'I said that of course I would be delighted.

'A glance then passed between them.

' "He requires – we require – some garments which perhaps may seem somewhat unusual," she went on, upon which he produced from a *portmanteau* a set of papers which he set before me. They were rough drawings of such garments indeed as I had not previously seen. I studied them for a while in silence.

' "Of course," my Lord remarked, "these are drawings which take no account of any problems of – er – construction which may arise; these, we must leave to you to solve, if indeed a solution is possible . . ."

' "There should be no difficulty, my Lord," I said. "I will however require some measurements."

' "Certainly," said Lady Darcy. "What better time than now, Tom?"

'She nodded to my Lord (and the informality of her address confirmed the impression given by the drawings – that their relationship was now upon grounds of intimacy no doubt provoked by the episode between them which I had observed at Hornyby House, and which clearly continued).

'Lord Pemberley rose to his feet, and without the least hesitation or ceremony, and encouraged perhaps by my giving no suggestion of offence, but merely busying myself with finding my tape and preparing a paper and pencil, divested himself of his clothing – not merely undressing to his shirt, but removing that before dispensing also with his trousers, and leaving himself entirely bared.

'The most intimate garment represented on the paper consisted merely of a triangle of leather into which it was meant the wearer should gather his *membrum virile*. Pictured only from the front, this article resembled a pair of trousers cut uncommonly short at the leg; but a drawing showing it from the rear revealed merely a string about the waist, and the problem of how it might be maintained in position was left to the imagination. I expressed my belief that the method of suspending the garment would prove inefficient, but after a moment's thought – and having ascertained that my Lady was of the view that the lack of a seat was essential (curious as that seemed to me) – I remarked that some additional secure fastening must be devised if my Lord's bulky equipment were not to . . . At that point I stopped, somewhat confused; but all naked as he was, my Lord made an elegant bow, and remarked that such flattery was always welcome.

'The gentleman was indeed remarkably well hung (indeed, I have since often considered myself rather fortunate in the circumstance, for the architectural problem which presented itself was of such a dimension that once I had solved it, it never concerned me more).

'Measuring the part of the body involved was by the way, I remarked; for I knew of no convention by which a garment could be shaped around it. It must be a matter of what might be called a practical fitting. Reaching therefore for a piece of cotton (not to waste the valuable leather) I cut a triangle of cloth to a size which seemed to me concomitant with the circumstances and placed it with the longest side stretching horizontally across my Lord's belly, passing the other corner through his legs; his prick and cods (you will forgive my using somewhat coarse expressions, but they are the ones which most easily fall from the tongue) were then caught up in the cloth, myself holding the two corners at the front, and my Lady, passing her hand between her friend's buttocks, sustained the remaining third.

'The occasion of two ladies busying themselves about his private parts now provoked a new difficulty, the circumstances giving rise to a change in the profile of the part of the body most intimately concerned, and making it impossible to estimate the form or indeed the size of the garment I was engaged in designing, presuming it to be required for use under less stimulating conditions. Indeed (I suspect through some impertinent movement of my Lady's fingers unobserved by me) it very rapidly became the case that the triangle or pouch previously entirely sufficient to contain the goods, now proved considerably too small; and indeed, on my Lady's suddenly relinquishing her corner, the piece of cloth sprang forward and upward, and I found myself holding the ends of a mere awning largely supported by a pole sufficiently substantial to carry a much heavier weight.

' "This is impossible, Tom," said my Lady; "we cannot proceed if you make this difficulty."

'Our attempts to continue were indeed entirely frustrated by my Lord's wanton prick, which stolidly declined to diminish in size. He showed no particular embarrassment at my having to regard him in this state, but merely apologized at holding up the proceedings. I cannot say that I was offended by the display, for apart from its arising quite naturally from unusual circumstances, he was – I must admit – a fine figure of a man, and having at that time had very small experience of gentlemen in a state of undress (those few lovers I had had preferring darkness for their manoeuvres) I was more interested than disgusted at the necessity to regard from only a few inches away a set of genitalia outstanding for its handsome proportions, generous size, and enthusiastic defiance of all requests that it should return to a less enlarged state.

' "Only one thing for it, my boy!" said my Lady eventually; "you will excuse us, Miss Nephrosyte . . ." and falling to her knees before my Lord, to my complete astonishment took his prick in her mouth and began to suck upon it as a child sucks upon a lollipop.

'The circumstance was entirely unexpected by me, for I had never conceived of such an action being either desirable or proper; but that my Lord found it pleasurable in the extreme there was no question, for placing his hands behind my Lady's head, he gently guided her in her movements, which within a very few moments, by his expression and the barely restrained bucking of his loins, had roused him to a point at which his emotions could not longer be contained.

'Rising to her feet, my Lady – wiping her lips with a handkerchief, but without any sign of that nausea with which (I must confess) through my naivety I had regarded her action – said: "I think, Miss Neophyte, you will now find the situation made easier . . ." And indeed, my Lord's intimate parts were already returning to that unexcited state which made the completion of my task possible.

'The conclusion I reached, after some thought, was that the garment (to dignify with such a name a piece of clothing barely large enough to sustain the description) could be kept in place by joining to the string about the waist a second, brought up between the legs from the lower corner of the material, and thus keeping it firmly about that area of the body it was formed to conceal.

'When I had quickly run up such a garment in cotton, my Lady entirely approved it, the single suggestion she made for its modification being that the strings should be joined in a bow which would instantly disintegrate upon one of them being pulled – for, she said, a sudden unveiling was occasionally desirable, and indeed necessary should the concealed weapon for any reason enlarge itself to such a degree that it was dangerous to the structure of the garment.

'We turned then to the other sketches which had been brought me – but I think rather than describe them to you now, or enlarge upon the problems I encountered in making them (this being my first essay in a kind of tailoring which was then new to me) I will pass on to the occasion for which they were devised.

'This was one which I believe even now is relatively unknown to the public, though from your expression ma'am [looking at Sophie], you are cognizant of it. It was my Lady who explained the occasion to me, upon my wondering for what purpose this strange clothing could possibly be required.

'It appears that every year since the turn of the century, an evening's entertainment has been devised at a great house to the west of London – the identity of it I had best perhaps conceal, since there would be a general misunderstanding should it become common knowledge, a number of ladies and gentlemen of quality, some of them high in the government of the country, being in the habit of attending the occasion, though it is of such a nature that their presence might be criticized should it become common knowledge.

'One of the chief features of the entertainment is the devising of original costumes – there being a contest for the best; but the difference between it and the more usual kind of costume ball is that the dresses shown at it are in particular supposed to arouse the sensual instincts of the lookers-on, and are shown as it were in action. Half a dozen couples each year are invited, upon application, to provide an entertainment, which is judged in accordance with popular applause; the reward being no more than the regard of those attending – the audience being such that this automatically allows them the titles of leaders of society for the season. Inspired by my Lady's dress, my Lord Pemberley had insisted that he could suggest such items, made in leather, which would result unquestionably in their walking away with the crown – and it was to this end that I was employed, at a fee (I may remark) unusual in its size, and which was to be doubled – I was promised – should my patrons be successful, for the social *cachet* of victory, in the company they kept, was considerable.

'On the evening in question I attended my Lord and my Lady, sharing their carriage to the country house near Henley upon Thames where the occasion was mounted; my presence was deemed necessary, it being impossible for them to dress unaided, such was the design of the garments contrived for them.

'The roads towards Henley were busy with fine equipages, and the drive of the house in question positively crowded with them; there was a buzzing also about the house itself, well-known faces abounding among the many we passed on our way to the room set aside for us. I did not see a great deal of the earlier part of the evening, for my patrons had by fortune been allotted the final place among the contestants, so that I must occupy my time in making sure that the costumes were in proper condition, and then assisting my Lord and my Lady to don them.

'My Lord, however – being a close friend of Lord X,

the owner of the house – was able to slip out and from a place of concealment glimpse the other entrants, the first four of which, he claimed, were insufficiently lubricious to bring a blush to the cheek of the most innocent maiden. The fifth pair he was unable to see, for it was time for him to dress.

'Having made sure that each was satisfactorily attired, and there still being (evidently) some time before they were to be called, I did beg of my Lord that he would direct me to the spying-place of which he knew, for I was eager to see the effect of my costumes – and indeed how my Lord and my Lady were to carry them off, for I knew nothing of their plans for the exhibition.

'Though somewhat hesitant, the vantage-point being in the private rooms of our hosts, my Lord finally gave me instructions; and, slipping from the bedroom where they awaited their summons I passed down a corridor, across the top of a staircase, along another corridor and then into what appeared to be the bedroom of the master and mistress of the house. A massive chamberlain's bed was hung with fine embroidered velvets and bore the crest of one of the most famous families in the land. In a corner, behind a screen, I found (as I had been told) a small window, concealed by a curtain; assuring myself that the screen was in place behind me, and that therefore there was insufficient light for me to be observed on the unlikely occasion of someone glancing in my direction, I seated myself.

'Through the window (almost too small to be so described) I looked down from a place perhaps twenty feet above the ballroom. About three of the sides of this huge room, lit by a thousand candles set in gilded sconces, sat the fashionable and excited crowd; upon the fourth side a low platform had been erected, upon which now a lady and gentlemen were disporting themselves. I assumed that they had been enacting a classical *tableau*, for on the stage lay two white sheets and a golden crown (so presumably one of them had represented a god); however at the moment the gentleman – whose thickset and muscular body suggested that he was of the working class (indeed, I was later informed that he was a manual labourer from Clerkenwell, hired for the occasion) – was strolling about the stage, his hands clasped under the buttocks of his lady, a handsome but thickset personage whose size explained the necessity of so muscular a partner. She, having her arms about his neck, was presumably impaled upon his prick, her ankles being crossed behind his waist and resting upon the platform of a jutting pair of hugeous buttocks.

'This feat was no doubt impressive as a demonstration of strength, but through its lack of variation was insufficiently stimulating to the sophisticates of the audience, who were hissing and whistling. This expression of disapproval not unnaturally had an unwonted effect upon the gentleman, for after a while that equipment which only could convince the audience of his sincerity shrank to such a point that it was clear the two were no longer amorously connected; and indeed the lady, losing her patience, boxed the fellow's ears, upon which he dropped her on her bottom on the stage and left it precipitately, necessarily however revealing as he did so his diminished prick (to renewed jeers). Picking herself up, red with a mixture of passion and embarrassment, the lady followed him without ceremony, leaving the audience rocking with laughter.

'This seemed to bode well for my Lord and my Lady, and I watched eagerly as, the discarded togas and crown having been removed by a menial, a large card was held up with the number 6 upon it, and after a pause a cloth at the back of the stage was whisked aside and revealed my lord standing, one hand raised above him, from which dangled a silver chain; while my lady reclined at his feet in an attitude of submission.

'This might have been tame stuff, except for the costumes they wore, entirely made in the leather they had brought me. Soft leather was tight about my lord's fine calves and thighs, and was cut off perhaps an inch below the groin – a strip of fine flesh being revealed between this and his loins, about which he wore the brief triangle whose design had first concerned me. Upon his turning, there was a spontaneous tribute of applause as the audience saw a handsome arse apparently entirely naked (the string passing between the cheeks having been made of a flesh-coloured material, so that even the inch or two which showed was invisible to the sight at a distance of more than a few feet).

'His jacket had no sleeves, and his sinewy arms were left bare – though fine black gloves were upon his hands; his breast was only partially covered, the jacket being without buttons, and cut to reveal both the top of the breast and the navel, below which his body was again bare to a point only perhaps half an inch above the root of his prick, where coarse black curls seemed almost an extension of his nether garment.

'The round of applause may have been however as much a tribute to my Lady's appearance as to his. Her lower limbs were covered by a full skirt of supple leather, slashed to the waist at each side – so that upon her moving, each leg was entirely exposed to view – while even now, as she lay, she had carefully disposed the garment so that it fell between her legs, revealing the limb on the audience's side as far as the waist, and making it clear that she wore no other garment upon her lower body. The arms of her jacket were slashed from cuff to shoulder, the white skin seeming to shine through the slits. The body of the jacket was cut high to the neck – but where her handsome breasts would normally have swelled the material, I had carefully cut two apertures, so shaped that her bosom was displayed to the gaze. She, too, wore black boots – though these extended only to below her knee.

'The applause dying down somewhat, my Lord now made a coarse gesture of command, and my Lady half rose – at which he leaned forward, thrust at her so that she turned, and, catching her arms behind her, secured them (or seemed to do so) with the silver chain. There then began the strangest dance; it was as though he bade to seduce her by the movements of his body, moving with immense grace though also with a masterful strength, while she swayed as though entranced, the skirt of her gown swinging to reveal first one limb and then the other, exposing the whiteness of her upper thighs and even, from time to time, a suggestion of the shadow between them.

'Gradually, she seemed despite her early repugnance to be charmed by my Lord; then excited; and finally almost unbearably interested, so that at last she could not resist pressing her body to his – when, fixing her teeth in the leather of his jacket, she contrived to remove it as he turned (ostensibly as part of his dance, but in fact to enable the disrobing). Then was revealed the extraordinary fact that through each nipple of his breast had been passed a gold ring of perhaps an inch in diameter: something which had been done, it seemed, since I had left the couple – and yet there was no sign of the blood which must surely accompany so cruel a piercing. If the sight was startling to me, the audience was astounded at it – yet their astonishment had the unmistakable sound of excitement, which soon quietened to the most profound silence.

'Seemingly contemptuous, my Lord now stood motionless, while it was his mistress's turn to become the temptress; approaching, she kissed him upon the lips, gently took the rings between her lips and seemed to twist them about and about, then trailed her tongue down through a sparse but pitch-black shading of hair, inserting it into his navel before descending to that part of him which, while remaining concealed, bade fair (to me, who knew the garment's shape) to burst from its covering.

'Insolently, he turned, presenting her with his bare arse – which, nothing loath, she licked and kissed, then finding with her teeth the bow of string which held in place his vestigial lower garment, pulled at it; upon which the tiny triangle sprang from its place as though propelled by a powerful spring – which no doubt was the case, though none could tell, for my Lord still had his back to the lady and his audience.

'She now redoubled her attention to that posterior whose fine proportions no doubt made it a pleasure to her (though

I remained innocently surprised at so voracious an appetite for such a site); little bites left blushing impressions upon the flesh, the titillation of which encouraged my Lord to lean forward and so spread his legs that she was able to worm her tongue into that part concealed except from the most intimate of companions, when despite himself (for I assume it was no planned part of the performance) a loud groan escaped his lips.

'The audience was now so still that a pin could have dropped, and the noise it made would have shattered the air. My Lord straightened, and turned: and a gasp came from the lips of every lady present – and, perhaps in tones of envy rather than admiration, from many of the gentlemen; even I, who had seen my Lord's prick extended under other circumstances could not but wonder once more not so much at its size as its elegant proportions. I have no means of knowing the ideal classical measurements of that part of man, though if my understanding of history is not imperfect, there was sufficient interest to make it almost certain that a theory of prick-proportion was devised in classical times. And it would be difficult to suppose other than that my Lord would have scored high in any competition founded upon such a theory, for his instrument, thick without ponderousness, long without disproportion, stood at an angle which best displayed it, the head proudly lifted, so that it seemed to stare straight at the object it most desired, the two balls beneath it tightly embraced by their retaining sack, and seeming to support and encourage it.

'My lady's eyes fixed themselves on this object (my Lord having turned toward her) with an appetite the voraciousness of which she managed to convey by their brightness alone. Leaning forward, she surrounded the tip of the handsome article with her moist lips, and with the very slightest movement merely grazed the bald head of it – a circumstance which provoked my Lord beyond endurance, for reaching down he rent her bodice completely from her, raised her to her feet and in another impatient gesture also deprived her of her skirts (the contrivance of remarkably weak stitching making these actions possible without irreparable damage to the fabric). Then with a sort of rough gentleness he laid her upon her back, spread her limbs, and fell upon her – her thighs opening to receive him and her legs closing around him so that her black boots were tight against his buttocks. Throwing back her head, she gave out a silent laugh; then, lowering it again – to my horror – fixed her teeth upon one of the rings which hung at my Lord's chest, and tore it away – when a gout of blood immediately appeared, which she licked up with every evidence of enjoyment.

'The movement broke the silence: there was a roar of what can only be termed lust, which soon became a regular clapping which encouraged my Lord to swive with an increasingly swift movement, until, no doubt roused by the approval of the mob no less than by all the other circumstances, a thin wail of pleasure came from my Lady's lips. She then fixed her teeth in the remaining ring and tore it from my Lord's nipple, a second gout of blood spurting between her lips as with a roar and a final pounce he expressed the apogee of his own pleasure, and lay still.

'The applause which followed upon their standing and bowing made it perfectly clear that they were in triumph; and pausing only in order that my Lord should resume those parts of his costume which had been removed, and that my lady should drop the chains with which she had pretended to be bond, they retired.

'Reappearing after a short time once more wearing their garments, they moved among the audience – the gentlemen admiring my Lady's dress, lifting the fabric of the skirts apparently to admire the softness of the leather, but perhaps also to give themselves the pleasure of glimpsing the body beneath; while few of the ladies omitted to examine closely my Lord's nether garment, which soon began again to show signs of strain as a result of many interested hands, many of which were passed behind him in order to ascertain just how the piece was supported. Neither could they resist drawing the lapels of the upper garment aside – when it was remarked with amazement that his chest had been entirely cleaned of blood, nor was there any sign of that devastation which might have been expected to be caused by the tearing away of those rings which had been passed through his nipples. These, slightly brown and erect through the pleasant excitement of so many ladies touching them – even with their lips – to ensure themselves of their wholeness, were entirely undamaged. (It was of course the case, as I learned later, that my Lord, a clever conjurer, had contrived a trick with hollow rings, red dye, and spirit of gum, which had given so interesting an impression of enjoyable violence.)

'I shut the window and returned to the bedroom, where, excited by the events of the night, I fell asleep, only to dream of an enormous leather phallus which His Majesty had commanded me to construct for a central position before St James's Palace, the erection of which was to be blessed by the Archbishop of Canterbury.

'I was awakened by my Lord and my Lady returning to the room. No sooner had they closed the door than my Lord threw off his jacket, removed his lower garment, and advanced on my Lady in complete readiness for a renewal of that act with which their performance had concluded – no doubt inspired by the approbation of his peers and their ladies.

' "No no, my Lord! Your tribute should be paid elsewhere! To whom should the triumph be accorded?" – indicating myself.

'My Lord turned, and with the utmost politeness advanced to the bed upon which I was lying, and standing over me enquired whether I would be averse to a corporeal expression of his gratitude?

'This may seem a mixture of impertinence and pride in him; but I can only say that I, somewhat heated by observing the events of the evening without the possibility of participating in them, might well have responded to the attempts of the merest footman; and upon seeing within inches of my eyes certainly the most handsome prick I had ever set eyes upon (indeed, as I have explained, the *only* prick I had ever set eyes on) could but nod; whereupon with a gentleness the opposite of that impetuosity he had expressed upon the stage, my Lord lifted my dress, parted my thighs with a tender hand, and climbing upon the bed slipped between my legs and inserted his prick into my compliant body with all the delicacy, skill and nicety with which a practised sailor would lay into dry-dock.

'Perhaps inferring from my attitude that I was to be swayed more by tenderness than roughness, his movements were of the most quiet and wooing kind; though so high were my feelings that I had too soon twice expressed my ultimate pleasure; when with a courteous smile he allowed himself to follow me to the heights, and then retired.

'The events of the evening (though not, naturally, that final one) having been witnessed by some of the most influential men and women of the time, it will perhaps not surprise anyone to hear that enquiries for leather garments flooded into my shop. It seems that that material is to some people peculiarly inspiriting, when employed as a stimulant to sensual activity; and I soon had more orders than I could cope with without assistance. I was soon required to travel hither and yon in order to design or take orders for clothing of that sort – and indeed am now bound for the town of Lichfield, where a descendant of Dr Johnson wishes me to make . . . but I must not betray a confidence, merely hoping that these details which I have felt able to give have proved of interest to our company.'

At which, Miss Nephrosyte made her bow to applause less in volume perhaps, but as considerable in gratitude and amusement as that which had greeted her two clients upon the first public appearance of those peculiar garments she now supplies to the nobility and gentry!

8

The Gardener's Tale

The next of our fellow-travellers to regale us with a story was one of the middle-aged men from the second coach – a quiet-mannered, pleasant enough fellow, with pale blue eyes, thinning hair which had once been more golden than it now was, and hands which, although sufficiently rough to suggest that he knew the meaning of manual labour, were at the same time well-shaped and sensitive. He opened as follows:

'My name is Gabriel Shore, and I was born in the west of Devonshire, the son of a farm worker. It was at first supposed that I would spend my life in the fields as my father and grandfather had done before me; but at an early age I showed an interest in the cultivation of plants, and working in the small cottage garden which was attached to our humble home, I soon filled it not only with fine vegetables but with sturdy and beautiful flowers – many of which I grew from seeds carefully and secretly garnered from the gardens of those of our neighbours who were sufficiently endowed with the world's goods to be able to afford to purchase plants.

'Upon my father's instigation, who had the percipience to see that my talent was sufficient to enable me to earn a good living should I be properly trained, I was placed at an early age as gardener's boy at a great house in the neighbourhood, where the head gardener, a Mr Williams, a kindly and generous enthusiast, was only too happy to pass on his store of knowledge; so that by the time I was fourteen I knew as much about the cultivation of gardens as many adults who had worked upon flowerbeds for a lifetime.

'I was fortunate in that Wordsley Manor had fine grounds – for the garden and park had been cultivated since the time of Queen Elizabeth, a fact which was known from the records upon yellowing papers which Mr Williams once persuaded Mr Philip Manship, the house's owner, to show me: the earliest of which, under the date 1575, described a park "thynle sett with oaks and some Beches and 72 deare" – while some thirty years later a map showed formal gardens of great elegance already set about the house.

'Though I could barely read, these maps and records struck so strong a chord in me that I was determined to study the history of the place; and by dint of continual reading, in time grasped the manner in which the gardens had been developed over the past two centuries – which (if I do not bore you) had depended in the main upon two men, the first being George London, who laid out a parterre and terraces cut into a hill to the east of the house and drove delightful birch walks through woods to the west; and the second being Mr Lancelot Brown – known as Capability Brown – who dammed a stream to make a great lake, built a large greenhouse or orangery, a bridge and a grotto, and a summer-house on a hill above the lake.

'It was Mr Williams's task and pleasure to keep these grounds in the finest state of repair, and he did so well enough to attract visitors from all over the county to admire them. In time (and I speak of the period when I was sixteen or seventeen years of age) it became a keen pleasure to me to assist him, for gardening became a passion with me – and especially the cultivation of roses. I was interested too in topiary, or the shaping of bushes and hedges, and greatly pleased Mr Manship by asking if might repair a fine maze which over the years had been allowed to fall into disrepair.

'He was delighted to give me permission to do so, and when it became clear that the task was within my capabilities Mr Williams allowed me sufficient leisure from my other duties to accomplish it.

'It was while I was at work upon the maze that the story which I tell had its beginnings.

'This maze was a very complicated one: I know not who designed it, but it was a masterpiece of its kind, the passage to the centre (once I had cleared it of a mass of overgrown greenery) being exquisitely convoluted. As soon as I began to clear the ancient pathways, I started also to make a map or drawing which enabled me to become familiar with their twistings and turnings.

'I first seriously attacked the maze in the early spring, when the fair young shoots began to appear; and by mid-summer, by dint of hard labour, had almost completed its restoration. Mr Williams, though he could I believe have made use of me elsewhere, respected my passion – and was also pleased by my efforts, seeing to what an extent the restoration of the maze would add lustre to the gardens, and would have allowed me to proceed even had Mr Manship not encouraged me.

'I should now admit that the maze was not my only passion. There had come to the house during the winter preceding my work upon it, a young girl who Mrs Manship – an elderly lady whose kindness to me upon the rare occasions when I saw her was at least the equal of her husband's – had brought from a village near Exeter, and trained as her personal maid. An elderly and somewhat cantankerous woman who had filled that position for many years was being persuaded into unwilling retirement, and grudgingly aided her mistress to train young Lillian Gandy (which was the girl's name) in her tasks. She proved a willing, able and pleasant pupil, whose innocence of proper manners (having grown up in a small community) was soon cured, and who within a few months was fully able to perform those tasks expected of her, and was popular in the servants' hall, of which I was as it were an honorary member, taking my meals there.

'Because Mr Manship's staff had been with him and his wife for many years, they were all elderly, and being by far the two youngest members of it Lillian and I felt a natural kinship. She was a lively and naturally intelligent girl who though she had lived all her life in the country knew nothing of flowers or plants – for which however she had a natural admiration; so it became my pleasure to instruct her in the names of the flora which grew in abundance at Wordsley. It became our custom to walk out together during those hours which were free to us; and during my work upon the maze Lillian would bring me, in the middle of the day, a basket containing some bread and meat, some fruit, and a jug of cold tea, which we would share as our luncheon.

'The difficulty that she could not find her way to me through the winding paths of the maze, where now the privet walls grew to a height of six or seven feet, was overcome by my laying a thread from the entrance, which, on her following it, led to the centre, where I was at work upon a little topiary bower whose protection from the sun – through cunningly placed shady walls – would be the reward of the intrepid explorer who eventually found his way there.

'For some time I enjoyed Lillian's company without quite knowing why. We had little in common, and though she was amiable enough I could not quite understand why I found her presence so agreeable. (If you wonder at this, remember that I was an only child, and had for the past several years been working entirely with adults, the youngest of whom was some thirty years older than myself.) To my perplexity, I began to dream about her, and in what seemed to me to be a strange way: it was in my dreams that I first became aware of the manner in which her body differed from my own – of those rounded areas of her chest which, in my dream, aroused admiration and a certain strange, even thrilling emotion. I would often wake, after such a dream, to find that my male member was enlarged and stiffened, and seemed in some strange way to have gathered to itself all the emotions I had felt, in my dream, on contemplating that young girl.

'Then one night I dreamed that I walked into the maze to go about my daily work, and at the centre came upon

Lillian, with her back to me, who as I watched stretched up her arms and lifted her dress above her head, revealing her naked body – which so startled me with pleasure that my whole lower part seemed to explode: upon which I awoke to find it stickily wet with a liquid which seemed to have been expelled by my member, which as I woke already was beginning to diminish in size.

'This was a circumstance which (as we have already heard from Mr Hawthorn) can puzzle a young fellow to an extreme. I could not bring myself to speak to anyone about it – though I am sure that Mr Williams, with his usual solicitude, would have explained (in however embarrassed a fashion) the cause of my dreams and of the physical phenomenon which I fond so perplexing. As it was, I nursed that perplexity to myself; and cannot say that it positively troubled me – though certainly I began to regard Lillian with a new interest, and could not prevent myself from speculating as to the shape of her body beneath her clothes (not having the advantage of some boys, born with sisters upon whom they can spy, or who at an early age are shown, or contrive to see, illustrations of the female form which prepare them for the reality – and no doubt provoke them to contrive an encounter with it).

'One midday in summer, then, I was working at the centre of the maze, carving from the privet a small vaulted aperture in the hedge where a little rustic seat might be placed. The sun being hot, I had as usual removed my shirt; but as I stretched for a high corner of the hedge the string which secured my breeches at my waist snapped and they descended without ceremony to my knees. From behind me, I heard a soft laugh – and upon turning (an action which in view of my state of undress it would have been wiser perhaps to avoid) I saw Lillian, who had just come upon the scene bearing the basket containing our lunch, and whose first view of my buttocks had been complemented almost immediately by the sight of my foreparts, which brought a blush to her cheeks (she being as ignorant as I of the appearance of the opposite sex).

'Her laughter was so natural and without ribaldry that it scarcely confused me, and it was with only the slightest embarrassment that I caught up my breeches and descended from the ladder on which I had been standing. Neither of us referred to the situation, other than for her to offer to repair the cord which had broken, which was no great problem, since it simply required the tying of a knot. This done, we settled to our bread and meat.

'The sun pouring down, we took refuge in the shadows at one side of the core of the maze; yet even so, it was extremely hot, and by the time we had finished our frugal meal we were both well heated. Lillian remarked that she envied my being able to remove my shirt. My reply was that 'twas private enough for her to remove hers, since none without my guidance could find their way to the centre of the maze. She objected that all a stranger would have to do would be to follow the clue I had laid to guide her – my answer to which was to pull at the cord, which was merely laid upon the ground, until the far end came around the end of the hedge nearest us and was in my hands.

'Lillian then remarked that there was another difficulty, which was that she wore no shirt, but a dress, which could not be removed in part.

'I will confess that my heart beat a little faster as I answered that she need not fear offending me should she wish to remove the whole.

'There was for a moment a pause, and then to my extreme interest and pleasure (which I did my best to disguise) the heat persuaded her to comply; she stood, turned her back to me, and in a scene which was the precise counterpart of that which I remembered from my dream, lifted her single garment above her head.

'If anything, the picture which I now contemplated was even more entrancing than that of my dream. She had stepped half into the sunlight, which shone brightly on that golden hair which fell to her white shoulders; there, the shadows of the hedge began to fall, laying a line across one shoulder and down almost to her hip, and throwing into relief the modelling of her back. Below, her nether region swelled to resemble the shape of a peach or an inverted heart, her buttocks full yet with the firmness of youth, and supported by shapely thighs – between which, as she bent to place her dress on the grass, I saw (which was a surprise to me, for how could my imagination have provided it in my dream?) a little triangle filled by a similitude of a fig, even to its being shaded with fine, fair hair, darkened about what seemed a slim cavity.

'Turning, the girl threw herself quickly upon her face on the grass, her head on her folded hands, and smiled at me. I, too, turned upon my belly, and though my face was toward her, pretended to close my eyes – but could not but continue to examine her person from beneath lowered eyelids, conscious as I admired the curves of her body that I was beginning to be extremely uncomfortable due to the pressure of my young cock, which vigorously attempted to enlarge itself, though confined between my loins and the ground.

'I doubt not that Lillian realized that I was watching her – and I do believe that woman's natural coquetry persuaded her to remark, after a while, that she would not object should I wish to remove the remainder of my clothing. Though I had some instinctive feeling that a display of my true physical state might insult her, another and stronger instinct made it impossible for me not to comply, and without any remark, I turned away from her upon my side and removed my breeches, after some fumbling necessitated by the enlarged state of my instrument. I then turned once more on my face, first holding my cock up against my belly, so that it fell more or less comfortably between it and the grass.

'After a while: "I have not seen a young man undressed, before," says Lillian.

' "Nor I, a girl," I confessed, first having to clear my throat, in which a giant frog had taken up residence.

'There was a pause.

' "Do you want to see, properly?" she next enquired,

lifting her chin upon her hands – a movement which resulted in my glimpsing a pair of rounded somethings depending from her chest.

'Finding it impossible to reply vocally, I simply nodded.

'Without speaking further, but simply smiling at me, Lillian turned over and lay upon her back.

'My natural curiosity speedily overcame any shyness which may have been residual; though not daring to touch her body, I leaned over it with the keenest interest, the prospect before me being (I must remind my auditors) entirely unfamiliar. It will not be doubted that my eye was first caught by those most enchanting of appurtenances, the female breasts, which in Lillian were perhaps at their most delightful, having been formed but a few years previously, and therefore – despite that domestic work which entails a number of attitudes (in much bending forward, for instance) which are unkind to the female figure and can result in its premature destruction – were as close to the ideal as is possible. It was certainly the case that since, it must be remembered, the girl was lying upon her back, they did not at first appear to their full advantage; yet they were sufficiently fleshy to provide a considerable contrast to my own bosom, not only in the absence of those few hairs which had so far ventured upon my chest, nor in the fuller flesh which even in that posture displayed itself, but in particular in the roseate nipples which, no doubt unconsciously interested by my approach, had formed themselves into perfect buds, which I could not but compare to those of a pink rose about to blow.

'Nor could I resist, having examined them, lifting a finger as though to test their resilience – and though hesitating at last to do so, I was given permission by Lillian's smile to go so far, and, placing the tip of my forefinger to the tip of her bosom, felt with pleasure its softness, complemented by the slight roughness which I almost insult by the adjective; it was rather a texture like that of coarse velvet, which was conveyed also by the aureole which surrounded each nipple, and was of a darker pink, almost to brownness.

'Some instinct now prompted me to bend my head and place a kiss upon each soft upstanding bud – and I even, I believe, felt the deep-seated longing to suck upon them; yet did not do so, for fear of giving offence to one so kind.

'Next, my eye was drawn to the centre of her body, even more different to my own than our breasts. There was no appurtenance like my own, even in its most limber and diminished state, but a little plain of silky hair at the centre of which was a dark opening. My eye, even at its closest, could see no detail of this other than a pair of soft pink lips whose colour was somewhat veiled by the golden haze; and on my reaching out and attempting with my forefinger to probe the mystery, Lillian's whole body shivered as though stung by some insect; and I almost rose to enquire whether this was so – and would no doubt have done so had the girl not immediately opened her thighs as though to welcome a further examination, which I was not hesitant to give. Now, I was able, by using the fingers of both hands, to draw her nether lips apart, revealing a cleft lined by clear pink flesh gleaming with a lubricant sheen; and, at the tip of the cleft where it broke into the sunshine, a tiny hooded finger (as it were) which seemed a miniature replica of the skin which surrounded the head of my own cock (which by this time, I may say, seemed likely to burst from the apprehensive blood being pumped into its tissues).

'I gently placed my finger upon this strange but interesting feature, at which my friend's body positively leaped, arching upon the grass so that for a moment it was supported only by her shoulders and heels.

'I was quick to enquire whether I had hurt her; a question whereto, her teeth being clenched upon her lower lip, she was unable to reply, but shook her head with a fierceness which seemed to beg me to continue.

'However, Miss was now eager that the favour she had allowed should be returned, and wriggling about disposed her body so that while my head was still about her middle parts, she was able to approach mine with a view to an inspection of the topography; and in a moment, I felt her inquisitive fingers about my person.

'It was the first time any person other than myself had laid a hand upon that part of my body, and that her touch had much the same effect upon me as mine upon her need not be said. Indeed, as I once more stroked the little nodule I had discovered, so I felt the tenderest touch upon my cock, as Lillian in turn stroked it, then gently drawing back the skin to inspect the head beneath, now grown to a size of which I had not suspected it capable.

'Wetting finger and thumb at her lips, she placed them upon that cap, and gently moved them about in much the same way as my forefinger now moved upon its miniature replica; and – you will have guessed it – at the same time we were both seized with what seemed a killing emotion, so keenly did it run through our limbs; I heard from her a shrill cry as another paroxysm lifted her body, almost throwing me off while an explosion in my loins resulted almost immediately in a second cry as she saw to her astonishment a fountain of creamy liquor burst from the tip of my cock, continuing in bursts or waves for some time before diminishing to a mere drop oozing from the tiny hole at the centre of the dome of my delighted instrument.

'It will be credibly supposed that the experience we had enjoyed was repeated subsequently upon many occasions during a long and warm summer; though whether I will as readily be believed when I assert that our experiments never went further than upon that first occasion, I cannot be confident. The truth was that neither of us having been informed what it was that a man and woman did together, it did not enter our heads to juxtapose our private parts in a more intimate manner; nor indeed did we desire it, gaining quite sufficient pleasure from our manual caresses, to which in time was joined another pleasure, when Lillian discovered that her placing my cock between her lips gave me quite inordinate delight – which encouraged me first to kiss and suck her nipples, and then to convey my tongue to that other part of her body where its touch – capable upon the one hand of a softer, and on the other of an equally firm caress gave even more pleasure.

'So often did we meet at the centre of the maze that our absence was remarked – and upon my being questioned about it with a somewhat stern air, I quickly invented the explanation that I was preparing a surprise for Mr Manship; and then had quickly to think of something to justify the promise. Lillian's admiration of my shaping of the arbour of privet gave me the idea to attempt to make a likeness of her body in that material; and there being a vertical growth of privet near the centre which I had intended to form into a sort of column, I turned my attention to it, and persuading Lillian to stand model for me, indeed turned out a very credible imitation of a woman, just at the side of the arbour.

'When the time came to admit Mr and Mrs Manship to see the work, I was rather saddened, for I must also release to them a plan of the maze, which ended the privacy Lillian and I had enjoyed there. However, the pleasure that was taken in my work was a reward, no less than the purse of money with which my master presented me. If there was some surprise at the work, it was not so much because of my natural talent, as that I should have chosen to depict – at my relatively tender age – an unclad woman, and a suspicious look or two was directed at Lillian and myself. However, nothing further was said; and if we could no longer disport ourselves in the maze, it was also now autumn and somewhat cool for such outdoor activities. I had, however, little difficulty in finding a way to Lillian's room, for though it was upon the first floor, at that corner of the house was a large tree which obligingly dropped its branches near the walls, from one of which it was a simple matter for an agile youngster like myself to convey himself to a window-sill and thence into his sweetheart's arms.

'That winter a sad event overtook us, which was to have yet sadder results. In October, Mr Manship was taken with a sudden stroke and within forty and eight hours was dead; upon which his wife, uncommonly devoted to him, also repined and sank into unconsciousness, from which she drifted almost imperceptibly into the grave.

'Their heir was a nephew, Mr Oswald Manship, and the household awaited his arrival with interest. He drove up to the mansion on the morning of the funeral in great haste and a four in hand, leaping from it and demanding liquor. Taking a flask of brandy into the very churchyard, he also found his way, that first evening, into his late uncle's cellar, an excellent one, and made considerable inroads on the good claret there, also sending into the town for more brandy (of which there was not a great supply in the house) which he consumed late into the evening.

'From the first he showed great impatience with the servants on grounds of their age and incompetence – the first of which charges was no doubt true, but the second unjustified except perhaps on the ground of their somewhat leisurely performance of their tasks – which did not suit Mr Oswald, whose impatient nature demanded the arrival of a bottle within a very few minutes of his ordering it up.

'Two days after his arrival, seeing me about my work in the garden and recognizing me as the only male about the place much beneath the age of fifty, he commanded me into the house to serve him; and would not brook refusal, despite my attempts to explain that not only was it my task to work in the gardens, but that I knew nothing of domestic service, nor was my manner sufficiently refined to accomplish it without offence.

'To this, his answer was a curt: " 'Twould take more than that to offend me," and ordered me that moment to fetch him a bottle of the '07 claret for his lunch. My having no livery did not concern him; all that interested him was that his orders should be carried out at the run. The vision of myself in my working clothes passing through the marble hall with its fine organ, serving in the dining room with its handsome carvings by Jonathan Ritson, or handing Mr Oswald his wine in the best silver-gilt cups (formerly used only for ornament) almost gave Mr Podson the butler a heart attack, and no doubt would have done so had he not been more concerned by the news that he was to be dismissed the week following.

'Within two months things had altogether changed: the old servants had almost all gone, only the outdoor staff continuing in the service of a master thoroughly unworthy of any man's service. Replacements had been brought largely from town, and were almost as unpleasant as their master, being also (as I now realize) extremely licentious. Happily in one way, Mr Oswald had insisted on my remaining in the house, so that I was able to prevent undue offence being given to Lillian, who to my relief had also been retained. We gave it out indeed that we were shortly to be married – which might indeed have been the truth, though we were now driven to it by circumstance rather more sharply and suddenly than might otherwise have been the case.

'There was now no mistress to be served; and it should have been a warning to us both that our new master insisted on Lillian being retained to tidy and care for his bedroom. There being no one of an older generation left to make us understand his probable reason for this, we gave it only small consideration; and it must be admitted that at first Mr Oswald offered no outward offence, and though often in bed when Lillian entered the room in the morning, did not in any way display himself improperly to her, always turning his back when rising unclad from the sheets, and never offering any untoward action or comment.

'She, however, expressed herself as unhappy in her new master's attitude; and when I asked why, remarked that he looked at her with the eye of a man regarding a horse he had bought and meant shortly to ride to death. I laughed at this, and teased her about it; though as it turned out, with an unjustified levity. For excuse, I can only say that it did not occur to me that any gentleman was likely to admire a mere servant, or to consider taking liberties with her person. (It was common knowledge that Mr Oswald made use of certain expensive wh*res from the nearby town, with whom he was known to converse at least once a week.)

'Towards Christmas, Mr Oswald now announced a large

dinner and ball, to which he invited every person of consequence in the surrounding district, including the Lord Lieutenant and his Lady. It was his intention, it was believed, to offer himself as a Parliamentary candidate at the next election, and in order to ensure his election he must make himself agreeable even to those people who by temperament he considered to be bores. The preparations for this evening were in hand when the events occurred which were to lead at first to distress and then to the making of my fortune.

'Two nights before the entertainment, Mr Oswald had dined well, and accompanied his meat with sufficient wine to heat his blood. On my coming in with a tray of brandy, I found him admiring a painting by an Italian artist which he had found in the attic and placed in the dining room. It represented the legend of Leda and the swan, and even to my eyes the placing of the neck and head of the swan between the unclad lady's ample thighs was sufficiently suggestive to make me understand why my late master had relegated it to a store room. Mr Oswald, however, whose colour was high, asked whether I did not wish I was in the place of the bird, and asked how I contrived to "put it away, regular?" to which I made no reply, nor could, for I could only vaguely infer the meaning of his remark.

'Excusing myself, I went out to the orangery, where I had some sensitive plants which I was hoping to nurse through the cold months, and did not return until late. Wanting no less to talk to Lillian than to share some warmth with her, I climbed the tree at about eleven o'clock and tapped at the window of her room. There was for a time no reply, and I was at the point of descending, believing her for some reason to be absent, when her figure appeared and she unlatched the window. On entering, I was surprised to find her shaking and confused, and her face tear-stained. She was clad in a fresh shift, and upon the floor by her bed lay her dress, crumpled and stained with what could only be blood.

'It took some time for me to comfort her sufficiently to persuade her to tell me what had passed. It appears that our master had met her upon the stairs, on his mounting to his room an hour ago. In passing her, he had seized her arm, and pulling her toward him had pressed a kiss upon her lips, at the same time thrusting his tongue into her mouth. This kind of exchange we had practised, it having occurred to us as a pleasant novelty; but Mr Oswald performed the action with a roughness which Lillian found distinctly unpleasant – and it was followed by the equally rough gesture of his thrusting his hand between her legs, at the same time enquiring whether she was not "ready for it".

'Confused and frightened, she thought to offer no resistance as he opened the door of his bedroom, dragged her into it, and threw her upon the bed, then in a moment tearing off his breeches, lifting her dress and . . .

'The listener will know what came next. To Lillian and myself it was at once a revelation and a matter for disgust. A revelation because we now instantly understood the nature of an action which we might ourselves have performed together in love, had we but known of it; a matter for disgust because not only was it offered roughly by a relative stranger, but because since there had been no offering of tenderness the very act of penetration was painful, while there was also some other pain – that almost of flesh being rent; and on Mr Oswald (after but two or three lunges of his loin) raising himself, Lillian saw indeed in fear and loathing an issue of blood between her thighs, and anointing his instrument.

'He was not however in the least dismayed – and seemed even proud; reaching for the sheet and wiping himself (while not offering the courtesy to her) he remarked something about the pleasure of taking a maidenhead (a phrase which meant nothing to us), and told Lillian she could go.

'I believe – though it may be nothing to be proud of – that my anger was as much at Mr Oswald's taking a place which should by all sentimental rights have been mine, as at his uncouth violence. But that I understood Lillian's distress and pitied her goes without saying; and it was as a matter of immediacy that I took her in my arms, and we went to her bed, where after a while I was able to comfort her.

'When her grief began to subside, the warmth of my body against hers persuaded her to invite those intimacies which could perhaps allow her to forget Mr Oswald's unpleasantness, and indeed, after perhaps twenty minutes, when we had become so engrossed in our tender gestures that other matters were at the back of our minds, she whispered to me that she would not be distressed were I to attempt that particular intimacy her master had so rudely offered.

'I was much concerned that I might injure her, for it seemed to me that my particular weapon was too thick to enter her without pain, especially since she must be tender from the recent rape (not that I knew enough to call the offence by its proper name). However, the pleasure we had had in our mutual caresses had conveyed itself in that lubrication which makes the ultimate gesture an easier one, and upon my carefully presenting the head of my cock at the gates I found that it slipped between them with ease, to be followed to my amazement by the entire length of the instrument, until our bellies were so close together that we could make no further effort at jointure.

'Lillian expressed herself equally astonished, for knowing the dimensions of my cock well, she could not have believed that it could so completely hide itself within her body; she could feel its tip, she said, almost at her heart.

'Though I had no knowledge of what was next expected, nature prompted me to withdraw somewhat from her, and then to press forward once more. The feeling of my cock being embraced by a sort of fleshy glove, pressing in upon every inch of it, was more delightful than anything I had hitherto experienced; while Lillian was delighted at the manner in which the inside of her cave was stroked upon all sides at once by the snugly fitting instrument – and soon we were swiving as though we had been practising for years, the soreness which she at first felt lost in the pleasure which movements gave her.

'I will not weary the listener by a further description of that act which is familiar to all lovers better educated than we were; I will merely say that by morning we had pleasured ourselves several times, and had almost reached the stage of being grateful to Mr Oswald for introducing us to such a delight. However, it was our mutual understanding that some way must be found to punish our master for his impertinence – and indeed a way had occurred to me.

'The moment dusk fell on the following day, perhaps four hours before the great dinner and ball was to be held, I excused myself and crept from the house while the other servants were making the final arrangements, and Mr Oswald Manship was in his room making himself fine.

'My labours were directed at the trimming of two large privet bushes, one of which grew upon each side of the house's main entrance, and which had so far simply been maintained in their natural uncouth state.

'At eight o'clock my master stood in the hall to receive his guests, and the first carriage rolled up to the house. Its occupants – who happened, by good luck, to be the Bishop of Exeter and his lady – descended. Six footmen – or rather men hired from the neighbouring farms for the purpose – stood with flaming *flambeaux*, and full in the pool of their light could be seen, one at each side of the steps leading up to the house, two enormous cocks, each supported by a pair of cods in proportion.

'On setting eyes on these, the Bishop's wife fainted clean away and had to be revived with *sal volatile* before insisting that they return immediately, though at great inconvenience, to the Bishop's Palace, whence an interdiction went out to the entire see: Mr Oswald Manship was beyond the pale.

'If this lady's was the most extreme reaction to my handiwork, everyone attending the occasion was affected by it. Many were shocked, some declining to enter the house of a man who could greet them in such a way. The Lord Lieutenant and his wife, high Tories to whom Mr Manship looked for support in the forthcoming election for which he was to be a candidate, came into the house, but were extremely distant, and after making the slightest possible gesture of politeness, left again.

'A few – particularly those young sparks who felt perhaps that the county needed enlivening – nudged each other with ill-disguised delight, and surprised Mr Oswald with comments which he failed to understand, himself knowing nothing of the matter. On the party thinning out far earlier than he expected, and the Lord Lieutenant making his excuses, he accompanied the latter to the front door when he was confronted for the first time by the twin sets of cock and balls. Though not the sort of man normally to be at a loss for words, he could find nothing to say, and his choleric splutterings did him no good – even with those guests who were left, and to whom he attempted to excuse himself.

'Meanwhile, below stairs, I had been spreading among the visiting coachmen and other servants the true state of affairs; so that even among those young men who shared his own attitude, regarding servant maids as proper targets for their libidinous activities, he was made a laughing-stock – and the tale went forth to the whole county. There may no doubt have been a few men of Mr Oswald's own class who felt no natural repugnance at the notion of a master so insulting his own servant; but for the most part the county joined both in scorning him and laughing at the manner of my revenge.

'I was of course prepared for my master's wrath, and before the end of the evening in question Lillian and I had left the house together. I had feared we might have some difficulty in finding a new position – but fortunately within a few days the news of my revenge had reached the ears of the Hon. John Pothkitt of Ellerslie in Somerset, who was in need of someone to renovate his extensive gardens, and being amused by my impertinence and also cognizant (through having visited the gardens at Wordsley while passing through Plymouth earlier that year) of my talents, engaged me, welcoming Lillian as my wife (which she became at the Church of St Hilarion, Exeter, three days after we left Wordsley, thus regularizing those nightly pleasures which we continued to enjoy).

'I cannot say that in retrospect, and despite his insulting behaviour, either of us feels much more than scorn for Mr Oswald Manship. His attack on Lillian certainly merited disapproval; but he had unwittingly introduced us to the full pleasure of matrimony, which we found constantly inspiriting – while but for the revenge which I took on him, I would probably still be a gardener at Wordsley rather than the celebrated designer of gardens and estates who you see before you, with a wife in a small but pleasant household of four daughters awaiting, in Devon, my return from a visit to my Lord Brolling in Northamptonshire, before whom I am to lay the plans for the renewal of his gardens.'

With those words, Mr Shore concluded his narrative, having held and delighted us all, and left me wondering whether it was the case that every man and woman in England, could one but imprison them all under such circumstances as we were caught, might be able to produce such ingenious and enjoyable stories as we were enjoying!

9

The Actress's Tale

The evening of the third day belonged to the most handsome of the women of the southern-bound coach, and after we had enjoyed to the full a magnificent repast prepared (as she had promised) by Mrs Allbig, we once more gathered in the chief room of the George, in order to attend to the narrator. It was no great surprise when she announced herself as Davina Dance, an actress – returning from Edinburgh to take up an offer from the manager of the theatre in Drury Lane to play the part of Gertrude in Shakespeare's tragedy of *Hamlet* – a part for which she was suited by her age, though still extremely handsome, and once without doubt a woman of great appeal (which she was still, though somewhat stricken in years).

'You know,' she began 'that the theatre has a reputation for lasciviousness: and indeed, it is often deserved – not only through the presence in the profession of men and women whose morals are not those of polite society (being expressed in a freedom of action only otherwise seen in the houses of the aristocracy) but through the necessity of performing in costumes which must frequently represent another age, when it was fashionable to show rather more of the female body than is now the case. This is the reason why in some quarters the profession is deprecated: the great Dr Johnson was one who did so – though as in many other cases it is fair to infer that it was his own emotions which disturbed him, for it will be remembered that his reason for declining to accompany his friend Hume behind the scenes was that the silk stockings of the actresses disturbed his amorous propensities.

'On my first going upon the stage, at a much more tender age than you now see me, I was under the protection of Miss Lydia Kelly the celebrated Irish actress, whose fine stage figure and expressive countenance together with great animal spirits made her extremely popular with the people of Portsmouth, which was the town near which I grew up, and in which stood the theatre where, when I was fifteen, I first stepped upon the boards in the part of Perdita, having been heard by Miss Kelly reciting one of the poems of Lord Byron at a *soirée* held by my mother.

'Miss Kelly was a frequent attender of such polite occasions, it being the policy of the theatre that its players should where possible move in the best society. A great favourite with the ladies of the town, for instance, was Mr John Baldwin Buckstone, the company's leading actor, who had embraced the profession at the age of nineteen at a theatre at Wokingham in Berkshire, where his services were required at half-an-hour's notice owing to the absence of the comedian of a travelling company who had been going to play the part of Gabriel in *Children of the Wood*. On my joining the company at Portsmouth, I found him popular with all audiences – not least with the Naval officers of the town, for having been originally destined for the Navy, he knew how to amuse them.

'Miss Kelly was perhaps twenty and two and Mr Buckstone of about the same age, and a fine pair they made – often appearing together: his Tony Lumpkin to her Miss Hardcastle, his Orlando to her Rosalind, his Captain Absolute to her Lydia. I admired them as much as any of their audience, and treated them with the utmost respect, being delighted to have the honour of appearing on the boards with them.

'Soon after my arrival, I made a curious observation of their distinctive method of preparing for a role. The occasion was their appearing as Romeo and Juliet. I should explain that Mr Buckstone admired, and to distraction, the work of that greatest actor of our time, Edmund Kean – and from him had gleaned the notion that a theatrical performance must be entirely informed by passion, which in Kean's case too frequently meant the use of whores summoned from the streets of Covent Garden, with whom he would perform the act of love even in intervals between the scenes – and certainly between the acts – of plays in which the utmost of his energy was required.

'Mr Buckstone concurred that in plays of passion it was especially the case that the stage lovers must experience a mutual closeness of emotion; and so it was that on arriving at the theatre to prepare for my minor role of Peter, servant to Juliet's Nurse, I entered the single dressing room which was all the mean building could afford, to find that half of it which was set aside for the ladies was completely deserted. However, as I set about changing into my man's breeches, there came from the men's quarters (behind a tall screen which divided the room) noises which betrayed a presence of some sort – but, I thought, scarcely human, for they consisted of grunts and panting breaths, little screams and throaty babblings, which almost frightened me.

'However, the mystery was soon resolved, for in an excess of emotion one of the noise-makers kicked out and threw down the screen, when Mr Buckstone and Miss Kelly were revealed, having removed their everyday clothes but not yet assumed their costumes. Being both unclad, it was somewhat puzzling to an innocent young girl that they should be in such close proximity – indeed, that she should be sitting upon his knee – and not side-saddle, as I had often occupied the lap of my uncles, but astride and facing her companion, seeming positively to embrace him with her legs!

'On seeing me, he reddened; but my friend, who seemed strangely moved, cried out: "Oh, 'tis only Davvy – plough on, Lothario!" and began to jump up and down on Mr Buckstone's knee with a violent motion which I believed hurt him severely, for he began to cry out, his cries mounting until, joining with her mewings (which had recommenced), they reached a climax, at which Lydia for a moment remained still, and then turning to me invited me to fetch her her make-up box; and on my doing so, climbed from her seat and enabled Mr Buckstone to turn away – this act of politeness depriving me of the sight of his organ, which would certainly have disturbed me, who was properly ignorant of the appearance of that masculine appendage even in its relaxed state, and much less when raised to action.

'The modesty of Lydia's behaviour only extended so far however, for slapping Mr Buckstone upon his naked posterior, she cried: "There's a lovely arse for you, Davvy! Never trust a man with a big arse – he'll always prove to have a small heart!" – a theory which, as a matter of fact I have found to be false, for a number of gentlemen I have known whose posteriors were of generous proportions have proved to be equally generous in their emotions.

'But I must not be diverted from the course of my narrative.

'Mr Buckstone and Miss Kelly having clothed themselves we went upon the stage and performed the play with all the vigour possible, the chief actor and actress addressing themselves to the scene in Juliet's bedroom with an enthusiasm which seemed remarkable considering the extent to which their emotions seemed to have been drained by the *scena* of which I had been a witness. I took care in future not to attend at the dressing room more than ten minutes before a performance, for despite my innocence I somehow felt that such scenes as that which I had previously interrupted should be enjoyed in private – little thought John and Lydia showed any sign of it, their every meeting off-stage being accompanied by some lascivious gesture or other. Mr Buckstone was perhaps the leader in this, for though capable of great nobility upon the boards he was in his everyday life extremely waggish, a *double entendre* lurking in each eye, and with a smirk which was a strong hint of an unclean presence.

'The amorous behaviour of this couple was not restricted to the dressing and green rooms; where it was possible, it extended even onto the stage, any scene containing a be-

rousing them to particularly ardent embraces. *Romeo and Juliet* ended, for example, with Miss Kelly lying upon Mr Buckstone in such an attitude that her middle parts and his were closely pressed together, with results that I did not at first comprehend, but later myself experienced, upon my standing up in the part of Juliet, on Miss Kelly's indisposition.

'I came to understand the situation more clearly on myself becoming a woman, my maidenhead being taken by a lieutenant of Marines upon the dock at Southampton when I was bidding him farewell on his ship sailing for the Mediterranean. Though rough enough, our bed being merely a heap of sacking at the back of a timber pile, the experience if a little painful was still sufficiently enjoyable to enable me to understand Miss Kelly's devotion to the act, and I could fill out the rest of this evening by recounting some of the adventures I experienced as a result of my introduction to the pleasures of amorous conversation between the sexes; but I think that a more amusing narrative follows the adventures of the couple to whom I have now introduced you.

'It will not perhaps surprise you to learn that much of the energy of many members of the theatrical profession – those at all events who know themselves not to be so far masters and mistresses of their art as to be confident of commanding a fine position and a matching income – is spent in seeking for a patron, and preferably a patron to whom it will be possible to link themselves for life. The number of actresses who have allied themselves to members of the aristocracy is legion, Miss Nell Gwynn being only one of the earliest.

'My friend Miss Kelly approached this task by what is termed in naval strategy "scattering her shot". Her reason was not only that in attempting to seduce the many she hoped to secure the one, but that quite apart from the chief aim of the operation, she had an appetite for amorous dalliance far beyond the normal. Many, perhaps even the majority, of men are most happy when they are swiving; few women share the taste to an excessive degree – but Lydia was certainly one of the most prominent of that band, and when – having myself discovered a moderate taste for the activity – I raised the matter with her, she readily agreed that she considered the emotion experienced in the arms of a fine lover to be such as in her experience had few rivals. Her enthusiasm was such that she (in vulgar parlance) "put herself about" with an absence of reserve that was positively startling, the only bar to a place in her bed (or upon whatever convenient structure offered a comfortable reclining place) being either total lack of means or extreme physical ugliness – even these disqualifications being ignored should the applicant possess a sufficiently vigorous talent for amorous play.

'Mr Buckstone was somewhat more discriminating; reserving his passages of love with Lydia to those occasions when the resulting stimulus would (as he believed) improve his theatrical performance, he otherwise set his cap resolutely and singlemindedly at heiresses – the term being used to describe any woman, young or old, whose income was (or would be upon marriage or the death of a member of her family) a thousand pound a year or more – for, he said, a smaller income would scarcely be worth leaving the boards for.

'During the first two months of my association with the company, he had been through a Miss Gifford (the daughter of a Portsmouth draper), a Miss Sykes (the widow of a prominent local lawyer) and a Miss Geddes, the sole child of an importer of fine china. Exercising his by no means insignificant charms, he contrived to seduce them all: Miss Gifford by making use of the supposed glamour of his profession, taking her triumphantly to bed after a splendid and affecting performance of Etherege's *The Comical Revenge*. But he found he must resign her to the superior claims of a rival draper's son – which he did without repining on the discovery that she would on her father's demise receive only a beggarly £750 a year and a cottage in Lyme.

'Miss Sykes was wooed in Buckstone's character as a man of sensitivity, an artist, a student of literature and the drama;

but while he was surprised (so he told Lydia) to discover in the widow an appetite for carnality which almost wore him out, he passed her over on her insistence on drawing up a marriage bond which would have made him entirely dependent upon her for every farthing he might desire to spend.

'Miss Geddes was after a long and arduous campaign persuaded to a late supper; but on Buckstone's falling upon his knees and announcing a strong disposition to death were she to refuse him her bed, she broke out into a fit of hysterics; he tried to comfort her, but undoing her dress in order to fan her, merely succeeded in provoking a second fit of the vapours – and on her recovery, she hastened from the inn in which the assignation had been made. And, next day, he received threat from her father of prosecution for a criminal connection.

'Buckstone's agility in escaping prosecution – and indeed in escaping the arms of those ladies who proved for pecuniary reasons to be unworthy of his attentions – was a source of wonder both to me and to Lydia. She feared the worst (she told me) when he began to pay resolute attention to Amelia Ormidale. This lady was the daughter of Admiral Sir Macfarlane Ormidale, and had travelled to Portsmouth to wave her father off on his departure for the antipodes in command of a ship bearing the new Governor of the settlement in Melbourne, Australia.

'Sir Macfarlane was an almost excessively rich widower devoid of any family other than Miss Ormidale, who was therefore considerably in demand in society, the *longueurs* of which many a young man was happy to endure for the sake of the fortune which would one day be hers. A fortune, indeed, she already had, for she had no difficulty in extracting from her adoring father any amount of money for which she expressed a wish.

'Much whispering was consequent upon her arrival in a box at the theatre when we were giving Aaron Hill's *Merope*, with Lydia in the title role and Buckstone appearing in the dramatic role of Polyphontes, General of Mycenae, which allowed scope for his splendid voice and noble mien. It also allowed him the opportunity to appear in the toga, and was keenly anticipated by his lady admirers as affording (through his own contrivance) opportunities to display his not unhandsome body, through wearing the robe over one shoulder, his bosom largely bare; and permitting a glimpse of leg and even of upper thigh, on his taking up an attitude with one foot planted upon a box especially placed for the purpose.

'On peering between the curtains and descrying Miss Ormidale in a stage box, he professed himself hopeful of making a conquest.

' "She has a keen and apprehensive eye," he told me (who was at his side) "and, I have no doubt, an appetite which I can sharpen."

'I was in no doubt as to the nature of the appetite he mentioned, and enquired how he could know it from a single glance.

' "Why," he said, " 'tis an instinct – a handsome woman ready for the game gives out a sort of . . . almost an aroma, a glow, which is unmistakable" – and at that point the orchestra giving the cue for the beginning of the play, made for the side of the stage while the curtain rose showing Lydia, in a becoming *déshabillé*, lying all mournful on a couch. Mr Buckstone, who could not leave the proximity of the stage (for his cue came shortly) to my astonishment reached beneath his toga and removed those short breeches which, for decency's sake, were normally worn in such period pieces.

'Catching my surprised glance, he winked.

' "Fotherington's not in tonight," he said (referring to our manager), "so I'll give the lady a glimpse of my quality!"

'The box occupied by Miss Ormidale was upon the extreme right of the stage – indeed, almost upon the platform itself – and to say that Mr Buckstone played his entire role to her alone, excluding the rest of the audience from his consideration, is to tell no more than the truth. He even contrived by moving close downstage to prevent any other member of the cast from a place between him and the object of his enthusiasm. I was not aware of the true reason for this until I found myself perforce in that position – from which he could not prevent me, through the construction of the scene; on his turning towards me and addressing himself once more to the lady (who stood behind me) I was astonished to see him hitch up his toga idly in one hand, thus exposing to her (and incidentally myself) an organ whose present dimensions made amply clear the nature of his admiration.

'My jaw, I believe, fell at the sight – to an extent that the rest of the players could not understand; however, on their questioning me, after the performance, I replied that I had been astonished by the command of emotion showed by Mr Buckstone in the scene; it was not my nature to interfere in what was not my business.

'A knock came upon the door of the dressing room after the performance, and a flunkey entered with a note for Mr Buckstone. Insisting on delivering it personally, he passed through the room in which we women were changing our clothes – without, I must say, repining at the sight, but indeed rather coming right up to Lydia, whose upper body was at the time completely unclothed, and asking her where the actor was to be found. On her directing him to the other end of the room, he proved unable to wrench his eyes from her bosom and knocked over a chair and a small occasional table before passing behind the screen, where he gave the note to Buckstone, who having perused it, enthusiastically accepted the invitation it conveyed.

'My information as to the nature of his engagement came, subsequently, from Mr Buckstone himself – so as to its truth I can guarantee nothing; however, he was not an habitual liar, nor does the tale set him in a particularly advantageous light, so I am confident of its probity. It appears that he was commanded to supper at the Rose Inn, where Sir Macfarlane had taken a suite which his daughter was continuing to occupy while she remained in town. There, he was shown into a room where he found a table decently set with cold chicken and pies, and several bottles of good French wine. After a few moments, a connecting door opened, and in walks Miss Ormidale, clad in a gown sufficiently loose to display her person almost to the extent to which Mr Buckstone's toga had previously displayed his.

'The sight was neither (Mr Buckstone said) unpleasant nor discouraging. He rose to his feet and taking the lady's hand bowed and pressed a kiss upon it; she returning the compliment with a curtsy which revealed, at its perigee, most of her upper body – which carried, he said, a pair of breasts of that monumental nature frequently to be exhibited upon the torsos of ships' figure-heads.

'He could not but fix his eyes for a moment upon these twin hills, when smiling she said: "You have been, sir, so free in displaying your single manly attribute that I should remind you of the extent to which the female sex is endowed with other attractions perhaps as amusing to the opposite sex, if not of the same utilitarian character."

'He bowed silently, his wit for once deserting him in the face of so forthright a statement.

'They dined well, the conversation being chiefly upon the play and players, for Miss Ormidale was, when in town, an assiduous visitor to the theatres, and had seen most of the performances of the season both at drama and opera – Mrs Wood in Rosina, Mrs Bradshaw in Ophelia, Mr Mathews in Rattleton and Hawk, Mr Kean in Olivia and Mr Phelps in Sir Pertinax Macsycophant.

'However, finally, emptying her glass and pushing back her chair, the lady exclaimed:

' "Enough of this tattle; you did not come here for such gossip – nor did I invite you simply to extend my knowledge of the play. You were eager to show the minor character who accompanied you upon the stage tonight – now is the time to see whether he is capable of a major role!" – and rising to her feet she led the way into the neighbouring bedroom, where she threw herself upon the bed in an indiscriminately lascivious posture while Buckstone, now entirely cognizant of what was expected of him, stripped off his clothes.

' "You know, Davvy," he said, "I am ever ready for a bout but the lady's outright invitation had come so suddenly that I must remove my breeches to reveal myself entirely loblolly."

'I looked my question.

' "Unprepared for congress," he explained; "through my instrument being limpsy, flaccid, soft, quaggy, unfirm, unfit, slack, lax, unstiff, marrowless, sinewless, pithless . . ."

'I indicated that I took his meaning.

'The lady looked scornfully at him – which did not improve the situation. He knelt upon the bed, in hopes (he said) that she might by some sensual attention or another raise his spirits; but she simply remained supine, a sardonic smile upon her lips.

'He stretched out his hand to place it upon that part of her person which, were it to prove receptive, might instill the spirit of concupiscence; but she dashed it aside.

' "Really, sir," she said; "can you expect to handle the goods without the means to pay for them?" – and with an even more disparaging gesture, smacked out with the back of her hand at his pendulous prick, which in response shrank to even smaller dimensions.

'Mr Buckstone realized (he said) that the evening was past rescue; turned, picked up his clothes and left the room. Immediately he was outside, the apprehension of the scene which had just been inflicted upon him had, ironically, its effect upon his spirits, and he began to rise at it. But by now he was too angry at his treatment to give her the pleasure she had anticipated. Instead, lubricating the palm of his hand with some butter which remained upon the table, he worked his cock to a firm, proud stand, then strode through the door and up to the foot of the bed.

' "Thank you, ma'am, for your entertainment," he said. "I regret that your person proved insufficiently stimulating to provoke me to such a state that I could fulfil your desires.

Since they are not so heated that you are willing to encourage me, but prefer disparagement, I must seek my comfort elsewhere."

'Then (he said) I sought out Lydia and fucked her silly until four in the morning.

'Mr Buckstone's sad experience I fear somewhat amused me; as did my observation of Lydia Kelly's equally enthusiastic efforts to seek out a rich lover. As had Mr Buckstone, she suffered some disappointments; her too forward inclination to leap upon any likely candidate resulted in her scaring off first the younger son of the Member of Parliament for Portsmouth, who was so shaken by her attacking him at an evening party that he left the town next day for a prolonged visit to an aunt in Bridport – while the Rev. the Rt Hon. Jeremiah Clippin, curate of St Margaret-without, and the only son of the Earl of Havant, and thus heir to his title and fortune, was surprised when she arrived for Evensong at his church clad in the costume devised for the seductress Perpetua from Fotheringay's *The Temptress of Orléans*, consisting of a great deal of scarlet and black silk, and a quantity of lace somewhat insufficient to conceal that splendid bosom of which I have already spoken. Throwing away his notes for a sermon upon the loaves and fishes, he preached vehemently on the text "Let not sin reign in your bodies" (Romans, VI, 12) and became so impassioned that he had to be helped from the pulpit by a verger and revived in the vestry by a glass of the excellent claret which he provided from his own cellar for the communion table.

'Just after Mr Buckstone's little *contretemps* with Miss Ormidale, Lydia drew me to the curtain with great enthusiasm and pointed out a young fellow seated in the very same box which had been occupied by that lady. He was a handsome, slim youngster, with no special mark of distinction about him, and dressed with restraint – though in clothes of obvious merit.

' "That," says she, "is none other than Roger Fitzwilliam!"

'My answer, I fear, was a simple "Well?" for to tell the truth I had never heard of the man, who proved to be (as Lydia explained) the immensely rich only child of a man who had made a fortune through the provision of running water to the citizens of Leeds; he had recently been sued for breach of promise by a well-known lady of fashion in London, and his likeness had been published in many of the papers, which explained Lydia's recognizing him.

' "I shall not make the mistake of a frontal attack," she said; "I shall be more discreet than you could believe possible."

'However, her good intentions did not preclude her from making a show which might catch the eye of that particular onlooker; for if she was not noticed immediately, the task of taking his eye might prove difficult – for who was to say that he would necessarily visit the theatre again?

'Happily, that evening we were playing Marlowe's *Dr Faustus*, in which Lydia played the wordless role of Helen of Troy, which involved her merely walking across the stage (dimmed to a gloom in which she was scarcely visible) in order to astound Mr Buckstone (as Faustus) with her beauty. To escape the condemnation of the more prudish members of the audience, and possibly the attentions of the local magistracy, she usually wore a tight-fitting costume which merely gave the impression of nudity; on this occasion however – not especially to my surprise, I must confess – she eschewed this covering as blurring the clean lines of her body, and Mr Buckstone, exclaiming (in his character)

> "Was this the face that launched a thousand ships
> And burnt the topless towers of Ilium?" –

and then stepping forward to embrace her, was astonished to discover her condition, and pronouncing the next line with considerably greater enthusiasm and ardour than usual –

> "Sweet Helen, make me immortal with a kiss!" –

threw his arms about her and with his lips upon hers could not restrain himself from taking a liberty which he would normally have taken only in the privacy of the dressing room – that is, placing both hands upon her bottom and pressing their middle parts vehemently together.

'Lydia's unclothed state may not have been obvious to the entire theatre, so dim was the light; but Mr Fitzwilliam, a mere five or six feet away, could scarcely have failed to be aware of it. However, Lydia was careful to display only her back and a fleeting front view as she left the stage (having prised herself from Mr Buckstone's embrace), hoping that this would whet the gentleman's appetite.

'She waited in vain, after the performance for a message from him. However, he returned on the following night, when she played Beatrice to Mr Buckstone's Benedict in *Much Ado About Nothing*, and though she had no excuse for exhibiting herself unclothed, she took care to impress the admired gentleman with her charms of personality, which were not inconsiderable – and evidently succeeded, for this time a message was delivered – but inviting her *and* Mr Buckstone to supper.

' "He is clearly of a nervous disposition," she said, "and wishes to employ a chaperone!"

'I was not present at the supper, but according to Lydia it went exceptionally well; Mr Fitzwilliam proved a charming companion and a generous one, attentive to both his guests but – she said – in particular to her, though despite her hints he showed no inclination to invite her to remain with him, or to return after she and her fellow actor had bid him goodnight.

' "He is," she said, "certainly uncommonly careful; but it may be that his recent trouble has taught him this. I am confident of a success, dear Davvy, and you shall be our first guest at Fitzwilliam Hall on our return from honeymoon, which I am determined to take on the continent of Europe, having always wished to see the sights it offers."

'On the following week she dined thrice with Fitzwilliam – always accompanied by Buckstone; but after the last occasion came to me in great excitement, for Fitzwilliam had asked – with a meaningful shake of the head – whether they were both free on the following, Saturday, evening. Taking the hint, she apologized for being unavailable; and tactfully, Buckstone had said nothing.

'I cannot say that Lydia paid much attention to the role of Cordelia in *King Lear*, which she played opposite Harmonthwaite Titherley, an ancient principal with the company and celebrated for the role; the piece was not improved by her mind being on the seduction scene she intended to play later at Mr Fitzwilliam's room at the Bull; and indeed she entirely forgot her cue in the last scene, and I had to be carried on to represent Cordelia dead, since my friend was in the dressing room titivating herself.

'Her account of the subsequent events was terse and ill-tempered. She arrived at the Bull; sneaked upstairs avoiding the eyes of the servants; found the door of Fitzwilliam's rooms undone; opened it and went in; crossed to the bedroom door; opened it; and saw before her her supposed lover – in the embrace of another! Not only that, but Mr Fitzwilliam was seated upon his lover's body in just that posture which would normally have been expected of the lady. She then saw to her chagrin that the body stretched beneath that of Mr Fitzwilliam was in fact that of – Mr Buckstone. I expressed a sort of ignorant surprise at the news, and Lydia was forced to explain to me that the posture in which the two gentlemen had been discovered was one of a repertoire employed by a male couple when one wished to . . . but I am sure I need not go on, for the present company will be more cognizant of the behaviour of buggers than I was at the tender age of seventeen.

' "Well, I beg your pardon, Lydia," said Mr Buckstone next evening, as they prepared for their *Romeo and Juliet*, which seemed likely to me to be less romantic than usual. "But you know all's fair in love and war."

'Lydia expressed herself as surprised to find Mr Buckstone a Miss Molly.

'Not entirely so, said Mr Buckstone, as she of all persons

must be aware; but he did not find the connexion entirely repugnant, Mr Fitzwilliam was a pleasant companion, and after all, he had a fortune of at least five thousand a year.

'Having no iota of jealousy in her nature, Lydia – despite her disappointment – congratulated her rival on his success – and even dined with the couple before they departed for Mr Fitzwilliam's London home; which I commend to everyone as the sensible attitude, life being too short to repine at another's success – even should it have been achieved in so unexpected a manner.'

One or two of the company appeared somewhat shocked at this liberal attitude; but in general, the actress's story was approved both as amusing and moral, and we took ourselves to bed in a thoughtful and contented mood. Thus ended the third day of our incarceration.

10

The Astrologer's Tale

The story-teller's lot on the morning of the Boxing Day fell first upon the somewhat curious figure of one of the outside passengers of our own coach – that apparently elderly man who upon closer acquaintance was not as old as he appeared: or so I was informed by Sophie, who had been standing that morning looking out of an upstairs gallery window upon the snowstorm outside, and had been greeted by him on his appearance from a nearby room.

Upon her remarking on the longevity of the hard weather, he made the observation that it would lift on that very day, when (he observed) Saturn with the Luminaries, Jupiter with Mercury, and Mars with Venus would make an *apertio portarum* or 'opening of the gates', and the weather would change. This sufficiently interesting statement was accompanied (she could not but notice) by the light but appreciative laying of a hand upon her buttocks; and on taking the opportunity to study the gentleman's visage she was clear by the glint in his eyes that his vitality was greater than might be expected in an old man, and that he appeared much older than his years, which might be as few as thirty or so, the greyness and fullness of his beard helping to disguise his relative youth. As she made her way down the stairs to breakfast she could not but observe the door of his room open once more, and one of the maids of the hotel make her exit in a state more crumpled than could be explained by any domestic activity in the way of bed-making or water-bearing.

When we had all broken our fast, our friend announced

himself as none other than Tarantabobus of the celebrated journal *The Straggling Astrologer* (sixteen pages for four pence), of the success of which even I, who have no special interest in that science, am aware; certainly Sophie was, who confessed to have consulted this same Tarantabobus some years ago, when she herself was dabbling in the art (as the result of her first marriage, the sad story of which is related in the first volume of our joint memoirs, sent into the world by a reputable firm of publishers domiciled in Gt Titchfield Street in London).

Might we know his true identity? enquired Sophie – upon which he named himself as plain Robert Cross Smith, born (he said) in Bristol, the only son of a moderately wealthy merchant of that city. He continued:

'My father raised me with the aid of servants, for my mother had died when I was very young. I was encouraged to study nothing in particular except mathematics – for it was expected that I would follow in my father's way. As it happened, I proved to be adept in numbers, and indeed had some interest in their mystery – but none at all in trade – though I was interested in everything else, and became an omnivorous reader, devouring every volume which fell into my hands. It was at the age of fifteen, when I had ceased my schooling and been set to work in my father's office of accounts, doing my best to escape from such drudgery whenever I could through the alchemy of books, that there fell into my hands a work entitled *The Astrologer's Magazine*, edited by one Ebenezer Sibly. This in turn led me on to that gentleman's *The Complete Illustration of the Celestial Art of Astrology*, a work of well over one thousand pages, which revealed to me the mathematical and philosophical basis of the great art which I immediately formed the ambition to study.

'That ability in mathematics which had been somewhat thrust upon me now proved useful, for I found it easy to calculate horoscopes, and discovered the ease with which the uttermost secrets of personality could be discovered by an examination of the positions of the planets and their relationship with each other in such aspects as the square, the trine, the opposition, the sesquiquadrate.

'Nothing would now suit me but that I should study the subject, which could only be done in London – for although there were quacks and pretenders in Bristol, none of them were of account. Though it seemed hardly worthwhile to put this proposition to my father, whose hardheaded disposition was opposed to any speculative activity, I at last mentioned my ambition to him – but indeed found him, as I expected, adamantly opposed to it. So, rising early one morning, I stole from his house together with the sum of fifty pounds which I lifted from his desk – not repining at the theft, which was only a tiny amount of that portion which would properly accrue to me upon his death.

'Once in London, I made myself the pupil of Mr G. W. Graham, in Upper Thames Street, a man whose chief interests in life were two: astrology, and the use of balloons for ascending into the air. He taught me all he knew of the former subject (I resisted his offers to instruct me in the latter) – and by the time I was eighteen had set myself up in Grub Street, and placing a notice in *The Straggling Astrologer* soon attracted a number of clients – perhaps due to the not altogether accurate nature of my notice, which claimed that I had been "honoured with some astrological MSS appertaining to the lot of individuals of the highest rank by Her Royal Highness the Princess of Cumberland, who has, we are persuaded, been most unjustly persecuted." The "princess" was a Mrs Olivia Serres, who claimed to be the legitimate daughter of the Duke of Cumberland, brother of King George II. Coming one day to consult Mr Graham, and his being absent on one of his ascents into the upper atmosphere, she found me alone, and as I now believed (but then was too innocent to notice) took a fancy to me, and told me some tall stories which I committed to paper. It was believed by the public that she had many secrets to convey – and my announcement that I was in possession of some of them brought the credulous to my door, where, though they found the secrets largely without interest, they found my advice and prognostications sufficiently useful to detain them, and to milk from them certain contributions to my purse.

'I was soon making an income commensurate with a decent style of life, and dealing with a number of clients every day. However, the troubles which they brought me were largely very dull: as, Where has my cat gone? – Whether I shall find my true love? – Whether I am poxed or no? The principle that all work and no play makes Jack a dull boy was proved in me, for I soon felt that my life was wasting away.

'I now know that it was not so much the absence of variation in the work I undertook that lowered my spirits, but the fact that first through continual study, and now continual work, I had been deprived of that female company which under usual circumstance occupies much of the time and energy of young men of my age. I had, of course, been moved by the disturbing and inarticulate longings of my puberty; but since father had never spoken to me of *amor*, I had no experience of it, and Mrs Hand and her five daughters had been my only companions in bed, and my imagination having little to fire it, the simple ecstasy conveyed by manual means – though pleasant enough – seemed a simple form of enjoyment, being without variation, devoid of any interest other than that of attaining the momentary ecstasy which for a time subdued my physical itch.

'Gradually, however, I found myself becoming increasingly interested in members of the opposite sex: and simply in order to inform myself consulted a bookseller behind St Paul's, who provided me with that admirable work Mr Cleland's *Memoirs of a Woman of Pleasure*, John Ashem's *How to Raise Love*, and a sheaf of coarse illustrations originating in Paris which, while aesthetically negligible, provided me at least with diagrammatic explanation of the nature of *coitus*. This, from the drawings, seemed at first to be a comic acrobatic sort of activity; but on giving the matter some thought, I found the prospect of placing my prick in juxtaposition with that part of a woman so far entirely unknown to me, definitely if obscurely exciting; and that fixing my mind on the attitudes illustrated brought a new zest to my masturbatory fantasies, and thence a keener pleasure.

'It was now my ambition to test new-found knowledge, and to that end I walked forth in Covent Garden in search of an agreeable companion. But the women I found there did not inspire me, being either old and blowsy or young but dirty. I would have been willing to spend a considerable sum to achieve my aim; but was ignorant of how to go about finding any of the upper class of whores. On my repairing once more to my bookseller, and with some hesitation explaining my problem, he retired to his back room and emerged with a copy of *Harris's List of Covent Garden Ladies*: on examination of which I believed my problem was solved.

'That admirable book listed a large number of females practising the art of prostitution in London: indeed, for amusement, I have kept the copy about me ever since, and perhaps it might interest my auditors.'

Mr Smith produced a well-thumbed book from his pocket, and read us a couple of entries:

' "Miss B—nf—ld, No. 9, Portland Street.

' "Miss B is about nineteen years old, tall, genteel, and very handsome, being quite fair, with blue eyes, light red hair, and fine regular teeth. She is a very agreeable companion upon all occasions, and approves herself in bed a *devotee* to Venus, who has well studied the mysteries of that Goddess. She is frequently mounted *à la militaire*, and as frequently performs the rites of the love-inspiring queen according to the *equestrian* order, in which style she is said to afford uncommon delight, being perfect in her paces, having studied under a professed riding-master who has taught her the *ménage* in the highest perfection. For these lessons, which she daily and nightly gives, she expects two or three guineas at least."

'She should have them, I thought,' said Mr Smith. 'Then there was Miss J—nson, at the Dog and Duck, Willow Walk.

' "This pretty filly is of middling size, near twenty. Norfolk gave her her birth. Her countenance is rather pleasant, with fine black eyes that are very attractive, good teeth, and a fine skin, and of so amorous a constitution that in the arms of an equally lewd partner she never wishes to fall into the arms of sleep; the *dairy hills* of delight are beautifully prominent, firm and elastic, the *sable coloured grot* below with its coral-lipped *janitor* is just adapted to the sons of Venus. She is a really delicious piece, and her *terra incognita* is so very agreeable to every traveller therein that it hath ceased to deserve that name, and is become a well known and much frequented country; freely taking in the stranger, raising up them that *fall*, making the *crooked straight*, and although she does not pretend to restore sight to the blind, she'll place him in such a direction that he cannot mistake the way; and for one guinea will engage he returns the same way back without any direction at all. She is the only girl that frequents the Dog and Duck worth mentioning; her price is from five shillings to half a guinea."

'It seemed to me that Miss J--nson was just precisely the mistress I required: and I took myself off instantly to the Dog and Duck, a public inn full of gentlemen drinking with some vehemence. Of only a few women present, one was sitting alone in a corner, and though she looked a respectable person, she was not entirely dissimilar from the description given, so, after taking a glass of brandy for courage, I approached her and asked whether she was not Miss J—nson, and would accept half a guinea for an hour's play.

'She immediately jumped to her feet and let loose a stream of vituperation, accusing me of insulting her; upon which uproar a large man joined her, having it seems been buying drink at the bar, and on his asking what was the matter was informed that I had accused his friend of being "that notorious ladybird, Prossy Johnson"; on which he gave a roar, and in a moment I found myself lying upon the pavement with a split in my lip.

'This somewhat dampened my amorous ambitions; however next evening, having convinced myself that the first unfortunate business had been an accident, I took myself off to Poland Street. The door of number nine was scarred and ill-painted and the knocker a mere nugget of iron attached to a nail by means of a piece of wire. I gave a good bang with it, however, and in a while heard footsteps along the hallway, when the door opened a half inch. I announced (taking an attitude which I trusted would be inoffensive should another mistake have been made) that I had come to enquire about a riding lesson.

'There was a moment's pause, when the door was swung open and a husky voice invited me to enter. I did so, and the door was closed behind me; then on turning, found the light of a candle shining upon the somewhat pockmarked face of someone who attempted to give the impression of youth, but was perhaps well over thirty. This did not entirely surprise me; but I was somewhat abashed to recognize that the person who now placed a hand welcomingly upon my shoulder, was of my own sex!

'That I made an excuse and left goes without saying – though I got away with some difficulty, the Molly concerned being enthusiastic in his welcome of someone he clearly believed to be a customer.

'On returning home, I was disposed to destroy my copy of the *List of Covent Garden Ladies*; but on taking a last look at it, discovered on inspection of the title page that the book had been published in 1783 – which meant that any of the young ladies advertised in it would by now be long past the age at which I would find them appetizing – and was certainly an explanation of the fact that the names and addresses given no longer applied.

'It was clear that I must turn my attention to some other way of finding female company: and a possible resolution of the problem occurred to me as I was searching through Lilly's *Christian Astrology*, that great textbook of the subject. I was looking for the indication of a possible answer to a query from a husband whose wife had deserted her, and came across the advice which Mr Lilly gives to those attempting to discover whether one person may be able to achieve marriage with another. I will not trouble you with the astrological significators – except to say for the interest of any of you who have some knowledge of the art that it concerns the Lord of the Ascendant or Moon and the Lord of the Seventh House.

'After a little examination of the great astrologer's work, I discovered a formula which I believed would assist me, and now only wanted time and good fortune in order to test it.

'The opportunity came sooner than I expected, when at ten o'clock one morning a knock came at my door and I found a young woman without – a Mrs Phillida Madden – who on being admitted wished to consult me as to the loss of her purse – whether it had been stolen or no, and whether it might be recovered.

'She was a very personable being, of little more than my own age, and though her dress was high at the neck, the swelling of her breast, the narrowness of her waist and the high carriage of her hips suggested an admirable figure.

'Ascertaining that she had little knowledge of astrology, I obtained from her not only those details which I needed in order to answer her query, but also the time and place of her own birth, then sent her away, making an appointment for her to return the following day at noon. On her leaving, I set about my charts, comparing her map to my own; and noted that according to Mr Lilly's receipt and my own theory, if I tried her on the following day I should be successful – the one problem being that the best time for my attempt would be at thirty-two minutes past four o'clock in the afternoon. I therefore sent a message by a boy I sometimes employed about my business, pleading the inconvenience of our previous appointment and asking that the time be changed to four fifteen (hoping that she would be punctual).

'She was. At precisely the time appointed, a knock came upon the door, and I admitted her. I had myself made some preparations: as, lugging my couch from the bedroom into my room of consultation, where I concealed it behind a screen; and as to my own person, washing most carefully and clothing myself in clean linen (which, it being summer, consisted solely of a shirt and breeches).

'I invited Mrs Madden to sit, pointing to a stool which I had placed with its back to the window of my room. She did this, when I straightway began to explain the nature of the planets' commentary upon her lost purse – which in my opinion was indeed merely mislaid, and would be found before the week was out, should she look in an easterly direction from where she last saw it, and in some low place. All this while I had through the window a clear view of the clock of St Duthac's church, and prolonged my explanation until I saw the hands approach the vital time.

'I must confess that my heart almost failed me: Mrs Madden, though from the brightness of her eyes a lady of some spirit, had addressed me politely and without any sign that she found me of interest except inasmuch as I could be of assistance to her. However, the planets are infallible in such matters. At thirty-one and a half minutes past the hour I made some excuse, rose and walked behind her; as the minute-hand of the clock came to the vertical position, I placed my hands upon her shoulders, and began softly to rub at the base of her neck with my thumbs, continuing as I did so to explain the basis of my advice about the recovery of her lost purse.

I half expected her to protest at the connection: but far from it – I felt the muscles of her neck first contract and then relax under the gentle pressure of my hands, and moving a little nearer, slipped them over her shoulders and on beneath the neck of her dress to the rise of her breasts, then to that position whence I felt at my fingertip the small protuberances of her nipples. As I touched each tip with a forefinger, I felt a shiver run through the woman's whole body; and had I not been confident in my prediction of the success of the moment would have been amazed at her response: reaching behind her she caught at my thighs and pulled me towards her, so that she could not but have felt at the lower part of her back the hard swelling of my prick, which – after some days of abstinence from self-abuse, was now over-ready for satisfaction.

'She made no objection to my unbuttoning of her dress, nor of my slipping it from her shoulders – and when by leaning further over her shoulder I plunged a hand into her lap, her immediate reaction was to part her thighs, when I was able manually to explore a cranny which though strange to me seemed so soft and welcoming that it now became impossible further to delay a more active conjunction.

'I was not slow to clamber from the clothes I wore – but by the time I had done so, she was as bare as I; and indeed on my thrusting down the screen which concealed my couch, proved so eager that she threw me down upon it and ignoring my protests (for my knowledge of the carnal act was restricted to the idea that it was the man who should mount the woman) clambered on top of me and straddling me with a pair of thighs whose strength belied their soft and tender appearance, lowered herself upon my eager rod and in a moment began to rise and fall at a positive canter.

'This was more than an untutored lad could be expected to bear for long at his first tumbling, and with a cry half of protest and half of delight I felt my very being erupting from my prick with a force which I half expected to lift the lady from me as a ball is lifted into the air by a jet of water! That she felt the force of it is unquestionable, for an angry look shot from her eyes; yet she was soon placated – for as is sometimes the case in the vigour of youth, my weapon remained in condition, failing by only an imperceptible (to her) degree to maintain its firmness; whereupon she continued her ride, no less than three times giving vent to an impassioned cry and leap as though lifting a horse over a jump. These motions I took merely as instances of vigorous enjoyment, for I was not at that time aware that it is in the nature of women to share the capacity for those moments of high pleasure which in men result in the eruption of the vital fluids, but in the fair sex merely signal the apogee of their delight.

'A second climax of my own finally did for my strength – but by then she was satisfied, and collapsed upon me, when positively stuck together by the mutual exhalation of joyous perspiration we lay for some time in a exhausted embrace.

'Climbing from the bed after a while, Mrs Madden expressed herself entirely satisfied with the consultation, paid my fee of five shillings without question, and left promising that she would recommend me to her friends – which she did on the grounds of her recovering her lost purse, with the enclosed coins, in just such a place as I had suggested.

'Following the instructions of Mr Lilly, somewhat adjusted through my own experience, resulted in my enjoying the favours of any of my women clients whose persons attracted me (which in my state of newly honed appetite, embraced almost all). Some returned for several additional consultations not always connected with astrology, for not to be immodest I must confess that I was no less handsome than the next lad, and was as quick to learn the intricacies of the art of pleasuring myself and my companion as I had been to learn the secrets of my other art. I had an appetite for shagging which speedily renewed itself: upon one occasion I enjoyed no less than four ladies in one day – though the last, I must confess, was of such remarkable beauty and eagerness that although already exhausted I could not bear to let the occasion pass. Happily, when I was slow to rise to her, she demonstrated an appetite for consuming the male member which she satisfied with such eager delight that she speedily contributed that additional stimulus which recovered me.

'The event to which I am leading by this preamble had its genesis upon my being consulted by Lord . . . well, I think I must even among friends disguise his name, for it will be well-known to many of you; so let me call him the Lord Mars. I recognized him immediately, for I had seen him at the play, most recently with Lady Venus, whom it was rumoured he was soon to marry. Her beauty is such that she by no means even now disgraces that title, while ten years ago her beauty shone even brighter. She was a prize to interest and excite the spirit of any man in the kingdom.

'My Lord came to me upon the recommendation of a friend who had for some years been the companion of his bed, but who was not of such rank as to expect to wed him; anticipating a continuation of their connection – for it was not to be supposed that so vigorous a man would restrict himself strictly to his wife's company – she had on hearing of the problem that perplexed him, advised him to consult me. (She had been for some time herself employing me on various matters, though our carnal connections had been relatively few, Lord Mars being a most demanding lover.)

'The gentleman came quickly to the point. Lady Venus, though all in body that a man could desire, would not fuck. He put the matter in so many words. A marriage having been proposed by their fathers, both had happily accepted the proposition; indeed, the lady had shown such warmth that my lord had scarcely been able to contain his delight that such a prize would be his.

'After a private dinner to celebrate the agreement, Lord Mars had supposed that he would be permitted those favours which any man would expect upon such an occasion. However, on his taking her hand, the lady had merely dropped him a curtsy, thanked him for supper, and left! Upon two subsequent occasions the same result had followed upon his approach, while even the light familiarity of stroking her thigh in the box at Drury Lane Theatre during a performance by Mr Kean of *King Lear* had met with coolness.

'What was he to do?

'He had come equipped with his lady's birth time, and I immediately drew up a map and saw that the problem was one of timing: the lady had no inveterate dislike of coupling but no compulsion to seek out the opportunity for it; indeed, it was clear that while at one time she would receive an approach with enthusiasm, should the offer be made without consulting the calendar and the clock it would be treated with coolness if not a positive contempt.

'My maps suggested two occasions in the near future on which an offered connection would undoubtedly succeed in its purpose. A horrible temptation now thrust itself upon me, and within half a second I had succumbed to it.

' "My lord," I said, "if you approach the lady at nine at night on the evening of August the thirteenth" (which was in ten days' time) "you will certainly be kindly received."

'Remarking that a supper could surely be contrived which would end at just such a time, he thanked me, and left after placing upon the table a handsome sum in gold.

'I now sat down before my maps, and considered the fact that at three thirty on the morning of that same day, August the thirteenth, the lady would be even more receptive than on the later occasion – Venus on its journey through Scorpio falling retrograde, and moving into such a relation with both Mars and Mercury that . . . but I must not bore you with astrological detail.

'You will perhaps believe that I did not find it easy to resist the implication of this discovery; indeed it may be understood that I did not long hesitate in making a decision which will perhaps only be regarded as reprehensible by those who have not found themselves so tempted as I was. Imagine it: here was a woman who was adored by everyone who had set eyes on her; whose eyes, shoulders, breasts had been admired and celebrated by every living poet; the possession of whose person was a fantasy which provoked – nay even tortured – every man of spirit who had found himself in her company – yet whose coolness, the spotlessness of whose reputation, the rigid propriety of whose behaviour could only discourage even the thought of inviting her to amorous play.

'I will not tediously rehearse my days of studious research: suffice it to say that by the proper date I had discovered (through the bribing of a servant girl who was paid not only in metal but in more fleshly coin for her information) behind which window Lady Venus slept in that great house by the river into whose grounds I was admitted in the early hours through the connivance of a watchman to whom I had made myself useful in an amorous endeavour of his own. My mounting of a convenient ivy which clung to the front of the house was made the more difficult by reason of there being no moon; but my previous close observation of the place, together with a drawing I had taken, facilitated my mounting to the first floor, where the window of my Lady's room had been left unbolted by my friend within the house.

'The opening of the window having with some difficulty been achieved, I crept through it as a distant clock struck the half hour: the period of time during which the starry influence favoured me was no more than an hour and twenty minutes. I trod lightly around the room towards the dim outline of the bed, upon which an equally dim form could be seen. At the bedside, I removed those few garments which decency rather than climate required (for it was a hot night), and slowly lowered myself to my lady's side.

'On my stretching out a hand, it met no covering, but warm flesh: in the heat of the night she had eschewed any clothing other than the sultry air itself. She did not wake at my touch. I raised myself, and bent over her; with a daring only rendered possible by my confidence in my studies, I placed my lips upon hers, which, slightly parted, exhaled a breath sweeter than roses. She woke at this, and with a start: now was the testing moment. Would she rouse the house with a shout of rape – or, influenced by the starry rays of those planets which incline to passion, welcome to her bed even someone unknown to her?

'I felt her lips move beneath mine and her breast rise and fall under that hand which I now placed upon its smooth, warm surface. As I lifted my face from hers, she breathed a name: it was that of Lord Mars!

'Though vanity for a moment prompted me to reveal my true self, I immediately recalled the fact that, as is acknowledged by all historians, even great Jove himself – *particularly* great Jove himself! – disguised his person in order to enjoy mortal women. Must I test his patience, should he exist in some pagan heaven, by refusing to follow his example when occasion arose? Surely not! I therefore bent and once more laid my lips upon the lady's, which opened now to admit my questing tongue and to greet it with her own; and sliding hands down her quiescent but welcoming body, laid one upon those other lips whence my ambition drew me.

'Before however I could venture further in that direction, my Lady, betraying a warmth which surprised me even though I knew it was lit by the planets, began to pass her hands over my person with remarkable freedom (so that I had reason to be grateful that in height and general features I was more or less of my Lord's size and shape). I cannot of course say whether I resembled him in that feature upon which my Lady now fixed, first admiring it with her fingers, which explored its every surface, lingering particularly upon its barrel, now as adamant as that of any gun, but not neglecting the mechanism beneath, her toying with which bade fair to set off the charge. However, by now I had had sufficient experience to be able to contain my ardour – though this was severely tested when, worming her body down along my own, her breasts brushing my breast and belly and momentarily embracing my prick itself before falling between my thighs, she applied her lips to that same barrel, and began to suck upon it with such lubricious riggishness that it was difficult to suppose that she had not met with a similar implement before.

'This, when I had later the opportunity to consider the matter under less urgent circumstances, was no doubt the case. It had long been noted that the lady was commonly attended by a particularly handsome footman. Any other woman would have fallen under suspicion from the inveterate companionship of this servant, whose livery enhanced rather than concealed the handsome proportions of his body. However, Lady Venus' reputation remained unsmirched, through her invariable refusal of the offers even of the most eligible admirer. My own researches however suggested the proposition that at particular times the urgency of an appetite more generally under control would demand satisfaction; and it is my view that the young man in question could have provided a list of dates and times which would have tallied with my own.

'However, this is beside the point – except that some of the tricks in which she engaged during the seventy and five minutes I was in her company were such as she could surely have learned only in low company – as the very phrase in which she invited me to apply my lips and tongue to her own quim; or later, the hope she expressed that I would "go up the chute" – which phrase I failed to understand, but which by kneeling before me and guiding my prick I learned was an invitation to an unnatural but not entirely unenjoyable perversion of the true nature of intercourse.

'To be short about it, my Lady, possessing in public the most retiring nature, proved at the proper time to be polymorphously perverse; and it was only with difficulty that I removed myself from her arms at the required time though by then suspecting that not even the setting of the specified planets would necessarily have curtailed her appetite much before dawn. So much did she enjoy the game, that she expressed no surprise that during the whole period I said not a single word: actions, after all, speak louder than these – especially when accompanied from time to time by that inarticulate growling or grunting which must accompany pleasure.

'To what extent my lady was astonished when her lover, after such a passionate passage, claimed her again only a few hours later – when Lord Mars made his own no doubt successful attempt – I cannot say. Nor should I have been surprised at the situation in general, for my lady's horoscope – in which the properties of Aquarius were mingled with the attributes of Scorpio – when I examined it betrayed the necessity to show a cool front to the world, while behind it lay depths of passion easily plumbed by any man who cared to present himself at the proper time with sufficient ardour – the mere pressure of a hand being too faint a spark to ignite the powder, but a more ardent and outright gesture invariably resulting in a conflagration.

'I end here.' said the magician, 'merely with the offer that any lady or gentleman who wishes to consult me may feel free to do so, and the assurance that, since we are all friends and sharing the same predicament, my charges will be most moderate.'

At this, the astrologer, amid general applause, left the room – accompanied by my friend Sophie, who no doubt wished to share with him her own experience in astrological matters, for Mr Lilly had been her own first master. Their discussions were keen enough to occupy the time until luncheon, and they did not reappear until past midday, and then appeared exhausted by their arguments – having missed the second tale of the day, which followed hard upon their disappearance.

11

The Dean's Wife's Tale

My friend Sophie and her astrological colleague, as I have remarked, failed to hear the next story. They were, I later discovered, busy testing the manner in which astrological significators can reveal the marks of a person's body – my friend, from her studies recalling Mr Lilly' receipt, theorized that since Mr Smith had Scorpio for his ascending sign, Saturn in the same sign as the Moon, and that same planet in the third house, there should be a black mole or mark upon his left buttock – which he was pleased to confirm by displaying it, going on to conjecture that the underside of my friend's left breast must bear a little red mark somewhat in the shape of a sickle, which also turned out to be the case. Their speculations then took a somewhat more personal turn, which delayed their reappearance among us.

We were meanwhile entertained by a finely dressed woman of some presence, from the second coach, who introduced herself as Mrs Aspasia Ryves. She felt, as she admitted, some hesitation at the prospect of revealing her tale to strangers. 'But,' she said, 'the forthright honesty of those who have so far spoken convinces me that I shall be heard sympathetically – and while it is true that some aspects of my history might be regarded by the puritanical as shameful, yet its felicitous outcome can only be seen to confirm the chance everyone has of happiness in this world, should they take the opportunity to seize it.

'I was born in the small village of Chelsea, almost in the shadow of that splendid hospital erected by Sir Stephen Fox for veterans battered in the wars. My father being a financier in a good way of business, we lived, my parents and I, in a house once occupied by Sir Robert Walpole, in which Dean Swift, John Gay, Alexander Pope and other luminaries were in former times wont to gather.

'My childhood was a delightful one: the hours I spent playing with neighbourhood children in the Physic Garden while mother sat reading upon a bench nearby, and other hours spent riding in the park upon my very own palfrey, belong to an anthology of childish memories upon which I was to draw when my life became, as I shall explain, less pleasant – which accident occurred just after my seventeenth birthday. My father's business failing, due to the villainous behaviour of a trusted partner, he – my father – regarded himself as having betrayed those friends who had placed their monies in his hands by way of speculation, and in despair threw himself into the Thames from the nearest bridge. My mother, equally despairing, died within the fortnight – and when those trusted with the administration of Papa's affairs had done their worst, and the house and all its possessions been sold, I was left with barely sufficient funds to rent a small room in a mean house within sight of my former abode.

'I was now faced with the prospect of earning my living, which was something for which I was ill prepared: believing themselves to be assured for ever of an income, and that they could leave me in no fear of want (should I remain unmarried), my parents had failed altogether to educate me, and other than learning to read and write, I was taught nothing apart from the rules of polite behaviour, which would be sufficient to commend me to any young man who admired me – most husbands (it was believed) being antagonistic to too clever a wife.

'No doubt my beauty (for honesty forces me to admit that my face and figure were universally commended) would in the natural course of things, being accompanied by a generous dowry, have impressed some young gentleman sufficiently to result in an offer of marriage; but who would now marry a girl bereft both of accomplishment *and* money? I was in despair.

'The woman in whose house I lodged, in a room furnished with those few sticks of furniture I had succeeded in saving from the wreck, was good enough to pass to me those newspapers and magazines which she took in, in order that I could search the advertisements for any position for which I might be suited. These, however, were chiefly for governesses (a position for which I was through lack of education completely unsuited) or companions to the elderly (which through pride I was reluctant to undertake until reduced to my last ha'penny). Failing after some time to find any suitable place, I determined to insert an advertisement myself: and so it was that in the pages of the *Chronicle* there appeared the following notice: "Young lady, 18 years, of presentable aspect, seeks rewarding position in which enthusiasm and goodwill may compensate for lack of experience. Kindly write to *Neophyte*, at this newspaper, when applications will be forwarded."

'I can see from the expression with which my auditors greet this turn of my tale' (said Mrs Ryves) 'that my next revelation will be no surprise. But you must remember that I was, as I have said, entirely ignorant of the ways of the world. No doubt my mother would on the eve of my marriage, have summoned the courage to refer in some way to what my husband would expect of me upon our wedding night. But her modesty was too complete for me to have learned anything from her other than a few comforting words at the time when my *menses* began; and I had learned nothing of any of the other qualities inherent in being a woman.

'At all events, the obvious happened: on the same day upon which the advertisement appeared, and before I was prepared for it, Mrs Hawkings (my landlady, in whom respectability was decidedly tempered by audaciousness) answered the door to a determined knock, and a moment later came to my room and announced that a gentleman desirous of conversation with me awaited me in the downstairs parlour – a room into which those of us who shared the bare amenities of the house were but rarely permitted to enter.

'Happily, I was so recently removed from my former state that my clothes were still decent, and I was able to descend the staircase confident that even were my visitor to be the Bishop of London, I could face him with equanimity.

'My first impression of him was such that it seemed unlikely that he was a bishop, or indeed a clergyman of any kind. He was a tall, youthful man of a strong, naturally commanding yet kindly demeanour, the separate features of whose face were nevertheless far from daunting, his full and perfectly curved lips turning up slightly at the corners, and a pair of black eyes beneath somewhat beetle brows enhanced by a sparkle of humour. He rose as I entered, and greeted me with a bow sufficiently friendly to be altogether lacking in condescension.

' "Miss Beadle," he said (for that was then my name), "I have had the pleasure of reading your notice in this morning's *Chronicle*, and was so impressed by it that I took advantage of a personal acquaintance with that newspaper's manager in order to obtain your address to facilitate my calling upon you personally, thus, I hope, circumventing any callers who might otherwise have out-bid me in engaging your interest."

'I acknowledged his words with a smile, flattered by the extent of his interest; whereupon he asked if we might be seated? – and on taking my place upon a *chaise-longue* which was the most remarkable piece of furniture in the room, I was perhaps a little surprised when he stepped forward to sit at my side, rather than occupying the chair most convenient to him. He then without further equivocation enquired whether I would be prepared to become one of a stable of ladies which he maintained in Kensington for the convenience of the gentlemen of the town.

'Needless to say, I was delighted by the offer – but took

the precaution of enquiring what duties would be required of me, lest they should prove beyond my capabilities. I would be able, I said, to converse with any gentleman on matters of politics and literature, and even perhaps on financial affairs, for my father had often talked to me on such matters, while my mother also had an interest in literature which had resulted in my being familiar not only with the works of Shakespeare, Milton and Pope, but those of the more recently deceased Keats, Shelley and Byron together with the novels of Miss Austen, Sir Walter Scot and Mr Peacock.

'Mr Albert Cowland – for that was the gentleman's name – seemed scarcely to know how to answer me, and looked for a moment even abashed; but then after a little spluttering remarked that the services he would expect were only occasionally connected with literature, and then but remotely.

'I was unable to enquire further, having no notion what he meant; and a silence fell, which he broke after a while to ask whether I had had no conversation with gentlemen?

'Often, I replied, for my father had kept a most hospitable house.

'Again, this seemed not to be the reply he expected; and in a moment he remarked that he had meant to ask rathe whether I had been made aware of what passed between a gentleman and a lady in the way of natural affection.

' "You are," he was good enough to remark, "a young person of such remarkable beauty and parts that I cannot believe that some chap has not been familiar with your charms" – and laid his palm upon my thigh. This latte action had a most curious effect upon my spirits, for though it was excessively familiar, I could not deny that it was remarkably warming, while upon his leaning forward and planting a kiss upon my cheek, I did not repine but rathe leaned towards him – whereupon, taking this for approbation, he turned my face with his palm and placed his lips firmly upon mine, when I felt his tongue invading my mouth – a most unexpected action resulting in a mor unexpected emotion, for my whole body now seemed to wish to cleave itself to his – for no rational reason of which I was aware.

'There can be no doubt that Mr Cowland by now recognized in me the lineaments of a naturally affectionate female, for without further delay he inserted one hand into my bosom and clasped my naked breast, while with the other he rummaged beneath my skirts and discovered another area of flesh which responded with an even fiercer ardour to his approaches.

'By now I was almost fainting with an emotion that a more experienced girl would have recognized as desire, but which I was incapable of acknowledging, for half-unconscious I slipped to the couch as he stood and released his lower limbs from their constricting garments, and I did not so much as glimpse the weapon with which he shortly made me a woman.

'The experience was painless – because, as I believe, my frequent exercise on horseback had some time since ruptured that barrier which normally resists the first assault of an eager prick; the lack of pain freed my emotions to concentrate solely on the pleasure, which on this first occasion consisted at least partially of the singularity of the experience – of the interesting knowledge that a gentleman could find so much pleasure in my company – then of the vigour with which this fine, large, smooth instrument was plunged into my person, and finally of the gradually rising apprehension of physical delight, which became so great that I actually lost consciousness as he brought me to my first crisis.

'I woke to find him standing over me, his instrument still vigorously at a stand, having withdrawn in anxiety that I had been taken with a sudden illness. The opposite was so far true that I seized him by the most interesting part of his body and by it, my eagerness no less than his, drew him once more between my thighs, where after some little while he satisfied us both at the culmination of a vigorous swiving.

'Having been introduced to the pleasures of love, it was explained to me that my task would be to continue to enjoy them; and that was all that was needed to persuade me to move my few belongings to a room in Mr Cowland's house in Kensington Square, where five other ladies of ages varying between my own and thirty years also lived, and were visited by only the most respectable gentlemen – those either in the infancy of desire, still experimenting in enlarging their understanding, those who required more variation in love making than their wives had command of, or those who simply required a holiday from the regular (however pleasant) diet of the marriage bed.

'Of these gentlemen, one or two particularly attached themselves to me, and would send their servants to the house of a morning, inviting me to make myself available to their masters at such-and-such a time. The other ladies equally had their own customers, who preferred them for one reason or another – some looking for plumpness, others for slimness, some for those with golden hair, others for those with black, some for active partners, others for more passive and compliant companions – and so on. A little conversation with my new friends educated me in the sophistication of an activity in which, it being so new to me I might otherwise have lacked skill or ingeniousness, and I soon was able to give complete satisfaction to most of those kind enough to invite me to perform a service for them

'Mr Cowland was kindness itself, generous in payment and in the provision of every comfort; he was also good enough to assure us that we were expected to provide onl those services which we felt ready to perform – so that upon a gentleman from some foreign country (I believe, Austria desiring to whip me, I had only to apply to my employe for Herr Braucht to be informed that he should take himsel off to the Haymarket, where prostitutes of the lower sor would be ready to assist him.

'I would not of course claim that I invariably enjoyed this life: there were some gentlemen who for reason of temperament or even of bodily form did not entirel commend themselves to me. But as most ladies of the game would confirm, we tended to be applied to on the whole by those we could fancy, and it was but rarely that I did not find the work both amusing and satisfying, and in the full meaning of that last word. In particular, I found myself attached (for what reason I could not entirely explain to myself) to gentlemen of a considerably more advanced age than my own. There was something to be said for those bouncing youngsters whose aim was to enjoy the favours of as many females as possible before settling into that married state which (as they naively believed) would preclude further experiment: their stamina was considerable, and their dexterity permitted them to assume, or at last try, the most original postures. These, however, were in the matter of amorous play more athletic than satisfying, the more adventurous contortions of the limbs – while often inspiriting to an onlooker – being but rarely conducive to actual physical pleasure; and the tendency of young men to reach the climactic moment within a shorter time than either they or we considered satisfactory, was a grave drawback.

'Those of our clientele who were of more advanced years had naturally, through experience, greater command of their emotions, and the more considerate of them concerned themselves with giving as well as receiving pleasure, which commended them to us no less as friends than lovers, no less as companions than patrons. They would frequently sit with us for some time in pleasant conversation over a bottle before at last rising to their feet and offering their arm; and upon the bedroom business being concluded, would accompany us downstairs where often a second bottle would be ordered, and if another gentleman were not waiting his turn, would be happy to sit late into the night in the most enjoyable social converse.

'Mr Cowland approached me one evening with just such an elderly gentleman of perhaps as many as fifty years, introducing him simply as Bruno – a somewhat peculiar name, though one which had run in the gentleman's family (as he explained) for two centuries and more. He was tall and slim, that brown hair which seemed to illustrate his name only slightly greying at the temples, his eyes a paler brown, his brow smooth and his mouth humorous.

' "May I introduce Miss Beadle," said my employer; "a young lady of the most perfect taste."

'The gentleman bowed over my hand, immediately ordered a bottle of the best Austrian wine, and sitting at my side filled a glass and handed it to me with the most perfect courtesy. He then began a conversation which – unlike that of many of my friends – embraced the latest exhibitions and shows, spoke of a recent recital of the works of the recently deceased German composer Herr van Beethoven, remarked upon the recent handsome edition of the works of Mr Milton as illustrated by the artist John Martin, and discussed the progress of the building of the great Museum in Russell Street which is to house the country's collection of antiquities.

'I have no doubt that had I proved uninterested in such topics, he would have turned the conversation into other passages; but on my proving able to speak on equal terms of the matters he broached, he showed some pleasure, and we got on famously.

'Gradually, and with a remarkable ease and grace, he became more personal, congratulating me upon my dress and the jewellery I wore (for, always interested in fashion, I took care of my appearance no less for my own pleasure than as a form of window dressing); then complimenting me most tactfully upon my personal charms – and with complete conviction, as I remarked from the obvious pleasure he took in regarding my bared arms and shoulders, while his eyes could be seen to glance from time to time at my breast, shown to advantage by a *décolletage* carefully contrived to flatter its roundness.

'At last, feeling that his delicacy might not permit him to be first to suggest it, I rose and invited him to accompany me to another place, where our discussion could more comfortably be continued.

' "If you consent to receive me in the capacity of a lover," he returned; and upon my smiling and offering my arm, he consented to accompany me to one of the private rooms. There, without more ado, I divested myself of my clothing – which was my habit unless the gentleman expressed a wish that I should remain somewhat covered, or indeed wished to unclothe me himself, some gentleman taking pleasure in personally unwrapping their gifts.

'In a leisurely fashion, he then also undressed, myself assisting him as a sort of female valet, taking and hanging his coat, unbuttoning and folding his shirt, placing his breeches neatly upon a chair. I was pleased to see that unclothed he was as handsome as in full fig: his body was unblemished by any weight of superfluous flesh, his belly merely somewhat rounded, and a little collar of plumpness at the waist no more than hinting at his seniority. His breast was flat, and without that suggestion of pendulousness about the paps which too often shows in the figures of elderly gentlemen who take no care of their diet; and upon it the hair, growing sparsely yet decoratively, was no more than flecked with grey. I was somewhat disappointed however to remark that between his thighs, where a shrub of hair was similarly peppered with grey, there was no sign of his purported admiration of my person.

'He evidently caught my disappointed glance, for, sitting upon the bed, he remarked that at his age the most poignant admiration of female beauty, unless accompanied by physical propinquity, no longer had the direct effect which had accompanied it in earlier years.

' "However," he remarked, "a closer acquaintance will have a result which I believe will not disappoint" – at which I sat at his side and leaning to kiss his lips permitted my hand to fall upon the pliant object of my disappointed gaze – which indeed immediately began to stir beneath my palm. On his fixing his own lips to my breast, I was left in no doubt that a prick of some fifty years' experience had as much life in it as one of ten; indeed, when in the natural course of events I was encouraged to inspect it more closely, I found it to be no less adamant than handsome – in size perhaps not extraordinary, but of the most perfect smoothness, while a careful trimming of the surrounding thicket set it off to perfection. The satin skin of the spheroids hanging beneath suggested a dextrous use of the razor, employed in order that one of his chiefest pleasures – that these should be mumbled and licked – should give no offence to a mistress.

'He accepted all my attentions with an approving gratitude; but then, as I prepared to permit him the final favour, urged me to lie back and insisted that he should spend some time pleasuring me – for, he said, it was a shame in any man to enjoy voluptuousness when he was not prepared to return it.

'He was as practised in this as any woman could hope, and more so than any boy could be; while, upon his finally entering me, when he had roused me to such a pitch of apprehension that my parts were lubricated to an extent which made the act easy and ready, he proved capable of prolonging the act almost indefinitely, so that I had in the end to beg him to permit me to bring him to his meridian. This was accomplished by pinching a nipple between my teeth on his inviting me to do it, it proving an action which gave him a pleasure sufficient to urge him over the final fence.

'His courteous thanks were no less chivalrous than his thoughtful preliminary conversation; and I was delighted to find that he was evidently as pleased with me as I with him. He returned within seven days, and then at regular intervals of a week or ten days, always at the middle of the week; sometimes arranging with Mr Cowland to remain for the entire night, when I could look forward to the most pleasurable attentions before his relapsing into sleep; after which, waking in the morning, he would do me the courtesy of shaving before returning to bed for a final enjoyable conclave preliminary to his taking his leave.

'I must confess that it was no less through infatuation than curiosity that I earnestly desired to discover my lover's identity; for within a month I was fathoms deep in love with him, and bitterly regretting my profession, which would necessarily make it impossible to form a regular union with him – though it was after all quite possible that I would never have met him had I not embraced it; while certainly had we met in a respectable drawing room there would surely have been little chance of our exchanging such embraces as would prove our suitability as lovers, for I doubted he would have felt able to pay public attention to one thirty and three years his junior.

'On his going, one morning, to Mr Cowland to settle his account before leaving, I must confess to reaching into the pockets of my lover's jacket in the hope of a clue; whereupon I found a letter addressed to the Very Rev. Bruno Ryves, at the deanery, Chichester! This affected me so strongly that my farewell must have seemed cooler than usual, for my lover enquired whether the strenuous nature of the morning's activity had incommoded me?

'After his departure, I considered the situation for some time; and going to Mr Cowland confessed all my emotions and enquired whether it was indeed possible that my lover could be so distinguished a figure. Happily, my employer was pleased with me, and we had over the past eighteen months achieved some degree of cordiality; he therefore had little hesitation in confirming the fact – which he had himself discovered only by accident. The Dean, he said, travelled each week to London for the express purpose of visiting the house, and had done so regularly during the ten years that had elapsed since the death of his spouse.

'On my confessing my love, Mr Cowland was somewhat disturbed, expressing himself as being doubtful whether it could possibly have a happy resolution; but I had by now an idea of my own, and on my explaining it, he was kind enough to give me what help I needed – which was chiefly in supplying clothes rather more decorous than those it had become my habit to wear, and in forwarding some little money which would permit me to travel respectably and stay at a decent inn. One of my companions at the house then helped me to dye my hair from its normal light brown colour to black – which, my eyes being dark, as you can see, looked by no means extraordinary, but, with the aid of a beauty spot upon my cheek, and my hair being dressed in a new style, would make me (as I hoped) unrecognizable even to a lover.

'Arriving at the city of Chichester late on Saturday evening, I took lodgings at the Dolphin Hotel, immediately opposite the cathedral, and the following morning, dressed in an elegant cloak of dark blue edged with fur, made my way to Matins, where I had the pleasure of observing my lover, looking as handsome in the gown, surplice and honours of Dean as in that less formal garb which was more familiar to me. His elegance and poise affected me strongly, as did the respect in which he was clearly held by those parishioners who clasped his hand at the door, after the service. When my turn came to do so, it was not without apprehension; and he may have felt my cold hand quiver somewhat, for he took it in both his hands and clasped it warmly, looking into my eyes with so kindly and poignant an expression – though it seemed to me, somewhat puzzled – that I almost gave myself away.

'Having taken lunch at the inn, though with small appetite, I enquired the whereabouts of Dean Ryves's home, which I found to be a handsome one only half a mile distant; and at four in the afternoon made my way there, and knocking upon the door asked the maid to announce to her master that a lady sought his advice. She showed a doubtful face; but a small reward persuaded her to perform the message. She showed me into a study in which, a few minutes later, I was joined by the Dean.

'On his enquiring what he could do for me, I (confident in my disguise and with the light of the window behind me) explained that I was in the difficulty of having an extreme admiration for a gentleman who was both considerably my senior and far above me in station; that my adoration for him was complete, almost to distress; and asked what I should do.

' "My dear lady," said the Dean without hesitation, "you can only declare yourself! Your demeanour and manner, the softness of your voice and the beauty of your person make clear the fact that any man would rejoice in your company; while as to age – what matters that, where love is in the question?"

'My answer could only take one form. Rising from the chair in which I had been seated, I slipped off my cloak, came towards him and, throwing my arms about him, addressed him by a diminutive which we only used together in the privacy of the bedchamber.

'To say that he was astonished would be to describe a mountain as a molehill; yet after only a moment's hesitation he clasped me in his arms, when the joining of our persons produced an effect (no doubt emphasized by the unexpected nature of my appearance) impossible to deny.

'The severely practical nature of clerical garb made an immediate response difficult; but the Dean, pausing only to lock the door (being far too impatient to take me up to the bedchamber) overcame this by the simple dint of removing it, then giving me ample proof that I had not been mistaken in believing that his natural affection for me would outweigh the shock of my appearance.

'To cut the story short, I walked with him to Evensong later that afternoon – when only the closest observer would have remarked on a slight unsteadiness in his dress which was the result of too rapid an assumption of coat and trousers – and was introduced as a friend from London; I then returned temporarily to Kensington Square while the banns were called at Chichester; and within the month was installed in that city as Mrs Dean Ryves – a position held until the unfortunate death of my dear husband some eighteen months' since, after almost twenty years of happy marriage.

'There is no doubt a moral to this story," Mrs Ryves concluded, "though I would not wish to be the one to draw it; you must learn what lesson you will from my tale – but certainly one assurance must be that innocence is not always ruined by experience!'

It was at this moment that the door opened and Sophie appeared with Mr Smith, the applause which greeted the end of Mrs Ryves's story suggesting to them (which was true) that whatever pleasurable conversation they had been enjoying, our own entertainment had not been much less keen.

12

The Young Man's Tale

The light which shone through the windows of the room in which we spent most of our time seemed perceptibly to have brightened during the course of the morning, and daring to step outside after partaking of the handsome fare with which, as usual, we were provided at noon, I found that while a cold, bright blue sky still hung above us, my breath no longer issued in a cloud from my lips, and there even seemed a suggestion of warmth in the air.

Finding at my side that rather sallow, dark young fellow who had been an outside passenger in our coach, I addressed to him the observation that it appeared to me that the weather was about to break.

'Doubtless our friend Tarantabobus would ascribe it to the movements of the planets,' he drily observed; but then went on to ask if he could confide in me.

These were almost the first words I had heard him speak, for he had kept himself very much apart, though attending all our meetings, sitting in a corner; but while clearly appreciative of the narratives, making no observation upon them.

Now that I was able to observe him more closely, I found him to be a gentleman of perhaps rather more years than a casual observer would credit him with; he was, it now seemed to me, perhaps nearer thirty than twenty – but of such personable appearance as would make a mistake credible. His skin was somewhat darker than is common, of an olive hue which gave him almost the appearance of a foreigner – though his speech was entirely English, if of a pattern difficult to place: he had a kind of neutral accent, neither of the common people nor of the aristocracy.

'Mr Archer,' he said, 'I have observed with some surprise the freedom with which the other members of our party have told their tales; but with increasing apprehension as my own turn approached – for I am down to be the next person to address the company, and to be frank with you I am not only unused to addressing any number of people, but have some doubt whether the story of my life might not be such as to give offence.'

'My dear sir,' I replied, 'can you be in any doubt of that after our reception of some of the other tales with which we have been regaled?'

'But this,' he insisted, 'is something of another matter – for to be frank with you, my fortune has been earned by way of . . . in a manner which . . . in short, has been the result of my . . .'

'You mean to say,' I intervened, 'in a manner which may seem disreputable?'

He nodded, grateful for my prompting.

'Be easy, my friend,' I said; 'this is no party of puritans, and if my observation is to be trusted, none would turn a hair should you turn out to be Bluebeard himself!'

He was somewhat, if not altogether, comforted, but still appeared ill at ease as we returned to the warmth of the chief room, under the approving gaze (as it seemed to me) of the portrait of the fattest man in England, one Daniel Lambert, who had died at Stamford only a few years previously, and was depicted at a time when he weighed no less than fifty-two stones and eight pounds – and looking remarkably cheerful considering the problems which such girth as his must necessarily have laid him under.

Our latest story-teller began in a somewhat halting manner, but gained confidence as he proceeded:

'My name is Gerry Trustworth; but to be honest with you – and I am determined on honesty, though some of the facts I must relate may impress you as disreputable – I was not born with it; the name given to me at birth, indeed, was

Geraldo de Hoyas, and I was born in northern Spain to the leader of a tribe of gypsies – within a family which was to that tribe as the British royal family is to their people; for my father was after a fashion a prince.

'But family feuds break out even in royal families – as was illustrated by the events surrounding the marriage of your own King George; and one such was, with us, of a ferocity so strong that upon my father losing the argument, he and his wife were bound hand and foot and set into a boat with poor me, his only child, then of only a year's age.

'That we survived the Bay of Biscay, which the experienced travellers among you will know to be a most dangerous place, was due entirely to our being picked up by a British ship – to the kindness of whose captain we owed our lives; for he fed us and kept us, and rather than setting us ashore once more on the coast of Spain, which would have meant our deaths almost as certainly as if he had left us adrift, took us to the small Cornish port of Mousehole, where my parents found themselves alone, speaking no English, and devoid of any means of making a living.

'The Cornish, though a rough breed, recognized my father as a fellow Celt, and those who spoke the Cornish tongue even proved capable of understanding a word or two of the language he spoke; this as well as their natural disposition made them sufficiently kindly as to assist my father to find work – though only as a farm labourer. We lived for the next fifteen years, securely if without luxury, in a hovel on a farm within a few miles of the Land's End – that rough promontory against which beat those waves whose birth is near the coast of the New World.

'Then, however, came a rough winter whose rude winds inflicted such a chill upon my poor parents that first my mother then my father were taken from me, and I was left alone in the world to fend for myself as best I might.

'The farmer who employed us was disinclined to send me packing, for I was now a healthy lad of almost seventeen years, who if not particularly muscular was wiry and strong and well able to cope with such tasks as clearing out pigsties, shovelling dung, milking, herding, and a hundred and one other matters of the farmyard.

'I knew nothing of life outside the few acres of land which surrounded the farm, for the nearest village – that of St Just – I had visited only once or twice in my life, and in any case offered no temptations to draw me thither. Neither, indeed, was I tempted by the only human female within reach – the slatternly wife of my employer. I observed with some interest the activities of rams with sheep, bulls with cows, and stallions with mares, and noticed that on occasions, when I woke in that nest of rags which was my bed, my own yard had grown to become a miniature replica of that massive instrument deployed by Tarow, our bull, but made nothing of it. Even had I recognized the strength of those vestigial emotions which occasionally tickled me, the only readily available means of slaking that appetite (apart from my mistress) was the farm animals, none of which attracted me in that manner – though my master was not so averse to them, and from time to time preferred one of his goats to his own wife – a preference which, if I did not share it, I entirely understood. My sympathy did not extend however to offering him similar hospitality, and on his once offering to insert his hand between my thighs (finding me alone, with my parents at work in his fields) I had kicked him between his own legs with such accuracy as had rendered him a hobbler for several days.

'The summer following my bereavement was as hot as the previous winter had been cold; and – for it is time that my narrative came to a point – it was on one of its hottest days, in the middle of July, that my affairs took a turn.

'I had been working since dawn in the farmyard, clearing out a barn in which five cows normally resided, and which bore a strong resemblance to those Augean stables which taxed even the strength of Heracles. Completing the task, I had awarded myself a few minutes' respite, and took the shadow of the farmyard's wall. I had been reluctant to soil those rags which were my everyday clothing with the shit of the yard, and had stripped to my skin, merely winding a length of cloth about my loins lest either the farmer or (how much worse!) his wife should find my undressed state a temptation. The muck, together with the heat, had rendered me a noisome object – offending even my own nose, so that only my weariness and the state of the farm's duckpond (the water so thick with dirt as to resemble some noxious soup) delayed me from cleansing myself; in a while, I thought, I would trudge to the sea, a few hundred yards away, and allow myself the luxury of washing in its water and renewing my spirits by swimming for a while.

'For a while, I must have drowsed upon the grass verge below the wall, for I awoke suddenly at a sharp pricking of my shoulder which at first I took to be the sting of a bee, but which proved to be the effect of the flick of a whip. I jumped to my feet with an imprecation – in the Cornish language, I may say (for my employer commonly spoke in a mixture of that tongue and an English which only very slightly resembled the language you would recognize as your own. This, with a smattering of Spanish, at that time was my only means of communication).

'I almost swallowed my oath, however, for on the board of the small cart or carriage which had drawn up in the lane, sat a lady, reins in one hand and a small whip in the other. She appeared to me a figure of such splendour that I was struck almost blind: yet should you set eyes on her now, you would recognize only a person of moderate means, the wife perhaps of a country squire. But to me, her dress, her equipage, her very manner appeared those almost of a goddess. I rose to my feet with a bound – alas, forgetting that for comfort I had loosened the filthy rag about my waist, with the result that as I stood, it slipped from my body – and being too confused to recover it, I stood before her with lowered eyes, completely unclothed; and a strange figure I must have made, my body brown with ordure except for a band of white about my centre parts, where my contrived loincloth had protected my skin from the worst of the dirt.

'Had I but known it, the insecurity of those vestigial breeches was to change the course of my life. After what seemed a long pause, on raising my eyes I could not but notice that the lady's seemed fixed on that part of me which from my tenderest years my mother had taught me – for she had a natural modesty – to veil even from her eyes. Swiftly, I bent, and recovering the rag, quickly wound it once more about my loins.

'My movement seemed to break the spell, for the lady now spoke.

' "I was about to enquire of the road to Grumbla," she said.

'Unable to muster words, I pointed down the road in the way she was going. I had never been to that place, but had heard it spoken of by my master with a respect uncommon in his normal conversation, as a mansion of impressive dimensions.

'She nodded.

' "As I thought," she said. "But tell me, you have a name?"

' "Gerry," I replied – for that was the nearest my master's rough tongue could come to Geraldo.

'She nodded again.

' "And you are employed in this . . . this place?' She looked at the farm with a far from admiring gaze.

'It was my turn to nod.

' "You are no doubt utterly devoted to the interests of your master?'

'Uneducated though I was, I recognized irony when I heard it. And, while to be truthful I had never considered the matter, upon her asking I immediately knew that not only did I not enjoy my present situation, but that I was violently attracted to any other world which contained ikons like herself.

'She opened a reticule at her waist, fumbled within it, and produced in a moment a coin which shone like silver –

which, on her throwing it at my feet, it proved to be.

' "If you care to be, you are from now on in my employ!" she said. "Follow on!" – and touching her pony with her whip, she encouraged him to move off down the road.

'I had but a moment to consider: yet consideration was unnecessary. I picked up the coin – I had never possessed a piece of money in my life – and disregarding my state, began to trot along at the side of the carriage.

'But what of my luggage? you may ask. The answer is simple: I had none. My parents had left only a stick or two of furniture in the single room which they had been allowed to inhabit; themselves cast naked upon the kingdom they had had no treasure to leave me; my master had fed and watered me like a beast, allowing me nothing. Presented with the sudden opportunity for escape, I did not hesitate to leave behind the single shirt and breeches which were my only clothing, and to set forth clad only and literally in rags – or, more accurately, a rag.

'Nor did my new mistress repine, it seemed, for she was careful to keep the speed of her carriage at a pace which a boy on foot could maintain, and the glances which from time to time she sent in my direction seemed to me (astonishing as it was) to be more admiring than admonishing – despite the fact that my appearance grew more and more disreputable as the sweat inspired by the hot day and the action of running coursed from my face and neck down breast, belly and thighs, leaving white runnels amid the brown dirt.

'Though it was only a matter of eight or ten miles to Grumbla, the place seemed to me almost to inhabit a new planet: the rough hedges and gnarled, twisted trees which had decorated my former master's ground gave way to what seemed exquisite gardens; the tumble-down farmhouse was in equal contrast to the palace which now stood before me – though in truth, it was only a decent house.

'The little carriage drew up at the front door; and not pausing to wait for a groom, my new mistress threw the reins of the pony over the long disused *torchère* by the steps, and seizing me by the hand strode through the front door, across the hall (which left the brief impression upon my mind of vast spaces bounded only by white marble), up a staircase, along a corridor, through another door, and into a room which, though a perfectly ordinary bedroom, seemed to me like a magician's cave, so rich were the hangings, so soft the carpets, so impressive the silver instruments upon the dressing table.

'Slamming the door, the lady paused for a moment, looking at me as I stood, dazed, in these strange surroundings – then, to my amazement, as swiftly as her hands could effect the task, she threw off every stitch of her clothing and, stepping towards me, clasped me, filthy and running with sweat as I was, in her arms.

'Not unnaturally, perhaps, I struggled – being unaccustomed to such actions from a female; and slippery as a fish with perspiration, easily escaped. The front of her white body now imprinted with some of the dirt acquired from my own, she gave chase – and in a moment we were engaged in a frantic game of catch-as-catch-can about the furniture: until there slid from beneath my feet one of the rugs upon the floor, and I fell to the ground, the lady immediately throwing herself on top of me.

'I was by now delirious with a kind of passionate laughter; she, however, only with passion – and now wriggled her body upon my own in an excess of what unconsciously I must have recognized as lust, and which (as her ample breast slithered to and fro across my chest) communicated itself to me in so lively a fashion that my young yard rose at it, and found as much pleasure as pain in the manner in which my lady's squirming ground it between my belly and hers.

'The vision of Tarow, our bull, assaulting one of his cows now set itself before me with such firmness that I attempted to throw the lady from me, in order that, turning her about, I could plough her from behind – that being the posture which recommended itself to me as the only manner in which my rampant prick could be set at her. She, however, was having none of it, but continuing to pin me to the floor now began slavering over my whole body with kisses, to my surprise and embarrassment licking at my neck, my shoulders, my paps, my belly and even – to my utter astonishment – my prick (which I must confess, no lessons in hygiene having been given me, was in no less noisome a state than the rest of me).

'Her face and lips now in just such a filthy state as the rest of her, madam raised herself and spitting into the palm of her hand and anointing with it those other lips which as yet had been inactive, placed my prick between them and with a great yell of pleasure sank down upon me in a squatting posture, and I watched with interest by no means unmixed with pleasure as the length of my yard disappeared into her belly.

'The instrument having been so completely sheathed that the curls at its base were confused with those which decorated her own most intimate parts, she began to ride me with the passion of a practised huntswoman, leaping two fences almost immediately, and at the second so raking my breast with her nails that the pain of it gave me an immediate fall; the stamina of youth however enabling me to support her in the saddle until she had flown over a final fence and came to rest panting and exhausted.

'After a while, and without a word, wrapping about her a gown which lay upon the bed, she rose and turning away from me pulled at a bell. Bending, she picked up the rag which she had seized from about my waist, and threw it at me; whereupon, confused anew, I covered myself with it – just before a maid appeared at the doorway.

'Again to cut the story short, the maid – who was known as Doll – took me away, and fortunately being of a kindly disposition showed me where I could wash myself, clean those scratches which my mistress had inflicted upon me, and then (presumably at the lady's behest) gave me a suit of clothes, indifferently clean, but infinitely preferable to what I had formerly possessed.

'The next two months continued confusingly. I was given

nothing to do either in house or garden. All my previous experience had been in menial work, chiefly caring for animals. Here there were others to perform that task, and no animals to care for – so I occupied myself as best I might by a little gardening. My sole responsibility was to present myself to my mistress perhaps twice or thrice a week, under what then seemed to me strange circumstances: she would send an instruction by Doll, who would take me into the kitchen garden and, inviting me to undress myself, with the aid of a bucket of water and the earth of the cabbage patch do her best to render my body in a state as filthy as that in which I had been found – after which she would escort me to the bedroom, where after just the same sort of scene as I had first experienced, my mistress would ravish me.

'It would be disingenuous of me to pretend that these scenes were not to an extent enjoyed by me; and yet the suspicion that they were unusual persuaded me to ask Doll whether her own proclivities were similar – in response to which enquiry she consented to demonstrate the fact that not all women were of a similar temperament, the form and manner of her embraces being such as would be generally recognized as more conventional.

'I must now make a claim which may seem boastful, but which is a truth necessary to state: I swiftly found that not only then but subsequently I possessed a talent for pleasing ladies in whatever way of love their preference lay. My mistress's attentions I was able not only to bear with equanimity, but – once I understood the nature of her desires – to enlarge: I gradually found that apart from the necessity to embrace an unclean lover, she also received much enjoyment from being treated roughly – and on the first occasion on which I succeeded in unseating her, and, pinning her to the ground, treated her almost in the manner of a rapist, she responded with a cry of pleasure so demonstrative that the rooks rose in great clouds from the trees outside the bedroom window.

'Not only that, but I found that by dint of merely concentrating my mind elsewhere, I was able to remain at stand for as long as might be required; and even to satisfy my Lady without myself coming off – a convenience when I had arranged, for variety, to bed young Doll immediately afterwards, whose longings I was also able to satisfy without repining.

'My sentimental education was, then, considerably advanced by the time that, at the end of September, a carriage brought from Bristol my mistress's husband. Setting eyes upon him furthered my education, for though not a ninny he was so fastidious in his manner and behaviour that it was immediately understandable why his wife, in his absence, sought out rougher trade.

'I have no means of knowing whether he later became aware of my activities in his bed – or rather more commonly upon his bedroom floor; certainly there was no intention on the part of his wife that he should; for at her command Doll presented me with a purse and instructions to leave the house and never to return to it.

'This might have been a serious blow to some young men; to myself it presented a challenge. Being (and here I must once more appear to boast) of natural intelligence, I had found out the small library which the house afforded, and though I was then unable to read, had from the engravings to be found there taught myself that the world was wider than I had supposed – or even than my parents, in the few years during which they had spent with me, had been able to impress upon me.

'Those depictions of fashionable cities, ladies and gentlemen of breeding, much impressed me; and I formed the ambition to be as like them as might be. I had also learned from Doll what little skill she had in the forming of letters, and had struggled to improve my form of speech at least to her level – which though low, could not but be higher than my own.

'On my questioning her, she believed that it was not common that ladies should pay for the services of a gentleman in the way of romantic companionship (or, as she put it, that they should pay good money for rantam scantam). Proficiency in said rantam scantam being my only skill, I hoped she might be wrong, and determined to investigate the possibility. In order to better my appearance I stole (and the word is, I fear, the only accurate one) some clothing from a press which I can only assume belonged to Mr Treleaven (as the head of the house was called) – consisting of two or three good white shirts and some plain breeches.

'I then walked to the town of St Ives, which Doll described as the very Sodom and Gomorrah of cities, especially in summer, when it was visited by the fashionable and fair. I hoped to be able to demonstrate to some likely female the fact that at least one of the young men of the neighbourhood was not skilled only in fishing or in agriculture.

'On my arrival in the vicinity of the town, I slept under a hedge; and next morning, having gone down to the sea and cleansed myself as best I might in its salty waters, made my way to the best inn in the place, and from a vantage point observed those coming and going there, marvelling at the fine clothing, the marvellously crafted *coiffeurs*, the polite manners of the great.

'There seemed however little possibility of my successfully trawling there, for all those ladies who entered or left the inn seemed to be accompanied. On my walking nearer the sea's margin, however, my eye fixed upon a woman who seemed to be of about my former mistress's age (which was perhaps thirty years and three or four more). She was unaccompanied by any partner, and upon her setting out along the shore, I followed her at a careful distance.

'In a short time, she settled herself with a book upon a rock near the sea's edge, in a little cove which broke in upon the coast about half a mile from the town. After perhaps five minutes, when no other person had appeared, I divested myself of my clothing and took to the water. The sea was calm and almost without waves, which was slightly disconcerting considering the plan I had formed; nevertheless, rounding the rocky corner where the lady was sitting, I began to flounder somewhat, as though in distress;

and seeing from the corner of my eye that I had attracted her attention, I gave the best imitation I could of someone at the point of drowning, and only after some time was able to gain a hand-hold upon a tiny promontory of that very rock upon which she sat.

'On witnessing what appeared to be my plight, she had laid down her book and risen to her feet, and now did not hesitate to stretch out a hand and help me from the water – nor did she repine when she found me to be entirely naked, though I fancied a slight blush coloured her cheeks.

'I took care to collapse, apparently breathless, at her feet, my limbs so asprawl that she could not but have full access to a view of my private parts – which, though somewhat shrunken by their immersion in the sea, were (the water not being very cold) still of such proportions as I hoped would commend them to her.

'I could see from below my lowered eyelids that she observed me more closely than perfect modesty would have allowed; and now allowed a feeble groan to escape my lips at which she knelt at my side in a display of concern so real that for a moment I felt almost guilty.

'With a strength that was surprising, she now seized me by the shoulders and turned me upon my face (the better to permit any water which I had swallowed in my extremity, to run from my mouth). The action was no doubt a wise one, and based upon sound medical principles; for me, however, it had the lucky advantage that it placed before the lady a view which she found irresistible. As I was later to learn, the prospect of a fair backside was the principal pleasure found in the close observation of a gentleman, next (that is) to the ultimate one; and happily for me, my own arse was of just such proportion and shape as most appealed to her: the cheeks small, smooth and hairless, and carried high, seemingly curved specifically to fit the palm of the hand – so that she could not, even under the circumstances, refrain from trying whether they would fit hers – for I almost immediately felt a warm hand laid upon me; and upon hearing that sigh of satisfaction which I allowed to escape me, it began to stroke my flesh with so appetizing a motion that I became immediately conscious of the fact that lying face downwards upon rocks was not a posture at all kindly to the male frame even when unaroused – while upon a manly interest being manifested, it became positively dangerous.

'I was thus forced to rearrange my posture – which I feared might break the spell; but by now the lady was in no mood to refrain from her examination of this particular merman, and did not hesitate to extend that examination to the rest of his body – and especially to that appendage with which a merman is not supposed to be equipped. She went so far, indeed – while I continued to feign faintness – as to lay a hand upon that now engorged limb which rose like a lighthouse from the still damp, dark weeds which were entangled about its base.

'The situation was promising – but before it could warm to an even more inspiriting caress, I heard approaching voices in conversation – and having no means of covering myself, and not wishing to embarrass the lady concerned by appearing naked in her company, could do nothing but slip swiftly back into that watery element from which I had so recently emerged – which I did with such celerity as to convince her (as she later confessed) that my former struggle with the sea had been less desperate than my feigning had suggested.

'Submerging myself completely, I clung to the edge of the rock so that only my nostrils and the top of my head were to be seen, and those hidden by a convenient projecting ledge. A lady and gentleman then walked past, the former complaining at the roughness of the path, while the latter's warm encouragement to continue upon it may, I believe, have proceeded from the hope that another secluded cove lay ahead – for the coast of Cornwall, especially beautiful to those who have a love of nature, also offers generous privacy to those who wish rather to contemplate the beauties of woman, and are used for that purpose on a regular basis by holiday makers who find their way thither.

'But to return to my narrative – it was with complete frankness that my own lady now once more held out her hands to lift me from the water. Touched, I believe, by my tact in preserving her from audacious comment resultant upon my naked proximity to her person, on my admitting that my clothes lay nearby she invited me to accompany her to rooms which she had taken, and overlooking the beach. There, she said, I could rest after my ordeal: though this excuse was so lamely offered that her real interest in my person was scarcely disguised.

'Outside the long window of her rooms was a little terrace overlooked only by sun and seagulls; and on my admitting to a certain chill from placing my clothes upon a wet body, she encouraged me to remove them and warm myself in the sun – herself contributing to a swift glowing of my blood by divesting herself, also, of her covering. The passage of love which she then offered me was much different from that I had been educated in by the energetic Mrs Treleaven: Miss Rodesley (as proved to be her name) was almost excessively gentle – indeed, my first approach to her, modelled on the preferences of my only former mistress, so alarmed her that she almost fled!

'Fortunately, however, my instinct was even in those early days quick in the apprehension of ladies' predispositions in the matter of love, and I soon learned that her greatest pleasure was to contemplate and caress my body – her particular interest being in my arse, which within four and twenty hours had received more kisses and caresses than had ever been hung upon my lips, while her tricks of tickling my fundament, warming my cods with her palm, and even inserting the tip of a finger within that orifice which (in view of the charm of the resulting sensation) too rarely receives such an attention, were in themselves a liberal education.

'My own part was to a great extent merely to lie at ease while her fingers and (after an initial and understandable diffidence) tongue complimented those areas of my body she most admired, and – for she was always keenly interested in giving as well as receiving pleasure – those where the application of a fine talent most roused my own passionate nature.

'Her pleasure in this – in seeing my colour rise, my breast begin to pant, in feeling between her lips the sceptre of my manhood grow yet more adamant – became in the end sufficiently keen for her to show, by lying back with an appealing look, that I must now take my own part in the play; whereupon, on my kneeling between her opened thighs, the mere placing of the tip of my prick between the apprehensive verges of her *vulva* resulted in a gasping moan which indicated the spontaneous release of her most private emotions.

'I was thus commonly deprived (for she insisted that the pattern be followed upon every occasion) of my own satisfaction, which must be obtained later, in private, and by boringly solitary means. In a wife, her tastes would have been irritating to the point of absurdity; in a patron – for Miss Rodesley invited me to return with her to Bristol, where she kept me for six months in rooms near the house in which she lived with her brother, a merchant – they were necessarily supportable.

'When the six months had elapsed, and Miss Rodesley's engagement in marriage had been announced to an alderman of the city, I was kindly given my *congé* together with a purse of twenty guineas and an introduction to a Miss Formby of Uxbridge – by way, I believe, of a joke; but she proved to find me acceptable on other than humorous grounds, and another six months' of pleasant intimacy was the result.

'Since that date, I have continued fortunate in discovering patrons in the same line, and have found my work in that line only moderately arduous – though always demanding thought, care, sensitivity and a lack of consideration for my own tastes, which are by no means always satisfied by those who *I* am employed to satisfy.

'My acceptance of the chief condition in my line of work – that my place must be to satisfy others rather than myself

– is one which has resulted (as perhaps you my guess) in a career which has now for twelve years afforded me a life of some luxury, if not one the circumstances of which I am prepared to boast of. In that time I have been the *confidant* of perhaps two dozen ladies of all ages from eighteen to fifty and five, and can confidently claim to have offered them all perfect satisfaction in that area of life which I have been employed to cater to.

'I hope,' concluded our friend, 'that I have not offended the ladies present by my narrative. Any who may feel mine an improper story should perhaps look into their hearts and consider why a career often followed by the gentler sex should necessarily be despicable when adopted by a man. It has at all events raised me from the farmyard to the drawing room, has taught me how to speak, how to behave, how to dress; when I cease to pursue it, I shall be prepared both socially and financially to adopt a situation in life for which my birth would certainly not have prepared me.'

Somewhat suddenly, the young man concluded; and after a short silence was congratulated by all present, the ladies perhaps showing more enthusiasm than the gentlemen, and my friend Sophie, among the most enthusiastic, capturing Mr Trustworth (though she called him 'Geraldo', and in the true Spanish accent, which delighted him) and (as I overheard) beginning to tell him the story of that establishment she had set up some years ago at Chiswick for the entertainment of the fashionable ladies of London (a circumstance related in our joint memoirs entitled *Eros in Town*, still to be obtained at the bookseller's for a negligible sum).

The extent to which her interest was engaged by his story, or by the predilection I know she has for young gentlemen with olive skins and small, tight arses, I cannot say; except that her glowing appearance at tea time persuaded me that she had succeeded in comparing Mr Trustworth's manly virtues with those of the members of her Chiswick stable – and not to his disadvantage. (Nor, I may say, do I believe that she had paid a fee for the pleasure, my friend being naturally averse to exchanging money for love except under the most necessitous of circumstances.)

But it was now Sophie's turn to regale us with a narrative: perhaps – from the speedy thaw which I now discerned, the dripping of water from the eaves clearly to be heard in the dark outside the window – the last of those tales with which our imprisonment had been lightened.

13

Sophie's Tale

It was with some interest that I realized that the time had come for my friend Sophie to relate an anecdote to the now attentive audience, whose interest in each story had grown keener by degrees, so that far from having to be mustered as the time came about for each new story to be told, it was now in attendance in ample time, its members even jostling for places!

Which of the many adventures would she elaborate, to which she had already made privy not only myself but the multitudinous readers of the joint accounts of our adventures published by the industrious – nay, indefatigable – firm of venturers known as the Headline Press, situate as it is in elegant premises in Great Titchfield Street, London West One?

To my astonishment and pleasure, I realized as soon as she began, that she was plucking from her memory a story I had never heard before – though I would have sworn that there were no secrets between us. The glint of humour in her eye as I caught it suggested that she took particular pleasure in the fact that her narrative was as new to me as to her other auditors – and it was certainly with increasing interest that I listened as the story was unfolded.

'The date of the occurrences I am about to relate was the year 1818, when I was staying at Alcovary House, not far from the city of Cambridge. The university of that city is one which has always been keenly interested in the advancement of science, and thus it was that (having several friends connected with the colleges) I frequently was among the first to hear rumours of some of those discoveries which were to revolutionize our lives. One, which became current in the first decade of the century, was of a remarkable engine devised by a Cornish gentleman, Mr Richard Trevithick, which was in some way set in motion by the pressure of steam raised by the boiling of water.

'It will be believed that at the time when they were first current, I paid little attention to such lunatic tales. However, as is so often the case, the world being not only stranger than we believe but stranger than we can believe, they turned out to be based on fact: and one day in 1818 *The Times* newspaper carried the following announcement:

' "We are credibly informed that there is a Steam Engine now preparing to run against any mare, horse or gelding that may be produced at the October meeting at Newmarket; the wagers at present are stated to be £10,000; the engine is the favourite. The most astonishing machine ever invented, this is supposed to gallop from fifteen to twenty mile an hour on any circle."

'This was a most interesting proposition, and my interest in it was strengthened when my half-brother and host, Sir Franklin Franklyn, Bart., returning from London, informed me that he had seen this remarkable instrument on exhibition, running upon a track of rails near Gower Street, the engine bearing the motto *Catch Me Who Can*. Upon payment of one shilling, my brother (ever rash in his search for new experiences) had mounted a carriage pulled by the machine, and, consulting his watch, had estimated its speed as no less than twelve miles an hour – while Mr Trevithick was confident it could reach twenty, up a lengthier track.

' " 'Tis the thing of the future, Soph!" said my brother, as we lay together in bed on the morning after his return (having spent the night, as was our wont in a friendly and intimate exchange of those courtesies current between man and wife or lover and mistress, and which we had enjoyed together since we were children and knew no better).

' "That is as may be," I said; "but is it sufficient to make our fortune?" – and in reply to Frank's puzzled look of enquiry, jumped from bed in that state of undress in which I normally slept, and crossing the room (for it had been my bed in which I had been hostess) reached *The Times* and placed it before him.

'The idea which had immediately occurred to me had also occurred to him. Though, if the report were true, the odds offered by bookmakers would be short enough, a successful wager would be pleasantly remunerative – while in any case (as Frank said, placing a kiss upon my breast) it would be interesting to watch as history was made – should that indeed be the case.

'The October meeting was due to begin that very day and the contest upon the morrow, so no time was to be lost if we were to find accommodation near Newmarket, where through the fashionable interest in racing, beds were at a premium during the season. In short, we were off within the hour, Frank's valet and my maid having thrown some small changes of clothes into trunks – for we proposed to be absent only for perhaps a week.

'The journey to Newmarket passed without any remarkable occurrence; but there, as might have been foreseen, the inns proved to be entirely full – perhaps in part due to the excitement generated by the contest between horse and steam engine – and no amount of enquiry could discover so much as a length of floor where we could lay ourselves. After spending several hours in the search, Frank sadly instructed his driver to set off once more for home.

'However, as we were running down the hill upon which the main street of the town is built, we were hailed by a fashionably dressed gentleman upon a fine steed, who was riding in the opposite direction.

' "Why, Saint!" exclaimed Frank – and immediately introduced me to St John Fenmore, a gentleman the sharpness of whose eye as he bowed suggested to me that he would welcome any opportunity of proving his nickname to be an inappropriate one.

'Not to make my tale tedious, Mr Fenmore, an acquaintance of Frank's during his time at university, and a gentleman for whom sport was more a way of life than a form of relaxation, always took a villa at Six Mile Bottom, on the London road, for the races; and hearing of our predicament immediately offered us hospitality – "though 'twill be somewhat crowded, for my party is an unexpectedly large one; and" (he turned to me) "I must also remark that it is exclusively male – if this will not embarrass your sister."

' "The man has not been born," said Frank (with what any other woman might have thought to be undue plainness), "who can embarrass my Soph!"

'And so we followed Mr Fenmore out of the town, past the racecourse, where a muck of the common people was already in a state of happy drunkenness staking claim to patches of land where they would sleep the time away until the first race on the following morning. They were likely to be largely uncomfortable, it occurred to me; for, almost before we were out of the town, the heavens opened and heavy rain began to fall – and even with our hood up, by the time we reached Fenmore's villa (which lay not far from the house of Colonel Leigh, the brother-in-law of the poet Lord Byron) we were wet through.

'Upon our entering the villa, we were immediately conscious that what Frank's friend had said was no less than the truth: for there seemed to be as many as a couple of dozen gentleman, mostly of his own age – that is, in the middle twenties – in one room or another.

'As we shook ourselves like dogs in the hallway, Fenmore joined us – equally wet.

' "Fence!" he shouted. "Where is that unregenerate b******? Fence!" – and on the said servant appearing, instructed him immediately to heat water "for a tub" – and taking us upstairs showed us into a bedroom where, in a corner, a place had been fitted out in the modern manner as somewhere where one could wash oneself.

' "Mrs Nelham, perhaps you would like to take advantage of a hot plunge," he said; "my people are practised in the provision of hot water as speedily as I require it, and since the weather has turned inclement, the failure to warm yourself from your present sodden state may be dangerous."

'I was of course delighted at the convenience, though it consisted only of a large metal bath with a screen about it. On the servants appearing with no less than three large pails of steaming water, I did not hesitate to retire behind the screen and, divesting myself of my wet clothing, plunged into a bath which was so hot that I could scarcely bear it, and which coloured my body in one roseate hue.

'Conscious that the gentlemen were waiting their turn and that the water would not remain hot for ever, I did not linger, but the moment I observed my limbs turn from a damp paleness to a rosy warmth, rose – and realized that I had no means of leaving the bath except wringing wet and in a state of nature, for I had stupidly neglected to bring with me the towel which had been handed me, but had left it hanging over the edge of the screen.

'Well, Frank had seen me sufficiently often in my present state for neither he nor myself to repine at the prospect, and I now invited him to pass me the towel.

'There was a silence; and on repeating the request, I was answered not by my brother but by Mr Fenmore.

' "Sir Frank has for a moment left the room to satisfy a call of nature," he said; "can I be of assistance?"

'I was fortunately sufficiently a woman of the world to recognize a gentleman when I saw one; and in any event Mr Fenmore was (not to beat about the bush) a young man of parts, whose person I found by no means repugnant. I therefore confessed my predicament, and asked whether he would find it embarrassing were I to ask him to pass me the towel.

' "I shall be honoured, ma'am," he replied, and in a moment appeared around the edge of the screen – and I discovered that he had, in preparation for following me into the warm water, undressed and was merely girded about the waist with his own towel.

'I saw this over my shoulder, for I had, not in a ridiculous display of prudity but in common politeness, turned my back on him. I could not but remark, as he stepped towards me, that the pupils of his eyes were large and luminous (an invariable sign, ladies, of a gentleman's amorous interest); and was not unprepared when, as he placed the towel about my shoulders, his hands lingered somewhat upon them, and then began gently to rub the towel over them.

'The warmth communicated by the friction, joined to the glow which the warm water had engendered, was extremely pleasant, and I was not overly inclined to rebuke him for what if it had not begun as a liberty could now perhaps be regarded as one, for not content with drying my shoulders, arms and back, he now reached about to pay the same attention to my breasts – while against my back I felt the cool propinquity of his own body: the slight roughness of a male chest decorated with a generous growth of wiry black hairs.

'If I must be honest, I must confess that my action in stepping from the bath was prompted as much by an interest in what might follow as by the need to leave the water; in doing so, I turned somewhat towards the gentleman, and by some accident my hand knocked against his waist, dislodging the mere tuck by which the towel hung there – which immediately dropped to the ground, revealing the lower portion of his body. This bore no less generous a decoration of black hair than his chest – indeed his belly and thighs were so covered that the white skin scarcely showed through. What did show with remarkable clarity was a splendidly upright prick of fine and well-proportioned dimensions, which being a wand entirely devoid of hair was thrown into sharp relief, so that even the most casual glance would have been arrested by its uncommon size, not only of length but of thickness.

'So impressive was this instrument – at that time by far the largest I had seen (though subsequent experience especially in certain foreign climes – has made the recollection somewhat less startling than was the original manifestation) – that my gaze remained fixed on it longer than many would in the circumstances have considered polite.

'Raising my eyes, I met his own, which had such a quizzical look that, rarely, I blushed.

' "Forgive me, ma'am," he said, as I lowered my gaze again – realized to what I had lowered it, and blushed anew. "Forgive me, but I am incapable of resisting that instinct which must express in the manner of which you are a witness my admiration of a beautiful woman."

'Though at the time young, I was more experienced than to find it apposite to rebuke him.

' "Sir," I replied, "I take it for nothing but a compliment, and—"

' "And?" he prompted.

' "And," I continued, "am even inclined to hope that your regard for my person may lead you to express it in a more corporeal fashion than by a mere oracular demonstration."

'My listeners may be startled at this: but it must be remembered that I was still of an age when experience is craved by any honest young person, and the prospect before me was so promising a one that I found myself incapable of not taking advantage of the situation: in that respect, I must admit to being as open and eager as any young person of the other sex, my emotions being so eager that I could never bring myself to be shocked or surprised when I was offered attentions by any gentleman of reasonable demeanour.

'If Mr Fenmore was startled by my readiness, he did not allow his emotions to delay his response which was to take me in his arms and – knocking the screen to the ground on his way – to carry me to the bed which occupied the other half of the room, where, lying me gently down, he knelt between my thighs and bent to discover, by application of his lips, whether I was ready to receive him without pain; this being obvious by the generous lubrication which had occurred in those parts ever receptive to the idea of congress, he inserted the bulbous tip of his prick between my lower lips, and with a steady, relentless and delicious pressure lowered himself until his breast was upon my breast, his belly upon mine, and the whole length of that admirable instrument which lay below it rammed me with its fine flesh, swollen to adamantine firmness.

'Gentlemen who by simple fortune are well endowed where their generative organs are concerned – who are in popular parlance "well hung" – sometimes fear to injure the female sex in the way of coitus; a moment's thought teaches how insubstantial is that fear, or how vain is perhaps the hope! If it is possible for us to expel a child, though with some discomfort, from that same aperture through which it is conceived, how unlikely is it that the most massive prick should cause any injury! Yet time and again one hears talk of "splitting", of "battering", of "stretching". 'Tis all vanity! But when we are young, we (not unnaturally) may ourselves share that misconception, and I must confess that I was somewhat apprehensive of a connexion with Mr Fenmore: yet with what pleasure was the apprehension proved false! Certainly, had his entry not been tenderly slow – the result no doubt of generous experience – there might have been some momentary discomfort; but as it was, my emotions were rather those of a person indulging in an admirable and filling meal than of someone being forcibly fed!

'Added to this, the delightfully lethargy of his movements, the relaxed and gentle manner in which he raised and lowered his buttocks, thus seeming to stroke with his instrument the unseen surfaces within, was inexpressibly delightful, so that sooner than I would have believed possible I felt my whole person contract in one paroxysm of pleasure; whereupon, with the greatest consideration in the world, he intimated to me in a whisper that were I to wish to conclude the episode, I would find that the insertion of my hand between our persons, in order to caress his cods, would immediately bring about his own climax.

'To be frank, this was not my wish, the experience having been far too pleasant for me not to wish to prolong it somewhat; and, encouraged to proceed, he now to my surprise withdrew his instrument, and began as it were to kiss my body all over with its length, drawing it down my thighs, beating it gently upon my belly, and drawing himself up, even to titillate with its tip the points of my breasts – thereby instigating a feeling entirely new to me.

'If my description of this passage seems to be more than a little *naive*, it should be remembered that although experienced I was still relatively an *ingénue*, my previous partners (even my dear brother) having been gentlemen of more enthusiasm than practise. This was almost my first experience of a lover who felt it his duty to give at least as much pleasure as he received – not even suggesting to me that I should myself devise the means of pleasing him in any other way than being the mere vessel of his pleasure.

'This, however, I speedily enough became, for on that admirable weapon again being sheathed, and having prompted me once more to a charming ecstasy, I did avail myself of his invitation, and no sooner felt the comfortable rotundity of his balls within my palm than I apprehended also a sort of twitching, married to a hot flow within me which I was not simple enough to mistake for anything other than the final expression of his passion.

'I had been so occupied and preoccupied with my pleasure that I had failed to notice that Frank had returned to the room, and, though having prepared himself for his bath had been entirely unable to ignore us, and now sat, himself bare as a needle, in a chair at the side of the bed, his own person expressive of the keen aphrodisiac effect of the scene.

'I was unable to see his discomfort without sympathy, and Mr Fenmore having relinquished his position afforded Frank the means to satisfy that instinct which, unwittingly, we had provoked; after which, the water in the bath being now cold, Mr Fenmore summoned his servants anew who, while we rested, emptied the bath and refilled it, after which we bathed ourselves and each other, and late but happy commissioned some food.

'Mr Fenmore had, he said, been about to propose that Frank and I should share the room to which we had in the first place been shown, while he slept in a chair before the kitchen fire; however, we would not, of course, hear of it, and the three of us spent the night together – the bed being sufficiently large to accommodate us without discomfort, our earlier exercise having tired and satisfied us to such an extent that none of the three but slept without so much as turning about.

'We awoke next morning to the sound of rain drumming upon the roof and windows; and Mr Fenmore was good enough to suggest, laying a hand upon my breast, that there were ways of spending such an inclement day which were much superior to watching a race between a tin kettle and a gelding. However, while never entirely disinclined to such exercise as he had in mind, my curiosity as to the nature of Mr Trevithick's steed was such as to encourage me to reject the suggestion, and so by half past the hour of nine, wrapped well in waterproofed clothing, we were making once more for Newmarket, where just outside the town a circular track had been laid.

'The crowd which had gathered to see the contest was smaller than might have been the case had the weather been more clement – many people preferring to remain at home, to await the news of the result of the race as relayed to them by the popular newspapers, and then to collect their winnings should they have betted upon the successful side. The town being a place almost entirely devoted to the breeding and racing of horses, the money in this vicinity was heavily upon the latter – though in general, I was given to suppose, the chief wagers were upon the side of Mr Trevithick and his engine – which now stood, panting heavily in bursts of steam, upon the track. On approaching a gentleman of the turf known to Frank, we succeeded in placing the sum of fifty guineas each upon Mr Trevithick's engine to win, at odds of five to one.

'By the side of the engine stood none other than the inventor himself, a strong and handsome Cornishman over six feet in height, broad-shouldered, with a massive head and bright blue eyes. He was descanting to anyone who would listen upon the nature of his invention – talking with some pride of the improvements he had been able to make over the effort of his principal rival, Mr Woolf – that is (as I understand it) his insistence upon a direct-acting pumping engine, with an inverted cylinder set over and in line with the pump rod, thus dispensing with the beam that had previously been essential in all forms of steam engine.

'Technicalities however did not really interest me, and I suspect will not interest the reader; the engine itself was a sufficiently handsome beast, though to my mind not to be compared with the beauty of the creature against which it was to race, and which stood now, carefully covered against the rain and jumping nervously at every noisy expulsion of steam from its inanimate rival. Its rider was exchanging cool glances with the driver of the engine, evidently an assistant to Trevithick – an exceptionally fine, lean young fellow clad in white trousers striped with black, white shirt, and a red kerchief – all now soaked with the rain which continued to pelt down, and provided some difficulty by wetting the wood which lay in a carrier behind the engine, and with which the young man continually stoked the fire.

'I must confess that there is something about the adherence of wet clothing to the body of the young male which I have always found peculiarly excitatory; and especially when, as in this case, the person concerned is sufficiently muscular; the relatively thin material of his shirt was like a second skin, each muscle sufficiently outlined to convey to the mind a distinct impression of what his appearance would be should he . . .

'But as my mind reached this point, as though he had been following my train of thought (and it my be so, for we had already exchanged eyes), with a mild imprecation directed at the skies, he threw off his shirt – displaying indeed a figure which would please any woman: broad shoulders and a breast whose platform was brown, wholesome, and decorated with a pair of delightful paps the tiny nipples of which stood out like little marbles against the cold rain, which gave his naked flesh a silver sheen from the reflection of the cold, grey light of a cloudy but bright sky.

'The latter seeming for a moment to reach its apogee, the young man turned to Trevithick and seemed to inform him that the opportunity should be taken to begin the race. This being quickly agreed between Trevithick and Lord Nettlesburn, the owner of the gelding, it and the engine were lined up, the jockey leaped to the saddle of his horse, the young man to the platform of his engine, and upon the firing of a shot from Nettlesburn's pistol, there was a violent hiss of steam, the horse reared up upon its hind legs (almost throwing its rider), and both beast and engine set off, the former upon a path of chippings which followed the curve of the circular track of rails upon which Trevithick's monster raced.

'The sight was a very exciting one; but though the horse stretched its legs to enormous effect, there was no doubt in my mind that the engine would be the winner – the impression of power it gave being irresistible. I began to wish that I had placed a heavier bet with one of the numerous gentlemen of the turf who were now beginning to excite themselves over their prospects of winning or losing . . . But all bets were to be off, for sadly, a calamity now ensued.

'The mistake had been made (though only shown a mistake by the sudden deterioration in the weather) of laying the track upon low ground; the soaking which the earth had received during the night had softened it to a greater degree than might have been supposed possible; and on the engine reaching a certain speed, the track beneath it began to give way – and on its reaching a point almost opposite where we were standing, the rails buckled, the wheels left them, and Mr Trevithick's fine contrivance fell with a dull crash upon its side – the young mechanic being fortuitously hurled from its platform some distance from the wreck, for otherwise he would no doubt have been scalded to death by the great expulsion of steam which accompanied the accident.

'Frank, Mr Fenmore and I immediately ran with others towards the recumbent body of the young driver, who lay now upon the wet ground silent and motionless. Having had some experience with injuries, I laid my head upon his chest and to my great relief heard the strong and unhesitant beat of a young heart; lifting my head, I placed my fingers upon his eyelid and raised it, revealing an eye in which there was no appearance of dullness; and indeed upon my releasing it, it gave what seemed an unmistakable wink, and at the same time I felt the firm pressure of a hand against my thigh, where my skirt had fallen across the young man's body, thus concealing it from view.

'I rose.

' "Frank, perhaps you and Mr Fenmore could carry this unfortunate young man into the tent?"

'Without hesitation, they lifted him and bore him beneath the small, convenient tarpaulin which had been erected for Mr Trevithick's convenience, and in which, in between much engineering equipment of this kind and of that, was sufficient space to enable us to lay the victim upon a dry pile of sacking.

' "Thank you, gentlemen," I said; "what is now required is a period of rest and quiet, after which I am sure . . ."

' "But is he to live?" enquired Trevithick, who had accompanied us, clearly more distressed at the state of his assistant than at the wreck of his engine, which still lay hissing gently upon its side.

' "He is stunned," I said, "and requires to lie quietly for a while, after which I am confident he will be completely recovered."

'Frank had been clearing the tent of onlookers, and now escorted Mr Fenmore and Trevithick to the entrance.

' "I will stand guard," he said to me, adding in a whisper (for he was sharp enough not to have missed our exchange of glances) that he had no doubt the *régime* the young man would be offered would expedite his recovery.

'The listener may suppose that I acted precipitately in kneeling, the moment the tent was empty, at the side of the victim and, placing my lips upon his own, offering him a tender kiss; but I had two reasons for so doing – one was that such an action would almost certainly, through its action upon the senses aid in the recovery of a semi-conscious victim; the second, that I wished to test whether I had properly interpreted the glance which had come from that dark brown eye.

'The manner in which the young man's lips parted beneath my own, and the way in which his returning my kiss was accompanied by a determined effort to slip a hand into my bosom, suggested that my interpretation had indeed been accurate.

' "You are an impertinent fellow," I said, as soon as I could persuade myself to relinquish lips which were as sweet as a girl's.

' "Right enough," said the boy, opening his eyes and, ensuring that no one else was in the vicinity, continuing his efforts to free my bosom from the constraints of a somewhat tightly buttoned garment. I was forced to help him, lest with that strength of whose bounds the young are often unaware, he should damage the material.

'The sight of my breasts as they were freed from encumbrance was clearly sufficiently efficacious medicine to clear his head of any slight dullness, for the boy's delightful lips – much more tender than the rather horny hands which were now attempting to loosen other areas of my clothing – fixed themselves to the most receptive points of my bosom, where I soon felt his tongue gently flicking.

'Time was against us, however; Mr Trevithick's anxiety as to the health of his assistant could not long be contained. Detaching the boy's grip, I rose to my feet and threw off what remained of my clothing – at which he was no less speedy to detach his wet breeches (the steam rising from which spoke of a body heated through excitement), revealing himself to be ready to stoke any fire which offered.

'He was, I realized, a great deal more knowing than his youth – or his upbringing in a remote part of the country – might have suggested; for though I was ready to teach him how to love, indeed he needed no instruction, persuading me without difficulty and with the most sensitive caresses to lay myself down upon the sacking and make available to him that haven into which he slipped without difficulty, and where he immediately began to raise a storm.

'Each union has its particular flavour: this was of youth and vigour accompanied by an ingenious and inventive spirit, for realizing that he had little time, he passed within ten minutes from merely reclining upon my body to kneeling while he supported me upon his thighs, then to raising my legs until my calves lay upon his shoulders (thus enabling him to plumb depths unavailable in other postures).

'Withdrawing for a moment his prick – which under the momentary caress of my fingers felt as adamant as any metal bar – he invited me to kneel, when he came at me from the rear (careful, however, in his choice of the conventional aperture), when his hands busied themselves about my breasts, then stroked my belly and back with a ticklish, smooth lightness which was irresistible in its intensity, so that I was forced, reaching behind me, to seize a pair of small but sinewy buttocks in an attempt to persuade my lover to yet more strenuous efforts.

'His reply was to withdraw yet again, and lie upon his back – when, with some difficulty persuading his prick to a vertical position (which otherwise lay flat against his belly, always a sign of a fine and comprehensive virility) I crouched over him and sank upon it, thus – as had been his kind intention – being able to control those movements which would now at any moment . . .

'I had the greatest difficulty in suppressing a shriek as I came with a paroxysm as intense as any I had experienced; while at the same time being sadly conscious that I had not returned the compliment by bringing his emotions to their height. However, gently persuading me to rise, he seized his instrument and with one or two strokes brought himself off – a jet rising with astonishing force from its tip, perhaps eighteen inches into the air, each successive gush falling only slightly short of the first, and the whole fountain continuing for longer than might have been thought possible.

'Just at that moment, I heard Frank's voice raised in argument; and had only just time to throw my clothes on and to cast a piece of sacking across the momentarily exhausted figure of my lover, before Trevithick entered.

'I placed my finger upon my lips.

' "He is sleeping soundly, sir," I said (and indeed the young villain was giving a fine counterfeit of satisfied slumber – which might even have been no counterfeit). I spread some more sackcloth upon him.

' "I have made sure he is dry and warm," I said; "if you leave him for an hour, I am sure you will find him completely recovered.

' "Ma'am," said Trevithick as we left the tent, "I am infinitely obliged to you. He is my only son, and it is so impossible to contain his spirits that I have long feared such an accident."

' "Of his high spirits I have no doubt," I said; "nor do I fear that they will be permanently affected by the present circumstances, though you may find him more than commonly tired during the rest of the day."

'Difficult though it was to get away from the grateful father, I eventually escaped – promising to attend his next demonstration of his engine in London in some months' time, when, Mr Trevithick was sure, his son would wish to thank me personally for my help – "for he will regret", said the father, "his inability to show his gratitude on this occasion."

'Whether in fact we met again it is not for me, at this time, to reveal; and I trust that those of you who may fear the potential danger of travel by what is known as "the railway" will not be put off by my present narrative; though I cannot promise that every engine driver will offer those personal attentions I received on my first experience of the machine that drives that convenient mode of transport.'

At this point Sophie ended her narrative – and, though it was only nine o'clock, proposed that we should all retire to bed – for, she said, she had been informed by our coachman that the thaw was proceeding apace, and we should be very likely able to recommence our journey on the following morning.

So we retired, eschewing any carnal connexion other than bidding each other good night with a kiss sufficiently innocent to have been exchanged by brother and sister – or, come to that, compared to the circumstances of which we had heard, more innocent. (Though I must remind the reader that Frank – then unmarried – was merely Sophie's half-brother, and that the connexion between them was one which is known to have occurred in many of the most celebrated families in the country!)

14

Andy's Tale

The morning was so bright that I thought perhaps it threatened more snow; but upon looking out of the window the sky proved to be cloudlessly blue, and we believed it possible our journey might be resumed. However, on our breakfasting we were informed by the coachman that since it was freezing hard it would be inadvisable to start out for the north until we had positive news that the roads were passable.

This was clearly a day on which – after so long an incarceration – it would be possible to take a little fresh air, and much though they had enjoyed their tale-tellings, our fellow-passengers were clearly inclined to blow the cobwebs from their heads and by ten o'clock most had made their way across the meadow to the river and were larking about like schoolboys, throwing snowballs, building snowmen, and our poet even – surely unwisely? – venturing upon the ice with a pair of bone skates strapped to his boots.

Myself, having spent the morning in packing those goods which during the past few days had been scattered about that room which had been our home, had decided to step it out in the afternoon for a good, long walk, and having borrowed heavy boots from the house (where a selection was kept piled in the hall for just such a circumstance) set off up the hill, past one of the many churches of the town, and into the country. In only a few hundred yards, I came to great gates which spoke of some fine park, and since they were set open, and the grounds looked enticing, saw no harm in entering.

The landscape was little short of magnificent – the grounds had clearly been designed not by the random hand of Nature but by a master gardener; trees stood, their branches still laden by snow, in carefully posed groups about the park, as heavily laden ships might sail across a frozen sea. My footprints stood out behind me, dark against virgin snow. Gradually, the mass of a great house loomed up. I seemed to be approaching it from the rear, for outbuildings reached out towards me.

Suddenly, I heard from the direction of the buildings a cry of distress, in a woman's voice, keen and shrill on the still air. I broke my stride and halted; the cry came again, even more distressed than at first. As quickly as I could in my heavy boots, I ran in the direction of the sound and coming around the edge of a wall, where a small hut stood separate from the main buildings, I saw to my distress the naked body of a girl rolled in the snow; from her lips came, again, cries of distress.

Quickly, I removed my cloak and wrapping it about her lifted her in my arms and made towards the hut, from a little chimney of which I saw some smoke arising. The girl struggled in my arms, seeming to protest; I could not hesitate, for fear of provoking whoever had attacked her, and who might now turn upon me while I was encumbered by his victim. I pushed at the door of the hut with my foot. Happily it sprung open, and I stepped into an interior, where a wall of heat struck me like a furnace. I set down my burden.

'Do not fear,' I said; 'whoever has reduced you to this state shall rue the day, if I set my hands upon him!'

A thin wail came from the girl's lips – for I could now see that she was a mere girl, and a pretty one at that; she collapsed upon a sort of bench which was set against a wall of the hut, and hid her face in her hands, continuing to weep most pitifully. I sat beside her and placed my arm about her.

'My dear,' I repeated, 'do not distress yourself. You now have a protector who will consider it an honour to set himself between you and . . .'

But now she raised her face, and though indeed tears were rolling down her cheeks – I saw them to be tears of laughter!

My face must have been a study of bewilderment, for on catching my eye she laughed yet again – her entire body shaking with it, so that my cloak was dislodged from her shoulders and fell about her waist, revealing a shapely person which, now rosy from the sudden warming of flesh chilled with the snow, was (I must confess) extremely attractive.

It took some little time for the girl to recover herself, for every time she governed her laughter, the sight of my face again brought it on; but at last, she managed to stutter her apologies.

'Believe me, sir, your chivalrous intentions are very much appreciated – but I was under no attack, but merely indulging in a course of refreshing snow bathing which, while uncommon in this country, is well known as a healthful resort in certain northern climes.'

On enquiring further, she told me that the owner of the estate, much given to foreign travel had observed in the country of Finland the habit those people indulge in of rushing from a heated room into the snow and rolling about in it, sometimes beating each other with the smaller branches of trees in order to promote (she said) the running of the blood in the veins. Some two years ago, having enjoyed the custom, he had had built on his estate a little cabin or *sauna* (as it was properly called) which he and his wife used when hard weather came upon them, as in this northern part of the country it did almost every winter; and guests at the house were encouraged, should they wish it, to use the convenience.

I looked about me, at this; and saw that in the corner of the cabin, which was all of wood, was a small hearth in which large stones lay upon the fire, warmed even to a red heat, and filling the interior of the place with a dry swelter which was almost insufferable – indeed, my face was all a muck of sweat, and my clothes began to stick to my body.

'Why, sir, do you not try the effect?' the young lady now

asked – at the same time setting aside my cloak, and folding it carefully and placing it in a corner where some other clothes (presumably her own) lay – by her action revealing, I may say, a plump posterior whose shape was inviting enough to be pleasing to the most critical observer.

I must confess that it was in the supposition that my action might lead to a closer familiarity with those enticing limbs that I was glad to accept her invitation, and in no time had removed my own clothing and was as naked as she. As I seated myself upon the bench at her side, she rose and taking a pail of water dashed some upon the stones – releasing a cloud of steam which instantly provoked a torrent of perspiration which drenched my body from head to toe.

It might be thought that a gentleman of my amorous disposition (I admit it, even were I not convinced that the reader, by now having some knowledge of my character, is already cognizant of the fact) finding himself seated next to a particularly beautiful young woman, and both in the state in which Adam introduced Eve to the bliss communicated by the first love apple, might take advantage of the fact; and I was indeed careful – having the excuse of the somewhat confined space available – to sit sufficiently close to the girl for our thighs and arms at least to be touching. Yet to my amazement that part of my body which would normally have expressed the pleasure I certainly felt at the contact, remained entirely limp and unexcited; and while I admired my companion quite sufficiently to encourage me to hope for a connexion, I remained in a state in which such a connexion would prove entirely ineffectual.

I felt myself to be in a pitiable condition: what would the young lady think of me? Hoping to better my chances, I took the liberty of placing an arm about her shoulders – when immediately a fresh sweat broke out at the contact, and water ran freely down her back, while a rivulet trickled from beneath my hand (the fingers of which rested upon her neck) down over the charming globe of her breast, from the centre of which it fell in large drops to her thigh –

though watching it, I could not but remark that the centre of that breast, far from indicating by a pert alertness any amorous interest in the situation, remained as unaroused and flaccid as my poor prick.

Meeting my eye, she smiled – and, I was relieved to see, not unkindly.

'I apologise, ma'am,' I said, 'for my slowness in appreciating your beauty, but . . .'

' 'Tis the heat, sir,' she said; 'our persons are not accustomed to such extremes, and the circumstances are certainly not conducive to what I believe you have in mind. Indeed, the most intimate caress would be fruitless . . .' At which, she reached out with her hand and positively gathered up with her fingers the limp apparatus between my legs – my poor, shrivelled cock lying upon her palm, no more animate than a dead mouse!

'Do not repine, sir,' she said; 'in a while I will suggest an excursion which may provoke a different response.'

We sat for some little time together. The heat became such that I was unable even to bear to touch her, though every inch of that delicious flesh invited the pressure of a hand or a pair of lips. At the moment when it seemed entirely insufferable, she rose, and held out her hand – and on my taking it, threw open the door of the hut and drew me out into the snow, which thereabouts was perhaps three feet deep upon the ground.

To my astonishment, on following her example and throwing my naked body into it, the effect was by no means as painful as might be thought – while the cold certainly took one's breath away, and to an extent was as inspiriting as to provoke those cries to which my companion now once more gave vent, the general impression was one of liveliness and well-being, and gave rise to a playfulness which was expressed in our tumbling each other again and again, when the propinquity of our persons resulted (to my delight) in the happy rising of that head which until now had been uncharacteristically bowed – a circumstance which my friend made even more notable by dint of taking a handful of snow and rubbing it over my belly and those parts adjacent.

On this happy occurrence, I made to demonstrate my manhood in the normal manner; but wisely she drew me back into the *sauna*, where she freely offered me her body, and while we were both immediately again swamped with sweat, the slipperiness of our skins added only a happy additional *frisson* (as the Frenchies say), and I found myself able to enjoy our amorous frolic, the only disadvantage being that our jointure must be a brief one, for due to the renewed heat I already felt my powers failing.

Having come with a pleasure quite sufficient to send my senses (weakened, perhaps, by the heat) reeling, I lifted myself from the body of my friend with what perhaps might have been regarded as undue haste, but which was no doubt as great a relief to her as to myself, in view of the warmth. Upon my sitting up, I felt an immediate draught of cold air, and saw to my amazement that the door was open and that a figure stood in it.

'Excuse me,' said the stranger, with a heavy irony; 'I was unaware, Maggie, that you had company. But you can get rid of your Romeo, for we're in trouble!'

He took a step forward – and even in the gloom (for the cabin was lit only by the flickering light of the fire) I recognized a face I knew – just as it recognized me

'F—k me!' said the man, with a freedom of language which did not seem to surprise Maggie in the least, 'if it ain't Andy!'

'David!' I cried, throwing my arms about the fellow. 'What do you do here?'

'You shall hear everything,' he said, pausing only to give me a smacking kiss full on the lips; 'but Maggie, you must come to the hall immediately. Fred has gone down with a pain in his belly, and what we shall do for tonight I cannot think!'

Maggie threw herself into her clothes with a celerity which seemed to suggest that dressing and undressing was with her a matter of business rather than pleasure; while I clothed myself with almost equal speed, and followed David Ham across the snow to the main building.

He was (I should explain for those few readers who have not previously encountered him in the pages of my memoirs) a cully I had first met as part of a travelling theatre company when I was a mere youth; he had taken a fancy to me – which in itself might have been a source of some embarrassment, since he was of that breed of gentleman unfortunate enough – at least, in the eyes of those of us who are lovers of the ladies – to have been born with a taste for members of his own sex. But happily, while not rejecting the opportunity to make an attempt upon my virtue he was extremely pleasant, unprejudiced, and without the desire to take advantage of an innocent who had any rooted objection to the process; and our friendship had been (apart from one or two occasions which I have detailed elsewhere) entirely platonic.

He had made a living in a multitude of ways – not least in the theatre; most recently in North America, where, encountering him as unexpectedly as upon the present occasion, I had commissioned him to manage a brothel on behalf of a young woman to whom the procedures followed in such a place were entirely unknown until she had inherited it from an uncle. But those are stories that, as I say, I have related elsewhere (in those volumes entitled *Eros in the Country* and *Eros in the New World*), so I will not enlarge upon them here. As we walked quickly to the big house, he quickly explained that he had been engaged by the celebrated nobleman whose home it was to provide an entertainment for a number of gentlemen gathered in the house for the Christmas season.

'They have their wives with 'em, Andy,' he said, 'but those ladies scarcely provide enough joy for the whole season, and so after a while milords need a little ginger if they are to satisfy miladies.'

What sort of entertainment did he provide? I asked – imagining, knowing my friend, that it involved those ladies and gentlemen who specialized in exhibitions of erotic behaviour (for my friend had something of a reputation for providing such shows).

'Something new and original,' said Davy. 'But excuse me if I do not explain at this moment, for I face a difficulty of some magnitude. Maggie here was to participate in a . . . a form of performance, with myself and her friend Fred, this very evening; but Fred is now overcome with some kind of sudden distemper, and . . .'

'Where is he?' asked Maggie; and we were taken immediately to a small bedroom where the unfortunate young man was laid upon a bed groaning in some pain. Throwing off the bedclothes without ceremony, Maggie revealed the sick man as a person of some presence, nobly formed, with parts which (while now at their least impressive, as a result of his discomfort) would in extension no doubt be satisfactory not only to herself but to an audience.

On her placing her hand upon his belly, the man groaned again; and on her attempting to lift his head, gave vent to such a cry that she immediately dropped it once more upon the pillow.

'My Lord's physician,' said David, 'assures me that it is merely a severe attack of indigestion; but clearly there is no possibility of Fred's participating in our show.'

Maggie sat herself down with a melancholy air, and David seemed for a moment equally disconsolate; until, his eyes falling upon me, he brightened.

'Unless . . .' he said.

'It is my impression,' he went on, 'from the circumstances in which I discovered you, that you are no more impervious to Maggie's charms than I know you to be in general to those of the sex.'

I could not deny it.

'And in the past you have been good enough to help me out when circumstances have demanded it.'

I blushed at this, for it recalled a time when I had been forced by a sudden emergency to take part in an exhibition which had included my introduction to that practice most enjoyed by gentlemen of my friend's taste, and which – though Davy himself had proved a not unkind demonstrator – I did not care to have known by a lady.

'No – this is not a similar circumstance,' said Davy; 'but let me show you.'

Rising, he led me from the room and, Maggie following us, through several corridors and eventually to a large and handsomely furnished hall where perhaps twenty-five chairs were set out facing a large white sheet which had been suspended by cords, and was surrounded by draped dark curtains.

Davy sat me in one of the chairs and invited me to remain while he and Maggie proceeded through the curtains.

After a while, I was astonished to see a bright light illuminate the white sheet – and in a moment, the unmistakable silhouettes of Davy and Maggie appeared on the screen, a little larger than life size, but as clearly delineated as those cut out in paper by the man at the corner of Burlington Arcade and Piccadilly.

A table, upon which was a container with some flowers, was similarly clearly depicted. For a brief moment the two actors stayed, Maggie curtsying and Davy bending to kiss her finger tips; then they vanished, and a voice called to me to join them.

Behind the screen, I found a raised table set behind the sheet, while facing it and some distance away was a machine in which five candles blazed, their light falling upon a glass lens producing a beam which, passing through a square aperture in the side of the lantern, was cast upon the screen: so that any person standing upon the table would be reflected in silhouette in just such a manner as I had seen.

I now entirely understood the situation – and Davy saw it.

'Well, Andy,' he said, 'indeed 'tis no more and no less than our old trick – but in a new form; and I was to set it before my Lord and twenty guests this evening – and now . . . Unless . . .'

I could not but laugh, and concur; for not only was he

a good friend to whom I owed a favour – and I was interested to test any new scientific device – but I must confess that I found young Maggie an entrancing companion with whose person I had already formed the ambition of being better acquainted than had been permitted by the somewhat unfavourable circumstances of our single encounter.

It took but a moment for Davy to explain what was to occur; and a moment or two longer for me to accustom myself to a proper mode of behaviour before the machine, or 'projector of light', as Davy described it – the chief thing to remember being that it was important to remain for the most part either in profile or full-face towards the light, for otherwise the picture was most confusing to the onlooker.

We now retired, and enjoyed a light meal together with some wine, though not so much as to invoke the memory of Shakespeare's warning in his Scottish play – that alcohol, while it provokes the desire, takes away the performance. As we ate, Davy went once more over what passed for the 'plot' of the performance in which I was shortly to take part; and we were joined by an elderly gentleman of more than usually repugnant appearance, who was to accompany us upon the harpsichord.

At just seven o'clock we returned through the corridors to the room where we were to act out our parts, but entering it by a door which took us immediately behind the screen. Happily the space was now heated by a fine fire in the fireplace, the sheet or 'screen' however being protected from its flickering light by a more conventional guard which had been unfolded before it. I also noted that half of the table before the screen was now occupied by a low bench or couch. From the other side of the hangings a chatter of voices signalled that the audience was already assembled, and Davy sending our musician out, a little applause greeted him as he sat down and began to play.

The three of us now prepared, by taking off our topcoats and retaining only our shirts and trousers, while Maggie remained in that single dress which appeared to be the only one she possessed. Davy picked up a stick, and putting it between the folds of the curtain, nudged the musician with it – at which signal he broke off his tune and struck up several chords, which were the signal for the candles in the main room to be put out, and those in our 'projector of light' lit.

Our play then began, by Davy and Maggie striding upon the table or stage, hand in hand, to that music by Mr Handel commonly used as an accompaniment to weddings. They embraced with what appeared to be happy joy, and with an enthusiasm which was a tribute to Davy's skill as an actor, for I knew that while he numbered many ladies among his friends, he was largely incapable of responding to their charms in the way of passion. However, he permitted Maggie to remove his shirt, and replied by lifting her dress from her – the silhouette of those delightful young breasts, fully curved below, but uplifted so that the charming nipples were gently tilted skywards, bringing a clamour of applause from our unseen audience.

Davy went so far as to kiss these, then, extruding his tongue, to touch the tip of each with it – so skilfully contriving to present the profile of the manoeuvre to the screen that I was confirmed in my understanding that these actors had performed their piece many times before.

Falling into an embrace, the pair remained for a moment clasped tightly in each other's arms. But what was this? Breaking away, Maggie now raised her hands in astonishment and even horror – then placed one firmly upon that part of Davy's body where, in a lover, there should by now have arisen a proper protuberance in tribute to her beauty. Hastily undoing his breeches and drawing them to the floor, she revealed to the onlookers (who responded with a comic groan of disappointment and disapprobation) the outline of a merely relaxed apparatus, in which cock and cods were so confused, one so indistinguishable from the others as to be disappointing to any mistress.

Falling on her knees before her lover, Maggie now did

her best to remedy the situation, first by dint of rubbing the offending squab between her palms, then by taking it between her lips and licking, mumbling and sucking it with the greatest enthusiasm. Yet still there was no response – the scene one which spoke of Davy's skill in contriving the narrative, for no man not of his own nature could have withstood such an attack from so practised a female without the natural reaction.

Now, despairing of success in their present posture, Maggie guided Davy to the couch, and laying him upon it lowered herself on to his recumbent body and as it were massaged it with her own; then covering his entire person with kisses, licking his nipples, and again giving all her female attentions to that disappointing area where her hopes still lay – all without effect.

The circumstances were such that even knowing the male protagonist as well as I did, I was astonished that he managed to remain unmoved. As for me who saw before me, unencumbered by the intervention of screen, the entrancing vision of a charming person placing herself in every lascivious position, my own discomfort was now acute, my trousers barely managing to confine my growing manhood – and that restriction positively painful.

However, now Maggie gave up in despair; and with a gesture that drew from the unseen audience a sympathetic patter of applause, rose and with a gesture demanded that her lover leave her, which he did with head and prick equally low.

Now, it was my turn: mounting the table, I rapped with my knuckles upon it – a sound echoed by the harpsichord. Maggie raised her head as though called by a familiar voice, and then threw up her hands in a joyful gesture as I strode upon the stage, and pausing but a moment, removed my clothing with such celerity as to raise a cheer from the audience, every manjack of which was clearly upon my side.

As I removed my trousers, my own man – relieved to be no longer confined – sprang up and knocked against my belly with a sound clearly audible. At the sight, Maggie again raised her hands in pleasure, and throwing herself to her knees kissed and caressed the prominent signal of my admiration with an enthusiasm almost too great to be borne; indeed, I had to whisper to her to refrain if the performance were not to be brought to a premature end.

Understanding the situation, she laid me upon the couch, and there for a time kept clear of that most sensitive evidence of my state, instead paying tribute to other parts of my person, sucking my toes and fingers, kissing each part of me from ankle to shoulder, then turning, knelt above me, top to toe, and lifting my knees until she could tuck them beneath her arms, bent her head and licked my cods with all the appreciative fervour of someone enjoying strange fruits, and by extruding her tongue to the utmost and watching, from the corner of her eyes the effect upon the screen, even gave the impression of thrusting it into my fundament.

I was myself lost in pleasure – too much so to pay a great deal of attention to the silhouettes upon the screen. Fortunately, Maggie was sufficiently professional to watch that for us both – a matter which was in some ways a shame, for it was necessary to withhold a full completion of certain acts in order that their similitude should be sufficiently effective when projected by the light. In order, for instance, for her to have given me the full pleasure of her attentions to my rear, her face would have so closely approached it that the visual aspect of the matter would have been indecipherable. Sensing my disappointment, she whispered to me that other opportunities would doubtless occur – and encouraged me in my own activity, which was to return her compliment by paying attention to her own centre of pleasure – and, on her digging me in the ribs, to mitigate this too, in order that the screen should receive the impression of what was occurring, rather than portray a less effective silhouette.

That we were succeeding in our efforts was clear from the silence in which they were received, the audience being thrown into a discreet passion in which each participated as though he alone was the spectator. I was somewhat complimented, too, by the sight of Davy who, standing at the side of the table, was so inspirited by the performance (I have no doubt, chiefly by my own part in it) that Maggie could no longer have complained of his lack of interest, a perfectly acceptable prick now standing between his thighs – though, as I knew, the aperture into which he longed to thrust it was not that into which, at this very moment, I was nudging my own member.

In order to offer the most delightful impression to the audience, Maggie posed herself now upon all fours while I approached her from behind – for in that position the full effect of the mechanical process could be observed, myself being careful to maintain the advantage by entering and withdrawing slowly and completely enough for the whole matter to be visible; and, on the climax approaching (as I had been instructed) withdrew my instrument entirely, when to a cascade of notes from the attentive harpsichord, I ejaculated the fluid of life in the full light of the lantern, and therefore in a manner which convinced the audience that my rapture had indeed been effected; which resulted in considerable applause, and a swift scuffling of feet which signalled the gentlemen's disappearance, presumably in search of their wives, or perhaps those of my Lord's female servants who could provide those corporeal pleasures to which our effects had roused them. On our descending from the couch, Davy embraced us both with enthusiasm – myself perhaps more enthusiastically than Maggie, a fact which did not unduly disturb me, since my recent pleasure had now entirely subsided, and I could not even equivocally have given him any suggestion of a passion in which he could have shared.

This he recognized with a wry smile, and contented himself with giving me another smacking kiss upon my lips, and once more thanking me for my assistance.

His invitation to another meal I declined; though it was made clear that the invitation would include the opportunity of passing the night with Maggie, whose charms were such that even so recent a fulfilment of my admiration of them had not entirely disposed of my interest in and admiration for her person. Having bidden my friends farewell I rather took myself off, leaving Maggie to tend to Fred, whose circumstances seemed slightly improved, and who tended to be slightly jealous of my taking his place – until it was made clear to him that this had been merely temporary, and until Maggie's continuing care for him was shown (by her insertion of her hand beneath the bedclothes, and in a southerly direction) to be unchanged.

I resisted Davy's attempts to press upon me some proportion of the remuneration that he had received for the evening. I did however request him not to reveal my identity either to Maggie, Fred or (most certainly) any members of the audience – for it was more than likely that some of them would know me as a Member of the Parliament, and might entertain some doubts whether such a person should (even in the way of helping a friend) participate in such an exhibition.

I returned to the George Inn at ten o'clock, finding Sophie already abed, since we were to set out early the following morning. As I crept in beside her, she stirred, and reaching out, seemed disposed to request a service which I might find it difficult, in the nature of things, to perform so soon after so passionate an evening. On my remaining still, however, she merely tucked her body into the curve of my arm, and, with her head upon my shoulder, we both fell asleep.

The next morning we climbed again on board our coach and, the horses' hooves slipping somewhat upon the icy road, climbed the hill out of Stamford; a fellow-feeling among those of us on the stage reminding us of a pleasant few days during which we had learned much of each other, and something of the interesting and various contrivances of human nature.

More Erotic Fiction from Headline:

EROS IN THE COUNTRY

Anonymous

Being the saucy adventures of sweet, virginal Sophie, her lusty brother Frank and young Andrew, the village lad with a taste for pleasure – a youthful trio who engage in some not-so-innocent bedplay.

Their enthusiastic experiments come to an abrupt halt when they are discovered in flagrante and sent from home in disgrace. And so begins an erotic odyssey of sensual discovery to titillate even the most jaded imagination . . .

Her tender flesh prey to lascivious lechers of both high and low estate, Sophie seeks refuge in the arms of the students of Cambridge, ever keen to enlarge on their worldly knowledge. Meanwhile Andrew is bound by the silken lash of desire, voluptuous ladies provoking him to ever more unbearable heights of ecstasy.

EROS IN THE COUNTRY – where every excess of lust and desire is encountered, experienced and surpassed . . .

FICTION/EROTICA 0 7472 3145 1

More Erotic Fiction from Headline:

EROS IN TOWN

Anonymous

When the aristocratic Sir Franklin Franklyn and his half-brother Andy arrive in London to claim their inheritance, they find not the respectable family home they expected but the most lascivious of brothels. Frank takes things into his own hands and transforms the town-house into the most luxurious, romantic house of pleasure in all London. Here, every desire is catered for, any amorous wish met.

Not to be outdone, Frank's saucy sister Sophie declares that women are as much slaves to desire as men, and to prove her point she establishes a stable of lusty lovers patronised by the most elegant ladies in the land.

Thus both brother and sister indulge themselves in an orgy of sensuality that surpasses even the wildest flights of erotic fantasy . . .

Also available from Headline – EROS IN THE COUNTRY – the first volume in the sensual adventures of a lady and gentleman of leisure.

FICTION/EROTICA 0 7472 3199 0

More Erotic Fiction from Headline:

EROS IN THE NEW WORLD

Anonymous

Provoked once more by their unquenchable appetites for delight, the exquisite Sophia and her beloved Andy set sail for pastures new and naughty: the Americas. With open minds and open arms they resolve to experience the land of the free, from the most salacious Southern gentleman to the sauciest slave girl.

And for Sophia another challenge beckons: the carnal sampling of a dozen young studs, each of a different astrological aspect – and of intriguingly diverse erotic inclinations. From New York to New Orleans, from Montreal to the Mississippi our enthusiastic duo reveal a lusty land, bursting with an amorous ingenuity and enterprise to inspire the most sated of Old World sensualists . . .

Don't miss the other amorous adventures of Andy and Sophia:

EROS IN THE COUNTRY
EROS IN TOWN
EROS ON THE GRAND TOUR

FICTION/EROTICA 0 7472 3310 1

More Erotic Fiction from Headline:

EROS IN THE FAR EAST

Anonymous

Recuperating from a dampening experience at the hands of one of London's most demanding ladies, the ever-dauntless Andy resolves to titil.ate his palate with foreign pleasures: namely a return passage to Siam. After a riotously libidinous ocean crossing, he finds himself in southern Africa, sampling a warm welcome from its delightfully unabashed natives.

Meanwhile, herself escaping an unsavoury encounter in the English lakes, his lovely cousin Sophia sets sail for Panama and thence to the intriguing islands of Hawaii – and a series of bizarrely erotic tribal initiations which challenge the limits of even her sensuous imagination!

After a string of energetically abandoned frolics, Andy and Sophia fetch up in the stately city of Singapore, a city which holds all the dangerously piquant pleasures of the mysterious East, and an adventure more outrageous than any our plucky pair have yet encountered. . .

Follow Andy and Sophia's other erotic exploits:
EROS IN THE COUNTRY EROS IN TOWN
EROS IN THE NEW WORLD EROS ON THE GRAND TOUR

FICTION/EROTICA 0 7472 3449 3

More Erotic Fiction from Headline:

Lustful Liaisons

Erotic adventures in the capital city of love!

Anonymous

PARIS 1912 – a city alive with the pursuit of pleasure, from the promenade of the Folies Bergère to the high-class brothels of the Left Bank. Everywhere business is booming in the oldest trade of all – the trade of love!

But now there is a new and flourishing activity to absorb the efforts of go-ahead men-about-town: the business of manufacturing motor cars. Men like Robert and Bertrand Laforge are pioneers in this field but their new automobile has a design defect that can only be rectified by some cunning industrial espionage. Which is where the new trade marries with the old, for the most reliable way of discovering information is to enlist the help of a lovely and compliant woman. A woman, for example, like the voluptuous Nellie Lebérigot whose soft creamy flesh and generous nature are guaranteed to uncover a man's most closely guarded secrets...

FICTION/EROTICA 0 7472 3710 7

More Erotic Fiction from Headline:

FAYE ROSSIGNOL

PEARL OF THE HAREEM

The sensational story of life in a high-class house of pleasure

'Here I am – the girl who hit Constantinople like a sexual earthquake!'

Kidnapped in Vienna in 1904, shipped to the Orient and sold into slavery by the most ruthless rogue in the land, though she does not yet know it, the beautiful young American Pearl Keefer is on her way to becoming the most famous courtesan of her day. Her new home is the French Hareem, the most fabulous brothel in Turkey, and it is there that her magical talent for the pleasuring of men is honed to the heights of artistry. Here is her story and these are the erotic secrets of a lifetime of love!

Also available from Headline by Faye Rossignol:
SWEET FANNY
SWEET FANNY'S DIARY
LORD HORNINGTON'S ACADEMY OF LOVE
A VICTORIAN LOVER OF WOMEN
FFRENCH PLEASURES
THE FFRENCH HOUSE

FICTION/EROTICA 0 7472 3779 4